The Complete Dr. Thorndyke

Volume VIII:

For the Defense: Dr. Thorndyke
The Penrose Mystery
Felo de se?

The Complete Dr. Thorndyke

Volume VIII:

For the Defense: Dr. Thorndyke
The Penrose Mystery
Felo de se?

by

R. Austin Freeman

Edited by
David Marcum

ISBN Hardback 978-1-78705-685-5
ISBN Paperback 978-1-78705-686-2
AUK ePub ISBN 978-1-78705-687-9
AUK PDF ISBN 978-1-78705-688-6

These works are in the Public Domain in Great Britain
Portrait of Dr. Thorndyke by H.M. Brock (1908)

Published in the UK by
MX Publishing
335 Princess Park Manor, Royal Drive,
London, N11 3GX
www.mxpublishing.co.uk

David Marcum can be reached at:
thepapersofsherlockholmes@gmail.com

Cover design by Brian Belanger
www.belangerbooks.com and *www.redbubble.com/people/zhahadun*

CONTENTS

Introductions

Adventures

For the Defense: Dr. Thorndyke

The Penrose Mystery

Book I: *Being the Narrative of Ernest Lockhart, Barrister at Law*

(Continued on the next page . . . .)

Book II: *Narrated by Christopher Jervis, M.D.*

Felo de se?

Part I: *The Gambler – Narrated by Robert Mortimer*

Part II: *The Case of John Gillum, Deceased –*
Narrated by Christopher Jervis, M.D.

(Continued on the next page . . . .)

The Complete Dr. Thorndyke

Volume VIII:

For the Defense: Dr. Thorndyke
The Penrose Mystery
Felo de se?

Dr. John Thorndyke

MR LPA KERSHAW
MR ?? BROXHOLM
MR WA MILNER
MR ?? HUDSON.

99

5A King's Bench Walk
in the late 1890's when
Thorndyke would have moved in

5A King's Bench Walk
Photographed by the Editor
during his
Sherlock Holmes Pilgrimage No. 3
(September 8th, 2016)

Meet Dr. Thorndyke
by R. Austin Freeman

My subject is Dr. John Thorndyke, the hero or central character of most of my detective stories. So I'll give you a short account of his real origin – of the way in which he did in fact come into existence.

To discover the origin of John Thorndyke I have to reach back into the past for at least fifty years, to the time when I was a medical student preparing for my final examination. For reasons which I need not go into I gave rather special attention to the legal aspects of medicine and the medical aspects of law. And as I read my text-books, and especially the illustrative cases, I was profoundly impressed by their dramatic quality. Medical jurisprudence deals with the human body in its relation to all kinds of legal problems. Thus its subject matter includes all sorts of crime against the person and all sorts of violent death and bodily injury: Hanging, drowning, poisons and their effects, problems of suicide and homicide, of personal identity and survivorship, and a host of other problems of the highest dramatic possibilities, though not always quite presentable for the purposes of fiction. And the reported cases which were given in illustration were often crime stories of the most thrilling interest. Cases of disputed identity such as the Tichbourne Case, famous poisoning cases such as the Rugeley Case and that of Madeline Smith, cases of mysterious disappearance or the detection of long-forgotten crimes such as that of Eugene Aram. All these, described and analysed with strict scientific accuracy, formed the matter of Medical Jurisprudence which thrilled me as I read and made an indelible impression.

But it produced no immediate results. I had to pass my examinations and get my diploma, and then look out for the means of earning my living. So all this curious lore was put away for the time being in the pigeon-holes of my mind – which Dr. Freud would call the *Unconscious* – not forgotten, but ready to come to the surface when the need for it should arise. And there it reposed for some twenty years, until failing health compelled me to abandon medical practice and take to literature as a profession.

It was then that my old studies recurred to my mind. A fellow doctor, Conan Doyle, had made a brilliant and well-deserved success by the creation of the immortal Sherlock Holmes. Considering that achievement, I asked myself whether it might not be possible to devise a

1

detective story of a slightly different kind – one based on the science of Medical Jurisprudence, in which, by the sacrifice of a certain amount of dramatic effect, one could keep entirely within the facts of real life, with nothing fictitious excepting the persons and the events. I came to the conclusion that it was, and began to turn the idea over in my mind.

But I think that the influence which finally determined the character of my detective stories, and incidentally the character of John Thorndyke, operated when I was working at the Westminster Ophthalmic Hospital. There I used to take the patients into the dark room, examine their eyes with the ophthalmoscope, estimate the errors of refraction, and construct an experimental pair of spectacles to correct those errors. When a perfect correction had been arrived at, the formula for it was embodied in a prescription which was sent to the optician who made the permanent spectacles.

Now when I was writing those prescriptions it was borne in on me that in many cases, especially the more complex, the formula for the spectacles, and consequently the spectacles themselves, furnished an infallible record of personal identity. If, for instance, such a pair of spectacles should have been found in a railway carriage, and the maker of those spectacles could be found, there would be practically conclusive evidence that a particular person had travelled by that train. About that time I drafted out a story based on a pair of spectacles, which was published some years later under the title of *The Mystery of 31 New Inn*, and the construction of that story determined, as I have said, not only the general character of my future work but of the hero around whom the plots were to be woven. But that story remained for some years in cold storage. My first published detective novel was *The Red Thumb-mark*, and in that book we may consider that John Thorndyke was born. And in passing on to describe him I may as well explain how and why he came to be the kind of person that he is.

I may begin by saying that he was not modelled after any real person. He was deliberately created to play a certain part, and the idea that was in my mind was that he should be such a person as would be likely and suitable to occupy such a position in real life. As he was to be a medico-legal expert, he had to be a doctor and a fully trained lawyer. On the physical side I endowed him with every kind of natural advantage. He is exceptionally tall, strong, and athletic because those qualities are useful in his vocation. For the same reason he has acute eyesight and hearing and considerable general manual skill, as every doctor ought to have. In appearance he is handsome and of an imposing presence, with a symmetrical face of the classical type and a Grecian nose. And here I may remark that his distinguished appearance is not merely a concession to my personal taste but is also a protest against the monsters of ugliness whom some detective writers have evolved.

These are quite opposed to natural truth. In real life a first-class man of any kind usually tends to be a good-looking man.

Mentally, Thorndyke is quite normal. He has no gifts of intuition or other supernormal mental qualities. He is just a highly intellectual man of great and varied knowledge with exceptionally acute reasoning powers and endowed with that invaluable asset, a scientific imagination (by a scientific imagination I mean that special faculty which marks the born investigator, the capacity to perceive the essential nature of a problem before the detailed evidence comes into sight). But he arrives at his conclusions by ordinary reasoning, which the reader can follow when he has been supplied with the facts, though the intricacy of the train of reasoning may at times call for an exposition at the end of the investigation.

Thorndyke has no eccentricities or oddities which might detract from the dignity of an eminent professional man, unless one excepts an unnatural liking for Trichinopoly cheroots. In manner he is quiet, reserved and self-contained, and rather markedly secretive, but of a kindly nature, though not sentimental, and addicted to occasional touches of dry humour. That is how Thorndyke appears to me.

As to his age. When he made his first bow to the reading public from the doorway of Number 4 King's Bench Walk he was between thirty-five and forty. As that was thirty years ago, he should now be over sixty-five. But he isn't. If I have to let him *grow old along with me*" I need not saddle him with the infirmities of age, and I can (in his case) put the brake on the passing years. Probably he is not more than fifty after all!

Now a few words as to how Thorndyke goes to work. His methods are rather different from those of the detectives of the Sherlock Holmes school. They are more technical and more specialized. He is an investigator of crime but he is not a detective. The technique of Scotland Yard would be neither suitable nor possible to him. He is a medico-legal expert, and his methods are those of medico-legal science. In the investigation of a crime there are two entirely different methods of approach. One consists in the careful and laborious examination of a vast mass of small and commonplace detail: Inquiring into the movements of suspected and other persons, interrogating witnesses and checking their statements particularly as to times and places, tracing missing persons, and so forth – the aim being to accumulate a great body of circumstantial evidence which will ultimately disclose the solution of the problem. It is an admirable method, as the success of our police proves, and it is used

3

with brilliant effect by at least one of our contemporary detective writers. But it is essentially a police method.

The other method consists in the search for some fact of high evidential value which can be demonstrated by physical methods and which constitutes conclusive proof of some important point. This method also is used by the police in suitable cases. Finger-prints are examples of this kind of evidence, and another instance is furnished by the Gutteridge murder. Here the microscopical examination of a cartridge-case proved conclusively that the murder had been committed with a particular revolver, a fact which incriminated the owner of that revolver and led to his conviction.

This is Thorndyke's procedure. It consists in the interrogation of things rather than persons, of the ascertainment of physical facts which can be made visible to eyes other than his own. And the facts which he seeks tend to be those which are apparent only to the trained eye of the medical practitioner.

I feel that I ought to say a few words about Thorndyke's two satellites, Jervis and Polton. As to the former, he is just the traditional narrator proper to this type of story. Some of my readers have complained that Dr. Jervis is rather slow in the uptake. But that is precisely his function. He is the expert misunderstander. His job is to observe and record all the facts, and to fail completely to perceive their significance. Thereby he gives the reader all the necessary information, and he affords Thorndyke the opportunity to expound its bearing on the case.

Polton is in a slightly different category. Although he is not drawn from any real person, he is associated in my mind with two actual individuals. One is a Mr. Pollard, who was the laboratory assistant in the hospital museum when I was a student, and who gave me many a valuable tip in matters of technique, and who, I hope, is still to the good. The other was a watch- and clock-maker of the name of Parsons – familiarly known as Uncle Parsons – who had premises in a basement near the Royal Exchange, and who was a man of boundless ingenuity and technical resource. Both of these I regard as collateral relatives, so to speak, of Nathaniel Polton. But his personality is not like either. His crinkly countenance is strictly his own copyright.

To return to Thorndyke, his rather technical methods have, for the purposes of fiction, advantages and disadvantages. The advantage is that his facts are demonstrably true, and often they are intrinsically interesting. The disadvantage is that they are frequently not matters of common knowledge, so that the reader may fail to recognize them or grasp their significance until they are explained. But this is the case with all classes of fiction. There is no type of character or story that can be made sympathetic and acceptable to every kind of reader. The personal equation affects the reading as well as the writing of a story.

R. Austin Freeman
(1862-1943)

5A King's Bench Walk
in the early 1900's when
Thorndyke was in practice

Dr. Thorndyke: In the Footsteps
of Sherlock Holmes
by David Marcum

When Sherlock Holmes began his practice as a "Consulting Detective", his ideas of scientific criminal investigations caused the London police to look upon him as a mere "theorist". He was perceived as an amateur to be tolerated, often with amusement – until, that is, his assistance was required. Then they were more than willing to come knocking upon his door, asking for whatever help that they could receive. And usually this help took the form of brilliant solutions to bizarre and otherwise insoluble problems.

Holmes espoused methods and ideas that were considered ludicrous in the late 1800's. For instance, his frustration knew no bounds when a crime scene was disturbed. Holmes realized that so much could be determined from the physical evidence – footprints, fibers, and spatters. The police were happy to trod into and disturb the evidence as if they were herds of field beasts, with the equivalent level of intelligence.

However, Holmes's methods, and the science behind catching criminals, eventually won out and became so important that it's hard to now imagine the world without them. Many of the exact same techniques and methods that he advocated are now standard practice. From being an amateur with unusual ideas, Holmes is now recognized around the world as The Great Detective. In 2002, Holmes received a posthumous Honorary Fellowship from the British Royal Society of Chemistry, based on the fact that he was beyond his time in using chemistry and chemical sciences as a means of solving crimes.

And before that, in 1985, Scotland Yard introduced *HOLMES* (*Home Office Large Major Enquiry System*), an elaborate computer system designed to process the masses of information collected and evaluated during a criminal investigation, in order to ensure that no vital clues are overlooked. This system, providing total compatibility and consistency between all the police forces of England, Scotland, Wales, and Northern Ireland, as well as the Royal Military Police, has since been upgraded by the improved *HOLMES 2* – and like the first version, there is absolutely no doubt as to who is being honored and memorialized for his work in dragging criminology out of the dark ages.

Many famous Great Detectives followed in Holmes's footsteps – Nero Wolfe and Ellery Queen, Hercule Poirot and Solar Pons – each with their own methods and techniques, but before they began their careers, and while Holmes was still in practice in Baker Street, another London consultant – Dr. John Thorndyke – opened his doors, using the scientific methods developed and perfected by Holmes and taking them to a whole new level of brilliance.

Meet Dr. Thorndyke

Dr. John Evelyn Thorndyke was born on July 4th, 1870. We don't know about where he was raised, or if he has any family. At no point will we be introduced to a more brilliant brother who sometimes *is* the British Government. He was educated at the medical school of St. Margaret's Hospital in London, and while there, he met fellow student Christopher Jervis. They became friends but, after completing school in 1895, they lost touch with one another. Over the next six years, Thorndyke remained at St. Margaret's, taking on various jobs, hanging "about the chemical and physical laboratories, the museum and *post mortem* room," and learning what he could. He obtained his M.D. and his Doctor of Sciences, and then was called to the bar in 1896.

He'd prepared himself with the hope of obtaining a position as a coroner, but he learned of the unexpected retirement of one of St. Margaret's lecturers in medical jurisprudence. He applied for the position and, rather to his own surprise, it was awarded to him. (He would continue to maintain his association with the hospital, going on to become the Medical Registrar, Pathologist, Curator of the Museum, and then Professor of Medical Jurisprudence, all while maintaining his own private consulting practice.

It was when Thorndyke was named lecturer that he obtained his chambers at 5A King's Bench Walk, in the Inner Temple, that amazing and historic area between Fleet Street and the River. Founded over eight-hundred years ago by the Knights Templar, it is one of the four Inns of Court, (along with the Middle Temple, Lincoln's Inn, and Gray's Inn.) The buildings along King's Bench Walk, and particularly No.'s 4, 5, and 6, have a great deal of historical significance – and not just because Dr. John Thorndyke practiced at 5A for a number of years.

Thorndyke was quite fortunate to obtain a suite of rooms on multiple floors at this location, which leads to speculation about his influence and resources – a question which has no answer. In any case, it was there that he opened his practice and began to wait for clients and cases. He also made the acquaintance of elderly Nathaniel Polton, that man-of-all-work with the crinkly smile who ran the household, as well as Thorndyke's upstairs laboratory.

Like Sherlock Holmes during those early years in the 1870's when he had rooms in Montague Street next to the British Museum and spent his vast amounts of free time learning his craft, Thorndyke also found a way to make the empty hours more useful. He had the unique idea of imagining increasingly complex crimes – often a murder or series of them, for instance – and then, when he had planned every single aspect of the crime, he would turn around and work out the solution from the other side. While doing this, he made extensive notes of each of these theoretical exercises, and retained them for their later usefulness when encountering real-life crimes.

His first legal case was *Regina v Gummer* in 1897. Sadly, no further information about this affair is ever revealed to us, but we may be certain that Thorndyke used his considerable skills to bring it to a satisfactory conclusion, adding to his reputation as he did so.

In the meantime, Jervis had a more unfortunate story. As his time at school ended, his funds ran out rather unexpectedly, and after paying his various fees, he was left with earning his living as a medical assistant, or sometimes serving as a *locum tenens*, moving from one low-paying and temporary job to another, with no prospects of improvement.

Jervis is unemployed on the morning of March 22nd, 1901 when he encounters Thorndyke a few doors up from 5A King's Bench Walk. The two friends are happy to see one another, and before long, Jervis is involved in an investigation that will change his life in several ways, as recounted in *The Red Thumb Mark*.

But it should not be assumed that every Thorndyke adventure is narrated by Jervis in a typical Watsonian manner. In fact, the very next book, *The Eye of Osiris*, is instead told from the perspective of one of Thorndyke's students, Dr. Paul Berkeley. It is one of several that provide a look at Thorndyke – and Jervis – from a different perspective. But Jervis returns as narrator in the third novel, *The Mystery of 31 New Inn*, and we see Thorndyke through his eyes for a good many of both the novels and short stories.

Here a word might be mentioned about the Chronology of the Thorndyke stories. For some this is an irrelevant factor, but for others – like me – understanding the correct chronological placement of the stories is very important. Like the volumes that make up the Sherlock Holmes Canon, the Thorndyke stories aren't published in chronological order – a case set in 1907 (such as "Percival Bland's Proxy") might be collected before one that occurs in 1908, ("The Missing Mortgagee"), or it might not. For instance, *The Red Thumb Mark* (1907) is set in March and April 1901. (This chronological placement, by the way, is determined by noticing that a specific date is given three times in the book – in the British fashion of day before month – *9.3.01* – or *March 9th, 1901*. The dates for the events of the rest of the book can be carefully worked out from this fixed point.)

The next book, *The Eye of Osiris* (1911) is primarily set in the summer of 1904 (with Chapter 1, something of a prologue, taking place in late 1902.) Then, the next book to follow, *The Mystery of 31 New Inn* (1912), jumps back to the spring of 1902, about a year after the events of *The Red Thumb Mark*, and before *The Eye of Osiris*. And one of the short stories, "The Man With the Nailed Shoes" occurs in September and October 1901, between the first two books. Clearly, there is a great deal of material for the chronologicist in the Thorndyke Chronicles.

As Jervis becomes a part of Thorndyke's world, following their reacquaintance in March 1901, he meets others in Thorndyke's circle, including policemen such as Superintendent Miller and Inspector Badger, lawyers like Robert Anstey, Marchmont, and Brodribb, and other physicians like Dr. Paul Berkeley and Dr. Humphrey Jardine. He also has more opportunity to learn from his friend as he begins his own studies in order to become a similar specialist in the medico-legal practice – although he'll never be another Thorndyke.

Through Jervis's eyes – as well as others along the way – we build up our knowledge of Dr. Thorndyke. In appearance, he is tall and athletic, just under six feet in height, slender, and weighing around one-hundred-and-eighty pounds. He is exceptionally handsome – and has been called the handsomest detective in literature. He has no vices, except – perhaps – that he enjoys a Trichinopoly cigar upon occasion when he is feeling especially triumphant – although there is one time when the criminal's knowledge of this fact leads to a clever attempt at Thorndyke's murder . . . .

There are several instances where Thorndyke displays a marked resemblance to Sherlock Holmes – and not just in his scientific approach to crime. The two men sometimes say similar things – such as when Holmes says "*It is quite a pretty little problem,*" (in "A Scandal in Bohemia") or "*. . . there are some pretty little problems among them*" (in "The Musgrave Ritual"). Thorndyke mimics this in *Felo de Se?* ("*There, Jervis,*" said he, "*is quite a pretty little problem for you to excogitate*") or "*Ah, there is a very pretty little problem for you to consider*" (in *The Eye of Osiris*).

And who can forget the many instances when Holmes refers to *data*:

- *"It is a capital mistake to theorize before one has data. Insensibly one begins to twist facts to suit theories, instead of theories to suit facts."* – "A Scandal in Bohemia"
- *"I had,"* said he, *"come to an entirely erroneous conclusion which shows, my dear Watson, how dangerous it always is to reason from insufficient data."* – "The Speckled Band"
- *"No data yet,"* he answered. *"It is a capital mistake to theorize before you have all the evidence. It biases the judgment."* – A Study in Scarlet
- *"The temptation to form premature theories upon insufficient data is the bane of our profession."* – The Valley of Fear
- *"Still, it is an error to argue in front of your data."* – "Wisteria Lodge"

Thorndyke's version? *". . . believe me, it is a capital error to decide beforehand what data are to be sought for."* – from *The Mystery of 31 New Inn*. There are others.

Then there is Holmes's quote from "The Man With the Twisted Lip":

> *"You have a grand gift of silence, Watson,"* said he. *"It makes you quite invaluable as a companion."*

Here's the Thorndyke equivalent:

> *"It has just been borne in upon me, Jervis,"* said he, *"that you are the most companionable fellow in the world. You have the heaven-sent gift of silence."*

And then there is the time, in "The Anthropologist at Large", that a client – expecting a Holmes-like performance as based on "The Blue Carbuncle" – presents Thorndyke with an object for examination:

> *"I understand,"* said he, *"that by examining a hat it is possible to deduce from it, not only the bodily characteristics of the wearer, but also his mental and moral qualities, his state of health, his pecuniary position, his past history, and even his domestic relations and the peculiarities of his place of abode. Am I right in this supposition?"*
>
> *The ghost of a smile flitted across Thorndyke's face as he laid the hat upon the remains of the newspaper. "We must*

11

not expect too much," he observed. "Hats, as you know, have a way of changing owners . . . ."

Another area of intersection between Holmes and Thorndyke is the assembly of information. Recall Holmes's *"ponderous commonplace books in which he placed his cuttings"* as mentioned in "The Engineer's Thumb". We find, also in "The Anthropologist at Large", that Thorndyke does the same thing:

> *[H]is method of dealing with [the morning newspaper] was characteristic. The paper was laid on the table after breakfast, together with a blue pencil and a pair of office shears. A preliminary glance through the sheets enabled him to mark with the pencil those paragraphs that were to be read, and these were presently cut out and looked through, after which they were either thrown away or set aside to be pasted in an indexed book.*

No doubt and examination of Thorndyke's lodgings at 5A King's Bench Walk would reveal – in addition to a series of indexed commonplace books filled with clippings – a number of other items and aspects that would remind one of 221b Baker Street.

Like many locations where the detective's residence is almost a character in and of itself – Sherlock Holmes's London address at 221 Baker Street, and the New York homes of Ellery Queen on West 87th Street and Nero Wolfe's Brownstone on West 35th Street – Thorndyke's rooms at 5A King's Bench Walk are a living and vibrant place – from the entry way, where a heavy door known as "The Oak" leads visitors into a most comfortable wood-paneled sitting room, located on the (British) first floor, one flight up from the ground floor. On the next floor up, Polton has his laboratory and workshop, containing everything that is needed (or what might be manufactured) in order to solve the case.

On the next floor, underneath the attic, are bedrooms belonging to Thorndyke, Jervis, and Polton. Even after Jervis has married – and now you know that he does get married! – he continues to reside a good deal of the time in King's Bench Walk. As he explains in *When Rogues Fall Out* (1932, with the U.S. title of *Dr. Thorndyke's Discovery*):

> *Here, perhaps, since my records of Thorndyke's practice have contained so little reference to my own personal affairs, I should say a few words concerning my domestic habits. As the circumstances of our practice often made it*

12

desirable for me to stay late at our chambers, I had retained there the bedroom that I had occupied before my marriage; and, as these circumstances could not always be foreseen, I had arranged with my wife the simple rule that the house closed at eleven o'clock. If I was unable to get home by that time, it was to be understood that I was staying at the Temple. It may sound like a rather undomestic arrangement, but it worked quite smoothly, and it was not without its advantages. For the brief absence gave to my homecomings a certain festive quality, and helped to keep alive the romantic element in my married life. It is possible for the most devoted husbands and wives to see too much of one another.

Thorndyke's Other Appearances

Through the years, Thorndyke's reputation continues to grow, as presented through a number of adventures. Surprisingly, in light of the tens of thousands of Post-Canonical Sherlock Holmes that have come to light over the years, as discovered by latter-day Literary Agents taking over Watson's first Literary Agent, Sir Arthur Conan Doyle, stopped literary-agenting, there have been almost no additional Thorndyke cases brought to the public's attention. The few exceptions to this statement are *Goodbye, Dr. Thorndyke* (1972) by Norman Donaldson, and *Dr. Thorndyke's Dilemma* (1974) by John H. Dirckx. Both narratives deal with Thorndyke and Jervis in their latter years, and each is written by an expert in the field of Thorndyke scholarship.

Donaldson also wrote what might be the final scholarly word on the subject, *In Search of Dr. Thorndyke* (1971). In fact, he had intended his pastiche, *Goodbye, Dr. Thorndyke*, to be published as the conclusion to this book, but it ended up appearing separately.

To my knowledge, "The Great Fathomer", as Thorndyke is sometimes known, has rarely appeared in other locations. He is mentioned in the Solar Pons tale "The Adventure of the Proper Comma" by August Derleth, which finds Dr. Parker returning "from Thorndyke & Polton with an analysis of the capsules Mrs. Buxton had carried with her . . . ."

In my own book of authorized Solar Pons stories, *The Papers of Solar Pons* (2017), Thorndyke makes two appearances. "The Adventure of the Additional Heirs" has Pons and Parker visiting King's Bench Walk:

13

At 5A, we learned that our friend Thorndyke, the medical juris-practitioner, was out on some investigation or other, but Pons handed the papers, sans photograph, into the care of Polton, his crinkly-faced laboratory technician, with a detailed explanation of what he wished to learn. The man nodded and smiled, and without any extraneous chit-chat, shut the door, freeing us to return to Fleet Street. We paused at the edge of the walk to look at the photograph, still in Pons's hand.

Later Thorndyke sends Pons a detailed report that helps toward the solution of the problem. And in "The Affair of the Distasteful Society", set in July 1921, Pons and Parker attend the first meeting of a group gathered to honor Sherlock Holmes, where the following conversation occurs:

"I see that you invited Thorndyke, and that little Belgian over on Farraway Street," said Rath.
"And Sexton Blake as well," replied Sir Amory.
"Sexton Blake is a fictional character, Sir Amory," said Pons with a smile.

In my story, "The Adventure of the Two Sisters", included in *The New Adventures of Solar Pons*, Dr. Parker writes:

Pons was not the only detective who offered his services to the London populace, although he might have been the most well-known. We were friends with several others, including the former Belgian policeman who lived in Farraway Street, and another rather mysterious fellow in nearby Bottle Street. And of course, Pons went way back with Thorndyke, whose chambers were across town. It wasn't unusual for Pons and the others to regularly confer on investigations, or simply to sit down and share a few drinks and professional anecdotes.

Thorndyke doesn't just appear in some of my Solar Pons adventures. He's also been referenced off-stage in a couple of Sherlock Holmes adventures that I've pulled from Watson's Tin Dispatch Box – and it's more than likely that others will follow. In "The "London Wheel", contained in *The MX Book of New Sherlock Holmes Stories* –

Part IV: 2016 Annual (2016), Holmes, looking through some documents, states:

> *"I believe," said Holmes, "that I have enough amateur legal training that I can get a sense of the implications of the clauses in question in both of these documents." He pulled the folded pages from his pocket. "I thought about sending a message to my* protégé *Thorndyke in King's Bench Walk for his opinion, as he could have been here very quickly, should he be at home at all and not out on his own business. However, I don't believe that will be necessary.*

Perhaps it is a point of interest that Thorndyke is referred to Holmes's protégé. Possibly more information will be forthcoming, such as that which is hinted in my story, "The Coombs Contrivance" (in *The Irregular Adventures of Sherlock Holmes!*). Set in 1889, when Thorndyke was nineteen years old, Holmes and Watson are discussing a precocious Baker Street Irregular:

> *[Holmes] pinched the bridge of his nose. "Do you trust Levi's judgment, Watson?"*
> *I considered. "For an eight-year-old, he's remarkably perceptive – as much as any of the other Irregulars who have assisted you. The Wiggins family, or the Peakes, or Thorndyke, before he went away to university."*

So was Thorndyke, perhaps, a gifted Irregular who learned from The Master, and then went on to create his own successful practice, taking what he learned to a next very successful level? Possibly. In my story "The Inner Temple Intruder", to be found in *Sherlock Holmes and the Great Detectives*, such an origin story is posited. As Robert Downey, Jr. succinctly stated when playing Holmes in 2009's *Sherlock Holmes*: "Food for thought!"

Thorndyke is also mentioned in Bob Byrne's Holmes story, "The Adventure of the Parson's Son" (*The MX Book of New Sherlock Holmes Stories – Part III: 1896-1929*), wherein Holmes, examining a piece of evidence, cries:

> *"Ha! I believe we have discredited the coat entirely. Though I wish I could get Thorndyke to examine it. Would that we were back in London."*

And it isn't just Thorndyke who has appeared elsewhere. His lawyer friend Marchmont has assisted Holmes and Watson in a small way a couple of my own: "The Coombs Contrivance" and the forthcoming adventure *Sherlock Holmes and The Eye of Heka.*

Although I have encouraged these Thorndyke cameos in my own stories or in Holmes and Pons books that I edit, his appearances elsewhere are much more fleeting. In the 2015 BBC radio series *The Rivals*, Inspector Lestrade, Holmes's most frequent associate at Scotland Yard, is placed into the events of the Thorndyke short story "The Moabite Cipher". And Thorndyke has only had a handful of other media appearances. In 1964, the BBC produced seven episodes (now lost) of *Thorndyke*, starring Peter Copley. The episodes were:

- "The Case of Oscar Brodski'
- "The Old Lag"
- "A Case of Premeditation"
- "The Mysterious Visitor"
- "The Case of Phyllis Annesley" – Adapted from "Phyllis Annesley's Peril"
- "Percival Bland's Brother" – Adapted from "Percival Bland's Proxy"
- "The Puzzle Lock"

From 1971 to 1973, Thames TV aired *The Rivals of Sherlock Holmes,* and two stories were adapted: "A Message from the Deep Sea" starring John Neville (who had also played Holmes in 1965's *A Study in Terror*), and "The Moabite Cipher" starring Barrie Ingram. Except for a 1963 BBC Radio adaption of *Mr. Pottermack's Oversight,* and a few on-air readings by a single performer, there have been no other Thorndyke adaptations – which is a terrible shame, as the stories certainly lend themselves to visual and audible interpretations. Perhaps a new generation will discover Thorndyke, Jervis, and the rest, and they will find popularity once again, as they did more than a century ago.

Copley, Neville, and Ingram as Thorndyke

A Few (Hundred) Words About R. Austin Freeman
Thorndyke's Chronicler

Richard Austin Freeman was born on April 11, 1862 in the Soho district of London. He was the son of a skilled tailor and the youngest of five children. As he grew, it was expected that he would become a tailor as well, but instead he had an interest in natural history and medicine, and so he obtained employment in a pharmacist's shop. While there, he qualified as an apothecary and could have gone on to manage the shop, but instead he began to study medicine at Middlesex Hospital.

Austin Freeman qualified as a physician in 1887, and in that same year he married. Faced with the twin facts of his new marital responsibilities and his very limited resources as a young doctor, he made the unusual decision to join the Colonial Service, spending the next seven years in Africa as an Assistant Colonial Surgeon. This continued until the early 1890's, when he contracted Blackwater Fever, an illness that eventually forced him to leave the service and return permanently to England.

For several years, he served as a *locum tenens* for various physicians, a bleak time in his life as he moved from job to job, his income low, and his health never quite recovered. (These experiences were reflected in the narratives of Doctors Jervis and Berkeley.) However, he supplemented his meager income and exercised his creativity during these years by beginning to write. His early publications included *Travels and Live in Ashanti and Jaman* (1898), recounting some of his African sojourns.

In 1900, Freeman obtained work as an assistant to Dr. John James Pitcairn (1860-1936) at Holloway Prison. Although he wasn't there for very long, the association between the two men was enough to turn Freeman's attention toward writing mysteries. Over the next few years, they co-wrote several under the pseudonym *Clifford Ashdown*, including *The Adventures of Romney Pringle* (1902), *The Further Adventures of Romney Pringle* (1903), *From a Surgeon's Diary* (1904-1905), and *The Queen's Treasure* (written around 1905-1906, and published posthumously in 1975.) The specifics of the two men's writing arrangement are unknown to the present day, although much research was carried out by Freeman scholar Percival Mason ("P.M.") Stone, who was actually able to confirm Pitcairn's involvement and influence. Following this association, which apparently helped to train Freeman to be a better writer and to focus on a recurring character, his luck changed, and he was able, within just a few years, to abandon the practice of

17

medicine, which had never been successful, and become a professional author.

In approximately 1904, Freeman began developing a mystery novella based on a short job that he had held at the Western Ophthalmic Hospital. This effort, "31 New Inn", was published in 1905, and it is the true first Dr. Thorndyke story. In it, we meet narrator Dr. Christopher Jervis, working as a *locum tenens*, moving from practice to practice in the same bleak existence that Freeman had experienced. Jervis becomes involved with a patient that may or may not be in danger. Unsure what to do, he recalls his former classmate, the brilliant Dr. John Thorndyke.

Curiously, this novella, (included in Volume II of this newly reissued collection *The Complete Dr. Thorndyke*), has numerous references to the events of the first Thorndyke novel, *The Red Thumb Mark*, which would not be published until 1907. Much of Freeman's life is obscure and unknown, including his writing processes and milestones, but clearly, with so much already clearly defined in this novella about Thorndyke and Jervis, he had firmly established not only fixed aspects of their histories, but the plot of *The Red Thumb Mark* as well, several years before the book's publication. One wonders why he chose to first publish "31 New Inn", since it occurs chronologically a whole year *after* the events of *The Red Thumb Mark*.

Interestingly – at least to a chronologicist such as myself – the original novella of "31 New Inn" is specifically set in April 1900, as indicated internally. However, when it was later revised to become the third Thorndyke novel, *The Mystery of 31 New Inn*, (1912, and included in Volume I of *The Complete Dr. Thorndyke*), the narrative's date is changed to 1902 – which fits, since the events definitely occur after *The Red Thumb Mark*, which takes place in March and April 1901.

Like Rex Stout's Nero Wolfe, who seemed to have sprung fully formed from his creator's brow, Thorndyke and his world are well-defined and immediately real. Although certain characters are added to the circle through the years, the basic layout – with Thorndyke, Jervis, and Polton (the man-of-all-work crinkly-smiled assistant) are always at 5A, ready to spring into action when Jervis – or one of the other varied narrators who show up throughout the series – arrive with a curious problem.

Freeman had found his voice with the Thorndyke books and short stories, and he was able to make use of his lifelong interest in medicine and natural science – often conducting extensive experiments to work out exactly how the solutions in his stories could be discovered. And in Thorndyke's early days, Freeman was able to turn the literary form inside out with the creation of the "Inverted Mystery Story", wherein the criminal is known from the beginning – the motive is explained, the planning and execution of the crime are observed, and the miscreant is left to believe that all is well and that he'll never be caught. And then, in the second part of the story, Thorndyke enters to inexorably follow the trail that is completely invisible to everyone else, scraping away, layer by layer and point by point, until the truth is inevitably revealed.

As Freeman explained:

> *Some years ago I devised, as an experiment, an inverted detective story in two parts. The first part was a minute and detailed description of a crime, setting forth the antecedents, motives, and all attendant circumstances. The reader had seen the crime committed, knew all about the criminal, and was in possession of all the facts. It would have seemed that there was nothing left to tell. But I calculated that the reader would be so occupied with the crime that he would overlook the evidence. And so it turned out. The second part, which described the investigation of the crime, had to most readers the effect of new matter.*

This format went on to be used by a great many authors through the years. For example several of the Lord Peter Wimsey narratives come close to being this type of story, and television's *Columbo* used this type of story-telling as its basis.

While these volumes are an attempt to reintroduce the modern reader to Thorndyke, and are a celebration of him and his world, it must be discussed at some point that Freeman held views that are unacceptable. Unlike Sir Arthur Conan Doyle, who spent his last decades championing spiritualism but never allowed it to creep into the Sherlock Holmes stories, Freeman sometimes did let his own prejudices make their way into the Thorndyke tales. In his book *Social Decay and Regeneration* (1921), he expressed his rather nationalistic view that England had become an "homogenized, restless, unionized working class". Worse, he inexcusably and detestably supported the eugenics movement, arguing that people with "undesirable" traits should not be allowed to reproduce by means such as "segregation, marriage restriction, and sterilization". He referred to immigrants as "Sub-Man", and argued that society needed to be protected from "degenerates of the destructive type."

Some have attempted to excuse his beliefs as being a product of his times. For instance, it has been written that he had a distrust of Jews because of the competition that his father, a tailor, had faced when Freeman was a boy. Later, he served in the Colonial Service in Africa during some of the worst years in terms of treatment of natives by the British, and as an older man, he existed in the Great Britain between the two wars when great upheavals disrupted much of what he had known and expected.

Sadly, there are occasional racial stereotypes and references in the Thorndyke books. As I explain in the *Editor's Caveat*, some of these stereotypes had to be unfortunately maintained within the story in order to accurately reflect the plot and the characters of those times. However, there are some words or phrases that were used in the original stories – vile racial epithets that have no business being repeated or perpetuated anywhere – that I have cheerfully and happily removed. (There weren't many of them, but any are too many.)

These books are intended to bring Dr. Thorndyke and his adventures to a new generation – and not to be an untouchable and sacred literary artifact, with every nasty stain preserved and archived for the historical record. As I warn in the *Caveat*, if readers find that they want to experience the original versions as they were first written, with those hateful words included, then they would be advised to go and seek out the original books, because you won't find that filth here. These versions celebrate Dr. Thorndyke and Dr. Jervis – who do not use the awful stereotyped language, I'm glad to say! – and as such, I felt no need whatsoever to include and perpetuate the objectionable and offensive material

From Thorndyke's creation until 1914, Freeman wrote four novels and two volumes of short stories. Then, with the commencement of the First World War, he entered military service. In February 1915, at the age of fifty-two, he joined the Royal Army Medical Corps. Due to his health, which had never entirely recovered from his time in Africa, he spent the duration of the war involved with various aspects of the ambulance corps, having been promoted very early to the rank of Captain. He wrote nothing about Thorndyke during this period, but he did publish one book concerning the adventures of a scoundrel, *The Exploits of Danby Croker* (1916).

Following the war, he resumed his previous life, writing approximately one Thorndyke novel per year, as well as three more volumes of Thorndyke short stories and a number of other unrelated items, until his death on September 28th, 1943 – likely related to Parkinson's Disease, which had plagued him in later years.

Upon learning the news, *Chicago Tribune* columnist Vincent Starrett wrote:

> *When all the bright young things have performed their appointed task of flatting the complexes of neurotic semi-literates, and have gone their way to oblivion, the best of the Thorndyke stories will live on – minor classics on the shelf that holds the good books the world.*

Raymond Chandler wrote in his famous essay, which initially appeared in a couple of magazines and then was published in the book of the same name, *The Simple Art of Murder* (1950):

> *This man Austin Freeman is a wonderful performer. He has no equal in his genre, and he is also a much better writer than you might think, if you were superficially inclined, because in spite of the immense leisure of his writing, he accomplishes an even suspense which is quite unexpected . . . There is even a gaslight charm about his Victorian love affairs, and those wonderful walks across London.*

In the introduction to *Great Stories of Detection, Mystery, and Horror* (1928), Dorothy L. Sayers, Chronicler of Lord Peter Wimsey, stated:

> *Thorndyke will cheerfully show you all the facts. You will be none the wiser . . . .*

Discovering Dr. Thorndyke

I first encountered Dr. Thorndyke in a rather backwards way – in passing only – and it took several decades to correct that mistake. In approximately 1980, my dad gave me Otto Penzler's *The Private Lives of Private Eyes, Spies, Crime Fighters, and Other Good Guys* (1977). This wonderful oversized book has biographies of twenty-five well-known heroes, along with lists of the original books featuring each one.

My dad bought it for me because it had a chapter about Sherlock Holmes. There were a few others in there that I recognized or had already read about– Ellery Queen and Perry Mason – and soon I would become fanatical about a few more – Nero Wolfe and Hercule Poirot. Over the next few years I would also find the chapters on James Bond and Lew Archer indispensable, and later than that I would come to appreciate the entries about Philip Marlowe, Sam Spade, Miss Marple, Philo Vance, and Lord Peter Wimsey. But there were a few that, to this day, I've never bothered to read – such as Modesty Blaise or Mr. Moto – and a few others that I skimmed but otherwise ignored. And one of these was the biography of Dr. Thorndyke.

That fact was easily understandable, as throughout the entire time that I was growing up in eastern Tennessee – and in the years since as well – I've never come across a Thorndyke book for sale here in the wild, either in a new bookstore or in a used one. If I'd found one, I might have bought and read it, liked it, and then sought out others. Instead, I was bound to discover Thorndyke by way of Sherlock Holmes.

I've been collecting traditional Sherlock Holmes pastiches since the same time that I discovered the Sherlockian Canon, when I was ten years old in 1975. Since that time, I've collected, read, and chronologicized literally thousands of them. It never gets old, and I'm constantly looking for more – and that means checking Amazon to see what new releases are on the horizon.

In 2012, someone – and I've never determined who – began releasing a variety of Holmes stories for Kindle under the author name *Dr. John H. Watson.* This wasn't too unusual – there have been a number of pastiches that officially list Watson as the author, rather than putting the editor of Watson's papers first. Of course, after determining that these latest entries weren't going to be available as real books, I bought the e-versions, and then printed them on real paper. (I cannot stand e-books – ephemeral electronic blips that you lease instead of buy. I'll only buy those titles if they aren't going to be released as legitimate books – and in this case, it's a good thing that I did, as each of these Kindle stories that I found and paid for were soon withdrawn.)

As I read these latest "Holmes" stories, I noticed that each had a definite style that captured the writing from the late 1800's or early 1900's. (No matter how modern pasticheurs try to achieve that, they never quite pull it off.) But in one of the first two or three titles that I read, I caught a couple of mistakes. In one story, Holmes and Watson leave 221 Baker Street and are immediately in the area around The Temple and Fleet Street, rather than in Marylebone, where Baker Street is properly located. On another occasion, the story's policeman – who had been identified up to that point as Inspector Lestrade – was inexplicably named *Superintendent Miller* – but only in one instance. And in another place in one of the stories, Holmes's address was stated to be *5A King's Bench Walk.*

It was then that some vague memory triggered in my head, and I realized why these stories had captured the style of the late Victorian and

22

early Edwardian eras: *It was because they had actually been written then*. I recalled – from reading Otto Penzler's book of biographies so long ago - that 5A King's Bench Walk belonged to Dr. Thorndyke, and not Sherlock Holmes. Someone was taking the original Thorndyke stories, which I had never before read, and simply changing names: Dr. Thorndyke, Dr. Jervis, and Superintendent Miller became Sherlock Holmes, Dr. Watson, and Inspector Lestrade, respectively.

Between 2012 and 2014, the anonymous author continued to load new Kindle editions on Amazon of Thorndyke-converted to-Holmes stories, and I continued to buy them. As soon as I had one, I would read it, and then try to figure out the original Thorndyke story from which it was taken. When I'd done so, I'd post a review, identifying what this editor was doing, from where he or she was taking the story, and urging that person, whoever it was, give credit to R. Austin Freeman instead of listing the author as Dr. John H. Watson.

Soon after each of my reviews would appear, the story would be withdrawn. I don't know if it was because the editor had made enough money from the initial sales, or if my reviews alerted him or her that they're game had been uncovered. In any case, I still have the printed copies of each of these converted stories – possibly the only copies that are still in existence.

For the record, over that two year period, this editor produced sixteen converted tales – four of the original Thorndyke novels, and twelve short stories. One of the original short stories, "The Mandarin's Pearl", was converted twice, with slight variations – initially published as "The Dragon Pearl", withdrawn, and later revised and reloaded as "The Oriental Pearl":

- "The Bloodied Thumbprint" – Originally the first Thorndyke novel, *The Red Thumb Mark*;
- "The Eye of Ra" – Originally the second Thorndyke novel, *The Eye of Osiris*;
- "The Cat's Eye Mystery" – Originally the sixth Thorndyke novel, *The Cat's Eye*;
- "The Julius Dalton Mystery" – Originally the ninth Thorndyke novel, *The D'Arblay Mystery*;
- "The Green Jacket Mystery" – Originally "The Green Check Jacket";
- "Mr. Crofton's Disappearance" – Originally "The Mysterious Visitor";
- "The Coded Lock" – Originally "The Puzzle Lock";

23

- "The Duplicated Letter" – Originally "The Stalking Horse";
- "The Bullion Robbery" – Originally "The Stolen Ingots";
- "The Talking Corpse" – Originally "The Contents of a Mare's Nest";
- "The Blue Diamond Mystery" – Originally "The Fisher of Men";
- "The Dragon Pearl" – Originally "The Mandarin's Pearl". (This story was also reworked and published again as a Holmes story under the title "The Oriental Pearl");
- "The Ingenious Murder" – Originally "The Aluminium Dagger";
- "The Bloodhound Superstition" – Originally "The Singing Bone"; *and*
- "The Magic Box" – Originally "The Magic Casket".

For quite a while, I was happy to have these as Holmes stories, and I even considered converting the rest of the Thorndyke adventures into additions to the extended Holmes Canon as well. (For at that time I cared nothing for Dr. Thorndyke.) It was partly with these converted stories in mind that I was motivated to go ahead and publish *Sherlock Holmes in Montague Street* (2014, 2016), which did the same thing to the Martin Hewitt stories, making them early adventures of Holmes before he met Watson and moved to Baker Street. I had long before decided to my own satisfaction that Martin Hewitt *was* a young Sherlock Holmes, with his identity changed through the preparations of a different literary agent than Sir Arthur Conan Doyle.

The taking of old public-domain stories featuring other detectives as the main protagonists and switching them so that Holmes is the main character has also been done by Alan Lance Andersen for his collection *The Affairs of Sherlock Holmes* (2015, 2016), wherein various non-series Sax Rohmer stories from nearly a hundred years ago were reworked as Holmes tales. Other non-Holmes authors have sometimes done the same thing. Raymond Chandler revised some of his early short stories so that the original characters' names were changed to Philip Marlowe. Ross MacDonald – (Kenneth Millar) also rewrote his old stories as well, making them into Lew Archer cases instead. More recently, the British

ITV series *Marple* has taken non-Miss Marple Agatha Christie stories and converted them into episodes featuring that character.

So I had no problems with this type of change – and still don't. In fact, in my foreword to *Sherlock Holmes of Montague Street*, I wrote that I would rather have these converted Thorndyke stories as Holmes adventures, because I would rather read about Holmes than Thorndyke. But gradually my mind began to change, and I became more curious about Thorndyke, as presented in the proper fashion.

In 2013, I was able to go to London, as well as other places in England and Scotland, on the first (of three so far) Holmes Pilgrimages. For the most part, if a location wasn't related to Holmes, I didn't visit it. There were a few exceptions – I did intentionally visit Solar Pons's house at 7B Praed Street, Hercule Poirot's two residences, James Bond's flat in Chelsea – but everything else was pretty much pure Holmes.

One day, during my Holmesian rambles, I was making my way east down Fleet Street, and I visited both of the possible locations of "Pope's Court" (as featured in "The Red-Headed League"), Poppin's Court and Mitre Court. (The latter is also one of the locations where Denis Nayland Smith and Dr. Petrie had quarters in some of the Fu Manchu books.) I decided that Mitre Court was certainly the original of "Pope's Court", and I passed through it to find myself unexpectedly in The Temple.

That's the amazing thing about a Holmes Pilgrimage to London – one travels to a site and finds two more very close by. I had planned to visit The Temple, but hadn't realized that I was so close. And now here I was – and more interesting was the fact that I was walking along King's Bench Walk, which runs downhill from the Miter Court passage. I recalled that Thorndyke had lived at 5A, so I made my way there – but without too much awe on that day, because I hadn't actually read any Thorndyke adventures yet – just some converted Holmes stories.

After I returned home, the thought of that side-trip to Thorndyke's front door stuck in my mind, and I sought out and read the first novel in the series, *The Red Thumb Mark.* I was so impressed that I kept going, and discovered a wonderful series of books and stories – fascinating characters and mysteries, and very evocative descriptions of both the London and the countryside of those times.

When I returned on my second Holmes Pilgrimage in 2015, I took the second Thorndyke book with me, reading it while there – while also reading Holmes stories too, of course! This one, *The Eye of Osiris*, has a great deal of London atmosphere, and I spent part of one late afternoon tracking down locations in this book – or what's now left of them – in the area around Fetter Lane to the north of Thorndyke's home in The Temple. It was truly unforgettable.

And of course I made an intentional stop at King's Bench Walk on that 2015 trip, and again on Holmes Pilgrimage No. 3 in 2016. By that point I was a Thorndyke fan, and I took the trouble to write to the current occupiers of 5A before I traveled to see if I could step inside and perhaps spend a moment in Thorndyke's old quarters. Sadly, they did not respond – either because it was simply beneath them to do so, or possibly because they get too many people like me who want to make a literary pilgrimage to what is a functioning and thriving business location.

While making photographs at Thorndyke's old doorway, I had several chances to go inside when someone else would enter or leave – My ever-present deerstalker and I could have simply been bold enough to slip in and then talk my way onward. It worked at other places on my Holmes Pilgrimages – the laboratory at Barts where Holmes and Watson met, for instance, and the site of the (former?) Diogenes Club at No. 78 Pall Mall, where they acted just oddly enough to make me think that the club is still there. But for some reason, barging into Thorndyke's old chambers without proper permission didn't feel quite right. But if or when I make Holmes Pilgrimage No. 4, I'll definitely make an even greater effort to see the doctor's former rooms.

The Editor and his Deerstalker at 5A King's Bench Walk
September 2016

With many thanks . . . .

These last few years have been an amazing ride, and I've been able to play in the Sherlockian sandbox more than I'd ever imagined. (And subsequently, the Solar Pons sandbox, and now Thorndyke, too! Along the way, I've been able to meet some incredible people, both in person and in the modern electronic way, and also I've been able to read several hundred new Holmes adventures, as well as to be able to share them with others.

Still, what is most important is my amazingly wonderful wife (of over thirty years!) Rebecca, and our truly awesome son and my friend, Dan. I love you both, and you are everything to me! I am the luckiest guy in the world.

I have all the gratitude in the world for everyone that I've encountered along the way – It's an undeniable fact that Sherlock Holmes authors are the *best* people! I'd like to thank those who offer support, encouragement, and friendship, sometimes patiently waiting on me to reply as my time is directed in many other directions. Many many thanks to (in alphabetical order): Brian Belanger, Derrick Belanger, Bob Byrne, Roger Johnson, Mark Mower, Denis Smith, Tom Turley, Dan Victor, and Marcia Wilson.

In particular, I'd also like to especially thank Steve Emecz, who is always supportive of every idea that I pitch. It's been my particular good fortune that he crossed my path – it changed my life in a way that would have never happened otherwise, and I'm grateful for every opportunity!

I hope that these books will provide pleasure to those discovering Dr. Thorndyke for the first time, and to others who have known him for a long time. As always, I approach these matters from a Sherlockian perspective, so of course these stories, to me, are a peripheral extension of Holmes's world, and as such they are just more tiny threads woven into the ongoing Great Holmes Tapestry. However, they are wonderful on their own, and however one reads them, I wish great joy upon the journey.

David Marcum
(Revised October 2020)

Questions, comments, and story submissions
may be addressed to David Marcum at
thepapersofsherlockholmes@gmail.com

5A King's Bench Walk
in the late 1890's when
Thorndyke was in residence

Editor's *Caveat*

These stories have been prepared using modern text-converting software, and as such, occasional deviations in punctuation have occurred. Those who absolutely must have the original version, down to each jot and dash, should understand that this version was created in order to present Dr. Thorndyke's adventures to a modern audience, and not to preserve an absolute pristine model for the historical archives.

Similarly, these stories were written in a time when racial prejudice and stereotypes were much more common than today. While some of these stereotypes must be unfortunately maintained within the story in order to accurately reflect the plot and the characters of those times, there are some words that were used in the original stories – vile racial epithets that have no business being repeated or perpetuated anywhere – that I have cheerfully removed. (There weren't many of them, but *any* are *too many*.)

If readers find that they want to experience the original versions as they were first written, with those hateful and ignorant words included, then they would be advised to seek out the original books. These versions celebrate Dr. Thorndyke and Dr. Jervis – who do *not* use the awful stereotyped language, I'm glad to say! – and as such, I felt no need whatsoever to include objectionable and offensive material simply for the sake of honoring or archiving the historical record.

David Marcum
Editor

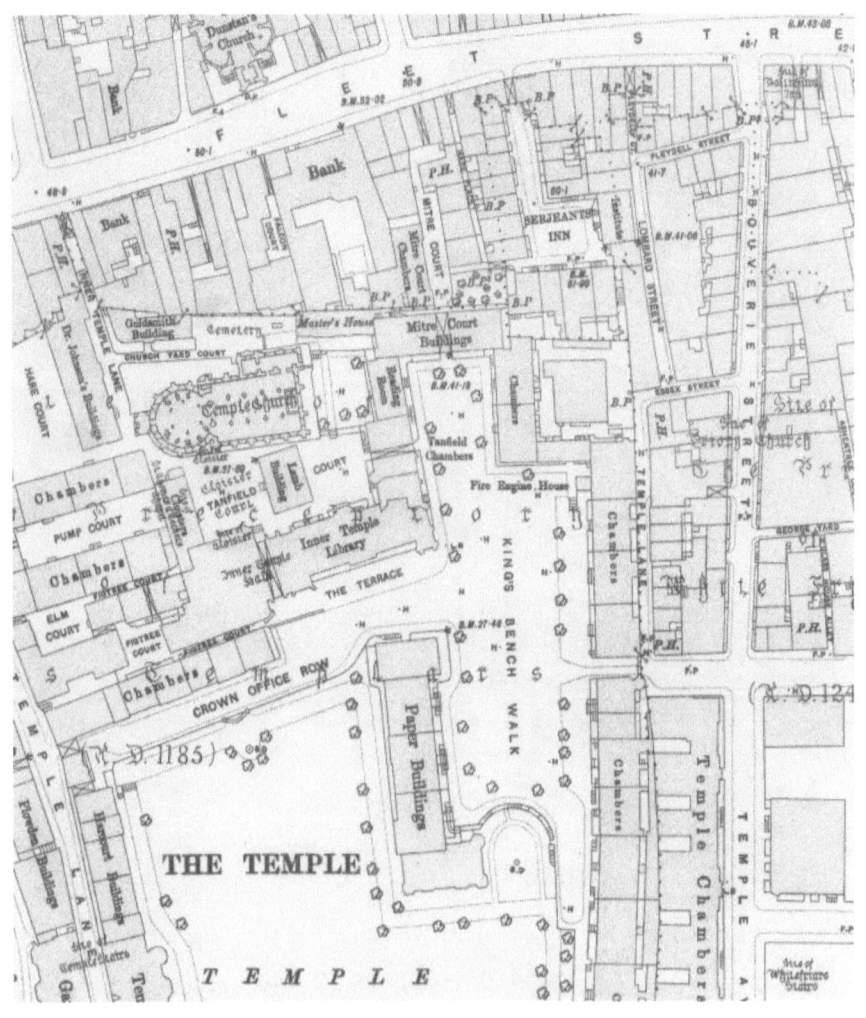

King's Bench Walk and the Temple, London
around 1900

33

FOR THE DEFENCE: DR. THORNDYKE

— and there, members of the jury, he watched unseen.

R.AUSTIN FREEMAN

1934 Hodder & Stoughton, London Cover

Chapter I
The Letter

It was about four o'clock on a summer afternoon when Andrew Barton, pipe in mouth and garden shears in hand, suspended for a moment his operations on the privet hedge in his front garden to glance down the lane at the postman, who had just turned into it from the road at the end. It was a glance of no special interest. He was not expecting any communication. But as there was no other house in the lane – which presently petered out into a foot-path across fields – it was obvious that his own residence was the goal of the postman's peregrinations.

He observed the man's approach intermittently, punctuating his observations with perfunctory snips at the hedge and speculating vaguely and incuriously on the source of the letter which the messenger was presumably coming to deliver. He was not particularly interested. Yet even a rural postman, though less portentous than the telegraph boy, embodies untold potentialities of good or evil, of joy or sorrow, of fortune or disaster. But Andrew was not particularly interested, and thus he watched, unmoved and unsuspecting, the approach of Fate's special messenger, charged with a message the significance of which was only by degrees to be unfolded.

The man strode up to the gate with a letter in his hand and ran his eye critically over the half-cropped hedge. "I see you are havin' a bit of a tidy-up, sir," he remarked as he handed the letter over the gate, "and none too soon. He was getting rare straggly. But Lord! How the stuff do grow in this weather! 'Tis out of bounds almost afore you've done a-trimmin' of it."

As Andrew showed no sign of rising to this conversational bait, beyond a vague assent, the postman wished him "Good afternoon", took another glance at the hedge, and turned back down the lane, a little disconcerted by Mr. Barton's unwonted taciturnity. "Didn't seem to like the look of that letter," he mused as he swung along in his heavy, nailed boots. "Someone dunning him for money, maybe."

It was a simple and reasonable explanation of the sudden change in Andrew's expression as he read the address on the envelope and glanced at the postmark, and not so very wide of the truth. But "dunning" was not quite the right word, since that implies a demand for payment of a lawful debt. Of such demands Andrew Barton had no experience, being a scrupulously prompt paymaster. But a glance at the too-familiar handwriting prepared him for a demand of another kind, and the only question was, "How much does he want this time?" He tore the envelope open with angry impatience and read the answer to that question.

16 Barleymow Street, Crompton-on-Sea. 21ˢᵗ August, 1928

My dear Old Chappie,

What a time it is since I had the felicity of looking at your blessed old mug! Years and years! I am just pining for the sight of you, and no doubt you are equally pining for the sight of me. I hope so. Because I am going to satisfy my yearning and I should like to satisfy yours at the same time. In short, I propose to pop over this day week and shed the light of my countenance on you and Molly. I shall turn up to lunch.

Your affectionate and devoted, though unfortunate cousin,

Ronald

P.S. I have just got the offer of a top-hole job in the North. £300 a year and commission. But the fly in the ointment is that they want me to deposit £50, and I haven't got it. I hope you will be able to help me to that extent, for it would be a thousand pities to miss a chance like this. Of course, I shall be able to let you have it back in a month or two, with five-per-cent interest if you like. Further particulars when we meet. By the way, if you should be writing to me, please address me as Mr. Walter Green. I am adopting that name temporarily, for business reasons. R.B.

Andrew read the letter through twice, returned it to its envelope, and put it away in his pocket-book. Then he resumed his operations on the hedge, with increased energy but diminished attention, whereby its symmetry was somewhat impaired but the job was more speedily completed. When the last savage snip had done its work, he hastily raked the cuttings together, conveyed them to the destructor in the back garden, and deposited the shears and the rake in the tool-shed. Then he sauntered down to the studio which he had built at the bottom of the garden and let himself in with his key. A half-finished picture stood on the water-colour easel, the palette, brushes and water-dipper reposed invitingly on the table alongside, and the Windsor chair seemed silently to offer its services. He sat down wearily. He even dipped a brush in the water. But it would not do. Painting is no occupation for a mentally preoccupied man. Finally he rose and, leaving the studio, walked up to the house, where he scribbled a note to his wife and laid it on the hall table – (They kept no maid, and the daily "help" had gone after lunch.) – put on his hat and went forth, turning to the right as he emerged from the gate and taking his way along the foot-path that led across the fields.

His cousin's letter had given him matter for serious and somewhat difficult thought. As to the money, the nominal loan – which would certainly never be repaid – was an inconvenience to a man of his modest means. But it was not that which disturbed him. He was used to being "milked" periodically by this thriftless scallywag, who was always in low water and always on the point of making his fortune. But these transactions had been conducted through the post. They involved no personal contact. It was the threatened visit that was the cause of his trouble and that gave him so difficult a problem to solve. For on one point he was resolved – that visit must not be allowed to take place. And furthermore, Molly must not become aware that it had been proposed. He would, if it must be, submit to the extortions of this wastrel, if not with pleasure, at least with resignation. But he would not have him in his house. And thereby hangs a tale which may as well be told now, to the end that the reader of this narrative may start with a clear understanding of all the circumstances.

Andrew Barton's life lay under the shadow of a tragedy. The origin of that tragedy was insignificant even to triviality. But so it is in the affairs of men, from the merest trifles consequences develop which bear no reasonable proportion to their determining antecedents. The chance burrowing of a mole robbed a nation of its king, a trivial error of our most remote ancestress *"Brought death into the world and all our woe."* The tragedy that darkened Andrew Barton's life was due to nothing more impressive than a misplaced cricket ball.

But on occasion, a cricket ball can be a formidable missile. This one, driven by a vigorous stroke of the bat, impinged with a terrific impact on Andrew's face between the eyes, just below the level of the brows, and laid him on the field insensible and gory. Perhaps something in the way of plastic surgery might have been done but, for a time, his condition was so critical as to occupy the whole of the doctor's attention in the effort to save his life, and when at length his recovery was assured it was too late. The fractured nasal bones had united firmly in their displaced position.

It was a tragedy indeed. The Andrew Barton who had gone to the cricket match was a rather strikingly handsome young man. The convalescent who came out of the hospital was one at whom the passing wayfarer cast one curious glance and then looked away. The fine Grecian nose was flattened level with the cheek-bones, excepting the uninjured tip, which jutted out from the face like a sparrow's beak.

The disfigurement alone was tragedy enough, especially to an artistic young man who had been accustomed to take an innocent pleasure in his own good looks. But his exaggerated disgust of his uncomely face and the self-consciousness that it engendered were not the worst results of the disaster. There was his wife. To do her justice, she made heroic efforts, in her pity and sympathy, to appear unaware of the change. But her efforts to seem not to notice the disfigurement were misinterpreted. To him, with his morbid conviction that he was a curiosity of hideousness, the fact that she seemed to avoid looking at his battered nose conveyed the impression that she could not bear the repulsive spectacle. In short, in respect of his personal appearance, Andrew suffered in an intense degree from what it is fashionable to call "an inferiority complex", and that complex led him to take a perverted view of his relations with his wife.

The marriage had been a typical love-match but, in its beginnings, very largely based on physical attraction. The beautiful girl and the handsome young man had fallen in love with each other's good looks which, as they were both amiable, kindly, and pleasant mannered, was not a bad start. But at that their relations had tended to remain. They continued to be lovers, mutually devoted, but the deeper comradeship of man and wife seemed slow to develop.

The fault was undoubtedly with Molly. Unconsciously, she made the fatal mistake of failing to enter into her husband's chief interest. Andrew was devoted to his art. She was aware of the fact and took it for granted, but she made no attempt to share his artistic interests. She admired his pictures, was pleased with the recognition that they received, and praised them in somewhat inexpert terms. Indeed, the rather naive and ignorant comments that she made jarred on him, so that he unobtrusively discouraged her from frequenting the studio. So she tended to live her woman's life apart, treating the studio and its activities as matters outside her province. The love and mutual admiration that had brought them together had continued unchanged and undiminished during their married life up to the time of the accident – nor was there, even then, any sign of a change. But still, they were little more than lovers.

Hence, it was not perhaps unnatural that, when the misfortune befell, Andrew should experience a certain sense of having failed to keep his covenant. Molly had married a handsome man and had given her beauty in exchange. And now the bargain was, on his side, unfulfilled. He still received, but had nothing to give. Still, he could delight in her loveliness and charm, but she must put up with a husband who was a monster of ugliness. It was rather unreasonable and perverse, and it was largely untrue. But that was what he felt. And he felt it bitterly.

But his fatal misadventure had yet another unfortunate effect, which brings us back to our story. Andrew had but one near relative – his cousin Ronald. Ronald, however, was a very near relative indeed. He was, in fact, a cousin twice over, for not only was his father a brother of Andrew's father, but his mother was a sister of Andrew's mother. In view of this double relationship, it is not surprising that the two men were a good deal alike. Actually they were as much alike as a pair of twins. But the remarkable resemblance was masked to some extent by the one point of difference. Andrew's nose had been of the straight, or Grecian type. Ronald's was curved on the bridge-a definite Roman nose. Now, a Roman nose imparts a very distinctive character to a face, particularly in profile, and hence this really trifling difference served effectually to disguise the fact that these two men were almost identically alike.

Nor was the resemblance limited to the facial characteristics. As in the case of twins, it pervaded the whole personality. They were of much the same colouring, stature, and figure. Their voices and intonations were recognizably similar, and even in those elusive muscular habits which express themselves in pose and gait, there was in each man a suggestion of the other.

Their mental similarity was less marked. But yet it was distinguishable. For Ronald was not devoid of artistic aptitude. He painted in a somewhat dilettante fashion, and could have done better if he had taken more trouble, and in other respects he showed a certain mental affinity to his cousin. But just as the almost uncanny physical resemblance was masked by a single salient dissimilarity, so, but in a much more marked degree, were the mental resemblances masked by a profound contrast in the moral qualities. It seemed as if, in Ronald, some "recessive" moral taint, which had lain dormant for a generation or two, had suddenly come to the surface. He was an undeniably "bad egg". To the precise, thrifty, conscientious Andrew, his thriftless, slippery cousin was an object of puzzled contempt and, moreover, a source of constant anxiety. For Ronald Barton was an inveterate cadger, a confirmed borrower and, as is the way of the habitual borrower, as soon as the loan

41

had been obtained, the transaction was finished and the incident closed so far as he was concerned. Thus it happened that at the end of each year, Andrew found his bank balance substantially eaten into by the "trifling loans" that this plausible rascal had wheedled out of him.

But, as we have already hinted, it was not the drain on his resources that was troubling him now. He had accepted Ronald – his only near kinsman – as a sort of troublesome younger brother and was resigned to his extortions. What was disturbing him so profoundly was the fear that he might not be able to stave off the proposed visit. He loathed the very idea of having his cousin under his roof, and especially did he loathe the idea of any association between Ronald and Molly.

That was the real trouble. It was not that he was in general a jealous man or that he had the slightest mistrust of his wife. But he distrusted Ronald profoundly. Of that gentleman's mode of life he knew nothing, but he suspected a good deal. And he was very clearly convinced that this shabby knave was no fit associate for Molly. And there were certain special reasons why he disliked the idea of their meeting.

They had met twice. The first time was shortly after the wedding, and then, Andrew had been not displeased by Molly's warm admiration of his cousin. For Ronald was an undeniably fine-looking young man, and he had been on his best behaviour.

But the second meeting had been a very different affair. The experience had been one of which Andrew could not bear to think. It had occurred soon after the accident, when the "inferiority complex" was at its worst, and Andrew had found himself constantly following Ronald with his eyes, noting with envy the strikingly handsome face and the swaggering, confident carriage, and contrasting them with his own hideousness and insignificance. And he suspected that Molly was making a like comparison, and he knew that Ronald was. For on this occasion, that gentleman had been somewhat less discreet. Ostentatiously respectful, with a certain oily civility, he was nevertheless disposed to assert the privileges of cousinship with an insinuating familiarity that made Andrew squirm. And beneath his deferential manner there seemed a sinister suggestion of a new consciousness of power – a suggestion that he had discovered a new way to put on the screw if the need should arise. Andrew had then and there determined that he should never come into the house again.

To that resolution he still held firmly. But the problem that he had to solve was how, decently, to evade the proposed visit. He could not write bluntly refusing it and, even if he did, the thick-skinned Ronald would pretty certainly come, notwithstanding. In any case, there would be a letter in reply, which Molly would probably see, and then he would have to tell her of the proposal, and it would be difficult to explain his objection. But he wanted to keep the whole affair from her knowledge. In this he was, perhaps, unwise. It would certainly have been simpler to accept the visit and prepare Molly with a few words of advice and caution. But he could not do it. Deep down in his soul was a feeling that bade him keep Ronald completely out of her life.

Thus he turned his difficulties over and over as he strode along the foot-path through the fields. And gradually a plan shaped itself in his mind. It was quite a simple one. He would first send Ronald a postcard acknowledging his letter but making no comment. Then, on the day before that of the proposed visit he would send a letter stating that he had some business in Crompton – which was only thirty miles distant – and would call on Ronald to talk over the financial situation. There would be no time for an answer to his letter and, if he agreed to the "loan" – which experience told him he probably would – the matter would be settled and the reason for the unwelcome visit would cease to exist.

There was only one detail at which he boggled. If he went to Crompton, he would be away from home all day, and he would have to give Molly some sort of explanation of his absence. And it could not be a true explanation. It seemed a small matter, but Andrew hated the making of a directly untrue statement at any time, and especially did he hate the idea of telling his wife a lie. However, it seemed that there was no choice. The only way in which his day's absence from home could be simply and naturally explained would be by saying that he was going up to London to show some of his work to a dealer, and that was the course that he decided to adopt.

When he arrived home, he found, rather to his relief, that Molly had not yet returned. With his decision fresh in his mind, he went straight to the writing table in the sitting-room and wrote a brief note to Ronald, acknowledging his letter. Having sealed and stamped it, he dropped it into his pocket, ready for posting later, and then went into the little kitchen to make preparations for tea. But still, as he filled the kettle and set it on the gas ring, collected the tea-things and arranged them on the tray, his perplexities and the plans he had made to solve them continued to revolve in his mind as a sort of background to his present occupation. Impatiently, he tried to dismiss them. He had decided what to do, and further thought was but a useless, purposeless travelling back and forth over the same ground. But the emotional jar that Ronald's letter had inflicted, with its vivid revival of unpleasant memories, had disturbed him profoundly and, strive as he would to concentrate his attention on what he was doing, he could not silence the running accompaniment of futile reflection. Nevertheless, he carried out his task quite efficiently and

43

with careful consideration of Molly's very definite views on the niceties of the tea-table. The embroidered tea-cloth was spread on the table in the sitting-room in exactly the correct manner and garnished with little top-heavy flower glasses, artfully disposed so as to develop the maximum of inconvenience and liability to capsize. The tray, symmetrically set with its proper appointments – excepting the teapot and hot-water jug, which lurked in the kitchen awaiting the co-operation of the kettle – was placed at the head of the table. Biscuit box, cake basket, butterdish, jam and preserve jars, and other minor articles of "family plate" were posted with the strictest regard to their customary stations (and with no regard at all to the fact that the biscuit box was empty and there was no cake). In Molly's mind the "five o'clock tea" tradition still lingered, and the occasion was one of some ceremony.

When he had laid the table, Andrew surveyed his work critically and, having decided that all was in order, proceeded to cut some wafery slices of brown bread and butter, which he adroitly rolled up into little sausage-like scrolls. Of these he prepared quite an imposing pile, in view of Molly's partiality for them and of the fact that she usually returned from her expeditions in a state of ravenous hunger. (She had gone over for an afternoon's shopping to the little town of Bunsford, some two miles away.)

At length he laid down his knife and, having taken a glance at the kettle, went out to the garden gate and looked down the lane. His wife had just turned into it from the road and was now advancing briskly with an enormous parcel in either hand and a smaller one tucked under her arm. For a moment he was disposed to run and meet her and relieve her of her burdens but, experience having taught him that Molly's parcels usually ran to bulk rather than weight, he turned back into the house, leaving the garden gate and the front door ajar, and went to the kitchen to make the tea.

He had just placed the silver teapot and hot-water jug on the tray when he heard her coming up the garden path, whistling cheerfully to announce her approach. He went out into the hall to welcome her and, when she had held up her face for the customary kiss, she tenderly deposited her parcels on the hall table. "You seem to have been going it," Andrew remarked, with an eye on the parcels.

"I have," she admitted. "I've had a lovely time – a regular beano. They were simply giving the things away, so, of course, economy suggested that one should take the opportunity. And I did. I've bought no end of things. You shall see what I have brought with me, presently. The rest are being sent. Do I smell tea? I hope so, for I am simply starving."

She entered the sitting-room and stood for a moment regarding the arrangements with smiling approval. "How nicely you've laid the table, Andy!" she exclaimed. "And, my word! What a heap of roly-polys you've cut."

She picked one up and bit off half. Then she continued, with slightly impaired enunciation, "There are some pastries in a box on the hall table. Puffs and things. I hope I haven't squashed them under my arm. I was nearly eating them in the train. Shopping does make you hungry."

Andrew fetched in the box and transferred its contents – bilious little tarts and cakes and three-cornered puffs, apparently produced with the aid of a pair of bellows – to the cake-basket. Then he lifted Molly's hat off – it came off quite easily, being of the coalscuttle-extinguisher type then in vogue – while she placidly poured out the tea with one hand and fed herself with the other, continuing her cheerful babbling, punctuated with mastication.

Andrew sat down at the table and, as he sipped his tea, looked thoughtfully at his wife. Perhaps a little furtively, too, with an unpleasant and guilty consciousness of the letter in his pocket. But principally his mind was occupied, half-unconsciously, in admiring contemplation of his beautiful wife. Her charm seemed to him always new, as something freshly discovered. To look at her was a pleasure that never staled. It was not only that he was as much, or even more, in love with her as ever, but as an artist, and a figure-painter at that, he was peculiarly sensitive and appreciative of human beauty, and especially the beauty of women. "So you've had a good day's sport," said Andrew.

"Rather!" she replied, in a tone of deep satisfaction. "Of course, Bunsford is not like London, but there are quite a lot of good shops there. And didn't I turn them upside down! And didn't I make the money fly! You'll have to hurry up and sell some more pictures or we shall be on the rocks."

Now, Andrew knew quite well that this was all nonsense. Molly's little raids on the Bunsford shops were dissipations of the most inexpensive sort. She never nearly spent the hundred pounds a year that had come to her on her father's death. Nevertheless, he seized the opportunity. "Yes," said he, "it is about time I raked in some fresh supplies. There are one or two small things that I have got on hand, ready for the market. I must take them up to Montagu and turn them into cash."

"You needn't, Andy," she said, with one of her delightful dimpling smiles. "I was only joking. I didn't really spend much, and I've got quite a lot in the bank."

"I know, dear," he replied. "I wasn't such a mug as to take you seriously. But still, I think I may as well take those things up to Monty.

45

It's no use keeping stuff in the studio cupboard. I think I will go up one day next week, probably Tuesday."

She made no comment on this proposal, and their talk drifted into other channels. After tea she produced the two hats – the principal spoils of the raid – and exhibited them to Andrew, who looked at them as Lord Dundreary looked at the chimpanzee, with surprise and incomprehension. (The feminine hat is usually outside the scope of the masculine intellect, and the hats of that period were beyond belief as things intentionally created.) Then Molly went about her lawful domestic occasions, and Andrew sneaked out to drop his letter into the post-box down in the village. It was a harmless letter, devoid of significance and committing him to nothing. Yet, as he held it in the slit of the post-box, he felt an unaccountable reluctance to let it go, and when at length he released it and heard it fall to the bottom of the box, he had the sense of having done something portentous and irrevocable.

Chapter II
Alarums and Excursions

The days that followed slipped by slowly and wearily, charged for Andrew with anxiety and unhappiness. Unhappiness because he had, for the first time in his married life, a secret which he was withholding from Molly. And in his heart he felt that it was a discreditable secret, of which he would be ashamed if it should ever leak out. This was the chief occasion of his anxiety. For there was the chance that something might upset his plan and, if it did, he would have to explain. But what could he say? To Molly it would appear as if he distrusted her, and who could say that she would be wrong? Was there not some distrust implied in his repugnance to her meeting Ronald? It was a dreadful thing to think of for, hitherto, the most perfect confidence had existed between him and his wife, and no woman could be more irreproachable in her conduct than Molly.

Still he went on making the few preparations that were necessary. From his bank at Bunsford he drew out fifty pounds in cash (paying in an equivalent cheque on his London bank) in case Ronald should be unable to deal with a cheque and, to meet the alternative case, he drew a cheque on the London account to the order of Ronald Barton, Esq., and put it in the attaché case that he kept in the studio cupboard. Then, with great care, he drafted the letter which he proposed to send to Ronald. He dated it the 26th of August – Sunday – though, in fact, he proposed to post it early on Monday, so that it should be delivered on Monday evening or by the first post on Tuesday morning – in either case in time to prevent Ronald from coming, but not in time to allow of a reply. It was but a short letter and, in its final form, ran thus:

Willow Cottage, Fairfield
26th August, 1928

My dear Ronald,

It happens by a fortunate chance that I have to run over to Crompton on business. I say "fortunate" because we shall have certain matters of a rather private nature to discuss and we can do that better in your rooms than here.

I don't know quite how long my business will take, but I shall turn up at your diggings punctually at one o'clock, when we may, perhaps, go somewhere and get some lunch, before beginning our discussions.

Yours ever,
Andrew

It was not without some qualms that he concocted this mendacious epistle, and when he had finished it and addressed and stamped the envelope, he hid it away securely in the attaché case until the time should come for posting it. Finally, into the same receptacle he put one or two small and trivial paintings-little more than sketches-which he had hardly thought worth offering to his dealer. Of course, he was not going to offer them now. Their presence in the attaché case was merely a concession to sentiment. He didn't want to tell more lies than were absolutely necessary.

Now that he had made all his preparations, it would have seemed reasonable for him to dismiss the matter from his mind until the time for action should arrive. But this he was quite unable to do. The emotional upset, which was at the root of the whole rather foolish business, kept his mind unsettled and exaggerated the effect of his guilty consciousness of his secret and his anxiety lest some unforeseen hitch should occur. The result was that he found himself everlastingly revolving the details of his plan, considering what he should say to Ronald and what he should do if, by any disastrous chance, his scheme should miscarry and his deception should become known to Molly.

In order to be alone and free to think his futile thoughts, he spent much of his time in the studio. He tried to work. He had a rather important picture well started and, in his normal state of mind, it would have been easy and pleasant to carry on. But after a single attempt he had to desist for fear of spoiling what he had already done.

In the evenings, his restlessness and a curious shyness of his wife's society drove him out to stride impatiently across the fields or along the little-frequented road, chewing the cud of useless and purposeless reflection. He had better have stayed at home and listened to Molly's cheerful gossip, for thereby he would have avoided a world of trouble. But no man can foresee the little surprises that Fate has in store for him, and so it was that Andrew, taking his way along the darkening road, walked straight into the ambush that chance had prepared.

48

The week had nearly run out, for it was the Monday evening, the evening before the appointed day of his visit to Crompton, when he set forth in his old studio jacket, hatless and unadorned by the spectacles that he wore in more populous places to mitigate the effects of his disfigurement, to tramp along the road and think out once again the details of his proceedings on the morrow. He had posted his letter to Ronald in time for the eleven o'clock collection, and everything was ready for his journey. By this time to-morrow, he thought, his difficulties would be over. He would have paid out the money, have disposed of his wastrel cousin, and would be free to take up again the normal course of his life.

Thus preoccupied he swung along, taking little note of his surroundings. At long intervals the head-lights of an approaching car started out of the gathering gloom, glared on him for a moment, and were gone, or overtaking him, cast his attenuated shadow along the lighted surface of the road with increasing intensity until it culminated in an instant of dazzle, a whizz, a hum of mechanism, and a dwindling red light fading into the darkness.

It was at the cross roads, known locally as Kibble's Cross, that the incredible affair happened. Preoccupied as he was, a stationary car drawn up at the corner of the side road made little impression on him, though he saw it and could hear the engine running, and was dimly aware of two men lurking near the car. But wrapped in his own thoughts, he gave them but a passing, inattentive glance and straightway forgot their existence. A few moments later, a bright light streamed past him from behind, then a car came abreast of him and drew up abruptly with a shriek of the brakes and an irritable voice demanded, "Well, what is it?"

Andrew gazed in astonishment at the speaker – a hard-faced elderly man who appeared to be addressing him – and stepped up to the open window to ask what he meant. As he put his head in at the window, the light of an electric torch flashed full in his face, but in spite of the dazzling light he could see that the man had his other hand thrust into his hip pocket. He could also see a middle-aged woman grasping the driving wheel and staring at him with an expression of consternation. He was about to put his question – in fact he had begun to speak – when he felt both his wrists seized in a vice-like grip and held together behind his back. Simultaneously, a hand grasping a pistol was thrust over his shoulder and a voice from behind him commanded, "Put 'em up. Both of you."

Exactly what happened during the next few seconds Andrew never clearly knew. As he felt his wrists grasped, he struggled to turn round and became aware of two men whose faces were hidden by black masks.

At the same moment, the man in the car made a quick movement with his farther hand. An instant later there was a double report with the sound of shattering glass, a piercing scream from the woman, a grinding noise from the engine, and the car leaped forward. In another moment it had gathered speed and was receding swiftly into the darkness. As the reports rang out, Andrew felt his wrists released and, turning quickly, he saw the two men running furiously towards their car and heard a whimpering voice exclaim, "You blasted fool! Couldn't you see it was the wrong man? And you've done him in."

Andrew stood, bewildered and half-stupefied, looking at the retreating bandits. They were still talking excitedly but he could not hear what they were saying. Soon they reached their car, tumbled in hurriedly, and slammed the door. Again, there was a grinding sound, the car started forward, turned up the side road, and was quickly lost to sight between the hedgerows. The hum of the engine soon died away and Andrew was left standing alone in the silence of the deserted road.

He tried to collect his scattered wits and to realize what had happened. It was an astounding affair. The audacity of these ruffians in attempting a highway robbery in the presence of a witness seemed amazing. Yet, but for the circumstance that the passenger in the car had been armed, it might easily have been done. The presence of an unarmed stranger would have offered no hindrance to two armed and masked men.

But what had really happened? Was it true that that stern-faced elderly man had been "done in", or was this only a frightened man's conjecture? Almost certainly the latter, for there had been no time to ascertain the effects of the shot. Perhaps there was no harm done, after all, beyond the smashing of the wind-screen. Meanwhile, the question arose as to what he ought to do. At first he was disposed to hurry back to Fairfield and give information to the police, but on reflection, that seemed a futile thing to do for, long before he could reach the village, the woman who was driving the car would have reported the outrage to the police at the next town. Moreover, there was no police station at Fairfield and only a police patrol who was sent out to the village from Bunsford. Finally, he decided to notify the police at Bunsford on the morrow, though even that would be of little use, seeing that he would be totally unable to identify either of the men or give any description of them.

While he had been turning these questions over in his mind, he had been retracing his steps along the road, for the shock that he had sustained had effectually diverted his thoughts from his domestic troubles and the solitary countryside ceased to attract him. Presently he came to a stile at the entrance to a foot-path which led in a nearly straight line to the village. Here he paused for a few moments and looked back

50

along the road. In the far distance the head-lights of a car appeared as bright sparks of light on the dark background. He watched them, as he stood with one foot on the lower step of the stile, with a feeling of faint dislike. At the moment, the idea of a motor-car seemed to have unpleasant associations. After looking for a few seconds at the distant lights, which grew brighter as he looked, he mounted the stile and, stepping down on to the foot-path, set forth on the short cut across the fields.

There was no lack of matter for conversation with Molly that night. As he poured out the thrilling story of his adventure, she almost lost interest in the hat, on which she was performing some kind of minor operation, in the wonder and horror of the tale. "But what impudence and bravado!" she exclaimed. "They seem to have gone on just as if you hadn't been there."

"I shouldn't have been much good in any case," said Andrew. "They were probably both armed. At any rate one of them was, and he was pretty ready with his pistol."

"Yes," said she. "I am glad you weren't able to interfere. You might have been lying dead at this moment. I wonder if that poor man in the car was really killed."

"I hope not," said Andrew, "but I am afraid he was hit. He could hardly fail to have been, seeing that the muzzle of the pistol was within a foot of him. I suppose I had better drop in to-morrow morning at the police station at Bunsford and give my name and address in case they want to call me as a witness."

Molly laid down her work and looked at him anxiously. "Do you know, Andy," she said, "I don't think I would if I were you. Why say anything about it to anybody? You have got nothing to tell that would help the police. You wouldn't know the men again if you saw them. It is a horrible affair. There may have been murder done. Don't you think it would be better for you to keep right out of it? Nobody knows that you were there, and nobody need ever know."

"The woman in the car saw me, you know," said Andrew.

"Yes," retorted Molly, whisking about with that mental agility which is the peculiar gift of woman, "and she probably took you for one of the gang. And if she did, she will swear through thick and thin that you were. You know how positive women are when they have got an idea into their heads."

He did – Molly, herself, having contributed some striking instances – and he realized that she had put her finger on the one possible complication. Nevertheless, he did not like the idea of lying low when it was certain that inquiries would presently be made. "Well," she urged, when he pointed this out, "wait till they are made, and see what sort of inquiries they are. If the police advertise for the witness who saw the attack, you can come forward. In the meantime, keep your own counsel, and don't go out of the house without your spectacles."

The serious view that she took of the matter tended to transfer itself to him, though the conclusion of their talk still left the question unsettled in his mind. But as to the wisdom of her advice in regard to the spectacles he had no doubt. Until he announced himself, he had better remain unrecognized. And the spectacles were a very efficient disguise, having, in fact, been designed expressly for that purpose. The horn rims enclosed lenses which were virtually plain glass, to offer the least possible obstruction to Andrew's excellent vision. The part of them which really functioned was the bridge, which was provided with a broad, saddle-shaped guard of flesh-coloured celluloid which occupied the hollow where the bridge of the nose should have been and, to a great extent, concealed the deficiency. He almost invariably wore them out of doors, and it was due only to the failing light and his mentally disturbed state that he had gone out this evening without them.

The morning found him still undecided as to what he should do, though Molly renewed her admonitions during breakfast. But now the unpleasant business that he had in hand once more began to occupy his thoughts to the exclusion of everything else. The guilty consciousness of the deception that he was practising on his wife worried him intensely and made him impatient to be gone. Immediately after breakfast, he fetched his attaché case-packed in readiness on the previous day-from the studio, put on his spectacles, and made ready to depart. "I suppose, dear," said Molly, as she accompanied him to the outer door and gave him a farewell kiss, "you won't be very late home to-night?"

"I don't expect to be," he replied. "Still, you had better not stay up if I am not home by about ten."

With this he kissed her again and, turning away, strode briskly down the path. At the gate he looked back and waved his hand. Then he started at a good pace towards the station, with a sense of relief at having got so far without a mishap. Only a few hours more, now, and he would be clear of his worries and would be his own man again. And once again as he swung along, he debated whether he should or should not call at Bunsford Police Station.

But the question was decided for him by circumstance. As the train on the little branch line from Fairfield drew up in Bunsford Station, he found that a train from London to Crompton was signalled and already in sight down the line. It was a full three-quarters-of-an-hour earlier than the one that he had intended to travel by and would bring him to

Crompton that much before his time. Nevertheless, in his impatience to get clear of his own neighbourhood, he welcomed it, and hurried across to the booking office. A couple of minutes later, the train drew up at the platform. It was only moderately full and he was able to secure a first-class smoking compartment to himself. While the train lingered in the station, he peered out anxiously, but no one came to disturb the solitude for which he yearned. At length, the guard's whistle sounded and the train began to move.

He heaved a deep sigh of relief, and as the train gathered speed he proceeded deliberately to fill his pipe. Then he took out Ronald's letter from his letter-case, read it through slowly from the address to the signature, and tore it into minute fragments, which he allowed to flutter out of the window. Then he opened his attaché case and carefully checked its contents, and when he had done this, he leaned back, relighted his pipe, and once more began to revolve in his mind the problem of how he should deal with Ronald.

The money question did not trouble him appreciably. He had in the attaché case in two blank envelopes, a cheque for fifty pounds drawn to Ronald's order, and a bundle of fifty pound notes. He took it for granted that one of those two envelopes would be transferred to Ronald – preferably the cheque or, if it had to be the notes, he would tear up the cheque and cancel the counterfoil. That was all plain sailing and, though it irked him to pour his earnings into the bottomless pocket of this worthless spendthrift, he would accept the loss with resignation. The real problem was how to keep Ronald away from Fairfield. Supposing that even after the money had been paid, he should persist in his intention of making the visit? What was to be done? Could Andrew tell him bluntly that his presence would not be acceptable? It would be very uncomfortable. And even so, Ronald was uncommonly thick-skinned.

He would not be easily put off if he wanted to come . . . It was a difficult problem, and Andrew had not solved it satisfactorily when the train rolled into the station at Crompton and came to rest at the platform.

Chapter III
In the Midst of Life

Andrew's first proceeding on coming out of the station was to make inquiries at the baker's shop, which was also a post office, for the address of a picture dealer. Of course he knew that there would be no picture dealer, as he understood the term, in a town like Crompton, nor had he any expectation of transacting any business whatever. The inquiry, like the pictures in his attaché case, was a mere concession to sentiment. He had told Ronald that he had business in Crompton, and he felt that he must make some pretence of business. It was mere foolish make-believe, and he knew it, but to a man habitually truthful, as he was, there is perhaps a shade of difference between a statement, true in the letter though false in the spirit, and one without even a foundation of truth. At any rate, that was how he felt about it. "A picture dealer," the woman in the shop repeated, reflectively, "I don't know of any regular picture dealer In Crompton. There's Mr. Cooper in the High Street, he sells pictures. He calls himself a carver and gilder. He's the only one I know of."

"I expect he will do," said Andrew, with literal truth this time and, having thanked the woman, he went forth in search of the High Street and Mr. Cooper.

The former was found easily enough, and the latter after a very brief exploration. Andrew stood for a while outside the shop and examined the contents of the window. There were a few brushes and tubes of colour, several empty frames and half-a-dozen "original water colours". As the most ambitious of these was priced at eighteen shillings the pair, including the frames, the prospect of any business grew still more remote. Nevertheless, Andrew entered the shop and, by way of breaking the matter gently, began with the request for a tube of Winsor and Newton's cobalt. When this had been handed to him, he laid his attaché case on the counter and opened his "business". "Do you do anything in the way of buying pictures?" he asked.

Mr. Cooper was cautious. "I don't buy a lot," said he, "but I am always ready to look at samples. Have you got any with you?"

Andrew opened his case and produced his "samples", which the dealer took in his hands and looked at suspiciously. "Are these originals?" he asked. "They look like reproductions."

"No," replied Andrew, "they are originals – my own work."

54

Mr. Cooper examined them again with renewed interest. After a prolonged inspection, he inquired, "How much?"

"Five guineas each," Andrew replied.

The dealer stiffened and cast a startled glance at the artist. "Did you say five guineas *each*?" he demanded, incredulously.

Andrew repeated the statement, whereupon the dealer hastily deposited the paintings in the open attaché case and shook his head sadly but emphatically. "I don't say they may not be worth it," said he, "but I have to sell pictures cheap, and find the frames myself. Five shillings a drawing is my outside price."

Andrew was not surprised or disappointed. The interview had served its purpose. It had been a business transaction and had conferred a quality of literal truth on his statement to Ronald. Satisfied with this make-believe, he repacked his pictures and closed his attaché case. Then, after a few minutes' amicable chat with the dealer, he wished him "Good morning" and took his leave.

His premature arrival at Crompton left him with a full hour to dispose of before keeping his tryst at Ronald's lodgings. He was not inclined to call there before he was due, with the chance of finding his cousin absent and being brought into undesired contact with the landlady and, moreover, he still had the foolish urge to consider over again what he would say to Ronald at the coming interview. Accordingly, he spent the time rambling up and down the streets, looking with rather wandering attention into the shop windows and examining the general features of the town.

First he proceeded to ascertain the whereabouts of the street in which his cousin lived and, having found it, to locate approximately the Number 16. Barleymow Street was a respectable though rather shabby street, mostly consisting of private houses with a few shops. Near one end was an archway leading into a kind of alley and above the arch was a blue lamp bearing the words, "*Police Station*", while, on the space of wall beside the arch was a large board covered with printed bills containing announcements of *Persons Missing*, *Wanted*, or *Found Drowned*, and other similar police notices. Here he lingered for a while, reading these rather gruesome advertisements and once more considering irresolutely whether he ought not to step in and make his report of the incident of the previous night.

It was a more momentous question than he realized, but, fortunately, he took the right decision, though whether that decision was due to Molly's admonitions or his preoccupation with his present business it is impossible to say. At any rate, he decided to wait until he was back in his own neighbourhood and turned away in search of further objects of interest.

Such an object he found near the opposite end of the street, and the oddity of it diverted his attention for the moment from his immediate anxieties and preoccupations. It was in a large window – a sort of hybrid between a shop and a private house – and consisted of a hand-written placard executed in bold Roman capitals announcing that these premises were occupied by no less a person than Professor Booley, late of Boston, U.S.A. (popularly believed to be the hub of the universe). It set forth that the said Professor was a specialist in the beautification of the Human Countenance, and gave in emphatic and even dictatorial terms a number of items of advice coupled with reasoned suggestions. Thus:

Good looks are the surest passports to success.

If nature hasn't given them to you,
Come in and let me make good her failure.

Why have eyebrows all awry when
the specialist can set them fair and even?

Why have a wrinkled face? Don't.

Come right in and have your skin
made smooth as a baby's.

Why have a crooked nose?
Don't. Let me straighten it out.

Don't be content with a back seat
because you were born homely.

Come into my parlor and be made fit
for a place in the front row.

Andrew stood before the window, reading these adjurations and commands with a faint smile, in which, however, there was more of wistfulness than amusement. Doubtless, the Professor was a quack of the deepest dye, but he had set forth a truth of which no one could be more sensible than the spectacled reader who stood before the window. Dimly as he had realized the value of good looks when the precious gift was his,

his loss had made it but too clear. What most men experience only with advancing years, he had experienced in the hey-day of his manhood.

He sauntered on, musing whimsically on the Professor's procedure. How did that redoubtable operator go about smoothing out wrinkles? A flat iron hardly seemed to meet the case. And how did he straighten out a crooked nose? The question evoked a ridiculous picture of the Professor tapping out the patient's proboscis on an anvil, or bringing it to a straight line by means of a screw clamp. If only the Professor's claims could be taken seriously! Though to be sure, even Professor Booley had not claimed to be able to create a new nose on the foundations of one that had been battered out of existence.

Slowly his saunterings and shop-gazings consumed the time, as he noted by an occasional glance at his watch, and punctually at two minutes to one he turned again into Barleymow Street. There was no need for him to check the numbers afresh for, at the middle of the street, where he had located Number Sixteen, his cousin was already waiting, slowly pacing up and down before his doorway, and at the moment with his back turned towards Andrew. Then he swung round and, catching sight of his cousin, started forward briskly with a smile of recognition and greeting.

As the two men approached, they regarded each other critically, and Andrew noted with something like a pang of envy what a really fine-looking man his cousin was. Such a man as he, himself, had been but a year or two ago. "Here you are, then," said Ronald, grasping his hand effusively, "punctual to the minute as usual. You ought to have been a business man instead of an artist."

"There is no reason why one should not be both," said Andrew.

"Answered with your customary wisdom," rejoined Ronald. "And, speaking of business, have you polished off the little affair that brought you to the unlikely region of Crompton-on-Sea?"

As he asked the question, Ronald's face exhibited a faint smirk which brought an angry flush to his cousin's cheek. Obviously, Ronald was slightly sceptical of the business appointment, but he might have kept his scepticism to himself. "Yes," Andrew replied, "it didn't take more than a few minutes."

"I hope you brought off the deal," said Ronald.

"No," replied Andrew, "there was nothing doing – at least, not at my price. Better luck next time, perhaps. Do you know of a likely place where we can get some lunch?"

"I know a place that will suit us exactly," answered Ronald. "But you won't want to lug that attaché case about with you all day. We shall probably go for a walk after lunch. Shall I plant it in my digs until you want it again?"

Andrew accepted the suggestion gladly, having already had enough of the case, and handed it to Ronald, who let himself into the house with a latchkey and disappeared for a few moments. When he reappeared, he linked his arm in Andrew's and led him a way in the direction of the approved restaurant, which was situated at the farther end of the High Street and turned out to be a place of some pretensions. As they walked, Ronald chatted with the easy volubility of an accomplished salesman or cheap-jack on every subject but the one which was the occasion of their meeting, while Andrew listened half-impatiently but with a certain grim amusement. He knew this trick of Ronald's of old. That slippery gentleman could never be brought to make a plain statement of the circumstances which called for the particular loan which he happened to be seeking. Instead, he managed with really remarkable skill to keep up a sort of conversational solo on all kinds of indifferent topics, always discreetly avoiding the one concerned with the financial transaction.

On this occasion, he got an excellent start as they passed the arched opening that led to the police station for, at that moment, a bare-headed policeman was engaged in sticking a new bill on the notice board. They had only a glimpse of it in passing, but they were able to see that it was headed in bold type: "*Wanted for Murder*". That bill furnished Ronald with material for discourse – one could hardly call it conversation – until they reached the restaurant.

Andrew made no attempt to counter these manoeuvres. In a contemptuous way he was slightly amused by his cousin's evasions, and he had no curiosity as to the "top hole opening" which was the nominal occasion of the need for fifty pounds. Probably it was a myth covering some gambling transaction. That was really of no consequence. He had brought the money with him and he knew that presently he would hand it over. The only thing that mattered was that there should be no arrangement for a visit to Fairfield.

The lunch was a complete success. Andrew, himself, was pretty sharp-set, and Ronald's exploits suggested a recent period of abstemiousness. In fact, his concentration on alimentary activities hindered his conversation to an extent that enabled Andrew to get in a question or two on the subject of the "opening". But Ronald was not to be drawn. "Yes, old chappie," said he, "we shall have to talk things over presently, though it's all pretty simple to a man of your business acumen. We might take a stroll in the country where we can talk at our ease. There's some quite pleasant country along the north coast. Quiet, too. Most of the visitors seem to keep to the south. By the way, those

58

spectacles of yours are an excellent idea. You hadn't got them when I saw you last. I suppose you don't really want them for your eyesight, but that wide bridge covers up the scar so that you look quite like your old self."

Andrew noted the evasion with amused exasperation, but he made no further attempt to "get down to brass tacks". He sipped his coffee and assented passively to Ronald's suggestion of a green Chartreuse "to give the festivity a final kick". Then he paid the bill and went forth with his companion to see what the country walk might bring in the way of explanations.

It brought what he had expected – an endless stream of talk on the most diverse topics with a discreet avoidance of any references to the golden opportunity. Only once was that subject approached, and then merely in respect of that aspect of the transaction which to Ronald was the only one that mattered. "By the way, old chappie," he said when Andrew had put out another feeler, "I suppose you have brought the rhino with you?"

"I have brought a cheque," Andrew replied.

Ronald's face fell. "That's a bit awkward," said he. "The fact is I haven't got a banking account at the moment. Didn't find my bank satisfactory and haven't got a new one yet."

Andrew made no comment, but a vision of the initials "*R.D.*" arose before "the eye of his mind". Bankers are apt to develop an "unsatisfactory" attitude towards customers whose cheques have to be "referred to drawer", which, as Andrew knew, had happened in Ronald's case on more than one occasion. "You see," Ronald continued, "it would hardly look well if I had to hand in your cheque for my deposit. They'd see that I had no banking account of my own, and that's just what I don't want them to know. I want to give the impression of a financially substantial person, as I shall have some of their money passing through my hands."

Andrew noted mentally the appropriateness of the phrase, "passing through my hands", and saw unpleasant possibilities looming in the future. He only hoped that "they", whoever they were – supposing them to have any real objective existence – would make suitable arrangements for "their" own security.

Meanwhile he replied, "It is an open cheque, but if that doesn't quite meet the case, I dare say I could manage to let you have cash. But I should like to know a little more about the business."

"Of course you would," Ronald agreed heartily, "though the essential fact is that I have to lay down fifty pounds as security before I can take up the appointment. Look at that jolly old windmill. What a pity they have taken the sails off! Makes it look such a ruinous affair. But they nearly always do, if they don't pull the whole thing down. Soon there won't be a complete windmill in the whole country."

Here he broke off into a discourse on windmills in particular and the deterioration of the countryside in general and, for the time being, the subject of the security lapsed – it being obvious that he did not mean to be drawn into any intelligible account of the business transaction, real or imaginary, Andrew resigned himself to the inevitable and accepted the conversational lead, with the reservation that no arrangements for a visit to Fairfield were entertained.

Apart from its unpleasant antecedents, the walk was agreeable enough. They had soon left the little town behind, and the country, though not romantically beautiful, offered a pleasant rural prospect. The cornfields, it is true, were denuded of their crops, which now, in the form of rows of ricks, lined the hedgerows at the bottom of the fields. But the stubble, now faded to a soft purplish grey, was enriched by the daisies that had sprung up since the harvest, and the groups of scarlet poppies. The only drawback to the landscape was the scarcity of trees and the lack of any relief from the glare of the hot afternoon sun. For, late as it was in the year, the summer continued with unabated heat and brilliancy. The sky was cloudless, a tremulous haze hung over the ground, and the sea, which was visible over the edge of the cliffs, was still of the clear summer blue. "It's deuced hot," said Ronald, taking off his hat to wipe his forehead. "How would it be to get down to the beach and have a stroll along the sands? It would be fresher there than up here."

"Can we get down?" asked Andrew.

"Yes," replied Ronald. "There is a sunken road leading to a gap-way that opens out on to the beach. I found it by following a couple of seaweed carts, and I've been there once or twice since for a bathe. Nobody ever seems to come there, so you don't have to bother about bathing suits."

He turned off the road and led the way across a stubble field and, after walking about a quarter-of-a-mile, they came to a shallow sunken road, marked by deep ruts in its chalky surface made by the wheels of the heavily laden seaweed carts. Gradually the road sank deeper as it declined towards the sea level until it took on the character of a narrow gully enclosed by lofty walls of chalk. Down this gully the two men picked their way over the rough road in the deep, cool shadow until they reached the bottom of the slope and stood looking out on the sun-lit sands.

Ronald cast a glance at the two lofty headlands which enclosed the little bay and remarked, "We shan't be able to walk very far along the beach. The tide is coming in, and it won't be long before it is up to the cliffs where they jut out. We mustn't get caught on the hop."

"Well," said Andrew, "there's a good stretch of smooth sand in the bay. It will be quite pleasant to walk up and down by the sea without going out of the bay, and it will seem cooler by the water's edge, even if it isn't."

"Yes," Ronald agreed, "there is something cooling in the very sound of the waves breaking on the beach. But I don't see why we need stop at the sound. A dip would be a good deal more refreshing. What do you say? The sea looks just perfect for a bathe."

Andrew cast an approving glance at the calm blue sea and the lines of creamy white where the little surf broke with a gentle murmur on the shore. "It does look rather inviting," he admitted, "but it seems a bit primitive – no bathing suits and no towels."

"As to the suits," said Ronald, beginning to slip off his jacket, "you can see for yourself that the place is as solitary as the Sahara, and what do you want with towels when you have got a roasting sun like this to dry you?"

He settled the question by backing into a shallow recess in the cliff and proceeding rapidly to divest himself of his clothes, when Andrew, after a moment's hesitation, followed suit. As both men were rather scantily clad in the ubiquitous grey flannel suits that were then the vogue, the process was not a long one. In a couple of minutes they were scampering across the sand towards the surf in a condition which Mr. Titmarsh would have described as "naked as a pair of Hottentots", Ronald taking a certain satisfaction in the defiance of convention and Andrew slightly self-conscious.

The breach of the proprieties, however, was only potential, for Ronald's description of the place was so far justified that the nearest approach to a spectator was a small fishing lugger with dark brown sails which was beating up the coast some three or four miles away. Meanwhile the two cousins swam up and down in the calm water outside the surf, with intervals of resting and wallowing in the shallows or basking in the sun on the dry sand before once more splashing into the water.

In these disports the best part of an hour passed. At length, Andrew suggested that it was time to be turning homeward, and they emerged for the last time, shaking themselves as they stepped out on to the wet sand, and took their way across the beach to the place where their clothes were deposited close under the cliff. Ronald led the way at a brisk run and, on arrival at the "dressing station", sat down and reclined at his ease on one of the heaps of clothes-it happened to be Andrew's, and the similarity of the two suits may possibly have misled him, but the enjoyment with which he rubbed his wet body on the dry garments strongly suggested an intentional "mistake". It would have been like Ronald. Andrew followed, shivering slightly, and sat down on the other heap in an upright posture, to catch as much of the sun's heat as possible, for the afternoon was drawing out and the sun was now appreciably lower.

For some time neither of the two men spoke. Ronald lay stretched at full length with his eyes closed, enjoying the warmth of the sunlight which played on his rapidly drying skin, while Andrew sat absently watching the fishing lugger, now tacking out to sea and now going about to make a tack in-shore. At length, Ronald spoke, in a drowsy tone and without opening his eyes. "So you think you will be able to manage cash in place of that cheque? I hope you will. It will be a lot more convenient for me."

"Well," replied Andrew, "I'll see what can be done. But you haven't given me any particulars, you know."

"What's the good?" protested Ronald. "I don't know much about it myself. It's an insurance job. I shall have to rout out new clients and, when I get a bite, I shall have to take the first premium. That's why they want a deposit. So that I shan't mizzle with the takings. Isn't that enough for you?"

As it was all the information he was likely to get, Andrew assented with a grunt and once more fixed his eyes on the distant lugger. Another interval of silence followed. Then Ronald inquired, sleepily, "Molly send me any message?"

"She doesn't know I was going to see you, and I don't want her to know anything about this transaction. She mightn't be best pleased at my dropping money in this way."

"Don't you believe it, dear boy," said Ronald, with a faint smile. "Molly is quite fond of her cousin. She would be only too delighted to help him out of a difficulty. She knows what an affection he has for her. And, by Jove! What a good-looking girl she is! I don't know of any girl that I admire so much. You're a lucky beggar. But I'll remember that mum's the word when I come over to see you."

"I think," Andrew said, huskily, "that it would be as well if you did not come over just at present. In fact, I would rather you did not."

Ronald opened his eyes and looked curiously at his cousin. Then he shut them again and smiled a smile of deep cunning. "So that's how you feel, is it?" said he. "I suspected something of the kind when you had this very opportune business appointment in Crompton. However, I can take a hint. I should be devilish obtuse if I couldn't take one of that breadth."

He spoke without anger but in a tone of undisguised contempt which brought the hot blood to Andrew's cheeks, and which made it clear that he grasped the position exactly. Andrew squirmed with shame and anger – shame of the paltry, unreasonable jealousy of which Ronald evidently suspected him, and anger at the suspicion. For a moment he looked down at the face of the man beside him, with its closed eyes and the sinister, cunning, insolent smile, and an impulse surged through him to batter it with his fists until it was even as his own. But he conquered the impulse and looked away, fixing his eyes once more on the lugger, which was now tacking in-shore and would soon be hidden by the projecting headland. He followed it with a dull interest as it drew nearer and nearer to the headland, idly watching for the moment when it should pass into eclipse, or should go about and head again out to sea.

Gradually the distance between the vessel's bows and the jutting promontory contracted, and Andrew still watched with a strange, foolish eagerness to see whether she would vanish or turn about. At last the dwindling space dwindled to extinction and the boat's bows and the dark brown mainsail began to slip out of sight behind the promontory, and at that moment, Andrew was startled by a heavy thud at his side, a rattle and clatter above and around him and a volley of falling fragments of chalk, one of which struck him a shrewd blow on the shoulder. With a cry of alarm, he scrambled to his feet and raced away for dear life across the sand, pausing only to look round when he had run a full thirty yards.

What he saw when he did at last look round, seemed to turn him to stone. Beside the place where he had been sitting was a litter of fragments of chalk and one great block which rested where Ronald's head had been. Out of the litter the naked legs projected, moving with a slow, twitching, purposeless motion which was horrible to look on, and which, even as he looked, slowly died away and gave place to a dreadful limp stillness.

For some moments, Andrew stood gazing with starting eyes at this awful spectacle without conscious or intelligible thought. He was literally stunned. Presently, regaining some semblance of consciousness, he began to creep back towards the place where his cousin lay with some vague idea of help or rescue. But when he drew nearer, that idea faded from his mind. The way in which the great block sat on the flattened clothing, to say nothing of the gory oozings around it, told the horrible story. That block, weighing perhaps a hundred-weight, had come down on the smiling face with the closed eyes with the impact of a steam hammer. It was useless to think of trying to move it, even if that had been within the compass of one man's strength. The head that had been there was a head no longer.

Still confused and bewildered by the suddenness of the catastrophe, Andrew stood with his eyes riveted on the great block, shaking like a man in the cold stage of an ague. He was aware of a dreadful feeling of faintness and nausea and of a cold sweat that had broken out on his face and trickled down in chilly drops. But for a time, his power of thought seemed to be in total abeyance. He could only stand and stare vacantly at the great block and the naked, motionless legs.

Suddenly, he became conscious of his own nude condition, and with that consciousness his faculties awoke. With a nervous glance up the face of the cliff to the white patch which marked the spot from which the block had fallen, he ran to the heap of clothes and, snatching them up, backed away from the cliff and began to huddle them on as quickly as his shaking limbs would permit. But still, his actions were those of an automaton for all the while, his eyes strayed continually to the motionless form under the litter of chalk fragments and the great block which rested where, but a few minutes ago, had been that comely head with the closed eyes and the sinister, insolent, smiling face.

When he had dressed himself, he looked around for his hat, but he could only see Ronald's panama. His own hat must be somewhere under that gory heap, which he would not even dare to approach. With a shudder at the very thought, he picked up the panama and flung it on his head, careless of the fact that it came down nearly to his ears. Then, with a last look at the figure that reposed with such dreadful stillness at the foot of the cliff, he turned and walked away quickly towards the gap that opened on to the sunken road. As he entered the now sombre and gloomy gully, the dark silhouette of the lugger stole out from behind the headland and began to shape a course towards the bay.

Chapter IV
The Shadow of the Gallows

Andrew stumbled up the rough sunken road with an appearance of haste and speed which was in curious contrast with his actual lack of conscious purpose. Vaguely, there was in his mind an intention to give information to somebody of the terrible mishap, and a desire to get back to the town to that end. But he was still shaken by the horror of what he had seen, was still haunted by the vision of that great block of chalk resting so flatly where a head had been that there had seemed to be no space underneath it. Quickly as he went, his knees trembled weakly, the faintness and nausea were only beginning to subside and a chaotic whirl of thoughts surged through his mind. To the bearing on the future of the thing that had happened, he was as yet unable to give any consideration. His whole attention was focused on the dreadful disaster that had befallen in the twinkling of an eye – the heavy thud of the falling block, the rattling down of the fragments and, above all, the sight of those horrible, twitching legs.

When the sunken road at length reached the surface, it strayed away across the fields as a rough, chalky cart-track which seemed to lead in the direction of a distant farm. As it was the only road visible, Andrew followed it automatically without giving any thought to its direction. At least, it led away from the sea and that terrible haunted bay. As to the whereabouts of the town he had only a confused idea, for during the walk out with Ronald, his mind had been so preoccupied that he had taken no note of the way they had come. Ronald had selected the route and he had followed Ronald. Now nothing impinged on his vision with any kind of familiarity. So, for a time, he walked on rather like one in a dream, clearly conscious of nothing and only dimly aware of a certain feeling of discomfort, particularly in his feet.

He had followed the cart-track for close upon a mile when it opened on a road – a small by-road enclosed by dust-whitened hedgerows. The necessity of deciding which way he should turn aroused him from his dreamy, half-conscious state. He wanted to get to Crompton, but he had only the vaguest idea as to the direction in which it lay, and the sinuous road, curving away on either hand, gave little indication as to whither it eventually led. After a few moments of hesitation, he turned towards the right and once more set forth at a quick pace, spurred on to haste by the agitation of his mind rather than by any conscious purpose.

He hurried on along the road for more than half-a-mile before he met any human creature. Truly, Ronald had been right as to the scarcity of wayfarers in this part of the country. At length there appeared at a bend of the road a miller's cart with its tarpaulin cover raised, in the old-fashioned way, on a sort of ridge-pole, and the driver dimly visible in the dark triangle underneath. As it came in sight, Andrew decided to hail the driver and ask for a direction to Crompton, and then, becoming aware for the first time that his spectacles were not on his face, he instinctively thrust his hand into the pocket in which he usually carried them. But they were not there. Instead, he brought out a cigarette case which was certainly not his.

For a few moments he stood staring foolishly at the case in his hand and wondering how it could have come into his pocket. Then his eye caught the wristband of the shirt which projected from the end of his sleeve, and he saw that the shirt also was not his. On this, with a sudden suspicion that something was amiss, he examined critically the clothes which he was wearing, including the shoes. Of them all, not a single item was his own. In his hurry and agitation, he had put on Ronald's clothes – indeed, he could not have done otherwise, for his own were under that dreadful heap which he could never have brought himself to disturb.

The discovery gave him a shock which was somewhat disproportionate to the occasion. Naturally, he was surprised, but there was really nothing in the affair that need have disturbed him. The clothes were almost exactly like his own, and they fitted him well enough to pass without attracting notice. The error could be easily explained, and he would probably be able to recover his own clothes, or at least the contents of the pockets. But the incident jarred on his already strained nerves as if there were something incriminating in it. Perhaps the need for explanation which would presently arise unnerved him, and certainly the loss of his spectacles and the necessity for going abroad with his hated disfigurement exposed affected him profoundly. So much so that he let the miller's cart pass unhailed and started forward once more, trusting to chance to find the right direction.

By this time, his thought had become a little more coherent, and he began to look about him with some anxiety, for the afternoon was waning and, at this time of year, the evenings begin to draw in. It was, therefore, with a sense of relief that he found himself approaching a cross-road and perceived at the crossing a four-armed finger-post. But, if he was relieved at the prospect of getting a reliable direction, he was rather disconcerted when he reached the post and read the inscription on the pointer, for it then became clear that he had been walking almost directly away from Crompton from the time when he emerged from the sunken road.

He turned away from the post and started on what appeared to be the direct road to the town, though even this was only a larger by-road. But its surface was better than that of the one on which he had been travelling, and he set forth at a swinging pace to cover the three miles that, according to the finger-post, lay between him and the town, regardless of the slight discomfort due to the strange shoes. In spite of the unpleasant surprise of finding himself in the wrong clothes, the halt and the necessity for thought had done him good by diverting his attention from the horrors of his late experience to his present condition and the question as to what he would be called upon to do. He had found a wrist-watch in one of the pockets of the coat and, as he now strapped it on his wrist and noted the lateness of the hour, he turned this latter question over in his mind.

Someone would have to be informed of the accident and, when he asked himself *Who?* the obvious answer was, *the police*. He knew where to find the police station, and he decided to make straight for it as soon as he entered the town. The story that he had to tell was perfectly simple. There would be no need for any elaborate questioning on the part of the police. At least, he hoped not, for he was conscious of a very definite shrinking from any discussion of his relations with Ronald. Perhaps he might take the opportunity to mention the incident of the motor bandits. He considered this point and, possibly influenced by Molly's warning, eventually decided that he had better keep to the subject of the accident and say nothing of the other matter.

Presently another question intruded itself on his mind. At the time of the disaster, the tide was coming in and the margin of the advancing waters was not so very distant from the base of the cliffs. Would there be time for the body to be recovered? And, if there were not – if the corpse should be borne away by the waves and carried out to sea, how would that affect the position? He considered this point at some length and not without a shade of uneasiness, but could arrive at no conclusion, excepting that it would involve disagreeable explanations to Molly. But in any case, he would have to account for his presence at Crompton.

So, as he strode along the road, his thoughts rambled from one to another of the innumerable consequences of the tragedy that came crowding into his consciousness. Mostly they were unpleasant to contemplate, and if, in the dim background of his thoughts, there was some faint feeling of relief at the disappearance from his life of this troublesome parasite, he put it away from him with something like a sense of guilt.

When at last he entered the town, the light was already failing. Nevertheless, he pulled his hat even further down over his face as he yearned for the protection of the lost spectacles, and looked about him furtively. At first, the place seemed to him completely unfamiliar but, after wandering up one thoroughfare and down another, he came into the High Street and was then able to take his bearings. The police station, he knew, was at the end of Barleymow Street, and thither he at once directed his steps. He found it without difficulty and turned into it gratefully out of the glare of the High Street with its illuminated shop windows. He crept along in the shade of the houses, glancing uncomfortably at Number 16 as he passed it, and thinking of the fine, manly figure that he had seen standing outside it when he arrived, and of the corpse around which the waves were perhaps already clamouring. But he hurried on and presently came to the archway that led into the passage or alley in which the station was situated.

Here he paused irresolutely, suddenly aware of an unaccountable feeling of nervousness and a reluctance to speak to strangers of the awful thing which he had witnessed. The lamp had been lit outside the arch and it cast its light brilliantly on the notice board and the various bills that were pasted or tacked on it. Conspicuous among these was the bill that he had seen the constable sticking up as he and Ronald had passed. Again his eye caught the heading, printed in bold type: "*Wanted for Murder*", but he was too much preoccupied with his present business to feel any curiosity as to this crime, whatever it might be – in fact, he was on the point of turning away when two other words in large type arrested his attention. Half-way down the sheet, occupying an entire line, were the words, "*Kibble's Cross*". Then there had been a murder, and he was a principal witness.

He turned back and rapidly ran his eye down the bill. Not the whole way though. After a brief and dry statement of the actual circumstances, the announcement went on:

> *It is believed that more than one man was concerned in the crime, but the only one who was seen was the man who actually fired the shot. He is described as a somewhat fair man with grey eyes, about thirty years of age, and easily recognizable by reason of a remarkably deformed nose, which appears to have been broken and is completely flat excepting at the tip, which is rather prominent.*

He read no farther but, backing away hastily from the area of light under the lamp, crept into the shadow of the houses and stole along the darkened street, trembling so violently that his legs seemed ready to double up beneath him. The description in the bill had struck him with the force of a thunderbolt. For the moment, he was on the point of mental and physical collapse, conscious of nothing but an overwhelming terror and a horrible feeling of sickness – indeed, so near was he to actually fainting that he was fain to lean against the wall of a house and rest awhile on the low sill of a darkened window.

His terror was natural enough and not without ample cause for, stunned as he was, the essential position presented itself clearly and unmistakably: There had been two persons in that car. One of them was dead – murdered, and the other, the woman, believed that she had seen him commit the murder. Even in his dazed condition, Molly's words recurred to him – when a woman holds a belief, she knows no doubts. This woman would be ready to go into the witness-box and swear that she saw him fire the shot that had killed her companion. But what answer could there be to the testimony of an eye-witness? There could be none. Nor could there be any extenuation. It had been a cold-blooded murder without provocation or excuse of any kind. He had but to be caught to be set forthwith on the direct road to the gallows. And caught he would assuredly be. The woman had given a correct description of him and she would recognize him instantly and with certainty. And as to escape – how was a man to escape arrest whose face advertised his identity to any chance stranger?

He rose shakily from the window-sill and began once more to creep along the street in the shadow, pulling down his hat over his eyes and lowering his head when he came within the range of a street lamp. His state was pitiable. He was as one already condemned. Hope he had none. He saw the rope dangling before his eyes, the drop of the gallows yawning at his feet. Like some hunted animal, he looked around wildly for some place in which to hide. But where could he hide in this wilderness of men? Where every stranger was a possible enemy? Supposing he should make his way back to the country and lurk in the unfrequented fields? To what purpose? Sooner or later he must be found. Someone would see him and report his meeting with the man with "the remarkably deformed nose". He could not hide in the fields forever. He must have food and drink, unless he could find some remote and obscure place where he could lie in hiding until he should die of starvation. It was a poor chance, though perhaps it was better than being hanged.

As his thoughts rambled on thus, he continued to creep cautiously along the street. In so far as his mind was capable of forming a decision, he had decided to make his way out of the town, and he began to look warily ahead and scan the corner of the street as he approached it, and at this moment he found himself passing a half-lighted window which he recognized by the still visible placards as that of the Beauty Specialist.

He paused and gazed at the placards. There was not enough light to read the inscriptions, but he had no need to read them. He remembered them quite clearly. And as he recalled those ridiculous promises and exhortations, a wild hope sprang up in his heart. Of course, the fellow was a mere quack. But was it possible that he could do something? It mattered not in the least what he did. An additional disfigurement even would answer the purpose if only his appearance could be in some way changed so that his face should cease to be the face which that woman had seen at the window of the car. It was a chance – the only chance that he could see of escape from the gallows.

He looked up and down the street. Not a living creature was in sight. He made an effort to pull himself together. The pallor of his face he could not control, but he could try to muster up some composure of manner. But even in that moment of agitated expectation, one cautionary idea stole into his mind. Supposing the Professor had seen the bill outside the police station! He must be prepared for that contingency. Nevertheless, he determined to take the risk. After another glance up and down the street, he approached the door and, gripping the handle firmly to control the tremor of his hand, turned it deliberately, pushed open the door, entered, and closed it after him. As he turned away from the door, he confronted a pleasant-faced elderly man in shirt-sleeves and a white apron, who was busily engaged in packing one or two large trunks, by the rather dim light of a single electric lamp.

At the sound of the closing door, the man looked up, and a shade of impatience or annoyance stole over his face. Andrew noted it with some misgiving as he inquired nervously, "Are you Professor Booley?"

"I am," was the reply, "or, perhaps, I should say I was, as my professional career in this country has now come to an end. I am just putting my goods together ready for a start to-morrow morning. In twenty-four hours, I hope to be in Liverpool, if not actually on board ship. May I ask what you wanted with me?"

At the Professor's announcement Andrew's heart sank. For a few moments he was unable to answer but, at length, recovering his outward composure with an effort, he replied, "I had come to ask for your professional help, and I hope you will not refuse to do what you can for me.

"I am afraid that is what I shall have to do," the Professor rejoined in a tone of courteous regret. "You see how things are with me. I have finished up and am just making my preparations for departure. I thought I had fastened the door when I turned the lights out. I am real sorry not to be able to do your business, whatever it is. By the way, what was it that you wanted me to do for you?"

"If you will look at my face," said Andrew, "I think that will answer your question, and I do hope you will try to help me if the thing is not absolutely impossible."

The Professor looked at him a little curiously. Then, suddenly, his attention sharpened and a somewhat startled expression appeared on his face, whereat Andrew experienced a spasm of alarm. Had this man seen the police bill, and was he recognizing "the man with the remarkably deformed nose"? His terror was not diminished when the Professor strode forward and fixed a look of intense scrutiny on that unfortunate member. But the next question reassured him to some extent. "You were not born like that?"

"No," replied Andrew. "I once had quite a decent-looking nose. This is the result of a blow from a cricket-ball."

"Ah!" said the Professor, "nasty, dangerous things. You must have been a fairly good-looking fellow before you caught that biff."

"I believe I was," Andrew replied, modestly.

The Professor continued to scrutinize the injured nose with the most profound interest and attention. Then from inspection he proceeded to palpation. With an unmistakably expert finger and thumb he explored the sunken bridge, delicately tracing the edges of the flattened nasal bones and pinching up the loose skin which lay over them. "It's an absolutely ideal case," he murmured, rather with the manner of a man speaking to himself. "A good firm base of solid bone and a fair amount of spare skin, all free, without any adhesions to the bone underneath. It's a case in a million."

Recognizing these observations as being of the nature of a soliloquy, Andrew forbore to interrupt. But when the Professor, subsiding into silence, stepped back a pace and stood, still with his eyes riveted on the deformed feature, as if taking in the general effect in relation to the rest of the face, he ventured once more to urge his case. "I hope you are going to relent, Professor," he pleaded, "and give me the benefit of your skill. It means a lot to me, as you can judge for yourself."

How much it meant to him, the Professor was, naturally, unable to judge, having, apparently, not seen the police bill. But the hideous disfigurement of an otherwise comely young man must have seemed to him a matter of sufficient urgency, for he replied in a tone of kindly sympathy, "I can see it does, sonny, and I can't find it in my heart to send you away like that when a bit of trouble on my part may make life a different thing for you. No, sir! We have our duties to one another, and my duty is to let the packing go to blazes and put all the skill and knowledge that I have at your disposal."

Andrew drew a deep breath of relief and, with a heart bursting with gratitude, he began to stammer out his thanks, when the Professor interrupted him. "Don't be too previous," said he. "When I tell you what I propose to do, perhaps you'll think better of it. If I get busy, you won't enjoy it a little bit. I tell you, it will hurt like blazes. It might be possible to use a local anaesthetic such as dentists use. I do sometimes, but I don't want to in this case because it might easily happen that the anaesthetic would just turn the scale the wrong way and make the operation a failure. And I don't want it to fail. But I give you fair warning. While I am working, you will feel as if you had molten lead running into your nose. And, mind you, you'll have to stick it and not move a muscle or the whole thing will be a failure. Now, what do you say? Can you stick it? It's up to you to decide."

Andrew had no hesitation. What the Professor was going to do, and what the result would be, he had no idea. But whatever the result might be, if only it were to alter his appearance, he would be saved from his present horrible peril. "You can take it," said he, "that I am prepared to put up with any pain that you have to inflict, and I promise you that I will keep absolutely still until you have finished."

"Good!" said the Professor. "I take you at your word, and I think it will be worth your while. But there is one other warning that I ought to give you. There is just the possibility that something may go wrong after the operation. It isn't at all likely, but it has happened in one or two cases, so I think it only right to mention it. Will you take the risk? It's only a small one."

Even to Andrew, the change in the Professor's attitude was apparent. From reluctance to be disturbed in his preparations for his journey, it had changed into an evident eagerness to proceed with the operation, whatever that might be and, when Andrew replied that he was fully prepared to accept the risk of subsequent failure and to hold the Professor unaccountable for any such failure, his answer was received with a grunt of satisfaction. "We won't want to be disturbed," said Booley, when this point had been settled, "so I will just lock up and switch out the light."

He locked the front door and retired into an inner room where he switched on the light and invited his patient to enter. Then, having extinguished the light in the outer premises, he closed the inner door. "Now," said he, "let me just explain in a general way what I propose to do. The method that I am going to employ is what is known as the subcutaneous wax method. I'll show you." He opened the drawer of a

72

cabinet and took out a circular cake of a colourless, glassy-looking material, which he exhibited to his patient. "Now, see here," said he, tapping the round mass with his knuckles, "this is paraffin wax, quite a hard substance, as you see, but not in the least brittle. Now, paraffin wax is a very remarkable material. It is one of the most inert substances known. It never changes of itself, it has practically no effect on any other substance, and it is not affected by contact with other materials. And it can be reduced to a liquid by heat – rather a lot of heat, unfortunately, in the case of hard wax like this. Now, what I am going to do is this: I shall melt some of this wax and, when it is quite liquid, I shall inject a quantity of it into the space under the loose skin of your nose. That will produce a shapeless swelling over the place where the bridge ought to be. Then while the wax is still soft, I shall model that shapeless lump to the shape that you want your nose to be. And now you will see why I am telling you this. I have got to do all the modelling while the wax is soft enough to pinch up into shape. When once it has set solid, it is finished for better or worse. Nothing more can be done. And it is only a matter of seconds before it sets. Consequently, the success or failure is in your hands. No matter how much it hurts, it is up to you to keep quite still until I have finished the modelling. You realize that?"

"Quite," replied Andrew, "and you can rely on me to stick it without moving, however bad it is."

"I believe I can," said the Professor. "You looked in a most almighty funk when you first came in but, you seem to be your own man now. Which is rather singular. Most people are as bold as brass at first, but get the horrors when it comes to actual business."

The Professor was quite correct in his observations, but he was not in possession of all the facts. What had revived Andrew's confidence was the information that, in any case, there would be some sort of hump over the sunken bridge of his nose. As to the shape of that hump he was not very much concerned. Any kind of hump would transform him so that the woman's description of him would be totally inapplicable. And the mere pain dismayed him not at all. Doubtless it would be extremely disagreeable, but it would be a good deal less disagreeable than being hanged.

Having delivered himself of the above admonitions, the Professor inducted the patient into a sort of modified dental chair and then proceeded to light the gas ring under a water-bath in which was a porcelain vessel containing a quantity of wax shavings. While the water was heating he made his other preparations, beginning by washing his hands very thoroughly in a lavatory basin and then laying out his instruments on a small swivel table such as dentists use. The most

73

conspicuous of them was a hypodermic syringe of large size but fitted with a rather fine needle. From time to time he examined a chemical thermometer which he had placed in the vessel containing the wax and, meanwhile, carried on encouraging conversation. "By the way," said he, "we haven't settled on the sort of nose that you would like me to build up. We must be quite clear on that point before we start. What was your nose like before that cricket-ball came bumbling along? Was it a straight nose, or was there a curve on the bridge?"

Even while the question was being propounded, Andrew had come to a decision, and a perfectly natural and reasonable one in the special circumstances. In his terror of the gallows, his one object was to shake off his identity-the identity of the man who was "wanted for murder". He would not go back even to what that man had been, if that had been possible. He wanted to break all connection with that man. "It was a slightly curved nose," he replied.

"I thought so," said the Professor, "a moderate Roman. And very becoming it must have been – and will be again. You'll think it cheap at the price of a few minutes' discomfort."

He bent down over the porcelain vessel and again inspected the thermometer. Apparently, the correct temperature had been reached, for he now turned out the gas and placed the water-bath on the little table, which he swung round close to the patient's head. Having lighted a spirit-lamp on the table, he held the needle of the syringe in the flame for a few seconds. Then, dipping the needle into the melted wax, he slowly filled the syringe, emptied it into the vessel, and very slowly and carefully re-filled it. "Now," said he, "get a grip on the arms of the chair and make up your mind to put up with a bit of pain. It will be over in less than a minute. Better shut your eyes."

The Professor had not exaggerated. It was an appalling experience. First, Andrew was aware of the prick of the needle in the loose skin over the nose. That was nothing to complain of. But it was followed immediately by the most horrible pain that he had ever experienced. The Professor's words exactly described it. He felt as if molten lead were being poured into his nose. In his agony, he held his breath and clutched the arms of the chair until his knuckles seemed to be bursting through the skin. His eyes were closed, but the tears welled up between the lids and trickled down his face in a little stream towards his ears. But, by a supreme effort, he resisted the natural impulse to shrink away from the torturing hand. Throughout the whole proceeding, he held his head rigidly still and uttered not a sound.

Meanwhile, the Professor, murmuring at intervals little phrases of sympathy and encouragement, went about his work with unhurried skill and concentrated attention, but yet with a certain air of suppressed excitement. Having completed the injection, he laid aside the syringe and made a critical inspection of the rounded, blister-like swelling which had arisen over the sunken bridge of the nose. After a few seconds, he began cautiously to manipulate it at the edges, persuading the liquid wax towards the middle line. Then, as the wax began to thicken, he proceeded quickly and deftly to model it to the desired shape, darting from one side of the chair to the other to view the growing member from its different aspects. Yet, in spite of his eagerness and excitement, his movements were quite deliberate and controlled. Evidently, in his mind, he had a perfectly clear picture of the state of the invisible wax and, as its consistency increased and it gradually approached the solid condition, the touch of the flexible, sensitive fingers became firmer and more decisive.

It was, as he had said, only a matter of seconds, but to the unfortunate patient, sitting with the muscles of his neck contracted into tense cords and his hands holding the arms of the chair in a vice-like grip, it seemed hours before the Professor, straightening himself up with a gentle sigh, announced, "There, my son, That's finished. The wax is set solid, though it won't be quite hard for an hour or two. How is it feeling?"

"Not as bad as it did," Andrew replied, faintly, "but it still hurts a good deal."

"I've no doubt that it does," the Professor rejoined, sympathetically, "but it will soon be all right now. You've been a good lad. You stuck it like a Trojan."

"What does it look like?" Andrew asked, without much eagerness and with his eyes still shut.

"You shall see for yourself presently," the Professor replied in a tone of deep satisfaction, regarding his work with his head on one side. "But don't move just for a minute. I must touch up the colour a trifle so that it shan't be too noticeable. At present it's as red as a strawberry."

Having recourse once more to the inexhaustible cabinet, he produced therefrom a stick of yellowish grease-paint and a little jar of powder. With the former he laid a fairly thick tint of opaque yellowish white over the restored nose (to the patient's extreme discomfort), smoothing it out with the tip of his finger until the tint was perfectly even. Then, with a tiny puff, he covered the greasy surface with a thin coating of powder, finishing off with a few delicate touches of a ball of cotton wool. "There," he said, "I think that will do. It looks quite a natural colour now. When the irritation from the heat goes off and the redness dies away, it will look a bit queer and tallowy. Then you'll have

75

to wash the paint off. And I need not warn you that, although the wax will be quite hard and firm, you've got to be careful in the way you handle that nose. It will stand any ordinary treatment in reason, but you've got to remember that it's only a lump of wax after all, and that if you knock it out of shape, it's going to remain out of shape. It can't be melted soft again."

"Yes," said Andrew, "I realize that, and you may take it that I shall keep out of the way of cricket-balls in the future. Can I see what it is like, now?"

"You can," replied the Professor, who still showed a tendency to dodge about from side to side of the chair and take ecstatic glances at the new nose from various points of view. "I am going to show it to you this instant."

As he spoke, he wheeled away the swivel table, and in its place wheeled up an appliance somewhat like a reading-stand with a largish mirror in the position usually' occupied by the book-rest. Deliberately, he trundled it up to the side of the chair, arranged the mirror at exactly the correct angle, and then swung the brass arm round so as to bring the glass precisely opposite the patient's face. "Now," said he triumphantly, "tell me what you think of the result."

Chapter V
Black Magic

In response to the Professor's invitation, Andrew sat up in the chair and looked into the mirror. But, as his eyes were still full of water, he got but a blurred impression of what was before him. Even so, he was aware that the face which confronted him was not the face to which he had of late years become accustomed – the face of the "man with the remarkably deformed nose".

He took out his handkerchief and carefully and thoroughly wiped away the still-exuding tears, while the Professor hovered around, watching him in a transport of delighted expectancy. When he had dried his eyes as completely as was possible in the circumstances, he looked again into the mirror. And then he sustained yet another shock. It is impossible to guess what he had expected – if he had expected anything. But most assuredly he had not expected what he saw. For the face that looked out at him from the mirror was the face of his cousin Ronald.

He stared at it in blank amazement with a bewildered sense of being in a dream, or suffering some sort of hallucination, or being the subject of some kind of wizardry or enchantment. And the Professor, watching him eagerly, rubbed his hands and smiled.

The thing was astounding, incredible. It was no mere resemblance or similarity. The face was Ronald's face, Doubtless, if Ronald had been there to furnish a comparison, some difference might have been discoverable. But Andrew could perceive none, and when he moved his head from side to side, exhibiting the half-profile with a view of the Roman nose, the effect was even more impressive. For that was the view of Ronald's face that he had always found most striking and characteristic.

The Professor, watching him with an expectant smile, noted his astonishment and was deeply gratified. Well might the patient be astonished at the miracle that had been wrought in the space of a few minutes. But his kindly soul yearned for something more than astonishment, and the joy that he had looked for did not seem to be there. "Well," he asked, at length, "what do you think of it? Will it do?"

Andrew pulled himself together with an effort and came back to the realities of the situation. "I beg your pardon," said he, "but I was so amazed at the result of your skill that I could find no words to thank you. I can't even now. When I look into the mirror, I can't believe my eyes."

"Your eyes are all right," said the Professor, "or will be when they have done watering. Meanwhile, you can trust mine, and I tell you that you have got a nose that any man might be proud of. And, if you don't mind me saying so – I'm talking business, not paying compliments – you are an uncommonly good-looking young man."

The compliment, which his own eyesight confirmed, fell pleasantly on Andrew's ears even in the midst of his confusion. Why not? His repulsive ugliness had been the haunting trouble of his later life, and he had known the satisfaction of conscious good looks in the golden past. It was pleasant to realize that he would have no more to sneak about in spectacles and hide himself from the common gaze. But, furthermore, and especially, the change assured him that his main purpose was achieved. The deadly peril that had encompassed him was dissipated. He was saved. That woman might now shout from the house-tops her vivid description of the murderer. The more vivid and exact it was, the less would it apply to him. "The man with the remarkably deformed nose" had ceased to be. The police might search for him as they pleased, it was no concern of Andrew's. "Naturally, I don't mind your saying so," he replied, "since the good looks – which I can see for myself – are your own creation. I only wish I could find words to thank you sufficiently. You can hardly imagine the misery of going about, an object of pity and disgust to every person whom one may meet, and the relief of having that disfigurement removed. I assure you that I am more grateful than I can tell you, and I do think it most generous of you to have put aside your own urgent affairs to render me this great service."

"Not in the least," said the Professor. "It has been a delight to me to exercise my art to such excellent purpose. We all like to succeed in what we try to do, and I feel that I have had a great success to-night, and I don't mind admitting that I'm mighty pleased with myself."

A less appreciative listener than Andrew might have felt a slight suspicion that the brilliant success was a somewhat novel experience for the Professor. But as the splendour of the achievement dawned on him by degrees and he realized its beneficent consequences, Andrew had no room in his mind for anything but gratitude. "You have reason to be," he replied. "It must be a glorious thing to wield the power to change for the better the whole course of a fellow creature's life. I shall be your debtor to my dying day, and I shall never forget what I owe you. Which reminds me that, apart from the debt of gratitude, which I can never repay, I am in your debt in a pecuniary sense. May I ask what the amount is? I know in advance that whatever your fee is, it is quite inadequate to the value of the benefit bestowed."

Even as he uttered the words, he experienced a sudden pang of alarm. For in that moment he remembered that he was not wearing his own clothes. He had not yet searched the pockets of the suit that he had put on in error but, as they were those of his thriftless and chronically impecunious cousin, it was quite conceivable that they might not contain the wherewith for him to pay even a modest fee. Hurriedly, he thrust his hand into the breast pocket of the coat and brought out the small wallet that he felt there. When he opened it he discovered, to his intense relief, that it contained two pound notes. They might not be enough, but they would be better than nothing.

As a matter of fact, they were more than enough, for the Professor, glancing at the wallet and possibly noting its scanty contents, held up his hand. "Put it away, sonny," said he. "There isn't any fee. It has been a labour of love, and I am not going to spoil it for myself by taking money for it. Let me have the luxury of giving you a free and willing service."

Andrew was disposed to demur, but the Professor would listen to no protests and, as he was obviously in earnest, Andrew refrained from pressing him any further. "Very well," said he. "I am so much in your debt that a little more makes no difference. But it would give me very great pleasure if you would come as my guest and let us celebrate your triumph and my resurrection with a little dinner – or perhaps we might call it supper. You won't refuse me, will you?"

The Professor reflected, with a gloating eye still fixed on his masterpiece. "I'd enjoy a little celebration," he said, at length, "if only for the pleasure of looking at you. But it will have to be a short one as far as I am concerned, for I still have my packing to finish. Where did you propose to dine?"

"I leave that to you," replied Andrew, "as you probably know the town better than I do."

The Professor knew of a respectable Italian cafe in the High Street close by and, when he had doffed his apron, turned down his shirt-sleeves, and put on a coat and hat, they went forth together, the guest leading the way and the host submitting to be led and secretly hoping that the cafe would not turn out to be the one at which he had lunched with Ronald. Not that it mattered much, since he had then been wearing his spectacles. But he was still under the influence of the police bill and accordingly anxious to avoid any connection with the man who was "wanted".

It was not the same restaurant, but a more modest establishment of the familiar Italian type. It resembled the other, however, in one respect: Its walls were lined with large mirrors, to the evident satisfaction of Professor Booley, who was thus enabled to inspect his masterpiece from several points of view, which he did with such persistence that he appeared to consume his food by a mere mechanical and half-conscious act of ingestion.

To Andrew that dinner was a most uncanny experience. His mind was still in a whirl of confusion from the crowding events and the repeated shocks that he had sustained and, above all, from the glimpse of his cousin's face looking out at him from the mirror. He had still the feeling of being in a dream or under some sort of spell of enchantment, of moving in a world of unrealities. The change that had been wrought in him had been too sudden and profound for complete realization. In the space of less than an hour he had become a different person. It was no mere matter of disguise. He was actually a different person. The Andrew Barton who had set forth from Fairfield that morning, had ceased to exist. In his place had been born an entirely new individual, and that individual was himself. It is not unnatural that an idea so opposed to all human experience should have been difficult to accept as a thing that had actually happened. It was not only amazing – it was incredible.

The sense of being in a dream or under some hallucination was intensified by the immediate circumstances. As he sat at the table he had a wall-mirror on either hand. By turning his head slightly in either direction, he was able to observe his cousin Ronald dining with Professor Booley. It was extremely uncanny. The first time he caught sight of that familiar figure, he started violently and looked away only to find that same apparition presented to his view in the mirror at his other hand. By degrees, however, his nervous tension relaxed and his mind became less confused, under the reviving influence of food and drink. He had, in fact, been badly in need of refreshment after his long walk, together with the repeated mental shocks finishing up with the severe pain of the operation, and though the latter had now subsided to a dull ache and a tenderness which made mastication slightly uncomfortable, he found distinct physical satisfaction in disposing of the carefully chosen dishes and the contents of a small bottle of claret.

He was but half-way through his meal when the Professor looked at his watch and stood up. "Don't let me disturb you," said he. "Make a good dinner and don't eat too fast. But I must run away now and finish my packing. I am sorry that you did not come to me sooner, so that I could have seen a bit more of you. But I'm mighty glad that you came at last. I shall look back on this as a red-letter day. You've given me the greatest opportunity I ever had. No, don't get up. Finish your dinner quietly and, as I told you before, be careful how you handle that nose."

The two men shook hands heartily and, after cordial expressions of mutual good will, said a final "Goodbye", when the Professor bustled away, pausing only for an instant at the door for a last fond look at his masterpiece.

When he had gone, Andrew resumed his attack on the food with a growing sense of bodily well-being. He even ordered a coffee and liqueur and, while these were being obtained, he stood up and stepped over to the mirror to view himself at close quarters, to the indulgent amusement of the elderly waiter, who wrote him down a vain young dog – but not without some excuse for his vanity.

He gazed long and earnestly at the tall handsome man who looked out at him from the mirror. But his original impression remained unshaken. The man was Ronald – and yet the man was himself. Well as he knew his cousin, he could see in the reflection not a single appreciable point of difference. He and Ronald had been as like as twins, excepting for their differently shaped noses. And now the wizardry of Professor Booley had extinguished even that difference.

He went back to his seat and, as he sipped his coffee and the liqueur, lit one of Ronald's cigarettes, and set himself to consider the amazing situation, and his own course of action whereby to meet it. And even then, he began to have some dawning perception of the complications that this situation might involve. But he was far from perceiving that the control of his future had passed out of his hands, that events were already shepherding him irresistibly in a particular direction without regard to his inclinations or desires. It was only by degrees, as he began to make his plans, that he realized how little choice he had, how completely he had become the creature of circumstance.

The first shock of discovery came to him when he essayed to settle his immediate proceedings. He had looked out the trains on the previous day and he knew that there was a train leaving Crompton at half-past-nine. That would get him home about eleven. By that time Molly would have gone to bed and, as he had no latch-key, he would have to knock her up. But the consideration that he had no latch-key – that his latch-key was in the clothes which were now, perhaps, washing about in the sea – brought him up against the realities of the situation. Suddenly, he realized that the Andrew who would appear at his door was not the Andrew who had left it in the morning. The figure that faced him in the mirror was the figure that would face Molly at the door. He would have to explain what had happened. But as the thought came to him, he put it away. The thing was impossible, absurd. Molly was not an intellectual woman, but she had a massive common sense. How would she react to the amazing story that he had to tell? He could not have a moment's doubt. She would see, standing on the door-step, a man who, to all outward seeming, was cousin Ronald. She would hear him explain that

81

he was her husband, strangely metamorphosed – that, having started for London, he had returned from Crompton, that he had, in error, put on another man's clothes, and that he had, in the course of a few hours, grown a new nose. Whether she would ever listen to such a statement was an open question, but it was quite certain that she would not allow him to enter the house at eleven o'clock at night.

Such being the case, it was obviously useless to think of going home that night. He would have to stay at Crompton, and he would have to make some arrangements for the night's lodging. As he debated this question, it suddenly occurred to him that Ronald's lodgings were available. He would have to go there to retrieve his attaché case, for that case contained a hundred pounds, and he began to perceive that he might want that hundred pounds rather badly in the course of the next few days. He felt in his pocket for the latch-key which he had seen Ronald use and, having found it, took it out, inspected it curiously, and returned it. But simple as it seemed to enter this house and take his place as the tenant, he viewed the project a little apprehensively and considered it at some length. And all the time, as he sat there considering, the Clock of Destiny was ticking on, the clock which no man can put back.

At last when he had screwed up his courage to the sticking point, he beckoned to the waiter and, having paid his bill, took up his hat and went out. He found his way easily back to Barleymow Street and, entering that secluded thoroughfare, walked briskly towards the house. Suddenly, it occurred to him that he was not certain as to which rooms his cousin had occupied. When Ronald had run in with the attaché case, he had been absent for but a few moments, and Andrew, looking in at the ground floor window, had thought that he saw someone moving within. But he was not quite certain, and the doubt gave him pause. It would be very awkward if he let himself into the house and then was unable to find his rooms.

He slowed down his pace to a saunter while he turned the problem over in his mind. As he passed Number 16 on the opposite side of the street, he looked across and noted a light moving about in a first-floor window. Otherwise, the house was in darkness. Still he could not bring himself to make the plunge and, as he wandered on irresolutely, he came to the archway leading to the police station. The lamp still threw its light on the portentous bill, and he was moved, partly by curiosity and partly by a certain bravado, to stop and read it. He could do so now with perfect safety.

At this moment three men issued forth from the police station, one of whom looked like a fisherman while the other two were policemen, and the latter carried between them a folded stretcher. They advanced together and came out of the archway, when the two stretcher-bearers halted, opened the stretcher, fixed its struts and deposited it on the pavement. Then the three men turned and looked up the street. "They ought to be here in a minute or two," said the fisherman. "I left 'em coming into the High Street." He stared into the gloom of the ill-lighted street for a few more seconds and then announced, "I think I hears 'em coming. Yes, here they are."

As he spoke, Andrew became aware of a faint rumbling in the distance, which suddenly grew more distinct as a dark object accompanied by a moving light appeared at the end of the street. With a sudden suspicion as to what that dark object might be, Andrew turned away from the archway and began to saunter up the street. Very soon the dark shape resolved itself into a two-wheeled farm cart, of which the horse was being led by a labourer, while two men, apparently fishermen, one of whom carried a ship's anchor-light, walked at the side.

As the rather funereal procession passed him, Andrew looked at it with a strangely detached interest. He could not see what was in the cart, but a few wisps of sea-wrack that clung to the spokes of the wheel told him that it was a seaweed-cart, on which he turned once more and slowly retraced his steps.

The cart drew up opposite to the stretcher, which the policemen, one of whom was a sergeant, dragged close alongside. Then the three fishermen and the labourer proceeded to draw from the cart an elongated object wrapped in a boat sail which they carried to the stretcher and deposited thereon with elaborate care, notwithstanding which, the canvas became slightly displaced and a bare foot projected at the end. The sergeant, observing the foot, stooped and tenderly replaced the canvas covering. Then he turned back the canvas at the other end, glanced inside, ejaculated "Good God!" and hurriedly replaced it.

Meanwhile one of the fishermen had climbed into the cart and now descended with a bundle of clothing in his arms. "Here's his clothes," said he, addressing the sergeant. "You'll want them to find out who he is."

"Yes, by the Lord!" the sergeant agreed. "There won't be much chance of identification otherwise. Bring them along."

Andrew watched with profound interest as the fisherman handed the clothes, garment by garment, to the sergeant, who, as he received them, laid them over the shrouded figure on the stretcher, excepting the shoes and the crushed hat, which he tucked under his arm. "That seems to be the lot," he remarked, as he took these last articles. "There was nothing else? No walking stick?"

"No, that's the lot," was the reply. "I suppose you don't know what is in the pockets?"

"No," the fisherman replied rather gruffly. "'Twasn't no business of ourn. We just grabbed 'em up and stowed 'em in the boat. Another five minutes and they'd have been awash."

"Well," said the sergeant, "we will go through them when we get them inside. Do you mind lending a hand with the stretcher, as I've got these things to carry?"

The fisherman took his place at the foot-end between the handles as the constable took his at the head. The latter gave the word, when they both stooped, grasped the handles, and lifted, and then the whole procession moved off under the arch and disappeared down the alley, excepting the carter, who remained in charge of the horse and was now engaged in adjusting the nosebag.

When he had seen the last of the procession, Andrew turned away and began to walk slowly up the street, his retreat being somewhat accelerated by signs of impending conversation on the part of the carter. It had been a strange experience and he was conscious of a certain surprise at his own state of mind. As the clothes – his own clothes – had been transferred, he had watched with a curiously detached interest, checking each garment and making a mental note of the contents of its pockets, not without a passing thought as to the information that they would convey to the observer who should presently turn them out. Yet he had felt no sense of proprietorship in them. Once they had been his, but now they belonged to the corpse on which they lay. They appertained to a past which had been blotted out and had no connection with the present – at least with his present. And his mental attitude towards the corpse itself also surprised him in a vague way. The thrill of horror which had affected him at the time of the catastrophe had now no counterpart. In the whirl of events which had followed it, the tragedy had dwindled to a mere incident, which concerned him only in respect of its consequences. And these consequences were what he would presently have to consider. But for the moment, there was the immediately important question of the night's lodging. When he arrived at the middle of the street, he perceived that there was now a light in the window of the ground-floor room of Number 16. This rather disconcerted him but, since the thing had to be done sooner or later, he screwed up his courage to make the attempt forthwith. Taking the key out of his pocket, he crossed the road and walked boldly up to the door.

It was evidently the right key, for it entered and turned in the lock without difficulty. He pushed the door open softly and stepped into the hall. There was no light in it excepting what came through the open door

84

of the room. He looked into the latter, which appeared to be a bed-sitting room, for it contained a bedstead, an easy-chair and a good-sized table. On the table was a shaded oil lamp and, what was of much more importance to him, his own attaché case.

As there could be no doubt that this was Ronald's room, he walked in confidently and was about to shut the door when a voice from somewhere upstairs called out, "Is that you, Mr. Green?"

He was on the point of replying "No," when he fortunately remembered Ronald's alias, whereupon he answered, "Yes."

"Oh!" said the voice, "so you have come back. I began to think you had gone for good."

The voice did not impress Andrew as an amicable voice, and when it took visible shape as a rather slatternly-looking middle-aged woman, the impression was confirmed. "I thought that perhaps you'd hopped off," she explained, standing in the doorway and regarding him with a truculent eye.

"Now, why should you think that?" he asked in a conciliatory tone and wondering what the deuce her name was.

"Well," she replied, "you are not usually so late as this. Mighty punctual for your meals you are as a rule, and nearly a fortnight's board and lodging owing, and no luggage to speak of excepting this – " indicating the attaché case " – if it belongs to you. I haven't seen it before."

Andrew thought it best not to discuss this point, but the arrears (which did not surprise him in the least) had better be settled at once. The difficulty was that the money was in the case and, as his ownership had been questioned, it might be a little awkward to produce it from that source in the lady's presence. "I am sorry to be so behind hand," he said, meekly, "but I can settle up now if you would be so kind as to let me have an account of what is owing."

"I gave you my bill days ago," said she. "You know I did."

"Yes," said Andrew, "but that was only for last week. I think I had better settle up for the fortnight, Would you mind making out a fresh bill?"

"Up to Thursday, the day after to-morrow? That will be the fortnight."

"Yes, I think that will be best."

The lady thought so too, by the light of experience, and in a slightly mollified frame of mind retired, shutting the door after her.

As soon as she was gone, Andrew proceeded with some anxiety to open the case, which, fortunately in the circumstances, had no lock. But his anxiety was relieved by the first glance. Whatever the landlady's shortcomings were, dishonesty was not one of them, for the contents of the case were exactly as he had left them. Hurriedly, he took ten of the pound-notes from the bundle and, having shut the case, bestowed the notes in his wallet. Then he began rapidly to consider his future movements.

There was no object in his remaining at Crompton and there was a very good reason why he should go up to London without delay. His main banking account was kept at the head office in Cornhill, and he was accustomed to keep a rather large balance there. The account at the Bunsford branch was only for local expenditure and he fed it with cheques on the London office. He had had to pay in a London cheque to get the fifty pound-notes.

Now, the cheque that he had drawn for Ronald was drawn on the London office, and there he would have to go to cash it. He did not know much about banking, but it occurred to him that if he was to cash that cheque, he must do so without delay. On the morrow at some time there would be a rumour of his death, and he presumed that with the death of the drawer the cheque would be unpayable at the bank, and he did not want to be referred to the executors. What he would do about the question of his death was a matter that he would have to consider later. At that moment, it was vitally important that he should have that fifty pounds.

By which it will be seen that his power of coherent thinking was reviving and also that he was beginning, even if half-unconsciously, to realize the compelling force of events.

The landlady's bill was not a masterpiece of calligraphy, but it supplied some indispensable information. It set forth that Mr. W. Green was indebted to Mrs. Sarah Baxter in the sum of four guineas, being two weeks' board residence at the rate of two guineas per week. It seemed a modest charge, and he suspected that Mrs. Baxter had not made an extravagant profit. He handed over the sum and, when the bill had been receipted, he dropped it into the attaché case. "Shall you be staying on after Thursday?" Mrs. Baxter asked.

"Well, no," he replied. "I have finished my business in Crompton and I have to go up to London to-morrow. Probably I shall have to stay there some time, so I shall take my luggage with me. If I should have occasion to come back, I will write to you."

"I can't keep the rooms vacant, you know," said she.

"Of course you can't," he agreed. "I must take my chance. Do you know how the morning trains for London go?"

"There's a fast train at eight-thirty-five," she replied. "It's the best train in the day, gets to London at a quarter-to-ten. I should go by that if I was you."

"I think I will," said he, "if my going so early will not inconvenience you."

She looked at him with amused surprise. "You're mighty considerate all of a sudden." she remarked. "But, Lord bless you, I am up before six every morning. You'll have your breakfast by seven o'clock and, if you'll put your shoes outside the door, I'll give them a brush. They look as if they wanted it."

Andrew thanked her (but not too profusely, as she seemed unaccustomed to excessive manifestations of politeness) whereupon she wished him "Good night" and retired.

When he was once more alone, he sat down in the easy-chair and tried to think out his position. But the fatigues and agitations of the day, combined with the effects of his recent meal, began to make themselves felt. A comfortable drowsiness stole over him. The cigarette which he had lighted, went out and fell from his fingers. His thoughts grew muddled, and he felt a growing desire for sleep. After nodding in his chair for half-an-hour he got up, searched for Ronald's pyjamas and, having found them hidden under the bedclothes, undressed and turned into bed.

Chapter VI
Two Inquests

It was but a quarter-of-an-hour after the time for opening when Andrew presented himself at the bank. He entered with a studiously assumed air of unconcern, but with a curious feeling of unreality and a distinct and unpleasant consciousness of the fact that he was falsely personating the payee of the cheque which he was about to present for payment. He knew the place well – his own bank, where he had kept an account for years and where he had at this moment some four hundred pounds to his credit – and most of the clerks and cashiers knew him well enough by sight. Yet he was entering in the guise of a stranger, for though some of the cashiers had seen Ronald, it was unlikely that any of them would remember him.

Nevertheless, he maintained a calm exterior and, selecting a cashier who was a stranger to him, laid his cheque on the counter and pushed it under the brass screen. He had already endorsed it with a copy from memory of the too-familiar signature.

The cashier took up the cheque, looked at the signature, turned it over to see that it was endorsed, and then retired, presumably to compare it with the recorded signature in the book. But Andrew watched him with a shade of uneasiness lest there should be some other kind of investigation. He had not seen the morning paper and could not, therefore, judge whether his assumed death had yet become publicly known, or whether, if it had, the bank would take notice of it. Hence he waited in anxious suspense while the formalities were being disposed of, and he breathed a sigh of relief when the man, reappearing from behind a screen, approached the counter, laid the cheque on it, and opened the drawer in evident preparation to pay. "How would you like it?" the cashier asked. "Five pound notes?"

"Thank you," said Andrew, "but I think pound-notes would be more convenient."

"Yes," the cashier agreed, "five pound Bank of England notes are not quite what they were when you could change them into gold."

He counted the notes out from a new bundle and passed them across the counter to Andrew, who counted them and bestowed them in his wallet. Then he wished the cashier "Good morning" and took his departure with a faint sense of having received yet another push from "circumstance" in a direction which was not that of his own choice. He had cashed Ronald's cheque, and thereby he had tacitly assumed the identity of the payee.

The sense of compulsion became more pronounced as he turned over once again the question of his immediate future. He had already decided that it was not practicable for him to go home at once. The identity of his clothes would have been already ascertained from the letters and visiting cards in the pockets and, by this time, it was probable that the police had communicated with Molly. He might even find them at the house and become involved in the inquiries. But the very thought of any kind of contact with the police filled him with horror. The risk was not to be entertained for a moment.

But after the initial inquiries, there would be the inquest. Of course, Molly would have to attend, and she would have to identify the body. That consideration gave him pause, for it opened up fresh possibilities. He knew of no recognizable differences between Ronald and himself, apart from their respective faces, and as the body had, apparently, no recognizable face, comparison in that respect was impossible. But might it be that he had some bodily peculiarity which Ronald had not, whereby Molly would be able to decide that the body was not that of her husband? The thing was conceivable. It was not even so very improbable. And if she did so decide, or even express a doubt as to the identity of the corpse, matters would be greatly simplified for him in regard to his explanations to her, though a doubt as to the identity of the body would be an element of danger.

The conclusion which emerged was that he had better wait and see what happened at the inquest. Meanwhile, he had to make some arrangements for food and lodging. Hotels he dismissed on the score of expense and especially of publicity – for he still had an instinctive urge to keep out of sight as far as was possible. The alternative was a bed-sitting-room or furnished apartments and, having decided on the latter, he bought a morning paper and betook himself to a tea-shop to study the advertisements over a cup of coffee.

His choice settled on three sets of apartments, all in the neighbourhood of Hampstead, a locality with which he had been familiar before he married. Having finished his coffee, he tucked the newspaper under his arm and made his way to the Broad Street terminus, where he took a ticket for the Heath Station and, selecting an empty compartment, opened the newspaper, and searched its pages vainly for some notice of the Crompton tragedy. Apparently the news had not reached London when the paper went to press.

In the matter of lodgings he was fortunate, for his first essay brought him to a pleasant, old-fashioned house in a small close off the High

Street, where he was offered a ground-floor room, with a bedroom over it, which seemed in every respect so desirable that he engaged them at once. Then, having paid a deposit to establish the tenancy, he returned to town to lunch and to collect his scanty luggage from the cloakroom at Cannon Street Station.

The latter part of the programme, however, he deferred until later in the day, for he had no object in returning to his lodgings before the evening, and he found some relief in walking about the crowded city streets while he turned over again and again the various possibilities of escape from the perplexities in which he was involved. He looked in, for a while, at the Guildhall Art Gallery and found some comfort in the companionship of the pictures. Then he had a late and leisurely tea, after which he repaired to Cannon Street Station and, having redeemed his luggage – Ronald's suit-case and his own attaché case – made his way to Broad Street Station. And here he had a most surprising and disturbing experience.

As he reached the top of the broad staircase, he observed that a train was waiting at the platform, and he judged by the hiss of escaping steam that it was ready to start, an opinion that was confirmed by the ticket collector who urged him to "look sharp" as "she was just off". On this, he started forward at a run, threading his way as well as he could through a dense crowd of people who were waiting for the next train. But he nearly missed his passage for, as he struggled towards the open door of an empty compartment, the engine-driver sounded his whistle and the train began to move. He barely managed to fling his luggage in at the open door and scramble up to the foot-board as the protesting guard rushed at him, pushed him in, and slammed the door.

As soon as he was shut in, he turned and thrust his head out of the window to compare his wrist-watch with the station clock. But the comparison was never made, for at that moment he met the eyes of a woman at the edge of the crowd and then only a few feet away, who was gazing at him with a most singular expression. As their eyes met, she uttered an exclamation and started forward, making as if she were about to try to board the train. She did, in fact, run alongside for a short distance until a porter, suspecting her intentions, firmly headed her off, and then Andrew, gazing at her in the utmost astonishment, saw her standing, still staring at him with that strange expression, until distance and a curve of the line hid her from his view.

It was an amazing affair. Who could she be? She was a total stranger to him – that is, to Andrew Barton. But he was Andrew Barton no longer. The reflection was a distinctly uncomfortable one. He had taken over the reversion of Ronald's nose. Might there be some other reversions of which he knew nothing? It seemed far from improbable, judging by the little that he knew of his late cousin's moral character and manner of life.

He tried to recall the woman's appearance. It was not difficult, for she was a somewhat unusual-looking woman – rather big, with a marked suggestion of energy and muscular strength and by no means uncomely. She had a good deal of hair of a coppery tint and eyes of a pale, bluish grey. Certainly not a woman whose appearance would be easily forgotten.

But what was the meaning of that singular expression? Astonishment undoubtedly. But the flushed face and the truculent grey eyes suggested emotions other than surprise. There was no denying that the woman's expression and manner had been definitely hostile. She was an unmistakably angry woman.

The incident, with its uncomfortable implications, supplied him with matter for thought until he reached his lodgings. And when he had unpacked the suit-case and went forth for a walk on the Heath, it continued to intrude itself as an added complication to the difficulties of his other problems.

But as he turned into the High Street on his way home, his attention was brought back to the main issues by the voice of a paper-boy announcing the contents of the late evening paper. As the boy came nearer, the generalized howl resolved itself into the words: "Kibble's Cross Murder – Inquest!"

In an instant the woman was forgotten, blotted out by the picture of the lonely road, the car with its two occupants, and the figures of the flying bandits. With a thrill of mingled curiosity and terror, Andrew stopped the boy, bought a copy of the paper and, having folded it and stowed it in an inner pocket, stole into his lodgings to read it in secret.

The report was complete to the inevitable verdict, for the inquest had been held in the morning and the proceedings had been comparatively brief. The deceased was a Mr. Oliver Hudson, the publisher of a technical journal, and the woman who was with him was his secretary. Miss Kate Booth. She, naturally, was the principal witness, and her evidence was taken first, and was to the following effect.

In the evening of Monday, the 27th of August, she was driving Mr. Hudson from his office to his home at Lenham. She was accustomed to drive him daily to and from his office and knew the road well. On the night of the murder, as they were approaching Kibble's Cross, she saw a closed car drawn up at the corner with its head pointing towards the side road. She thought she saw a man standing by it, but was not certain as, owing to the speed at which she was driving – about forty miles an hour

– she had to keep her attention fixed on the road. But someone must have made a signal of some kind for her car to stop, though she did not see it, for the deceased exclaimed, "Confound them! Pull up and see what they want."

She put on the brakes and stopped the car. A man came to the window and the deceased said, "Well, what is it?" and put his hand into the pocket in which he carried his revolver. The man said, "Put 'em up, both of you!" and pointed a revolver at the deceased, who, almost at the same moment, drew his revolver from his pocket.

She had only a rather confused recollection of what followed. Both revolvers seemed to go off almost at the same moment, and the bullet from one – it must have been Mr. Hudson's – made a hole through the wind-screen. The deceased uttered a cry and lurched up against her. When the revolvers were fired, she instinctively put down the accelerator pedal and the car jumped forward. She did not look back through the rear window as she had accelerated to over fifty-miles-an-hour, and she had to keep her eyes on the road.

At Padsworth, four miles farther on, she halted at the Welbeck Hotel and sent for a doctor and the police, but the deceased was already dead. A police patrol came in a few minutes and she told him what had happened. "Can you describe the man whom you saw at the window?" the coroner asked.

"Yes," she replied, "I saw him very distinctly, because, as he appeared at the window, the deceased threw the light of a torch full on his face, and it was a most extraordinary face – one that I could never forget. His nose appeared to have been broken, at any rate, it had no bridge. It was perfectly flat excepting at the tip, which was of the ordinary length and stuck out from his face like a bird's beak. He had grey eyes and I should say he was about thirty years of age."

"Could you see how he was dressed?"

"No – at least, I didn't notice anything about his clothing excepting that he had no hat on."

"Was he the only person present, or were there others?"

"I had an impression that there was someone behind him, but I did not actually see anyone. My eyes were fixed on the face that was lighted up by the torch."

"Are you quite sure that the man whom you have described is the man who fired the shot?"

"Yes, quite sure. There was no one else that I could see. And I saw the revolver pushed in over the edge of the window."

"Do you think you would recognize this man if you were to see him again?"

"I am certain that I should. It was a face that you could never forget."

"Did the deceased usually carry a revolver?"

"Only, I think, when he was motoring at night. Then he always did, and he declared that he meant to use it if he was stopped by an armed robber."

"Do you know of any reason for this attack? Had you anything of value in the car?"

"No, there was nothing of any value in the car beyond the money in our pockets."

"Did you notice if any cars overtook and passed you on the road?"

"Yes, several cars overtook us and passed ahead near London. I always drive at a very moderate speed until I am clear of the town and let the faster cars go by."

"Do you remember any car in particular?"

"Yes, there was one which passed us at great speed just as we were approaching the open country road. Mr. Hudson remarked upon it as it flew past."

That was the sum of the secretary's evidence. It was followed by that of the medical witness, who deposed that death was due to a gunshot wound penetrating the heart, and must have been practically instantaneous. Then came the patrol officer, who had not much to tell, and finally a detective-inspector with a remarkable gift for keeping his own counsel. But if somewhat elusive in regard to matters of fact, he was prepared to offer certain rather guarded opinions. Thus, when asked by the coroner if the circumstances of the attack were not very unusual and surprising, he agreed, and continued in explanation, "The police are inclined to believe that the whole affair was a mistake. There is reason for suspecting that it was a carefully planned robbery concerned with certain very valuable property which was being conveyed in a car along this road at about this time but, at the last moment, the thieves got flurried and attacked the wrong car. It is a pity," the inspector added, "that the deceased produced his revolver, because that probably flurried them still more, and led to the disaster."

The coroner discreetly refrained from further questions on this subject but, turning to another, asked, "With regard to the man who has been stated to have fired the fatal shot – is there any clue to his identity?"

Here, the inspector became once more distinctly elusive, but he was of opinion that, having regard to the man's very unusual and distinctive appearance, there ought not to be much difficulty in finding him and, once found, the witness, Miss Booth, would be able to identify him beyond any reasonable doubt.

This completed the evidence. If the police knew any more about the case, they were reserving their knowledge, and the coroner was wise enough to ask no questions that were not strictly relevant to the inquiry. There was no doubt as to how the deceased had met his death, and the verdict of wilful murder by a person unknown was a foregone conclusion.

The reading of this report had no other effect upon Andrew than to confirm him in his resolve to abandon for ever his original personality. The guarded tone of the inspector's evidence left him in little doubt that "the man with the deformed nose" had already been identified as Mr. Andrew Barton, and that the police were in hot pursuit. What would have happened if they had been able to run him to earth? The woman, Booth, was evidently prepared to swear that she saw him fire the fatal shot, and to this, the clear testimony of a competent eye-witness, there appeared to him no possible answer. Of course he was wrong, and in his peculiar state of mind, he was ignoring the strength of his defence. But even if he was mistaken as to his position if he were brought to trial, who can say that he was wrong in his choice of action? Who would accept the chances of a trial for murder – and an atrocious murder at that – when he could, by lying *perdu*, avoid even the accusation. In the character of Ronald Barton he lay under no suspicion whatever. His security was complete. If there were any incidental disadvantages, he had yet to discover them.

When he had finished the report, he turned over the leaves of the paper in search of some notice of the discovery of Ronald's body. He found it near the bottom of the page, headed, "*A Mystery of the Sea*", and the brief account read as follows:

> *Yesterday afternoon, a party of fishermen, sailing along the coast near Crompton, made a strange and gruesome discovery. Looking shorewards, they saw what appeared to be a pair of nude human legs protruding from under a heap of chalk which seemed to have fallen recently from the cliff. On this, they ran their boat in-shore and landed to investigate, when they found the nude body of a man buried under a mass of chalk fragments. The largest of the fragments, a mass weighing fully a hundred-weight, had fallen on his head and crushed it so completely as to render the face unrecognizable. The man had apparently been bathing, as a complete set of clothes was under the body, and from articles found in the pockets, it is inferred that the*

94

remains are those of Mr. Andrew Barton, of Fairfield near Bunsford. The inquest is to be held at Crompton to-morrow.

He laid the newspaper aside and fell into a train of deep but uneasy thought. And once again, the sense of unreality, of illusion, which had never quite left him since Professor Booley had waved the magician's wand to such amazing purpose, came over him with renewed intensity. He repeated the statement to himself: *"The inquest is to be held to-morrow."* The inquest! The inquiry into his own death! And he, the deceased, would read the report of the proceedings! It was an incredible situation, and the more he thought of it, the more impossible and unbelievable did it appear.

Yet he knew that it was a reality, and presently, as his thoughts settled down into a more orderly train, he began to be aware of certain possibilities which might affect his future and influence his conduct most profoundly. At present the position was that the body of Mr. Andrew Barton had been found on the shore. The identification by the clothing was not legally conclusive, but it would have occurred to nobody to doubt whose body it was. And the suggestion which had influenced others would doubtless take effect also on Molly. Her husband was missing, and here was a dead man – unrecognizable, but of similar age, size, and general appearance – who had been wearing her husband's clothes. Would the idea that this might possibly be another man even enter her head? It was practically certain that it would not. She, like the others, would take the appearances at their obvious face value, unless –

He sat up with suddenly sharpened attention to consider the position more critically. Yes, undoubtedly there were counter possibilities that had to be reckoned with. A single item of positive evidence would shatter the whole illusion. It need be but the merest trifle – a mole, a wart, a scar, a tattoo mark, any permanent characteristic on that body, which was not on the body of Andrew Barton, would be enough to destroy the suggestion effect of the clothing. And when once the question of identity was raised, all the mysterious and abnormal circumstances would combine to confirm the suspicion of a substitution.

And how would that affect him? On the whole, favourably, for it would simplify his task when he sought to convince Molly of his changed identity. True, it would set the police once more searching for the man with the deformed nose. But that need cause him no concern. That man was dead. If he had not died at the foot of the cliffs, he had at least died in Professor Booley's "beauty parlour". And, mercifully, the Professor would be on the high seas before the inquest opened.

95

But when the report of the inquest appeared, it raised questions of a somewhat different kind from those which Andrew had anticipated. The evening paper of Thursday contained only the opening of the proceedings, but *The Daily Telegraph* of the following morning had a full report, given in considerable detail, and this Andrew studied with the closest attention.

The first witness was Samuel Sharpin, the skipper of the fishing lugger, who deposed as follows: "On Tuesday, the 28th of August, I was aboard my boat, the *Sunflower*. We was beating up for Meregate Cove, where we berths. About four o'clock in the afternoon we was opposite Hunstone Gap when I noticed that some of the cliff had fallen down and I remarked to my mate that it was a good job that no one was underneath when it came down. Then the apprentice, Joe Todd, said he thought someone had been underneath, because he seemed to see what looked like a pair of legs sticking out from under the heap of chalk. So I got my glass and looked, and then I saw a pair of naked legs sticking out. So we put the boat about and turned her head inshore and, when we was near enough in, we dropped the anchor and pulled ashore in the dinghy. Then we saw a man lying under a heap of chalk with his legs sticking out. It wasn't a big fall. But one large lump of chalk, nearly half the size of a fish trunk, had come right down on the man's head, and there it sat, resting on his face, with the blood and stuff oozing out at the sides.

"My mate, who is a pretty hefty lad, hove the block of chalk off the man's face, though it must have weighed well over a hundred-weight, and then we could see that his head was smashed as flat as a turbot and his face hadn't got no more features than a skate. It was an awful sight. Gave us all a reg'lar turn.

"We took up the body and carried it to the dinghy – it wasn't far to go, for the tide was up and beginning to wash round the corpse when we came ashore. Then we carefully collected the clothes and put them in the boat, and then we just had a look round before we went back aboard."

The Coroner: "You had a look round. What were you looking for?"

Witness: "We wanted to see if the man had come to the place by himself. Because, as he was naked, and seemed to have been bathing and sitting on his clothes to dry himself, it seemed funny that he should have come there all by himself. So we had a look round."

"And what did you find?"

"We found that he hadn't. There was only a small strip of clear sand left opposite the Gap, but we could see quite plainly that there were two sets of footmarks coming down to the shore from the cart-track that leads down to the Gap, but there was only one set going up. So he must have come there with someone else."

Coroner: "This is very remarkable and very important. Are you quite sure about the two sets of footprints? I mean, are you sure that they were the footprints of two persons walking together and not merely the footprints of two persons who had come to the place separately?"

Witness: "No, they looked like the footprints of two persons who were walking together. So far as we could see them, they went on side by side, keeping at the same distance – about two foot apart.

"Well, when we had got the body on board, we up anchor and beat up for Meregate Cove. When we got there, we brought up at our berth and I sent Joe Todd up to Meregate Farm and told him to ask Farmer Blewitt for the loan of a seaweed cart to take the body into Crompton. So Mr. Blewitt he sends a man down with a cart and we brought the body into Crompton and handed it and the clothes over to the police."

The coroner thanked the witness for the clear way in which he had given his evidence and was about to dismiss him when Mrs. Barton, the wife of the deceased (if the identification is correct) asked to be allowed to put a question to him.

Coroner: "Certainly you may. What is it that you wish to ask?"

Mrs. Barton: "He has said that he saw two sets of footprints going down to the shore. I want to ask him if either of those two sets were the footprints of the – the deceased."

The coroner looked interrogatively at the witness, who replied, "Well, ma'am, I really can't say. How would I know whether they were his footprints or no?"

Mrs. Barton: "You found the shoes with the body. Did you not compare those shoes with the footprints?"

Witness: "No, ma'am, I never thought of it, like a dam' fool – begging your pardon."

Coroner: "What makes you ask that question? Is there anything special in your mind?"

Mrs. Barton: "Yes. I find it impossible to believe that my husband came there of his own free will."

Coroner: "We must consider that question presently. I think there is nothing more that we need ask this witness."

The next witnesses were the rest of the crew of the *Sunflower* who, however, had nothing fresh to tell. They merely confirmed the evidence of the skipper. They were followed by Mrs. Barton, the dead man's wife. As she took her place, the coroner expressed his sympathy and that of the jury, and his regret at having to subject her to the distress of giving evidence on so painful an occasion. He then proceeded with his examination. "You have seen the body of the deceased. Do you recognize it as the body of your husband, Andrew Barton?"

"No. It might be his body, but the dreadful injuries make it impossible for me to recognize it."

"Have you any doubt that it is the body of your husband?"

Here the witness was somewhat overcome but, after a pause, she replied, "No, I am afraid not. The clothes are his, and the things from the pockets are his, and the body might be his. There is nothing to suggest that it is not. But it is all very mysterious."

"In what way mysterious?"

"That he should be there at all, in that strange place. He left home in the morning to go to London on definite business, taking with him an attaché case containing some of his paintings, and he is found here, miles away from home and from London, apparently behaving in a way in which I don't believe he would ever have behaved – I mean bathing without bathing-clothes or towels – and accompanied by at least one unknown person. And the attaché case seems to be missing. I think there is something very suspicious about the whole affair."

"When you say 'suspicious', do you mean to suggest that your husband met with foul play?"

"That is what it looks like to me."

"But do you think that the mode of death is compatible with such a suspicion?"

"I don't know what to think. It is all so strange and unnatural."

"We can quite understand your feeling about it. The circumstances are, in fact, very remarkable. But now, to pass on to another matter, can you give us a description of your husband?"

"He was just under thirty years of age, about five-feet-eleven in height, of medium complexion with grey eyes and darkish brown hair. His nose had been struck by a cricket-ball which broke the bridge and caused some little disfigurement."

"I am sorry to have to refer to a subject that will be painful, but which is relevant to this inquiry. Are you aware that a man answering to the description of your husband has been accused of complicity in an attack on a motor-car when a Mr. Hudson was killed?"

"Yes. A police officer called on me to make inquiries and I told him all I knew about the affair. Of course, it is a mistake. The thing is ridiculous. My husband was a gentleman of reputation and of substantial means. He happened to be present when the attack was made. He told me all about it when he came home that night, and I repeated what he told me to the police officer."

"When he came home that night, did he seem at all agitated?"

"Not in the least. Of course, he was rather excited, though, at that time, he did not know that any one had been killed."

"And in the morning when he left home?"

"He was in his usual spirits. I understood that he proposed to call at the police station to report what he had seen."

"And do you connect his disappearance with the circumstances of that crime?"

"Certainly not. There was no reason why he should run away. He had nothing to fear."

"Is there anything more that you can tell us that would help the jury in arriving at their verdict?"

"No, I have told you all I know."

"Then I think we need not trouble you any further. We thank you for the very clear way in which you have given your evidence in circumstances which must have been very painful to you, and we should wish once more to offer you our most sincere sympathy."

The rest of the evidence was of little significance. The medical witness gave a brief description of the injuries and stated that death must have been practically instantaneous. The police superintendent described the reception of the body and the articles found in the pockets, by which the remains were identified in the first place, and mentioned as a curious coincidence that a bill containing the description of the deceased was posted up outside the station when the body was brought in. He was the last witness and, when he had given his evidence, the coroner proceeded to sum up the case for the jury to the following effect: "This inquiry is in some respects perfectly simple and in others rather obscure. Death was obviously caused by the fall of a heavy mass of chalk on the head of the deceased, and it is difficult to see how the fall of that mass could be other than accidental. On the other hand, an element of obscurity is introduced into the case by the fact that the deceased was apparently accompanied to the shore by some other person, that that person never reported the accident and has not come forward to give any information. There is no denying that the behaviour of that person to some extent justifies the suspicion that has been expressed by the wife of the deceased. If the cause of death were such as to admit of the idea of homicide, the conduct of that person would expose him to the gravest suspicion. As no such idea appears possible, his behaviour is quite incomprehensible.

"With regard to the strange conduct of the deceased, the circumstances connected with the murder of Mr. Hudson may offer some explanation. The superintendent has told us that at the very moment when the body was brought to the station, there was a bill posted outside giving a description of the deceased and stating that he was wanted for the murder. Such bills must have been posted outside all other police stations, and it may easily have happened that the deceased had seen one.

Then, even though he were innocent, he might have become seized by panic and fled to hide himself. It is rather an alarming thing to see one's description outside a police station and to learn that one is wanted for murder.

"That, however, is only a surmise. What we have to decide is when, where and by what means the deceased met his death. You have heard the evidence, and on that you must form your decision."

The jury eventually returned an open verdict. They were not entirely satisfied, the foreman said, that it was a case of death by misadventure. The presence of an unknown person, who had absconded and made no sign, suggested that there might be more in the case than met the eye. And to this, after some demur, the coroner assented.

Chapter VII
Molly

Andrew had read the report of the inquest on his own supposed remains with profound interest but with rather mixed feelings. The possibilities which he had envisaged had not been realized, and certain facts which he had overlooked had come into view. The double set of footprints, for instance, introducing an undoubted element of suspicion, came to him as a something quite unexpected. His attention had been so completely focused on the question of identity that he was unprepared for the new issues that had been raised.

Another matter of surprise to him was the shrewdness and strength of character displayed by his wife. It dawned on him that he had considerably under-rated her intelligence. In spite of the agitation that she must have suffered from the terrible circumstances in which she was suddenly placed, she had not only kept her wits unclouded, but had shown a quick perception of the significance of the facts which had transpired. She had, indeed, accepted the identity of the corpse – no reason had been shown for doubting it – but, with her ready common sense, she had instantly detected the abnormal character of the whole set of circumstances, and refused to take them at their face value.

The conclusions, then, which emerged were these. First, Molly had no doubt that her husband was dead. Second, that she utterly refused to regard that death as due to a mere accident. She was clearly convinced that some unknown person or persons were implicated in it. In short, that there had been some sort of foul play. Incidentally, it was clear that she did not take the murder charge seriously. To her, it appeared simply as a ridiculous mistake which would be instantly disposed of when suitable explanations were given. That he could have taken fright at the accusation and gone into hiding would appear to her incredible.

These were the data which he had to consider in forming his decision as to what line of action he should adopt. Hitherto he had responded passively to the pressure of events. He had simply gone whither he had been driven. But he could drift passively no longer. He had got to make up his mind as to what course he would steer through the amazing complications with which he was encompassed. So, for the first time, he set himself fairly to face the realities and decide what it was possible to do.

But to all his cogitations, as he tramped along the secluded paths of the Heath where he could think uninterrupted and turned over one plan after another, there was a permanent background. The tremendous shock that he had sustained from the police bill at Crompton had established in his mind an abiding horror – a sort of "gallows-phobia". And not, perhaps, quite unreasonably. Innocent men have been hanged on worse evidence than that which Miss Booth was prepared confidently to swear to. The man whom she had described had been identified as the artist, Andrew Barton, and since Andrew Barton was conveniently dead, dead he had got to remain. That was the undeniable postulate on which all his plans were based. There could be no resurrection of Andrew, for the instant he appeared, the police would pounce on him. But that postulate seemed to block every avenue of escape.

Thus the idea of going home and taking up the old life was obviously unthinkable, for Molly's husband was dead, and he was a visibly different person. The explanation which would have made it possible could not be given, for that would bring Andrew to life – and death. Some other plan would have to be thought of – when he had made things clear to Molly. And the question was: How was that to be done?

His first idea was to write her a long letter telling her all that had happened, signing his own name and announcing his intention to come home. She would recognize his handwriting, and that would make the story credible enough to prepare her for his changed appearance. But would she recognize his handwriting? It was not so very characteristic, and there was an awkward complication. It often happens that a similarity of handwriting runs in families, and his was a case in point. Ronald's handwriting had borne a distinct resemblance to his. Molly had noticed it and remarked on it. Then the handwriting would not be conclusive, and the fantastic story would have to rest on its merits. Then there was the complication of Ronald's character. Molly had admired Ronald, and had been indulgent in regard to his faults. Perhaps she liked him, but she had no delusions as to his character. She knew him to be a slippery rascal whose word was of no value whatever. She might – and probably would – reject the letter as an impudent imposture, an attempt on Ronald's part to personate her dead husband. And when he appeared, miraculously transformed into the outward semblance of Ronald, her suspicions would be instantly confirmed, and she would probably refuse to let him enter the house or to listen to anything that he might wish to say.

But that was not the worst. Molly had expressed her suspicion that there had been foul play of some kind. Now, if he wrote such a letter, he would have to admit that he had been on the shore at the time of the catastrophe – in short, that one of the sets of footprints had been his. What more likely than that she should suspect him (in the character of Ronald) of having made away with her husband? And once the suspicion of foul play was aroused, the letter itself would seem to supply the motive for the crime. It would suggest to her that Ronald, relying on his resemblance to her husband, had made away with Andrew with the deliberate purpose of stepping into Andrew's shoes.

Then what would she do? There was very little doubt. Molly had certain very pronounced feminine characteristics: She was quick to decide, confident when she had decided, and quick to act on her decision. If she disbelieved the wildly improbable story and wrote the letter down as a fraudulent attempt on Ronald's part to personate her husband, she would, without waiting for him to appear in person, at once communicate her suspicions to the police and show them the letter.

And what then? In spite of his anxieties, Andrew smiled grimly at the thought of the dilemma which would be created. He would stand to be accused of having murdered himself, and his only defence would be to prove his real identity – that of a person who was already accused of having murdered someone else.

Evidently, the letter would not do, nor would an unannounced visit, with verbal explanations, be much safer. The story that he had to tell was so preposterous that she would probably dismiss it off-hand as an imposture, and then there would be the same trouble as in the case of the letter.

So once again, Andrew found himself shepherded by inexorable circumstance in the direction in which he did not want to go. For in the end, he had to fall back on a compromise, and not a very good one at that. He decided, instead of committing himself either by letter or word of mouth, to feel his way cautiously and see if any opportunity offered. He would write to Molly, signing himself "Ronald", and proposing to call on her. When he met her, he would be better able to judge what was possible. Perhaps it might be easier than it looked. It was actually possible that she might recognize him in spite of the disguise. He had examined himself repeatedly in the mirror and had thought he had detected some small differences between himself and Ronald. Perhaps, after all, they were not so much alike as he had thought, and there might be some little peculiarities in his own face and person of which he was not aware, but which might be familiar to her. At any rate, he would see what happened, and if he failed the first time, at least he would not be landed in the net of the police.

But he would not write for a day or two. He would give her time to settle down after the inquest. And then, of course, there was the funeral.

The funeral! He had not thought of that before. Now the idea came upon him with devastating effect, imparting a horrible reality to the whole hideous farce. It was an appalling thing to think of his beloved wife standing in tears beside the grave of what was in effect a dummy corpse. It was an obscene outrage. But even in his anger, he realized how that dreadful farce seemed to set the seal of finality on his changed condition, what a formidable obstacle it raised to his attempts to dispel the illusion.

A couple of days later he dispatched the momentous letter, quite a short one, suggesting a call about tea-time on the following Wednesday, which elicited a still briefer reply agreeing to the date and time. Brief and rather colourless as it was, Andrew read it again and again. For it was Molly's own writing, and though it was addressed to a fictitious person, yet it seemed to bring him, for the first time since the transformation, into some sort of touch with real life – his own real life.

The days passed in a fever of impatience mingled with anxiety, of longing to stand once more within his own house and to see and talk with the woman who had become to him the centre and focus of life, of anxiety lest he should, after all, fail to break the spell that circumstance had cast over him. And when at last the day of the visit came, he set forth on his adventure thrilling with the strangest mixture of emotions, with love and yearning for the woman who was at once his wife and his lover, with hope and apprehension and even a queer, irrational tinge of jealousy. For it was Ronald, and not he, who was going to meet and talk with Molly. Any tokens of kindliness or affection that she might bestow would be for Ronald, not for him. And thus his thoughts, swaying back and forth to the contending pull of two opposing sets of emotions, oscillated continually between the intense yearning to give expression to the love that was welling up in his heart and a jealous fear lest the rival whom he was impersonating should be received with undue warmth.

At Bunsford, he changed on to the branch line and, alighting presently at the little wayside station of Fairfield, set forth to walk the familiar road that led to his home. It was a strange experience, that walk from the station. He had the feeling of a traveller, returning after a long absence, treading the well-remembered ways and looking on the familiar scenes of long ago. It seemed as if years had passed since he last turned into the lane. He found it unbelievable that it was but a week and a day since he had kissed Molly at the door and waved his hand to her from the gate. Once more the sense of illusion and enchantment came over him and, as he approached the cottage and his eyes were greeted by the fresh gashes that his hastily-wielded shears had made in the privet hedge, the conflict between his inner sensations and the visible and undeniable facts became positively bewildering.

Like a man in a dream, he opened the gate, stole unsteadily up the path, and plied the little knocker with a shaking hand. And all the while, he was trying confusedly to think what he should say to her, while in the background of his consciousness there lurked a dim hope that she might recognize him despite the transformation.

A few seconds passed. Then a light footstep in the hall, at the sound of which his heart seemed to stand still. The door opened and there she stood, his dearest Molly, his own beloved wife, garbed in a simple black dress, and looking pale and tired, but sweeter and more lovely than ever. At the sight of her, a flood of passionate love surged through him, a wild impulse to take her in his arms and kiss the roses back into her cheeks. It was but a momentary impulse, instantly chocked, not only by reason but by something in the way in which she looked at him. She greeted him cordially enough, but yet there was in her manner something new to him, a quiet self-possession with, perhaps, just a shade of chilliness.

He took the proffered hand with a deep sense of anticlimax. She had not recognized him. Of course she had not. How could he have expected it? But the initial failure left him with all his difficulties before him. He could do no more than wait and see if any opening offered. "Go and sit down, Ronald, while I make the tea," she said in a friendly, matter-of-fact tone, still with that faint suggestion of coolness, "I won't be a minute. You know the way. No, you don't, though. You have never been in this house before. It's in here."

She threw open the door of the dining-room and bustled away towards the kitchen, leaving him to enter alone. He stepped in through the open doorway and stood for a few seconds at the threshold, looking, with a lump in his throat, at the familiar room – his own room, where he had passed so many delightful hours, and where he now stood, a mere visitor, almost a stranger.

He ran his eye over the table, fondly taking in all the little, trivial details: The foolish little flower vases, the cake-basket, the biscuit-box, the jam-jars, all set out in correct array just as he, himself, had set them out on that *dies irae* in the irrevocable past when Fate, in the garb of a postman, had delivered his summons. And yet Fate had not been unkindly, for its messenger had forestalled another kind of summons, uttered in the King's name to the jingling of hand-cuffs. The reflection came to him as an opportune reminder just as Molly entered with the teapot and hot-water jug on the little tray.

She took her seat at the head of the table and he drew up his chair, but as he did so, he noted that it was not his own particular chair in which he had always been used to sit. That was drawn back against the wall. And the place that was "laid" for him was not his customary place,

105

but was on the opposite side of the table. It was a small matter but it defined his position as a visitor. "It is nice of you to come and see me, Ronald," she said, as she poured out the tea. "I couldn't write to you because I didn't know your address. I suppose you saw it in the papers?"

"Yes," he replied. "It was a dreadful shock, even to me. I can't bear to think of what it must have been to you."

She made no comment on this, and he continued. "I would have written sooner but I thought it better to wait until the – er – the – "

"Yes," she replied quietly, "I understand. It was on Saturday. In Fairfield churchyard. I brought him from Crompton. Everybody was awfully kind, especially the police."

She finished a little unsteadily with a catch in her voice, and Andrew, deeply moved, stole a furtive glance at her, marvelling admiringly at her quiet dignity and self-restraint. She made no parade of grief nor showed any outward sign other than the pale, weary face, the set composure of which smote him to the heart.

For some time neither of them spoke. She sipped her tea mechanically, seeming to be wrapped in thought while he searched his mind frantically for some suitable words but could think of none. At length she asked, "When did you see him last?"

He started, and his gorge rose at the lie that he would have to tell. But he made it as near the truth as he could. "I think," he faltered, "it was about two years ago, when I met him by chance in London."

"I remember," said she. "He told me he had met you. But I thought you might have seen him recently. I noticed that he had drawn a cheque for you – I am his executrix, you know – so I thought you might have met. He never mentioned the cheque to me."

"No," stammered Andrew, "I suppose he would not. It was a – a loan, you know, to enable me to – a – to pay a deposit. But I must refund it as soon as I can."

"You needn't worry, Ronald," she replied. "I don't suppose he intended you to repay it. At any rate, there is nothing to show that it was a loan, and if there were, I, as executrix, can use my own discretion in regard to debts. And I shall do what he would have wished me to do."

"That is very good of you, Molly," he said. "But things are different now. I ought to repay that loan when I am able to – though," he added, with a sudden realization of his present plight, "I don't know when that will be."

"As to that, Ronald," she said, in the same curiously quiet, level tone, "you know there is something to come to you when the will has been proved – or had you forgotten?"

106

He did know, of course, but he had completely forgotten until this moment. Now he gazed at her in dismay as she went on, without raising her eyes from her teacup. "There is a legacy of five hundred pounds. It was a separate insurance that he made in your favour in case he should die before you. He knew that his death would rob you of a faithful and generous friend, and this was to compensate you."

Andrew was thunderstruck. Here was an appalling complication! This money would presently be paid to him. He could not refuse it without disclosing the whole deception. Yet to accept it was to commit a blatant fraud on the Insurance Society, a fraud for which, if it were discovered, he could be sent to penal servitude. And that was not all. There was the principal insurance, which would be paid to Molly with his connivance. The whole affair was plainly and grossly fraudulent.

He was so overwhelmed by this new complication that he could only mumble incoherent acknowledgments and then once more subside into silence. Molly, having given the explanation, let the subject drop and, since he sat in dumb confusion, she made shift to keep up some sort of conversation, with long intervals of silence, avoiding, as far as possible, any references to the tragedy or her own immediate affairs. She spoke just in the colourless way in which she might have spoken to some chance stranger who had come to make a ceremonial call.

Meanwhile Andrew, returning such banal answers as fitted the indifferent, semi-formal character of the conversation, was inwardly fermenting with suppressed emotion with surprise, bewilderment, and exasperation. The position was preposterous. The woman who was making polite conversation and so obviously, though tactfully, holding him at arm's length, was his wife! His own wife, whom he loved passionately and who loved him with answering passion! He was starving for her love, filled with a devouring desire to fold her in his arms, to cover her pale face with kisses and murmur into her ear those soft endearments that had always evoked such sweetly frank response. If only he could shake off this bewitchment, how gladly and with what lavish affection would she fall into his arms! He knew it, and yet he could only sit like a fool, talking commonplace drawing-room stuff and even doing that badly.

But he could see no way out. The opening for which he had hoped had failed to present itself. Not only had there been no glimmer of recognition but, what was worse, she had accepted him as Ronald without a sign of doubt or hesitation. And civil and even kindly as was her bearing towards him, she was evidently on her guard. He could see clearly that she did not trust cousin Ronald, and he realized that she had understood that gentleman's character better than he had supposed.

But this wariness on her part was a complete bar to the revelation that he wanted to make. At the first word her suspicion would light up and, as the preposterous tale unfolded, she would listen – if she listened at all – with angry impatience to what would seem like a mere crude, silly imposture. It was useless to think of making the attempt, for failure seemed inevitable, and the probable consequences of failure were too appalling to contemplate.

Nevertheless, he tried to pull himself together and at least find something to say. From time to time, as they had been talking, he had caught her looking at him with a rather curious expression, an expression of faint surprise, as if she were "sizing him up" and found something in his manner a little puzzling. This he put down to his deplorably bad acting, for assuredly the real Ronald – the voluble, ready talker, suave, genial, and self-possessed – would not have sat mumchance at the table opposite his pretty cousin. He must rouse himself and, if he could not be Andrew, then he must be a reasonably convincing Ronald. "I suppose," he ventured, "you will shut up the studio now?"

"No," she answered, "I have taken it as my sitting-room."

He was slightly surprised. She had always left him in undisputed possession of the studio as a place that was entirely outside her province. "I have never seen this studio," said he (reconciling the blatant untruth to his conscience by the fiction that he was speaking in the character of Ronald). "Would you let me have a look at it presently? Andrew's pictures were always a great delight to me."

"Were they?" she exclaimed, in evident surprise. "I didn't know that you took any interest in them at all. Certainly I will show you the studio. We will go down there as soon as we have finished tea. Can I give you another cup?"

"No, thank you," he replied. "I have finished."

"Then," said she, rising, "we may as well go now, and I shall be able to show you one or two of his later works."

As they made their way to the back door and down the garden path, Andrew was impressed by a distinct change in her manner. She was still grave and a trifle prim but, ever since his reference to the pictures, a new note of cordiality had come into her voice. At the studio door, she produced her little key-wallet and, taking from it the well-remembered Yale key, inserted it, turned it, and pushed the door open. "You see," she said, as they entered, glancing at him for a moment with a wan smile, "I am keeping the nest warm."

He looked round the place, choking with emotion. Everything in it hailed him in a familiar voice and called to him to come back. Nothing was changed – with one exception. Formerly, the walls had borne only a few sketches given him by brother artists, and one or two of their paintings which he had bought from Montagu. Now these had been removed, and every available space was occupied by his own work. Every finished picture of his that they possessed had been collected from the house – excepting those which he, himself, had hung in the drawing-room – and put on the wall, and a number of sketches from his portfolio had been affixed to the match-boarding with drawing-pins – carefully placed at the edges to avoid making holes in the paper – and he noted with surprise the judgment with which they had been selected. His workshop had become a one-man exhibition.

Otherwise the place was just as he had left it. The half-finished picture stood on the easel, protected by its paper dust-cover, the "models" that he had been using – an old wooden-faced clock, the dismembered remains of another clock, and a number of tools and implements – were on a side table, together with the studies that he had made for the details of the picture. His big folding palette lay on the table beside the painting-chair with the brushes set out tidily on the rough wooden rack that he had made. Even the water dipper, he noticed, was full of clean water. "This is the picture he was at work on when he went away," said Molly, carefully turning back the dust-cover. "I think it was to be called 'The Clock-Jobber'. I don't know where he did the sketch for the interior, but the old man is our village cobbler. It is quite a good likeness, too."

Andrew looked at the picture with profound interest, trying vainly to realize that he had actually been working at it but little more than a week ago. The figure and part of the detail were nearly finished, but the background, the general lighting and colour scheme were only indicated. The most interesting part of the work was waiting to be done – waiting for him, who had the completed picture in his mind's eye. Would it wait forever?

He made a few appreciative but critical comments on the picture, to which she listened respectfully, and then (still in the character of Ronald) said, "I suppose his pictures have always been a great interest and pleasure to you."

"No," she replied. "That is what I now look back on with astonishment and bitter self-reproach. I never interested myself in his work, though it meant so much to him. Somehow, I let it become a thing apart, outside my own life and personal interests. I used to let him go off to this studio to do his day's work, just as if he were going off to a bank or an office. I was satisfied to hear what he had done and to see the pictures when they were finished, and I feel that I didn't understand them or appreciate them a bit. They were just our livelihood, and I used to see them packed up to go to Mr. Montagu – the dealer, you know – without a pang of regret. It seems very strange now when I think of it. It was a great opportunity. I might have been his good comrade in what he cared for most. And I let it go."

As she concluded, her voice sank almost to a whisper and her eyes filled with tears. He looked at her with adoring sympathy, and a flood of affectionate yearning surged through him. The impulse to take her in his arms and kiss away her tears was almost irresistible. He could hardly restrain himself. And yet his reason held him back. He realized that this was no opportunity, that her very preoccupation with her lost husband would make her proof against the grotesque story that he had to tell.

But what an exasperating absurdity it was! She was his own wife, his sweet Molly, sweeter than ever and still more dear, and he was her loved husband for whom her poor heart was hungering. And here they stood, held apart by this preposterous make-believe! The thing was monstrous! "I suppose," she resumed, reflectively, "it was because he was so interesting in himself and so sympathetic, because he entered so keenly into all my little feminine pleasures and interests as if they were his own, that I never realized that he might want some sympathy from me in the work that he loved. And he never obtruded his own personal affairs on me. There was not a grain of egotism in his nature. And, oh! Ronald! He was such a perfect husband, such a dear companion! In all the years of our married life, never an unkind word passed between us."

"No," Andrew said, huskily, "I know how fond he was of you and how happy you made him. He would like to think of you living here with his pictures to keep you company."

"Yes," she said, "that is just what they do. When I look round at them, I feel that he isn't quite lost to me. Because each of them is, in a way, a part of himself. The little figures in them were his friends, his children. They are acting his thoughts, just as he used to express them in words. And the places – the rooms and gardens and inn-parlours – are places that he knew, because he built them up out of his own imaginings. They, too, are really part of him."

"Yes," said Andrew, "that is quite true. A picture is, in a way, a detached piece of the painter's personality, just as a book is a sort of spiritual bud or outgrowth from the mind of the man who wrote it. And I think you will find the pictures grow more friendly and intimate the longer you live with them."

"But I do!" she exclaimed. "Already, I am beginning to see them with a new eye. At first it was the little stories that they tell that impressed me most. But now I begin to see that the story was only the subject, the peg, as it were, on which the real picture was hung. And I try to see how he did them and what he was thinking about and aiming at as he worked."

"Yes," said Andrew, "that is the way to look at pictures. Try to see what the artist had in his mind, what he wanted to do and what he wanted you to see – especially the composition, the pattern of form and colour and light and shade – the effect of the picture as a whole."

"That is what I am trying to do," said she, "and I think I am getting on." She glanced fondly round at the walls and murmured, "The dear things! They grow on me from day to day."

When they had examined the unfinished painting, she brought out the portfolio and they looked through the collection of sketches and studies, one or two of which he picked out to replace some of those on the wall. She adopted his suggestions readily and listened attentively to his comments and criticisms. "I didn't realize, Ronald," she said, "that you knew so much about painting. I never heard you talk about it to Andrew."

From the subject of pictures the conversation turned to her own domestic affairs, directed thereto by Andrew. But she was not very expansive and, somehow, her new-born cordiality of manner seemed to fade somewhat, especially when he ventured to proffer his assistance in setting her affairs in order. And, indeed, he was conscious of the incongruity of such a suggestion coming from the feckless, unthrifty Ronald. "I really don't need any help," she said. "Andrew had made such complete provision for me and left his affairs in such perfect order that there is hardly anything for me to do."

"Well," he said, "if I can't give you any help in that way, I hope you will let me look you up from time to time. I think we ought to see more of each other in the future than we have in the past."

She did not reply immediately, but he could see that the suggestion was not received enthusiastically, and that she was rather carefully considering her answer. At length in an earnestly apologetic tone, she replied, "Later, perhaps, Ronald, but not just at present. It was kind of you to come and I am glad you came. But it has been a painful experience. You are so dreadfully like Andrew. I had no idea you were so much alike. I suppose when I saw you together I only noticed the differences, but now everything about you reminds me of him, and I feel I can hardly bear it."

"But," he urged, "don't you like to be reminded of him?"

"In some ways," she replied. "In his pictures, for instance. But they are really himself. But this resemblance is different. There is something awful and uncanny about it, something ghostly and unreal. You've no idea, Ronald, how strangely like him you are. Even your face is his face."

"I should have thought we were quite unlike in that respect," he said.

"You are thinking of that dent on his nose," said she. "That troubled him so much, poor boy. But he exaggerated the disfigurement. It was only an accidental mark. It really didn't make any difference, at least to me. I was sorry that he let it worry him so much – principally on my account, I am afraid. And now, as I look at you, I see how little difference it did make. But you are like him in every way. You move like him, you write like him – your handwriting is his handwriting, and your voice! When you speak, I could shut my eyes and believe it was Andrew speaking."

His heart leapt. She had recognized him, after all! True, she thought she had only recognized his ghost. She was deluded by the false circumstances. But he could explain them away. His opportunity had come. And as she continued, he tried to think how he should approach the revelation. "You mustn't misunderstand me, Ronald. It is not that I am not your friend as I always was. Try to put yourself in my place. Remember what Andrew was to me – my dear husband, my faithful and loving friend, the very centre and focus of my life – and think what it must be to me to be in the presence of a counterfeit of him – now that he has gone forever – mimicking his looks, his movements, the very tones of his dear voice. Don't you understand how it wrings my heart?"

He listened, entranced and yet bewildered, still fumbling for the words which would enable him to open his revelation without setting up an immediate barrier of suspicion. "It is hard enough to bear," she went on, "to know that I shall never see him again, without having it driven home by a presence which mocks at my grief – a presence which seems to be his and yet is not his. Forgive me if I am unreasonable, but I am a broken woman. I have been robbed of all that I cared for and I cannot endure it patiently. My soul is in revolt. I ask myself: Can there be a God of Justice if such horrible wickedness is permitted?"

Her sudden change of mood disconcerted him. "You mean," he stammered feebly, "that dreadful, most deplorable accident?"

"Accident!" she repeated, and her voice, ringing out like a pistol-shot, made him start as if he had been struck. "No! I mean that crime. You don't suppose it was an accident, do you?"

"That was what I understood," he murmured uncomfortably. "I thought a block of chalk fell on him."

"A block of chalk was found resting on his poor battered head, and they assumed that it fell on him by chance. But did it? I don't believe it for a moment. A man – a good, kind fisherman – was able to lift it off by himself. Then another man could have lifted it on – to cover up the marks of murder. That is what happened. I am convinced of it."

"Why are you?" he asked.

"Why!" she repeated. "Because everything about the horrible affair shouts of murder. You know he was not alone. The footprints prove that – two sets going to the place and only one coming away. Somebody was with him. Who was it? Who was that secret wretch who sneaked away and hid himself like Cain? Nobody knows. But he shall be found. I will never rest, or let the police rest, until he is found. And when we find him, he shall pay his debt. He shall pay it to the uttermost farthing!"

Andrew looked at her in astonishment and dismay. This was a new Molly who confronted him with blazing eyes and hard-set mouth as she poured out her fierce denunciations. Never before had he seen her even ruffled, and he found it hard to realize that this stern-faced, resolute woman was his soft, gentle, girlish wife. But, as he gazed at her, all his new-born confidence and optimism melted away like snow before the sunshine. For he saw clearly that his opportunity – if there had ever been one – was gone. How, after what he had heard, could he tell her that he had been there? That those retreating footprints were *his* footprints? He dared not. As to the rest of his fantastic story, if she listened to it at all – which she probably would not – she would dismiss it with angry contempt, and denounce him to the police.

There was nothing more to say or do. His mission had failed and, since he had received more than a hint that his presence was not acceptable, there was no reason for prolonging his visit. Silently and gloomily he followed his unconscious wife up the garden to the house and, without re-entering the dining-room, prepared to take his leave. "If I mustn't come and see you, Molly," he said, as he took up his hat and stick, "I hope you will let me write to you sometimes. I hate the idea of dropping out of your life."

"Oh, I didn't mean that, Ronald," she replied. "Don't think I want to cut you. Perhaps, later, when I have got more used to – to my new condition, I shall be able to see and talk with you without having this awful ghostly feeling. At any rate, there is no reason why you should not send me a letter now and again. I should like to hear how you are getting on."

With this she opened the outer door and, apparently with some not unnatural feeling of compunction, shook his hand quite cordially, though her eyes remained averted from his face. He held her hand for a second or two, gazing, with a bursting heart, into the pale, sweet face that he was forbidden henceforth to look upon. Then, with a huskily murmured

"Good-bye!" he turned away and plunged down the flagged path, pausing, by habit, at the gate to look back and wave his hand in the old familiar way.

It was a grievous journey to the station. All the well-remembered objects that had greeted his arrival, now seemed, as he passed them and left them behind, to give him a sad and solemn farewell and, when he turned out of the homely little lane into the road, it was with something of the feeling of our earliest ancestors when they passed out through the gates of Paradise.

Chapter VIII
The Deserted Wife

It was in a mood of the deepest depression, combined with a sort of angry bewilderment, that Andrew reviewed his affairs as the train bore him back to London. To a permanent separation from Molly his mind refused assent as a thing to be seriously considered. He could not, and did not, for a moment entertain the idea of giving her up. Yet what could he do? For the time being, the barrier that she had placed between them seemed insurmountable. One plan only seemed possible, and for a few moments he was actually disposed to adopt it – the plan of going boldly to the police, proclaiming his identity, and taking the chances of his trial for the murder of Mr. Hudson.

But a very brief reflection convinced him of the futility of any such proceeding. For he was still obsessed with the infallibility of an eye-witness. There, at his trial, would be Miss Booth, who would swear that she actually saw him commit the murder. What answer could he give to that but a bare denial? And what weight would that denial have? It would have none. He would be found guilty and most certainly hanged.

No. There was no escape that way. He would have to put up with his false identity, even for Molly's sake. For she was, at least, better off as the widow of a man who had possibly been murdered than as the widow of one who had certainly been hanged. So he must wait and hope that some other way of escape from his intolerable dilemma might present itself.

But it was a maddening situation. Apart from the hideous illusion which cut him off from his wife, were other incidental and subordinate perplexities. There was, for instance, the life insurance. If he allowed the money to be paid, he would be not merely a party but the principal in a most blatant fraud. Yet he could not prevent the payment without disclosing his identity. Again, there was the probate of the will. It must be a criminal offence to connive at the probate of the will of a living man.

It was all very bewildering. Little did Professor Booley foresee the intricate train of consequences that the stroke of his syringe had set in motion! Nor was it possible for Andrew, himself, to foresee what further links in this extraordinary chain of causation might presently come into view, and as he realized this, he was disposed to speculate very

115

uncomfortably on the possible surprises that might yet be awaiting him in the incalculable future.

But at least one good result followed from his disappointing visit. The sight of his studio and his pictures had set his thoughts moving along the old, familiar channels. The artist in him had awakened. Once more, he was aware of the impulse to paint. And the impulse was not only artistic. He would have to earn his living somehow, and he knew that he could earn it by his brush. The painting would come, not only as a relief but as the necessary means of livelihood. Before he had reached the end of his journey, he had decided to set to work without delay.

Thus deeply preoccupied with his present difficulties and his plans for the future, he walked unguardedly into the first ambush that Fate had prepared for him. From Cannon Street he took his way through the fast-emptying streets to the terminus of the North London Railway, where he bought a first-class ticket for Hampstead Heath. Still wrapped in profound thought, he ascended the stairs to the platform and, worming his way through the throng of passengers, sought an empty compartment in the waiting train.

The guard was slamming the doors in preparation for departure as he reached the forward part of the train. Selecting one of several vacant compartments, he entered it and shut himself in. As he sat down, by a natural train of association, his thoughts reverted to the curious incident that had occurred on the last occasion when he had travelled on this line. He was even tempted to rise and look out of the window to see if that strange woman was by any chance on the platform.

But there was no need. At the very moment when the shrill screech of the guard's whistle rang out and the train began to move, a woman darted at the door, wrenched it open, bounced into the carriage, and slammed the door after her. Then she sat down in the seat opposite his and fixed her eyes on him with an unwinking, truculent stare.

He had recognized her in the first, instantaneous glance, and immediately averted his gaze to look out of the window. Not that he expected that manoeuvre to be of any avail. And it was not. There she sat, facing him with a stare as immovable as that of a waxwork figure. He avoided looking at her, but he was fully conscious of that basilisk stare, and it seemed to stir the very marrow of his bones. As the train gathered speed, he waited in fearful expectation for the next development.

It came after some three minutes of appalling silence. "Well. Haven't you anything to say to me?"

The voice was not unmusical, but it had a peculiar suppressed, menacing quality, as if the speaker were restraining herself with

116

difficulty from shouting. Andrew turned his head and met the gaze of the pale, truculent, wide-open eyes. "I think, madam," he replied, fully conscious of the futility of his answer, "that you must be mistaking me for some other person. I have no recollection of having had the honour of meeting you before."

The effect was very much what he had expected. She gave a shrill yelp of extremely mirthless laughter and then exclaimed, "Well, I'm damned! I really am, Tony! I knew you had the cheek of the devil, but this is a record performance, even for you. So you have no recollection of having had the honour of meeting your lawful wife before! Haven't you, indeed? Don't happen to remember meeting her at the prison gate at Wormwood Scrubbs on Easter Sunday three years ago, when she wasn't too thin-skinned to ask for Mr. Septimus Neville, the swindler, then due for discharge? Eh? You recognized her quickly enough then, didn't you, when she took you home and gave you your first square meal? But now your memory has given out. You are looking pretty prosperous. Perhaps you have got another wife, with a bit of money. Hey? Have you?"

As she ran off this string of questions, Andrew looked at her with very mixed feelings. For himself, he was frankly terrified, but he would have given a great deal to be able to speak some comforting words to her. For, in spite of her harsh tones and fierce manner, there was a faint undertone of tenderness in her voice and a suggestion of wistfulness in the way she looked in his eyes. He was profoundly sorry for her, and it was with real regret that he repeated – unavoidably – his futile disclaimer. "I assure you, most solemnly, Mrs. Neville – if that is your name – "

"Oh, drop it, Tony!" she interrupted impatiently. "Don't be a fool! What's the use of this play-acting? There's nobody here but ourselves. Now, listen to me. If I had any sense, I should be only too glad to be quit of you. But I'm not. Women are fools, and I'm one of the biggest of them. You've been a regular bad egg. You had all my money and spent it – and you know how that money was got. You've given me the slip over and over again and left me to get my own living as best I could. You've gone off philandering with other women, and you may have one or two other wives for all I know. I ought to hate you but, as I said, I am a fool. I am ready now to forget it all if you will only come back to me."

As she paused, Andrew gazed at her helplessly, utterly at a loss what to say. He was deeply moved and would have offered consolation, but that, he realized, would only have enraged her. But his silence and the sympathy and pity that his looks expressed led only to further misunderstanding. The fierceness died out of her face and her eyes filled. "Come back to me, Tony," she urged in soft, coaxing tones, "and we will

117

let bygones be bygones. I won't reproach you with what is past. You used to be fond of me, and I've never ceased to be fond of you. Come back and let us be as we were in the old days. I've got quite a decent job in the City, and I've made a nice little home out Brondesbury way. Come back to me, Tony, and I'll promise to make you as happy as you used to be. What do you say, Tony dear?"

The pitiful appeal in her swimming eyes and in the soft, wheedling tones of her voice wrung his heart. But he had to say something, and what could he say? It was a dreadful situation. At length, he stammered, "My dear lady, pray try to believe me when I assure you that there is some strange mistake, due no doubt, to an extraordinary resemblance. On my honour, you are a complete stranger to me."

The result was inevitable and clearly foreseen. In a moment all the softness faded out of her eyes, the blood rushed to her face, and she drew herself up, formidable and menacing. "Now, listen," she commanded in a stern voice. "I give you one more chance, and it is the last. Drop this foolery instantly and do as I said. The door is still open. But go on with this mumming for another instant and the door will slam. And, by God, it is not the only door that will slam. You know what I mean, and you know me well enough to be aware that when I start to fight, the gloves are off. Now, what do you say?"

"I can only say what I said before," he replied miserably. "If you would only try to believe – "

"That will do!" she interrupted furiously. "I've given you fair warning, and now it's a fight to a finish."

She flung herself back on her seat and for the short remainder of the journey sat silent, crimson-faced and scowling, perfectly still, but with a stillness suggestive of violence repressed to bursting-point. Andrew felt as if he were travelling with a Mills bomb.

As the train approached his destination, he watched her with furtive anxiety. His expectation was that when he got out, she would follow him to ascertain where he lived. But, to his surprise and relief, she did not. When the train stopped at Hampstead Heath station and he rose to alight, she made no move, and when he opened the door and wished her a civil "Good evening," she gave him one quick glance of concentrated anger and hatred and then averted her face.

Nevertheless, he walked very slowly along the platform, lingering at the farther end to see the train start, and it was not until it was well on the move that he turned towards the exit. And, even then, he waited at the foot of the stairs to see her carriage pass, and caught a fleeting glimpse of her face at the window, now glaring out at him like the face of some avenging Fury.

118

He drew a deep breath when the guard's van passed out and left the station empty. At least she was fairly out of his neighbourhood – for the present – and he was at liberty to consider precautions to avoid any future meetings. But so deep was the impression that she had made on him that, on leaving the station, instead of making his way directly to the town, he took the foot-path that leads past the ponds and made a wide detour of the Heath, approaching the town – or "village" – eventually from the Vale of Health. And as he strode across the open expanse of the Heath, with an occasional nervous glance behind him, and sneaked back towards his lodgings, he turned over in his mind the possible significance, as to the past and the future, of this ominous encounter, so ominous as, for the moment, to oust from his thoughts all his other difficulties and embarrassments.

Who was this woman? – this Mrs. Septimus Neville, if that was her name? He could have little doubt. She was Ronald's wife and, therefore, in the existing circumstances, his wife. It was a very awkward situation. As he reflected on the grim farce, he could not but be struck by the malignant perversity of Fate. From what insignificant causes do the most portentous consequences ensue! When Professor Booley had consulted him as to the type of nose that was to be created, he had hardly taken the question seriously. He had expected no more than a more or less shapeless lump, and all that he had desired in that moment of panic was to be made as unlike Andrew Barton, the missing murderer, as might be. And so he had asked for a curved nose-and had straightway been transformed into the likeness of his cousin Ronald. It had turned out to be a fatal decision. If he had only asked for a straight nose, all would have been well. He would have ceased to be the murderer and yet he would have been no one else, merely a person with a good deal of resemblance to the late Andrew Barton. Then he would probably have had no difficulty with Molly, and with her help he could have lived, under an assumed name, in peace and security.

However, the deed was done and could not be undone. In slipping out of his own personality, he had slipped into that of another person, and thereby had taken over the reversion of that other person's crop of wild oats. And it seemed that those wild oats were now ripe for the harvest. This woman certainly meant mischief – very naturally, as Andrew felt. And she was no contemptible antagonist. She was a fine woman, picturesque and rather handsome in a way, and obviously strong, energetic, and resolute. Obviously too, a woman of strong passions.

What was she planning to do? In his ignorance of her past – and his own, in his new character – he found her threats somewhat obscure. She had hinted darkly at some unlawful acts on his part, and had referred to the slamming of doors. What doors? The most probable answer was not a pleasant one.

His instinctive caution was not relaxed even when he approached his lodgings. On entering the little close, instead of going straight to the house in which he lived, he walked on to the extreme end that he might look back at the entrance and make sure that he had not been followed. And here he made a very welcome discovery. He had supposed that the close was a cul-de-sac with only one entrance. Now, he found at what he had thought to be the blind end, an arched opening like a doorway, giving entrance to a narrow alley. Following this, he emerged into a quiet by-street which presently brought him to Well Walk and so out on to the Heath. Having explored thus far, he retraced his steps, greatly encouraged, for here was almost complete security from the possibility of being followed, and tracked to his abode. He decided henceforth to adopt this approach to his lodgings and avoid the danger of entering the close from the High Street.

In the peace and security of his pleasant sitting-room he spent the evening in considering his position and making plans to meet the new complications that had arisen. Prudence suggested that he would be wise to migrate from Hampstead to some safer locality. But he was unwilling to move. His present quarters suited him perfectly. His landlady, Mrs. Pendlewick, was a delightful old woman with whom he was already on terms that were almost affectionate and, in view of his intention to resume his painting, the little old house was quite a valuable asset. The old-world room in which he sat, with its picturesque bay window and antique furniture, gave him an ideal cottage interior which would supply the backgrounds for a dozen pictures. So he decided to stay where he was, at least for the present, and avoid, as far as possible, exposing himself to view in frequented places, and having reached this decision, he spent the rest of the evening in making out a list of the things which he would need to enable him to get to work.

On the following morning, with the list in his pocket, he set forth (after a cautious inspection of the close from his bay window) by way of the back exit and the alley and along the open Heath to the tram terminus, walking warily, like a Red Indian upon the warpath, with an alert and suspicious eye on every human being who came into sight, especially on those of the feminine gender. Arrived at the terminus, he took up a sheltered and retired position to watch the waiting tram and observe the passengers as they took their places, and only when it was on the point of starting did he enter and select a seat near the door, whence he could escape easily if the need should arise.

It was all very irksome and disturbing to the mind, this furtiveness and incessant watchfulness. As he sat in his corner with the feeling of a fugitive from justice, while the tram rumbled on its way southward, Andrew reflected almost incredulously that but a fortnight ago he had been a reputable gentleman, living an ordered, peaceful life without a single enemy in the world. However, as the journey passed without incident, his mind became gradually more at ease, and he alighted in the Hampstead Road opposite the premises of the artist's colourman ready to give his attention to the business of the moment.

The outfit of a water-colour painter is a good deal more portable than that of a painter in oil, but as Andrew's purchases amounted to the entire stock-in-trade, including a substantial folding easel, a stool, drawing-boards, palette, brushes, tubes of colour, a supply of paper, and various other items, they resulted in two bulky and heavy parcels, burdened with which he went forth (having regretfully declined the salesman's offer to send them, as that would have involved disclosing his address) and waited in some anxiety for the tram. The chances that his pursuer – as he assumed her to be – would happen to be on that tram were infinitesimal to the point of absurdity. Nevertheless, when the vehicle drew up in response to his hail, he scanned the faces of the female passengers nervously as he stepped up to the footboard.

Similarly, but with more reason, he looked about him apprehensively as he alighted at the terminus, and disregarding the weight of his burden, struck out across the Heath with elaborate precaution and an occasional glance to the rear, before making the final turn into Well Walk. At the mouth of the alley he paused for a moment to make sure that the close contained no enemy and that no one was looking in from the High Street, and when, at length, he let himself in with his latchkey and closed the door, he experienced a sense of relief which he himself recognized as slightly ridiculous.

Having deposited his parcels in his sitting-room, he walked through to the back room, half-kitchen and half-parlour, to report his return and exchange a few-words with his landlady. And here he had a genuine stroke of luck. At intervals, amidst his distractions, he had been trying to think of a subject to fit into the background of his own room. Now, as he opened the door, after a perfunctory tap with his knuckles, behold a subject almost ready made. By the low, small-paned window sat Mrs. Pendlewick in a Windsor arm-chair with a little gate-leg table by her side and a lace pillow on her lap.

She looked up with a smile of welcome, viewing him over the tops of her spectacles as he stood in the doorway regarding her with delighted surprise. She made a charming picture. Figure, lighting, and accessories made up just such an ensemble as the old "genre" painters would have loved, and Andrew, being a belated survivor of that school, felt a like enthusiasm. For a while he stood, taking in the effect of the group – the old-world figure with its silky-white hair and antique cap, the black pillow with its covering of lace and rows of bobbins, the simple, elegant chair, and the ancient table-until the old lady became quite puzzled. "I am taking the liberty of admiring you, Mrs. Pendlewick," he said at length.

"Law!" she exclaimed, "I thought I had got beyond that."

"But this is a new accomplishment," said he. "I didn't know you were a lace-maker."

"New!" she chuckled. "I was a lace-maker before I was eight year old. Had my own pillow and bobbins and used to play at making lace. All the girls did down at my home – began it as child's play, and that's how we learnt. Down where I come from – I'm a Buckinghamshire woman, born and brought up at Wendover – down there you wouldn't meet a woman, no, nor a girl over ten, that couldn't make bone lace. They usually began to learn when they were about four or five."

"Why do you call it bone lace?" he asked.

"It's on account of these," she explained, indicating the bewildering multitude of little bobbins that dangled by their threads from the edge of the work. "They were mostly made of bone, though sometimes they used horn or hard wood. But bone was the regular thing because it was easy to come by. The lads used to make 'em for their sweethearts, carved 'em out with their pocket knives, they did, and some of them were uncommonly pretty bits of work. There's one that my grandfather made when he was courting my grandmother more than a hundred years ago, and it's as good as new now."

She picked out the historic bobbin – a little bone stick elaborately decorated with shallow carving – and held it up proudly for his inspection, and as he examined it she babbled on. "Yes, we're all of a piece, me and my belongings. We are all getting on. This chair that I'm sitting in was made by my Uncle James. He was a chair maker at High Wycombe, and they used to work out in the open beech-woods. And this little table was made by my grandfather – him that made that bobbin. He was a wheelwright, but he used to make furniture in the winter when the wagons was laid up and work was slack."

So she rambled on, but not to the hindrance of her work for, as she talked, her fingers were busy with their task, the right hand managing the pins while the left manipulated the bobbins, and all with an effortless dexterity that was delightful to watch. Nor were her babblings of the old country life in the Vale of Aylesbury without interest, and Andrew,

122

looking on and listening, found himself gathering the sentiment and atmosphere that he hoped presently to express in his picture.

After a spell of somewhat one-sided conversation, he ventured cautiously to approach the subject of that picture. But his caution was unnecessary, for Mrs. Pendlewick was all agog to "have her likeness drawn", as she expressed it. "Not but what I should have thought," she remarked, "that you might have found someone better worth drawing. Who wants to look at the likeness of an old woman like me?"

"You are too modest, Mrs. Pendlewick," he replied. "You don't appreciate your own beauty. Wait until you see my picture – you'll be surprised to find how handsome you are."

With this he retired – leaving her chuckling over her work – to unpack his parcels and to spend what was left of the morning in straining a sheet of paper on one of the boards and making one or two preliminary sketches to settle the composition and arrangement of the projected picture. Then, after the simple mid-day meal, he set up his easel in the kitchen, arranged the accessories and, while Mrs. Pendlewick went about her household activities, he drew in the background – the interior of the room, the window and the furniture, finishing with a short sitting until it was time for the model to lay the pillow on the table, spread a handkerchief over her face, and compose herself for her afternoon nap.

The painting of that picture did Andrew a world of good. It kept him indoors during the daylight hours and enabled him partly to forget the Avenger who was on his track and, as a normal and customary occupation, it brought him back out of the nightmare world in which he had been living, into the region of sane and ordinary human life. He worked with intense enjoyment. Painting was at all times the passion of his life, but now, to the pleasure that he always found in his work, was added a certain feeling of novelty, due to the nightmare interregnum. And as the work progressed and he perceived with some surprise that he was painting "at the top of his form", the discovery engendered a sense of power which was very pleasant in contrast to the sense of feebleness and futility by which he had been oppressed.

He worked steadily for four days, by which time the background was well advanced and the figure practically finished, and a most excellent portrait of the old lady it turned out, though he had not specially aimed at a likeness. They had been happy days, days of blessed relief from his troubles and distractions. But now, as the finishing work could be done at his own time without the model's assistance, his thoughts turned to an out-door subject or a study which would serve as the background for a studio composition. By this time his terror of the mysterious woman had subsided to a great extent. After all, what was the

123

risk of her shadowing him? She lived at Brondesbury and she had a job in the City. It was hardly possible that she could be haunting the neighbourhood of Hampstead.

Thus reassuring himself, and tempted out by a brilliant autumn morning, he set forth with his sketching kit to look for a subject. Sneaking out with his usual caution by the back way, he made for Well Walk and then struck out across the Heath to the Vale of Health. Here, on the high ground above the pond, he paused to look about him and consider which direction he should take, laying down his easel and stool the more conveniently to fill his pipe. But as he felt for his pouch, its lean and deflated condition reminded him that his stock of tobacco had run out.

It was very annoying, for his tobacconist's shop was at the lower end of High Street, a locality which he preferred to avoid by daylight. However, his stock would have to be replenished and, as he habitually smoked as he worked, he decided to brave the terrors of the High Street rather than go on with an empty pouch. Accordingly he picked up his easel and, turning his face westward, re-entered the village by way of Heath Street, walking quickly down that thoroughfare and the High Street and keeping a bright look-out for any suspicious figures of the feminine gender.

Having arrived safely at the tobacconist's and made his purchase, he began once more to turn over in his mind the most likely spots in which to look for a subject, and as the High Street and its northward continuations would, if he followed them, eventually bring him to the West Heath, he decided to explore that locality and particularly the neighbourhood of the Leg of Mutton Pond, in spite of the fact that this route involved the passage of close upon a mile of fairly frequented streets and roads. But the acute alarm which had affected him on the day following the encounter in the train had to a great extent subsided, notwithstanding which, as he strode along, pipe in mouth, he kept a wary eye ahead and around and even paused from time to time to look back and scrutinize such wayfarers as happened to be coming in the same direction. It was only when he had at length emerged from the village on to the rustic road known as Rotten Row, with the open Heath on all sides of him, that he was able to dismiss from his mind the idea of a possible "shadower" and give his attention to the search for a subject.

The search did not, in fact, take up very much time. He knew the place pretty well and was able to make his way almost at once to a suitable spot, which he found within a short distance from the pond. Here he spent a quarter-of-an-hour circling round and trying various points of view with the aid of a little cardboard view-finder, and having, at length, decided on the most satisfactory composition, he set up his easel and stool, refilled his pipe, and set to work with his open satchel hitched to the foot of the easel so that his materials were all conveniently within reach.

For upwards of an hour he worked away in uninterrupted peace, becoming more and more absorbed in his occupation as he proceeded from the preliminary drawing to the stage of colour. From time to time, solitary wayfarers had passed along the road below him and once a horseman had gone by at a canter. But although they all looked up at him as they passed, they had made no nearer approach. His pitch might have been in some remote country district rather than in a populous London suburb.

But his peace was not to remain entirely undisturbed. Pausing in his work to squeeze out on to his palette a fresh supply of colour from a tube, he became aware of a phenomenon familiar to out-door painters and designated in the slang of the craft a "snooper". The peculiarity of this type of onlooker is in his mode of approach. The simple rustic spectator regards the artist frankly as a public entertainer. He approaches boldly, takes up his position with an air of permanence and stares with undissembled wonder, sometimes at the painting but more usually at the painter. Not so the snooper. His approach is devious and unpredictable as to direction – excepting that it will inevitably bring him within a yard or so of the easel. He maintains an ostentatious unawareness of the painter's existence until, by some unforeseen chance, his sinuous advance (at a gradually diminishing speed) has brought him abreast of the easel, when he takes one long, hungry, side-long look and passes on.

As he squeezed out the little blob of pigment, Andrew observed a man approaching from the high ground above him and, by the manner of his advance was able to make a provisional diagnosis. Not that he minded in the least. He had no prejudice against the snooper who, after all, is actuated only by a reasonable curiosity tempered by good manners. It is only the unseasoned amateur who quails at the snooper's approach.

The man drew nearer by degrees, meandering down the slope, and still profoundly unconscious of Andrew's existence, until he had reached the inevitable spot a yard or two from the artist's pitch, when he suddenly "unsnooped" (if I may use the expression) and became a normal spectator. "Mind my having a look?" he asked civilly, with his eye on the painting.

"Not at all," Andrew replied, "but there isn't much to look at. I have only just begun."

With this permission, the man stepped forward and took up a position close beside the artist, making a show of examining the painting,

125

though, in fact, he seemed more interested in the painter, judging by the frequent and somewhat furtive glances that he stole at Andrew's profile. "A lovely scene!" he remarked. "Don't you think so?"

"Well," replied Andrew, "I would rather say 'pleasant'. It is not romantically beautiful."

"No," the other agreed, "not romantic but, as you say, very pleasant, extremely so. You are making a pretty big sketch, aren't you?"

"It isn't a sketch," Andrew explained, "it is going to be a rather detailed study, so it has to be a good size."

"I see. But there will be a lot of work in it, won't there? If you are going to paint all the detail?"

"Yes," Andrew replied, "there will be plenty to do. But I rather like a subject with a fair amount of matter in it."

"But won't it take a deuce of a time to do? I should think there will be a week's work in it, at least."

"No," said Andrew, "not as much as that. I shall probably get it finished in three or four sittings."

"Will you, indeed? Three or four sittings? And how long do you generally work at a sitting?"

"As long as the light will let me," Andrew replied. "Three hours, at the outside. It doesn't do to go on too long, or you get the light and shade all wrong."

Here Andrew paused rather definitely. He was a naturally polite and civil man, but he disliked interruptions of his work and he felt that the conversation had gone on long enough. Apparently, he had managed to convey a hint to this effect, for the man stepped back a pace and remarked apologetically, "I am afraid I am hindering you, and that won't do. Perhaps I shall be passing this way again before you have finished your study. I should like to see the completed work. In the meantime I will wish you 'Good morning' and many thanks for letting me see it in its early stage."

With this he turned away and walked off towards the road, and Andrew, glancing at his retreating figure, was struck by the contrast between the brisk, purposive manner of his retirement and his aimless, sauntering approach. Apparently he was making up for the time that he had spent in the conversation, and Andrew, turning once more to his painting, proceeded to do likewise.

But in spite of his growing interest in his work as the picture progressed, the incident had left a slightly disagreeable impression. Perhaps it was natural that the disturbing and insecure circumstances in which he was living should cause him to view with a critical and suspicious eye any chance contacts with strangers. So he persuaded

126

himself and tried to dismiss the matter from his thoughts. Nevertheless, he could not quite get rid of the impression. Little details of the incident tended obstinately to recur. He recalled the elaborate, leisurely, snooperesque manoeuvres by which the man had managed to establish the contact, and then the quick, definite way in which he had departed, with the air of having accomplished some specific object. Again there was the rather futile conversation. Obviously, the man neither knew nor cared anything about painting. Yet he had made a very evident pretext to open the conversation.

Then there was the appearance of the man. Once or twice as they were talking Andrew had looked in his face, and his artist's eye had been quick to note certain slight anomalies. The hair was sleek and black and had somewhat the appearance of a wig, and the eyebrows were black and heavy, like little moustaches. But the eyes were pale blue and the skin was fair and slightly freckled. Now, the black-haired blond is a recognized type, and is not so very rare. Still, there was an anomaly, and to a man in Andrew's circumstances, it tended to attract uneasy notice. Oddly enough, the one really significant point in the incident escaped him entirely. It was only by the light of subsequent events that he was able to perceive the relevancy of that apparently futile conversation.

He worked on for nearly an hour beyond his allotted time in order to get the painting well started and, by degrees, as he became more and more engrossed in his task, the incident faded into the background of his mind. But the impression tended to revive when, the day's work finished, he packed up his kit and started on his way home, manifesting itself in a long detour, punctuated by searching glances around, before the final plunge into Well Walk.

Chapter IX
The Axe Falls

Andrew's forecast was so far correct that, by the end of the third sitting, his picture was virtually finished. Another short sitting to "pull it together" would see the work complete. He leaned back on his stool and viewed the painting critically and not without satisfaction. For the work of one who was not a professed landscape painter, it was quite a creditable performance and, as the material for future studio subjects, it should be of some value.

He had sat thus for a minute or two, inspecting his work and comparing it with the landscape before him when he became conscious of someone standing behind him. Assuming that it was some stranger who had crept up to have a look at the painting, he took no notice and remained still, in the hope that the spectator would presently depart without attempting to open a conversation. But as the time ran on and the onlooker remained immovable, he began unostentatiously to put his kit together, for he had finished work, and certain internal sensations associated themselves pleasantly with the lamb cutlets which he happened to know would be awaiting him at his lodgings.

He disposed of his colours, put the brushes away tidily in their case, emptied the dipper, and put it into its special pocket, and still the person behind him made no move. Finally, he took the pin-frame board, on which the painting was stretched, off the easel and slipped it into its compartment in the satchel. Then he stood up and turned round to face the spectator and instantly he realized that some kind of mischief was brewing. There was not one spectator, but three: Two tall, massive men and one shorter, and though the latter had close-cropped reddish hair and no eyebrows to speak of, Andrew had no difficulty in recognizing the "snooper" of two days ago.

The shorter man looked at him insolently and asked, "Well, have you quite finished?"

"I have finished work for to-day," Andrew answered.

"Good!" the other rejoined. "Now we can get to business. I don't think you spotted me a couple of days ago."

"I did not," Andrew replied, "and I don't spot you now. Who are you?"

The man laughed, contemptuously. "Well, I'm damned. Tony!" he exclaimed. "Lizzie's right. You've got the cheek of the devil. Pretending to my face that you don't know who I am!"

"It is no pretence at all," said Andrew. "You are a complete stranger to me."

The man laughed again, more savagely, and was about to make some further rejoinder when one of the tall men interposed. "There's no use in wasting time on talk," said he. "Is this the man?"

"Yes," was the reply. "This is the man."

Thereupon the tall man took a pace forward and, touching Andrew lightly on the arm, said, "I am a police officer, and I arrest you, Anthony Kempster, on a charge of fraud and personation."

"But," protested Andrew, "my name is not Anthony Kempster."

"That may be," replied the officer, "but my information is that you are Anthony Kempster and I hold a warrant for your arrest. You can see it if you like."

"There is no need," said Andrew. "I am not disputing your authority to arrest Anthony Kempster. My point is that I am not Anthony Kempster. This gentleman has made a mistake."

"Well, you know," the officer replied, not uncivilly, "we can't go into that here. You must come with me to the station. Then the Inspector will read the charge over to you and you can say anything that you want to say. I can't listen to any statements. My duty is simply to arrest you and hand you over to the proper authorities. And you had better not say anything until you get to the station. May I take it that you are coming along quietly?"

Andrew smiled sourly. "It doesn't seem as if I had much choice," said he. "I'm certainly not going to make a scene, and I hope you are not going to."

"No," replied the officer, "you will not be subjected to any unnecessary indignities if you don't give any trouble. We've got a car waiting down the road. We shan't have to walk you through the streets. Are you ready?"

"I shall be when I have strapped my easel and stool together," Andrew replied.

"Very well," the officer agreed. "Be as quick as you can."

Andrew folded up the easel and the stool and strapped them together. Then, grasping the handle of the strap, and slinging the satchel over his shoulder, he turned to the officer. "I am at your service now," said he, whereupon the two officers placed themselves one on either side and, as the informer walked on ahead down the slope, they followed in his wake. Looking forward in the direction which the red-headed man was taking, Andrew now saw, on the road below, just at the entrance to Rotten Row, a large car and, a few yards ahead of it, a taxi-cab. As they bore down on the car, Andrew observed that the driver, who wore some kind of official uniform, had emerged from his place by the wheel and was standing by the door, which he was holding open and, glancing at the taxi-cab, he could see, though not very distinctly the face of some person peering out through the rear window. But he had not much time for observation, for when they reached the car one of the officers immediately stepped in and directed him to follow, which he did. Then the other officer entered and was shut in by the driver, who now walked round to the front and took his place at the wheel, and Andrew, glancing out through the front window, saw the redheaded man getting into the taxi, which started as he slammed the door. After a few seconds the car – the engine of which was already running – started forward and the mysterious and not very promising journey had commenced.

It was not in any sense an agreeable journey. Sitting jammed in between the two rather bulky officers, Andrew's bodily discomfort was swallowed up by his mental distress, for he could not view the immediate future without the gravest forebodings. He had disclaimed all knowledge of the red-headed man but, as he recalled his features and his colouring, he was conscious of a distinct reminiscence of the woman who had threatened him with retribution. With those threats he naturally associated the present proceedings, and although the whole affair was founded on a mistake, he had grave misgivings as to the possibility of rectifying that mistake. "I take it," said he, "that that man who was with you is not a police officer?"

"No," was the reply, "he is a civilian. Name of Blake. Said you knew him."

"I don't know either the name or the man," said Andrew.

"Well," the officer rejoined, "he knew you – unless, as you say, he has made a mistake. However, we'd better not discuss that now, and if you take my advice you won't do any talking until we get to the station, because whatever you may say will be taken down in writing and used in evidence, and then, perhaps, you will wish you hadn't spoken."

Andrew thanked the officer for his advice, and in pursuance of it relapsed into silence. He had plenty to think about but, oddly enough, his thoughts tended principally to concern themselves with Mrs. Pendlewick. At this moment she was probably laying aside her lace pillow and considering, with an eye on the old wooden-faced clock, whether it was yet time to commence operations on the lamb cutlets. His direct, physical interest in those cutlets had suddenly become extinct, but his thoughts turned wistfully to the peaceful little room, the table with its snowy cloth and immaculate china, and the picturesque little brown jug which gave the beer an added flavour. He could see it all vividly in his mind's eye, and already he began to wonder gloomily when he should look on it again in the flesh.

But his chief concern was for Mrs. Pendlewick. He thought of her with all her preparations made for his entertainment, awaiting him, at first impatiently, then anxiously, and then, as the time ran on, and it became evident that something out of the ordinary had happened, in real alarm. He was very troubled about her and wondered vaguely what she would do when night came and still he did not return. Would she set inquiries on foot? And if so, how would she go about it? Perhaps she would apply to the police. He hoped not, because it was his intention, at present, not to disclose the whereabouts of his abode. He didn't want the police to get access to his rooms to rummage among his possessions and possibly establish a connection between Molly and the alleged Anthony Kempster. That would be intolerable in any case but, if he should be unable to dispel the illusion as to his identity, it would be absolutely disastrous.

So his thoughts rambled on until the slowing down of the car in a rather narrow street recalled him suddenly to his present business. He had taken no note of the route that the car had followed and had no idea as to his present whereabouts, but when the car stopped opposite a building with a large doorway and a constable in the uniform of the City Police came forward to open the door, he realized that he must be somewhere in the City of London.

The senior officer stepped out and halted to wait for him, and he followed immediately with the other officer close on his heels. They entered through the wide doorway and passed into a large, bare room furnished with some benches and a few plain Windsor chairs. On two of the latter were seated the only occupants of the room, the red-headed man and the woman whom he had met in the train. The former greeted him with an insolent stare and a half-suppressed grin. The latter – to whom he bowed stiffly, raising his hat – gave him one swift glance and averted her face. It was evident to him that she was greatly distressed and agitated, for not only were there traces of tears on her pale and drawn face, but her hands, resting on her lap, trembled visibly. It was easy to see that already she was being torn by pangs of remorse.

The senior officer had gone out of the room immediately on their arrival. He now returned and took charge of Andrew, beckoning to the woman to follow. "Not you," he added, as the red-headed man rose from his chair. "You stay where you are. I'll send for you if I want you."

With this, he conducted Andrew out of the room, along a passage, and into a large, barely furnished office where an inspector sat at a desk with a number of papers before him, a grave, scholarly-looking man with a bald head and a pair of round-eyed, horn-rimmed spectacles. As they entered, he motioned the woman to a chair and cast an inquisitive glance at Andrew. "Is this Kempster?" he asked.

"Yes, sir," was the reply.

"Has he made any statement?"

"No, sir, excepting that he denies that he is Anthony Kempster."

The inspector nodded and, pulling out a drawer of the desk, selected a paper from a number of other documents and turned to Andrew. "You will want to know exactly what you are charged with. I will read out the charge and then hear if you have anything to say. It is that you, Anthony Kempster, did, on the 20th of April, 1919, and on divers other occasions, falsely personate one Francis Redwood, deceased, for the purpose of effecting a fraudulent life insurance. That is the charge. Now, is there anything that you wish to say? You are not bound to say anything, but if you do, I have to caution you that anything that you may say will be taken down in writing and used in evidence."

"All that I have to say," said Andrew, "is that I am not Anthony Kempster."

The inspector looked round at the woman and asked, "What do you say to that, Mrs. Kempster? Is this man your husband or is he not?"

"I say that he is," she replied in a low voice.

The inspector turned to Andrew. "Now," said he, "what do you say to that? Do you say that this lady is making a false statement?"

"No, not at all," Andrew replied earnestly. "I have not the least doubt that she is speaking in perfect good faith. But she is mistaken. She is, indeed. I can only suppose that I bear a remarkable resemblance to her husband, but I assure you that I never met her until a few days ago when she spoke to me in the train. I beg you, madam, to look at me again and see if you are not mistaken."

As he spoke, he looked appealingly in the woman's face, and as he did so, he saw that it had taken on a very curious expression – an expression of which he could make nothing. Whether it denoted doubt or hope or relief or merely bewilderment he was unable to judge. But it was a very singular expression, so singular that the inspector noticed it, for he remarked, "I suppose there isn't any mistake? I don't see how there could be, but still, we want to be sure. Are you sure, Mrs. Kempster?"

She hesitated for a few moments and then replied, doggedly, "Yes. He is Anthony Kempster."

132

The inspector turned once more to Andrew and said in a patient, persuasive tone, "You hear that. What do you say now?"

"I say again that this lady is mistaken."

"Very well," said the inspector, in the same quiet, persuasive tone, "let us suppose that she is. Then, you see, if you are not Anthony Kempster, you must be someone else. You see that, don't you?"

Andrew had to admit that the inspector's logic was unimpeachable. "Then," the inspector pursued, "all that you have got to do is to prove that you are someone else and we shall know that you can't be Anthony Kempster. Come, now. Tell us who you are."

Andrew was, naturally, not unprepared for this question, and had already decided on his reply. "I think," he said, "that, under the present circumstances, I would rather not give my real name."

"Very well," said the inspector, without the slightest trace of irritation, "then, for the present, we will call you Anthony Kempster. Any objection to telling us where you live?"

"I would rather not give any address, at present," Andrew replied.

"Quite so," said the inspector. "Not a very communicative gentleman. But if you won't tell us anything about yourself, we shall have to find out as best we can. Perhaps you have got something in your pockets that will help us."

He glanced significantly at the officer who was standing by, who immediately stepped forward and laid an expert hand on Andrew's coat in the region of the right breast. "What's this?" said he. "Feels like a pocket-book."

He slipped his hand into the pocket and adroitly fished out a wallet, which he handed to the inspector and, as Andrew saw it transferred, his heart sank. For it was Ronald's wallet, the one which he had found in the pocket of the coat on that fatal day at Crompton. He had used it ever since, but merely as a receptacle for notes, and exactly what else it now contained he had no clear idea. There were one or two closed compartments, which he had opened and glanced into in case one of them should contain his own or any other letter which might have to be burned. But there were no letters, and the few scraps of crumpled paper that were in them he had carelessly left there unexamined. It was a singularly foolish thing to have done, as he now realized, and he watched the inspector's proceedings with growing alarm. "Four pound-notes," the latter remarked, laying them out on the desk. "Clean ones. Look as if they had come from a bank." He looked into the open compartments and, seeing that they were empty, went on to the two closed ones. Opening one, he apparently drew a blank, for he reclosed it and passed on to the other. From this he extracted three crumpled pieces of thin paper, one of which he smoothed out carefully and studied with evident interest. Turning to Mrs. Kempster, he asked, "Do you know the names Bailey and Warman?"

"Yes," she replied. "They are wine merchants at Ipswich."

"Did you ever live at Ipswich? And if so, at what address?"

"I lived at Ipswich with my husband at Number 23, Beckton Street."

The inspector nodded. Then, taking up the piece of paper, he held it out towards Andrew for his inspection. "Just take a glance at that," said he.

Andrew took a glance at it, and instantly realized that he was lost. It was a tradesman's bill ("*Account Rendered*"), and it set forth that A. Kempster, Esq., 23, Beckton Street, was a debtor to Bailey and Warman, Wine and Spirit Merchants, Ipswich, in the sum of four pounds. "Well," said the inspector, "that seems to dispose of the mistaken identity racket. I presume you agree with me?"

"I agree with you that it seems to," Andrew replied. "But I still maintain that I am not Anthony Kempster."

The inspector smiled sardonically. "You certainly know your own mind," said he, "but you have got to explain how you come to have a bill in your pocket addressed to A. Kempster, Esq. Can you explain that?"

"I am afraid I can't," Andrew had to admit.

"No," said the inspector. "I don't suppose you can. And that, I think, completes our business for the present. You will remember, Mrs. Kempster, that you are bound over to give evidence. You had better come back here about three o'clock. We shall take Kempster before the magistrate as soon as possible. Say a quarter-to-three."

While these directions were being given Andrew looked at his alleged wife. Her expression had changed and was more inscrutable to him than ever. There was nothing in it in the least suggestive of elation or triumph. Rather did it suggest disappointment and the most profound dejection. As the inspector finished speaking, she rose and, without a glance at Andrew, turned away and walked slowly towards the door. Suddenly she snatched out her handkerchief and held it to her face, and there came to his ear the sound of muffled sobs.

The inspector followed her with an impassive, but not unkindly eye and, as she disappeared, he proceeded to moralize. "Women," he remarked, "are kittle-cattle. She started the ball, all agog to get it moving, and now she'd like to stop it. And she can't. She doesn't know her own mind as well as you do, Kempster."

He smoothed out the other pieces of paper and, having glanced at them, attached them to certain other documents which he put away in a tray. Then he copied on a slip of paper the numbers of the notes and,

134

having put this slip with the other papers, replaced the notes in the wallet and handed the latter back to Andrew. "You may as well keep that for the present," he remarked. "You will be detained here until we are able to bring you before the magistrate, which we shall do this afternoon."

With this, he drew his chair up to the desk and resumed the studious pursuits in which he had been "discovered", as the playwrights express it, and Andrew reverted to the custody of the attendant officer, who proceeded to pilot him out of the room, and presently to transfer him to the care of a uniformed constable, who conducted him to a passage in which were a couple of rows of black-painted doors, each distinguished by a number. One of these doors the constable unlocked and opened and, having thrust in his head and sniffed, shut it again and passed on to the next. Here, the result being apparently satisfactory, he threw the door wide open and invited Andrew to enter. "I may as well relieve you of your kit," he remarked, assisting his charge to remove the satchel from his shoulder and taking possession of the easel and stool. "The things will be taken care of and given back to you at the proper time. And I must just see what you have got in your pockets. It is only a formality, but there are certain things that you are not allowed to have about you while you are in custody. Just put them out on the table and let me look through them."

Andrew emptied his pockets, laying the various objects on the little fixed table. These the constable glanced through and, having satisfied himself that the pockets had been really emptied, selected from the collection a pocket knife and a small bundle of string. "You can put the rest back for the present," said he, "and I hope you'll be able to keep them and have the others back. And now, what about grub? When did you have your last meal?"

"About eight o'clock this morning," Andrew replied. "But I don't really feel as if I could manage any food."

The constable shook his head. "That won't do," said he. "Mustn't give way. You'll be going before the magistrate presently, and you'd better not go on an empty stomach. Take my advice and get a square meal while you can. You'll feel better after it. You have got some money, and you can have anything in reason that you want. Better let me send out for something."

Andrew accepted the well-meant and obviously sensible advice, handing over the modest sum that his custodian suggested as sufficient. Then the constable retired, locking the door and leaving him to his own reflections. Those reflections were, naturally, not of the most agreeable kind and were singularly confused. The attitude of the constable impressed him with mild surprise. He might have been a nurse or attendant in some Erewhonian convalescent home for moral invalids, so solicitous did he seem for the welfare of his charge. And even the dry, impersonal civility of the other officers was not what he would have expected.

But once more, his thoughts reverted to Mrs. Pendlewick. By this time, the lamb cutlets were ruined beyond redemption, but she would not have given him up. He pictured her sitting, working automatically at her lace, looking up from time to time at the clock and painfully aware of the aroma of the half-cremated cutlets.

His meditations were interrupted by the arrival of his meal and, acting on the further exhortations of the constable, he made a determined and moderately successful effort to dispose of it, with the result foreseen by that experienced officer. He felt better in a bodily sense. The physical depression left him, and even his mental state seemed to be improved.

But his mind was still in a state of utter confusion. Presently he would be brought before a magistrate and charged with a crime that he knew nothing about. What was he to say? Of course, he would declare his innocence, and he would continue to deny that he was the person charged. That he must do, since it was the actual truth. But he realized the utter futility of it. The wine merchant's bill had labelled him Anthony Kempster, and to that "attribution" he had no answer. It was even doubtful whether he would not further prejudice his case by saying anything at all.

At any rate, there was nothing that he could do. When the time came, he would have to stand passively and watch this tragedy of errors working itself out to its illogical conclusion. He felt like a swimmer in some swift stream, borne along by the irresistible force of the torrent. Ahead of him the rapids were roaring, but he could do no more than drift passively to his destruction.

Chapter X
Gaol

As Andrew took his place in the dock at the police court, he looked around him with a sort of dull, impersonal curiosity. He had never been in a police court before and had but a vague idea as to the nature of the proceedings that were conducted in such places. First, he noted the persons present. Of those whom he knew, the one who instantly caught his eye was his accuser, Mrs. Kempster, and as he looked commiseratingly at her pale, haggard face and the restless hands that were incessantly clasping and unclasping themselves, he realized the truth of the inspector's remarks. It was easy to see that she would have given a good deal to be able to undo the knot that she had tied.

Sitting beside her on the same bench was the redheaded man and, now that he saw them together, the likeness between them which he had detected at the morning's meeting was still more noticeable. From them his eyes wandered to the inspector and the two officers who had arrested him and, passing quickly over the background of mostly squalid strangers who had loafed in to look on, he looked lastly at the magistrate, a wooden-faced elderly man of a pronounced legal type.

The proceedings were opened by a senior police officer, apparently a superintendent. He began by intimating that he was proposing only to produce evidence of arrest and identification and that he would ask for a remand to enable the necessary evidence to be obtained and the witnesses notified. Then he went on to give a general outline of the case, to which Andrew listened with profound interest, having up to this time only the most obscure notion as to what he was accused of. "This," said the superintendent, "is a prosecution under the False Personation Act. The prosecutors are the Griffin Insurance Society, but it has not been possible for them to be represented on this occasion. The facts of the case are, in broad outline, as follows:

"In February, 1919, the accused, Anthony Kempster, came to live as a boarder with Mr and Mrs. Francis Redwood at Colchester. Francis Redwood was a retired builder who had given up his business on account of bad health. He was more or less an invalid and, in addition, he suffered from an aneurism, from which it appeared certain that he would die in the course of a year or two. He had saved a little money on which he lived, but his means were very small and he took a boarder to eke them out. In view of his bad health, and especially of the aneurism, he

137

had some time previously made a will, leaving the little property that he had to his wife and making her sole executrix.

"When the accused had been living with them about a month, he began to urge Mrs. Redwood to insure her husband's life, pointing out how very little provision there was for her under the will. But of course, Redwood was uninsurable by reason of his aneurism, as she explained to him, the question of insurance having been already considered. Then Kempster suggested to her that he thought he could manage the insurance if she left the business to him, but stipulated that nothing should be said about the matter to her husband. She did not at all clearly understand what it was that he proposed to do but, as he assured her that he would take the whole responsibility, she agreed and promised to keep the affair secret from her husband.

"Then Kempster left Colchester for a time and went to live at Dartford under the name of Francis Redwood. There he consulted a Dr. Croft about his health – which was quite good – and mentioned that he was thinking of insuring his life. Now, Dr. Croft was the local examiner for the Griffin Insurance Society, and he naturally recommended his office and, at Kempster's request, gave him a proposal form. This Kempster filled up – in the name of Francis Redwood – giving the name of Dr. Croft as his ordinary medical attendant. Then he went up to the London office for the medical examination and in the end managed to effect an insurance in the sum of two-thousand pounds.

"As soon as the business was concluded, he went back to Colchester and took up residence with the Redwoods. After a month or two, he notified the Insurance Company of his change of address, still in the name of Francis Redwood, although he had by now resumed his own name of Anthony Kempster, imitating Redwood's signature as he had done on the proposal form.

"In April 1921, shortly after the second premium had been paid, Francis Redwood died. But he did not die of the aneurism. He died of pneumonia following influenza, and a death certificate was given to that effect. Accordingly, as there was nothing unusual in the circumstances of the death, no inquiries were made but when the will was proved, the two thousand pounds were paid to the executrix in the ordinary way.

"About six months after the death of Francis Redwood, Kempster proposed marriage to the widow, Elizabeth Redwood, and was accepted. They were married at Ipswich and went to live there, having sold the Colchester house. After the marriage, Kempster managed to persuade his wife to allow him to put all their money into his bank with a view to making some investments. But those investments were never made. What became of the money, Mrs. Kempster never knew. In some way it disappeared, and then Kempster himself disappeared, and from that time until a week or two ago she never set eyes on him again.

"Then one day she got a passing glimpse of him getting into a train and was subsequently able, with the assistance of her brother, Joseph Blake, to locate him as living in the neighbourhood of Hampstead. There he was arrested this morning by Detective Sergeant Morton. On his arrest, he stated that his name was not Anthony Kempster and that he had never heard of such a person. At the police station he was confronted with Mrs. Kempster, who identified him as her husband, Anthony Kempster, but he still denied that that was his name and insisted that she was mistaking him for someone else."

"Apart from the identification by Mrs. Kempster," said the magistrate, "is there any evidence that he is Anthony Kempster?"

"Yes, your Worship," replied the superintendent. "As he refused to give any name or address or any sort of account of himself, it was necessary to search him. Then there was found in his pocket a bill addressed to A. Kempster, but he still denied that that was his name. That is a summary of the case, your Worship, and I shall now call the witnesses to prove the arrest and the identity."

The first witness was Detective Sergeant Roger Morton who deposed that, acting on information received, he had that morning proceeded to Hampstead Heath where he had arrested the accused, who was then engaged in making a sketch of the Heath, in execution of a warrant. He had administered the usual caution and the accused had made no statement beyond a flat denial that he was the person named in the warrant. The accused had not, however, resisted arrest.

The next witness was Inspector Frank Butt. He deposed that the accused had been brought to the station by the last witness at 1:45 pm. He (the inspector) had read the charge to him and administered the usual caution. The accused was then confronted with Elizabeth Kempster, who identified him as her husband, Anthony Kempster. The accused declared that she was mistaken and that he was not Kempster, but he would not say who he was or give any address or any account of himself whatever. He was then searched and there was found in his pocket a wine merchant's bill (produced and handed to the magistrate), addressed to A. Kempster. He could not account for his having this bill in his pocket, but he still maintained that the charge was a mistake and that he was not Kempster.

When the inspector had retired, the superintendent intimated that that was all the evidence that he was producing on this occasion, that he was asking for a remand to enable him to produce the other evidence and

139

summon the witnesses, and that, as the accused refused to give any account of himself and his place of abode was unknown, he opposed bail.

The magistrate looked curiously at Andrew for a few moments and then said, "You have heard the evidence that has been given. Do you wish to say anything? You are not bound to. But – " and here followed the inevitable caution.

"I don't wish to say anything at present," Andrew replied, "excepting that my name is not Anthony Kempster and that Mrs. Kempster is mistaken in believing me to be her husband."

"What do you say that your name is?" the magistrate asked.

"I prefer not to give my name, at present." Andrew answered.

"Nor your address or occupation?"

"No, your Worship."

"Then," said the magistrate, in the calm, impersonal tones to which Andrew was becoming accustomed, "you will have to be remanded in custody. You are remanded for seven days."

Thereupon Andrew was taken in custody by two constables and removed from the court. But he was not taken back to the police cells. Instead, he was conducted out of the building by a side passage and, on emerging into the street, found a prison van drawn up at the kerb. Passing – like a wedding guest, but with certain differences – between two rows of spectators, he was conducted to the van and assisted up the back steps into the dim and rather malodorous interior.

He had often wondered what the inside of a prison van was like. Now his curiosity was satisfied. It consisted of a dark and narrow passage with a row of doors on either side. Each door was furnished with a keyhole and a small grated window like the inspection trap in a convent gate. When one of the doors was opened, it disclosed a narrow compartment suggesting something between a sentry box and an extremely ascetic sedan chair, with a fixed seat, polished by friction with the persons of dynasties of disreputable occupants, and a small space in front of it to accommodate the feet of the sitter. On this uncommodious seat Andrew sat down gingerly, not without some uncomfortable speculations as to the characteristics and personal habits of the last occupant, and as soon as he was seated, the door was closed and locked.

It was a strange experience and far from an agreeable one. On the closing of the door, he seemed to be plunged into almost total darkness, excepting a faint glimmer from a ventilator over his head and the little square of twilight before him which indicated the position of the tiny grated window. For the back door of this criminal omnibus, when it was closed, admitted no more light than what was able to struggle through a very moderate-sized grated opening, and even this was largely obscured by the person of the "conductor".

But any deficiency in the matter of light was more than made up in smell. The whole vehicle was pervaded by the peculiar and distinctive odour of unwashed humanity and, as the van proceeded on its round, picking up from time to time fresh consignments (which were fresh only in a limited sense), the flavour of the "imperfect ablutioner" became ever more pronounced. Yet these halts were not altogether unwelcome, for then, for a few moments, the back door was flung open and the depressing darkness was relieved by a flood of light, by which Andrew, peering out through the little grating, could get a glimpse of the new arrivals and could observe that the few other gratings which were within the range of his vision were each occupied by an eye similarly engaged in inspecting the new tenants.

But even the round of a prison van comes at last to an end. The termination of this journey was indicated to Andrew by a slowing down of the vehicle, a sudden increase of darkness, and then, as the van stopped, a clang from the rear as of the shutting of a heavy gate. After a brief interval there came a sound from the front like the opening of another gate, the van moved on, the light reappeared, and the gate – now behind – clanged to and its closure was immediately followed by the click of a large lock. Finally the van stopped once more, the back door was opened, the doors of the respective cells were unlocked, and the process of unloading began.

As he took his place in the queue that filed in at the prison gate, Andrew glanced curiously at his fellow sufferers. Assuming with more probability than charity that they were mostly criminals, their appearance was no advertisement for crime as a profession. Nor did it suggest that the profession was favoured by the elite of mankind. Manifest poverty and physical unclean-ness were the distinguishing characteristics of the immense majority and, taken as a random sample of the population, even this small group was noticeably below the average both in physique and in the outward signs of intelligence. It looked as if crime were not a "paying proposition", though, to be sure, it might be argued that the present assembly represented only the unsuccessful practitioners.

Meditating this question as he followed the shuffling crowd, Andrew was yet again impressed by the civil and tolerant attitude of the officials. In the reception ward, the officer who presided over the ceremonies instructed him quite kindly in the necessary preparations, and the doctor who examined him might have been the medical referee of an insurance office. Nevertheless, the general atmosphere of the place was unspeakably grim and forbidding. Never for a moment was the inmate allowed to forget that he was a prisoner in the custody of the law. As he followed the warder from "Receptions" to his final resting-place in a faraway gallery, every one of the innumerable light iron gates which they passed had to be unlocked to admit them and was immediately locked behind them, and when, tramping along the iron-floored gallery, they came to a door bearing a number corresponding to that on the label which had been attached to his coat, that door had to be unlocked to admit him to his cell, though being furnished with a spring lock, it fastened him in without the aid of a key. But before it was closed the warder, having gathered that he was a "green hand", lingered to give him a few general instructions, to explain the use of the bell by which an attendant could be summoned, and to caution him against the improper use of this important appliance. Then he retired from the cell, the heavy door slammed, the spring lock snapped audibly, and the sounds from the galleries without suddenly became muffled and remote.

When Andrew was left alone he proceeded to do what every man probably does when he finds himself in prison for the first time: He made a tour of inspection of his apartment and examined its furniture and appointments. There was little of the picturesque dungeon in the appearance of the cell. It was just a small, bare room with whitewashed walls and a fair-sized iron-framed window with very small panes. The furniture consisted of a small fixed table, a solid stool, and a plank bed with the bedding – mattress, pillow, blanket, sheets, rug, and pillow-slip – neatly rolled up into a cylindrical bundle, not without regard to the decorative possibilities of the variously-coloured items. There was a tin jug, filled with water, a drinking vessel (officially known as a "pint"), a tin plate, a salt cellar, and a wooden spoon. Other conveniences included a tin basin, a comb and brush, a dust pan, a queer little sweeping brush like a tiny besom without a handle, and a slate with a stump of pencil attachéd by a length of string. A bell push communicated with the warder's room and actuated a sort of semaphore arm outside the cell and, lastly, the massive door was furnished with a tiny round window of thick glass covered by a sliding shutter – but the shutter was outside and beyond the prisoner's control.

Having made his inspection, he looked round for other objects of interest. The slate did not attract him. As a writing or drawing medium it was a poor substitute for the excellent paper to which he was accustomed, and the stump of pencil was worn to a shapeless end which repelled him. He would have liked to sharpen it, but his knife had been taken from him. Then he transferred his attention to the walls of the cell. In one respect they conformed to the traditional ideas of a dungeon, for they were covered with the comments and lamentations inscribed by former tenants and, as these were written in lead pencil, it was obvious that they were the work of "remands" like himself. He wandered round idly reading them and filled with an ever-increasing wonder at their amazing puerility and the almost incredibly low intelligence that they suggested. He was surprised, too, to notice the almost complete absence of any tendency to obscenity in them. They seemed to be just the harmless outpourings of perfectly vacant minds. Most of them might have been the work of backward children of eight or nine.

Some were mere pathetic expressions of self-pity, such as "*Poor Old Blower*", repeated more than a dozen times on different parts of the walls. Others gave bald particulars of their offences with rough estimates of their expectations. Thus, "*Joe Viney from Wood Green expects a stretch for stabbing*", "*Moley from Upper Rathbone Place, Oxford St. W. Committed for trial North London Sessions for a Byke*", "*Nobble in for a bust*", "*Jim Brads from Rathbone Place fullied for a bust*", "*T. Savage from Chapel St expects 6 wks.*", "*J. Williams expects 3 years*", and so on. Others made complaints or accusations, as "*Charles Kemp was put away for deserting by Mr. Goldstein of Hackney road*", or "*Jackson is the one. Hurry up and catch HIM. Jackson you have ruined me. Jackson will get 300 years*", while yet others merely recorded names, as "*Mikey from the Boro.*", written in reverse in six places with several unfinished attempts, and "*Hymey from Brick Lane and Ginger Jim*".

Andrew studied these curious memorials gravely and with deep interest. They were certainly quaint, and to some they might have been amusing. But not to Andrew. To him their significance was too sinister. They labelled their writers the refuse, the "throw-outs", of humanity. And what was he but one of them? He drew the stool up against the wall to provide a back and, seating himself, fell into a train of vague reflection on the dismal prospects that were opening out before him. His feeling was one of utter helplessness. He was the victim of a whole complex of illusions, and he did not in the least see how those illusions could be dispelled. Perhaps some ideas might come to him later. There was plenty of time to think over matters – seven days before he had to make his next appearance before the magistrate. And so his mind rambled off to other subjects, to thoughts of Molly, and especially to Mrs. Pendlewick.

His reflections were interrupted by the arrival of his supper, a hunk of brown bread and a mug of cocoa, both excellent and very welcome. Refreshed by his meal, he took a little exercise pacing up and down his cell. Finally, having laid his mattress and made his bed, he took off his shoes and some of his clothes and laid himself down on his not very resilient couch.

Naturally, in the early part of the night, he slept little if at all. The day's excitements and the unusual surroundings tended to keep him awake, as did the lack of the customary darkness for, when the daylight faded, the cell was lighted by a square of ground glass illuminated by a lamp outside the cell, which threw in its unwelcome rays throughout the night. And then there was the "Judas" – the little round spy-hole in the door. To Andrew that was the most disturbing influence of all. He found himself continually watching it with expectant nervousness and straining his ears to catch the foot-falls of the warder on his rounds and to be ready to see it open. Later he learned that the night warders wear shoes with list soles, which explained why, on each occasion, the uncanny, secret "blink" of the Judas-like the opening and closing of a bird's eye-startled him by occurring silently and without warning. And each time it left him more nervous and more profoundly humiliated.

But even a prisoner's night is not endless. He heard midnight strike on some clock in the world of freedom without, and then he knew no more until he was roused to clean up his cell and get ready for breakfast. And so began a day which was like all the succeeding days. He washed himself in the tin basin and even brushed his hair gingerly with the official brush. When he was summoned out for exercise, he tidied himself up as well as he could and, having taken his number label, or badge, down from the hook on which it hung when he was "in residence", he attached it to his coat in the prescribed manner and was ready to take his place in the ranks of the other occupants of the gallery and be marched off to the prison yard.

The process of taking exercise was doubtless beneficial, but it was not exhilarating. The surroundings of the exercise ground of a local prison are hardly romantic. Still, to Andrew, on his first morning, the experience had the charm of novelty. He found himself embedded in a long and squalid procession trailing interminably at a quick, mechanical stride along narrow, sinuous paved paths just wide enough to accommodate the single file that moved along them, supervised by a number of warders, each of whom stood, statue-like, on a low stone pedestal, from which he could look over the heads of the exercisers. Nominally, the march was conducted in absolute silence. Actually, there was a more or less continuous hum of conversation of a very curious ventriloquial quality due to the fact that the "old hand" can talk without moving his face. From time to time a warder would call out sternly to the conversationalists to "stop that talking", but still the mumble went on. Even the most experienced officer is baffled by a talker who stares straight before him and preserves a face of wood.

144

The experiences of this first day included two that were not repeated. The first was connected with the prison photographer, who, having looked him over critically, proceeded to execute a couple of portraits of him, one full face and one in profile. The other brought him within the province of the officer who took the finger-prints of His Majesty's guests and entered their descriptions and other "particulars" on the prescribed form for deposit at the Criminal Record Office, to all of which procedure Andrew submitted without demur, although, as an unconvicted, and therefore nominally innocent man, he was entitled to object. But he saw no reason for objecting – indeed, he was fast settling down into a state of dull fatalism, apprehensive of the future but hopeless of any means of controlling it.

This fatalistic attitude was viewed with deep disapproval by the fatherly middle-aged officer who looked after him by day. Andrew, as we have said, was a naturally polite man, instinctively suave and courteous in manner, with the obvious appearance and habits of a gentleman, circumstances which commended him to Officer Bolton, who had been in the Army and had something of the old soldier's social exclusiveness. Moreover, Andrew gave no trouble. He obeyed the rules, accepted the discipline, made no complaints as to his food or otherwise, and was in all respects a model prisoner and, as such, was duly appreciated by the staff who had to deal with him.

But his passive attitude, apparently taking no measures for his defence, caused the good-natured warder great concern and, in the course of his official visitations, he took the opportunity to offer advice and admonitions which became more urgent as the days passed. "Look here, Kempster," he said, "you ought to have legal assistance. Get a decent solicitor, tell him all about it, and let him make out the best case he can."

"I don't see what he could do for me," replied Andrew, "as I don't choose to give my real name."

"I can understand that," said Bolton (who, to Andrew's astonishment, seemed quite prepared to entertain his innocence). "But it's no use being thin-skinned. The name is bound to come out, sooner or later, if you get sent to prison. You know, you are not taking this affair seriously enough. You are charged with personation. Now, that's a felony, and the magistrate can't deal with it. He will commit you for trial at the Old Bailey if you can't make a proper defence, and you may get a nasty sentence. Don't wait for that. Get a solicitor and tell him the whole truth. Don't you see, my lad, it's no use your going into court and telling them that you didn't commit the crime and they've arrested the wrong man. That's what every accused man says, and nobody takes any notice. You've got to get someone who knows the ropes to manage your little business. And you've got to look sharp about it. Time's running on. In three days more the remand expires, and then you'll be up before the magistrate for the second hearing and, if you haven't got something definite to say, you'll be "fullied" as the crooks call it – committed for trial. Now, you think over what I've said, and don't take too long thinking over it."

Accordingly, Andrew did think over it, but his thinking brought him no more forward. Once more he considered the advisability of boldly proclaiming his real identity. But the plan did not commend itself for two reasons. First, it would be useless. No one would believe him. There was Elizabeth Kempster, ready to swear to him as her husband and probably there would be other witnesses who would swear to his identity as Anthony Kempster. And what evidence could he produce in support of his statement that he was the late Andrew Barton? To call Molly would be obviously useless. Her manner towards him when he had visited her had shown evident mistrust. She would certainly scout his claim to be her dead husband as a transparent and impudent fraud. The only witness who would be of any use – Professor Booley – was on the high seas or in some inaccessible part of the United States.

But even if he were able to prove his real identity, how would that help him? He would merely prove that instead of Anthony Kempster, charged with personation, he was Andrew Barton, charged with murder. It was the old dilemma and, so far as he could see, there was no way out.

So, once more, he was thrown back on his original position. Fate had him fast in its clutches. He had no choice but to accept whatever might befall. And in this frame of mind he waited in dull expectation for the second hearing, waited to see what Fate really had in store for him.

The second hearing impressed him as something compounded of a nightmare and a chapter from *The Arabian Nights*. In spite of Bolton's exhortations, he was unrepresented by a lawyer. As he did not mean to disclose his identity, he had nothing to tell the solicitor, and he could make his bald denial without legal aid.

But it was a strange and bewildering experience. Standing in the dock, he listened to the evidence with a feeling of stupefaction. He heard a gentleman from the insurance office read out the proposal form for the insurance of Francis Redwood and give the particulars of the transaction, including the payment of £2,000. He heard the doctor from Dartford identify him as the man whom he had treated under the name of Francis Redwood, to whom he had given a proposal form made out in the same name, whom he had examined in connection with the said proposal form and whom he had, in the character of the proposer's usual medical attendant, certified as a first class life, still under the name of Francis

146

Redwood. He heard a person of the name of Baines, who appeared to be Redwood's successor in the business, describe the late Francis Redwood, whom he had known long and intimately, as a feeble, sickly man, extremely unlike the accused, and further declare most positively that the accused was certainly not Francis Redwood but was one Anthony Kempster, well known to him as a man who had lodged in Redwood's house.

And so on. It was a most conclusive and convincing mass of evidence, and the mere fact that it was all totally untrue was known to Andrew alone, and could not be communicated by him to anyone else excepting in the unconvincing form of a comprehensive denial. But it was all rolled out with exhaustive and tedious thoroughness. Each deposition was taken down verbatim by the clerk, read over to the witness, and signed by him as well as by the magistrate. And even that was not the end of it, for when the whole of the evidence had been given, the depositions of all the witnesses were solemnly read over again for Andrew's special benefit. Then the magistrate addressed him in the usual formal terms. "Having heard the evidence, do you wish to say anything in answer to the charge? You are not obliged to say anything unless you desire to do so, but whatever you say will be taken down in writing and may be given in evidence upon your trial. And you are also clearly to understand that you have nothing to hope from any promise of favour, and nothing to fear from any threat which may have been holden out to you to induce you to make any admission or confession of your guilt, but whatever you now say may be given in evidence against you upon your trial, notwithstanding such promise or threat."

"All I wish to say," replied Andrew, with a perfect recognition of the fatuousness of his reply, "is that I am not Anthony Kempster, and that the evidence which has been given does not apply to me."

The magistrate wrote this down and then asked, "Do you wish to say who you are?"

"Not on this occasion," Andrew answered.

"Nor to give any account of yourself?"

"No," was the hopeless reply, on which the magistrate, having written down the answers and signed them, informed the accused that he stood committed for trial at the Central Criminal Court, and he was forthwith removed from the dock and taken back "to the place from whence he had come".

Chapter XI
The Last Straw

As Andrew sat in his cell, recalling again and again the incredible proceedings of the police court, he was conscious of the first stirrings of revolt against the malignity of Fate. The wild absurdity of the whole affair tended to dispel his apathy and rouse a spirit of resistance.

After all, the final blow had not fallen. He was not condemned, he was only committed for trial. There was still time for him to set up a defence, and Bolton's indelicately broad hints as to what he might expect from the judge if he made no reasonable defence spurred him on to reconsider his tactics. It was no question, the worthy officer pointed out, of a few months in prison. The crime of false personation is a felony and may carry a substantial term of penal servitude. That was an appalling prospect. It meant several years cut out of the best part of his life, to say nothing of the misery of those years, and at the end of it he would be no better off. For he would come out of prison with the label of Anthony Kempster affixed to him immovably and forever.

Something would have to be done. But the question was, what? Perhaps there was something in Bolton's idea after all. To a reputable solicitor he could safely tell his story, for a lawyer is entitled to hold sacred the secrets of his client. But when he had told his story, what then? His lawyer would be involved in the old dilemma. His client was either Anthony Kempster or Andrew Barton. If he was Kempster, he was guilty of personation, if he was Barton, he was guilty of the murder of Oliver Hudson. It was a hopeless position, and he did not see how any amount of legal acumen could steer a course between the two impossible alternatives.

So, ineffectively, he struggled to find a way out of the labyrinth of perplexities in which he had become involved. How long he would have continued to struggle and what he would eventually have done, it is impossible to say. For the problem of Anthony Kempster suddenly receded into the background. Fate had another little selection from its repertoire to offer for his consideration and a new problem to submit for solution.

It was the second day after the police court hearing, early in the afternoon, when the door of his cell was thrown open, disclosing his usual custodian and a couple of gentlemen standing in the gallery outside, one of whom he recognized as Inspector Butt and the other as

Superintendent Barnes, the officer who had opened the case against him at the first hearing. The two men entered the cell and the warder retired into the gallery, leaving the door ajar. It was the superintendent who addressed him. "We have come here," said he, "to discharge a disagreeable duty, to convey to you the information that you are charged with murder."

"With murder!" Andrew exclaimed, gazing at the officer in amazement. He could hardly believe his ears.

It seemed incredible that even the police should have penetrated his disguise. This was the very last thing that he had expected or been prepared for. "The charge is," the officer continued, "that on the 28th of August, 1928, at a place called Hunstone Gap, you, Ronald Barton, alias Anthony Kempster, alias Walter Green, feloniously did kill and murder one Andrew Barton. That is the charge. I don't know whether you wish to say anything, but it is my duty to caution you that anything you may say will be taken down in writing and used in evidence at your trial."

As the superintendent read out the charge, Andrew's feelings underwent a curious revulsion. Somehow, he experienced a sense of relief, almost of amusement. For the thing was so utterly preposterous. He was actually accused of having murdered himself! "May I ask," he said, "what reasons there are for supposing that I murdered Andrew Barton?"

"A summary of the evidence against you," the superintendent replied, "will be supplied for your use or that of your lawyers, if you obtain legal assistance, as I suppose you will, and as you certainly ought to, but I will give you the main facts that are in the possession of the police.

"First, on the day of Andrew Barton's death, you were seen in his company, and you appear to have been the last person who saw him alive, as you were seen walking with him in the direction of Hunstone Gap.

"Second, there was found in your possession, in your lodgings at Hampstead, an attaché case containing ninety pounds in money and certain valuable property. This case, and the property in it, has been identified as the property of the deceased Andrew Barton, which he had with him on the day of his death. It has also been ascertained that this case was seen in your possession, in your lodgings at Crompton on the evening of that same day.

"Third, it is known that, on the day following the death of the deceased, you cashed a cheque at the deceased's London bank, which cheque was either in the case or on the person of the deceased when he left home. Those are the principal points in the evidence at present available, and I now ask you if you wish to make any statement, bearing in mind the caution that I have just given you."

Andrew reflected rapidly. He was not disposed to make any statement until he had given some thought to the new developments. But there was one thing which instantly struck him. The case must have been identified by Molly and, if that were so, she would be called to give evidence as to its identity at his trial. But the idea was so repugnant to him that he was prepared to compromise himself to some extent if by so doing he could prevent her from being called. "May I ask who identified the case?" he inquired.

"Mrs. Barton, the wife of the deceased," was the reply, "and she is prepared to swear that the case was in the deceased's possession when he left home on the morning of his death."

"Yes," said Andrew. "It will be very disagreeable for her to appear as a witness. Would it simplify matters if I were to admit that the case is the property of Andrew Barton? Would that render it unnecessary for her to be called?"

"It might," the superintendent replied, "but I can give no promise or make any kind of conditions. Do I understand that you admit that the case that was found in your lodgings at Hampstead was the property of the late Andrew Barton?"

Again Andrew reflected, with a new mental alertness. He could not accept the superintendent's wording, but yet he did not wish to alter it conspicuously until he had considered his course of action. Eventually he said, "I admit that the case which you found in my rooms at Hampstead is the case which Andrew Barton was carrying when he left home on the morning of the 28th of August. Will you write that down?"

The superintendent, with a look of obvious surprise, wrote the statement down in his note-book and then asked, "Do you wish to state how the case came into your possession?"

"No," Andrew replied, "I do not wish to make any further statement."

"Very well," said the superintendent, "then I will ask you to read the statement and, if you find it correct, to sign your name underneath."

He handed the book and his fountain pen to Andrew, who read the statement and, finding it faithfully set down in his own words, affixed his signature and returned the book to its owner who, having added his own signature as a witness, pocketed it. "I think that is all there is to say at present," said the superintendent. "You will be given all necessary facilities for preparing your defence if you apply to the Governor of the prison, and you will be brought before the magistrate as soon as possible. You are sure you don't want to make any further statement?"

"Quite sure," Andrew replied, whereupon the two officers retired, and Bolton, with a wistful look into the cell, slammed the door and left the prisoner to his own thoughts.

The immediate effect of this bolt which had fallen, not, indeed, out of the blue, but out of an uncommonly stormy sky, was to bring Andrew abruptly to his senses. Curiously enough, he was not particularly alarmed by this new charge. He was still under the influence of Miss Booth's accusation and was more afraid of being charged with the murder of Mr. Hudson than with that of Andrew Barton. Nevertheless, he realized that this was a charge of murder and that, if he made no effective answer to it, he stood to be hanged. And to being hanged he had as great an objection as ever. To a term of imprisonment he might have resigned himself if there had been no way of avoiding it. But to the rope he could not resign himself at all. Some effective defence he would have to set up, though at the moment he could think of none, seeing that the evidence that the superintendent had recited was all true in fact, but already he was beginning dimly to recognize that he was receiving yet another shove from circumstance – that Miss Booth's accusation notwithstanding, he would be forced to make an effort to recover his own identity.

Indeed, the more he reflected on the matter, the more did the motor crime tend to recede into a second place. A bird in the hand is worth two in the bush. The murder of Andrew Barton was a criminal charge that was very much in the hand, whereas the Hudson murder was still in the bush, even though that bush was uncomfortably near. Moreover, as he compared the two cases, he began to see that the new charge was the more formidable of the two. For the first time, he realized that Miss Booth's accusation was opposed to all reasonable probabilities and that he really had something weighty and material to offer in reply. In fact, with the clarity of vision that the new danger had produced, he began to suspect that he might have exaggerated the former danger.

On the other hand, the more he considered the new charge, the more did its formidable character tend to make itself felt. For here all the probabilities were against him. The absurdity of the charge was beside the mark – indeed, it was an added element of danger when the incredible nature of his own story was taken into consideration. Now that it had been ascertained that he had been present at Hunstone Gap when the death occurred and that he had "sneaked away like Cain", as Molly had expressed it, he could see that his subsequent conduct in keeping out of sight and offering no word of explanation was in the highest degree suspicious.

These cogitations led him to the inevitable conclusion. He would have to proclaim his real identity and he would have to tell the whole of

151

his preposterous story. He would tell it to a lawyer and trust to his capacity to present it to the court in as plausible and credible a form as was possible. But the difficulty was that the lawyer would, at least in his own mind, reject it as a mere silly fable. It was even possible that a reputable lawyer might refuse to undertake a defence which was based on such a mass of absurdities, while the type of lawyer who would be ready to undertake any kind of case, good or bad, would probably have neither the skill nor the personal credit which would be necessary to give so unconvincing a case a fair chance. And there was the further difficulty that he knew no lawyers excepting his family solicitor, Mr. Wakefield, a respectable provincial practitioner who had no experience of criminal practice and who would pretty certainly flatly refuse to have anything to do with a man whom he would regard as his late client's murderer.

Eventually, he decided, as a preliminary measure, to discuss the position with Bolton. But it presently appeared that that kindly and conscientious officer, in his anxieties at the new position, had made representations in higher quarters. The fact transpired when the Medical Officer made one of his periodical visits to inspect his charge and inquire if there were "any complaints". When he had finished his professional business, instead of bustling away in his usual fashion, he lingered with a somewhat hesitating air and a thoughtful eye on his patient, and at length opened the subject that was in his mind. "I don't want to meddle in your affairs, Barton – your name is Barton, isn't it?"

"Yes," Andrew replied, "my name is Barton."

"Well," said the doctor, "as I said, I don't want to meddle, but your day officer, Bolton, is rather concerned about you, and he has spoken to me, suggesting that I might have a few words with you. He thinks that you have not given yourself a chance, so far – that you have had no legal assistance and taken no measures for your defence. Now, if that is so, it is a serious matter. Judges and magistrates will do all they can to see that you get fair play, but they can't conduct your defence. You have got to help them by giving them the facts on your side, facts which are known only to you. But perhaps you would rather that I did not interfere."

"On the contrary," Andrew replied, earnestly, "I am most grateful to you, and would thankfully accept your advice if you are not compromising yourself officially by giving it."

"Good Lord!" exclaimed the doctor, "of course I am not. Everyone wants you to have a fair trial. Even the police don't want a conviction against an innocent man, and as to me, it is perfectly correct for me, or any other prison official, to advise a prisoner if he wants advice."

"I am glad of that," said Andrew, "because I want advice very badly. I realize that I ought to have legal assistance, but appearances are so hopelessly against me that I doubt if a lawyer could help me."

"But," the doctor protested, "the more appearances are against you, the more do you need the help of a lawyer. I take it that you are not going to plead guilty?"

"Certainly not. I am absolutely innocent of both of the charges against me."

"Then," said the doctor, "if you are innocent, there must be facts producible which would form an answer to the charges."

"There are," said Andrew, "but they are known only to me, and they are so extraordinary and incredible that no one would believe them. That is my difficulty. I have a perfectly complete and consistent story, but if I should tell that story to a lawyer, he would think I was merely romancing."

"Your lawyer isn't going to try you," the doctor remarked, adding with a queer, one-sided smile, "and you mustn't misunderstand his position. The function of an advocate is not to experience belief in his own person but to be the occasion of belief in others."

"Still," Andrew persisted, "it is rather hopeless to be defended by a lawyer who believes one to be guilty. I should have liked to convince him that, at least, I might possibly be innocent."

"Naturally, and very properly. But why not? The truth of those facts which are known to you must be susceptible of proof or disproof. If they are true, it is for your lawyer to ascertain and demonstrate their truth." He paused for a moment and then, speaking with marked emphasis, said, "Now tell me, Barton – supposing a competent lawyer should undertake your defence, would you be prepared to give him all the facts in your possession – to tell him everything that you know, truthfully and without any reservation whatever?"

"Certainly," Andrew replied. "I would promise to hide nothing from him."

The doctor reflected for a few moments. Then he asked, "Have you any lawyer in your mind whom you would like to consult?"

"No," Andrew answered. "I know of no lawyer. That is a point on which I was going to ask for your advice. Is there anyone whom you can recommend me to apply to?"

"I think there is," the doctor replied, "but I am not quite sure whether all the circumstances are suitable. When I was a student I had the good fortune to be the pupil of a very great man. His name is Dr. John Thorndyke – perhaps you may have heard of him."

"I seem to have heard the name," said Andrew, "but I know nothing about him. I take it that he is a doctor, not a lawyer."

"He is both, and he was our lecturer on Medical Jurisprudence – that is the legal aspect of medicine or the medical aspect of law. He practices as a barrister but he is not an advocate in the sense in which I was speaking just now. His speciality is the examination and analysis of evidence, and it seems to me that your case might interest him. You see, Barton, that I am taking your statement at its face value. I am assuming that you are an innocent man who is the victim of misleading appearances."

"That," said Andrew, "I swear most solemnly is the absolute truth."

"I hope it is, and I accept your statement. Now, would you like me to see Dr. Thorndyke and explain your position and find out whether he would be prepared to consider the question of his conducting your defence?"

"I should be profoundly grateful if you would. But do you think he would believe my story?"

The doctor smiled his queer, lop-sided smile. "I don't think, Barton. I *know*. He wouldn't. But neither would he disbelieve it. He would just treat it as material for investigation. He would pick out the alleged facts which were capable of being verified or disproved and he would proceed to verify or disprove them. If he found your statements to be true, he would go on with the case. If he found them untrue, he would decline the brief and pass you on to a counsel who would conduct the defence without prejudice as to his personal convictions."

"That seems to me a very reasonable and proper method," said Andrew. "I ask for nothing more. But I don't see how he is going to find out whether my story is true or false."

"You can leave that to him," the doctor replied. "But," he added, emphatically, "understand once and for all, Barton, I am assuming that your story, whatever it is, is a true story. If it isn't, don't send me on a fool's errand. I assure you that it is impossible to bluff Thorndyke. If he starts on the case, he will have you turned inside out in a twinkling, and if you tell him anything that isn't true, you'll be bowled out first ball. Now, Barton, what do you say? Would you like me to put the case to him?"

"If you would be so very kind," replied Andrew. "It seems to me that Dr. Thorndyke is exactly the kind of lawyer that I want."

"I am glad to hear you say that," the doctor rejoined, with obvious satisfaction. "Then I will call on him without delay and use what persuasion I can. But I shall want a written authority from you to offer

154

him the brief. A leaf of my note-book will do to write it on. He won't be unduly critical of the stationery in the special circumstances."

With this and a trace of his quaint smile, he produced his note-book and a fountain pen, and when Andrew had drawn up the stool to the little fixed table and seated himself, he dictated a brief authorization which Andrew wrote and signed "Ronald Barton", enclosing the signature between quotation marks. Then he turned the book and pen to their owner who glanced through the few lines of writing and then looked up sharply. "Why have you put your signature between inverted commas?" he asked.

"Because I am signing as a prisoner in my prison name, which is not my real name. I am not Ronald Barton."

"Oh, aren't you?" said the doctor, in a tone of surprise and looking at Andrew a little dubiously. "I thought you said your name was Barton."

"So it is," replied Andrew, "but not Ronald."

The doctor continued for some seconds to look at him with a puzzled and somewhat dissatisfied expression. At length he said, as he put away the note-book, "Well, the facts of the case are no concern of mine, but I hope you will be able to make them clear to Dr. Thorndyke, if he is willing to listen to them."

With this parting remark, of which the dry and even dubious tone was not lost on Andrew, the doctor pushed open the door, which had (necessarily since there was no inside keyhole) stood ajar during the interview and, stepping out, closed it behind him.

The clang of the closing door and the snap of the lock suddenly put Andrew back in his place, from which the brief spell of civilized conversation seemed for the time to have liberated him, even as the loop of key-chain that peeped below the hem of the doctor's coat as he retired, served to remind him that this kindly gentleman was, after all, a prison officer, one of whose duties was to hold the captive in secure custody.

Chapter XII
Dr. Thorndyke

The visible results of the doctor's mission appeared early in the afternoon of the following day when the door of Andrew's cell was thrown open and Bolton looked in on his charge. "Your lawyer is waiting down below," said he. "Just tidy yourself up a bit and come along with me. And look sharp."

There was not much to be done, since razors were forbidden by the regulations. Andrew gave his hair a perfunctory brush, extended the operation to his coat and announced that he was ready. "You've forgotten your badge," said the officer, and Andrew, with a grim smile, took it down from its hook and fastened it to his coat, remarking that "One might as well look the part". Then they set forth on their journey by innumerable iron staircases and through a long succession of iron gates, each of which had to be unlocked to give them passage and locked again when they had passed. Eventually, they reached their destination, a smallish, very bare room with one door, of which the upper half consisted of a single panel of plate glass through which the warder, posted outside, could keep the prisoner under observation without intruding on the conference. Here, Bolton delivered his charge and shut him in.

There were two persons in the room. One was the doctor and the other was a tall stranger, at whom Andrew looked with deep interest and a certain amount of awe. For this stranger was a very impressive person with a distinctly imposing presence, due not alone to the stature, the upright, dignified carriage, and the suggestion of physical strength. In the handsome, intellectual face was a subtle quality that instantly conveyed the impression of power, an impression that was reinforced by a singularly quiet, contained, reposeful and unemotional bearing. His hair was tinged with grey, but the calm, unlined face was almost that of a young man. "Well, Barton," the Medical Officer said as Andrew entered, "Dr. Thorndyke is willing to listen to your story, or as much of it as may be necessary to make clear the nature of the defence and, as I have done my part by inducing him to come, I will take myself off and leave you to your consultation."

With this he took his departure, carefully shutting the door after him and pausing to say a few words to the warder who was posted outside. Then Dr. Thorndyke drew one of the two chairs up to the table and, indicating the other, said, "Pray be seated, Mr. Barton," (Andrew noted the "Mr." appreciatively), "and draw your chair close to the table so that we need not raise our voices." He opened a case which looked like a small suit-case and, taking out a block of ruled paper, placed it on the table before him and continued, "Dr. Blackford, your Medical Officer, has indicated to me in very general terms the nature of your difficulties, and I understand from him that you have a remarkable and rather incredible story to tell me. We must have that story in detail presently, but before we begin, there is one point which I should like to have cleared up. In this authorization which you gave Dr. Blackford," – here he laid it on the table – "you have signed your name, Ronald Barton, between inverted commas, and the doctor quoted you as having explained this on the ground that Ronald Barton is not your name. Is that correct?"

"Quite correct, sir. My name is not Ronald Barton."

"Then," said Dr. Thorndyke, "let us start fair with the genuine name."

"My name," replied Andrew, a little hesitatingly and in uncommon trepidation now that the climax was reached, abruptly and all unprepared, "my name is Andrew Barton."

Dr. Thorndyke looked slightly surprised. "Your name, then," said he, "is the same as that of the man whom you are accused of having murdered."

"Not only the same name, sir," said Andrew, with his heart in his mouth. "The same person. I am Andrew Barton. The man who was killed was Ronald Barton."

On receiving this statement. Dr. Thorndyke laid down his pen, leaned back in his chair and regarded Andrew with an expression that made his flesh creep. "I read the report of the inquest at Crompton," he said, in quiet, level tones, "and I filed it. Last night, after seeing Dr. Blackford, I read it again with great care. I noted that Andrew Barton was described – by his wife – as a man whose nose had been injured by an accident, with the result that the bridge was broken and rendered completely fiat. I need not point out that that description does not apply to you."

"No, it does not," Andrew admitted, "and that is the cause of all the confusion and error."

"Then you still maintain," said Dr. Thorndyke, "in spite of the total disagreement between your appearance and the description, that you are Andrew Barton, the husband of the woman who gave that description."

"I do," replied Andrew, "because it is the literal truth."

"And are you proposing to offer a reasonable explanation of this extraordinary discrepancy between the description and the visible facts?"

"Certainly I am," Andrew replied. "It is the essence of my defence. Shall I give you the explanation first, or shall I take it in its proper place in my story?"

"I think," said Thorndyke, "that, as your statement appears to postulate an impossibility, no useful purpose would be served by going into any other matters until this apparent contradiction in facts has been disposed of. Let us begin with the explanation."

Accordingly Andrew launched out into a detailed account of his dealings with Professor Booley, beginning with his panic on reading the description of himself in the police notice and finishing with the shock that he sustained on looking at his reflection in the mirror. To this account Dr. Thorndyke listened with the closest attention, jotting down an occasional note on his pad but uttering no word until the whole story was told. Then he put one or two questions, including the exact whereabouts of Professor Booley's premises, and wrote down the answers, finally requesting Andrew to put his finger on the spot at which the Professor had inserted the needle. "That," said he, "is a very remarkable story. Before we go any further, I should like to make a preliminary examination of your nose. You understand that I am a doctor of medicine as well as a lawyer?"

He opened the case on the table and took from it a small electric lamp and, by the light of this, and with the aid of a pocket lens, he made a minute examination of the bridge of Andrew's nose, especially in the region in which the entry of the needle had been indicated. Then, laying the edge of his open hand on the bridge of the nose, he brought the lamp close to one side while he scrutinized the other. Finally, he put the lamp on the table and proceeded to explore the nose with the tips of his fingers, winding up by taking the base of the bridge between his finger and thumb (a proceeding that was observed with profound astonishment by the warder on duty outside).

Having made his examination, Dr. Thorndyke went back to his chair and made one or two brief notes. Then he looked up, and Andrew, catching his eye, was sensible of a subtle change of expression. And he thought he detected a similarly subtle change of tone when Dr. Thorndyke said, "And now let us have the story."

Andrew hesitated in some slight embarrassment. "I hardly know where to begin," said he. "It is rather a long story."

"You had better begin," said Thorndyke, "with the first event which had any causal bearing on your present predicament. What took you to Crompton?"

"I went to see my cousin about a letter that he had written to me."

"Then begin with that letter. And never mind the length of the story. We have got to have it all, either now or in installments. But I want now at least an outline of the whole set of circumstances."

Thus encouraged, Andrew embarked on the strange history of his misadventures from the moment when the fatal letter had been put into his hands. As before, Dr. Thorndyke listened without comment or question but making numerous notes – in shorthand, as Andrew subsequently learned. Only twice did he interrupt the narration. The first time was shortly after it had started and was in the nature of a general instruction. "Don't epitomize, Mr. Barton," said he. "Tell the story in detail, and don't be afraid of being prolix. The details may be more significant than they appear to you."

The second interruption occurred when Andrew was recounting the meeting in the train with Elizabeth Kempster. "She was very angry and indignant," he was saying, "and reproached me for my ingratitude for all that she had done for me – "

It was at this point that Thorndyke held up his hand. "That won't do, Mr. Barton," he exclaimed. "I want the conversation verbatim, the very words that were spoken by you and by her – especially by her. You must try to recall them, fully and accurately."

Andrew had little difficulty in doing so, for that terrible interview had burned itself into his memory, though he felt some qualms in retailing to another that unfortunate woman's emotional outpourings. But Dr. Thorndyke had no such qualms, for he took down a verbatim report of the entire conversation with a care and minuteness that seemed to Andrew beyond the merits of the matter.

When the narrative came to an end with the narrator's committal for trial. Dr. Thorndyke remarked, "A very strange story, Mr. Barton, and I certainly agree with you that it is not one to put to a jury in its raw state. And not such a very long story, but we will now proceed to amplify it a little."

With this he glanced over his notes and then opened a cross-examination, taking the narrative point by point from the beginning. And a very curious cross-examination Andrew thought it. For to him, it appeared that Dr. Thorndyke passed over all the important points and dredged deep for the most exhaustive details of things which did not matter at all. To the murder of Mr. Hudson he made no reference whatever, nor did he show any special interest in the tragic events that befell at Hunstone Gap. But his interest in the history and relationships of the Barton family was so profound that, having elicited all that

Andrew knew, he not only wrote it down but illustrated it with a sketched pedigree.

Then he was strangely inquisitive as to Andrew's professional career, and especially as to the details of his dealings with Mr. Montagu, and his interest in Mrs. Pendlewick and her bone lace and the sittings she had given him for his picture filled Andrew with astonishment. What on earth could Mrs. Pendlewick have to do with the alleged murder at Hunstone Gap? Nevertheless, he answered the questions with conscientious completeness, and if he was puzzled by their apparent irrelevance to the great issue, he never had a moment's doubt that some good purpose, invisible to him, lay behind them.

When the cross-examination was finished and Thorndyke, having collected his notes, stood up, Andrew plucked up courage to inquire, "You have now heard my story, sir. May I ask if you find it possible to believe that it is a true story?"

Thorndyke looked at him for a few moments without speaking, and for the first time, his impassive, rather severe face relaxed into a faint smile which seemed to let some inner, unsuspected kindliness show for a moment on the surface. "I am not going to let you cross-examine me, Mr. Barton," said he. "And I am not committing myself to any opinions until I have checked and verified certain facts affirmed in your statement. You have told me a complete and consistent story and I have at present no reason to disbelieve it. But remember that, even if my investigations convince me of its truth, that is only a beginning. The problem will be to transfer my conviction to those who will have to make the decision."

It was a cautious statement but somehow, Andrew was not discouraged by its tone of caution. And as to the checking of his alleged facts, since he had told nothing but the truth, they were all in his favour. "Before I go," said Thorndyke, "I must ask you to sign one or two little documents. I want your written authority to conduct your defence, if I decide to do so, and to make all arrangements to that end at my sole discretion. Then I want your authority to take custody of any of your property at present held by the police, if necessary and if they consent, and I want a similar authority in respect of property of yours in Mrs. Pendlewick's possession. The arrangements for the defence will include the selection of a solicitor. In this case it is a mere formality, but the usage in English practice is that a counsel must be instructed by a solicitor. I will arrange with a friend to instruct me, in a technical sense."

He wrote out the three documents and presented them to Andrew for his signature. When he had signed them, Andrew ventured to raise another question. "We have said nothing about the financial arrangements," said he, and was about to enlarge on the unsatisfactory

160

nature of his resources when Thorndyke interrupted him. "We had better leave those matters for the present," he suggested. "I shall take it for granted that you will discharge your liabilities if you are in a position to do so. But the costs are really a side issue. And now I must be off. I shall proceed at once with the necessary verification of your statements and when I see you again, I shall be able to tell you exactly how we stand."

With this he picked up his case and, being released by the warder, took his departure, and Andrew was, in due course, conducted back to his apartment, where he presently consumed his evening meal of brown bread and cocoa with unwonted relish and thereafter spent the short remainder of the prison day in curious tranquillity of spirit.

This state of mental relief, with a new-born feeling of hope and security, was surprising even to himself. To what was it due? Certainly, he had at last unbosomed himself of his preposterous story and had not been denounced as a liar and an impostor. He had been given a hearing and promised an investigation. That was all to the good. But that did not account for the strange manner in which his fears and his anxieties seemed suddenly to have gone to rest. What was it? And when he asked himself the question, the answer that came to him was – Dr. Thorndyke.

And yet it was strange. Nothing could have been more unemotional than the bearing of this calm, quiet, self-contained man. Not a word of sympathy or encouragement had he uttered. By no hair's breadth had he deviated from the most strictly judicial attitude. There he had sat with a face like a mask of stone, listening impassively without sign of belief or disbelief, speaking only to put some searching question or to check some statement. Only one when, for a moment, that faint smile had lighted up his face with a gleam of kindliness, had he manifested any trace of human feeling. And yet, in some mysterious way, some virtue had come out of him and communicated itself to Andrew. Behind that immovable calm, he had had a sense of power, of energy, and of incorruptible justice – of justice that would try him impartially in the balance, of power to enforce it, if he was not found wanting.

This restful feeling of having, in a sense, passed on his troubles and responsibilities to another, remained in the days that followed. In the results of Dr. Thorndyke's investigations he had perfect confidence, for he knew that they must, of necessity, confirm the truth of his story. So as the time passed, he waited patiently with sustained courage for the next developments. But it was not until the fifth day that his patience was rewarded by the announcement of Thorndyke's decision.

On entering the room in which the previous interview had taken place, he found Dr. Thorndyke in company with another tall and athletic-looking gentleman who was introduced to him as Dr. Jervis. Both men shook hands with him and Dr. Thorndyke proceeded to state the position. "I have checked such of your statements as it was possible to check and have been able to confirm them and am now satisfied that the story you told me is a true story. Accordingly, I am prepared to undertake your defence and I have, in fact, made all the necessary arrangements. My friend, Mr. Marchmont, a very experienced solicitor, has agreed to act for you and I have asked him to call here and make your acquaintance. So everything is now in order. I suppose you have not thought of anything else that you wish to tell me? No additions to or amplifications of your statement?"

"No," replied Andrew, "I think you squeezed me pretty dry last time."

"Well," said Thorndyke, "I have no questions to ask, but perhaps Mr. Marchmont may want some detail filled in. A solicitor sees a case from a slightly different angle and has his own special experiences. And here, I think, he is."

As he spoke, the footsteps of two persons were heard approaching down the corridor, and the warder on guard threw open the glazed door, through which another warder ushered the visitor and then retired after shutting him in.

Mr. Marchmont was an elderly gentleman, prim, precise but suave in manner and a lawyer to the finger-tips. When the introductions had been effected and a few civilities exchanged, he turned to Thorndyke. "I have read your summary," said he, "and note that my role is that of a figure-head, as it usually is when I act with you. But there are one or two points on which I want more information. First, as to procedure. I presume that the preliminary investigation will take place before the justices at Crompton and the trial at the Maidstone Assizes. Is that so?"

"No," replied Thorndyke. "The case has been transferred to the Central Criminal Court – "

"By a *writ of certiorari?*"

"No. Under the new procedure provided for in the Criminal Justice Act of 1925."

"Ah!" said Marchmont, "I had overlooked that. Criminal practice is rather out of my province. And as to the preliminary investigation?"

"There isn't going to be any. I am informed that the Director of Public Prosecutions intends to present a voluntary bill to the Grand Jury."

"But that is rather unusual, isn't it?" said Marchmont.

"It will save a great deal of time and trouble and expense," replied Thorndyke, "and I, certainly, shall not complain. It extricates us from quite an awkward dilemma."

162

"What dilemma?" asked Marchmont.

"My difficulty," Thorndyke replied, "was this: If there had been an investigation before a magistrate, I should have had either to produce all my evidence, which I should not want to do, or to reserve my defence, which I should not have been justified in doing and could not, in fact, have done."

Dr. Jervis chuckled softly and, glancing at Marchmont, remarked, "It is a let-off from Thorndyke's point of view. Can't you imagine how he would have hated letting the cat out of the bag prematurely?"

Marchmont laughed in a dry, forensic fashion. "Yes," he agreed, "it wouldn't have suited his tactics, for when once the cat is out, she is out. You can't put her back and repeat the performance. But the effect of this move on the Director's part is that the trial may begin quite soon. However, I shall receive due notice of the date. And now, having made our client's acquaintance and gleaned these particulars, I will take myself off and leave you to your occupations, whatever they may be."

He shook hands with them all round, and as the warder, observing this sign of farewell, opened the door, he bustled out and was taken in tow by the other officer. He had hardly disappeared when yet another official arrived with a message for Thorndyke to the effect that, "Dr. Blackford sends his compliments and the room is now available."

Andrew looked inquiringly at Thorndyke, who explained briefly, "The doctor has kindly given us facilities for certain experiments which may help us. You will hear all about them later if their bearing is not apparent at the moment." Then, addressing the officer, he asked, "Do we come with you?"

"If you please, sir," was the reply, and the procession, having formed up, was personally conducted by the officer on a tour of the prison, coming to a halt at last in the neighbourhood of the infirmary where Dr. Blackford was awaiting them. "I have had all your traps put into this room," he said, opening a door as he spoke. "If you should want me, I shall be close at hand."

"Aren't you coming in with us?" asked Jervis.

"No," replied the doctor. "I should like to, for I am devoured with curiosity as to what the deuce you are going to be up to. But I am not sure that it would be quite in order. And, besides, it is just as well for me not to know too much about Barton's affairs."

This was evidently Thorndyke's view for, without comment beyond a few words of thanks, he led Andrew into the room and, when Jervis had followed, shut the door.

It was a rather small room, apparently some kind of annexe to the infirmary to judge by its appointments, which included a plain deal table and a bare, ascetic-looking couch with a distinct suggestion of surgery in its appearance. Looking about him curiously, Andrew noted that the table bore a pile of about a dozen large black envelopes and that at the head of the couch was reared a formidable-looking apparatus of which he could make nothing (scientific knowledge was not his strong point), but which aroused a faint and rather uncomfortable reminiscence of Professor Booley.

He watched, with the rather vague interest of the entirely non-scientific person, while his two friends busied themselves with various preparations and adjustments of the apparatus, speculating a trifle uneasily on the nature of the experiment which was about to be performed and of which it seemed that he was to be the subject. He saw Dr. Thorndyke take two of the black paper envelopes from the table and place them carefully on a slab of wood that lay near the head of the couch, and he noted that the envelopes were rigid as if they contained plates of metal or some hard substance. Then he saw him adjust the position of a rather odd-looking electric lamp-bulb, which was fixed on a movable arm, placing it with great care immediately above the black envelopes. At length it appeared that all the preparations were complete, for Thorndyke, stepping back from the couch and taking a last fond look at the apparatus, announced, "I think we are all ready now, and I suggest that we begin with you, Jervis. What do you say?"

"Yes," replied Jervis. "It is always wise to begin by trying it on the dog. And Barton can watch the procedure."

He took a small rug from the foot of the couch and, folding it, laid it on the black envelopes. Then he lay down on the couch, resting his head on the folded rug. Thorndyke raised the corner of the rug, apparently to ascertain the position of the head on the envelopes, and once more made a slight adjustment of the lamp overhead. "Ready?" said he, with his hand on a switch, and as Jervis responded, he turned the switch with a snap. Instantly the apparatus emitted a growl which rapidly rose up the scale until it settled into a high-pitched droning like the piping of a giant mosquito. At the same moment the lamp began to glow with a green light at the centre of which appeared a bright spot of red. "Keep perfectly still, Barton," said Thorndyke, who stood rigid as a statue with his watch in his hand. "It is most important that there should not be the slightest vibration."

Andrew stood, resting with one hand on the table, listening to the curious high-pitched hum of the apparatus, wondering what these mysterious rites and ceremonies might have to do with a charge of murder and sensible of a perverse desire to change his position. At length Thorndyke put away his watch and turned the switch, whereupon the light of the lamp faded out, the whine of the apparatus swept down an octave or two until it died away in a low growl, and Jervis rose from the couch. "Quite a harmless proceeding, you see, Barton," said he. "Nothing of the Booley Touch about us."

He took the two envelopes from the couch and, having written his name with a pencil on each, added his signature and the date and handed them to Thorndyke, who counter-signed them and placed them apart on the table, while Jervis took another two of the envelopes and, having placed them in position on the couch laid the folded rug on them. "Now, Barton," said Thorndyke, "you saw what Dr. Jervis did. Go thou and do likewise. And remember that you have to keep perfectly still, to which end, you must settle yourself comfortably in a position which you can maintain without effort."

Accordingly Andrew laid himself down on the couch in as restful a pose as he could manage, and when Thorndyke had made some slight alteration in the placing of the head, the switch was turned, the apparatus uttered its plaintive whine, the mysterious green light glowed afresh, and the previous proceedings were repeated. "You heard what we were saying to Mr. Marchmont," said Thorndyke when Andrew had risen from the couch and the envelopes had been signed and put away. "The trial may open quite soon, and in the meanwhile, I would urge you to be very careful to keep your own counsel. Give no information to anybody either as to what we have been doing here or as to anything in any way connected with your case. The special arrangements for presenting the bill of indictment direct to the Grand Jury give us the advantage of going into court without having disclosed the details of the defence. Let us keep that advantage. There may be nothing in it. But it is usually good tactics to let the enemy bring his heavy guns to bear on the place that you don't need to defend. So I say again, don't discuss your case with anybody, no matter how friendly."

Andrew promised to bear this caution in mind, adding, "I suppose I shall get due notice of the date of the trial."

"Certainly," replied Thorndyke. "You will be kept informed of everything that you ought to know, and if you should want to confer with me or Dr. Jervis or Mr. Marchmont, you have only to send one of us a line to that effect. Is there anything that you would like to be advised upon now?"

"Yes," Andrew replied, "there is one rather important question that does not seem to have been raised. It is concerned with the Hudson case. When Andrew Barton disappeared, he had been accused of having committed that murder. If he should reappear, it would seem that that accusation will be revived. Isn't that so?"

"No," Thorndyke replied promptly. "You can dismiss the Hudson case from your mind, and you need never have taken the charge seriously. At first, the police, naturally enough, took Miss Booth's statement at its face value. But as soon as they began to make inquiries they realized that she had made a mistake – the common mistake of confusing what she had seen with what she had inferred. She saw a face at the window and she saw a revolver, and she inferred that the revolver and the face appertained to the same person. But when the police ascertained that the face was that of Mr. Andrew Barton, and when they had heard his wife's account of the affair, they were satisfied that he was merely a chance spectator of the crime. As a matter of fact, they had some fairly definite information as to who the perpetrators really were. So Andrew Barton's connection with the case will be no more than that of a witness."

Andrew breathed a sigh of relief. "You have lifted a great weight off my mind," said he. "It may have been unreasonable of me, but I think I was more afraid of that accusation than of the charge that has actually been brought against me. It is an immense relief to know that I am free of it."

"I can easily understand that," said Jervis. "One doesn't want to step down from the dock after a triumphant acquittal, to fall into the arms of a detective-sergeant with a fresh warrant. And that isn't going to happen, Barton. When you are acquitted, you will be acquitted completely. Both indictments, murder and personation, for the greater includes the less and our evidence covers both. So keep a good heart and don't be discouraged or alarmed by any signs of preparation, such as identification parades or other movements of the enemy."

"You speak," said Andrew, "as if you were quite confident of an acquittal."

"I am," said Jervis, "and so, I think, is my learned senior. Aren't you, Thorndyke?"

"I certainly expect an acquittal," replied Thorndyke. "The case for the prosecution can't be a strong one, in any event. In fact," he added, with a smile, "my principal anxiety is lest the Grand Jury should throw out the bill."

"That would be rather an anti-climax," said Jervis, "and would crab a most promising defence. But still, it would be, in effect, equivalent to an acquittal."

"Not altogether," Thorndyke dissented, "for it would not cover the personation charge. But you see, Jervis, that a mere acquittal would not be enough for us. We are concerned with something more than the alleged murder. You remember the old schoolboy verses, *Pistor erat*

166

quondam, which were, I think, rendered, '*There was a baker heretofore, with labour and great pain, Did break his neck and break his neck and break his neck again.*'

"Now that is what Barton has done. He has gone on piling illusions and false appearances on top of one another until he has got himself charged with his own murder, and we, like the baker's medical attendant, have got to deal with the whole series. We have got to reduce, not only the final fracture, but all the others as well. And the defence to the murder charge will give us the opportunity we want."

"Then," said Jervis, picking up the signed envelopes and bestowing them tenderly in a suit-case, "let us hope the Grand Jury will not be too critical in respect of the evidence for the prosecution."

Chapter XIII
Prisoner at the Bar

The sands of time, which trickle out grudgingly enough within the prison walls alike for the just and the unjust, had run through the glass to the last grain, and it was Jervis's hopes rather than Thorndyke's fears that had been justified by circumstances. For the Grand Jury had returned a true bill, and Andrew Barton stood in the dock at the Central Criminal Court to answer the charge of Wilful Murder.

His state of mind was very peculiar for that of a prisoner arraigned on such a charge. He realized it, himself, and was faintly surprised at it – particularly when he contrasted the abject panic of the terror-stricken wretch who had staggered away from the police bill at Crompton with the serenity of the prisoner at the bar who stood waiting to watch the throw of the dice in the game which was presently to be played between Thorndyke and his accusers – a game of which his life was the stake. The bare possibility that this thing might happen had then paralysed him with horror, and now that the reality was upon him, he seemed to face the terrible chances almost unmoved.

He looked about the court with somewhat of the interest of a spectator. He had never before been in a criminal court and the various objects and persons and the solemn procedure all had the attraction of novelty. He inspected the scarlet-robed judge approvingly, excepting as to his wig, which he found disappointing. Like most uninformed persons, he had supposed that judges wore full-bottomed wigs when they sat in court. He observed the Clerk of the Court sitting in wig and gown behind his desk below the judge's dais, he counted the jury, who were waiting to be sworn, and noted that two of them were women. Then his eye roamed along the counsels' seats, where Dr. Thorndyke sat placidly looking over his brief, and he endeavoured to pick out Sir Oliver Blizzard, who, he had been informed, was to lead for the prosecution, eventually fixing – correctly, as it turned out – upon a clerical-looking gentleman with a monocle firmly jammed in his eye unsecured by any cord or other support.

But all the time he was imperfectly conscious of his actual position. The old feeling of unreality still possessed him, the sense of being in a dream or under some sort of spell, which had first come on him when he looked into Professor Booley's mirror and saw the face of his cousin Ronald looking out at him. Only at intervals, by some special occurrence

– as, for instance, when a woman juror asked to be excused from serving, on the grounds that she objected to capital punishment – was he startled out of his curious mental lethargy into a vivid realization of his actual position.

At length his wandering thoughts were interrupted by the Clerk of the Court, who had risen and was addressing him, apparently in the words of a document which lay before him on his desk. "Ronald Barton, you are charged with the murder of Andrew Barton on the 28th of August, 1928. Are you guilty or not guilty?"

"Not guilty," Andrew replied.

The Clerk noted the answer and then once more addressed him. "Prisoner at the Bar, if you wish to object to any of the persons whose names I am about to call to form the jury to try you, you must do so as they severally come to the book to be sworn, and before they are sworn, and you will be heard."

There being obviously nothing to say to this, Andrew bowed to the Clerk and resumed his reflections, but in a somewhat more disturbed frame of mind. For there was something deadly realistic in the wording of the charge, and the address which had followed brought home to him vividly that the men and women whose names were now being called out would presently hold his life in the hollow of their hands. They were to be his judges who would decide whether he was or was not guilty of the crime with which he was charged. On their intelligence and capacity to understand evidence, even on their individual temperaments, would depend the decision whether he should go forth a free man or should be hauled away to the gallows. It was not a very comfortable thought. As each juror "came to the book", Andrew scanned his or her face anxiously for indications of stupidity, or, still worse, of obstinacy. One man or woman who "knew his or her own mind" might turn the scale against him.

Thus he was reflecting when the process of swearing-in came to an end. The jury were then counted and asked by the Clerk of the Court if they were all sworn. When these formalities had been completed, an official of the Court (the Bailiff and Crier) rose and proclaimed in resonant tones and with profound gravity of manner: "If anyone can inform my Lords the King's Justices, or the King's Attorney General, ere this Inquest be taken between our Sovereign Lord the King and the Prisoner at the Bar, of any Treasons, Murders, Felonies, or Misdemeanours, done or committed by the Prisoner at the Bar, let him come forth, and he shall be heard, for the Prisoner now stands at the Bar on his deliverance. And all persons who are bound by recognizance to prosecute or give evidence against the Prisoner at the Bar, let them come forth, prosecute and give evidence, or they shall forfeit their recognizances. God save the King!"

To this proclamation Andrew listened with profound interest, tempered with a slightly uncomfortable feeling of awe. For the Old World dignity and solemnity of the phrasing served but to emphasize and intensify the tone of menace that ran through it, and to bring home to "the Prisoner at the Bar" the dreadful reality of his position.

Almost as the tones of the Crier's voice died away, the witnesses filed into the Court and took their places in the seats reserved for them. And at this point he was really startled by the appearance of Molly, who had just entered and was being ushered across to her seat. For some reason, he had assumed that she would avoid being present at his trial, and he had admitted the ownership of the attaché case to the express end that she might not have to be called as a witness, and he now speculated anxiously as to what had brought her there and whether she would have to give evidence against him. Apparently she would, since she had come in with the other witnesses and, as she walked across the floor of the Court, he followed her wistfully with his eyes. As she sat down, she took one quick glance at him and looked away. But brief as was the moment in which their eyes met, the expression in hers was unmistakable. There was no gleam of pity or compunction. Her pale face was grave and stern and hard as a mask of stone.

He was pondering on her state of mind and how it would be affected by the evidence which he was presently to give when his thoughts were interrupted by the voice of the Clerk of the Court, who had risen and, turning towards the jury, proceeded to "give the Prisoner in charge" to them. "Members of the jury, the Prisoner at the Bar is charged with the murder of Andrew Barton on the 28th August, 1928. To this indictment he has pleaded 'Not Guilty', and it is your charge to inquire, having heard the evidence, whether he be guilty or not."

This was the end of the preliminaries. The Clerk sat down behind his desk and the judge, who had inspected the prisoner narrowly from time to time, now turned towards the counsels' bench and, with a little formal bow, invited the leader for the Crown to open his case. Thereupon Sir Oliver Blizzard rose and, having fixed his monocle securely in position, looked steadily across at the jury and began. "The case, my Lord and members of the jury, which you are about to try has certain unusual features to which I wish to draw your attention before entering into any details. In the majority of cases of murder, the fact of the homicide is obvious and undeniable, and the matter in issue is the connection of the accused person with that homicide. A body is found, or a person is known to have died, and the condition of the body is such that it is obvious that the death was caused by the act of some person, and the question that the jury have to decide is whether the prisoner is, or is not, the person who committed or did that act.

"But in the case which you are going to try, the conditions are exactly the converse of those which I have described. Here, there is no question as to the connection of the prisoner with the death of the deceased Andrew Barton. If Andrew Barton was murdered, there can be no reasonable doubt that he was murdered by the prisoner. The matter in issue, the question on which you have to form a decision, is whether Andrew Barton did, in fact, meet his death by the homicidal act of some person, or whether that death was due to what old-fashioned people call 'the act of God' – that is, to some natural accident.

"To this question, which is the crucial question in the case, the medical witness can give no decisive answer. He can tell us that Andrew Barton died a violent death, but there is nothing in the appearance of the body that enables him to decide whether the violence was due to human or to natural agencies. Either is equally possible, from which it follows that the question of murder, on the one hand, or a natural accident on the other, will have to be decided by you from a most careful consideration of all the attendant conditions. You will have to examine the strange circumstances in which Andrew Barton met his death, and you will have to consider the conduct of the prisoner at the time of that death and subsequently, and ask yourselves whether such conduct is or is not consistent with his innocence.

"I have put the position before you at the start so that you may realize that your decision is to be formed on all the facts taken together, and I shall now proceed to put you in possession of those facts, first as relating to the deceased Andrew Barton and then as relating to the prisoner. I think it better to take them separately in the first place, as we shall thus get a clearer impression of the sequence of events.

"We begin, then, by following the movements of Andrew Barton on that fatal day at the end of August. And at the very outset, we are confronted by a mystery which we have no means of solving. For on the morning of that day, this unfortunate man set forth from his home on a definite mission and with a specific purpose which he never attempted to accomplish. The object of his journey, as he informed his wife, was to take some pictures to his dealer in London. But instead of taking the train to London, he took one to Crompton-on-Sea. Why he made this curious change in his plans we shall probably never know. Whether something unforeseen happened after he had left home, or whether he had, for some reason, deliberately misinformed his wife, we can only speculate. But he certainly had the paintings in the attaché case which he carried with him,

171

and his wife will tell you that he was, in general, a most scrupulously truthful man. At any rate, he set out from home carrying an attaché case in which were not only the paintings but, as we now know, a cheque for fifty pounds drawn in favour of his cousin, Ronald Barton, and a bundle of fifty pound-notes. The suggestion certainly is that he expected to meet his cousin but, as I have said, we shall never know, and the point is, in fact, more curious than important.

"His movements on arriving at Crompton are also rather mysterious, for he appears to have made his way direct to the shop of a frame-maker named Cooper, where he made a small purchase and then offered his paintings for Cooper's inspection, which was a very singular proceeding if we remember that a Bond Street dealer was prepared to take the whole of his work and pay high prices for it. But again, this mystery has no direct bearing on the question which you have to decide. The real importance of the incident is that Mr. Cooper, having had some conversation with the deceased, was able later to identify him and to give a most weighty piece of evidence.

"Our next view of Andrew Barton is at the Excelsior Restaurant, where he lunched in company with the prisoner. The waiter, Albert Wood, who waited on the two men, will describe their appearance to you, and evidence will be given that he picked the prisoner out without hesitation from a row of over twenty. Both he and Mr. Cooper noticed the deceased particularly on account of the rather peculiar spectacles that he wore. I may mention in passing that Andrew Barton had suffered an injury to his nose which resulted in considerable disfigurement, concerning which he was rather sensitive, and these spectacles were specially made to cover up the disfigurement by means of an extra broad bridge.

"On leaving the restaurant, the two men, the prisoner and the deceased, appear to have gone for a walk in the country, along a road which leads to Hunstone Gap, a place of which you will hear more presently. It is here that Mr. Cooper's evidence is of such vital importance. For this gentleman happened to have some business at the outskirts of the town, and just as he came out into the street after finishing his business, he saw the two men passing on the opposite side of the road. He recognized Andrew Barton instantly, and his attention was attracted to the other man by the curious resemblance between the two men, which was noticeable in spite of the spectacles. When they had passed and he got a back view of them, the resemblance was so remarkable that he walked some distance after them the better to observe it. These two men were not only dressed almost exactly alike, and of the same height, colour, and figure, but they seemed to him to have precisely

172

the same gait or manner of walking. This similarity in the two men is of no special interest for us, excepting in that it attracted the attention of this witness and caused him to make some further observations which are of the most vital interest. For, following them to observe their gait and gestures, he saw that they took the road which leads out into the country and to Hunstone Gap and, at the corner of the road, he stood watching them until they disappeared round a bend. And thus, members of the jury, did Andrew Barton pass for ever out of human ken. Thereafter, no eye, save that of the prisoner, looked upon him as a living man. The next eye that looked on him saw, not a young man in the very prime of life, full of vitality and manly strength, but a battered corpse, lying in a dreadful solitude at the foot of a cliff in a remote little bay called Hunstone Gap.

"The discovery was made late in the afternoon by the master of a fishing lugger called the *Sunflower*. Sailing past the Gap, he noticed that there had been a fall of chalk from the cliff, and when he came to examine the place through his glass, he saw a pair of naked legs protruding from under the heap of fragments. Thereupon he steered his craft inshore and, when she was near enough, he put out the boat and rowed ashore. And there, at the foot of the cliff, he saw the nude body of a man lying on the beach, partly covered with fragments of chalk and with one large block resting on the face. They removed the fragments and then the mate of the lugger, William Cox, lifted the great block off the face, when it was seen that the dead man's head was so horribly battered that it was practically flat. They carried the body to the boat and they then collected the clothing – the dead man had apparently been bathing – and they put the body and the clothes on board the lugger. But before he returned on board, the skipper, Samuel Sharpin by name, and a most intelligent man, had the good sense to examine the beach to see if the dead man had come there alone, or whether he had had any companions. There was only a small space of sand left, for the tide was rising and had already covered the greater part of the beach. But the little patch that was still left uncovered was quite smooth, and on that smooth surface were clearly visible two tracks of human feet. One track consisted of the footprints of two persons, walking side by side and advancing from the sunken road which led down to the beach towards the sea, the other track consisted of the footprints of one person only, and that person was returning across the beach towards the sunken road.

"Now, whose footprints were these? Since there were no others, it is evident that one set of them must have been the footprints of Andrew Barton and, since he never came away from that fatal place, it is obvious that the returning footprints could not have been his. Two men walked down together into the Gap and one of them returned from the Gap alone. One of those two men was certainly Andrew Barton. Who was the other – the one who came away alone? Can there possibly be a moment's doubt? When Andrew Barton was last seen alive, he was seen walking towards Hunstone Gap in company with the prisoner. I affirm that it is certain, in so far as certainty is possible in human affairs, that the person who walked down into the Gap with Andrew Barton and who afterwards stole away alone, was the prisoner, Ronald Barton.

"We have followed Andrew Barton to the place where he met his death. There is little more to tell. The body was conveyed by these good fishermen to the place where they berthed the lugger and there they put it ashore. Then they borrowed a seaweed cart and in this they carried the corpse into the town and delivered it to the police together with the clothing. And by the police it was deposited in the mortuary.

"And now let us, in the same manner, follow the movements of the prisoner on that fatal day and thereafter. His first appearance in this tragic history is at the Excelsior Restaurant where the waiter, Albert Wood, saw him as I have described, lunching with the deceased. Then we see him again, as described by Mr. Cooper, walking with the deceased towards Hunstone Gap. After this, there is an interval of several hours, for it is not until late in the evening, about nine o'clock, that we hear of him again. At this time, he was seen by one Frederick Barnard, a waiter at Mason's Restaurant, to enter that establishment and take his seat at a table. Now, however, he was not alone. He was accompanied by an American who was known to Barnard by sight but not by name but who has since been identified as a beauty specialist who described himself as Professor Booley. Unfortunately, this person is not available as a witness as it has been ascertained that he left Crompton on the following morning for Liverpool, where he embarked to return to America.

"The connection of the prisoner with this man Booley is rather mysterious, but there is some suggestion that he may have received some sort of treatment from this charlatan. Barnard observed that the American was the prisoner's guest and that he seemed to take a remarkable interest in the prisoner's appearance, for he watched him almost continuously and with a curious air of satisfaction. Moreover, after the American had left – which he did quite early – Barnard saw the prisoner rise from his chair, walk up to a large mirror, and examine himself in it with extraordinary interest and attention.

"However, as I have said, the connection between the prisoner and Booley remains somewhat of a mystery. Presently we shall consider whether it has any bearing on the problem which you have to solve. Of

174

more interest to us are certain other observations made by the observant Barnard. Thus, he noticed instantly when the prisoner entered that he looked ill and distressed and showed evident signs of fatigue, that he hardly spoke a word to his guest, that he improved remarkably in appearance after a substantial meal and a small bottle of wine, and that after dinner, while he was taking his coffee and a liqueur, he seemed to be wrapped in deep and anxious thought.

"The next appearance of the prisoner is most surprising and significant. For it seems that, on leaving the restaurant, he must have made his way directly to the police station. At any rate, there he was seen by no less than four persons and in the most astonishing circumstances. We have seen that the fishermen brought the body of Andrew Barton to the town in a seaweed cart and delivered it to the police. But the skipper, Samuel Sharpin, hurried on in advance to give notice of what had happened and of the approach of the cart with its tragic burden. On receiving this notice, the sergeant procured a stretcher which he and a constable, accompanied by Sharpin, carried out and laid in readiness on the pavement. And there, incredible as it may appear, they found the prisoner, ostensibly reading the notices on the wall, but apparently waiting for the arrival of the cart. For, as the cart turned into the street and the rumble of the wheels became audible, the prisoner turned and looked directly up the street – in fact, he walked part of the way as if to meet it, turning about when he met it and walking with it to its halting-place. And there, members of the jury, he stood, placidly watching while the body of his cousin was lifted from the cart and placed on the stretcher, noting the several garments as they were handed out, each of which he must have recognised, and making no sign and speaking no word. Indeed, when the poor remains had been carried away and the carter who stood by the horse approached to talk to him, he turned away and walked up the street.

"The account sounds incredible, but it is true. This secret watcher was seen by four persons, each of whom has since identified him without hesitation. There can be no doubt that this astonishing thing really happened. It is vouched for by the evidence of Sharpin, of Sergeant Steel, of Constable Willis, and of the carter, Walter Hood.

"From the police station, the prisoner seems to have gone straight to his lodgings, which were in the same street, and where he was living under the name of Walter Green. And here also some very significant events befell. His landlady, Mrs. Baxter, will tell you that at this time, Mr. Walter Green was nearly a fortnight in arrear in his rent. She had made several applications for payment, but her lodger was, at the moment, not in a position to pay the very modest sum that he owed.

175

When he came in on this evening, she reminded him of the debt. But now his attitude was entirely different. He seemed to be hard up no longer, for not only was he ready to pay what was owing, but he offered to pay in advance for the remainder of the fortnight, an offer which she discreetly accepted and was duly paid with clean, new Treasury notes.

"Now, this sudden change from penury to comparative affluence would in itself be remarkable. But much more so are the accompanying circumstances. It was on this occasion that Mrs. Baxter noticed for the first time an attaché case in the prisoner's possession. She had never seen it before, and when she mentioned the fact to him and asked if it was his, he returned no answer. But the answer to her question can be given to us by Andrew Barton's banker. Those clean, new notes with which Mr. Green paid his rent were selections from a bundle of fifty pound-notes which had been paid to Andrew Barton by his banker at Bunsford. They were a consecutive series the numbers of which had been noted and their issue to customers recorded, and the police have since been able to trace the four pound-notes paid by the prisoner to Mrs. Baxter.

"From this witness we also learn that the prisoner suddenly changed his plans. He decided to leave his lodgings on the following morning and go to London, and he was very anxious to catch an early train. That he did catch that train we have other evidence for, on the following morning, the 29th of August, he presented himself at the London office of Andrew Barton's bank in Cornhill shortly after the doors had been opened. He endorsed and presented an open cheque drawn in favour of Ronald Barton, Esq., for the sum of fifty pounds and signed Andrew Barton and, having received that sum in Treasury notes, he left the bank.

"From thence he seems to have gone straight to Hampstead, where he engaged lodgings at a house in Vineyard Place occupied by a Mrs. Martha Pendlewick, and there he was living up to the time of his arrest. But, before coming to this closing scene, we have to note one more incident which, if it is of no great importance, is of considerable interest. This was his visit to his cousin's widow. He wrote to her from Hampstead proposing to call, and on Wednesday, the 6th of September, he made his appearance at her house.

"We need not go into details of what passed at that visit. But there are two incidents which we may notice. The first is that, when Mrs. Barton asked him when he had last seen her husband, he considered for a while and then mentioned a date about two years previously. Thus, in effect, he denied having met him at Crompton. The other incident occurred shortly before he left. He then suggested that he should repeat his visit at an early date, and expressed the hope that they would see more of each other than they had done in the past, to which Mrs. Barton replied quite frankly that she would rather that he did not repeat his visit, at least for a considerable time. The reason that she gave for this wish on her part was that his remarkable resemblance to her dead husband made his presence painful to her. That is what she said, and what she still says, and it is quite understandable, but members of the jury may feel, as I confess I do, that there may have been something more subtle in her dislike to having this man in her presence.

"We now come to his arrest, and concerning the circumstances in which that arrest took place it would not be proper for me to say more than that he was arrested when he was engaged calmly in making a sketch on Hampstead Heath. And now, having followed his movements from the moment when he was first seen in company with Andrew Barton, to that when he was taken into custody, we are in a position to take a general view of the whole set of circumstances and consider their significance in relation to the charge which has been brought against him. The prisoner is accused of having murdered his cousin, Andrew Barton, at Hunstone Gap, and the question that you have to decide is: Do all these circumstances, taken together, lead convincingly to the conclusion that he is guilty of that crime, or do they not? If you decide that they do, it will be your duty to return a verdict to that effect. If, on the other hand, you feel any reasonable doubt as to whether he did commit that crime, it will be your duty to give him the benefit of that doubt and pronounce him 'Not Guilty'. Let us now examine these circumstances and see what conclusion emerges from them.

"We have seen that Andrew Barton met his death by violence, but the medical witness cannot tell us with certainty whether that violence was inflicted by natural agencies or by the murderous act of some person. Either is possible, and both are equally consistent with the appearance of the body as observed by the medical examiner. Then, since the most expert examination cannot furnish a decision as to whether death was due to accident or homicide, we must consider what light is thrown on the question from other directions.

"First there is the conduct of the prisoner. Was it that of an innocent or of a guilty man? Remember that when Andrew Barton met his death, the prisoner was present. Of that there can be no doubt. If Andrew Barton's death was due to an accident, the prisoner saw that accident happen. If Andrew Barton was murdered, he was murdered by the prisoner. Now I ask: What was the behaviour of the prisoner on that terrible occasion? Was it the behaviour of a man who has witnessed a dreadful accident? Or was it that of a man who has committed a crime?

"How would a man behave in these respective circumstances? Let us take the case of an accident. Supposing that the prisoner had seen that great block of chalk fall with a crash on his cousin's head. What would it have been natural for him to do? Would he not have hurried away in search of help, or at least have given notice of the dreadful thing that had happened? Why should he not? No one would have suspected him of being in any way to blame. Indeed, no suspicion did arise in this case until it was engendered by the prisoner's own conduct. We may say with confidence that if the prisoner had gone at once to the police station and given information, this charge would never have been brought against him.

"But suppose that the prisoner had murdered Andrew Barton. How would he have behaved? Doubtless, if he had been a man of sufficient nerve and sufficient judgment, he would have gone and reported an alleged accident. But that is not usually the way of those who commit crimes. The instinct of the criminal is to keep out of sight, to avoid the appearance of any connection with the crime.

"Now let us observe the prisoner's behaviour. With his cousin's battered corpse lying under the cliff, he steals away secretly and is lost to sight for several hours. He makes no communication to anyone. The tide is rising, and presently the waves will be washing round that corpse. But he takes no measures for its recovery before it shall be borne out to sea. He just steals away alone and hides himself.

"He next comes into view several hours later at Mason's Restaurant, and at once we are impressed by certain remarkable and significant facts. First, his appearance as described by the waiter, Barnard, is that of a man who has been exposed to some unusual strain. He shows signs of fatigue and exhaustion. He looks ill and seems to be suffering from mental distress, but he revives under the influence of food and wine. Then he is accompanied by a stranger who turns out to be what is called a 'beauty doctor', and Barnard's evidence suggests in the strongest manner that there had been some professional transactions between this man Booley, and the prisoner. Booley appeared to be intensely interested in the prisoner's face. He kept his eyes riveted on it to the neglect of his own food. But it was not the beauty doctor only who was interested in the prisoner's face. When Booley had gone, the prisoner was seen to walk up to the mirror and make a minute inspection of his own countenance.

"Now what can this mean? The suggestion is, as I have said, that Booley had done something to the prisoner's face. But what could he have done? If you will look at the prisoner, you will see that he has no need of the services of a beauty doctor. What, then, could it be that Booley had done to the prisoner's face? Could it be that the tragedy that had been enacted at Hunstone Gap had left its traces on the prisoner's face? That those tell-tale marks had prevented him from giving

178

information of the catastrophe? And that he had invoked the aid of the beauty doctor – skilled in the art of make-up – to paint out, or otherwise obliterate those incriminating marks? That, I submit, is the inference which instantly arises in the mind of any reasonable person. Andrew Barton was a young and strong man and, unless he had been taken completely by surprise, he would assuredly have left some marks of the conflict on his assailant. Admittedly, this is only an inference. But it is a reasonable inference, and the facts seem to admit of no other explanation.

"I pass over the further fact that, after Booley had left, the prisoner remained wrapped in profound thought, for he had matter enough for reflection if no murder had been committed. Let us proceed to the amazing, the appalling incident described by Sergeant Steel and the others in connection with the arrival of the body in the seaweed cart. I have told you what happened, and no comment seems adequate or necessary. You have to think of this man standing there, a calm and unmoved spectator, while the mutilated corpse of his cousin is lifted from the cart and borne away to the mortuary, looking on with the detached interest of a chance stranger and keeping his knowledge of the dead man's identity locked in his own breast. Think of this amazing callousness and secrecy, and ask yourselves what can be the explanation of it. Is this the conduct of a man who has seen his kinsman killed by a natural accident? Or is it that of one whose guilty knowledge bids him hold his peace? Is it, in short, the conduct of an innocent man? Or is it that of a murderer who is looking on the corpse of his victim?

"When he has seen his cousin's body disposed of, he goes home to his lodgings and forthwith proceeds to take possession of the dead man's property. Andrew Barton's attaché case is already on his table. When or how it came there we do not know, but we do know that, within a few minutes of his return, even while the unburdened seaweed cart was rumbling back up the street, he had possessed himself of some of its contents. For it was with Andrew Barton's money that he paid his debt to the landlady. The cheque we may admit to have been his lawful property, but the cheque had not been cashed. The money with which Mrs. Baxter's bill was paid was money that had been stolen from the dead. And again I ask: Is this calm and callous appropriation of the dead man's money the act of an innocent man?

"But the same eager greed is apparent in the actions which followed. As soon as he had paid the landlady, he came to the sudden decision to go to London early on the following morning. For the cheque had to be cashed before the tidings of Andrew Barton's death reached his bank. Otherwise it would have been returned to the payee endorsed '*Drawer*

Deceased'. And once out of the neighbourhood, he decided to stay out. Regardless of his cousin's corpse, lying in the mortuary, and of the poor wife, waiting for the husband whose voice she was never to hear again, he goes off to Hampstead, there to lie in hiding until things had settled down and all danger might be considered to be over.

"The sordid avidity for money that we have noted on the part of the prisoner leads us to another point: The will of Andrew Barton contains a clause bequeathing to the prisoner the sum of five-hundred pounds. The widow, who is the executrix, will tell you that her husband had been in the constant habit of making loans to the prisoner – loans which, it may be remarked, were never repaid and never expected to be repaid. Now, it seems that Andrew Barton, having regard to the fact that, if he should die, these gifts would necessarily cease, decided to make a provision for his cousin. Accordingly, he effected a separate insurance on behalf of his cousin in the sum of five-hundred pounds and in his will directed that this sum should be paid to the prisoner. Thus the prisoner, who was aware of the provision, knew that he stood to benefit by the death of Andrew Barton to the extent of five-hundred pounds, a fact which, when we consider his avaricious seizure of his dead cousin's money, we cannot but find profoundly significant.

"And now, to sum up in a few words: Taking the prisoner's conduct as a whole, is it that of an innocent man who has nothing on his conscience, or is it that of a man who has a burden of guilt on his conscience and is harbouring in his soul a guilty secret? Did Andrew Barton die by the chance fall on him of a block of chalk? Or was that block used by murderous hands as a terrible weapon to cover the traces, and perhaps complete the work, of some other weapon? The body has no decisive message for us. We must decide from the conduct of the prisoner. And I submit that the prisoner's conduct answers the question conclusively, especially when considered in connection with the substantial sum of money which he stood to gain by his cousin's death. He had a motive – a strong motive to an avaricious man. He was present when the death occurred. He had the opportunity to commit murder, and when the death had occurred, he stole away and instantly laid hands on the dead man's property, thereafter not only hiding himself, but denying to his cousin's widow that he had seen that dead man for many months. I repeat, he had a motive to commit the crime, he had the opportunity to commit it, and his subsequent conduct has been, in a striking degree, that of a man who has committed a crime.

"Accordingly, I submit that you can come to no other conclusion but that he did, in fact, commit that crime, and that it will be your duty to return a verdict of 'Guilty'."

Chapter XIV
The Evidence for the Prosecution

The conclusion of Sir Oliver's opening speech was succeeded by a brief pause before the calling of the witnesses, during which Andrew reflected in a dull, bewildered fashion on what he had heard. It was all surprisingly plausible, even convincing, and the speaker had contrived, in spite of a studied moderation, to convey the feeling that he, himself, was convinced of the prisoner's guilt. Of course, it was all quite unreal, but no one besides himself – and perhaps Thorndyke – knew the real facts. Sir Oliver had in no respect exaggerated or distorted the known facts, and the conclusion that he had suggested as inferable from those facts was a fair, reasonable, and logical conclusion.

And now the witnesses would be called, and Andrew knew in advance what they would say. They would fully bear out the counsel's statement, and what they would say would be the truth which no cross-examination would shake. It did not look promising, but yet Dr. Thorndyke (who knew all that the prosecution knew) had seemed to be quite confident. But at this point, his reflections were broken in upon by a voice, calling the name of Molly Barton. His eyes had been resting almost continuously on her, and he now saw her rise from her seat and walk resolutely towards the witness-box. He noted that she was pale and haggard and obviously distressed, but her face was set in an expression of hard, stern resolution that he found it difficult to connect with the gentle, kindly Molly whom he had known in the days of his happy and peaceful married life.

Her evidence, as elicited by the "examination in chief", followed the lines of Sir Oliver's opening. There was a brief reference to the Hudson murder and to a visit on the 28th of August of a certain Inspector Sands, who had come to make inquiries as to the personal appearance, habits, and occupation of her husband, and whom she had referred to her husband's banker in London and to Mr. Montagu, his agent and dealer. Then there was the more tragic reference to another visit from the inspector on the following morning, to inform her of the finding of a body believed to be that of her husband, and to request her to go to Crompton to confirm the identification, and her dreadful experiences in the Crompton Mortuary when she was confronted with that terrible corpse.

The examination was conducted with the utmost delicacy and consideration that was possible, and Molly rose bravely to the occasion, though now and again there came a break in the clear voice, and her steady answer petered out into something very like a sob. But the counsel passed as quickly as he could over the most distressing incidents and, when he proceeded to the prisoner's visit to Fairfield, she recovered her self-possession completely. "When the prisoner came to see you," said Sir Oliver, "did he mention when he had last seen your husband?"

"Yes, I asked him. At first he seemed not to remember, but afterwards he said that he had not seen him for about two years."

"With reference to the benefit which the prisoner receives under your husband's will, was anything said about that?"

"Yes. I reminded him of the special life insurance that my husband had effected on his behalf."

"You say you reminded him. That seems to imply that he knew that the arrangement had been made. Can you say, of your own knowledge, that he was aware of it?"

"Yes. When my husband took out the policy and made his will, he wrote to his cousin, Ronald, and told him exactly what he had done. I saw the letter and read it."

"In that letter, was the amount mentioned?"

"Yes. It was clearly stated that, in the event of my husband dying before Ronald, the latter would receive five-hundred pounds free of legacy duty."

"In the course of your interview with the prisoner on this occasion – on the 6th of September – was anything said about future visits?"

"Yes. He said that he should come and see me again soon, and that he thought we ought to see more of each other than we had done in the past."

"And what did you reply to that?"

"I told him that I would rather that he did not come to see me again just at present, as I found that his great resemblance to my husband made his presence painful to me."

"You found it painful to be in his society?"

"Yes. His likeness to my husband got on my nerves. I felt that I could not bear to have him in the house."

"Are you sure that it was the likeness only that caused this feeling of repulsion? Was there nothing else in your mind?"

"I know of nothing else. He seemed unconsciously to be mimicking my husband, and I felt that I could not bear it."

On receiving this reply, Sir Oliver paused to take a glance at his brief. Then he reached down below the bench and produced an attaché case which he handed to an attendant who conveyed it to the witness. "Can you tell us anything about the case which has just been handed to you?" the counsel asked.

"It belonged to my husband," was the reply. "He was carrying it when he left home on the morning of the 28th of August."

"You have no doubt that it was your husband's case?"

"None whatever. The letters stamped on the lid are his initials, *A. B.* He stamped them himself with book-binder's letters. I have the tools here, and you can see that they fit the stamped initials."

She produced from a hand-bag three brass "handled letters", an *A*, a *B*, and a *stop*, which were taken by the attendant, with the attaché case, and passed round for inspection by the judge and jury. "Can you tell us," Sir Oliver continued, "what the case contained when your husband left home?"

"I understood that it contained one or two small water colours, but I did not see them. Of the other contents I know nothing."

The case and the tools made their round, being eventually deposited as "exhibits". Meanwhile, Sir Oliver took another glance at his brief, and finding, apparently, that he had exhausted his matter, sat down, whereupon Dr. Thorndyke rose to cross-examine. "You have told us," he began, "that on the 29th of August, you went to Crompton Mortuary for the purpose of inspecting and, if possible, identifying a body which was lying there and which was believed to be the body of your husband, Andrew Barton. I deeply regret the necessity of recalling to your memory what must have been a very terrible experience, but it is essential that we should be quite clear as to the facts. Were you able to identify that body?"

"No," Molly replied, with a visible shudder. "It was quite unrecognizable. But the clothes were my husband's clothes."

"Yes," said Thorndyke. "You identified the clothes as your husband's but, apart from the clothes, were you able to form any opinion as to whether the body was or was not that of your husband?"

"No," Molly replied. "I was not. I said so."

"So far as you know, was any evidence as to the identity of the body, apart from the clothing, given at the inquest?"

"No. The identity of the body was established by means of the clothing."

"You referred just now to a severe injury to the nose from which your husband had suffered. Did the medical witness at the inquest mention having found any traces of that injury?"

"No. I don't think he knew about it when he made his examination. At any rate, he said nothing about it."

"Did you ever learn what was the exact nature of that injury?"

"Yes. The surgeon at the hospital gave me a certificate for the insurance office. It described the injury as a depressed and comminuted fracture of the nasal bones."

"You have spoken of your alarm when your husband did not come home on the night of the 28th of August. May we take it that he was not in the habit of staying away from home without notice?"

"He never stayed away from home without notice," Molly replied, emphatically. "He hardly ever stayed away at all."

"Did he ever stay away from home, and away from you, for a considerable period, say for more than a month?"

"Never. We used, occasionally, to go away together, but he never went away by himself for longer than a week-end."

"Now, Mrs. Barton," Thorndyke said in a persuasive tone, "I want you to try to give me a statement of your husband's whereabouts on a particular date. Can you remember where he was on Good Friday in the year 1925?"

Molly looked at him in evident surprise, but replied, after a few moments' thought, "I believe he was at home – at any rate, I have no recollection of our having been away at that time."

Thorndyke was manifestly dissatisfied with the reply and pressed for a more precise answer. "Take a little time to think," he urged, "and see if you cannot recall the circumstances. It is only three years ago, and Good Friday is a very distinctive date. You will surely be able to remember where you spent your Easter."

Again she reflected with knitted brows. Suddenly she exclaimed, "Oh, yes, I remember. He was at home."

"Something has recalled it to your memory," he suggested.

"Yes. In that year I undertook to decorate the parish church, and my husband helped me. In fact, he did most of the decoration."

Thorndyke paused to make a note of the answer and then proceeded. "With reference to the prisoner's visit to you on the 6th of September, you have said that his resemblance to your husband was so close as to cause you great distress. In what respect did he appear to resemble your husband?"

"In every respect," Molly replied, "excepting, of course, that his nose was different. Otherwise, he seemed exactly like my husband, even in the face, in spite of the difference in the shape of the nose. And his figure was the same and he had the same tricks of movement with his hands and the same rather unusual way of picking up his tea-cup without using the handle."

"And what about the voice?"

"That was the worst of all. It was exactly like my husband's. If I had shut my eyes, I could have thought that it was my husband speaking."

"To what extent had you been acquainted with Ronald Barton? Had you previously seen much of him?"

"No. I had met him only twice, when he came to see us. The second occasion was a little over two years ago."

"When you were in his society on that occasion, were you greatly impressed by his resemblance to your husband?"

"Not so much. I could see, of course, they they were very much alike, but the resemblance did not strike me as so very extraordinary when I saw them together and could compare them."

"When the prisoner came to see you in September, did his great resemblance to your husband come upon you in any way as a surprise?"

"Yes, very much so. I had no idea that the two men were so much alike. It was quite a shock to me."

"Did it appear to you that he was in any respects different from the Ronald Barton whom you remembered? Did he seem to have changed in any way?"

"Yes, he did seem to have changed in some respects. He was quieter in manner, less boisterous. In fact, he was not boisterous at all, as he used to be. But I put that down to the sad circumstances in which his visit was made. It was only a few days after the funeral."

"Did you notice any other differences from what you remembered of him previously?"

"There was one thing that surprised me. He seemed to know so much more about pictures and painting than I had supposed he did, and he was so much more interested in them. On the previous occasions, he had not seemed to be interested at all in my husband's work or in painting in general."

"Then, taking your impressions as a whole, would it be correct to say that the Ronald Barton who came to see you in September did not seem to be quite the same kind of person as the Ronald Barton whom you remembered having met formerly?"

"Yes, I think that would be correct."

"And would it further be correct to say that such changes as seemed to have occurred, increased his resemblance to your husband?"

"Yes, I think that is so."

On receiving this answer, Thorndyke sat down, and Andrew took a deep breath. He was beginning to understand his counsel's tactics. But he was the only person present who did. Throughout the cross-examination, the judge had listened attentively with an obviously puzzled expression, and Sir Oliver and his junior, Mr. Horace Black, had looked frankly

185

bewildered. Even Molly, though she answered readily and with conscientious care, was evidently surprised at the apparent irrelevancy of the questions. There was no re-examination, the two prosecuting counsel being clearly of the opinion that no point had been made and that there was nothing to contest. Accordingly, Molly was released from the witness-box and went back to her seat.

The next witness was Mr. Cooper, the carver and gilder, whose evidence repeated in detail the account which had been given by Sir Oliver in his opening address. Having regard to the importance and damaging character of that evidence, it was obviously a matter of surprise to the judge and the prosecuting counsel that Thorndyke allowed the witness to leave the box without any attempt at cross-examination. He was followed by Albert Wood, the waiter at the Excelsior Restaurant, whose evidence was also ignored by Thorndyke. Then the name of Samuel Sharpin was called, and a copper-faced elderly man in a stiff suit of blue cloth, rolled into the witness-box and fixed a seafaring blue eye on Sir Oliver's monocle. In much the same terms as he had used at the inquest, he described the circumstances in which he had observed the body through his glass, had put inshore and salvaged it, and had conveyed it in the seaweed cart to the police station at Crompton. When the narrative was completed, Sir Oliver, having taken out his monocle, wiped it with his handkerchief and refixed it securely, addressed the witness in quiet but impressive tones, pointing his hand towards the dock. "Look attentively at the prisoner and tell me if you have ever seen him before."

The witness turned slowly and with seeming reluctance and cast a commiserating glance at the prisoner. "Yes," he said. "I've seen him before."

"Where did you see him?" Sir Oliver demanded, with something of a dramatic flourish.

"I see him." replied Sharpin, "in the prison yard, yonder, along of a lot of other fellows in a row. I was told to see if I could pick him out."

"And could you?" asked Sir Oliver, making the best of the slight anti-climax.

"Easily," replied Sharpin. "He was the only decent-looking man there."

"And where and when had you seen him before that?"

"I see him the night we brought the dead man in from Hunstone Gap. He was a-standing on the pavement outside the police station, a-watching of us as we unloaded the dead man out of the cart and set him on the stretcher."

186

"Are you certain that the prisoner is the man you saw watching you as you took the body out of the cart?"

"Yes," Sharpin replied doggedly. "He's the man."

"Do you swear that he is the man whom you saw there on that night?"

"I ain't much given to swearing," said Sharpin. "Don't hold with it. I've said he is the man, and he is the man."

"Did that man speak to anybody when you were moving the body?"

"Never spoke a word to nobody," was the slightly ambiguous reply.

"Did he seem agitated or upset in any way?"

"He didn't seem to be, but I didn't notice him very much. I was attending to what I was doing."

Having noted this reply. Sir Oliver relinquished his prey and Thorndyke rose. "When you came ashore and saw the block of chalk resting on the dead man's head, did you look up to see where the block had come from?"

"Yes, I did, in case there might be some more coming down. You could see where the block had broken out. Left a sort of square hole."

"And did you notice whether that hole was straight over the body, or whether it was to one or other side?"

"It was straight overhead, and I kept an eye on the place while we was a-moving of the body."

"You said that your mate, William Cox, lifted the rock off the dead man's head. Should you describe Cox as a strong man?"

"Ay. Will Cox is an uncommon beefy lad."

"Should you say that he is an unusually strong man?"

"Yes, strong as a young elephant he is. I gives him all the heavy jobs to do, and he don't never turn a hair and he don't never grumble."

"You seem to be fortunate in your mate," Thorndyke remarked with a smile.

"I am that," agreed Sharpin. "Worth his weight in gold is Will Cox, and he turns the scale at fourteen stone."

This completed Samuel Sharpin's evidence, and on his retirement he was succeeded by his much-appreciated mate, a good-looking young giant with a mahogany complexion, bright blue eyes, and a mop of curly hair. His skipper's commendations, which he had necessarily overheard, seemed to have covered him with confusion, for he swung shyly into the witness-box and, having taken up a negligent pose, greeted the judge with an embarrassed grin and then fixed an expectant eye on Sir Oliver, being, apparently, like his skipper, fascinated by the learned counsel's "dead-light".

But whatever might have been his worth to his commander, he was of little to the prosecution, and when they observed the way in which Thorndyke pounced on him, they may have regretted the necessity for calling him. His evidence merely confirmed and amplified that of the previous witness and, after a brief and matter-of-fact examination, Sir Oliver resigned him to the defence. "You have said," Thorndyke began, "that you lifted the block of chalk off the dead man's head. Did you find it easy to lift?"

"No, I did not," replied Cox, with a shake of his curly head. "'Twas most uncommon awkward to lift. Heavy, too, it was."

"You are accustomed, I suppose, to lifting heavy weights? Fish-trunks, for instance?"

"Ay, but d'ye see, fish-trunks is fitted with rope beckets for to catch hold of. They are easy enough for to hoist. 'Tis only a matter of weight. But this here block of chalk wasn't no sort of shape. There wasn't nothing for to lay hold of or to hook your fingers under."

"What are the usual weights of fish-trunks?"

"They runs five, seven, eight, or ten stone."

"And a stone, in your trade, is how many pounds?"

"Fourteen pounds goes to a stone of fish."

"What should you say was the weight of that block of chalk?"

"Somewhere between eight and nine stone, as near as I can judge."

"And how near can you judge a weight of this kind, say a fish-trunk?"

"I can judge the weight of a trunk of fish within two or three pounds."

"You say that you found that block difficult to lift. How high did you lift it from the ground?"

"Only an inch or two. I just hoisted it clear and dropped it alongside."

"Could you have lifted it higher, so far as you could judge? Say two or three feet above the ground?"

"I might have been able to, but I shouldn't have liked to try. Not more than a foot, anyway. He was mighty slippery and difficult to hold, and you don't want eight or nine stone of chalk on your toe."

"Do you find any difficulty in lifting a ten-stone trunk?"

"Lord, no sir! Wouldn't be much good in our trade if I did. But as I was telling you, a trunk has got beckets – rope handles, you know – and if you've got hold of them, the trunk can't slip."

"So you can lift ten stone – a hundred-and-forty pounds – without difficulty?"

"Yes, and a tidy bit more if need be and if I'd got a proper hand-grip."

Having received and noted this answer, Thorndyke sat down and Sir Oliver rose to re-examine. "Does it require a specially strong man to lift an ordinary fish-trunk?"

"Not if he's used to it. Them as ain't don't make much of it."

"Take the case of an eight stone trunk. Do you say that a young man of the prisoner's height and build would have any difficulty in lifting it?"

"No, I suppose he could lift it if he put his back into it. But he'd find it a tidy weight if he wasn't used to hoisting."

Apparently, Sir Oliver judged it wise to let well alone for, having got this qualified assent to his question, he sat down. Then William Cox descended from the witness-box and the name of Frederick Barnard was called.

Frederick Barnard, having been sworn, deposed that he was the senior waiter at Mason's Restaurant, Crompton-on-Sea. He had identified the prisoner among a number of other men at the prison. He recognized him as a man who had come to the restaurant at about half-past-eight in the evening of the 28th of August. He had noticed him particularly because he looked pale and ill and had a drawn expression as if he were in pain or in some serious trouble. He also looked very tired. Seemed "dead beat". His manner was peculiar. He had a companion with him but hardly spoke a word to him. He improved very much when he had taken some food and wine, but he ate very slowly and carefully, as a man might who had a tender tooth, and he used his napkin as if he was afraid of hurting his mouth.

His companion was an American gentleman whom the witness knew well by sight, as he had frequently come to the restaurant, sometimes alone and sometimes with a friend. The witness did not, at that time, know the American gentleman's name, but he had since ascertained from the friend who used to come with him that he was a Professor Booley, who described himself as a 'beauty specialist'.

"Do you know what Professor Booley did for a living?"

"I only know what his friend told me – that his work consisted principally in making up ladies' faces, touching up their complexions and eyebrows and covering up any blemishes."

"Did you notice anything peculiar in Booley's behaviour?"

"Yes, his manner was very peculiar. He ate very little, but very fast, and he hardly talked at all. But he sat looking at the prisoner's face as if he couldn't take his eyes off it. It was most singular. Sometimes he would lean back or move his head sideways to get a different view, and sometimes he would look in the big mirror on the wall and then back at

189

the prisoner's face as if he was comparing the reflection in the glass with the original. And he seemed to be extraordinarily pleased with both of them and quite excited about them."

"And did the prisoner show any special interest in his face?"

"Yes. I saw him looking at himself in the glass from time to time and, after Mr. Booley had gone – which he did before the prisoner had finished his dinner – he got up from the table and walked up to the mirror and stood there looking at himself for quite a long time."

"And what did he do after that?"

"He sat for close on half-an-hour over his coffee and a green Chartreuse. He looked quite natural by this time, but he seemed to have something on his mind – at least, he looked as if he was thinking very hard about something."

"Did you see anything about the prisoner's face that might have accounted for the interest that he and Professor Booley seemed to take in it?"

"I didn't then. I just thought that he was a good-looking young man who was rather pleased with himself. I didn't know who Professor Booley was, then. But since I've known what his trade was, I've been disposed to suspect that – "

"Ah!" Sir Oliver interrupted, "but you mustn't tell us what you suspect, though I daresay you may be right. We are dealing with the facts that are known to you. We must not go beyond what you saw or heard."

"Well," said Barnard, slightly crestfallen and even huffy, "I've told you all I saw and heard. I can't remember anything more."

Thereupon Sir Oliver sat down and proceeded thoughtfully to polish his eye-glass. The judge cast an inquiring glance towards Thorndyke, but as the latter made no sign, the witness was released and the name of Thomas Steel was called.

The new witness was a sergeant in the Crompton police force and he gave his evidence with professional tidiness and precision. But it did not amount to very much. He had picked the prisoner out of a row of twenty men, and he identified him as the man who had stood outside the police station watching the removal of the body from the seaweed cart. That man had made no sign of recognizing the body and had not spoken to anyone. Did not appear in any way agitated or greatly concerned. Had seemed to be just an ordinary spectator. The witness was quite sure prisoner was the man. He was used to recognizing persons, and the prisoner was a rather striking person who would be easy to remember and recognize.

From this incident Sir Oliver turned his attention to Professor Booley, referring to the evidence of Frederick Barnard. "Do you know anything about this man Booley?"

"I knew him by name and by sight," the sergeant replied, "and I knew his premises in Barleymow Street. He described himself as a beauty specialist, and he had a big card in his window setting forth what he could do. I took a photograph of it to keep in case any question of fraud or false pretences should be raised."

"Have you got a copy of that photograph?"

"Yes. I have here an enlarged copy from the small negative." He produced from an attaché case a whole-plate photograph which was passed across to Sir Oliver, who took out his eye-glass to read it, and then, with an indulgent smile, returned it to the usher who passed it up to the judge. From his lordship it was conveyed to the jury, who studied it with broad and appreciative grins, and back to the Counsels' bench, finding its way eventually to the Clerk's table, where it remained. "Have you any knowledge," Sir Oliver asked, "as to the success of the Professor's methods? Have you, for instance, met anyone who had had a crooked nose straightened out by him?"

The sergeant admitted, amidst a murmur of merriment, that he had not. "But," he added, "I know that he was very clever at painting out black eyes."

"Did you ever see a specimen of his skill?"

"Yes. Our court missionary got a black eye when he was trying to separate two drunken sailors. It was such a bad one that he didn't like to show his face out of doors. But one of our constables took him round to Booley's to have it painted out with grease-paint, and when he came back you couldn't see a trace of the discolouration. It looked perfectly natural."

"So far as you know, did Booley get much work of this kind?"

"I have no personal knowledge beyond this one case. The constable told me that Booley did an extensive trade in painting out black eyes and bruises and pimples and blotches, but I can't verify his statement from my own knowledge."

This concluded the examination in chief. When Sir Oliver sat down, Thorndyke rose to cross-examine. "You have said that when you came out of the police station with the stretcher, you found the prisoner waiting there and making a show of reading a bill that was affixed to the notice board. Do you recall anything remarkable about that bill?"

"Yes. By a most extraordinary coincidence, that bill contained a description of the man whose body was in the seaweed cart."

"What was the heading of that bill?"

191

"It was headed, '*Wanted for Murder*'."

"And who was it that was wanted for murder?"

"The dead man. Andrew Barton."

"For the murder of whom was he wanted?"

"For the murder of Mr. Hudson at Kibble's Cross."

"Can you remember the exact terms of the description?"

"I cannot remember the exact wording, but I could give you the substance of it."

"I will read you a portion of the bill and you shall tell me whether what I have read is correct. This is the passage:

> *It is believed that more than one man was concerned in the crime, but the only one who was seen was the man who actually fired the shot. He is described as somewhat fair man with grey eyes, about thirty years of age, and easily recognizable by reason of a remarkably deformed nose, which appears to have been broken and is completely flat excepting at the tip, which is rather prominent.*

"Is that a correct quotation from the bill?"

"To the best of my recollection and belief it is quite correct."

"You say that the description in the bill was that of the dead man, Andrew Barton. When did you first learn that the man described in the bill was Andrew Barton?"

"On the following morning, the 28th. A telephone message came through from Bunsford directing us to take down the bill and call in any copies that we had circulated. I took the telephone call."

"Was any reason given for the withdrawal of the bill?"

"Not officially. But I had a few words with the officer at the other end and was informed by him that inquiries had been made and that it appeared that there had been some mistake. It turned out that the man described in the bill was not concerned in the murder at all. I then reported the finding of the body of Andrew Barton of Fairfield, and the officer at Bunsford then informed me that Andrew Barton of Fairfield was the man described in the bill."

"So far as you know, was any public announcement made by the police that the accusation of Andrew Barton was a mistake due to an error in identification?"

"No such announcement ever came to my knowledge and, as no name had been mentioned and the man was dead, it would seem to have been unnecessary."

"That," remarked the judge, "seems to be a rather easy-going view to take. There had been a public accusation of a particular person and there ought to have been a public withdrawal of it."

The sergeant agreed that some such announcement ought to have been made, but pointed out that he had merely said that he was not aware of its having been made. It was possible that there had been a public withdrawal which had escaped his notice, and this observation brought his evidence to an end.

The next witness was Mrs. Susan Baxter of 16 Barleymow Street, Crompton, who identified the prisoner as her late lodger, Mr. Walter Green. She deposed that, on the night of the 28th of August, Mr. Green who had previously been quite impecunious and unable to pay his rent, seemed suddenly to have become flush of money and anxious to discharge his debt. He paid her with four pound notes which were quite clean and new, but she had not noticed their numbers and could not identify them. On that occasion she had seen an attaché case on the table in prisoner's room. She had never seen it before and was certain that it had not been in the room until that night. Had asked prisoner if it was his but he had not answered. The case produced and handed to her was like the one she had seen, but she would not swear that it was the same one. The prisoner announced that night that he was going to London the next day and he seemed very anxious to catch an early train. He went away next morning at a little past eight o'clock, and she had not seen him since until she picked him out of a row of men at the prison.

When the examination in chief was finished. Thorndyke rose. But he raised only a single point. "When you were talking to the prisoner on that last night, did you notice anything in his manner that was unusual or different from what you had been accustomed to?"

"Well, yes, I did," Mrs. Baxter replied. "He was quieter in his way of speaking, and much more polite and considerate. I noticed it particularly, because he had usually been rather loud-spoken and gave his orders like a Lord. And he was a decidedly selfish and inconsiderate lodger."

"Did you notice a great difference in his manner on this occasion?"

"I did. He spoke like a perfect gentleman, most respectful and polite. And he was quite anxious not to put me out by going away so early. I was quite took aback. He seemed like a different gentleman."

Having elicited this answer, Thorndyke sat down, and once more the judge cast a speculative and rather puzzled glance in his direction. Evidently his Lordship was endeavouring to trace through these seeming irrelevancies some intelligible line of defence. To him, as to the prosecuting counsel, these questions of Thorndyke's must have seemed to have no bearing whatever on the issue which was being tried. But experience would have told him that Dr. John Thorndyke was not a gentleman who asked irrelevant questions, and a suspicion may have begun to filter into his judicial mind that the defence was going to take the form of a counter-attack – and a flank attack at that. Andrew alone, listening with growing interest and a queer sense of detachment, could recognize the logical structure which his champion was building up, brick by brick.

The evidence of Mrs. Baxter was followed by that of the cashier at the London Bank and, when this had been disposed of, Sir Oliver proceeded to bring up his big gun. And a very big gun it was and, to tell the truth, the gunner seemed just a shade nervous about "letting it off". For – to drop metaphor – the new witness was no less a person than Sir Artemus Pope, M.D., F.R.S., the eminent pathologist, and the evidence of Sir Artemus Pope was the foundation on which the whole super-structure of the prosecution rested. And the counsel's opening address had made it clear that Sir Artemus was neither an enthusiastic nor a pliable witness. It was certain in advance that he would not budge a hair's-breadth from bald, literal, demonstrable fact.

Sir Oliver approached him cautiously with the introductory questions. "You have made an examination of the body of the deceased, Andrew Barton, whose death is the subject of the present proceedings. Is that so?"

"Yes," replied Sir Artemus. "On the 6th of November, acting on instructions from the Home Office, I conducted an exhumation at Fairfield Churchyard of the body of Andrew Barton and made a careful examination of the said body."

"What was the object of the examination?"

"To check the findings of the medical witness at the inquest and to determine, if possible, the cause of death, particularly in connection with the present proceedings."

"Were you given full particulars of the circumstances in which the death occurred?"

"Yes, including the depositions taken at the inquest."

"What were the conditions that your examination revealed?"

"I found extensive multiple fractures of the skull and the bones of the face. Practically all the bones were broken and the head appeared to have been crushed flat. The injuries were of such a kind as would have been produced by an extremely heavy blow from some hard and ponderous object, delivered when the head was lying on the ground, face upwards."

"What conclusions did you reach as to the cause of death?"

"If the man were alive at the moment when the blow took effect, it would certainly have killed him instantly. As there was nothing to suggest that he was not alive at that moment, I concluded that the blow was the cause of death."

"Would the very gross injuries which you have described be sufficient to cover up and obliterate the traces of any lesser injuries which might have been previously inflicted?"

"That would depend on the nature of the previous injuries. If they had been inflicted with a sharp instrument, such as an axe, the incised wounds would be recognizable even after the subsequent smashing. But if they had been inflicted with a blunt implement, all traces of them would probably have been obliterated by the blow which flattened the skull."

"Is it possible that such previous injuries may actually have been inflicted and their traces destroyed by the major injuries?"

"It is *possible*," Sir Artemus replied, with distinct emphasis on the final word.

"From your examination, did you form any opinion as to whether the injuries were due to accident or homicide?"

"The examination informed me only of the nature of the injuries. I have no personal knowledge of the circumstances in which they were inflicted. The information supplied to me set forth that they were produced by a block of chalk, weighing about a hundred-weight, which had fallen from the cliff. If it had fallen on to the head of the deceased when he was lying face upwards, it would have produced injuries such as those which I found. And in that case, death would be due to accident."

"Precisely," said Sir Oliver. "That is one possibility. Now let us consider another. Suppose that the block had already fallen and was lying on the beach. Suppose that the deceased had been killed or rendered insensible by a blow on the head with a heavy stone or some other blunt instrument. Suppose, then, that his assailant picked up the block of chalk and dropped it on his head as he lay. In that case, would the appearances be such as you found?"

"No," replied Sir Artemus. "A man could not lift such a block more than two or three feet, and a fall from that height would not smash the skull into fragments as I found it to be smashed."

"Not with one single blow. But suppose the blow to have been repeated several times?"

"In that case, it is possible that the skull might ultimately have been completely crushed."

"And would it then have presented the appearance which you observed when you examined it?"

195

"Probably it would, so far as I can judge. But that is merely an opinion. I cannot say definitely that it would."

"Is it possible that the injuries which you found could have been produced by homicidal violence?"

"It is physically possible that they might have been."

"You agree that the appearances which you observed were consistent with the theory that the death of the deceased was due to homicidal violence?"

Sir Artemus did not appear to like the form of the question, but eventually gave a grudging assent, on which Sir Oliver, having got the utmost agreement that he was likely to get, promptly sat down, and Thorndyke rose to cross-examine. "You have said that the injuries which you found were such as would have been produced if the block of chalk had fallen on the head of the deceased when he was lying face upwards. Did you find anything that was in the least degree inconsistent with the belief that death was caused in that way?"

"I did not," Sir Artemus replied, promptly.

"It has been suggested that death or insensibility may have been caused by a blow, or blows, with a blunt instrument. Did you find any traces or any appearances of any kind which led you to believe that such blow, or blows, might have been inflicted?"

"I did not."

"Did you observe anything which suggested to you that the injuries had been produced by human agency rather than by the accidental fall of the block?"

"I did not."

"Did you observe anything, or ascertain any fact, which offered a positive suggestion that death might have been due to homicide?"

"I did not."

"Would it be correct to say that the conditions which you found were entirely consistent with death by accident?"

"It would."

"And that your examination disclosed no positive evidence or any suggestion of any kind that death was due to homicide?"

"Yes. That would be quite correct."

Thorndyke, having squeezed the witness dry (and he had not seemed unwilling to be squeezed), noted the replies and then proceeded. "Were you supplied with a description of the person of the deceased?"

"I was given a copy of the depositions taken at the inquest. They contained a description of the person of the deceased."

"Had you any instructions to verify the identity of the deceased?"

"No. My instructions were to ascertain the cause of death and consider the possible alternatives of accident or homicide. The question of identity was not raised. The body which I examined was described to me as the body of Andrew Barton, and such I assumed it to be."

"But you had a description of the person of Andrew Barton. Now, when you made your examination, did you find that the body which you were examining corresponded completely with that description?"

The question seemed to put Sir Artemus on the alert, and he gave himself a few seconds to consider it. But he was not the only person who roused at the question. The judge seemed to have found a possible clue to the mystery that had been puzzling him, for he leaned forward with eager interest to catch the reply. The prisoner in the dock, too, perceived a ray of light from an unexpected quarter and, glancing at Molly, he saw that she had fixed a startled eye on the questioner. "What do you say, Sir Artemus?" Thorndyke inquired, placidly.

"The deceased," Sir Artemus replied cautiously, "was personally unknown to me, so I was dependent on the description. There did appear to me to be a slight discrepancy between that description and the body which I was examining. The description set forth that the deceased had suffered from a severe injury to the nose resulting in complete flattening of the bridge. The conditions which I found were not exactly what I should have expected from that description."

"You have heard the evidence which was given by Mrs. Barton that the surgeon's certificate described the injury as a depressed and comminuted fracture of the nasal bones?"

"Yes, I heard that evidence. It agrees with the description that was given to me."

"Did you make a careful examination of the nasal bones of the deceased?"

"I did. They were both fractured, but not very extensively. They had been driven bodily into the nasal cavity."

"In a case of comminuted fracture with a depression which remained permanently, what conditions would you expect to find?"

"As the fragments must have united in a false position, I should expect to find the bones distorted in shape and associated with a good deal of callus or new bone."

"What did you actually find?"

"The bones were fractured, as I have said. But when the fragments were put together, they did not appear to be in any way abnormal. I was not able to recognize any callus or traces of repair."

"What conclusions did your observations suggest?"

"I concluded that the original injury could not have been as great as had been supposed – that there must have been some exaggeration, due to error."

"Does that conclusion seem to you to be supported by the evidence which you have heard to-day?"

"I am hardly prepared to pronounce an opinion on that question. My examination was not concerned with the issue of identity, which you seem to be raising, and I did not give it sufficient attention to enable me to make a perfectly definite statement."

"Are you prepared to admit that, if the description given to you of the person of Andrew Barton was a true and faithfully correct description, the body which you examined could not have been the body of Andrew Barton?"

"That seems rather sweeping," the witness objected. "I don't think I can commit myself to that. But I will admit that, if the description was correct, there were disagreements between that description and the visible facts which I am unable to account for."

As this amounted, in effect, to an affirmative answer to the question, Thorndyke pushed the cross-examination no farther. As he resumed his seat, Sir Oliver rose to re-examine and, as he could evidently make nothing of Thorndyke's later questions, he set himself to mitigate the effects of the earlier ones. "You have said, Sir Artemus, that you found no positive indications of homicide. Did you find any positive indications that excluded homicide?"

"I did not," was the reply.

"Can you say whether Andrew Barton met his death by accident or by homicide?"

"I cannot. I have said that either is physically possible. I have no means of comparing the probabilities."

Sir Oliver noted the reply. Then, turning towards the judge, he informed the court that that was his case. Thereupon Thorndyke rose and announced, "I call witnesses." And a few seconds later the name of Ronald Barton was called, and the prisoner was conducted from the dock to the witness-box.

Chapter XV
The Witnesses for the Defence

As Andrew made his short journey across the court from the ignominy of the dock to the comparative respectability of the witness-box, he was aware of a curious and unexpected sense of confidence. For now, at last, he was about to make his long-dreaded revelation – to tell, before judge and jury and the crowded court, his preposterous story with all its outrageous improbabilities. And yet, to his surprise, he did not shrink from the ordeal. What had once seemed almost an impossibility had now come within the compass of the possible.

But his surprise was unwarranted, as he himself partially realized. For there is all the difference in the world between making an astounding revelation to an audience that is utterly unprepared for it and making the same revelation to hearers who are already waiting for the solution of a puzzle. And that was his position now. By his skilfully conducted cross-examination, Thorndyke had thoroughly prepared the way for Andrew's statement, ignoring the apparently important issues and building up a fabric of evidence which would immediately drop into its place as soon as Andrew began to tell his story. And when he stood up and faced his witness, it was not the judge alone who leaned forward all agog to hear what the defence really was. "You are indicted," he began, "in the name of Ronald Barton for the murder of Andrew Barton. Is your name Ronald Barton?"

"No," replied Andrew, "it is not."

"What is your real name?"

"My name is Andrew Barton."

As the answer was given, a startled cry mingled with the universal murmur of astonishment. Glancing quickly at Molly, Andrew could see that she had swung round on her seat and was gazing at him with an expression of the wildest amazement. The judge, after a quick glance towards the interrupter, fixed a look of critical scrutiny on the witness. "Is this a coincidence in names?" he asked, "or do you mean that you are the Andrew Barton whom you are accused of having murdered?"

"I am that Andrew Barton, my Lord," was the reply.

"The same Andrew Barton whose description has been read out to us from the police bill?"

"The same, my lord."

The judge continued to look at him for two or three seconds. Then, with a slight shrug, he bowed to Thorndyke with a manner that seemed to invite him to "get on with it". Meanwhile the jury, suddenly reminded of the police bill, looked first at the prisoner and then at one another, some with frank incredulity and others with undisguised grins. Unperturbed by those grins, Thorndyke proceeded. "The evidence relating to the alleged crime of which you are accused covers a certain period of time and a certain succession of events. What is the starting-point of that series of events?"

"They began with a letter which I received from my cousin Ronald. It was dated the 21st of August and reached me on the 23rd. Its principal purpose was to ask for a loan of fifty pounds, but it also announced his intention to pay me a visit on the 28th." Andrew then went on, urged by Thorndyke, to give the minutest details, even to the cutting of the privet hedge, of the circumstances connected with the letter, and his difficulties in staving off Ronald's visit.

"What was your objection to this visit?"

"From what I knew and suspected of my cousin's mode of life, I did not consider him a suitable person to associate with my wife, and I had also found his manner towards her distinctly objectionable."

"Why did you not tell your wife about this letter?"

"I was afraid that she would misunderstand my motives in objecting to Ronald's visit – that she might feel that I had not complete confidence in her discretion in dealing with him."

"Had you any such fear as to her discretion?"

"Not the least. I had perfect confidence in her. But I thought she did not quite realize what kind of man Ronald was, and might not be completely on her guard if he should try to establish relations of a kind that I considered undesirable."

When the arrangements for the pretended visit to London had been described, Thorndyke proceeded to the incident of the murder of Mr. Hudson and led Andrew through it in the closest detail. "When you went home after the attack, were you at all alarmed or uneasy as to your connection with the affair?"

"Not at all. I did not know that any murder had been committed and, of course, I was only a spectator. I told my wife exactly what had occurred and we discussed what I had better do. I was inclined to go over to Bunsford and give information at once. But my wife thought that, as I could not tell the police anything that they did not know already, I had better wait until some inquiries were made. But I intended to call on the police on the following day and tell them what I knew, and I should have done so had not the train come in sooner than I had expected."

There followed a description of the visit to Crompton in the same minute detail, including the inspection of Professor Booley's window and the remarkable announcements on his advertisement card, of which Andrew was able to remember nearly the whole, and the recital of which was received with murmurs of amusement. "When you read the list of Professor Booley's accomplishments, did it occur to you to give him a trial and see if you could not dispense with the spectacles which you have described to us?"

"No. I did not take his claims seriously. I thought he was merely an advertising quack."

The account of the day's doings, almost from minute to minute, was continued until the incident of the seabathing at Hunstone Gap was reached. Then Thorndyke pressed for even more exhaustive details. "You say that your cousin ran up before you to the place where your clothes were lying and that he took possession of the heap that belonged to you. Is it not remarkable that he should have mistaken your clothes for his own?"

"I don't think so. The outer clothes were almost exactly alike in the two suits. But I don't think that it was really a mistake on his part. I think it was a practical joke. It was just the kind of joke that I should have expected from him."

"What makes you think that it was a joke?"

"I have since remembered that, before sitting down, he turned the clothes over, putting the coat on top. And then he proceeded to wipe himself on my coat."

"Can you account for the circumstance that you did not notice that you were sitting down on the wrong clothes?"

"As I have said, the two suits were almost exactly alike. They were both ordinary grey flannels. But apart from that, I was in a very disturbed state of mind. I was trying to think how I could decently put him off the visit to Fairfield, which he still seemed to be bent on."

The account now approached the tragic incident of the falling block of chalk. The silence in the court was profound, and still Thorndyke insisted on tracing events from moment to moment. "Did you actually see the block fall?"

"No. I was much agitated by the unpleasant turn the conversation had taken and was avoiding looking at my cousin. I was watching a fishing lugger which was beating up the bay. When the chalk came rattling down, I jumped up and ran away from the cliff. When I stopped and looked round, Ronald was lying in the same place, covered with small lumps of chalk and with the large block resting on his head."

"Was he already dead?"

201

"He must have been, but his legs were moving slightly with a sort of twitching movement. They continued to move for nearly half-a-minute."

"Can you explain how it happened that you did not notice that you were putting on the wrong clothes?"

"There was not much to notice. The clothes were almost identical with my own, and they fitted me. But I was so shaken and horrified by what had just happened that I hardly knew what I was doing. As I was dressing, I still had my eyes on the corpse. The only thing that I noticed was the hat, and I did not stop to ask myself how it happened that Ronald was lying on mine."

Andrew then described how he had hurried away from the Gap intending to seek assistance or give information, and how he had missed the road and wandered about in the country, reaching Crompton only after night had fallen, and how he had made his way straight to the police station and had encountered the police notice.

"Did you stop to read the bill?"

"No. I was feeling very confused and shaken and I stopped to think over what I had to tell, and how I should explain my presence in Crompton, and also whether I ought to say anything about the affair of the motor bandits. Then, as I was standing opposite the bill, my eye caught the words, '*Kibble's Cross*', and I glanced quickly through the notice to see what had happened. Then I saw the heading, '*Wanted for Murder*', and reading down further, I read the description of myself and the statement that I had been seen to fire the shot."

"You read the notice which directly accused you of having committed the murder. Were you particularly alarmed?"

"I was terrified. For the notice not only accused me but stated, on the evidence of an eye-witness, that I had been seen to fire the shot that had killed the man."

"Did you think that you were likely to be convicted of this murder?"

"I thought that I was certain to be. This lady was prepared to swear that she had seen me fire the shot, and I had no answer but a bare denial. I thought that if I was caught I was bound to be condemned."

"And did you think it likely that you would be caught?"

"I considered it a certainty that I should be, as the disfigurement of my nose, which was described on the bill, made me so very easy to recognize. Anyone who had read the bill who should see me would know instantly who I was. And my spectacles, which were the only means of any sort of disguise, were in the pocket of the clothes that had been under the body of my cousin."

The account went on to relate how Andrew had sneaked up the dark street, keeping in the deepest shadow and avoiding the street lamps, and

202

how he had stumbled on the premises of Professor Booley and had then had the sudden idea that the Professor might be able to produce some sort of disguise. "Had you anything definite in your mind when you decided to apply to Professor Booley?"

"No. I realized that the disfigurement of my nose was the great source of danger as I could not cover it up and anyone would notice it at the first glance. I thought it possible that Professor Booley might be able to do something – even a temporary disguise – which would give me a chance to escape."

"So you decided to see if he could do anything for you. Now tell us exactly what happened."

Andrew proceeded with the description of his interview with the Professor, brought up repeatedly by Thorndyke for the filling in of some apparently trivial detail. He spoke confidently and clearly and, as he told that strange story, the entire court, judge, jury and spectators alike, listened in breathless silence. He described the Professor's reluctance, changing suddenly into enthusiasm and even eagerness, the consulting-room with its chair and instruments and the cake of wax that had been shown to him and the various preparations for the operation, the operation itself, his agonies in the operating-chair, and the climax, when the Professor bade him look in the mirror. "And when you looked in the mirror, what did you see?"

"I saw the face of my cousin Ronald."

"You mean that your face now resembled the face of your cousin?"

"That, I suppose, is the fact. It must have been. But the resemblance was so complete that it seemed like some magical illusion. What I saw was not my own face but Ronald's. I could hardly believe my eyes."

"Do you now think that the transformation was so very wonderful?"

"No. Since I have had time to think it over, I have realized that it was quite natural. Ronald and I were extraordinarily alike in every respect but our noses. Ronald had a Roman nose and my nose was straight, and after my accident, the difference was much more striking. But Professor Booley, in filling up the notch in my nose, happened to model the patch which he put in so that the repaired bridge was almost exactly the shape of Ronald's. The result was that the only appreciable difference between us was done away with. If Ronald had been alive, he and I would have looked like a pair of twins."

"Professor Booley's magic has had some rather embarrassing effects. What did you do when you recovered from the operation?"

Andrew described the visit to the restaurant and his examination of himself in the mirror, and explained how the complete transformation in his appearance made it impossible for him to go home, how the necessity for recovering his attaché case compelled him to go to Ronald's lodgings, and how, while waiting for an opportunity to enter unobserved, he had halted at the police station to read the bill and had thus been present when the cart arrived bearing his cousin's body. With occasional assistance from Thorndyke in explaining and elucidating the incidents and emphasizing their significance, he continued the narrative, including his life at Hampstead, his visit to Molly, his meeting with Mrs. Kempster and so on up to the moment of his arrest and his committal for trial on the charge of fraud and personation.

When the examination-in-chief had thus brought the story up to his consignment to prison, Thorndyke sat down and Sir Oliver rose to cross-examine, and Andrew realized that the period of plain-sailing was over. He had to brace himself up for some difficult questions. The learned counsel discreetly refrained from challenging statements of fact and attacked the evidence from the psychological side. "Your explanation of the mystery that was made about the visit to Crompton is difficult to follow. What prevented you from giving your wife a straightforward statement of what you intended to do?"

"Nothing but my own stupidity," replied Andrew. "There was not the least necessity for any deception."

"You have described your state of extreme panic on reading the police notice. But what occasion was there for panic? You would surely know that a charge of this kind could not be entertained in the case of a man of good position and known respectability?"

"I did not know it. I supposed that the sworn evidence of a respectable eye-witness would be conclusive. This lady said that she saw me kill Mr. Hudson. There seemed no answer to that!"

"Can you explain why, in all this time, you made no attempt to communicate with your wife?"

"Seeing that I was wanted for murder, I did not dare to disclose my identity. I felt sure that, if I told this story to her, she would reject it as an attempt at imposture and communicate with the police, and I could not risk any dealings with them."

"Again, you actually state that you had an interview with your wife and that she did not recognize you, though she noticed your resemblance to her husband. It seems perfectly incredible that she should have failed to recognize her own husband. But allowing that she did, what prevented you from simply telling her who you were?"

"In the first place, she evidently recognized me as Ronald, and she appeared to be distinctly distrustful of Ronald. Then she believed that she had seen the dead body of her husband, and she had attended his funeral only a few days before. Moreover, I found that she was convinced that

204

the person who was with him at Hunstone had murdered him. But I should have had to begin by telling her that I was one of the two persons who were at Hunstone. I thought, and still think, that she would have gone straight out and informed the police."

"There is then the case of the woman, Elizabeth Kempster. You admit that she, having seen and talked with you, was firmly convinced that you were her husband, Anthony Kempster. You admit that there can be no doubt that Anthony Kempster and Ronald Barton are one and the same person. You admit that this woman still believes that you are her husband, Ronald Barton. See, then, what it is that you are asking us to believe. On the one hand, you assert that you had a long interview with your own wife and that she never even suspected that you were her husband. On the other hand, you had an interview of some length with Elizabeth Kempster and she was then convinced, and still remains convinced, that you are her husband. And both these women are convinced that you are Ronald Barton. Do you still maintain and ask the jury to believe that you are not Ronald Barton, which both of these women are convinced that you are, and that you are Andrew Barton, which Andrew Barton's wife is convinced that you are not?"

"I have declared on oath, and I repeat, that I am Andrew Barton."

The learned counsel raised his eyebrows (whereby it became necessary for him to catch his eyeglass as it dropped from his eye, which he did with an expertness born of long practice and, after a pause to give effect to that gesture of incredulity, continued his cross-examination, skilfully picking out all the improbabilities and apparent contradictions. It was cleverly done and it served, at least, to save the face of the prosecution. But it was all very inconclusive since it left all the evidence on the main questions of fact untouched. Those questions Sir Oliver was too wise to attack. His long experience in the courts would have taught him that technical evidence from Dr. John Thorndyke was best left alone. Moreover, he probably suspected that Thorndyke had not played his last card.

And so it turned out when the long cross-examination was ended. For the next witness whose name was called was Dr. Christopher Jervis, and it soon appeared that Dr. Jervis belonged to the heavy division of the defence's artillery. Having elicited his name and qualifications, Thorndyke began. "Can you tell us anything about the block of chalk which was found on the body of the dead man who has been described as Andrew Barton?"

"Yes. On the 13th of November, I went to Hunstone Gap with the witness, William Cox. He showed me the place where the body was found and the position of the head, which was marked by some splashes of blood which had soaked into the chalk at the foot of the cliff. He also showed me the block of chalk, which was still lying where he had dropped it. Looking up the cliff, I could see the spot from which the block had broken away. It was quite clearly distinguishable as a squarish cavity. I measured, with a sextant, the height of this cavity above the beach and found it to be sixty-three feet. I tested, with a plumb-line, the position of this cavity in relation to the blood-mark at the foot of the cliff and found that they were both exactly in the same vertical line. The head of the deceased must, therefore, have been exactly on the spot on to which the block would have fallen. I tested the weight of the block by lifting it. With great difficulty, I was able to lift it a few inches from the ground, but was able to hold it for only a very few seconds owing to the absence of anything for the fingers to grasp."

"Could you have lifted it two or three feet?"

"No, certainly not."

"Are you a fairly strong man?"

"Yes. I am rather above the average of strength for a man of my size. I am just under six-feet-two-inches in height."

"You have heard the suggestions of the prosecution as to the method employed in committing this alleged murder. Do you consider, judging by your experience of the block, that the method suggested is physically practicable?"

"No. I am certain that it would be impossible for even a strong man to lift that block two or three feet from the ground several times in succession."

"Were you present when Sir Artemus Pope made his examination of the body which is alleged to be that of Andrew Barton?"

"Yes, and I was authorized to make any independent examination that I considered necessary."

"What observations did you make?"

"I paid particular attention to the condition of the nasal bones. The description of Andrew Barton made it clear that he had suffered from a severe depressed fracture of the nasal bones, caused by a blow from a cricket-ball. I searched carefully for traces of that fracture and the callus thrown up in the processes of bone repair. I could find no such traces. The bones were fractured in several places, but these were new fractures. There was not a sign that the bones had ever been fractured before. I carefully separated out the broken pieces and fitted them together on a wax support. I had no authority to bring them away to produce in evidence but I made a plaster cast of the joined fragments on the wax. I produce the cast for inspection, and I have also brought a normal skull for comparison. The cast shows clearly the new fractures in the bones, but it also shows clearly that there are no traces whatever of any old fractures or of any callus or signs of repair. The bones in the cast are perfectly normal, as can be seen by comparing them with the uninjured bones of the skull."

"What do you infer from this?"

"I infer that it is quite impossible that the body which I examined could have been the body of Andrew Barton."

"Are you quite certain that it was not the body of Andrew Barton?"

"I am quite certain that it was not. It is a physical impossibility that his nasal bones could have been perfectly normal in appearance as the bones are seen to be in the cast."

On receiving this answer, Thorndyke paused for a few moments to complete his notes and then proceeded. "Have you made any examination of the prisoner?"

"Yes. I have examined his nose with the naked eye, with ordinary electric light and with X-rays, and also by the sense of touch. To the naked eye it appears to be a completely normal nose of the Roman type with a rather high bridge. To the sense of touch it is hard and smooth in the upper part with some irregular masses at the base. I was unable to feel the lower edges of the nasal bones or the median cartilage. On examination with electric light or sunlight, it is seen that the bridge of the nose is not composed of bone, but of some translucent substance which I believe to be paraffin wax."

"What are your reasons for believing it to be paraffin wax?"

"It has all the properties of paraffin wax and no other substance is known to me which could be introduced into that situation and formed into that shape."

"What methods did you use in respect of the X-rays?"

"I took an X-ray photograph of the prisoner and another of myself for comparison as our noses are somewhat alike in shape. I produce those photographs. Each is signed by me and countersigned by John Thorndyke, and I swear that they are the photographs of the persons whose names are written on them. On the one of myself it can be seen that the nasal bones are clearly visible occupying the bridge of the nose and corresponding to its outline. In the photograph of the prisoner the outline of the bridge is faintly seen but there are no nasal bones there. At the base is an irregular mass of bone which corresponds to no normal structure. It looks like an old depressed fracture of which the fragments are cemented together with callus, or new bone."

"What conclusions do you draw from these photographs?"

"The photograph of the prisoner shows a condition which exactly agrees with the description of Andrew Barton, plus the shadowy indication of the mass of wax forming the bridge. Disregarding the wax, which is really a foreign body and no part of the prisoner's person, the photograph is that of a man who is identical in appearance with Andrew Barton, according to the various descriptions of him which have been given in evidence, including the surgeon's certificate referred to by Mrs. Barton."

This completed the examination in chief. As Thorndyke sat down, Mr. Horace Black, Sir Oliver's junior, rose to cross-examine. But he had a thankless task, for Jervis's evidence dealt almost entirely with observed facts which could not be disputed or even questioned, and when the learned counsel mildly hinted at errors of observation or mistaken inferences, Jervis blandly offered him the cast or the photographs, which the counsel smilingly waved away as matters outside the province of a mere lawyer.

The next witness came as a surprise to most of the persons present, including Andrew, for the name that was called was that of Elizabeth Kempster. As the lady stepped into the box and looked nervously at Thorndyke, a certain redness around the eyes and a handkerchief held in the hand suggested that the occasion was, for her, not a happy one. When the preliminaries had been disposed of, Thorndyke opened his examination with the request. "Will you kindly look at the prisoner, Mrs. Kempster, and tell us whether you recognize him?"

The witness cast a deprecating glance at Andrew and replied, "Yes, I recognize him."

"Can you tell us who he is?"

"I don't think I can," she replied. "He looks like my husband, Anthony Kempster, but from what I have just heard, he can't be."

"But, disregarding the evidence that you have heard, who do you say he is?"

"Well, he looks exactly like my husband."

"Have you previously identified him on oath as your husband?"

"Yes. I swore to him as my husband at the police station and in the police court. But," she added with a catch in her voice and an application of her handkerchief to her eyes, "I didn't know that I was letting him in for this."

"When you identified him at the police court, had you at any time any doubt that he was really your husband?"

"Yes. I did think, just for a moment or two, that I might have made a mistake. But then they found in his pocket-book a tradesman's bill addressed to A. Kempster, Esq., and that convinced me that I was not mistaken."

"What was it that caused you that momentary doubt?"

"It was the way he spoke and behaved. He was quite polite to me, and he didn't reproach me for having given information against him. That was not at all like my husband. He was accustomed to talk loud and bluster when he was put out."

"And what about the voice? Was it exactly like your husband's?"

"No, it was rather like, but not exactly. I noticed then that it seemed a little different from what I remembered, and I noticed it again when he was giving evidence."

"I need not ask you whether your husband was in the habit of absenting himself from home, but I should be glad if you could give us some information as to a particular date. Do you know where your husband was on Good Friday in the year 1925?"

"Yes, I remember very well. He was in Wormwood Scrubbs Prison. He came out on Easter Sunday."

Here the judge interposed, though without any great emphasis. "It is hardly necessary for me to remind learned counsel that it is not admissible to refer to previous convictions or delinquencies of the prisoner until the jury have given their verdict."

"That is so, my lord," Thorndyke agreed. "But the submission is that the prisoner is not the person named in the indictment and that the previous convictions of that person do not, therefore, affect him. And I may say that the point which I am trying to elicit is highly material to the defence."

"If you say that the point is material to the defence," the judge rejoined, "I must allow the questions to be put."

Whereupon Thorndyke resumed his examination. "Do you know how long your husband had been in prison?"

"Yes. Six months. I had notice when he was going to be discharged and I went and met him at the prison gate."

"Have you any doubt that the man whom you met at the prison gate was your husband?"

"No, none whatever. I recognized him and he recognized me, and I took him home and gave him a good dinner. Besides, I had been present in the police court when he got his sentence."

"At the police court and in the prison, was he known by the name of Anthony Kempster?"

"No. When he was arrested, he gave the name of Septimus Neville, and he stuck to it. They never knew his real name."

"You speak of his real name. Do you know what his real name was, or is?"

"I am not sure. He married me under the name of Anthony Kempster, but I sometimes suspected that that was not his real name. He was very much in the habit of changing his name."

"Did you ever meet with the name of Barton in connection with him?"

"Yes. I think he had a cousin of that name. He was very secret about his letters, as a rule, but I happened to see one that he had left in the pocket of a coat that I had to mend for him, and I saw that it was signed, '*Your affectionate cousin, Andrew Barton*'. But, of course, I didn't know that his name was the same as his cousin's."

This concluded Thorndyke's examination and, as the prosecution had no inkling of the bearing of this witness's evidence on the issue, the cross-examination was tentative and brief. When it was finished and Mrs. Kempster left the box, with a commiserating glance at the prisoner and a final wipe of her eyes, the court, and Andrew, had another surprise, for the witness who followed her was no less a person than Andrew's old friend, Mr. Samuel Montagu.

The new witness, having given his name, deposed that he was a dealer in works of art and that his premises were in New Bond Street. He was a good judge of pictures – he had to be – and his own personal preference was for water-colour paintings, especially interiors and subject pictures of high finish and fine execution. When he had got so far, Thorndyke produced from under his bench a framed and glazed water-colour painting which was conveyed to the witness-box, and handed to the witness, who examined it with profound attention and evident interest. "Have you ever seen that picture before, Mr. Montagu?" Thorndyke asked.

"I have not," was the reply.

"There is, as you see, no signature to the picture. Can you give any opinion as to who the painter was?"

"I can. This picture was painted by Andrew Barton."

"You speak quite positively, as if you were certain."

"I am certain. I was for many years Andrew Barton's agent and dealer. Nearly all of his work passed through my hands, and I have always had a great admiration for it. I have two of his paintings in my permanent gallery and three of them in my private house."

"You feel that you can say quite definitely that this picture was painted by Andrew Barton?"

"Yes. Quite definitely. I have not the shadow of a doubt."

At this point, Thorndyke sat down and Mr. Horace Black rose to cross-examine. At his request, the picture was passed across to him and he examined it critically for a while before beginning. At length, he opened fire on the witness.

"You have stated, as if it were a fact known to you, that this picture was painted by Andrew Barton. Are you not offering us a mere conjecture as a statement of fact?"

"It is not a conjecture," replied Montagu. "It is an expert opinion, and a very expert opinion considering my great experience of Andrew Barton's work. And I feel perfectly certain that it is a correct opinion."

"You are extremely confident. But looking at this picture, it seems to me that there is nothing very highly distinctive about it. It seems to me to be a picture of the kind that is sometimes called photographic, such as could be produced by any skilful draughtsman."

"The people," said Montagu, "who call highly finished paintings photographic are people who don't know much about either painting or photography. There is no analogy between a work of imagination and a photograph."

"Still, I submit that a simple, realistic style like this could be easily imitated by any competent painter."

"That is not so," said Montagu. "A first-class professional copyist might be able to make a copy of this picture which would deceive any person but an expert. But imitation is quite a different matter from copying. To begin with, every artist has his own manner of thinking and working. Now the imitator would have to drop his own manner – which he couldn't do – and adopt not only the technique but the mental and emotional character of the man he was imitating. And then, if he was trying to imitate a first-class artist like Andrew Barton, he would have to be a first-class artist himself. But if he were, he wouldn't want to imitate anybody, and what's more, he couldn't do it, because he would have an unmistakable style of his own."

"And do you say that this simple, literal representation of an old woman making lace shows an unmistakable style which nobody could possibly imitate?"

"I do. I say that any genuine expert could pick out Andrew Barton's work at a glance. Of course, he was not like some of the present-day painters who play monkey tricks to give the art critics something to write about. It was genuine, honest painting done as well as he could do it, and nobody could do it better."

"We are straying away from the issue," said the counsel. "I am not contesting the quality of the work. My point is that you have sworn that this picture was painted by Andrew Barton, a fact which cannot possibly be within your knowledge since you admit that you never saw the picture before. Do you still swear that it was painted by Andrew Barton?"

211

"I said I felt certain, and I do feel certain, and I am ready to buy it for fifty pounds with the certainty of being able to sell it at a profit."

Here the counsel smilingly abandoned the contest and sat down. The picture was handed up to the judge, who inspected it with deep interest, and Mr. Montagu retired triumphantly from the box.

The next name called was less of a surprise to Andrew, who had been following closely the drift of the evidence, and the name of Martha Pendlewick associated itself naturally with the picture. The old lady stepped up into the box with a bland smile on her face and, having curtsied to the judge – who graciously acknowledged the salutation – turned and saluted the prisoner in the same deferential manner. "I want you, Mrs. Pendlewick," said Thorndyke, "to look at the prisoner and tell us whether you recognize him."

"Lord bless you, yes, sir," said Mrs. Pendlewick. "The poor young gentleman was lodging with me at the very time that the police arrested him. And a nicer and more considerate lodger no one could wish for."

As the old lady was speaking, the judge repeatedly glanced from her to the picture, which he was still holding, and back, apparently comparing the real with the painted figure, and meanwhile he listened attentively to the evidence. Then, at Thorndyke's request, the picture was handed down and presented to the witness, who nodded at it with a smile of friendly recognition. "Have you ever seen that picture before?" Thorndyke asked.

"To be sure I have," she replied with a surprised air. "Why 'tis a likeness of myself a-making bone lace in my own kitchen."

"Do you know who painted that picture?"

"Certainly I do. 'Twas the young gentleman, himself, Mr. Barton."

"Can you tell us when he painted it?"

"He took several days over it. I can't give you the exact date, but he finished it only a few days before the police made that unfortunate mistake."

"Can you say positively that you saw him paint the whole of it from beginning to end?"

"Yes. I saw him begin it on the white paper and draw it with a lead pencil. And then he put on the colours. It took him the best part of a week and he finished it, as I said, a few days before he was took away to prison."

Mrs. Pendlewick's evidence was listened to with intense interest by the Court and spectators alike. But its effect on Mr. Montagu was most remarkable. From his place among the "witnesses in waiting", he craned forward with bulging eyes to stare, first at Mrs. Pendlewick and then at the prisoner. Evidently, he was in a state of complete mental

212

bewilderment. He had sworn that the picture could have been painted by no one but Andrew Barton. But clearly it had been painted since Andrew Barton's death, and it had been painted by the Roman-nosed gentleman in the dock. He could make nothing of it.

His bewilderment did not escape the notice of Thorndyke who, even while he was questioning the witnesses, kept a sharp eye, not only on the jury but also on the spectators. For long experience had taught him that, in practice, the final test of evidence is its effect on the non-expert listener. Now, Mr. Montagu was in a dilemma. The evidence of his eyesight told him that the picture had been painted by Andrew Barton. But it also told him that the man in the dock was not the Andrew Barton whom he had known. Yet there seemed no escape from Mrs. Pendlewick's evidence that the picture had been painted by the man in the dock. It was a puzzle to which he could find no solution.

Thorndyke then noted Mr. Montagu's state of mind and congratulated himself on having taken the precaution to put Montagu in the box before Mrs. Pendlewick for, evidently, if he had gone into the box after her, his evidence would have been worth nothing. He would never have sworn to the authorship of the picture. The observation, therefore, of Montagu's apparent immunity to the evidence of the change of personality came as a very useful reminder that that evidence had still to be driven home to the jury, and further, that it must be driven home to them through the evidence of their own eyesight. Fortunately, the next witness gave him the opportunity.

That witness was a quiet, resolute-looking gentleman who gave the name of Martin Burwood and stated that he was an Inspector in the Criminal Investigation Department of the Metropolitan Police. His duties were connected with the keeping of Criminal Records at Scotland Yard and especially with the Finger-print Department. "When the prisoner was arrested," said Thorndyke, "were his finger-prints taken?"

"They were," replied the inspector.

"Were those finger-prints already known to you?"

"They were not. On receiving them from the prison, I examined them and I then searched the files to see whether we had any duplicates. I found that there were no duplicates in the files."

"What does that prove?"

"It proves that the prisoner has never previously been convicted of any offence."

"Have you in your records any relating to a man named Septimus Neville? And, if so, of what do those records consist?"

"We have the records of Septimus Neville in the files. They consist of descriptive and other particulars, a complete set of finger-prints and two photographs, one in profile and one full face."

"Have you compared the finger-prints of Septimus Neville with those of the prisoner?"

"I have. They are not the same finger-prints."

"Are you quite sure that they are not the same?"

"I am perfectly sure. There is not even any resemblance."

"Is it possible that Septimus Neville and the prisoner can be one and the same person?"

"It is quite impossible."

"Have you compared the record photographs of Septimus Neville with those of the prisoner?"

"I have."

"Do you find anything remarkable about them?"

"I do. The photographs show that the two men are extraordinarily alike. They are so much alike that it is hardly possible to distinguish one from the other. I produce the photographs of both men."

He did so, and they were passed up to the judge, who inspected them with amused surprise. They were then handed round to the jury who, in their turn, viewed them with undisguised astonishment. "You have shown us," said Thorndyke, when he had examined them and passed them on to the other counsel, "four photographs, two of each of these men. They appear exactly alike, but you say that they are the photographs of two different men. Do you swear that they cannot be four photographs of the same man?"

"I do. The finger-prints, which were taken at the same time as the photographs, prove conclusively that they must be two different men."

Thereupon Thorndyke sat down, and Mr. Black, with more valour than discretion, rose to cross-examine. But it was quite futile, for the evidence was unshakeable and the officer was a seasoned and experienced witness. The usual questions were asked as to the possible fallibility of finger-prints, and received the usual answers. As a wind-up, the counsel asked, "Do you swear that it is impossible for two men to have the same, or similar, finger-prints?"

"I swear that it is quite impossible," was the withering reply.

"And I suppose," the judge interposed dryly, "that we may assume it to be impossible for one man to have two different sets of finger-prints?"

The witness grinned and agreed that it was impossible, and the learned counsel, hiding his blushes under an appreciative smile, hurriedly sat down.

Then Thorndyke rose and, having announced that all the witnesses for the defence had now been heard, prepared to address the jury.

Chapter XVI
Thorndyke's Address to the Jury

"In view," Thorndyke began, "of the mass of evidence that has been produced and of its remarkable and convincing character, it seemed almost unnecessary that I should address you. But this is a trial on a capital charge and the prisoner's life is forfeit if it should be held to have been proved against him. I cannot, therefore, take any risks of a miscarriage. I shall, however, occupy as little time as possible. You are sworn to give a true verdict according to the evidence, and I shall confine myself to an examination of that evidence and to pointing out what has actually been proved. The prisoner is indicted in the name of Ronald Barton for the murder of Andrew Barton. The words of the indictment, therefore, contain four affirmative propositions:

"1. That a murder has been committed.

"2. That the person who was murdered was Andrew Barton.

"3. That he was murdered by Ronald Barton.

"4. That the prisoner is Ronald Barton.

"Now, in order that a verdict of guilty should be returned against the prisoner, it is necessary that each and all of those propositions should be proved to be true. If any one of them should be proved to be untrue, the case against the prisoner would fall to the ground. I am not referring to any legal questions which might arise in respect of defects in the indictment, on which subject His Lordship will give you the necessary direction. I shall deal with the plain and simple issue: Whether the prisoner is or is not guilty of the crime with which he is charged. To enable you to decide on that question, I shall ask you to examine critically those four propositions.

"First, has it been proved that a murder was, in fact, committed? So far as direct evidence is concerned, I can dismiss that question quite summarily, for no direct evidence was produced. You heard Sir Artemus Pope declare definitely that not only did he find no positive evidence that the deceased met his death by homicide, but that he found nothing that tended to suggest or raise any suspicion of homicide. There is, therefore, no direct evidence that any murder was, in fact, committed, and I submit that on that alone, the prisoner is entitled to a verdict of 'Not Guilty'.

"We now come to the indirect evidence, which consists in certain considerations of motive and conduct. The motives that are suggested for the alleged murder are, first, that Ronald Barton stood to gain five-hundred pounds by the death of Andrew Barton and, second, that Andrew Barton had in his possession certain valuable property which Ronald coveted and subsequently stole, and which was found in the prisoner's possession when he was arrested. It is further suggested that the conduct of the prisoner was such as to lead to the belief that he had murdered the man whose body was found at Hunstone Gap.

"And now we see the importance of the other three propositions. For if the person whose body was found was *not* Andrew Barton, then no insurance was payable, and the suggested motive ceases to exist. Again, if the prisoner is *not* Ronald Barton, he is entitled to no benefit under Andrew's will, and again the motive disappears. Further, if the prisoner *is* proved to be Andrew Barton, the property found in his possession is his own lawful property, and the other motive disappears.

"Thus, you will see that the issue that you are trying is really the issue of personal identity. The questions which you have to decide are, first, who was the person whose body was found at the foot of the cliff at Hunstone Gap? And, second, who is the prisoner? I will take these questions in their order.

"First, who was the dead man? Now, we have the evidence of Mr. Cooper that two men were seen walking towards Hunstone Gap, and we may accept it as certain that the body which was found there was the body of one of these two men – for with that body was found the clothing of a man who corresponds exactly in appearance to one of them and who is known to have been in Crompton on that day and to have worn similar clothing.

"Of those two men, one had a broken nose and wore spectacles to conceal the disfigurement. The other had a normal and well-shaped Roman nose. The clothing was that of the man with the broken nose. But was the body also his? That is what you have to decide. Now I wish to impress on you the fact, which seems to have been somewhat overlooked, that that body was never identified. Mrs. Barton saw it and was unable to say whether it was or was not the body of her husband, and there was no one else who was competent to give an opinion. The clothes which were found with it were the clothes of Andrew Barton. Of that there can be no doubt. And from that fact the reasonable inference was drawn that the body was that of Andrew Barton. But I repeat that *the body itself was not identified.*

"Later, that body was re-examined by Sir Artemus Pope and by Dr. Jervis. Sir Artemus was naturally unwilling to pronounce on the identity of the body since his examination was not concerned with that question. But he admitted that the conditions which he found seemed to be irreconcilable with the personal description of Andrew Barton. On the

217

other hand, Dr. Jervis, who examined the body with the express purpose of ascertaining its identity, gave a clear, definite, and emphatic statement that the body was that of a man with a normal and uninjured nose, and furthermore, he produced a plaster cast of the dead man's nasal bones, which was shown to you and from which, by comparison with the normal skull which was also shown to you, it was quite evident that the nasal bones of the deceased had never been broken until the chalk block fell on them. On these facts, Dr. Jervis declared positively that the body could not possibly be the body of Andrew Barton. The evidence before you, therefore, of your own eyesight, confirmed by the testimony of an expert witness, is that the body found at Hunstone Gap could not possibly have been the body of Andrew Barton.

"But, so far, we have decided only who he was *not*. We have now to consider the question, who he *was*. And here you will see that I am not depending on the prisoner's evidence to decide questions of fact. That evidence is, of course, entitled to the same credit as that of the other witnesses, but I think you will agree with me that it will be more satisfactory if I can show you that the facts can be proved by independent evidence, reserving that of the prisoner to co-ordinate and explain facts that are otherwise difficult to understand.

"Now who was this dead man? We have agreed that he was one of the two men who were seen walking towards Hunstone Gap. All the known facts support this belief. Two men had been bathing in the Gap, for we find the nude body of one and the clothes of the other. The clothes were Andrew Barton's, but the body was not his body. Then, since there were no other clothes, it is clear that Andrew must have gone off in the other man's clothes. That he could hardly have done so by deliberate choice but presumably by mistake, suggests that those clothes were, in size and appearance similar to his own. But the two men who were seen together were extremely similar in size and figure and were dressed in almost exactly similar clothes. Thus everything goes to prove that the body was that of one of these two men.

"Now of these two men, one is known, and has been proved to have been Andrew Barton. Who was the other? From the evidence of the only two witnesses who saw the two men, Mr. Cooper and the waiter, Albert Smith, we know that the other man – Andrew Barton's companion – was extraordinarily like the prisoner, so like that both these witnesses instantly identified the prisoner and swore that he was the man whom they had seen. But the prisoner is indistinguishably like Ronald Barton. So like that Mrs. Barton, when he visited her at her house, had no doubt that he was Ronald Barton, and still had no doubt when she was giving evidence in this court.

"The unavoidable conclusion is that the man who was seen with Andrew Barton must have been Ronald Barton. And this conclusion is strongly supported by the fact that Ronald and Andrew were cousins. It was a natural and probable circumstance that Andrew's companion should be his cousin Ronald.

"But if the body that was found was that of Andrew's companion, then it was the body of Ronald Barton, in which case it is unnecessary to point out that the prisoner cannot be Ronald Barton, but must be some other person.

"And now let us approach this question from another direction. The prisoner was arrested, in the first place, in the name of Anthony Kempster on an information sworn by Elizabeth Kempster, who identified him as her husband, Anthony Kempster, and swore to his identity as such. It is, therefore, obvious that the prisoner is either Anthony Kempster or someone who is indistinguishably like him. But who is Anthony Kempster? He is someone who is the indistinguishable double of the prisoner. But the prisoner is indistinguishably like Ronald Barton. Then it follows that Kempster must also be indistinguishably like Ronald Barton. As such indistinguishable likenesses are excessively rare, there is an obvious probability that these three men, Kempster, Ronald, and the prisoner, are one and the same person, namely, Ronald Barton. And the fact that Kempster had a cousin named Andrew Barton confirms this probability so far that we may conclude confidently that Kempster was, or is, Ronald Barton.

"The question that we now have to decide is whether or not the prisoner is Anthony Kempster. For if we agree that Kempster is Ronald and the prisoner is Kempster, then the prisoner must be Ronald Barton. But we have evidence that Anthony Kempster served a term of imprisonment under the name of Septimus Neville. There is no doubt that Septimus Neville and Anthony Kempster are one and the same person, for we have the evidence of Kempster's wife to that effect. But we have the evidence of the officer from the Fingerprint Department that Neville and the prisoner cannot possibly be the same person. The prison photographs show these two men were extraordinarily alike, so much so that it would have been hardly possible to distinguish one from the other. But their finger-prints are totally different. It is therefore certain that the prisoner cannot possibly be Septimus Neville. But since Neville and Kempster are one and the same person, the prisoner cannot be Anthony Kempster, and since Kempster is Ronald Barton, the prisoner cannot be Ronald Barton.

"So far, we have answered the question: Who is the prisoner? from the negative side. We have shown who he cannot be. He cannot be the person in whose name he stands indicted. Now let us approach the question from the positive side. Who can the prisoner be? Who is it possible for him to be?

"He is not Ronald Barton, but he is someone so like Ronald that those who knew Ronald well, including his wife, have mistaken him for Ronald. The prisoner and Ronald have that curious resemblance that is usually associated with what are called 'identical twins'. Now there is only one person who is known to us who has this strange resemblance to Ronald – his cousin, Andrew. The only possible inference seems, therefore, to be that the prisoner is Andrew Barton. For if he is not, then he must be some third person who is indistinguishably like the other two. But this is against all reasonable probabilities. It is a sufficiently strange coincidence that we should have this pair of identical twins. It would be outrageous to turn them into identical triplets by postulating the existence of a hypothetical third person who is indistinguishably like them both.

"But we have still more convincing evidence that the prisoner must be Andrew Barton. We know that Andrew suffered from a depressed fracture of the nasal bones. Now, to the eye, the prisoner appears to have a well-shaped Roman nose. But the X-ray photograph shows that he has suffered, and still suffers, from a depressed fracture of the nasal bones, that the symmetrical appearance of the nose is due to a filling of a translucent substance, which must be paraffin wax since there is no other known substance which it can be, which fills up the deep notch caused by the injury and has restored the bridge of the nose. In short, the X-ray photograph shows us a condition of the nasal bones which is known to have existed in Andrew Barton, which was peculiar to him, and by which he could be distinguished from all other human beings. Even alone, it would be enough to identify him as Andrew Barton.

"Thus you see that, without referring to the prisoner's evidence, the case against him has been completely disproved. With that evidence I do not propose to deal. It would be useless for me to occupy your time by flogging a dead horse. You heard his evidence and it will be fresh in your memories. All that it is necessary for me to do is to point out to you that, strange as was the story that he told you, it was an entirely consistent story and that you have every reason to believe that it was a true story. It did not conflict in any way with any other evidence that you have heard. On the contrary, its truth has been confirmed in the most striking manner by the evidence of all the other witnesses – not only of the witnesses for the defence, but also of those for the prosecution, and even by the able opening address of my learned friend, the counsel for the Crown. I shall, therefore, conclude by reminding you briefly of the facts which have been proved.

220

"The charge against the prisoner is that he, Ronald Barton, murdered his cousin, Andrew Barton. What has been proved is:

"First – that there is not the slightest reason to believe that any murder was committed by anybody.

"Second – that the body which was found was not the body of Andrew Barton.

"Third – that the prisoner is not Ronald Barton.

"Fourth – that he is Andrew Barton, the person whom he is accused of having murdered.

"Thus the charge set forth in the indictment has been disproved at every point and in every detail. It has been made abundantly and convincingly clear that the prisoner is innocent of the crime named in that charge, and I, accordingly, claim for him a verdict of 'Not Guilty'."

Chapter XVII
The Verdict

As Thorndyke sat down, a low murmur pervaded the court, and the judge glanced furtively and a little wistfully towards the jury. After a brief interval, Sir Oliver rose without alacrity and proceeded to polish his eyeglass with a thoughtful and somewhat hesitating air. As Thorndyke had really left him nothing to say, his reply could be little more than an empty formality, and he was apparently considering how he could best dispatch it when the foreman of the jury came to his relief with the intimation that the jury had heard as much as they considered necessary for their purpose. Thereupon, the Clerk of the court rose and inquired whether they had agreed on their verdict, to which the foreman replied that they had. The Clerk then put the momentous question: "Do you find the prisoner 'Guilty' or 'Not Guilty'?"

"'Not Guilty'," was the reply, delivered with some emphasis, and even as the words were spoken, the court resounded with thunders of applause and Molly buried her face in her handkerchief. After a few moments, the judge held up his hand and the applause instantly died away, giving place to a profound silence. Then His Lordship leaned back in his chair and, regarding Andrew with a quizzical smile, addressed him thus:

"Mr. Barton – I can safely address you by that name, though I will not venture to be more particular – the jury have found you to be 'Not Guilty' of the crime with which you were charged. I consider it a very proper verdict and I concur unreservedly. You are accordingly discharged and are free to go your ways, and I hope that your troubles are now at an end. There are a few loose strands which you will have to gather up with the Insurance Society, and perhaps with the Probate Court, but they will probably present no serious difficulties. But before you depart, I will counsel you most earnestly, the next time you are accused of murder or any other crime, to seek legal assistance rather more promptly than you did on the last occasion."

He concluded with a smile and a friendly nod, the gate of the dock was thrown open, the officer at Andrew's side wished him "Good luck", and the prisoner stepped down to the floor of the court where Molly was waiting for him. While the judge had been speaking, she had risen and stolen across to the dock, and now, as he stepped down, she raised her eyes to his and silently held out her hands. Both were too overwhelmed for speech, or even to be conscious of the multitude of inquisitive eyes that were eagerly watching them. Passively, they allowed themselves to be shepherded by the discreet Jervis – who was acutely conscious of the curious though sympathetic spectators – out of the court and into a small room that opened off from the great corridor. Only then, when Jervis had slipped away with an excuse, did Molly trust herself to speak. "Oh, Andy!" she exclaimed shakily, "is it really you? Can it really be you, or is this only a tantalizing dream?"

"It isn't a dream, Molly dear," he replied. "It is an awakening from a nightmare – a nightmare of my own creating. I am the very prince of idiots. Say your husband is a fool, Molly."

She laughed a little hysterically. "Shall I?" she said. "Then I will. Andy, you have, really and truly, behaved like a – perfect – old – *Donkey*! But never mind that, darling. Only a few hours ago, I was a miserable widow. And now – "

She broke off with a sob and, laying her head on his shoulder, wept quietly and happily.

At this moment the door opened and Jervis entered, accompanied by Thorndyke, bearing the attaché case and the picture and followed by Mrs. Kempster. The latter, still red-eyed and somewhat emotional, advanced shyly and addressed herself to Andrew. "I have come," said she, "to ask for your forgiveness for all the mischief I have made. I never supposed – "

"Forgiveness!" interrupted Molly, seizing both her hands impulsively. "Why, you dear creature, you have been our good angel! It was you who broke the spell and brought us all back to realities. We can never be grateful enough to you. And don't forget that you are our cousin."

Here the door opened again to admit two more visitors, none other than Sir Oliver and his junior, Mr. Black. They both shook Andrew's hand heartily, and Sir Oliver, having carefully inserted his eyeglass, spoke for them both. "We congratulate you most warmly, Mr. Barton. You have given us a magnificent entertainment and we glory in our defeat. Your champion has displayed his usual invincible form, and we, the Philistines, have been smitten hip and thigh. But *not* with the jawbone of an ass."

The End

1936 Hodder & Stoughton, London Cover

Book I – Being the Narrative of Ernest Lockhart, Barrister at Law

Chapter I
A Gossipy Chapter in Which Coming Events Cast Their Shadows Before Them

I have been asked to make my contribution to the curious history of the disappearance of Mr. Daniel Penrose, and I accordingly do so, but not without reluctance and a feeling that my contribution is but a retailing of the smallest of small beer. For the truth is that of that strange disappearance I knew nothing at the time and, even now, my knowledge is limited to what I have learned from those who were directly concerned in the investigation. Still, I am assured that the little that I have to tell will elucidate the accounts which the investigators will presently render of the affair, and I shall, therefore, with the above disclaimer, proceed with my somewhat trivial narrative.

Whenever my thoughts turn to that extraordinary case, there rises before me the picture of a certain antique shop in a by-street of Soho. And quite naturally, for it was in that shop that I first set eyes on Daniel Penrose, and it was in connection with that that my not very intimate relations with Penrose existed.

It was a queer little shop, an antique shop in both senses. For not only were the goods that it contained one and all survivors from the past, but the shop was an antique in itself. Indeed, it was probably a more genuine museum piece than anything in its varied and venerable stock, with its small-paned window bulging in a double curve – as shop-fitters could make them in the eighteenth century – and glazed with the original crown glass, greenish in tone and faintly streaked, like an oyster-shell, with concentric lines. I dated the shop at the first half of the eighteenth century, basing my estimate on a pedimented stone tablet at the corner of the street, which set forth the name, *"Nassau Street in Whetten's Buildings"*, and the date, *"1734"*. It was a pleasant and friendly shop, though dingy, dignified, and reticent, too, for the fascia above the

227

window bore only, in dull gilt letters, the name of the proprietor, *"D. Parrott"*.

For some time I remained under the belief that this superscription referred to some former incumbent of the premises whose name was retained for the sake of continuity, since the only persons whom I encountered in my early visits were Mrs. Pettigrew, who appeared to manage the business and, more rarely, her daughter, Joan, a strikingly good-looking girl of about twenty, a very modern young lady, frank, friendly, and self-possessed, quite well-informed on the subject of antiques, though openly contemptuous of the whole *genus*.

Presently, however, I discovered that Parrott, so far from being a mere disembodied name, was a very real person. He was, in fact, the mainspring of the establishment, for he was not only the buyer – and an uncommonly good buyer – but he had quite a genius for converting mere dismembered carcasses into hale and hearty pieces of furniture. Somewhere in the regions behind the shop he had a workshop where, with the aid of an incredibly aged cabinet-maker named Tims, he carried out the necessary restorations. And they were real restorations, not fakes – honest repairs carried out for structural reasons and left open and undisguised. I came to have a great respect for Mr. Parrott.

My first visit was undoubtedly due to the ancient shop-front. But when I crossed the narrow street to examine it and discovered in the window a court cupboard and a couple of Jacobean chairs, I decided to avail myself of the courteous invitation, written on a card, to enter and inspect and indulge a mild passion for ancient furniture.

There were three persons in the shop: A comely woman of about fifty, who greeted me with a smile and a little bow, and thereafter took no further notice of me, a stout, jovial, rather foxy-looking gentleman who was inspecting a trayful of old silver, and a small clerical-looking gentleman who appeared to be disembowelling a bloated verge watch and prying into its interior through a watchmaker's eye-glass, which stuck miraculously in his eye, giving him somewhat the appearance of a one-eyed lobster.

"Now," said the stout gentleman, "that's quite an elegant little milk-jug, in my opinion. Don't you agree with me, Mrs. Pettigrew?"

I looked at him in some surprise, for the thing was not a milk-jug. It was a coffee-pot. However, Mrs. Pettigrew did not contest the description. She merely agreed that the shape was pleasant and graceful.

"I am glad, Mrs. Pettigrew," said the stout gentleman, regarding the coffee-pot with his head on one side, "that you regard the lactiferous receptacle with favour. I am encouraged and confirmed. The next question is that of the date of its birthday. I am reluctant to interrupt the erudite Mr. Polton in his studies of the internal anatomy of the Carolean warming-pan, but I have no skill in galactophorous genealogies. May I venture?"

He held out the coffee-pot engagingly towards the small gentleman, who thereupon laid the watch down tenderly, removed the eye-glass from his eye, and smiled. And I found Mr. Polton's smile almost as astonishing as the other gentleman's vocabulary. It was the most amazingly wrinkly smile that I have ever seen, but yet singularly genial and pleasant. And here I may remark that this amiable little gentleman was for some time a profound mystery to me. I could make nothing of him. I could not place him socially or otherwise. By his appearance, he might – in different raiment – have been a dignitary of the Church. His deferential manner suggested some superlative kind of manservant, but his hands and his comprehensive and inexhaustible knowledge of the products of the ancient crafts hinted at the dealer or expert collector. It was only after I had known him some months that the mystery was resolved through the medium of a legal friend, as will be related in due course. To return to the present incident, Mr. Polton took the coffee-pot in his curiously prehensile hands, beamed on it approvingly and, having stuck his eye-glass in his eye, examined the hall-mark and the maker's "touch".

"It was made," he reported, "in 1765 by a man named John Hammond, who had a shop in Water Lane, Fleet Street. And an excellent tradesman he must have been."

"There, now!" exclaimed the stout gentleman. "Just listen to that! It's my belief that Mr. Polton carries in his head a complete directory of all the artful craftsmen and crafty artists who ever made anything, with the dates of every piece they made. Don't you agree, Mrs. Pettigrew?"

"Yes, indeed!" she replied. "His knowledge is perfectly wonderful. Perhaps," she added, addressing Mr. Polton, "you can tell us something about that watch. It is said to have belonged to Prince Charlie and, of course, that would add to its value if it were really the fact. What do you think, Mr. Polton?"

"Well, ma'am," was the cautious reply, "I see no reason why it should not have belonged to him, if he was not a very punctual gentleman. It was made in Edinburgh in 1735, and there is a crucifix engraved inside the outer case. I don't know what the significance of that may be."

"Neither do I," said the lady. "What do you think, Mr. Penrose?"

"I should say," replied the stout gentleman, "that the evidence is conclusive. Charles Edward, being a Scotchman, would have a Scottish

229

watch, and being a papistical Romanist would naturally have a crucifix engraved in it. *Q.E.D.*"

Mrs. Pettigrew smiled indulgently and, as Mr. Penrose had indicated his adoption of the coffee-pot, she proceeded to swathe it in tissue-paper and make it up into a presentable parcel and, meanwhile, I browsed round the premises and inspected those specimens of the stock which were more particularly within my province. But it was not a very peaceful inspection, for Mr. Penrose persisted in accompanying me and expounding and commenting upon the various pieces in terms which I found rather distracting. For Mr. Penrose, as the reader has probably observed, was a wag, and his waggery took the form of calling things by quaintly erroneous names and of using odd and facetious circumlocutions, which was all very well at first and was even mildly amusing, but it very soon became tiresome. A constant effort was necessary to arrive at what he really meant.

However, in the end, I lighted upon a bible-box of dark-brown oak, pleasantly carved and bearing the incised date, *1653* and, as the little chest rather took my fancy and the price marked on the attached ticket seemed less than its value, I closed with Mrs. Pettigrew and, having paid for my purchase and given the address to which it was to be sent, took my departure. And, as I strolled at a leisurely pace in the direction of Wardour Street, I reflected idly on my late experience, and especially on the three rather unusual persons whose acquaintance I had just made. I am not in general a curious man, but I found in each of these three persons matter for speculation. There was Mrs. Pettigrew, for instance. Admirably as she played her part in the economy of the shop, she did not completely fit her surroundings. One is accustomed nowadays to finding women of a very superior class serving in shops. But not quite of Mrs. Pettigrew's type. She gave me the impression of being very definitely a lady, and I found myself speculating on the turn of the wheel of Fortune that had brought her there.

Then there was the enigmatical Mr. Polton with his strangely prehensile hands and his astonishing memory for hall-marks. And there was the facetious Penrose. And at this point, being then about halfway along Gerrard Street, the subject of my reflections overtook me and announced himself characteristically by expressing the hope that I was pleased with my bacon cupboard. I replied that I was quite pleased with my purchase and had thought it decidedly cheap.

"So did I," said he. "But our *psittacoid* friend has the wisdom to temper the breeze to the shorn collector."

"Our *psittacoid* friend?" I repeated.

230

"I refer to the tropic bird who presides over the museum of domestic archaeology," he explained and, as I still looked at him questioningly, he added, by way of elucidation, "The proprietor of the treasure-house of antiquities in which you discovered the repository of ancestral piety."

"Oh!" I exclaimed. "You mean Mr. Parrott."

"Certainly!" he replied. "Did I not say so?"

"Perhaps you did," I admitted, with a slightly sour laugh, at which he smiled his peculiar, foxy smile, looking at me out of the corners of his eyes, and evidently pleased at having "stumped" me. It was a pleasure that he must have enjoyed pretty often.

"I take it," he resumed, after a short pause, "that you, like myself, are a devotee of St. Margaret Pie?"

I considered this fresh puzzle and decided that the solution was "magpie", and apparently I was right as he did not correct me.

"No," I replied, "there is nothing of the magpie about me. I don't accumulate old things for the sake of forming a collection. I buy old furniture and use it. One must have furniture of some kind, old or new, and I prefer the old. It was made by men who knew all about it and who enjoyed making it and took their time. It is much more companionable to live with than new machine-made stuff, turned out by the thousand by people who don't care a straw what it is like. But my object is quite utilitarian. I am no collector."

"Ah!" said he, "that isn't my case. I am a convinced disciple of the great John Daw, a snapper-up of unconsidered trifles, a hoarder of miscellaneous treasure. Nothing comes amiss to me, from a blue diamond to a Staffordshire dog."

"Have you no special fancy?" I asked.

"I have a special fancy for any relic of the past that I can lay hands on," he replied. "But perhaps, like the burglars, I have a particular leaning towards precious stones – those and the other kind of stones – the siliceous variety – with which our impolite forefathers used to fracture one another's craniums."

"Your collection must take up a lot of space," I remarked.

"It does," said he. "That's the trouble. John Daw's nest has a tendency to overflow. And still they come. I'm always finding fresh treasures."

"By the way," said I, "where do you find the stuff?"

"Oh, call it not 'stuff'," he protested, regarding me with a foxy smile. "I spoke of treasures. As to where I discover them – well, well, surely there is a mine for silver and a place for gold where they refine it, a place also – many places, mostly cottage parlours – that no bird of prey knoweth, neither hath the travelling dealer's eye seen them, where may be found ancestral Wrotham pots and Staffordshire figures, to say nothing of venerable tickers and crocks from far Cathay. These the wise collector makes a note of – and locks up the note."

I was half-amused and half-exasperated by his evasive verbiage and his unabashed – and quite unnecessary – caution. A mighty secretive gentleman, this, I reflected, and proceeded to fire a return shot.

"In effect," said I, "you go rooting about in cottage parlours, snapping up rustic heirlooms, probably at a fraction of their value."

"Undoubtedly," he agreed, with a snigger. "That is the essence of the sport. I once, in a labourer's cottage, picked up a genuine '*Vicar and Moses*' by Ralph Wood for five shillings. But that was a windfall."

"It wasn't much of a windfall for the owner," I remarked.

"He was quite satisfied," said Penrose, "and so was I. What more would you have? But windfalls are not frequent, and when they fail, I fall back on the popinjay."

"The pop – Oh, you mean Mr. Parrott?"

"Exactly," said he. "Our friend Monsieur le Perroquet. Actually, I let him do most of the rooting about. He knows all the ropes and, as we agreed, he doesn't demand payment through the proboscis."

"No," said I, "he doesn't appear to be grasping, to judge by the price of my own purchase, and I gather that you have got most of your stuff – I beg pardon, *treasure* – from him."

"Oh, I wouldn't say that," he replied. "Mere purchase from a dealer is a dull affair, though necessary. But one wants the sport as well, the pleasure of the chase – not to mention those of the pick and shovel."

"The pick and shovel!" I repeated. "That sounds as if you did a little in the resurrection line. You are not a tomb-robber, I trust?"

I was, of course, only jesting, but he took me up quite seriously.

"But why not? We may grant the impropriety of disturbing the repose of the freeholders in Finchley Cemetery. Besides, they have nothing but their bones, which, at present, are not collector's pieces. But our rude forefathers had a foolish – but, for us, convenient – habit of taking their goods and chattels to bed with them, so to speak. Now, a man's title to his goods, after his decease, does not extend to an indefinite period. When a deceased gentleman has enjoyed the possession of his chattels for a couple-of-thousand years or more, I think he ought to be satisfied. His title has lapsed by the effluxion of time, and my title, by right of discovery, has come into being. The expression 'tomb-robber' is not applicable to an archaeological excavator. Don't you agree?"

I admitted that excavation for scientific purposes seemed to be a permissible proceeding, though I had secret doubts as to whether the expression was properly applicable to his activities. He did not impress me as a scientific investigator.

"But," I asked, "what sort of things do you turn up when you go a-digging?"

"All sorts of things," he replied. "Mostly preposterous stone substitutes for cutlery, decayed and fragmentary pots and pans, with an occasional – very occasional – torque or brooch and portions of the deceased proprietor. But I leave those. I don't collect proprietors."

"And I suppose," said I, "that when you find a gold or silver ornament you notify the coroner of the discovery of treasure trove?"

"That," he replied with his queer, foxy smile, "is indispensable. But you seem to be interested in my miscellaneous gleanings. I wonder if you would care to cast a supercilious eye on my little hoard. I don't often display my treasures because your regular collector is usually a man of one idea – indefinitely repeated – and he is disappointed to find that I am not. But you, like myself, are more eclectic in taste and I should have great pleasure in introducing you to Aladdin's Cave, if you would care to inspect its contents."

I was not, really, particularly interested, but yet I was faintly curious as to the nature of his "hoard". It sounded like a very queer collection, and might include some objects of real interest. Besides which, the man, himself, despite his exasperating verbosity and obscurities of speech, rather attracted me. Accordingly, I accepted his invitation and, when we had exchanged visiting cards and arranged the day and hour of my visit, we separated, he shaping a course in a westerly direction and I bearing east, towards my chambers in Lincoln's Inn.

Chapter II
Aladdin's Cave

Mr. Penrose's residence, or John Daw's Nest, as he would have called it, was situated in Queen Square, Bloomsbury and, what is more, it was one of the few remaining original houses, dating back to the time when residents could look out of their windows through the open end of the square, across the meadows to the heights of Highgate. Appropriately to the house of a collector of antiquities, its door was garnished with a pair of link-extinguishers, as well as with a fine brass knocker and an old-fashioned bell-handle.

A flourish on the knocker, reinforced by a hearty tug at the bell-pull, resulted in the opening of the door and the appearance thereat of an elderly man of depressed and nephritic aspect, with puffy eyelids and a complexion like that of a suet pudding. He received the announcement of my identity with resignation and, having admitted me, took my hat and stick and silently introduced me to a small room, the window of which commanded a view of the leaden statue of Her late Majesty, Queen Anne. At this window I had taken up a position from which I could contemplate that rather neglected example of an extinct art when the door opened briskly and Mr. Penrose entered.

"Ha!" said he, "I see you are admiring the mimic rendering of our proverbially deceased twenty-shilling Lady."

"I am afraid," said I, as we shook hands, "that your paraphrase fails in precision. You would have to pay thirty shillings to-day to buy a sovereign, if you could find one."

"There," he retorted, "is exemplified the pedantic accuracy of the legal mind. But I spoke in terms of the past. The aureous reality is now as dead as madame herself. But what think you of that masterpiece of the plumber's art? I rather like it, and it is the genuine metal. I have tried it with my pocket-knife. To tell you a little secret, I had thought of making an offer for it."

"Do you mean," I exclaimed, "that you want to buy it?"

"If it should come into the market," he replied. "Unfortunately it has not, up to the present."

"But what on earth could you do with a leaden statue?" I protested.

"Put it in my gallery," he replied, "if the floor would stand it."

"You can take it," said I, "that it would not. Why, the thing must weigh tons. Besides, it is much better in the place that it was made to occupy and which it does really adorn in its rather mouldy way."

"In short," said he, "you think me a bit of a vandal" (which was the literal truth). "Well, you needn't be alarmed. It is safe from my acquisitive instincts for the present."

He turned to a nondescript piece of furniture, half-cupboard and half-armoire and, opening a door, took out a decanter and two glasses, which he placed on the table.

"Before we venture into Aladdin's Cave," said he, taking out the stopper of the decanter, "shall we fortify ourselves with a morsel of cake?"

He looked at me interrogatively as he picked up the decanter. Of course, there was no cake visible, but my growing skill in interpreting his verbal puzzles enabled me to diagnose the dark-brown wine as Madeira.

Without giving me time to refuse, he filled the two glasses and, having handed me one, proceeded in a very deliberate and workmanlike fashion to empty the other.

"The vintages of the Fortunate Isles," said he, as he refilled his glass, "have always commended themselves to me, rivalled only in my affection by the product of the vines of Xeres – " (He pronounced the name in the Spanish manner, "*Hereth*", as a slight additional precaution against being too readily understood.) " – preferably the elderly and fuscous variety."

I noted the fact – while he filled his third glass – as explaining the vinous aroma which I had noticed in Parrott's shop as apparently exhaling from his person. It turned out later to be not without significance. Madeira and old brown sherry by no means share the innocuousness of what Penrose would probably have called "the celestial herb".

When I had resolutely declined a refill, he reluctantly returned the decanter to its abiding-place and locked the door thereof.

"And now," said he, "we shall proceed to explore the secret recesses of the cavern."

He conducted me out into the fine, spacious hall, from which a noble staircase gave access to the upper floors. In one swift glance I noted that the appointments were not worthy of the architecture, for the furniture – of which there was a good deal too much – consisted of undeniable "dentist's oak", and there were one or two shabby-looking busts, the obvious plaster of which had been varnished by some optimist in the hope that they might thereby be mistaken for bronze. But I had little opportunity for detailed inspection, for my host threw open, with something of a flourish, an adjacent door and motioned to me to enter, which I did, and found myself in one of a pair of great, lofty communicating rooms, and forthwith began my tour of inspection.

I had expected to find Mr. Penrose's collection something of an oddity, but the reality far exceeded my expectations. It was an amazing hoard. Alike, in respect of matter and manner, it was astonishing and bewildering. Of the ordinary collector's fastidious selection, prim tidiness and orderly arrangement there was no trace. The things that jostled one another on the crowded shelves and tables were in every respect incongruous, for, on the one hand, rare and valuable pieces, such as the "*Vicar and Moses*" and a fine slip-ware tyg, stood check by jowl with common, worthless oddments and, on the other, the objects themselves were devoid of any sort of kinship or relation. The "*Vicar*", for instance, was accompanied by a broken Roman pot, a few worthless fragments of Samian ware, a dried crab covered with acorn barnacles, and half-a-dozen horse-brasses, while the tyg had as its immediate neighbour a Sheffield coffee-pot, a Tunbridge-ware wafer-box, a pewter candlestick, and one or two flint implements.

The confusion and disorder that prevailed were perfectly astounding. These fine old rooms, with such splendid possibilities, suggested nothing more or less than the store of some curio dealer or the premises of an auctioneer on the day preceding a sale of miscellaneous property. I ventured tentatively to comment on the lack of arrangement.

"You have certainly got a very remarkable collection," said I, "but don't you think that its interest would be increased if you adopted some sort of classification? Here, for instance, is a wine-glass – a Jacobite glass, apparently."

"Not apparently," he objected. "Actually. An undoubtedly genuine piece. An appropriate memorial, too. '*Charlie loved good ale and wine*'.

"So he did, as '*his nose doth show*' in the portraits. But why put this glass next to that barbaric-looking pot? There is no relation whatever between the two things."

"There is the relation of unlikeness," he replied. "And don't disparage that rare and precious pot. It is extremely ancient. Prehistoric. Neolithic, I believe, is the correct word."

"But why not put all the prehistoric pots together instead of mixing them up with table-glass and Scandinavian carvings?"

"That would seem a dull arrangement," said he. "You would lose the effect of variety, the thrill of unexpectedness. How delightful, for instance, after considering this Book of Hours and this highly ornate sternutatorium – " He indicated a handsome tortoise-shell snuff-box. " –

to come upon these siliceous relics of the childhood of the race – also neolithic, I believe – the products of my own fossatory activities."

The "relics" referred to consisted of half-a-dozen rough flint nodules which looked as if they might have been gathered from a road-mender's heap. They may have been genuine flint implements, but they were certainly not neolithic. No one with the most elementary knowledge of stone implements could have supposed that they were. But my host's easy-going acceptance of them, and his indifference as to the actual facts, brought home to me a state of mind at which I wondered more and more as I examined this amazing collection.

For, in the first place, Mr. Penrose displayed the most complete and comprehensive ignorance of "antiques" of every kind. He knew no more of them than their names, and he frequently got those wrong. But not only was he ignorant. He was quite indifferent. He seemed to be totally devoid of interest in the individual things which he had accumulated, and the question that I asked myself was what earthly object he could have had in making this enormous and miscellaneous collection. Apparently, he was possessed by an insatiable acquisitiveness, with no other motive behind it. Mere possession seemed to be the object of his desire, and with mere possession he appeared to be satisfied. Not without reason had he likened himself to "The Great John Daw".

My long tour of inspection came at last to an end. I had examined the collection very thoroughly, not only to please my host – though he was evidently gratified and flattered by the interest that I displayed in his "hoard" – but because it contained, mingled with a good deal of rubbish, many curious and beautiful objects that invited examination. The last piece that I inspected was an ancient gold brooch, richly decorated with gilt filigree work and set with garnets. I lifted it tenderly from the dusty scrap of paper (marked in pencil with the number *963*) on which it rested and carried it to the window to look at it in a better light.

"This is a very fine piece of work, Mr. Penrose," I remarked.

"Ha!" said he, "the papistical fibula commends itself. I am glad you like it."

"A Roman fibula!" I exclaimed in surprise. "I should have taken it for a Saxon brooch."

"You may be right," he admitted. "In fact, I am inclined to think that you are. At any rate, it is one or the other."

"But," I protested, "surely you keep some sort of record. I see that the pieces are numbered. Haven't you a catalogue?"

"To be sure I have," he replied. "Excellent idea! We'll get out the Domesday Book and see which of us is right."

He pulled out the drawer of a table and produced therefrom a manuscript book which he opened and began to turn over the leaves. Still holding the brooch, I stepped across to him and looked over his shoulder. And then I got a fresh surprise, though I ought to have been prepared for something unusual. For if the collection was eccentric, the catalogue was positively fantastic. It seemed to be (and probably was) expressly designed to be as completely unintelligible as possible. The brief entries, scribbled illegibly in pencil, were apparently worded in Mr. Penrose's peculiar, cryptic dialect and, for the most part, I could make nothing of them. Running my eye down the pages, I deciphered with difficulty such entries as: "*Up +. Mudlarks*", "*Sammy. Pot sand. Sinbad*", "*Funereal flower-pot, Julie-Polly*", "*Carver, Jul. Pop*".

I stood gazing in speechless astonishment at this amazing record while Penrose slowly turned the leaves, glancing slyly at me from time to time, apparently to see how I took it. At length – at unnecessary length – Number *963* was found, but it was not very illuminating – to me – for it consisted only of the laconic statement, "*Sweeney's resurrection*". Apparently, however, it conveyed something to him, for he said, "Yes, you are right. I recollect now." But he did not enter into any particulars.

I laid the brooch down on its slip of paper and began to think of departing, and meanwhile he looked at me with a very odd expression, an expression of mingled anxiety and hesitation.

"I have to thank you, Mr. Penrose," said I, "for a very pleasant and profitable afternoon. It was very good of you to let me see all your treasures. I have seen them all, I suppose?"

He did not reply for a few moments, but continued to look at me in that queer, anxious, irresolute fashion. Suddenly, his hesitation gave way and he burst out in low, impressive tones, in a manner of the deepest secrecy, "The fact is that you haven't. There is another little hoard, which I don't show to anyone, but just float over in secret. I don't even mention its existence. But, somehow I feel tempted to make an exception in your case. What do you say? Would you like to have a peep at the contents of Bluebeard's Chamber?"

"This sounds rather alarming," said I. "Were there not certain penalties for undue curiosity?"

"I hold you immune from those," he replied. "Only I stipulate that this private view shall be a really private view, to be spoken of to nobody. I can rely on you to keep my secret?"

I did not much like this. Like most lawyers, I am a cautious man, and cautious men do not care to be made the unprivileged repositories of other people's secrets. But I could hardly refuse, and when I had, rather reluctantly, given the required undertaking, he moved off towards a door in a corner of the room and I followed, wondering anxiously what he was going to show me and whether it would commit me to any unlawful knowledge.

The room into which he led me – and of which he closed and bolted the door – was a smallish apartment, at one end of which was a massive mahogany cupboard or armoire. When he had unlocked this and thrown open the doors, there was revealed the steel front of a large safe or small strongroom. Apparently the safe-key was not in his bunch, for he returned the latter to his pocket and then, retiring a few paces, stood with his back to me while he dived into some secret recesses of his clothing. In a few moments he turned round, rather red from his exertions, and stepped up to the safe with the key in his hand, while I watched with growing curiosity.

The lock clicked softly, a turn of the handle withdrew the bolts, and the ponderous door swung open, disclosing a range of shallow drawers which occupied the whole of the interior. My host, first withdrawing the key and slipping it into his waistcoat pocket, proceeded to pull out the top drawer and carry it to a table under the window. And then I breathed a sigh of relief. There was nothing incriminating, after all. The drawer was simply filled with jewellery, looking, indeed, like a tray from a jeweller's window. My host's secrecy was naturally and reasonably explained by the value of his treasures and their highly portable and negotiable character.

I looked over the contents of the drawer with keen interest, for I am rather fond of gems, though I have no special knowledge of them. My host, too, showed a pleasure and enthusiasm in regard to the things themselves, which contrasted strikingly with the indifference that he had displayed towards the general collection.

Yet even here, there was no glimmer of connoisseur-ship. His manner suggested mere miserly gloating, and his ignorance of these beautiful baubles astonished me. It was suggested by the absence of any classification, by the way in which totally unrelated stones were jumbled together, and the suggestion was confirmed by his comments. For instance, in this first drawer were two cat's-eyes placed side by side, but they belonged to totally different categories. One, a dark yellowish-green stone with a bright band of bluish light, was a cymophane or true cat's-eye – a chrysoberyl. The other, a charming stone of the hue known as "honey yellow", was a quartz cat's-eye and should have been placed with the other quartz gems. I ventured to comment on the fact, referring to the cymophane as a chrysoberyl, but he interrupted me with the protest, "Chrysoberyl! Violin-bows, my dear sir! Gall not the optic of the fair Tabitha a chrysoberyl."

As he obviously knew – and cared – nothing of the actual characters of precious stones, I did not pursue the question, but continued my inspection of the really interesting and remarkable collection. The admiration that I expressed evidently gave him considerable pleasure and he also made admiring comments from time to time, though without much appearance of taste or discrimination. But his enthusiasm did really wake up when he brought forth the third drawer, which was devoted entirely to opals, and as these beautiful gems are special favourites of mine, we examined them with sympathetic pleasure.

It was a really magnificent collection, and what rather surprised me (considering the collector's comprehensive ignorance) was its genuinely representative character. There were specimens of every variety of the gem. Of the noble, or precious, opal a long range of examples was shown, of all the varied rainbow hues and of various sizes up to nearly an inch in diameter, some in plain mounts but most of them encircled with borders of rose diamonds or brilliants. There were harlequin opals, Mexican fire opals, glowing like blazing coals, black opals, a large series of the common non-prismatic form of various hues, and one or two examples of the dark, pitchy "root" or matrix, streaked and speckled with points of prismatic colour.

But the gem of the collection, in interest if not in beauty, was a cameo, cut in a disc of precious opal embedded in its dark matrix. The oval slab of matrix, carrying the glowing cameo, was worked into a pendant with a broad border of small rose diamonds and coloured stones forming the design of a rose, a thistle and a central star, while, at the bottom, worked in tiny diamonds, was the word "*Fiat*", which, with the engraved portrait of a middle-aged gentleman in a wig, gave a clue to the significance of the jewel.

As I pored over this curious memorial, Penrose watched me with a smile of evident gratification.

"My favourite child," he remarked, taking it out of its compartment and handing it to me, together with a magnifying glass. "Just look at the detail of the face."

I examined it through the lens and was greatly impressed by the perfection of the modelling on so minute a scale.

"Yes," I said, "it is quite a wonderful piece of work. One gets the impression that it might be a really good portrait. And now I know," I added, as I returned the jewel to him, "why you swore me to secrecy."

He paused with the trinket in his hand, looking at me with a distinctly startled expression.

"What do you mean?" he demanded.

"Well," I replied, "you must admit that it is a rather incriminating object to have in your possession."

He gazed at me uneasily, almost with an appearance of alarm, and rejoined, "I don't understand you. How, incriminating?"

I chuckled with mischievous satisfaction. For an inveterate joker, he seemed decidedly "slow in the uptake".

"Doesn't it occur to you," I replied, "that a portrait of James Francis Edward, the King over the water, cherished secretly by a presumably loyal subject of His Majesty George the Fifth, tends to suggest highly improper political sentiments? I call it rank sedition."

"Oh, I see what you mean," said he, with an uneasy laugh, apparently relieved – and slightly annoyed – at my schoolboy jest, "but sedition of that kind is a trifle threadbare in these days."

He returned the jewel to its place in the drawer and carried the latter back to the safe. As he slid it in, he remarked, "That's the last of the gem collection. The other drawers contain coins. You may as well see them, too."

I went through the coin collection and was rather surprised at its range, for it included ancient coins, Greek, Roman, Gaulish and British and English coins from the Middle Ages, down to the late spade guineas. But all that remains in my memory concerning them is that the different periods seemed to be mixed up, with an almost total lack of order, and that there appeared to be an abnormal proportion of gold coins. When the last of the drawers had been examined and returned and the safe and its enclosing cupboard had been closed and locked, I began once more to think of taking my leave. But my host pressed me to stay and take a cup of tea with him and, when I had accepted his invitation, he conducted me back through the large gallery to the room into which I had first been shown. Here, the melancholy manservant – who answered to the name of Kickweed – presently brought us tea and drew a couple of arm-chairs up to the table.

"This collection of yours," I remarked, as my host poured out the tea, "must represent a large amount of sunk capital."

"I hardly regard it as sunk," he replied, "seeing that I have the use and enjoyment of my treasures, but the collection is worth a lot of money – at least, I hope it is. It has cost a lot."

"So I should suppose," said I, "and it must cost you something quite substantial in the matter of insurance."

"Ah!" said he, "I am glad you raised that question. For the fact is that the collection is not insured at all. I have intended to go into the matter, but there are certain difficulties that have put me off. Now, I dare say you know a good deal about insurance."

241

"I know something about the legal aspects," I replied, "and such knowledge as I possess is at your disposal. You certainly ought to be secured against what might be a very heavy loss. What are the difficulties that you refer to?"

"Well," he answered in a low voice, leaning across the table, "I don't want to go about proclaiming myself as the owner of a priceless collection. Might arouse interest in the wrong quarter, you see. And as to the gems, as I told you, they are a secret hoard the existence of which I disclose to nobody excepting yourself. You are the only person to whom I have shown them."

"But," I protested, "somebody must have sold them to you and must be aware that you have them."

"They know that I have – or had – the individual jewels that they sold me, but they don't know that I have a great and valuable collection. And I don't want them to know, but that is the difficulty about the insurance. Before I could insure the collection, I should have to get it valued, and the valuer would have to see the gems, and then the cat would be out of the bag. At least, that is what I suppose. Perhaps I am wrong. Could I effect an insurance for a certain definite sum without calling in a valuer?"

"You mean," I replied, "on a declaration that you had certain property of a certain value? No. I think a Company would want evidence that the property insured actually existed and was of the value alleged, and in the event of a fire or a burglary, they certainly would not pay on property alleged to have been lost but which had never been proved to exist. But I think you are raising imaginary difficulties. You could stipulate that the valuation should be a strictly confidential transaction. Remember that the company's interests are the same as your own. If they insure you against burglary, they won't want you to be burgled."

"No, that is true," he admitted. "And you think I could rely on the secrecy of the valuer?"

"I have no doubt of it," I replied, "particularly if you made clear your reasons for insisting on secrecy."

"I am glad you think that," said he, "and I shall act on your advice without delay. I will put the case to the manager of the Society which has insured this house."

"I think you ought to do so at once," I urged. "There must be many thousands of pounds' worth of property in your collections, and a fire or a burglary might sweep away the bulk of it in a night."

He repeated, with emphasis, his intention to attend to the matter without further delay, and the subject then dropped. After a little more desultory conversation, I rose to take my leave, and the lugubrious

Kickweed, having presented me with my hat and stick, let me out at the street door with the air of admitting me to the family vault.

As I wended homewards I found ample matter for reflection in the incidents of my visit, but chiefly my thoughts concerned themselves with my eccentric host. Mr. Penrose was certainly a very strange man, and the more I thought about him, the less did I feel able to understand him. He had so many oddities, and each of them suggested problems to which I could find no solution. There was the collection, for instance. Including the gems and coins, it must have been of very great value, and its accumulation must have entailed a vast expenditure of time and effort, to say nothing of the prodigious sums of money that must have been spent. But with what object? He had none of the ordinary collector's expertness and enthusiasm. He had no special knowledge of any single class of objects, not even of the gems for which he professed so much affection. The motive force that impelled him to collect seemed to be simple acquisitiveness, the mere *cupiditas habendi*.

But the outstanding feature of his character was secretiveness. He was a secret man of the very deepest dye. His inveterate habit of secrecy coloured every word and action. The ridiculous jargon that he used, his silly circumlocutions and ellipses and paraphrases, were but phases of the tendency, as if he grudged to disclose the whole of his meaning. Even the preposterous catalogue revealed the same trait for, while it seemed to have been made deliberately unintelligible, it was clear that the absurd entries held some hidden meaning which was intelligible to him.

It was not an endearing trait. None of us likes a secret man. And very naturally. For secrecy implies distrust and, moreover, we are apt – again very naturally – to assume some reason for the secrecy, and to suspect that it is a discreditable reason. Thus it was with me in the present case, and my general dislike of the secret habit of mind was aggravated by the fact that I had become involved in the secrecy. The promise that had been exacted from me in regard to the gems recurred to me with a certain distaste and resentment. I was committed to the concealment of a fact which was no concern of mine and of the bearings of which I knew nothing. The explanations that Penrose had given for keeping secret his precious hoard were not unreasonable. But suppose there were other reasons. The thing was possible. Some collectors are not over-scrupulous, and I recalled not for the first time, the singular, startled expression with which he had looked at me when I made my foolish joke about the Jacobite jewel.

In short, I was not quite comfortable about that promise. There is something a little disturbing about a secret hoard of valuable gems and, but for the fact that Penrose was obviously a man of ample means, my professional experiences might have caused me to ask myself whether this very odd collection might not cover some activities of a more questionable kind.

Chapter III
Exit Mr. Penrose

I did not see Penrose again for about a fortnight. Then, having occasion to call at Parrott's shop to inquire after a gate-leg table which I had purchased and which was undergoing some necessary restorations, I encountered him, standing opposite to a lantern clock which had been fixed on a temporary bracket and was ticking cheerfully with every sign of robust health. Noting his evident interest in the venerable timepiece, I stopped to discuss it with him.

"You are looking at that clock, Mr. Penrose," said I, "as if you contemplated making an investment."

"I don't contemplate," he replied. "I investigated in it some time ago. It is a poor thing, but mine own."

"I shouldn't call it a poor thing," said I. "It is quite a good clock and it looks to me as if it were absolutely intact and in its original condition – which is unusual in the case of lantern clocks. People will tinker at them and spoil them. You were lucky to find an untouched specimen."

"I didn't," said he. "When it came to me – through the usual *psittacoid* channel – it was a mere wreck. Some misbegotten Daedalus had eviscerated it and wrought havoc with its entrails. Thereupon I sought medicinal advice for the invalid and had it put under treatment."

"You sent it to a clockmaker?" I suggested.

"I did not," he replied. "It had had too much clockmaker already. I consulted the erudite and podophthalmate horologer, and behold! – It has renewed its youth like the eagle."

I must confess that this stumped me for the moment, until a flash of supernormal intelligence associated the word "*podophthalmate*" with Mr. Polton's protuberant eye-glass.

"I didn't know that Mr. Polton was a practical mechanic," I remarked.

"Oh, don't call him that!" Penrose protested. "He is a magician, a wizard, a worker of miracles. By the way, Mrs. Pettigrew, I rather expected to find him here. He promised to see this clock safely established in my gallery."

"He is here," replied Mrs. Pettigrew. "He is in the workshop, doing something to Mr. Tims's lathe. Would you like to walk across and let him know that you have arrived? You know the way. And perhaps, Mr.

Lockhart, you would like to go and inspect your table? I think Tims wants you to see it."

I accepted the invitation and, following Penrose, passed out at the back of the shop and crossed a small paved yard to a wide doorway. Passing through this, I entered a roomy workshop, lighted by a skylight and littered with articles of ancient furniture in all stages of decay and dismemberment. There were three persons in the workshop. First, there was Mr. Tims, a tall, aged man, frail and decrepit of aspect – until he picked up a tool, when he seemed suddenly to develop fresh strength and vitality. Next, there was Mr. Polton in shirt-sleeves and an apron (which appeared by its length to have been borrowed from Tims), engaged at the moment in re-fixing the head-stock of a wood-turner's lathe. The third person was Mr. Parrott, as I learned when Penrose greeted him and, as this was the first time that I had encountered him in the flesh, I looked at him with some curiosity.

"Monsieur le Perroquet" was a somewhat unusual-looking man and not at all the type of a shopkeeper. Dark, clean-shaved, and blue-jowled, he had rather the appearance of an actor, and this suggestion was heightened by a certain precision of speech and clearness of enunciation, and especially by a tendency to the use of studied and appropriate gestures. Obviously, he was not only an educated man but what one would call a gentleman, easy and pleasant in manner, with that combination of deference and dignity that is attainable only by a well-bred man.

When I had introduced myself, Mr. Tims produced the dismembered table and exhibited the repairs on the damaged leg.

"You see, sir," he explained, "I've cut out the worm-eaten part and let in a patch of sound oak. Do you think he'll do?"

"Do you propose to stain the patch?" I inquired.

"That's as you please," replied Tims. "I wouldn't. A mend's a mend, but a stained mend looks like a fake."

"I think Tims is right," said Parrott. "Better leave the patch to darken naturally."

To this I assented, and thereupon Mr. Tims proceeded to assemble the separated parts while Parrott and I looked on, and Penrose divided his attention between the table and Mr. Polton's operations on the lathe.

"By the way, Mr. Penrose," said I, suddenly remembering our last conversation, "how goes the insurance scheme? Have you solved the difficulty of the valuer?"

Penrose turned to me quickly with a look of annoyance, so that I was sorry I had spoken.

246

"There is nothing to report at present," he replied with unwonted shortness of manner and, as if to close the subject, he stepped across to the lathe and manifested a sudden and not very intelligent interest in its mechanism. However, Mr. Polton's job was apparently completed for, when he had replaced the band on the pulley, tested the centres, and given the fly-wheel a trial spin, he proceeded to shed the apron and put on his coat, and was forthwith spirited away by Penrose.

I had noticed that when I spoke of the insurance, Mr. Parrott had seemed to prick up his ears (which, perhaps, explained the annoyance of the secretive Penrose). But he made no remark while the latter was present, though he had evidently heard and noted what had been said for, when Penrose had gone, he asked, "Do I understand that Mr. Penrose has actually decided to insure his collection? I have repeatedly urged him to, but he has always agreed with me and then let the matter slide."

"I am afraid," said I, "that my experience is the same as yours. I advised him to insure without delay, but you heard what he said."

"I heard what he said," Parrott replied, "but it didn't convey much to me, excepting that he is still putting the business off. Which is rather foolish of him. His collection is of no great value, as collections go, but still, it represents a good deal of money, and he would suffer a substantial loss if he had a fire."

"Or a burglary," I suggested.

"There is not much risk of that," said he. "Burglars wouldn't be tempted by a collection of miscellaneous bric-a-brac, most of it identifiable and none of any considerable value. Burglars like more portable goods and things that are intrinsically valuable, such as precious metals and jewellery."

"You have seen his collection, of course?" said I.

"Yes. As a matter of fact, I supplied the greater part of it. And I gather that you have seen it, too?"

"Yes. He was good enough to show me his treasures. That was how I came to advise him about the insurance. It seemed to me very unsafe for valuable property like that to be quite unprotected."

"I shouldn't have called it very valuable property," said he. "But perhaps he has some things that I haven't seen. It would be like Mr. Penrose to keep his court-cards up his sleeve. Did he show you any really valuable pieces?"

Now, here was the very difficulty that I had foreseen. Obviously, Parrott was unaware of the existence of the hoard of jewels and coins, but he evidently suspected Penrose of possessing something more than he had disclosed. It was very unpleasant, but my promise of secrecy left me no choice. I must either lie or prevaricate.

247

"It is difficult for me to estimate values," said I, adopting the less objectionable alternative, "but some of the things that I saw must have been worth a good deal of money. There was a Saxon gold ornament, for instance. Wouldn't that be rather valuable?"

"Oh, certainly," he agreed, "but only in a modest way. I don't know what such a thing would fetch, say, at Christie's. But I think you said he was employing a valuer, and having some difficulty with him, apparently?"

"No," I replied. "His difficulty is that a regular valuation would have to be made, which would involve an inspection of his goods and the making of an inventory. He seems to object to having a valuer nosing round his premises."

"He would, naturally," said Parrott. "I have never met such an extraordinarily secretive man. But really, the valuer would not be necessary. I could draw up an estimate that would satisfy the Company – that is, if the property to be insured is only what I have seen. But, as I said, he may have some other things which he has not disclosed to me. Do you think he has?"

Here I must needs prevaricate again, but I kept as near to the truth as I could.

"It is impossible for me to guess what property he has," I said. "You know the man. I know only what he showed me."

Parrott looked dissatisfied with my answer, which was, indeed, pretty obviously evasive, and he seemed disposed to press the matter further but, at this point, Mr. Tims, having completed the assembling of the parts of the table, offered the completed work for my inspection and approval. I looked it over quickly and, having pronounced it satisfactory, took the opportunity to make my escape before Parrott should have time to propound any more questions.

As I re-entered the shop from the yard, Penrose and Polton were just passing out at the front door, the latter carrying the body of the clock and the former bearing a large parcel, which presumably contained the weights, the pendulum and the bracket. I went to the door and watched them receding down the street until they reached the corner, when Penrose, happening to glance back, observed me and greeted me with a flourish of his free hand. Then they turned the corner and disappeared from my sight, and thus, though I little guessed it at the time, did Mr. Penrose pass out of my ken forever.

For I never saw him again. A few days later, I joined the South-Eastern circuit, and thenceforth, for the next few months, passed most of my time in the county towns in which the assizes were held, and when I came back, Mr. Penrose had disappeared.

The fact was communicated to me by Mrs. Pettigrew, who, in her kindly and discreet fashion, tried to minimise the abnormal features of the affair.

"Do you mean, Mrs. Pettigrew," I exclaimed, "that he has gone away from his home and left no address or indication as to where he is to be found?"

"So I understand," she replied, "but I don't really know any of the particulars."

"But," said I, "it is a very extraordinary affair."

"It would be," said she, "in the case of any ordinary man. But you know what Mr. Penrose is. It would be quite like him, if he had occasion, say, to go abroad, to go and keep his own counsel as to where he had gone to. I believe he has done it before, though not for so long a time. I understand that on more than one occasion he has gone out in his car and driven away into the country without saying anything to his servant as to his intentions – just gone out and returned after a few days, saying nothing to anybody as to where he had been."

"Amazing!" said I. "He can't be quite in his right mind. But this affair seems rather different from the other escapades. You say he has been gone for a couple of months. It looks very much as if he had gone for good."

"It does," she agreed, and then, after a pause, she continued, "It has been a great blow to Mr. Parrott, for Mr. Penrose was by far our best customer. He was really the mainstay of the business, and now that he has gone and that we have lost poor Mr. Tims, it is very doubtful if we can carry on."

"Why, what has happened to Tims?" I asked.

"He is dead, poor old thing," she replied. "He got influenza and went out like the snuff of a candle. He was very old and frail, you know. But he was invaluable to Mr. Parrott. He was such a wonderful workman."

"Still," I said, "I suppose he can be replaced."

"Mr. Parrott thinks not," said she, "and I am afraid he is right. It is very difficult to find a real cabinet-maker in these days. The few that are left are mostly old men, and even they don't understand old furniture as Mr. Tims did. But without a skilled restorer, we can't get on at all. Mr. Parrott is an excellent judge, but he is no workman."

In short, what the absent Penrose would have called "the *psittacoid* emporium" was in a bad way. It had never been a very prosperous concern, I gathered, and indeed, I had seldom seen a stranger in the shop, but with the aid of Penrose's numerous purchases (or "investigations," as he would have described them) and the prestige of Tims's skilful restorations, it had just managed to keep afloat.

"I do hope," Mrs. Pettigrew said, rather dismally, "that we shall be able to struggle on. It will be an awful disaster for poor Joan and me if the business collapses. Of course, Mr. Parrott has not been in a position to pay me much of a salary, but Joan and I have the use of the rooms over the shop, and with her earnings as a secretary we have rubbed along quite comfortably. But it will be very different if I am earning nothing and we have only her little salary to live on, and rent to pay as well. And it will be so unfair to the poor girl, who ought to be considering her own future, to have to carry the burden of a superannuated mother."

I was very sorry for Mrs. Pettigrew and I tried to present a more hopeful picture of the financial possibilities. I also reminded her that she had my address and that it was the address of a friend. And so we parted. A little way down the street – but on the opposite side – I met Miss Joan wending homewards and observed her with a new interest. With her short hair and short skirts, her horn-rimmed spectacles and her attaché case, she was the typical Miss Twentieth Century. But as she swung along manfully, she conveyed a pleasant impression of pluck and energy and buoyant spirits, with mighty little of the "poor girl" in her aspect or bearing and, raising my hat in response to her friendly nod, I hoped that the gathering clouds might pass over her harmlessly.

But when I next visited London the blow had fallen. I made my way to the dingy little street, only to find a gang of painters disfiguring the empty shop with garish adornments. The Tropic Bird had flown. The Popinjay was no more. The vacant window greeted me with a dull, unwelcoming stare. The pleasant little rendezvous had gone out, like poor Mr. Tims, with hardly a final flicker, and Mrs. Pettigrew and Joan and Penrose and the mysterious Mr. Polton seemed to have faded out of my life like the actors in a play when the curtain has fallen.

Book II: Narrated by
Christopher Jervis, M.D.

Chapter IV
The Burglar at
Queen Square

My introduction to the strange and puzzling circumstances connected
with the disappearance of Mr. Daniel Penrose occurred in a rather casual,
almost accidental fashion. On a certain evening, at the close of the day's
work in the Law Courts, I had walked up with my colleague, Dr. John
Thorndyke, to New Square, Lincoln's Inn, to restore to our old friend,
Mr. Brodribb, some documents which it had been necessary to produce
in Court. Finding Mr. Brodribb in his office, apparently up to his eyes in
business, we handed the documents to him and, when he had checked
them, were about to depart when our friend laid down his pen, took off
his spectacles, and held up his hand to detain us.

"One moment, Thorndyke," said he. "Before you go, there is a little
matter that I should like to take your opinion on. I'll just pop on my hat
and walk with you to the corner of the Square. It is quite a trifling affair
– at least – well, I'll tell you about it as we go." He rose and, putting on
the immaculate top hat which he invariably wore in defiance of modern
fashions, stepped through into the outer office.

"I shall be back in a few minutes, Jarrett," said he, addressing his
managing clerk, and with that he led the way out.

"The matter," he began, as we emerged on to the broad pavement of
the Square, "relates to a burglary, or attempted burglary, at the house of a
man whom I may call my client, a man named Daniel Penrose, though,
actually, I am being consulted by his executor, a Mr. Horridge."

"Penrose, then, I take it, is deceased," said Thorndyke.

"No. Penrose is alive, but he is absent from his home and no one
knows where he is at the moment. So Horridge is assuming that his
position as executor authorises him to take action in the absence of the
testator."

"That doesn't seem a very sound position," Thorndyke remarked.
"But what action does he propose to take?"

251

"I had better explain the circumstances," said Brodribb. "In the first place, the man Penrose, who has a biggish house in Queen Square, is the owner of a collection, a very miscellaneous collection, I understand, all sorts of trash from old clocks to china dogs. This stuff is kept in two large rooms on the ground floor, but adjoining the main rooms is a small room which contains nothing but a table, a chair and a large cupboard or armoire. This room is usually kept locked but, by a fortunate chance, when Penrose went away he left the key in the door, and the butler, a man named Kickweed, finding it there, very properly took possession of it.

"Now, the alleged burglary occurred about ten days ago. It seems that Kickweed, making his morning round of the premises, unlocked the door of the small room to go in and inspect, when, to his astonishment, he found it bolted on the inside. Thereupon he took a pair of library steps round to the side of the house where the window of the small room looks on a narrow uncovered passage. On climbing up the steps he found the window unfastened and was able to slide it up and step over into the room. There he confirmed the fact that the door was bolted on the inside, but that, and the unfastened window, were the only signs of anything out of the ordinary. The cupboard was perfectly intact, with no traces whatever of its having been tampered with and, although there were some scratches on the table by the window, as if some hard objects had been put on it and moved about, there was nothing to show when those marks had been made."

"The cupboard, I presume, was locked?" said Thorndyke.

"Yes, and with a Chubb lock."

"And what was in the cupboard?"

"Ah!" said Brodribb, "that is the problem. No one knows what it contained or whether it contained anything. But having regard to the facts that Penrose is a collector, that he always kept this room locked and that the cupboard was fitted with a Chubb lock, the reasonable assumption is that it contained something of value."

"Yes," Thorndyke agreed, "that seems probable. But what does Mr. Horridge propose to do?"

"He would like, with my consent – I am co-executor – to have the lock picked and explore the inside of the cupboard."

"That plan seems to present difficulties," said Thorndyke. "To say nothing of the fact that a Chubb lock takes a good deal of picking, there is the objection that, as you don't know what was in the cupboard, you couldn't judge whether anything had been taken. Suppose you find it empty – you don't know that it was not empty previously. Suppose you find valuable property in it – you still don't know that nothing has been taken and, by having forced the lock, you assume a slightly uncomfortable responsibility for the safety of the contents. Why not just seal the cupboard and let Penrose do the investigating when he returns?"

"Yes," said Brodribb, with a rather dissatisfied air, as he halted at the corner of the Square and looked up at the clock above the library. "But suppose he doesn't return?" He paused for a few moments and then burst out: "The fact is, Thorndyke, that this burglary is only an incident in a most complicated and puzzling affair. There is no time to go into it now, but I should very much like, some time when you have an hour or so to spare, to put the whole case before you and hear what you have to suggest."

"I shall have an hour or so to spare – for you – this evening," said Thorndyke, "if that will suit you."

Brodribb brightened visibly. "It will suit me admirably," said he. "I will get a bit of dinner and then I will trot along to King's Bench Walk."

"You needn't do that," said Thorndyke. "Jervis and I are dining at our chambers this evening. Come along and join us. Then we shall be able to get into our conversational stride with the aid of food and a glass of wine."

Brodribb accepted gleefully and, when we had settled the time for him to arrive, he turned away towards his office. But suddenly he stopped, searching frantically in a bulging pocket-book.

"Here," said he, holding out a small piece of paper, "is something to occupy your mighty brains until we meet at dinner, when I will ask you to let me have it back."

As Thorndyke took the paper from him, he broke out into a broad smile and, turning away once more, hurried off to relieve the waiting Jarrett. My colleague looked at the paper, considered for a few moments, turned it over to glance at the back, held it up to the light and passed it to me without comment. It was a small scrap of paper – about three inches square – apparently cut off a sheet with a paper-knife, and it bore three words untidily scribbled on it with a hard pencil: "*Lobster (Hortus petasafus)*".

"Well," I exclaimed, gazing at the paper with mild astonishment, "I suppose this has some meaning, but I'm hanged if I can make any sense of it. Can you?"

He shook his head and, taking the little document from me, put it away carefully in his wallet.

"Do you suppose it is some sort of clue?" I asked.

"I don't suppose anything," he replied. "Let us wait and hear what Brodribb has to say about it. His expression suggested what school-boys call a leg-pull. But I suspect that he has something quite interesting to tell us about the absent Penrose."

Thorndyke's suspicion turned out to be correct, for, when Mr. Brodribb arrived at our chambers, dressed immaculately and accompanied by a clerk carrying a brown-paper parcel, he gave us to understand that he had some rather surprising facts to communicate.

"But," he added, "I haven't come here just to eat your dinner and waste your time with idle talk. I want you to regard this as a professional consultation."

"We will consider that question later," said Thorndyke. "Our immediate purpose is to dine but, meanwhile, I will return your rather cryptic document. I have kept a copy of it in case it may have a bearing on anything, and Jervis has made a minute study of its ostensible meaning."

"I am glad you say '*ostensible*'," chuckled Brodribb, as he stowed the document away in his pocket-book. "And what conclusions has the learned Jervis arrived at?"

"My conclusions," said I, "are not very illuminating. Broadly speaking, the inscription is damned nonsense."

"I am with you there," said Brodribb.

"Then, as to the ostensible meaning, I take it that the word '*Lobster*' means – well, it means *lobster* – "

"I'll take my Bible Oath it doesn't," Brodribb interposed.

"And as to the Latin words, *hortus*, of course, is a *garden* and *petasatus*, according to the erudite Dr. William Smith, means '*having on a travelling cap*' or, alternatively, in more general terms, '*dressed in readiness for a journey*'. Which doesn't make any sort of sense. You can't imagine a garden wearing a travelling-cap or being dressed in readiness for a journey."

"Perhaps it was the lobster that wore the cap," Thorndyke suggested, regardless of syntax. "But what is the significance of this document? I presume that it has some connection with the burglary."

"Yes, it has," Brodribb replied, "and if we could only find out what the devil it means, it might be quite an important clue. The paper was found by Kickweed, when he was examining the small room, under the table by the window. He thinks that it came from inside the cupboard, and if he is right, it furnishes evidence that the cupboard had been opened. And if we could only make any sense of the damned thing, it might give us a hint as to what had been taken."

"Yes," Thorndyke agreed, "but this is all very hypothetical. There is no evidence as to when the paper was dropped. It is quite possible that it may have been dropped by Penrose himself. But as to this cryptic inscription – As Jervis says, it probably has some meaning. Does it convey anything at all to you?"

"As to meaning, most emphatically *No*. But," Brodribb continued, grasping his wine-glass fiercely, "it impresses on me what I have always thought, is that that Daniel Penrose is an exasperating ass!"

At this outburst, Polton (our laboratory assistant and general factotum), who had just removed the covers and was in the act of re-filling Brodribb's glass, looked at the speaker with an expression of surprised interest. He even seemed disposed to linger, but as there was no excuse for his doing so, he retired slowly as if reluctant to go.

"Perhaps," Thorndyke suggested when Polton had withdrawn, "that statement might be amplified and its bearings explained. You seem to imply that the cryptic inscription was written by Penrose."

"Undoubtedly it was," Brodribb replied. "It is typical of the man. Let me explain to you what sort of fellow Penrose is, and I want you to bear his peculiarities in mind when I come to tell you my story, because they probably have an important bearing on it. Now Penrose has two outstanding oddities of character. In the first place, he is an inveterate joker. He seems incapable of speaking seriously, and the form that his facetiousness takes is in calling everything by its wrong name. The tendency seems to have grown on him until it has become a fixed habit and now his conversation is a sort of everlasting cross-word puzzle. You have to cudgel your brains when he is speaking, to guess what he really means, and the only certainty that you have is that whatever he says, you know that he means something else."

"It sounds a bit confusing," said I. "But I suppose there is some method in his madness. Could you give us an illustrative example?"

"His method," replied Brodribb, "consists in using allusive phrases, equivalents in sound or sense, or distortions or perversions of words. He would not invest his money – he would investigate it. He would not call our friend 'John Thorndyke'. He would probably describe him as 'Giovanni Brambleditch'."

"I must bear that name in mind," said I, "for use on suitable occasions. But I think I grasp the principle. It is a sort of mixture of puns and metaphors."

"Yes," agreed Brodribb, "that is roughly what it amounts to. And now as to his other eccentricity. Penrose is an extraordinarily secret man. I use the word 'extraordinarily' advisedly. We are all, as lawyers, in the habit of keeping our own counsel. But we don't make secrets of our common and simple doings. If Thorndyke wants to go to the Law Courts, he doesn't sneak out on tip-toe when there is nobody about and leave no information as to where he has gone. But that is what Penrose would do.

His habit of secrecy is as inveterate as his habit of facetiousness. He has been known to set forth from his house in his car without giving any notice to his butler or anybody else, to drive away into the country and stay away for several days – probably rooting about for bargains for his 'collection' – and come back without a word of explanation as to where he had been. I assure you that when I had to draft his will, I had the greatest difficulty in extracting from him any intelligible particulars of the property that was to be disposed of."

"It is rather remarkable," said Thorndyke, "that he should have made a will at all."

"It is," agreed Brodribb. "Men of that type usually die intestate. And thereby hangs another part of the tale that I have to tell. But I repeat that it is most necessary to bear these oddities of character in mind in connection with what has happened. And now, I will drop Penrose for the present and let you finish your dinners in peace."

I think that Brodribb's resolution to change the subject occasioned some disappointment to Polton, for that cunning artificer developed an unprecedented degree of attentiveness, which caused him to make frequent incursions into the room for the ostensible purpose of filling wine-glasses and performing other unnecessary services. His obvious interest in our rather trivial conversation caused me some slight surprise at the time. But later events explained his curiosity.

When we had finished dinner, and before removing the debris, he drew the three easy chairs up to the fire, placed a small table by that which was assigned to Brodribb, and deposited on it the invariable decanter of port and three wine-glasses. Then he proceeded to clear the table by small instalments and by methods strikingly at variance with his usual swift economy of time and labour. But his procrastination was all in vain, for not until the table was cleared to the last vestige and Polton had made his final and reluctant disappearance, did Brodribb make the slightest allusion to the subject of our consultation.

Then, when the door had closed, the glasses had been filled and Thorndyke and I had produced our pipes, he extracted a slip of paper from his pocket-book and laid it on the table by his side, fortified himself with a sip of wine, and opened the proceedings.

Chapter V
Mr. Brodribb
Propounds a Problem

"The circumstances connected with Penrose's disappearance," Mr. Brodribb began, "are so complicated that I hardly know in what order I should present them."

"Probably," suggested Thorndyke, "the simplest plan would be to deal with the events in their chronological sequence."

"Yes," Brodribb agreed, "that would probably be the best way. I can refer back to previous occurrences if necessary. Then we will begin with the seventeenth of last October, roughly three months ago. On that day, in the early afternoon, he started out from home in his car and, contrary to his usual practice, he told Kickweed that he did not expect to be back until rather late. He directed that no one should sit up for him, but that a cold supper should be left in the dining room. As to where he was going or on what business, he naturally gave no hint, but we are justified in assuming that he started forth with the intention of returning that night. But he did not return and, so far as we know, he was never seen again by anybody who was acquainted with him."

"Your description," said Thorndyke, "seems to suggest that he is a bachelor."

"Yes," replied Brodribb, "he is a bachelor and, with the exception of an aged father, to whom I shall refer presently, he seems to have no very near relations. Horridge, his executor, is a somewhat distant cousin and a good deal younger man. Well, then, to repeat, on the day that I have mentioned, having given this very vague information to his butler, he went off to his garage, got his car out, closed up the garage and departed. Kickweed saw him drive away past the house, and that was the last that was seen of him by any person who knew him.

"His next appearance was in very remarkable circumstances. At midnight on that same day, or in the early hours of the next, a gentleman, a resident of Gravesend, who was returning home from Chatham in his car, saw a man lying face downwards on a heap of gravel by the roadside. The gentleman pulled up and got out to see what had happened, and as the man seemed to be either dead or unconscious, and there was nobody about excepting a rather squiffy labourer, he carefully lifted the man, with the labourer's assistance, put him into his car, and conveyed him to the hospital at Gravesend, which was about a mile-and-a-half from the place where he picked him up. At the hospital it was found that the man was alive though insensible, and on this the gentleman, a Mr. Barnaby, went away, leaving the hospital authorities to give information to the police.

"The injured man appeared to be suffering from concussion. He had evidently fallen on the gravel with great violence, for his face was a mass of bruises and both his eyes were completely closed by the swelling due to the contusions. There was a deep, ragged wound across his right eyebrow in which the house surgeon had to put a couple of stitches, and there were various other bruises about his person, suggesting that he had been knocked down by some passing vehicle, but there appeared to be no broken bones or other severe injuries. The visiting surgeon, however, seems to have suspected the existence of a fracture of the base of the skull and, on this account, directed that the patient should be kept very quiet and not questioned or disturbed in any way.

"The next day he still appeared to be unconscious, or nearly so, though he took the small amount of nourishment that was offered. But he answered no questions and, by reason of the suspected fracture, no particular attempts were made to rouse him. And so the day passed. On the following day, the nineteenth, he remained in much the same condition, speechless and somnolent, lying nearly motionless, taking no notice of anything that was occurring around him and giving no answers to questions.

"But about eight o'clock at night he roused quite suddenly and very completely, for he seemed at once to be in full possession of his senses. But what is more, he proceeded to get out of bed and demanded his clothes, declaring that he was quite well and intended to leave the hospital and go about his business. As you may suppose, there was a mighty hubbub.

"The house surgeon absolutely forbade the patient to leave the hospital and at first refused to let him have his clothes. But the man persisted that he was going, clothes or no clothes. Well, of course, they had no power to detain him, so the end of it was that they produced his clothes, and when he had dressed himself they gave him a light meal and took the particulars of his name and address and what little he could tell them of the circumstances of his accident. But of this he knew practically nothing. All he could tell them was that some vehicle had come on him from behind and knocked him down, and he remembered no more.

"When he had finished his meal and made his statement, such as it was, he asked for his overcoat. But there was no overcoat with his clothes, though the ward sister remembered that he was wearing one when he was brought in. Apparently, a patient who had been discharged earlier in the evening must have taken it by mistake, for there was a spare overcoat of the same kind – the ordinary raincoat, such as you may see by the dozen in any street, and it was suggested that he should take this in exchange for his own. But he would not agree to this, and eventually, as it was a mild night, he was allowed to go as he was.

"Now, he had not been gone more than an hour when the man who had taken the wrong coat brought it back. He had discovered his mistake by finding in the pocket a motorist's driving licence. But the odd thing was that the name and address on the licence did not agree with those that the departed patient had given. And yet there seemed to be no doubt that it was the missing coat, for the night nurse remembered the daubs of mud that she had noticed on it when she had undressed the patient. Moreover, she now recalled that the collar which she had taken off him had borne the initials '*D.P.*' in Roman capitals, apparently written with a marking-ink pencil.

"But there was an evident discrepancy. The patient had given the name of Joseph Blewitt, with an address somewhere in Camden Town, but the name on the licence was Daniel Penrose and the address was his address in Queen Square.

"It was certainly a facer. The coat had to be returned to its owner. But who was its owner? The secretary decided that it was not his business to solve that problem and, moreover, as there seemed to be something a trifle queer about the affair, he thought it best to communicate with the police. But as it was rather late and there seemed to be no urgency in the matter, he put it off until the following morning, and when the morning came, the police saved him the trouble by calling to make inquiries. And then something still more queer came to light.

"That morning, early, a patrol had discovered an abandoned car backed into the bushes at the bottom of an unfrequented lane leading down to the marshes a mile or so outside Gravesend. On making inquiries, he learned that it had been there all the previous day, for it had been seen by some boys who had gone down to the marshes on their probably unlawful occasions. They had taken no special notice of it, assuming that the owner had gone off on some business into the village in the irresponsible way that motorists have of leaving their cars unattended. But the boys could not say when it had arrived, as they had not been to the marshes on the day before. However, when the patrol pushed his inquiries in the village, he heard of the accident and of the man who had been picked up on the road not very far away. Thereupon, he took possession of the car and brought it into the town, lodging it, for the time being, in the garage belonging to the police station. And then he came on to the hospital to interview the injured man. But the bird had flown and only the coat with the driving licence remained.

"And then, once more, the plot thickened. For the name on the insurance certificate which was found in the car was the same as that on the licence, and if – as seemed nearly certain – the coat belonged to the departed patient, then that patient had given a false name and address. And this turned out to be the fact. No such person as Joseph Blewitt was known at the Camden Town address, and on inquiring at Daniel Penrose's house, it was ascertained that the said Daniel had left home in his car in the early afternoon of the day on which the injured man had been brought into the hospital and had not since been seen or heard of.

"As to what had become of that injured man, all that they could discover was that he – or, at least, a man with two black eyes and generally answering to the description – had taken a first-class ticket to London shortly after the time at which the patient had left the hospital, and that a man, apparently the same, had got out at New Cross. But they could get no farther. From the time when he passed the barrier at New Cross all trace of him was lost."

"Did the police make any efforts to follow him up?" Thorndyke asked.

"At the moment, I don't think they did. Why should they? So far as they then knew, the man had committed no offence. He was no business of theirs. If he chose to vamoose, he was quite entitled to."

"I need not ask if you know of any reason that he may have had for disappearing?"

"Ah!" said Brodribb, "now we come to the inwardness of the affair. I have told the story in the actual order of events and, at the time when he bolted from the hospital, there seemed no reason for his sneaking off and hiding himself. But, a day or two later, some other facts transpired which threw an entirely new light on his behaviour.

"It appeared that early in the morning of the eighteenth, the day after that on which he left home – and, incidentally, was picked up on the road – the dead body of an old woman was found in a dry ditch at the side of a by-road leading to the main road from Ashford to Maidstone. From the condition of the body as to *rigor mortis* and temperature, the police surgeon inferred that she had been dead about six hours, which, as the body was discovered at about five o'clock in the morning, roughly fixes the time of her death at eleven o'clock on the previous night. Of the cause of death there seemed to be no doubt. She had been knocked down by a motor, the driver of which had either been unaware of what had happened or had cleared off to avoid trouble. The latter seemed the more probable for, not only must the force of the impact have been terrific to fling the poor old creature right across the grass verge into the ditch, but the tracks of a car, which were plainly visible in the lane, showed it to have been zigzagging wildly and to have actually struck the grass verge at the point where the accident must have occurred.

"At first, it looked as if the motorist had got away without leaving a recognisable trace. But when the police came to make inquiries, they picked up some important information from the attendant at a filling station at Maidstone. He recalled that, a little after eleven o'clock on the night of the old woman's death, a car had come to his establishment for a refill of petrol. It was apparently travelling from the direction of Ashford, and there were certain circumstances connected with the car and the driver which had attracted his attention. He had noticed, for instance, that the near-side mudguard was badly bent, and there was earth on the wheels, as if the car had been run over a ploughed field. He had also observed that the driver – who was alone in the car – looked rather pale and shaken, and seemed to be excited or agitated. Moreover, he smelt strongly of drink, and the man was of opinion that the liquor was not whisky, but smelt more like '*sherry wine*'. These facts, taken together, made him suspect that the motorist had been in trouble and he very wisely made a note of the number of the car and had a good look at the driver. His description of the man is not very illuminating, excepting that he noticed the muddy state of the raincoat, which the nurse had mentioned. But the number of the car gave all the necessary information. It was that of Daniel Penrose's car and, sure enough, in confirmation of the identity, was the fact that the left mud-guard of Penrose's car was badly bent and there was a quantity of earth on the wheels. And there is a bit of further evidence, for it appears that Penrose was stopped by a police patrol on the top of Bluebell Hill, on the Maidstone-Rochester Road, and asked to show his licence, which explains how the licence came to be in his raincoat pocket. When you consider the devil of a hurry that he was in, you can understand that he would just shove it into the nearest pocket.

"Well, the final phase of the affair – so far – was the inquest on the old woman. Naturally, when they had heard the evidence of the police and the man from the petrol-filling station, the jury found a verdict of manslaughter against some person unknown."

"Unknown!" I repeated. "Then they did not mention Penrose by name?"

"No," replied Brodribb. "The coroner knew his business better than many coroners do. He directed the jury to confine their finding to the facts that had been definitely proved and leave the identification of the offender to the police. But I need not say that the police are keeping a bright look-out for Daniel Penrose.

"So there, you see, we have an explanation of the initial disappearance. Perhaps, not a very reasonable one, but then Penrose is not a very reasonable man. But that explanation does not quite clear up the mystery. He disappeared about three months ago and since then has made no sign. Now, we can understand his bolting off in a panic, but it is less easy to understand his remaining in hiding. On reflection he must have seen that he was really in no great danger, even if he did actually knock the poor old woman down, which is by no means certainly the case. There were no witnesses of the accident. If he chose to deny that he was in any way concerned in it, it would be impossible to prove that he was. He might even have denied that he was ever on that particular road at all."

"You mentioned," said Thorndyke, "that there were distinct tracks of motor tyres. Probably they would be identifiable."

"That would not be conclusive," Brodribb replied. "It would only prove that the tyres were of the same make. But, even if he admitted that he had caused the old woman's death, still, in the absence of witnesses, he could give any account that he pleased of the disaster. Carelessness on the part of the pedestrian is usually quite satisfactory to a coroner or his jury."

"I don't think the matter is as simple as that," Thorndyke objected. "I agree with you that there has been a most amazing indifference to the value of human life since the coming of the motor car. But this was an exceptionally bad case. The man had been drinking, he must have known that he had knocked the woman down, but yet he drove on callously, leaving her to die uncared for, and did not even report the accident. Whatever the coroner's verdict might have been, the police would certainly have prosecuted, and the man would almost inevitably have been committed for trial. But at the assizes he would have had to deal with a judge, and judges, as a rule – to which there are, I admit, one or two remarkable exceptions – take a reasonable and legal view of the killing of a human being."

"Well, even so," Brodribb rejoined, "what does it amount to? Supposing he had been convicted of manslaughter? It might have been a matter of six months' hard labour, or even twelve. It could hardly have been more. Killing with a motor car is accepted as something different from any other kind of killing."

"But," said I, "he would not be particularly keen on twelve months' imprisonment with hard labour."

"No," Brodribb agreed, "but what is the alternative? To say nothing of the fact that he is pretty certain to be caught, sooner or later, what is his present condition? He – a well-to-do man, accustomed to every luxury – is a wanderer and a fugitive, hiding in obscure places by day and sneaking out in terror by night. It must be a dreadful existence, and how the devil he is living and what he is living on, is beyond my powers to imagine, seeing that, when he went off, he had, presumably, nothing more about him than the few pounds that he would ordinarily carry in his pockets."

"I suppose," Thorndyke said, reflectively, "it has not occurred to you to connect that fact with the burglary?"

Brodribb looked at him in evident surprise.

"I don't think," said he, "that I quite understand what you mean. What connection could there be?"

"'I am only throwing out the suggestion," replied Thorndyke, "as a bare possibility. But the house seems undoubtedly to have been entered, and entered by a person who appears to have been acquainted with it. The entry was made into the small room, and that room was clearly the objective, as is proved by the fact that the door was bolted on the inside. Then the person who entered apparently knew what was in that room. But, so far as we know, the contents of that room were known only to Penrose. If the cupboard was opened, it was opened with a key, for it is practically impossible to pick a Chubb lock, and a burglar would not have tried. He would have used his jemmy and forced the door."

"By Jove, Thorndyke!" Brodribb exclaimed, slapping the table, at the risk of spilling the wine, "you have solved the mystery! It never occurred to me that the burglar might be Penrose himself. But your suggestion fits the case to a T. Here is poor old Penrose, penniless and perhaps starving. He knows that in that cupboard is portable property of very substantial value. He has the key of the cupboard in his pocket and he knows that he can get into the room easily by just slipping back the catch of the window with a knife. Of course it was Penrose. I was a damned blockhead not to have thought of it before. But you see, Thorndyke, I haven't got your criminal mind."

But Thorndyke, having made the suggestion, proceeded to sprinkle a little cold water on Brodribb's enthusiasm.

"It isn't a certainty," said he, "and we mustn't treat it as one. It is a reasonable and probable hypothesis, but we may think of others when we consider the matter further. However, the immediate question is what you want me to do."

"You can guess that," chuckled Brodribb, as I refilled his glass. "What do I always want you to do when I come here taking up your

263

valuable time and drinking your excellent port? I want you to perform miracles and do impossibilities. It seems a pretty large order, I admit, even for you, seeing that the police are unable to locate Penrose, but I am going to ask you to exercise your remarkable power of resolving insoluble riddles and just tell us where he is."

"But why trouble to hunt him up?" Thorndyke objected. "He probably knows his own business best."

"I am not so sure that he does," Brodribb retorted. "But, in any case, it is not his business that is specially agitating me. There are some other people whose interests are affected and one of them is keeping me very effectively stirred up. However, I suppose I mustn't inflict on you details of the purely civil aspects of the case."

It was easy to gather from the apologetic tone of the concluding sentence and the wistful glance that he cast at Thorndyke that he wanted very much to inflict those details, and I was not surprised when my colleague replied, "It wouldn't be an infliction, Brodribb. On the contrary, it would be both interesting and helpful to have a complete picture of the case."

"I suspect," said Brodribb, "that you are only being beastly polite, but I will take you at your word. After all, the civil aspects are part of the problem and they may be more relevant than I realise. So here goes.

"I spoke just now of Daniel Penrose's aged father and I mentioned that there were no other near relations. Now, Penrose Senior, Oliver by name, is a very remarkable old gentleman. He is over ninety years of age, but surprisingly well preserved. Up to a week or two ago, he was, mentally and physically, the equal of an ordinary man of sixty. That was his condition at the time of Daniel's disappearance, lively and active, apparently going strong for his hundredth birthday.

"But, within the last fortnight, the old man has been taken ill – a slight touch of influenza. It appeared at first, that seemed to offer no particular cause for anxiety. But you know what these hale and robust nonagenarians are. They dodder along peacefully, looking as if they were going to live forever, until, one fine day, something gives them a shake up and puts them out of their stride, and then they just quietly fade away. Well, that is what is happening to old Penrose. He doesn't seem particularly ill. But he shows no sign of recovering. Suddenly, the weight of his years seems to have descended on him and he is gradually fading out. It is practically certain that he will die within the next few weeks and, when he does die, some very curious complications are going to arise.

"Oliver Penrose is what we humble professional people would call a rather rich man. Nothing on the commercial scale of wealth. Nothing of the millionaire order. But there will be an estate, mostly personal, of over a hundred-and-fifty-thousand pounds. And so far as we know, that estate is not disposed of by will. The old man was rather obstinate about it, though there was some reason in his contention that it was a waste of trouble to make a will leaving the estate to the next of kin, who would inherit without a will. However, that question is of no importance for, in any case, Penrose Junior would come into the property. If there is a will, he will be the principal beneficiary, and if there is no will, he is the next of kin and, being the only child, will take the bulk of the estate.

"And now you see the difficulty. Daniel has made a will leaving a considerable proportion of his property to his cousin, Francis Horridge, who is also one of the executors and the residuary legatee. Daniel is not as rich as his father, but they are a well-to-do family and he has some fifty-thousand pounds of his own. So Horridge will not do so badly if he should survive Daniel, which he is likely to do, as he is over twenty years younger. But he wants to do better. On the old man's death, the bulk of his property will, as I said, come to Daniel and, as Daniel's will at present stands, it will fall into the residue of the estate and thus, eventually, come to Horridge.

"But there is a snag. Daniel has disappeared, but the old man is still alive. Now, suppose that Daniel elects to disappear for good. The thing is possible. He may have some resources that are unknown to us. It would be like him to have a secret banking account in a false name, and he may be in such a funk of criminal prosecution that he may never dare to come to the surface again. Well, suppose he remains in hiding. Suppose he has gone abroad or into some entirely new surroundings and has the means to go on living there, just see what a hideous mess will be created. In the first place, there will be an indefinite delay in distributing the old man's estate. Daniel is the next of kin (or else the principal beneficiary, if there should be a will). But his share cannot be allotted until it is proved that he is alive, and it cannot be otherwise disposed of until he is either proved or presumed to be dead. And, similarly, his own will cannot be administered so long as he is presumably alive."

"If he remains absent long enough," Thorndyke remarked, "the interested parties will probably apply for permission to presume his death."

"Well," retorted Brodribb, "they certainly wouldn't get it at present, or for a long time to come. If Daniel remains in hiding, the whole business may be hung up for years. But even if they do, later, succeed in getting his death presumed, another and still worse complication will have to be dealt with. For, of course, the question of survivorship will be raised. Oliver's next of kin will naturally contend that Daniel died before the old man and that he could, therefore, not have inherited the old man's property, in which case, Horridge stands to lose the best part of a hundred-and--housand pounds. And that, I may say, is where I come in. Horridge is in a most frightful twitter for fear Daniel should slip away for good and perhaps die somewhere under a false name. He wants to find Daniel, or at least ascertain that he is alive, and he is prepared to spend untold gold on the search. He has tried to ginger up the police and induce them to set up a hue-and-cry, regardless of poor old Daniel's feelings. But the police are not enthusiastic, as they have no conclusive evidence against him, even if they were able to locate him. So he has fallen back on me, and I have fallen back on you. And now the question is, are you prepared to take up the case?"

I had expected that Thorndyke would return a prompt refusal, for there seemed absolutely nothing to go on. To my surprise, he replied with a qualified acceptance, though he was careful to point out the difficulties.

"It is not very clear to me," said he, "that I can give you much help. You must see for yourself that this is really a police case. For the tracing of a missing man, the police have all the facilities as well as the necessary knowledge and experience. I have no facilities at all. Any inquiries that I may wish to make I must make through them."

"Yes, I see that," said Brodribb, "and, of course, I am not really asking you to perform miracles. I don't expect you to go outside and put your nose down on the pavement and forthwith make a bee-line for Daniel's hiding-place. But it occurs to me that you may be able to approach the matter from a different direction and by different methods from those of the police."

"That is possible," Thorndyke admitted, "but even a medico-legal investigator cannot get on without evidence of some kind, and there seems to be practically nothing to lay hold of. Do you know where the car is?"

"In Daniel's garage. It was taken there and locked up as soon as the police had made their examination of it."

"Do you know whether anything was found in it?"

"I have heard of nothing excepting a large empty flask which had, apparently, once contained brown sherry."

"Do you know whether the car has been cleaned since it was returned?"

"I am pretty sure that it has not. Penrose was his own chauffeur and did all the cleaning himself."

"Then you spoke of a raincoat. What has become of that?"

"It is in the parcel that I brought with me and which I put on the table in the lobby. It was delivered at Daniel's house by the police when they had looked it over, and Kickweed handed it to Horridge, who at once locked it up, and later, at my request, transferred it to me. I knew you would want to see it."

"Was anything found in the pockets?"

"There was the driving licence, as I told you. Beyond that there was nothing but the stump of a lead pencil, a wooden cigarette-holder, and what looked like a fragment of a broken flower-pot. And I may say that those things are still in the pockets. So far as I know, the coat is in exactly the condition in which it was found."

"We will have a look at it presently," said Thorndyke, "though it doesn't seem likely that we shall extract much information from it."

"It certainly does not," I agreed, heartily, "and the little information it may yield can hardly have much bearing on what we want to know. It won't tell us what Penrose's intentions may have been, or where he is now."

"Oh, don't say that!" exclaimed Brodribb. "I had hoped that Thorndyke would practise some of his wizardry on that coat and make it tell us all that we want to know about Daniel. And I hope so still, notwithstanding your pessimism. At any rate," he added, glancing at my colleague, "you are going to give us a run for our money? You agree to that?"

"Yes," Thorndyke replied, "just as a forlorn hope. It is nothing more, and it is unlikely that I shall have more success than the police. Still, I will sort out the facts, such as they are, and see if they offer us any kind of opening for an investigation. I suppose I can see the car?"

"Certainly, you can. I will tell Kickweed to let you have the key of the garage and to give you any help that you may ask for. Is there anything that you will want me to do?"

"I think," replied Thorndyke, "that, as Penrose is quite unknown to me, I had better have a description of his person, and it should be as minute and exhaustive as possible, and if a photograph of him is available, I should like to have that, too."

"Very well," said Brodribb, "I will get a description of Daniel from Horridge and Kickweed, separately, and write out another from my own observations. I will let you have the three, so that you can compare them, and I will try to get you a photograph. And that," he concluded, emptying his glass with relish, and rising, "is all, for the present, and I may say that, despite Jervis's pessimism, you have taken a load of anxiety off my shoulders. Experience has taught me that when John Thorndyke starts an investigation, the problem is as good as solved."

Chapter VI
Thorndyke Examines
the Relics

As we returned from the landing to which we had escorted Mr. Brodribb, I took up the parcel from the lobby table and conveyed it to the sitting room.

"Well, Thorndyke," I remarked, as I deposited it on the table under the electric light, "you seem to have let yourself in for a proper wild-goose chase."

He paused in the act of digging out his pipe to regard me with an approving smile.

"That is rather happily expressed, Jervis," said he, "having regard to the personal peculiarities of our quarry. But we are not actually committed to chasing him."

"I can't imagine why you undertook the case," I continued. "There is absolutely nothing to go on."

"That is how it strikes me," he agreed placidly, blowing through the pipe preparatory to refilling. "But we couldn't refuse Brodribb."

"The few facts that we have," I went on doggedly, "are all totally irrelevant. Our information stops short exactly at the point where the problem begins. Take this coat, for instance. Here is a fool – and a frightened, artful, secretive fool at that – who does a bolt and leaves his coat behind, and we are offered that coat as a guide to the particular bolt-hole that he has gone down. The thing is ridiculous. If it had been a question of where he had come from, the coat might have told us something. But obviously it can bear no traces of the place that he intended to go to."

"That is perfectly true," Thorndyke admitted, "but it might be worthwhile to find out whence he had come, if that were possible."

"I don't see why," I objected, adding hurriedly, to anticipate the inevitable reply, "Of course you will say that the significance of a fact cannot be judged until the fact is known, but still, I really cannot see any possible connection between the place whence he came and the place whither he went, especially as the circumstances had changed in the interval."

"Nor can I," said Thorndyke. "But yet it is possible that there may be some connection. It is evident that Penrose started out with a definite objective. He was going to a particular place with some defined purpose, and it seems to me at least conceivable that if we could discover whither he went and on what business, that knowledge might be helpful. Of course, it probably would not, but seeing that we know nothing of the habits and mode of life of this curious, eccentric, and secretive man, our only course is to pick up any stray facts concerning him that may come within our reach."

"Yes," I agreed, without much conviction, "and I take it that what is in your mind is that when he bolted he probably made for some place that was known to him and where he believed that he could hide in safety."

"Exactly," Thorndyke agreed. "If we could discover some of his haunts, we might have a clue to a possible hiding-place."

"It may be so," I rejoined, "and if that is your view, I suppose you will begin by seeing what you can glean from this coat." And with this I proceeded to untie the string and open the parcel.

The coat, when I lifted it out and unrolled it, was seen to be amazingly dirty. It was not merely splashed with mud. On the sleeves and around the bottom of the skirt were great daubs of thick dirt mingled with a number of whitish marks such as might have been produced by contact with wet chalk.

"It is extraordinary," said I, holding the coat up for Thorndyke's inspection. "The fellow seems to have been positively wallowing in the mire."

"Not exactly in the mire," said Thorndyke, looking closely at the great daubs. "This is not road dirt. It is earth, and the earth seems to have been mixed with particles of chalk. Perhaps we had better empty the pockets before we proceed with the examination of the coat."

I thrust my hand into the two pockets and drew out from one the driving licence, crumpled, smeared, and marked with the prints of dirty fingers, and from the other a stump of lead pencil, a cigarette-holder, and what looked like a fragment of a broken tile. But it was so encrusted with earth that it was difficult to see exactly what it was.

"Brodribb's description," said I, as I handed it to Thorndyke, "doesn't seem to fit. This is certainly not a fragment of a flower-pot. It is too dark in colour. It looks to me more like part of a tile."

Thorndyke took it from me and examined it closely in the bright light of the electric lamp.

"I don't think it is a tile, Jervis," said he, "but we shall see better when we get it clean. The interesting point about it is that the earth in which it is embedded seems to be similar to that on the coat, a mixture of loam and small fragments of chalk – a sort of chalk rubble. We will brush off the earth when we have looked over the other things."

He laid it in a small cardboard tray and put it aside on the mantel-shelf. Then he turned his attention to the cigarette-tube which I held in my hand.

"There," said I, handing it to him, "is another example of excellent but quite irrelevant clues."

"How irrelevant?" he asked. "And irrelevant to what?"

"To the subject of our inquiry," I replied. "Here is a highly distinctive object, for it was certainly never bought at a shop. As evidence in a case of doubtful identity, it would be quite valuable. But it is of no use to us. It gives us no hint as to where its owner is at present hiding."

Thorndyke smiled indulgently. "We mustn't expect too much, Jervis," said he. "In fact, we have no reason to expect anything. We are just looking over this jetsam as a matter of routine to note any facts that it may seem to suggest, without regard to their apparent relevancy or irrelevancy to our inquiry. You cannot judge the relevancy of an isolated fact. Experience has taught me, and must have taught you, that the most trivial, commonplace, and seemingly irrelevant facts have a way of suddenly assuming a crucial importance by connecting, explaining, or filling in the detail of later discoveries.

"Take this cigarette-tube, for instance. It appears to be the property of Daniel Penrose. But how did he come by it? As you say, it was certainly not bought in the ordinary way at a shop. There is no suggestion of mass-production about it. It is an individual thing made by a particular person, and probably there is not another like it in the world. But if we look at it attentively, we can form some idea of the kind of person who made it, and can even suggest the probable circumstances in which it was made. Thus, it is composed of a very hard, heavy, black wood, much like ebony in character, but with a slight brownish tinge instead of the characteristic dead black. Probably it is African ebony. It is competently turned but with no special display of skill. The mouthpiece has been shaped with a chisel, whereas you or I would have used a file on such a very hard material. The suggestion is that the chisel was a tool to which the maker was accustomed and which he used with facility. Then the rather artless but quite pleasant decoration consists of a pattern of circular white spots, each an eighth-of-an-inch in diameter, made, apparently, by boring holes probably with a Morse drill – right through the half-finished piece and driving into them little dowels of holly or some other white hardwood, which would be cut off flush when the work was finished in the lathe. Then there is the suggestion that the tube was made from odd scrap of wood, left over from some larger work."

"How do you arrive at that? I asked.

"I think," he replied, "it is suggested by this little streak of sapwood. It is a distinct blemish, and one feels that it would have been avoided if a larger piece of wood had been available. So you see that the impression we get is of a workman who was handy with a paring-chisel but also had some skill as a turner, possibly a joiner or cabinet-maker, who had a lathe in his workshop."

"Yes," I agreed, "he may have been and, on the other hand, he may not. I don't see that it matters. He is not our pigeon. What seems to me of more interest – though mighty little at that – is that there is a good-sized stump of a cigarette still in the tube. It looks as if Penrose had dropped the holder in his pocket with the cigarette still alight, and if he did that – in a motor car, with plenty of petrol vapour about – he must have been either drunk or frightened out of his wits.

"What is the next proceeding?"

"I think," said he, as he deposited the licence, the cigarette-tube, and the stump of pencil provisionally in a cardboard box, "we had better collect as much earth as we can get off the coat to examine at our leisure. We shall want one or two photographic dishes, a clean toothbrush, a glass funnel, a wide-mouthed jar, and a few filter-papers. Do you mind getting them while I damp the coat?"

I ran up to the laboratory and collected these articles, and when I returned with them I found Thorndyke with the coat spread out on the table, cautiously damping the larger mud-stains with a sponge, and we at once fell to work on the rather dirty and not very thrilling task of transferring the mud from the coat to one of the dishes, which I had partly filled with water. But the quantity that we collected by scraping with a paper-knife and brushing off into the water was quite surprising, and when, from the state of liquid mud in the dish, it was transformed into wet earth on a filter-paper, it at once took on the character of a definite and recognisable type of soil.

"That," said Thorndyke as he carefully removed the filter-paper from the funnel and set it on a blotting-pad to drain, "we can examine later and, if necessary, with the aid of an expert geological opinion. It appears to be a rather fine reddish loam a little like the Thanet sands, with a few minute white particles, apparently chalk. But we shall see. And now let us take a look at Brodribb's alleged flower-pot."

He brought the tray from the mantelpiece and, taking out the fragment, cautiously wetted its surface. Then, having first carefully washed the toothbrush, he proceeded to brush the earth from the pottery fragment into a small dish until it was completely clean and, having dried its surface with blotting-paper and his handkerchief, put it aside while he collected the detached earth-on a filter-paper.

"You notice, Jervis," said he as he opened out the filter-paper on the blotting-pad, "that it seems to be the same soil as that on the coat. There are more chalk particles and they are larger, but that is what we should expect, as the larger particles would have less tendency to adhere to the coat. And now let us have your considered opinion on this fragment."

I took it from him and examined it with a decent pretence of interest (and an inward conviction that it didn't matter tuppence what it was).

"I still think," said I, "that it looks like a piece of tile. The material is as coarse as brick and it has a slight curvature like that of an old hand-made tile. But I don't quite understand what those marks are. They are evidently not accidental."

"No," he agreed, "and I think they exclude your diagnosis, and so does the definite thickening at the edge. But let us proceed systematically. I find it a help to a thorough examination of an object to describe it in detail as if one were preparing an entry in a museum catalogue."

I agreed warmly and invited him to go ahead.

"Very well," said he. "If you feel unequal to the effort, the task devolves upon me. We will take the physical properties in regular order, beginning with the general character.

"This is a fragment of pottery of excessively coarse and crude quality, consisting of a reddish buff matrix in which are embedded numerous angular white particles which have the appearance of burnt flint. The texture is somewhat porous, and there is no trace of a glaze on either surface. On taking it in the hand, and allowing for the fact that it is wet, we find it noticeably heavy.

"Size and shape: The fragment forms an irregular oblong, approximately an inch-and-a-half long by three-quarters wide. Of the four sides, three are fractured – recently, you notice – and the fourth – one of the long sides – is thickened into a definite flange or rim, roughly T-shaped in section. The thickness, as shown by the calliper gauge, varies from five-thirty-seconds-of-an-inch at the thinnest broken edge to eleven-thirty-seconds on the thick unbroken edge.

"On the thick edge are five indented marks such as might have been made with a blunt knife on the soft clay, roughly a quarter-of-an-inch apart, and on the convex surface, next to the long broken edge, are four similar linear indentations, roughly half-an-inch apart and at right angles to the thickened edge.

"The fragment is curved in both diameters, rather irregularly, but still quite definitely. Let us see, approximately, what those curvatures amount to."

272

He took a sheet of writing-paper and placed the fragment on it, standing up on its thick edge and, with a sharp pencil, carefully traced the outline. The tracing showed the curvature very distinctly, and it became still more obvious when he placed a straightedge against the concave side and connected the two ends with a ruled line. Then he produced a pair of compasses furnished with a pencil and, setting the pencil-point on one end of the ruled line, was able, after one or two trials, to strike an arc which passed through both ends of the line and followed the curve of the tracing. On measuring the distance from the centre to the arc, it was found to be three inches and an eighth.

"We see, then," said he, "that the curve has a radius of three-inches-and-an-eighth, so that it seems to be part of a circle, six-inches-and-a-quarter in diameter. Now, let us try the other curvature."

He stood the fragment up on one of its short ends and made a tracing as before. Measurement of this showed a curve with a radius of two-inches-three-quarters.

"We can't take this last measurement very seriously," said he, "as the curve is so very short and irregular. But you see that we now have the material for a fairly reliable reconstruction of the object of which this fragment formed a part. It appears to have been an earthenware vessel of the very coarsest and crudest type, with curved sides – some kind of bowl or pot – approximately six inches across the top, or mouth, and possibly about three inches high. But the height is a matter of mere guess-work. The irregularity in the curvature of the mouth makes it pretty certain that the vessel was built by hand, not thrown on the wheel, and this suggestion is confirmed by the extremely crude and primitive decoration. The thickened rim of the mouth is ornamented by a series of linear markings about a quarter-of-an-inch apart, made, apparently, by indenting with a blunt knife, or perhaps a long thumb-nail, on the soft clay, and there is another series of similar markings, a little wider apart, which encircles the vessel about half-an-inch below the rim.

"There, Jervis, is a summary of the characteristics which enable us to form a reasonably exact picture of the object which yielded this fragment. Taking them together and in conjunction with the fact that the fragment was found in the pocket of a man who is known to be a collector of antiquities, what conclusion do you arrive at?"

"Concerning the object? Well, I suppose we must conclude that the pot or bowl must have been an extremely ancient vessel, perhaps prehistoric. It would hardly be Roman."

"No," he agreed. "Roman pottery was the product of a developed industry with quite advanced technical methods. This was quite a primitive piece of work, certainly pre-Roman, I should say, and more probably neolithic than Bronze Age. But that is a question which we can easily settle by inquiries or reference to published work."

"Yes," said I, "and when you have settled it, you will be exactly where you are now, so far as the abiding-place of Daniel Penrose is concerned, and where you were before you carried out this very interesting little investigation. You will have established a fact that can have no possible bearing on the problem that you are asked to solve."

"Who knows?" he retorted. "We have learned that Penrose had in his pocket a fragment of ancient pottery. It is not likely that he picked it up by chance on the road, and if he did not, it is possible that we may have here a clue to the purpose with which he set out on his travels on the day when he disappeared."

"But," I persisted, "even if you knew that, you would be no more forward. He certainly did not set out with the purpose of killing an old woman and becoming a fugitive from the law. You would just have another irrelevant fact."

He smiled as he dropped the fragment into the box, together with the two filter-papers. "It is quite likely that you are right, Jervis," said he. "But we have already agreed that the relevancy of a fact often fails to be perceived until the appearance of some further facts brings its significance into view. It is always much easier to be wise after the event."

With this, he deposited the cardboard box in the drawer of a cabinet, while I hung the wet coat on a peg in the lobby. Then we disposed ourselves in our respective chairs to smoke the final pipe before turning in and, dismissing the affairs of Daniel Penrose, chatted somewhat discursively on the morning's doings in court. But, in the intervals of our talk I found my thoughts drifting back to the cardboard box and to the occupations with which it was associated. And not only then but in the days that followed did that curious little investigation furnish me with matter for reflection.

Of course, Thorndyke was perfectly right in his contention. It is impossible to decide in advance whether a particular item of knowledge may or may not prove at some future time to be of value, and it was a fact that Thorndyke made a rule of acquiring every item of knowledge that was obtainable in connection with a case, without regard to its apparent relevancy. But still, I had the feeling that, in this present case, he was not merely acting on this rather academic principle. The care and thoroughness and the appearance of interest with which he had made this examination conveyed to me the impression that the facts elicited meant more to him than they did to me.

Yet what could they mean? The disappearance of Penrose had the hospital as its starting-point, or, at the earliest, the accident to the old woman. But the mud and the pottery fragment were related to events that had occurred before the accident, and which were, therefore, totally unconnected with the disappearance. Then how could they possibly throw any light on the present whereabouts of the missing man, which was the problem that we had to solve?

That was the question that I asked myself again and again. But by no amount of cogitation could I find any answer.

Chapter VII
A Visit of Inspection

The dubious and slightly bewildered state of mind to which I have referred induced me to observe Thorndyke's proceedings with a little closer attention than was usual with me. Not that there was really any occasion, for Thorndyke appeared to go out of his way to make me a party to any doings connected with the Penrose case, which tended to increase my suspicion that I had missed some point of evidential importance.

It was some two or three days after Brodribb's visit to us, when we seemed to have a few hours at our disposal, that Thorndyke suggested a call at Queen Square to examine Penrose's car. I had been expecting this suggestion and, with the hope of getting some new light on the purpose of his investigations, assented cheerfully. Accordingly, when Thorndyke had slipped a good-sized notebook and some other small necessaries into his pocket, we set forth on our quest.

I have always liked Queen Square, and have watched, regretfully, its gradual deterioration – or "improvement", as the optimistic modern phrase has it. When I first knew the place, it was nearly intact, with its satellites, Great Ormond Street, The Foundling Hospital, and the group of other pleasant old squares adjacent. As we walked towards it we discussed the changes that the years had wrought. Thorndyke, as an old Londoner, sympathised warmly with my regrets.

"Yes," he agreed, "the works of man tell us more about him than we can gather from volumes of history. Every generation leaves, in the products of its activities, a faithful picture of its capabilities, its standard of taste and its outlook on life. The people who conceived and created these delightful, dignified haunts of peace and quiet had never heard of town-planning and did not talk much about architecture. But they planned towns by instinctive taste and they built charming houses, the dismembered fragments of which we can now study in our museums. There is a beautiful wooden portico at South Kensington which I used to admire when it stood in Great Ormond Street."

"I remember it," said I. "But in the museum they have scraped off the paint and gilding to show the construction, which is all very interesting and instructive, but is not quite what the architect had in view when he designed it. It is rather as if one should offer the anatomical exhibits in the Hunterian museum as illustrations of the beauty of the

276

human figure. They might have restored the painting and gilding so that visitors could see what a fine London door-way was like in the time of Good Queen Anne."

As I spoke, we turned out of Great Ormond Street and crossed the square, passing the ancient pump with its surmounting lantern and its encircling posts, and directing our steps towards Penrose's house, which had been described as nearly opposite the statue of Queen Anne. As we approached the latter, Thorndyke remarked, continuing our discussion, "There is another example of what is practically a lost art. It seems to me a pity that leadwork should have been allowed to fall into such a state of decay. Lead may not be an ideal material for statues, but it is imperishable, it is cheap, and it is easy to work. In the eighteenth century, the Piccadilly foundries, from which this statue probably came, turned out thousands of works – urns and vases, shepherds and shepherdesses and other rustic figures for use in parks and formal gardens or as architectural ornaments. But they have nearly all gone – melted down, I suppose, to form sheet lead or water pipes. This looks like the house, and a fine old house it is, one of the last survivors of its family."

We ascended to the broad door-step, enclosed by forged railings bearing a pair of link-extinguishers and the standard for an oil lamp, gave a tug at the old-fashioned bell-pull, and executed a flourish on the handsome brass knocker. After a decent interval, the door was opened by a smart-looking maid-servant to whom Thorndyke communicated the purpose of our visit.

"We have called to see Mr. Kickweed on certain legal business. I think he is expecting a visit from me. I am Dr. Thorndyke."

On this the maid opened the door wide and, inviting us to enter, conducted us to a small room adjacent to the hall, where she requested us to wait while she informed Mr. Kickweed of our arrival. When she had gone, I cast an inquisitive glance round the room, which contained a table, two chairs, and a piece of furniture which might have been regarded either as a cupboard or as some kind of sideboard.

"This can hardly be the room in which the burglary took place," said I, "though it fits the description to some extent, but the window seems in the wrong place."

"Very much so," said Thorndyke, "as it looks out on the square and is over the area. And it is the wrong sort of cupboard with the wrong sort of lock. No, this is not the mysterious chamber."

Here the door opened slowly and discreetly to admit a pale-faced, rather unwholesome-looking elderly man who bowed deferentially and introduced himself by name as Mr. Kickweed, though the introduction was hardly necessary, for he might have served, in a museum of social anthropology, as a type specimen of the *genus* upper manservant.

"Mr. Brodribb wrote to me, sir," he continued in a melancholy tone, "to say that you would probably call and instructing me to give you any assistance that I could. In what way can I have the pleasure of carrying out those instructions?"

"My immediate object," replied Thorndyke, "is to inspect Mr. Penrose's car. Has anything been done to it since it came back?"

"Nothing whatever, sir," Kickweed replied. "I suppose it ought to be cleaned, but I know nothing about cars. Mr. Penrose always attended to it himself excepting when it went out for repairs, and he always kept the garage locked up. In fact, it was locked when they brought the car back."

"Then how did you get the car in?" Thorndyke asked.

"The police officer, sir, who came with the car, fortunately had a few odd keys with him, and one of them happened to fit the lock. He was good enough to leave it with me, so I shall be able to let you in. If you would like to go round there now I will just get my hat and show you the way."

"Thank you," said Thorndyke. "If it is not troubling you – "

"It is no trouble at all, sir," interrupted Kickweed, and thereupon he stole out of the room with the light, noiseless tread that seems to be almost characteristic of heavy, bulky men. A few minutes later he reappeared in correct morning dress, including a slightly rusty top hat, and we set forth together. The garage was not far away, being situated in a sort of mews, approached from Guilford Street. As we halted at the door and Kickweed produced the key, I noticed that Thorndyke cast an inquisitive glance at it, and I guessed what was in his mind, because it was also in mine. But we were both wrong. The key was not of the filed or skeleton variety but was just a normal warded key of a simple type. However, it turned in the lock, after a good deal of persuasion and, the doors being flung open, we entered.

It was a roomy place and fairly well lighted by a wide window above the doors. The car stood in the middle, leaving ample space on either side and still more at the end, where a rough bench had been placed, with a vice and a number of rather rusty tools together with various oddments in the way of bolts, nuts, and miscellaneous scrap.

"I take it," said Thorndyke, glancing at the littered bench, "that Mr. Penrose is not a skilled mechanic."

"No, sir," Kickweed admitted. "I don't think he is much of a workman. And yet he used to spend a good deal of time here. I don't know what he would have been doing."

"You did not assist him, then?"

"No, sir. I have only been in here once or twice, and then only for a few minutes with Mr. Penrose. I never came here by myself, nor, I think, did anybody else. There was only one key, until I got this one, and Mr. Penrose kept that himself, and has it still."

"I suppose you don't know of any reason why he should have objected to your coming here alone?"

"No, sir. And I don't think there was any. It was just his way. He has rather a habit of making secrets of nothing."

"So I have understood," said Thorndyke, "and a very bad habit it is, leading to all sorts of unnecessary suspicions and surmises. However, we came here primarily to inspect the car, so perhaps we had better get on with that."

Accordingly, he proceeded to make a systematic and detailed survey of the vehicle, beginning with the bent mudguard, the leading edge of which he examined minutely with the aid of a lens. But if there had ever been any fibres or other traces of the collision, they had been removed by the police. He then transferred his attention to the wheels and, after a preliminary glance at them, produced one or two envelopes from his pocket and laid them on the bench.

"The dirt on the face of the tyres," he remarked, "is of no interest to us, as it will have changed from moment to moment. But that on the inside and on the rims of the wheels is more significant. Its presence there suggests that, at one time, the car had been driven over quite soft earth, and that earth was a natural soil, not a road material, a reddish loam similar to that on the coat."

"Yes," I agreed, "it is evident that the wheels sank in pretty deep by the quantity of soil on the rims. And I think," I added, stooping low to look under the car, "that I can see a leaf sticking to the rim of the wheel."

With some difficulty I managed to reach in and pick it off, together with the lump of dry loam in which it was embedded.

"A dead leaf," Thorndyke pronounced when I handed it to him, "I mean a last-year's leaf, and it looks like a hornbeam. But we shall see better when we wet it and flatten it out."

He deposited the leaf and earth in an envelope, on which he wrote a brief memorandum of the source of the specimen, and then continued his examination. But there was nothing more to be seen from the outside excepting a general dirtiness, suggestive of a not very fastidious owner. Nor was there anything very significant to be seen when I opened the door. The interior showed no signs of anything unusual. The floor was moderately clean excepting that under the driver's seat, which was thickly plastered with loam. But this was what we should have expected, and the evidence that it furnished that there was almost certainly only one person in the car during that last drive, merely confirmed what we already knew. There were no loose articles in any of the pockets or receptacles other than the insurance certificate, and the rather scanty outfit of tools. In fact, the only discovery – and a very modest one at that – was another dead leaf, apparently also hornbeam, trodden flat into the dirt by the driver's seat.

Having finished with the car, Thorndyke once more glanced round the garage and I could see that he was making a mental inventory of the various objects that it contained. But his next question reverted to the car.

"I understood," said he, "that the police found an empty flask in the car."

"Yes, sir," replied Kickweed. "I took that away to wash it and polish it up. It is a silver flask and it seemed a pity to leave it in the dirty state in which it was found. I have cleaned it thoroughly and put it away among the plate. Did you wish to see it?"

"No," replied Thorndyke, "but I should like a few particulars. About how much does it hold?"

"It holds the best part of a bottle. About an imperial pint."

"That is a large flask," Thorndyke remarked. "Did Mr. Penrose usually carry it in the car?"

"Do you know, sir, I really can't say. I have only seen it once before. That was about two years ago when I happened to be brushing Mr. Penrose's overcoat and found it in the pocket. But I have the impression that he usually carried it with him when he went away from home. He would be likely to because he is rather fastidious about his wine. He drinks nothing but Madeira and old brown sherry, and you can't get good Madeira or brown sherry at roadside inns."

"And as to quantity? It has been stated that when he was last seen he appeared to be under the influence of liquor. Was that at all usual?"

Kickweed shook his head emphatically. "No, sir," he replied. "That must have been a mistake. He may have smelt of sherry. He often does. But sherry has a very strong aroma and a little of it goes a long way in the matter of smell. But in all the years that I have known Mr. Penrose, I have never seen him in the slightest degree the worse for drink. He does certainly take a good deal, as I can judge by the wine merchant's deliveries and the empty bottles, but then he takes no beer or spirits or any other kind of wine. They must have been misled by the odour."

"That seems quite likely," said Thorndyke. "By the way, I notice a couple of hazel twigs hanging up there under that hat. Do you happen to know whether Mr. Penrose is a dowser?"

"A dowser, sir?" Kickweed repeated with mystified air.

280

"A water-finder," Thorndyke explained. "That is what those forked twigs are used for." He took the hat from the peg and laid it on the bench and, taking down one of the twigs, held it by its two ends and continued, "The specially gifted persons – known as dowsers – who search for underground streams or springs, hold the twig in this way and walk to-and-fro over the land where they expect to find water, and when they pass over a hidden spring – so it is stated – they become aware of the presence of underground water by a movement of the twig in their hands. It looks as if Mr. Penrose had practised the dowser's art.

"Ah!" exclaimed Kickweed, "I remember now that Mr. Penrose once showed me one of these things and told me about it. But I thought it was one of his little jokes, for it was not water that he professed to be able to find with it. He said that it was an infallible guide to buried treasure. It would show the treasure-seeker exactly where to dig. But I never supposed that he was speaking seriously. You see, sir, Mr. Penrose is rather a jocular gentleman, and it is sometimes a little difficult to be quite sure what he really does mean."

"So I understand," said Thorndyke, "and he may have been joking in this case. But the idea of digging seems to have been in his mind. Now so far as you know, did he ever engage in any sort of digging activities in his search for antiquities?"

"Well, sir," replied Kickweed, "it is rather difficult to say. He is so very facetious. But I have known him to bring home certain articles – lumps of flint and bits of crockery, they looked like to me – which were covered with earth and which I have helped him to scrub clean at the scullery sink. I supposed that he must have dug them up somewhere as he referred to them as 'Treasure Trove' and 'the resurrectionist's loot' and other similar expressions."

"Yes," Thorndyke agreed, "those expressions and the condition of the objects certainly suggest something in the way of excavations. But I don't see any tools suitable for the purpose, and I should suppose that if he had had any he would have kept them here. Do you happen to remember having seen any picks, shovels, or similar tools here or elsewhere?"

Mr. Kickweed reflected as he ran an inquiring glance round the walls. "As I said, sir," he replied, "I have only been in here once or twice before Mr. Penrose went away. But I seem to remember a sort of pick – I think it is called a trenching tool – which I don't see now. And there was a small spade, pointed like the ace of hearts, with a leather case for the blade. But I don't see that either. It hung, I think, on one of those pegs. But that was over a year ago."

"It looks," I suggested, remembering the pottery fragment, "as if Mr. Penrose may have taken them with him when he left home. They were not in the car when it was found, but it had then been lying unattended for a couple of days. Loose property has rather a way of disappearing from derelict cars."

"It is quite possible," said Thorndyke, and he then appeared to dismiss the subject, for he replaced the hazel twig on its peg and picked up the hat to return that also, but paused, looking with a faint smile into its dusty and decayed interior.

"Mr. Penrose," he remarked, "seems to have attached undue value to this relic. But perhaps the marking was done when it was in a more presentable condition."

He exhibited the interior of the hat, on the crown of which the name "D. Penrose" had been carefully printed with a rubber stamp.

"Yes, sir," said Kickweed, "the name was probably stamped when the hat was new. Not that that would have made any difference, for Mr. Penrose stamped his name on everything that he possessed, not only on his underclothing and handkerchiefs and the things that are usually marked, but his hats, shoes, books, paper-knives – everything that was movable. It always seemed to me a little inconsistent."

"How inconsistent?" I asked.

"I mean," replied Kickweed, "he is in general a very secret gentleman. He makes a secret of the most simple and ordinary things. And yet he prints his full name, not just his initials as most men do, inside his hat and his shoes and his waistcoat lining, and even on his pocket-knife. Now, if a stranger asked him his name he would probably avoid telling him, but yet, as soon as he takes his hat off, he discloses his identity to all the world."

"I take it," said Thorndyke, "that he usually does the stamping himself?"

"Lord bless you, yes, sir! That rubber stamp has always been kept under lock and key as if it had been the Koh-i-noor, or as if it could have been used for forging his signature. I have never even seen it. But, of course, that signifies nothing. It is just his way."

"Yes," said Thorndyke, "and you are a wise man, to accept his harmless oddities and not let them worry you." He hung the hat on its peg and then, turning to Kickweed, opened a fresh subject.

"Mr. Brodribb consulted me about a burglary that occurred in your house a short time ago. There was a question of calling in the police and getting the cupboard opened. How does that suggestion strike you?"

"It strikes me," Kickweed replied severely, "as an improper and a foolish suggestion. It would be improper to tamper with Mr. Penrose's property in his absence and without his consent, sir, and it would be foolish because we should be none the wiser when we had opened the cupboard as we don't know what it contained, or whether it contained anything."

Here I interposed rather rashly.

"The suggestion has been made that it is just possible that the person who entered the room may have been Mr. Penrose himself."

Kickweed looked, and professed to be, deeply shocked. But I had, nevertheless, a strong suspicion that that was his own opinion.

"But, you know, Mr. Kickweed," said I, "there is nothing immoral or even improper in a gentleman's entering his own house to take his own property if he happens to have need of it. Most men, it is true, would prefer to enter by the front door. But Mr. Penrose was not like most men, and if he preferred the window, he was entirely within his rights. It was his own window."

I had the feeling that my observations were received with approval and even with some relief. But Mr. Kickweed, if he secretly concurred, as I believed that he did, was not committing himself.

"No doubt, sir," said he, "you are perfectly right. But I couldn't imagine Mr. Penrose doing anything so undignified, especially as he had the key of the front door in his pocket. And," he added, with a pensive smile, "it was his own front door."

"You were saying just now," said Thorndyke, "that nothing is known as to the contents of that cupboard. Have you no idea at all as to what it contained, or contains?"

"I said knowledge, sir," replied Kickweed. "I know nothing at all as to what is, or has been, in that cupboard."

He spoke with an emphasis that gave us clearly to understand that he was not going beyond his actual knowledge. He was going to hazard no opinions.

"And it is the fact, Mr. Kickweed," Thorndyke pursued, "that there is no one in the world who knows, or could form any reasonable judgement as to what that cupboard did, does or might contain?"

Mr. Kickweed reflected, a trifle uneasily, I thought. But Thorndyke's question admitted of no evasion, and he at length replied with some reluctance, "Well, sir, I wouldn't say that, for there is one person who may possibly know. I have not spoken of him to anyone hitherto, because Mr. Penrose was very secret about that room, and he is my employer and it is my duty to abide by his wishes, whether expressed or not. But you ask me a definite question and I suppose you are entitled to an answer. I think it possible that Mr. Penrose may have confided his secret to a certain friend of his, a gentleman named Lockhart."

"What makes you think that Mr. Lockhart may know what is or was, in the cupboard?" Thorndyke asked.

"The discovery – if it was one – " Kickweed replied, "was quite accidental. Mr. Lockhart came to the house by appointment to look over the collection, and Mr. Penrose took him into the great gallery. When they had been there some considerable time, I ventured to look in to ask if I should bring them up some tea. But when I entered the big gallery they were not there, but I could hear them talking, and the voices seemed to come from the small room, though the door of that room was shut. But they must have been in there because there was no other room that opened out of the great gallery. Now the small room contained nothing but the cupboard, so that if Mr. Penrose took Mr. Lockhart into that room, it could only have been to show him what was in the cupboard. And I did, in fact, hear sounds of movement in the room as if drawers were being pulled out. But of course, as soon as I realised what was happening, I went away.

"But there was another circumstance that made me think that Mr. Penrose might have let Mr. Lockhart into the secret of the small room. When they had finished with the collection they went into the morning room – the little front room that you went into – and I took them up some tea, and there they were for quite a long time before Mr. Lockhart went away. Afterwards I learned from Mr. Penrose, himself, that Mr. Lockhart had been advising him about insuring the collection, which made it seem likely that Mr. Lockhart had been shown all that there was to insure."

"Yes," said Thorndyke, "that seems a reasonable inference. Is Mr. Lockhart connected with insurance business?"

"No, sir. He is a legal gentleman – a barrister."

"Ah!" said Thorndyke. "Lockhart. Now I wonder if that would be – you don't happen to know what inn he belongs to?"

"Yes, sir. He belongs to Lincoln's Inn – at least, that is his address. I happen to know by having seen a card of his which Mr. Penrose left on his dressing-table."

"Is Mr. Lockhart an intimate friend of Mr. Penrose?"

"No, sir. Quite a recent acquaintance, I believe, though Mr. Penrose seemed to take to him more than he usually does to strangers. Still, I was rather surprised at his taking him into the small room. I have never known him to do such a thing before."

Thorndyke made no immediate rejoinder, but stood apparently considering this last statement and letting his glance travel about the place as if searching for some further objects of interest. But it seemed that he had squeezed both the garage and Mr. Kickweed dry, for he said, at length, "Well, I think we have learned all that there is to learn here, and I must thank you, Mr. Kickweed, for having been so extremely helpful."

Kickweed smiled a somewhat dreary smile. "I hope I have not been too much so, sir," said he. "I am not a willing helper, though I feel bound to carry out Mr. Brodribb's instructions. I understand from him that you are trying to find out where Mr. Penrose has gone to and, if you will pardon me for saying so, I hope you won't succeed."

Thorndyke smiled appreciatively. "Now, why do you say that?" he asked.

"Because, sir," Kickweed replied earnestly, "I feel that this pursuit is not justifiable. Mr. Penrose, as I understand, has had a little mishap and thinks it best to keep out of sight for a time. But if he thinks so, it is his own affair, and I don't consider it just or proper that other people, for their own purposes, should hunt him up and perhaps get him into difficulties."

I must confess that I sympathised heartily with Mr. Kickweed's sentiments, and so, apparently, did Thorndyke, for he replied, "That is precisely what I pointed out to Mr. Brodribb. But there are legal reasons for ascertaining Mr. Penrose's whereabouts, though there are none for disclosing them to others. You may take it from me, Mr. Kickweed, that nothing which may come to my knowledge will be used in any way to his disadvantage."

"I am very relieved to hear you say that, sir," Kickweed rejoined with evident sincerity, "because I have felt that there are others who take a different view. Mr. Horridge, for instance has, to my knowledge, been in communication with the police."

"Well," I said, as we retired from the garage and Kickweed locked the door, "I don't suppose he has done any harm if he has no more to tell them than we have been told."

As our way home led through Queen Square, we walked thither with Mr. Kickweed, and Thorndyke took the opportunity to ask a few questions concerning Mr. Penrose's collection.

"I don't know much about the things," said Kickweed, "excepting that there is a rare lot of them and that they take a terrible amount of dusting. I do most of it with a pair of bellows when Mr. Penrose is not about. But if you feel any interest in them, why not step in, as you are here, and have a look at them yourself?"

Now I have no doubt whatever that this was precisely what Thorndyke had intended to do but, in his queer, secretive way, had preferred that the inspection should seem to occur by chance. At any rate, he accepted the invitation, and we followed Kickweed to the door of the house and were by him admitted to the hall.

285

Chapter VIII
Mr. Horridge

$\mathbf{M}$r. Kickweed, as has been mentioned, had a light tread, and his movements in general tended to be silent. Thus our entry into the hall of the old house and the subsequent closing of the door, were almost noiseless. Nevertheless, our arrival was not unobserved for, even as Kickweed was pocketing his latch-key, the door of the morning room opened slowly and quietly and a large, distinctly fat gentleman appeared framed in the doorway.

There was something slightly odd and even ridiculous in the sudden and silent manner in which he became visible, and in the sly, inquisitive glance that he turned on us, as if he had been a plain-clothes officer and we a surprised party of burglars.

"How did you know I was here, Kickweed?" he demanded.

"I didn't, sir," was the reply.

"Oh," rejoined the other, "I thought these gentlemen might have come on some business with me."

"No, sir. They have been inspecting the car. They are Dr. Thorndyke and Dr. Jervis."

The fat man bowed stiffly. "Ah!" said he, "they have inspected the car. And now?"

"Dr. Thorndyke thought he would like to take a look at the collection," Kickweed replied frigidly, evidently resentful of the other man's manner, "so I invited him to step in and look over it."

"Ha!" said the fat gentleman. "You thought it quite in order to do that? Well, if Dr. Thorndyke wants to see the collection, there is no reason why he should not. I will show him round the gallery, myself. My name," he added, turning to us, "is Horridge. You have probably heard of me. I am Mr. Penrose's executor and, in his absence, am keeping an eye on his property."

Now, the tone of his remarks filled me with a burning desire to kick Mr. Horridge, but that being impracticable, I should certainly, if left to myself, have told him to go to the devil and forthwith walked out of the house. Thorndyke, however, was completely unruffled, and having once more thanked Kickweed, who was slinking away in dudgeon, he accepted the invitation with a suavity bordering on meekness (whereby I judged that he had definite reasons for wishing to see the collection).

286

"So," said Mr. Horridge, as he conducted us along the hall, "you have been examining the car. Now, what did you expect to find out from the car?"

"I did not expect anything," Thorndyke replied.

Horridge giggled. "And did your examination answer your expectations?" he inquired.

"Substantially," replied Thorndyke, "I may say that it did."

Horridge giggled again and, throwing open a door which opened from the hall, invited us to enter. We accordingly passed in and found ourselves in an immense and lofty room communicating with another of similarly magnificent proportions by an opening from which the original folding doors had been removed.

I looked around me with surprise and extreme distaste, for the noble apartments had been degraded to the status of a mere lumber-room. Of the trim and orderly character of a museum there was not a trace. The walls were occupied by interminable ranges of open shelves and the floor was crowded with plain deal tables, coarsely stained and varnished to disguise their humble material, and shelves and tables were littered with a chaos of miscellaneous objects, all exposed baldly to the air and dust. There was not a single glazed case in the room, and the only article of comely furniture was a lantern clock, perched on a bracket, which ticked sedately and actually showed the approximately correct time.

"This is a very singular collection," Thorndyke remarked, casting a puzzled glance over the shelves and tables. "One doesn't quite see what its purpose is – what it is intended to illustrate."

Horridge giggled again in his unpleasant way. "Whatever the intention is," said he, "it illustrates very perfectly poor old Pen's usual state of mind – muddle. But may I ask what is the object of this inspection? Is it just a matter of curiosity, or is it connected with the inquiry into Pen's disappearance? Because I don't see how the inspection is going to help you."

"It is not very obvious, certainly," Thorndyke admitted. "But one never knows what light chance facts may throw on the problem. I think it will be worthwhile for me to see what things Mr. Penrose has collected and where he obtained them."

Horridge grinned – and the explanation of the grin was presently forthcoming. Meanwhile he rejoined, "Well, cast your eye over the oddments and see what takes your fancy. Then you can go into the question of where they came from. What would you like to start with?"

Thorndyke glanced once more along the shelves and then announced his choice.

"I see there is a good deal of ancient pottery, mixed up with other exhibits. Perhaps it would be well to sort that out and see where the pieces were found. Now, here is a little dish of Gaulish red ware. The slip of paper that it rests on bears the number, 201. That, I presume, refers to a catalogue."

"It does," replied Horridge, giggling delightedly. "I will get you the catalogue and then you will be able to find out all about the specimen."

He went to a table near the end of the room and pulled out a drawer from which he extracted a stout quarto volume. This he brought to Thorndyke and, having handed it to him with something of a flourish, stood looking at him and giggling like a fool. But the reason for his merriment became apparent when Thorndyke opened the book and turned to the number. Observing the slow smile which spread over my colleague's face, I looked over his shoulder and read the entry, scrawled, not very legibly, in pencil:

201. Sammy. Pot Sand. Sinbad.

"This is not very illuminating," Thorndyke remarked, on which Horridge burst into a roar of laughter.

"Oh, don't say that!" he gurgled. "I understood from old Brodribb that you could see through a brick wall. Well, here's your chance. The whole catalogue is written in the same damn silly sort of jargon. Of course, Pen knows what it means, but he doesn't intend that anyone else shall. Perhaps you would like to note down a few samples to think over at your leisure."

Thorndyke instantly grasped the opportunity.

"Thank you," said he. "A most excellent suggestion. If you will be so very kind as to show Dr. Jervis the collection, I will make a few notes on the pottery and extract the entries from the catalogue. If we could identify some of the localities, we might get quite a useful hint."

This suggestion did not at all meet the views of Mr. Horridge, who was evidently as curious as to Thorndyke's proceedings as I was, myself. But he could not very well refuse, for Thorndyke, seeing a chance of carrying out his investigations – whatever they might be – uninterrupted by Horridge's chatter and free from his inquisitive observation, was quietly persistent and, of course, had his way, as he usually did.

"Very well," Horridge at length agreed, with a rather bad grace, "then I'll just take Dr. Jervis round the shelves and show him the curios. But I don't know much about them, and I don't suppose he cares much."

Accordingly, we set forth on a voyage of exploration round the crowded, disorderly shelves and, realising that my function was to keep

Horridge's attention distracted from Thorndyke's activities, I plied him with questions about the exhibits and commented on their interest and beauty with the utmost prolixity and tediousness at my command. But it was a wretched make-believe on both sides for, while Horridge was answering my questions (usually quite ignorantly and all wrong, as even I knew) he kept one eye cocked in Thorndyke's direction, and my own attention was similarly occupied.

But Thorndyke gave us but a poor entertainment. Drawing a chair up to a table near the window, he seated himself with his back to us and the catalogue before him. This he pored over for some time, making occasional entries in his notebook. Then he rose and, having taken a survey of the shelves, began to select pieces of pottery, each of which he took in turn to the table where he examined it critically, compared it with the entry in the catalogue and copied the latter into his notebook. He began with the Roman pottery but, from long acquaintance with his habits and methods, I suspected that this was only a tactical move to conceal from Horridge his actual purpose, for I knew that it was his invariable habit, when he had to work in the presence of inquisitive observers, to confuse the issues in their minds by actions which had no bearing on the matter in hand.

As to his real purpose, I had no doubt that it was in some way connected with the fragment which we had examined, and as Horridge conducted me round the loaded shelves, I kept a sharp look-out for pottery exhibits which might correspond to the hypothetical vessel which Thorndyke had sketched in his reconstruction. There were two pieces (in different places and among totally unrelated objects) which, so far as I could see without close inspection, answered the description: One, a largish, rather shallow bowl of which a large part was missing, and the other a deeper pot which had been broken and rather unskilfully mended, and which was complete save for a small part of the rim. This pot corresponded very closely both in shape and size with Thorndyke's reconstruction, and it seemed to me, even, that the piece which was missing from the rim was about the size of our fragment. Accordingly, I gave that pot my special attention.

One after another Thorndyke gravely examined specimens of Roman, Saxon, and Iron Age pottery in which I felt sure he could have no interest whatever. At last, after circling round, so to speak, he arrived at this pot, picked it up, and with a glance at the number on its paper, bore it over to the table. As he set it down and seated himself, I saw him take something from his pocket, but as his back was towards us I could not see what it was, or what he did with it. I assumed, however, that it was some measuring instrument and that he was ascertaining the dimensions of the piece that was missing. At any rate, his examination was quite brief and, when he had copied the entry in the catalogue, he carried the pot back to its place and proceeded to look about for further objects for study.

By this time, however, Horridge had begun to be rather bored and was disposed to make no secret of the fact.

"I should think," said he, with an undisguised yawn, "that you've got enough material to occupy you for a month or two, and I'll wager that you don't make any sense of it then."

Thorndyke looked thoughtfully at his open notebook. "Perhaps you are right," he agreed. "These entries will take a good deal of deciphering and probably will yield no information, after all. I don't think we need trespass on your patience any longer."

"Oh, that's all right," said Horridge, "but, before you go – if you've seen all that you want to see – perhaps you might as well have a look at the small room – the one that was broken into, you know. You heard about that burglary, I think? Old Brodribb said he was going to consult you about it."

"Mr. Brodribb did consult me," Thorndyke replied, "on the question of opening the cupboard by force or otherwise. I advised him that, in the absence of Mr. Penrose, it would not be proper to force the cupboard and that, as the contents of the cupboard were unknown, the proceeding would be useless as well as improper."

"But what about calling in the police?" Horridge suggested.

"I don't think the police would force a cupboard, without the owner's knowledge or consent, if it were locked and showed no signs of having been tampered with."

"Well," Horridge grumbled, "it's very unsatisfactory. Someone may have got away with a whole lot of valuable property and able to dispose of it at their leisure. However – if you have finished with the catalogue, do you mind putting it back in its drawer?"

As Thorndyke complied with this rather odd request, our host walked quickly up the long room to a door in the corner, and I had the impression that he inserted a key and turned it. But, as he stood half-turned towards us and in front of the handle and keyhole, I could not see distinctly, nor did I give the matter any particular attention.

"It is odd," he remarked, still standing before the door, grasping the handle, "that Pen should have left the key in this door when he went away. He was always so deadly secret about Bluebeard's chamber, as he called it in his silly way. He never let me see into it. I always thought he had something very precious in it, and I'm inclined to think so still."

With this, he opened the door and we all entered the mysterious chamber, a smallish room and very bare of furniture, for it contained only a single chair, a mahogany table, placed under the window, and a massive cupboard, also of mahogany, with a pair of doors like a wardrobe.

"So this is the famous cupboard," said Thorndyke, standing before it and looking it over critically, "the repository of hidden treasure, as you believe. Well, looking at it, one would say that whatever precious things were once in it, are in it still. But one might be wrong."

Having made this rather ambiguous pronouncement, he proceeded to a more particular inspection. The escutcheon of the Chubb lock was examined with the aid of a lens, and the interior of the keyhole with the tiny electric lamp that he always carried. From the lock he transferred his attention to the cupboard itself, closely examining the sides, standing on the chair to inspect the top and, finally, setting his shoulder to one corner and his foot against the skirting of the wall, tried to test its weight by tilting it. But beyond eliciting a complaining creak, he could make no impression on it. "I've tried that," said Horridge. "It's like shoving against the Eddystone lighthouse. The thing is a most ungodly weight, unless it is screwed to the floor. It can hardly be the stuff inside."

"Unless," I suggested, "Mr. Penrose indulged in the hobby of collecting gold ingots. But even a collection of plate can be pretty heavy if there is enough of it."

"At any rate," said Thorndyke, "one thing is clear. That cupboard has not been opened unless it was opened with its own key."

"Don't think the lock could have been picked?" said Horridge.

Thorndyke shook his head. "Burglars don't try to pick Chubb locks," said he. "They use the jemmy, or else cut the lock out with centre-bits."

Horridge grunted and then amplified the grunt with the remark, "Looks a bit as if our friend Kick had raised a false alarm."

"That can hardly be," Thorndyke objected. "I understood that he found the door bolted on the inside and had to enter through the window."

"Yes, that was what he said," Horridge admitted grudgingly in a tone that seemed to imply some scepticism as to the statement.

"It is conceivable," Thorndyke suggested, "that the visitor may have been disturbed, or that he gave up the attempt when he found it impossible to pick the lock. You see, there is no evidence that he was a skilled burglar. No difficulties were overcome. He simply opened the window and stepped in. The really astonishing thing is that Penrose should have left the place so insecure – that is, assuming that there actually was some valuable property here. The window, as you can see, has no shutters, or even screws or stops, and it looks on to an alley which I understand is invisible from the street. Let us see what that alley is like."

He moved the table away from the window, glancing at a number of parallel scratches on its polished surface, slid up the window and looked out.

"It is quite remarkable," said he. "The window is only a few feet from the ground and the alley is closed by a small wooden gate which has no bolt or latch and seems to be secured only by a lock, which is probably a simple builder's lock which could be easily opened with a skeleton key or a common pick-lock. There is no security whatever. That stout bolt on the room door is, of course, useless, as it is on the inside, and the lock is probably a simple affair."

As he spoke, he opened the door and plucked out the key, which he held out for our inspection.

"You see?" he said. "Just a plain warded lock which a skilled operator could turn with a bit of stiff wire. Penrose seems to have pinned his faith to the Chubb lock, and perhaps events have justified him."

He slipped the key back into the lock, and this seemed to bring the proceedings to an end. After a few perfunctory expressions of hope that our visit had satisfied us and that we had seen all that we wished to see, our host escorted us through the great gallery and the hall and finally launched us into the street.

Chapter IX
Thorndyke Tests
a Theory

As we took our way homeward I tried to arrange in my mind the rather confusing experiences of the last hour or two. Those hours, it seemed to me, had been virtually wasted, for we had learned nothing new that bore directly on our problem. This view I ventured to propound to Thorndyke, beginning, naturally, with Mr. Horridge, who had made a deep and disagreeable impression on me.

"Yes," Thorndyke agreed, "he is not a prepossessing person. A bad-mannered man and distinctly sly and suspicious. You probably noted his mental attitude towards Kickweed."

"Yes, distinctly hostile, and I gathered that he is inclined to suspect him of having faked that burglary for his own ends. I suppose, by the way, that it is not possible that he may be right?"

"It is not actually impossible," Thorndyke replied, "but there is nothing to support such a suspicion. Kickweed impressed me very favourably, especially by his loyalty to Penrose. If he is not a liar, the position with regard to the small room is this: Someone entered that room, that someone either knew or thought he knew what it contained. He either failed to open that cupboard or he opened it with its own key. The only evidence that he did open it is the piece of paper that was found, which, you notice, was similar to the slips of paper under the specimens in the gallery, excepting that it bore no catalogue number but had an inscription similar to those in the catalogue. That paper strongly suggests that the cupboard had been opened, but is not conclusive, since it might have been dropped by Penrose on some other occasion. But, as I said, its presence is strongly suggestive of a hurried opening of the cupboard at night. There were one or two other points that probably did not escape you."

"You mean the extraordinary weight of the cupboard? That certainly impressed me as significant, though I am not quite clear as to what it signifies. It might be due to some ponderous contents, but it seemed to me to suggest an iron safe inside."

"Yes," said Thorndyke, "that is undoubtedly the explanation. The cupboard is a mere wooden case enclosing a large iron safe. That was quite clear from the construction, which is very much like that of an organ case. The sides and top are fixed in position by large screws

293

instead of being keyed in with proper cabinet-maker's joints. The wooden case was built on after the safe had been placed in position."

"Then," said I, "the Chubb lock is a mere hollow pretence."

"Exactly. The wooden case could have been taken off with a common screw-driver. You noticed the scratches on the table?"

"Yes. But, of course, there is no evidence as to when they were made."

"No," he agreed. "Probably they were made at various times. But they are of interest in relation to the arrangement of the cupboard. You must have noticed that they were in two groups, roughly two feet six inches apart and all approximately parallel. They looked like the scratches that would be made by the runners of drawers of that width, and comparing them with the cupboard, one saw that, allowing for the space taken up by the wooden case, there would just be room for a range of drawers of that width. The reasonable inference is that the iron safe houses a range of largish drawers and that these have been taken out from time to time and placed on the table so that their contents could be looked at by the light from the window."

I agreed that this appeared to be the case, but I could not see that it mattered very much whether it was so or not.

"It seems to me," I added, "that we are acquiring a lot of oddments of information, none of which has the slightest bearing on the one question that we are asked to answer: Where is Penrose hiding at the present moment?"

"It would be safer," said he, "to say, 'seems to have'. I am picking up all the information that I can in the hope that some of it may turn out to have a bearing on our problem."

"By the way," said I, "why were you so keen on seeing the collection? You were, you know, or you would not have put up with Horridge's insolence. You had some definite point to clear up respecting that pottery fragment. What was it?"

"The point," he replied, "was this. To an archaeologist, that fragment alone would have been an object of interest, since, as you saw, it was possible to make from it a rough, but quite reliable reconstruction. But Penrose is not an archaeologist. He is, as we understood, a mere collector of curios. To such a man, a tiny fragment would be of no interest by itself.

"On the other hand, to an archaeologist, a broken pot is, practically, of the same scientific value as a complete pot. But to the mere collector, or curio-monger, the completeness of a specimen is a matter of cardinal importance. If he has an incomplete specimen, he will spare no trouble or expense to make it complete. He is not concerned with its scientific interest but with its value as a curio.

"Knowing, then, what we did of Penrose, it occurred to me as a bare possibility that this apparently worthless fragment that we found in his pocket might be the product of a definite search *ad hoc*. That he might have re-visited some place from which he had obtained an incomplete specimen with the express purpose of searching for the fragment which would make it complete. The edges of the fragment were freshly fractured. It had been broken off the pot in the course of digging it out. Therefore, the missing piece of the pot was still in the place where the digging had taken place and was certainly recoverable, It was just a speculative possibility, but it was worth testing as we are so short of data, so I decided to look over the collection when I got a chance."

"And I gather," said I, "that you obtained confirmation of your very ingenious theory?"

"I am hoping that I did," he replied, "but we shall see when we get home. If I have, we shall have some sort of a clue to the place from which that disastrous homeward journey started."

I forbore to remark that it did not seem to me to matter two straws where it started from, since it was evident that he thought the information worth acquiring. So I merely asked what the clue amounted to.

"Unfortunately," he replied, "it amounts to very little. This is the entry in the catalogue corresponding to the pot which I examined."

He indicated the entry in his notebook, and I read:

Moulin a vent. Julie (Polly)

"What a perfect and complete ass the fellow must be," I exclaimed, returning the notebook in disgust, "to write meaningless twaddle like that in what purports to be a museum catalogue!"

"I agree with you most warmly," he replied. "But the man's oddities are an element in our problem. And of course, these preposterous entries in the catalogue are not meaningless. They have a meaning which is deliberately concealed and which we have got to extract."

"In the case of this one?" I asked, "can you make any sense of it? Can you, for instance, discover any connection between an earthen pot and a windmill?"

"Yes," he replied, "I think that is fairly clear, though it doesn't help us much. There is a place in Wiltshire, near Avebury, known as Windmill Hill, where a certain distinctive kind of neolithic pottery has been found and which has been named the Windmill Hill type. Probably this pot is an example of that type, but that is a question that we can easily settle, though it doesn't seem to be an important one. The information that we want is probably contained in the other two words and, at present, I can make nothing of them."

"No," I agreed, "they are pretty obscure. Who is Julie? What is she? And likewise: Who is Polly? Good God! What damned nonsense it is!"

He smiled at my exasperation. "You are quite right, Jervis," said he. "It is monstrous that two learned medical jurists should have to expend their time and intellect in solving a set of silly puzzles. But it is part of our present job."

"Do you find any method in this fellow's madness?" I asked. "I noticed you copying out a lot of this balderdash."

"There is a little method," he replied. "Not much. But this entry, relating to that little embossed red-ware dish that you saw, will illustrate Penrose's method. You see, it reads: '*Sammy. Pot Sand. Sinbad*'. Now, this Gaulish red ware is usually described as Samian ware, so we may take it that '*Sammy*' means '*Samian*'. The interpretation of '*Pot Sand*' is also fairly obvious. There is a shoal in the Thames Estuary off Whitstable on which it is believed that a Roman ship, laden with pottery, went aground and broke up. From time immemorial, oyster dredgers working over that shoal have brought up quantities of Roman pottery, including Samian ware, whence the shoal has been named 'The Pan Sand', and is so marked on the Admiralty charts. Penrose's '*Pot Sand*' is therefore, presumably The Pan Sand, and as to Sinbad, we may assume him to have been a sailor, probably an oyster dredger or a whelk fisher."

"I have no doubt that you are right," said I, "but it is difficult to consider such childish twaddle with patience. I should like to kick the fellow."

"I should be delighted if you could," said he, "for, since you would have to catch him before you could kick him, that would mean that our problem would be solved. By the way, we shall have to contrive, somehow, to make the acquaintance of Mr. Lockhart. I wonder if Brodribb knows him."

"You think he could tell us what was in that small room. But I doubt if he would. Penrose would probably have sworn him to secrecy and, in any case, it would be a matter of professional confidence. But it seems to me that the burglary is a side issue, though I know you will say that we can't judge which issues are side issues."

"At any rate," he retorted, "the burglary is not one. It is very material. For if Penrose was the burglar, he must be in possession of property which he intends to dispose of, by which, if we knew what it was, we might be able to trace him. And if the burglar was *not* Penrose, we should very much like to know who he was."

I did not quite see why but, as our discussion had now brought us to our doorstep, there was no opportunity to pursue the question, for, as I had expected, Thorndyke made straight for the laboratory, and I followed, with mild curiosity as to the test that I assumed to be in view. As we entered, the sound of Polton's lathe in the adjacent workshop informed us that he had some job on hand there, but his quick ear had noted our arrival and he came in at once to see if his services were required.

"I need not disturb you, Polton," said Thorndyke. "It is only a matter of a small plaster mould."

"You are not disturbing me, sir," replied Polton. "I am just turning up a few spare tool handles to pass the time. You would like the quick-setting plaster, I suppose?"

"If you please," Thorndyke replied, and as Polton retired to fetch the materials, he produced from his pocket a small tin box from which he tenderly shook out into his hand a slab of moulding wax. Looking at it as it lay on his palm, I saw that it was a "squeeze" of the edge of the pot, the gap in the broken rim being represented by a wart-like swelling of the shape of the missing piece. Noting the exact correspondence, I remarked, "You hardly want the plaster. The shape of the squeeze is exact enough for comparison."

"Yes," he agreed, "but an actual measurement is always better than a judgement of resemblance."

Here, Polton returned with a jar of the special plaster, a rubber bowl, a jug of water and the other necessaries for the operation. Unobtrusively but firmly taking possession of the squeeze, he laid it in one of the little paper trays that he used for making small moulds or casts, brushed it over lightly with a camel-hair brush containing a trace of oil, and then proceeded to mix the plaster. This had to be done quickly, since the special plaster set solid in about five minutes, and I could not but admire the calm, unhurried way in which Polton carried the process through its various stages. At exactly the right moment, the plaster was dropped on to the squeeze, blown with the breath into all the interstices, and then the remainder poured on until the little tray was full to the brim, and even as the last drops were being persuaded out of the bowl with a spoon, the change began which transformed the creamy liquid into a white solid like the "icing" on a wedding cake.

At this point Thorndyke retired to fetch the fragment, and Polton and I took the opportunity to clean the bowl and spoon and spread on the bench a sheet of newspaper to receive the inevitable crumbs and scrapings, a most necessary precaution, for plaster, in spite of its delicate whiteness, is one of the dirtiest of materials. The particles which detach themselves from a cast seem to spread themselves over a whole room, with a special predilection for the soles of shoes, whence they distribute impressions on stairs and passages in the most surprising and unexpected fashion. But a sheet of paper collects the particles and enables them to be removed tidily before they have the opportunity to develop their diabolical tendencies.

When Thorndyke returned our labours were completed, and the little tray reposed on the paper with the plaster tools beside it.

"Is it hard enough to open?" Thorndyke asked.

Polton tested with his finger-nail the smooth, white mass that bulged up from the tray and, having reported that it was "set as hard as stone", proceeded carefully to shell it out of the paper container. Then he scraped away the projecting edges until the wax was free all round. A little cautious persuading with the thumb induced the squeeze to separate from the plaster, when Polton laid them down side by side and looked expectantly at Thorndyke. The cast was now clearly recognisable as the replica of a portion of the outside surface of the pot, including the rim and the gap where a piece of the rim had been broken away.

Thorndyke now produced the fragment of pottery and, holding it delicately between his finger and thumb – for the plaster was still moist and tender – very carefully inserted it into the gap, and as it dropped in, exactly filling the space, with a perfect fit at every point, he remarked, "I think that settles the question of identity. This fragment is the piece that is missing from the museum pot."

"Yes," I agreed. "The proof is absolutely conclusive. What is not quite obvious to me is the importance of the fact which is proved. I see that it strongly supports your theory that the fragment was the product of a definite search, but it is not clear to me that even the confirmation of your theory has any particular value."

"It has now very little value," he replied. "The importance of the fact which this experiment has established is that it carries us out of the region of the unknown into that of the known. If this fragment was part of the museum pot, then the place from which that pot came is the place from which this fragment came."

"Yes," said I, "that is clear enough. And it is fair to assume that the place whence this fragment came is the place from which Penrose started on his homeward journey. But, as we don't know where the pot came from, I can't see that we have got so very far from the unknown. We have simply connected one unknown with another unknown."

Thorndyke smiled indulgently. "You are a proper pessimist, Jervis," said he. "But you will, at least, admit that we have narrowed the unknown down to a very small area. We have got to find out where that pot came from, and I don't think we shall have very much difficulty. Probably the catalogue entry embodies some clue."

"But," I persisted, "even if you discover that, I don't see that you will be any further advanced. You will know where Penrose came from, but that knowledge will not help you to discover where he has gone to. At least, that is how it appears to me. But perhaps there is some point that I have overlooked."

"My impression is," Thorndyke replied, "that you have not given any serious consideration to this curious and puzzling case. If you would turn it over in your mind carefully and try to see the connections between the various facts that are known to us, you would realise that we have got to begin by re-tracing that last journey to its starting-point."

With this, he picked up the cast with the embedded fragment of pottery to put them into the box with the other "exhibits" and, as he retired, Polton (who had been listening with a curious intentness to our conversation) gathered up the newspaper and the plaster appliances and went back to his lathe.

Chapter X
Introduces Mr. Crabbe

Thorndyke's rather cryptic observation gave me considerable food for thought. But it was not very nourishing food, for no conclusion emerged. He was quite right in believing that I had given little serious consideration to the case of Daniel Penrose. It had not greatly interested me, and I had seen no practical method by which the problem could be approached. Nor did I now, and the only result of my cogitations was to confirm my previous opinion that I had missed some crucial point in the evidence and to make me suspect that there was in this case something more than met the eye.

This latter suspicion deepened when I reflected on Thorndyke's concluding statement. "You would realise that we have got to begin by re-tracing that last journey to its starting-point." But I did not realise anything of the sort. The problem, as I understood it, was to discover the present whereabouts of Daniel Penrose, and to this problem, the starting-point of his last known journey seemed completely irrelevant. But in that I knew that I must be wrong, a conviction which merely brought me back to the unsatisfactory conclusion that I had failed to take account of some vital element in the case.

But it was not only in respect of that disastrous return journey that I was puzzled by Thorndyke's proceedings. There was his unaccountable interest in the burglary at Queen Square. Apparently, he believed the burglar to have been Penrose himself, and in this I was disposed to concur. But suppose that we were able to establish the fact with certainty, what help would it give us in tracing Penrose to his hiding-place? So far as I could see, it would not help us at all, and Thorndyke's keenness in regard to the burglary only increased my bewilderment.

Naturally, then, I was all agog when, a few days later, Thorndyke announced that Mr. Lockhart was coming in to smoke a pipe with us on the following evening, for here seemed to be a chance of getting some fresh light on the subject. Lockhart was being lured to our chambers to be pumped, little as he probably suspected it, and if I listened attentively, I might catch some of the drippings.

"You haven't forgotten," said I, "that Miller is likely to call to-morrow evening?"

"'No,'" he replied, "but we have no appointment so he may choose some other time. At any rate, we must take our chance, and it won't matter so very much if he does drop in."

It seemed to me that the superintendent would be very much in the way and I sincerely hoped that he would choose some other evening for his visit. But Thorndyke presumably knew his own business.

"How did you get hold of Lockhart?" I asked. "Did Brodribb know him?"

"I didn't ask him," Thorndyke replied. "I saw Lockhart's name in the list of cases at the Central Criminal Court so I dropped in there and introduced myself. When I told him that I was looking into Penrose's affairs, he was very ready to come in and hear all about the case."

I laughed aloud. "So," said I, "this poor deluded gentleman is coming with the belief that he is going to be the recipient of information. It is a rank imposition."

"Not at all," he protested. "We shall tell him what we know of the case, and no doubt we shall learn something from him in exchange. At least, I hope we shall."

"Then," said I, "you are an optimist. If he knows anything that you don't, you can be pretty certain that he learned it under the seal of the confessional."

Thorndyke agreed that I was probably right. "But," he added hopefully, "we shall see. It is sometimes possible to learn something from what a man refuses to disclose."

I made a mental note of this observation and kept it in mind when our visitor arrived on the following evening, for it suggested to me that Thorndyke's questions might be more illuminating than the answers that they might evoke, particularly if our friend should turn out to be uncommunicative. But this did not, at first, appear to be the case, for, after a little general conversation, he led up to the subject of Daniel Penrose of his own accord.

"I did not quite gather what it was," said he, "that your clients expected you to do. If it is a permissible question, what sort of inquiry are you engaged in?"

"It is a perfectly permissible question," replied Thorndyke. "I can tell you all about the case without any breach of professional confidence as the main facts are already in the public domain. What I am expected to do is to discover the place in which Mr. Penrose is at present hiding, or at least to locate him sufficiently to make it possible to produce him, if necessary."

"And apparently he doesn't want to be produced? But why not? Why has he gone into hiding? My very discreet informant told me that he had gone away from home and left no address, but she didn't mention any reasons for his disappearing. Are there any substantial reasons?"

"He thinks that there are," replied Thorndyke. "But, if you are interested, I will give you a sketch of the circumstances of his disappearance, so far as they are known to me."

"I am very much interested," said Lockhart. "Penrose is a queer fellow – the sort of fellow who might do queer things – and I don't know that I am so violently fond of him. But he always interested me as a human oddity, and I should like to hear what has happened to him."

Thereupon, Thorndyke embarked on a concise but detailed account of the strange circumstances which surrounded Penrose's disappearance from human ken, and I listened with almost as much attention as Lockhart himself. For Thorndyke's clear summary of the events in their due order was a useful refresher to my own memory. But what specially amused and delighted me was the masterly tactical approach to the cross-examination which I felt pretty sure was to follow. Thorndyke's perfectly open and unreserved narrative, treating the whole affair as one generally known, in respect of which there was not the slightest occasion for secrecy, was an admirable preparation for a few discreet questions. It would be difficult for Lockhart to adopt a reticent attitude after being treated with such complete confidence.

"Well," said Lockhart, when the story was told, "it is a queer affair but, as I remarked, Penrose is a queer fellow. Still, there are some points that rather surprise me."

"For instance?" Thorndyke suggested.

"It is a small matter," replied Lockhart, "and I may be mistaken in the man, but I shouldn't have expected him to be the worse for liquor. You seemed to imply that he was definitely squiffy."

"It is only hearsay," Thorndyke reminded him, "and an inexpert opinion at that. The report may have been exaggerated. But, in your experience of him, should you say that he is a strictly temperate man?"

"I wouldn't go so far as that," said Lockhart. "He is most uncommonly fond of what he calls '*the vintages of the Fortunate Isles*' and the '*elderly and fuscous wine of Jerez*', and I should think that he gets through a fair amount of them, But he impressed me as a man who would take a glass, or two or three glasses, of sherry or Madeira pretty often, but not a great quantity at once. Your regular nipper, especially of wine, doesn't often get drunk."

"No," Thorndyke agreed, "though sherry and Madeira are strong wines. What were the other points?"

"Well," replied Lockhart, "doesn't it strike you that the actions of Penrose are rather disproportionate to the cause? He seems to have been abnormally funky. After all, it was only a motor accident, and there isn't any clear evidence that it was his car. He could have denied that he was there. And in any case, it doesn't seem worth his while to bolt off and abandon his home and all his worldly possessions. If he had committed a murder or arson or something really serious, it would have been different."

"It was manslaughter," I remarked, "'and a rather bad case. And the vintages of the Fortunate Isles didn't make it any less culpable. He might have got a longish term of hard labour, even if he escaped penal servitude."

"I don't think it was as bad as that," said Lockhart. "At any rate, if I had been in his place, I would have stayed and faced the music, and I would have left it to the prosecution to prove that I was on that road."

"That," said Thorndyke, "is a matter of temperament. From your knowledge of Penrose, should you have taken him for a nervous, panicky man?"

Lockhart reflected for a few moments. "You speak," said he, "of my knowledge of Penrose. But, really, I hardly know him at all. I made his acquaintance quite recently, and I have not met him half-a-dozen times."

"You don't know his people, then?"

"No. I know nothing about his family affairs. Our acquaintance arose out of a chance meeting at a curio shop in Soho. We walked away from the shop together, discussing collecting and antiques, and he then invited me to go and inspect his treasures. Which I did, and that is the only occasion on which I was ever in his house. But I must say that it was a memorable experience."

"In what way?" Thorndyke asked.

"Well," replied Lockhart, "there was the man, himself – one of the oddest fishes that I have ever encountered. But I dare say you have heard about his peculiarities."

"I understand that he is a most inconveniently secretive gentleman, and also that he has an inveterate habit of calling things by their wrong names."

"Yes," said Lockhart, "that is what I mean. He speaks, not in parables, but in a sort of cross-word puzzles, leaving you to make out his meaning by the exercise of your wits. You can imagine what it was like to be shown round a collection by a man who called all the specimens by utterly and ridiculously inappropriate names."

"Yes," said Thorndyke, "rather confusing, I should suppose. But you did see the collection, and perhaps he showed you the catalogue too?"

"He did. In fact, he made a point of letting me see it in order, I think, to enjoy my astonishment. What an amazing document it is! If ever he should have to plead insanity, I should think that the production of that catalogue would make medical testimony unnecessary. I take it that you have seen it and the collection, too?"

"Yes," said Thorndyke, "I examined the catalogue and made a few extracts with notes of the pieces to which they referred. And I was shown round the collection by Mr. Horridge, Penrose's executor. But I have an idea that he did not show us the whole collection. We saw only the collection in the great gallery, but probably you were more favoured, as you were shown round by the proprietor?"

The question was very adroitly thrown out but, at this point, Mr. Lockhart, as I had expected, developed a sudden evasiveness.

"It is impossible for me to say," he replied, "as I don't know what the whole collection consisted of. I assumed that he had shown me all that there was to see."

"Probably you were right," said Thorndyke, and then, coming boldly to the real issue, he asked, "Did he show you the contents of the small room?"

For some moments Lockhart did not reply, but sat looking profoundly uncomfortable. At length, he answered in an apologetic tone. "It's a ridiculous situation, but you know what sort of man Penrose is. The fact is that when he showed me his collection, he made it a condition that I should regard the transaction as a strictly confidential one, and that I should not discuss his possessions or communicate their nature or amount to any person whatsoever. It is an absurd condition, but I accepted it and consequently I am not in a position to tell you what he did actually show me. But I don't suppose that it is of any consequence. I take it that you have no special interest in his collection."

"On the contrary," said Thorndyke, "we have a very special interest in the collection, and particularly that part of it which was kept in the small room. Since Penrose went away, there has been a burglary – or a suspected burglary – at his house. The small room was undoubtedly entered one night, and there is a suspicion that the big cupboard was opened. But, if it was, it was opened with a key, as there was no trace of any injury to the doors. On the other hand, it is possible that the burglar failed to pick the lock and was disturbed. But Penrose has the only key of the cupboard, so there are no means of ascertaining, without picking the lock or forcing the door, whether there has or has not been a robbery, and we have decided that it would not be admissible to do either in Penrose's absence. Nevertheless, it is important for us to know what was in that cupboard."

"I don't see why," said Lockhart. "If it is not admissible to force the door – and I entirely agree with you that it is not – I don't see that it would help you to know what was in the cupboard – or whether it contained anything at all. Supposing that it had certain contents. You cannot ascertain without opening it whether those contents are still there or whether they have been stolen. But if you say that the lock has not been picked nor the door forced, and Penrose has the only key, doesn't that prove pretty conclusively that no burglary has taken place?"

At this moment, a familiar sound came to justify my fears of an interruption. I had taken the precaution to shut the outer oak door when Lockhart had entered. But the light from our windows must have been visible from without. At any rate, the well known six taps with a walking-stick – in three pairs, like the strokes of a ship's bell – spelled out the name of the visitor who stood on our threshold. Accordingly, I rose and threw open the doors, closing them again as the superintendent walked in.

"Now, don't let me disturb anyone," exclaimed Miller, observing that, at his entrance, Lockhart had risen with the air of taking his departure. "I am only a bird of passage. I have just dropped in to collect those documents and hear if the doctor has any remarks to make on them."

Thorndyke walked over to a cabinet and, unlocking it, took out a small bundle of papers which he handed to the superintendent.

"I can't give a very decided opinion on them," said he. "It is really a case for a handwriting expert. All that I can say is that there are none of the regular signs of forgery, no indications of tracing, or of very deliberate writing. The separate words seem to have been written quickly and freely. But I got the impression – it is only an impression – that there is a slight lack of continuity, as if each word had been executed as a separate act."

"I don't quite follow that," said Miller.

"I mean," Thorndyke explained, "that – assuming it, for the moment, to be a forgery – the forger's method might have been, instead of copying words continuously from an original, to take one word, copy it two or three times so as to get to know it thoroughly, then write it quickly on the document and go on to the next word. Written in that way, the words would not form such completely continuous lines as if the whole were written at a single operation. But you had better get the opinion of a first-class expert."

"Very well," said Miller, "I will, and I will tell him what you have suggested. And now, I had better take myself off and leave you to your conference."

"You need not run away, Miller," Thorndyke protested, very much to my surprise. "There is no conference. Fill up a glass of grog and light a cigar like a Christian."

He indicated the whisky decanter and siphon and the box of cigars, which had been offered to, and declined by, Lockhart, and drew up a chair.

"Well," said Miller, seating himself and selecting a cigar, "if you are sure that I am not breaking in on a consultation, I shall be delighted to spend half-an-hour or so in your intellectual society." He thoughtfully mixed himself a temperate whisky-and-soda, and then, with a quizzical glance at Thorndyke inquired, "Was there any little item of information that you were requiring?"

"Really, Miller," Thorndyke protested, "you under-estimate your personal charms. When I ask for the pleasure of your society, need you look for an ulterior motive?"

Miller regarded me with a crafty smile and solemnly closed one eye.

"I'm not looking for one," he replied. "I merely asked a question."

"And I am glad you did," said Thorndyke, "because you have reminded me that there was a little matter that I wanted to ask you about."

Miller grinned at me again. "Ah," he chuckled. "Now we are coming to it. What was the question?"

"It was concerned with a man named Crabbe. Jonathan Crabbe of Hatton Garden. Do you know him?"

"He is not a personal friend," Miller replied. "And he is not Mr. Crabbe of Hatton Garden just at present. He is Mr. Crabbe of Maidstone Jail. What did you want to know about him?"

"Anything that you can tell me. And you needn't mind Mr. Lockhart. He is one of the Devil's own, like the rest of us."

"I know Mr. Lockhart very well by sight and by reputation," said the superintendent. "Now, with regard to this man Crabbe: He had a place, as you say, in Hatton Garden where he professed to carry on the business of a diamond broker and dealer in precious stones. I don't know anything about the diamond brokery, but he was a dealer in precious stones all right. That's why he is at Maidstone. He got two years for receiving."

"Do you remember when he was convicted?"

"I can't give you the exact date off hand," replied Miller. "It wasn't my case. I was only an interested onlooker. But it was somewhere about the end of last September. Is that near enough?"

"Quite near enough for my purpose," Thorndyke replied. "Do you know anything more about him? Is he an old hand?"

"There," replied Miller, "you are asking me a question that I can't answer with certainty. There were no previous convictions against him, but it was clear that he had been carrying on as a fence for a considerable time. There was definite evidence of that. But there was another little affair which never got beyond suspicion. I looked into that myself, and I may say that I was half-inclined then to collar the worthy Jonathan. But when we came to talk the case over, we came to the conclusion that there was not enough evidence and no chance of getting any more, so we put our notes of the case into cold storage in the hope that something fresh might turn up some day. And I still hope that it may, for it was an important case and we got considerable discredit for not being able to spot the chappies who did the job."

"Is there any reason why you should not tell us about the case?" Thorndyke asked.

"Well, you know," Miller replied, "it was only a case of suspicion, though in my own mind, I feel pretty cock-sure that our suspicions were justified. Still, I don't think there would be any harm in my just giving you an outline of the case, on the understanding that this is in strict confidence."

"I think you can take that for granted," said Thorndyke. "We are all lawyers and used to keeping our own counsel."

"Then," said Miller, "I will give you a sketch of the case, what we know and what I think. It's just possible that you may remember the case as it made a good deal of stir at the time. The papers referred to it as '*The Billington Jewel Robbery*'."

"I have just a faint recollection of the affair," Thorndyke replied, "but I can't recall any of the details."

"It was a remarkable case in some respects," Miller proceeded, "and the most remarkable feature was the ridiculous softness of the job. Billington was a silly fool. He had an important collection of jewellery, which is a stupid thing in itself. No man ought to keep in a private house a collection of property of such value – and portable property, too – as to offer a continual temptation to the criminal class. But he did, and what is more, he kept the whole lot of jewels in a set of mahogany cabinets that you could have opened with a pen-knife. It is astonishing that he went on so long without a burglary.

"However, he got what he deserved at last. He had gone across to Paris, to buy some more of the stuff, I believe, when, some fine night, some cracksmen dropped in and did the job. It was perfectly simple. They just let themselves in, prised the drawers open with a jemmy, cleared them out, and went off quietly with the whole collection. Nobody knew anything about it until the servants came down in the morning and found the drawers all gaping open.

"Then, of course, there was a rare philaloo. The police were called in and our people made a careful inspection of the premises, but it had been such an easy job that anybody might have done it. There was nothing that was characteristic of any known burglar. But on taking impressions of the jemmy-marks and a few other trifles, we were inclined to connect it with one or two other jobs of a similar type in which jewels had been taken. But we had not been able to fix those cases on any particular crooks, though we had a growing suspicion of two men who were also suspected of receiving. Of those two men, one was Jonathan Crabbe, and the other was a man named Wingate. So we kept those two gentlemen under pretty close observation and made a few discreet inquiries. But it was a long time before we could get anything definite, and when, at last, we did manage to drop on Mr. Crabbe, it was only on a charge of receiving. The Billington job still remained in the air. And that's where it is still."

"And what about Wingate?" asked Thorndyke.

"Oh, he disappeared. Apparently, he rumbled the fact that he was getting a bit of attention from the police, and didn't like it. So he cut his connection with Crabbe and went away."

"And have you lost sight of him?" Thorndyke asked.

"Yes. You see, we never had anything against him but his association with Crabbe, and that may have been a perfectly innocent business connection. And our inquiries seemed to show that he belonged to quite a respectable family, and the man, himself, was of a decidedly superior type – a smart, dressy sort of fellow with a waxed moustache and an eye-glass. Quite a toff, in fact. The only thing about him that seemed at all fishy was the fact that he was using an assumed name. But there was not so very much even in that, for we ascertained that he had been on the stage for a time, and he had probably taken the name of Wingate in preference to his family name, which was rather an odd one – Deodatus Pettigrew."

"You never traced any of the proceeds of the robbery?" Thorndyke suggested.

"No. Of course, jewellery is often difficult to trace if the stones are taken out of their settings and the mounts melted down. But these jewels of Billington's ought to have been easier than most to trace, as a good many of them were quite unusual and could only have been disguised by re-cutting, which would have brought down their value a lot. And there was one that couldn't have been disguised at all. I remember the description of it quite well. It was rather a famous piece, known as the

Jacobite Jewel. It consisted principally of a lump of black opal matrix with a fire opal in the centre, and on this fire opal was carved a portrait of the Old Pretender, who called himself James the Third. I believe there was quite a little history attached to it. But the whole collection was rather famous. Billington was particularly keen on opals, and I believe that his collection of them was one of the finest known."

"Had you any inkling as to what had become of this loot?" Thorndyke asked. "The thieves could hardly have been able to afford to put the whole of it away into storage for an indefinite time."

"No," agreed Miller. "They would have had to get rid of the stuff somehow. We thought it just possible that there might be some collector behind the affair."

"But," I objected, "a collector would probably know all about the specimens in other collections, and particularly a famous piece like this Jacobite Jewel. And he would be almost certain to have heard of the robbery. It would be a matter of special interest to him."

"Yes, I know," said Miller. "But collectors are queer people. Some of them are mighty unscrupulous. When a man has got the itch to possess, there is no saying what he will not do to gratify it. Some of the rich Americans who have made their fortunes by pretty sharp practice are not above a little sharp practice in spending them. And your millionaire collector is dead keen on getting something that is unique, something of which he can say that it is the only one of its kind in the world. And if it has a history attached to it, so much the better. I shouldn't be at all surprised if that Jacobite Jewel had been smuggled out of the country together with the great collection of opals. It is even possible that Crabbe had negotiated the sale before the robbery was committed but, of course, it is also possible that I may be mistaken and that Crabbe may have had nothing to do with the robbery. We are all liable to make mistakes."

Here the superintendent, having come to the end of his story, emptied his glass, re-lit his cigar, and looked at his watch.

"Dear me!" he exclaimed, "how the time does go when you are enjoying intellectual conversation – especially if it is your own. It's time I made a move. No, thank you, not another drop. But, well, yes, I will take another of these excellent cigars. You have listened very attentively to my yarn, and I hope you have picked up something useful from my chatter."

"I always pick up something useful from your chatter, as you call it," replied Thorndyke, rising as the superintendent rose to depart, "but on this occasion you have given me quite a lot to think about."

He walked to the door with Miller and even escorted him out on to the landing, and meanwhile, I occupied myself in restraining, with exaggerated hospitality, a strong tendency on the part of our guest to rise and follow the superintendent – for I could not let him go until I had seen what Thorndyke's next move was to be.

The superintendent's narrative had given me a very curious experience, in respect of its effect on Lockhart. At first, he had listened with lively interest, probably comparing the Billington collection with that of Penrose. But presently he began to look distinctly uncomfortable and to steal furtive glances at Thorndyke and me. I kept him unobtrusively under observation, and Thorndyke, I know, was watching him narrowly, though no one who did not know him would have suspected it, and we both observed the change of manner. But when Miller mentioned the Jacobite Jewel and went on to describe its appearance, the expression on Lockhart's face was unmistakable. It was that of a man who has suffered a severe shock.

Having seen the last of the superintendent, Thorndyke closed both the doors and went back to his chair.

"That was a queer story of Miller's," he remarked, addressing Lockhart. "One does not often hear of a receiver including burglary in his accomplishments. I am disposed to think that Miller's surmise as to the destination of the swag from the Billington robbery is about correct. What do you think, Lockhart?"

"You mean," the latter replied, "that it was smuggled out of the country."

"No," said Thorndyke, "I don't mean that, Lockhart, and you know I don't. What I am suggesting is that the Billington opals, including the Jacobite Jewel, are, or were, in Penrose's possession, that they were in the cupboard in the small room, and that you saw them there."

Lockhart flushed hotly, but he kept his temper, replying with mild facetiousness, "Now, you know, Thorndyke, it's of no use for you to try the suggesting dodge on me. I am a practising barrister, and I have used it too often myself. I have told you that I gave an undertaking to Penrose not to discuss his collection with anybody, and I intend to honour that undertaking to the letter and in the spirit."

"Very well, Lockhart," Thorndyke rejoined, "we will leave it at that. Probably, I should adopt the same attitude if I were in your position, though I doubt if I should have given the undertaking. We will let the collection go, unless you would consider it admissible to discuss the source of some of the things in the big room, which we all saw. The question as to where he got some of those things has a direct bearing on the further question as to where he is lurking at the present moment."

"I don't see the connection," said Lockhart, "but if you do, that is all that matters. What is it that you want to know?"

"I should like to know," Thorndyke replied, "what his methods of collection are. Has he been in the habit of attending farmhouse auctions, or prowling about in labourer's cottages? Or did he get his pieces through regular dealers?"

"As to that," said Lockhart, "I can only tell you what he told me. He professed to have discovered many of his treasures in cottage parlours and in country inns and elsewhere, and to have practised on quite an extensive scale what he called '*resurrectionist activities*', but he was mighty secret about the actual localities. My impression is that his explorations were largely bunkum. I suspect that the bulk of his collection came from the dealers, and particularly from the antique shop that I mentioned to you. In fact, he almost admitted as much, for he told me that when his explorations drew a blank, he was accustomed to fall back on the Popinjay."

"The Popinjay?" I repeated.

"The proprietor of the antique shop was a man named Parrott, but I need not say that Penrose never referred to him by that name. He was always '*our* psittacoid *friend*', or '*Monsieur le Perroquet*' or '*the Popinjay*'. You will even find him referred to in those terms in the catalogue."

"That is useful to know," said Thorndyke. "I met with some entries containing the words, '*Psitt*', '*le Perro*' and '*Pop*' and could make nothing of them. Now I realise that they represented purchases from Mr. Parrott. And there was an entry, '*Sweeney's resurrection*'. That, I suppose, had a similar meaning. Do you know who Sweeney is?"

Lockhart laughed as he replied, "No, I have never heard of him, though I remember the entry. The only thing that I feel sure of is that his name is not Sweeney. Possibly it is Todd, and he is probably a dealer in antiquities. The piece, I remember, is an Anglo-Saxon brooch, and we may guess that Mr. Sweeney Todd got it from a Saxon burial ground in the course of some unauthorised excavations."

"That seems likely," said Thorndyke. "I must look up the list of dealers in antiquities in the directory and see if I can find out who he is."

"But does it matter who he is?" asked Lockhart. "If you are trying to discover the whereabouts of our elusive friend, I don't quite follow your methods."

"My dear Lockhart," Thorndyke replied, "my methods are of the utmost simplicity. I know practically nothing about Penrose, his habits and his customs, and I am out to pick up any items of information on the subject that I can gather, in the hope that some of them may prove to have some bearing on my quest. After all, it is only the ordinary legal method which you yourself are in the habit of practising."

311

"I suppose it is," Lockhart admitted. "But, fortunately for me, I have never had a problem of this kind to deal with. I can't imagine a more hopeless task than trying to find a very artful, secretive man who doesn't mean to be found."

At this moment, I heard the sound of a key being inserted in the outer door. Then the inner door opened and Polton entered with an apologetic crinkle.

"I have just looked in, sir," he announced, "to see if there is anything that you wanted before I go out. I shall be away about a couple of hours."

"Thank you, Polton," Thorndyke replied. "No, there is nothing that I shall want that I can't get for myself."

As Thorndyke spoke, Lockhart looked round quickly and then stood up, holding out his hand.

"This is a very unexpected pleasure, Mr. Polton," said he. "I didn't know that you were a denizen of the Temple, and I was afraid that I had lost sight of you for good, now that Parrott's is no more." He shook hands heartily with our ingenious friend and explained to us, "Mr. Polton and I are quite old acquaintances. He also, was a frequenter of Parrott's establishment, and the leading authority on clocks, watches, hallmarks, and other recondite matters."

"You speak of Parrott's shop," said Thorndyke, "as a thing of the past. Is our *psittacoid* friend deceased, or has he gone out of business?"

"Parrott is still to the good, so far as I know," replied Lockhart, "'but the business is defunct. I suspect that it was never more than half-alive. Then poor Parrott had a double misfortune. Penrose, who was by far his best customer, disappeared, and then his cabinetmaker – a remarkably clever old man named Tims – died and could not be replaced. So there was no one left to do the restorations which were the mainstay of the business. I was sorry to find the shop closed when I came back from my travels on circuit. It was quite a loss, wasn't it, Mr. Polton?"

"It was to me," replied Polton, regretfully. "Many a pleasant and profitable hour have I spent in the workshop. To a man who uses his hands, it was a liberal education to watch Mr. Tims at work. I have never seen any man use wood-working tools as he did."

With this, Polton wished our guest "Good evening!" and took himself off. As the outer door closed, Lockhart asked, "If it is not an impertinent question, what is Mr. Polton's connection with this establishment? He has always been rather a mystery to me."

"He is rather a mystery to me," Thorndyke replied, with a laugh. "He says that he is my servant. I say that he is my faithful friend and

312

Jervis's. Nominally, he is our laboratory assistant and artificer. Actually, since he can do or make anything and insists on doing everything that is to be done, he is a sort of universal fairy godmother to us both – and I can assure you that he is not unappreciated."

"I am glad to know that," said Lockhart. "We all – the frequenters of Parrott's, I mean – held him in the greatest respect, and none more so than Penrose."

"Oh, he knew Penrose, did he?" said I, suddenly enlightened as to Polton's interest in our conversations respecting the missing man. "He has never mentioned the fact."

"Perhaps you have never given him an opening," Lockhart suggested, not unreasonably. "But they were quite well acquainted. In fact, the very last time that I saw Penrose, he and Mr. Polton were walking away from the shop together, carrying a lantern clock that Mr. Polton had been restoring."

We continued for some time to discuss Polton's remarkable personality and his versatile gifts and abilities, in which Lockhart appeared to be deeply interested. At length the latter glanced at his watch and rose.

"I have made an unconscionably long visit," said he, as he prepared to depart, "but it is your fault for making the time pass so agreeably."

"You certainly have not out-stayed your welcome," Thorndyke replied, "and I hope you will stay longer next time."

With this exchange of civilities, we escorted our guest out to the landing and, having wished him "Good night!" returned to our chamber to discuss the events of the evening.

Chapter XI
Re-Enter
Mr. Kickweed

When I had closed the door and drifted back towards my chair, I cast an expectant glance at Thorndyke but, as he maintained a placidly reflective air, and thoughtfully re-filled his pipe in silence, I ventured to open the inevitable discussion.

"May I take it that my revered senior is satisfied with the evening's entertainment?"

"Eminently so," he replied. "In fact, considerably beyond my most sanguine expectations. We have made appreciable progress."

"In what direction?" I asked. "Does Miller's story throw any light on the case?"

"I think so," he answered. "What he told us, in conjunction with what Lockhart refused to tell us, seems to help us to this extent, that it appears to disclose a motive for the burglary, or the attempt."

"Do you mean that it establishes the probability that there was something there worth stealing and that somebody besides Penrose knew of it?"

"No," he replied, "though that also is true. But, what is in my mind is this: When Penrose disappeared, either for good or for some considerable time, there arose the probability that, sooner or later, the cupboard in the small room would be opened for inspection by Horridge or some other person claiming authority. But if that cupboard contained – as I have no doubt it did – a quantity of stolen property, the identifiable proceeds of a known robbery, a very awkward situation would be created."

"Yes," I agreed. "It would be awkward for Penrose when Miller caught the scent. There would be a hue-and-cry with a vengeance. And it might be unpleasant for Mr. Crabbe if any connection could be traced between him and Penrose. I suppose there can be no doubt that the stuff was really there?"

"It is only an inference," Thorndyke replied, "but I am convinced that the Billington jewels were in that cupboard and that Lockhart saw them there. Everything points to that conclusion. You saw how intensely uncomfortable Lockhart looked when Miller described the stolen jewels, and you must have noticed that he was perfectly willing to discuss the general collection. From which we may reasonably infer that his promise

314

of secrecy referred only to the contents of the small room. Besides, if the stolen jewels had not been there, or he had not seen them, he would certainly have said so when I challenged him. The denial would have been no breach of his promise."

"No," I agreed, "I think you are right in assuming that he saw them, though how Penrose could have been such an idiot as to show them at all is beyond my comprehension – that is, if he knew that they were stolen goods, which I gather is your opinion."

"It is not by any means certain that he did," said Thorndyke. "Evidently he is quite ignorant of the things that he collects. The promise may have been only a manifestation of his habitual secrecy, accentuated by the knowledge that he had acquired the jewels from some rather shady dealer. The evidence seems a little contradictory."

"At any rate," said I, "it was a lucky chance that Miller happened to drop in this evening. Or wasn't it a chance at all? There was just a suspicion of arrangement in the way things fell out. Did you know that Miller would select this evening for his call?"

"In effect, I may say that I did. I had good reason to believe that he would call this evening and, as you suggest, I made my arrangements accordingly. But those arrangements did not work out according to plan, for I knew nothing of the Billington robbery. Miller's disclosure was a windfall and it made the rest of my plan unnecessary."

"Then what had you proposed to do?"

"My intention was," Thorndyke replied, "to demonstrate to Lockhart that there had been transactions between Crabbe and Penrose. Of course, I could have done this without Miller's help, but I thought that if he heard of Crabbe's misdeeds from a police officer he would be more impressed and, therefore, more amenable to questions. But, as I said, Miller's story did all that was necessary."

"Then," said I, "there *was* a connection between Crabbe and Penrose, and that connection was known to you. How did you find that out? And, by the way, how did you come by your knowledge of Mr. Crabbe? I had never heard of him until you mentioned his name."

Thorndyke chuckled in his exasperating way. "My learned friend is forgetting," said he. "Are we not decipherers of cross-word puzzles and interpreters of dark sayings?"

"I am not," said I. "So you may as well come straight to the point."

"You have not forgotten the scrap of paper with the cryptic inscription which was found in the small room?"

"Ha!" I exclaimed, suddenly recalling the ridiculous inscription, "I begin, as Miller would say, to rumble you. But not very completely. The

315

inscription read: '*Lobster: hortus petasatus*'. But I still don't see how you arrived at it. Crabs are not the only crustaceans – besides lobsters."

"Very true, Jervis," said he. "Lobster is ambiguous as to its possible alternatives. Evidently, the more specific character was contained in the other term, '*hortus petasatus*'. Now, the learned Dr. Smith translates *petasatus* as '*wearing, or having on, a travelling-cap, ready for a journey*'. But the word '*petasus*' means either a cap or a hat, so the adjective, *petasatus*, may be rendered as '*hatted*' or '*having a hat on*'."

"Yes, I see," said I, with a sour grin. "So *hortus petasatus* would be a *hat on garden*. But what puerile balderdash it is. That man, Penrose, ought to be certified."

"Still," said Thorndyke, "you see that it was worthwhile to study his jargon for, when I had deciphered the inscription so far, the rest of the inquiry was perfectly simple. I looked up Hatton Garden in the directory and ran through the names of occupants in search of one that seemed related to the term '*lobster*'. Among them I found the name of Jonathan Crabbe (the only one, in fact, who answered the description), and as he was described as a diamond broker and dealer in precious stones, I decided that he was probably the man referred to by Penrose. Accordingly, I paid a visit to Hatton Garden and made a few discreet inquiries, which elicited the fact that Mr. Crabbe was absent from his premises and was in some sort of trouble in connection with a charge of receiving. Whereupon I made arrangements to give Lockhart a shock."

"And very completely you succeeded," said I. "He is in a deuce of a twitter, and well he may be, knowing quite well that he is making himself an accessory after the fact."

"Yes," Thorndyke agreed, "he is in a very unpleasant dilemma. But I don't think we can interfere, at least for the present. He is a lawyer and knows exactly what his position is and, meanwhile, his reticence suits us well enough. I don't want a premature hue-and-cry raised."

Here the discussion appeared to have petered out, but it seemed that the evening's experiences were not yet finished, for, in the silence which followed Thorndyke's rejoinder, there came to my ear the sound of soft and rather stealthy footsteps ascending the stairs, and at the same moment I suddenly remembered that I had not shut the outer door when we came in after seeing Lockhart off.

The steps continued slowly to ascend. Then they crossed the landing and paused opposite our door. There was a brief interval followed by a very elaborate flourish, softly and skilfully executed, on the little brass knocker of the inner door, very much in the style of the old-fashioned footman's knock. I rose and, striding across the room, threw open the door, when my astonished gaze encountered no less a person than Mr.

Kickweed. He broke out at once into profuse apologies for disturbing us at so untimely an hour. "But," he explained, "the matter seemed to me of some importance, and I thought it best not to call in the daytime in case you might not wish my visit to become known."

This sounded rather mysterious so, in accordance with his hint, I closed both the doors before ushering him across the room to the chair lately vacated by Miller.

"You needn't be apologetic, Mr. Kickweed," said Thorndyke, as he shook his visitor's hand. "It is very good of you to turn out at night to come and see us. Sit down and mix yourself a whisky-and-soda. Will you light a cigar as an aid to business discussion?"

Kickweed declined the refreshments but was obviously gratified by the manner of his reception and, having expressed his thanks, he came at once to the object of his visit.

"I am the bearer of news, sir, which I think you will be glad to hear. I have received a letter from Mr. Penrose."

There did not, to me, appear to be anything particularly surprising in this statement. But it was evidently otherwise with Thorndyke, for he received the announcement with more astonishment than I had ever known him to show – though, even so, it needed my expert and accustomed eye to detect his surprise.

"When did you receive the letter?" he asked.

"It came by the first post this morning," Kickweed replied. "I thought you would like to know about it and, perhaps, like to see it, so I have brought it along for your inspection."

He produced from his pocket a bulging letter-case, from which he extracted a letter in its envelope and handed it to Thorndyke, who took out the letter, opened it, and read it through. When he had finished the reading, he proceeded, according to his invariable custom when dealing with strange letters, to scrutinise its various parts, especially the signature and the date, to examine the paper, holding it up to the light and, finally, to make a minute inspection of the envelope.

"The letter, I see," said he, "is dated with yesterday's date but gives no address, but the postmark is Canterbury and is dated yesterday afternoon. Do you suppose Mr. Penrose is staying at Canterbury?"

"Well, no, sir," replied Kickweed, "I do not, though he used rather frequently to stay there. But from my knowledge of Mr. Penrose, I don't think he would have posted the letter in the town where he was staying. Still, he can hardly be far away from there. I think he knows that neighbourhood rather well."

"Does anyone else know about this letter?"

317

"No, sir. I took it from the letter-box myself, and I have not spoken of it to anybody."

"I think," said Thorndyke, "that Mr. Brodribb ought to be told. In fact, I think that the letter ought – with your consent – to be handed to him for safe keeping. You probably realise that it may become of considerable legal importance."

"Yes, sir, I realise that and that it ought to be taken great care of. What I proposed was to hand it to you, if you will take custody of it. Of course, you will dispose of it as you think best, but I brought it to you because you seemed to take a more sympathetic view of poor Mr. Penrose than anyone else has done. And I may say, sir, that I should be more happy if you would keep it in your possession for the present. I shouldn't like it to be used to help the police to worry Mr. Penrose by searching in his neighbourhood."

"Very well, Mr. Kickweed," said Thorndyke. "I will keep the letter for the present on the understanding that it shall be produced only if circumstances should arise which would make its production necessary in the interests of justice. Do you agree to that?"

"Oh, certainly, sir," replied Kickweed. "You will, of course, make any use of it that you think proper and necessary, other than the one I mentioned."

"You may take it," said Thorndyke, "that no attempt will be made by me, or with my connivance, to harass Mr. Penrose, and that you may safely leave the letter in my custody. And I may say that I am greatly obliged to you for letting me have it and for having taken the trouble to report the matter to me."

Kickweed mildly deprecated these acknowledgments, and Thorndyke continued. "On reading this letter I am struck by certain peculiarities on which I should like to hear your opinion. It is a rather odd letter."

"It is," Kickweed admitted, "but then you know, sir, Mr. Penrose is a rather odd man, if I may venture to say so."

Here Thorndyke handed me the document and I rapidly read it through. It was certainly a very odd letter. Secretly, I pronounced it the letter of a born fool or a lunatic, but I made no audible comments. Its precious contents were as follows:

26th March, 1935
Cerastium Vulgatum, *Esq.*

Respected Cer,

These presents are to inform you that, some time after my departure from Her Deceased Majesty's Equilateral Rectangle, I dish-covered that the key of the small room was not in my pocket. Thereupon I reflected, and after profound cogitation decided that it must be somewhere else. Peradventure, when I sarahed forth on that infelicitous occasion, I may have left it in the door, where it may have presented itself to your penetrating vision and been taken into protective custardy. This is my surmise, and if I have reason and you are now seised or possessed of the said key, I will ask you to convey the same to my bank and deliver it into the hand of the manager, in my name, to have and to hold until such time as I shall demand it from him. But first, fasten the window and lock the door. The room contains nothing but a few unconsidered trifles of merely scentimental value, but I wish it to remain undisturbed until I shall return carrying my sheaves and ready to do justice to the obese calf.

Hoping that you are in your usual boisterous spirits
Yours in saecula saeculorum,
Daniel Penrose

"You will agree with me, Jervis," said Thorndyke, when I returned the document, "that this is a very odd letter?"

I agreed with him in the most emphatic and unmistakable terms.

"We are all, by now," he continued, "accustomed to Mr. Penrose's oddities of speech. But this seems to go rather beyond even his usual eccentricity. What do you think, Mr. Kickweed?"

"I am disposed to think you are right, sir," replied Kickweed, a little to my surprise, for the letter contained just the sort of twaddle that I should have expected from Penrose.

"I think," said Thorndyke, "that you mentioned, when we last met, having noticed a gradual change in Mr. Penrose, a growing tendency to oddity and obscurity of speech."

"I think I did say," replied Kickweed, "that the habit of jocularity had been growing and becoming more confirmed. But habits usually do tend to grow, and I don't know that he was changed in any other respect. And as to this letter, we must bear the circumstances in mind. He is probably very much upset and he may have been a little more facetious than usual by way of keeping up his spirits."

319

"Yes," said Thorndyke, "that has to be considered. But a tendency to increasing eccentricity is a very significant thing, especially in the case of a man who has rather unaccountably disappeared. Any recent change in Mr. Penrose's mental condition might have an important bearing on his recent conduct, and I am inclined to believe that there has been some such change. Now take this letter. Is it the kind of letter that you have been in the habit of receiving from him?"

"Well, no, sir," Kickweed admitted. "He did not often have occasion to write to me, and when he did, his letters were usually quite short and to the point. They were not written in a jocular vein."

"In this letter," Thorndyke continued, "he addresses you by the style and title of *Cerastium Vulgatum, Esq.* Has he ever done that before?"

"No, sir, and it doesn't convey much to me now."

"*Cerastium vulgatum,*" said Thorndyke, "is the botanical name of the common chickweed."

"Oh, indeed," said Kickweed, with a sad and rather disapproving smile. "I supposed it was some kind of a joke, but I did not connect it with my somewhat unfortunate name."

"Has Mr. Penrose ever before made any kind of joke on your surname?" Thorndyke asked.

"No, sir," Kickweed replied, promptly and emphatically. "Mr. Penrose has his oddities, but he is a gentleman, and in all his dealings with me he has always been scrupulously correct and courteous. I am almost disposed to think that you may be right, sir, after all, in believing that his troubles have affected his mind."

Evidently, the botanical joke had produced a profoundly unfavourable impression.

"By the way," said Thorndyke, "have you delivered the key to the bank manager?"

"Not yet," replied Kickweed. "Of course, I must carry out Mr. Penrose's instructions, but I don't at all like the idea of having a locked room – possibly containing valuable property – with no means of access in case of an emergency."

"No," said Thorndyke, "it is a bad and unsafe arrangement. I suppose you have kept the key in your own possession?"

"Always," was the reply, "excepting on one occasion when I let Mr. Horridge have it for a few minutes to examine the window of the room. I was just going out to post a letter when he asked for it, and he gave it back to me when I returned from the post."

"I certainly think," said Thorndyke, "that you ought to have the means of access to that room. Do you happen to have the key about you?"

By way of reply, Kickweed thrust his fingers into his waistcoat pocket and withdrew them holding a key, which he held out to Thorndyke, who took it from him and inspected it.

"An extraordinarily simple key," he remarked, "for the lock of so important a room. It looks very like the key of my office cupboard. Would you mind if I tried it in the lock?"

"Not in the least," replied Kickweed, whereupon Thorndyke bore the key away to the office, the door of which he closed after him, a proceeding that somehow associated itself in my mind with the idea of moulding wax. In a couple of minutes he returned and, handing the key back to Kickweed, announced, "It fits the lock quite fairly, which is not surprising as it is of quite a common pattern. But it is a fortunate circumstance, for now, if the need should arise, I could supply you with a key that would open the small room door."

"That is very kind of you, sir," said Kickweed, "and I will bear your offer in mind. And now I mustn't detain you any longer. It is exceedingly good of you to have given me so much of your time."

With this he rose and, once more declining our offer of refreshment, took up his hat and stick and was duly escorted out on to the landing. When he had gone, and we were once more within closed doors, I delivered myself of a matter that had rather puzzled me.

"There seems to be something a little queer about that key. You haven't forgotten that Horridge had it – or a duplicate – in his possession when he showed us the small room?"

"I remember that he had a key," replied Thorndyke, "and the feeble and clumsy efforts that he made to keep it out of sight made me suspect that it was a duplicate. Now we know that it was."

"I presume that you took a squeeze of Kickweed's key?"

"Yes," he replied, "and I shall ask Polton to make a key from the pattern. If it is good enough for Horridge to have a duplicate, it is good enough for us to have one, too."

"Why do you suppose Horridge had his made?"

"It is difficult to say. Horridge, as you observed, is convinced that the mysterious cupboard contains something of enormous value – which it undoubtedly did at one time, and may still – and he is highly suspicious of Kickweed. He may want to try the cupboard lock at his leisure, or he may simply want to see that Kickweed does not. I doubt whether he has any very definite purpose."

"You seem," said I, "to be pretty confident that the Billington jewels were in that cupboard and that they are not there now. Have you formed an opinion as to who the burglar was?"

"We haven't much to go on," he replied. "We know that Crabbe could not have been the man, as he was in prison when the burglary occurred, and we know – or may fairly assume – that the Chubb key was in Penrose's possession. Those are all the facts that we have, and they lead to no certain conclusion. But now we have another problem to consider."

"You mean that idiot Penrose's letter. But what is its importance, apart from the internal evidence that the writer is certainly a fool and possibly a lunatic?"

"That is precisely what we have to discover. How important is it? Perhaps we had better begin with the obituary columns of *The Times*."

We did not keep a complete file of *The Times* on account of its enormous bulk, but it was our custom to retain our copies for three months, which usually answered our purpose. And it did on this occasion, for, on opening the file and scanning the obituary columns, we presently came upon a notice announcing that Oliver Penrose passed away peacefully in his sleep on the 16th of March, a few days before his ninetieth birthday.

"There," said Thorndyke, carefully replacing the papers and closing the file, "you have the answer to our question. Penrose's letter is dated – and was posted – ten days after his father's death. That is a fact of cardinal importance. It anticipates any possible question of survivorship. If Penrose should never be heard of again, if he should die and neither the time nor place of his death should ever be known, this letter could be produced as decisive proof that he was alive ten days after his father's death. Its immediate effect is to enable Brodribb to deal with Oliver's estate. If there is a will, it can be proved and administered, if there is no will, the intestacy proceedings can be set going."

"Yes," I said, "it is a mighty important letter in spite of its ridiculous contents, and its arrival will be hailed with profound relief by Brodribb. But it is a remarkably opportune letter, too. Doesn't it strike you as rather singularly opportune?"

"It does," he replied. "That is what immediately impresses one. So much so that one asks oneself whether its arrival can be no more than a coincidence."

"To me," said I, "it suggests that Penrose is not such a fool as his letter would imply. He has been keeping his eye on the obituary columns of *The Times* and, when he read the notice of the old gentleman's death, he made a pretext to write to Kickweed and thus put it on record that he was alive. That is how it strikes me. And that view is supported by the letter, itself. It was a perfectly unnecessary letter. Kickweed had had the key for months and there was no reason why he should not have continued to keep it, and every reason why he should. It looks as if the key had been a mere pretext for writing a letter. Don't you agree with me?"

"I do," he replied, "so far as the character of the letter is concerned. But we have to remember that when Penrose went away, his father was quite well, so that there was no need for him to watch the obituary columns. However, this is all rather speculative. The material fact is that the letter has arrived, and that fact will have to be communicated to Brodribb. I shall take the letter round and show it to him to-morrow morning."

Chapter XII
Mr. Elmhurst

Between Thorndyke and me there existed a rather unusual convention, which the reader of this narrative may have noticed. In the cases on which we worked together, he was always most scrupulous in keeping me informed as to the facts, and making me, if possible, a partner in the investigation by which they were ascertained. But he expected me to make my own inferences. Any attempt of mine to elicit from him a statement of opinion, or of his interpretation of the facts that were known to us both, met with the inevitable response: "My dear fellow, you know as much about the case as I do, and you have only to make use of your excellent reasoning faculties to extract the significance of what is known to us." The convention had been established when I first joined Thorndyke as his partner or understudy, as part of my training in the art and science of medico-legal investigation. But, apparently, my education was to continue indefinitely, for Thorndyke's attitude continued unchanged. He would tell me everything that he knew, but he was uncommunicative, even to secretiveness, as to what he thought.

But a habit of secretiveness sets up certain natural reactions. If Thorndyke would not tell me what he thought, it was admissible for me to find out, if I could, and I occasionally got quite a useful hint by observing the books that he was reading – for, unlike most lawyers, he dealt comparatively little in legal literature. His peculiar type of practice demanded a wide range of knowledge other than legal, and frequently it happened that his knowledge required amplification on some particular point. But by observing the direction in which he was seeking to enlarge his knowledge, I was able, at least, to judge which of the facts seemed to him the most significant.

Now I had noticed, of late, the appearance in our chambers of a number of books on prehistoric archaeology, a subject in which, so far as I knew, Thorndyke was not specially interested. There was, for instance, Jessup's *Archeology of Kent*, into which I dipped lightly, and there was a copy of the *Archaeological Journal*, containing a paper by Stuart Piggott on the "Neolithic Pottery of the British Isles". In this a slip of paper had been inserted as a book-mark and, on opening it, I found that it was marked at the section headed "Pottery of the Windmill Hill Type", and opposite, a page of drawings representing the characteristic forms of vessels and their decorative markings. And there were others of different characters, but all agreeing in giving descriptions and illustrations of neolithic pottery.

From these facts it was evident to me that Thorndyke's attention was still occupied by the ridiculous fragment of pottery that we had found in the pocket of Penrose's raincoat, and the object of his researches was, I had no doubt, the discovery of some likely place from which that fragment might have come. But why he wished to discover that place or what light it would throw, if found, on the present whereabouts of Daniel Penrose, I was utterly unable to imagine. That the question was one of importance I did not doubt for a moment. Thorndyke was not in the least addicted to the finding of mares' nests or the pursuit of that interesting phenomenon, the Will-of-the-Wisp. He wanted to discover the place which had been the starting-point of that wild journey in the motor car. Therefore, the identity of that place had some profound significance, and for several days I continued, at intervals, to cudgel my brains in a vain effort to reason out its bearing on our quest.

About a week after the receipt of the mysterious letter from Mr. Penrose, our inquiry entered on a new stage. Hitherto, Thorndyke's attitude had been mainly that of a passive observer. The visit to Queen Square, the examination of the coat and the pottery fragment, and the unearthing of Mr. Crabbe were the only instances of anything like active investigation. Otherwise, he had listened to the reports from Brodribb, Miller, and Lockhart and, while he had, no doubt, turned them over thoroughly in his mind, had made no positive move. But now he showed signs of a kind of activity which I associated, by the light of experience, with a definite objective.

I became aware of the change when, on a certain evening, coming home after a long day's work, I found a visitor seated by the fire, apparently in close consultation with Thorndyke. A glance at the little table with the decanter, wine glasses, and box of cigars told me that he was certainly a welcome and probably an invited guest, and a sheet of the six-inch ordnance map, on which lay the pottery fragment, hinted at the nature of the consultation.

The visitor, who rose as I entered, was a young man of grave and studious aspect, whose face – adorned with an impressive pair of tortoise-shell rimmed spectacles – seemed familiar, but yet I could not place him until Thorndyke came to my aid.

"You haven't forgotten Mr. Elmhurst, surely, Jervis?" said he.

"Of course, I haven't," I replied, as we shook hands. "You are the dene hole gentleman and the discoverer of headless corpses."

Mr. Elmhurst did not repudiate the dene hole, but protested that he had not actually made a habit of discovering headless corpses, at least in

325

the recent state. "The corpses that come my way," he explained, "are usually prehistoric corpses, in which the presence or absence of the head is of no special significance."

"In short," said Thorndyke, "Mr. Elmhurst is an archaeologist who is kindly allowing us to benefit by his special knowledge, as we did in the case of the dene hole."

"That," said Elmhurst, "is very nicely put, but it gives me undeserved credit. I am not an altruist at all. I am agreeing to do something that I have long wanted to do, but have been deterred by the cost. But now Dr. Thorndyke wants this thing done and is prepared to bear the expense, or at least part of it. You see, it is a case of enlightened self-interest on both sides."

"And what is this job?" I asked. "Something in the resurrection line, I suspect."

"Yes," said Elmhurst, "it is an excavation. The doctor has here a fragment of what seems to have been a neolithic pot of the Windmill Hill type, as it is usually described. He thinks it possible that this fragment was found in a certain long barrow in Kent. I don't know why he thinks so, but it is not improbable that he is right. At any rate, if that barrow contains any pottery, it is pretty certain to be of this type."

"That doesn't carry you very far," said I. "Supposing you found some pottery of this kind in the barrow, would that enable you to say that this fragment must have come from that barrow?"

"No," he replied. "It would only enable one to say that this fragment was of the same type as that it found in the barrow."

"But you know that already," said I.

"Believe," Elmhurst corrected.

"You said it was pretty certain to be of this type, and if you would repeat that on oath in the witness-box, I should think it would be sufficient. The excavation seems to be unnecessary."

"Oh, don't say that!" exclaimed Elmhurst. "You would degrade me from the rank of an investigator to that of a mere expert witness."

"My learned friend," said Thorndyke, "in spite of his great experience in court, seems to fail to appreciate the vast difference, in their effects on a jury, between an expert opinion – and a qualified one at that – and a pair of exhibits which the expert can declare, and the jury can see for themselves, are identically similar."

"Still," I persisted, "even if you could prove them to be identically similar, that would not be evidence that they came from the same barrow. You admit that, Elmhurst?"

"I admit nothing," he replied. "You know more about evidence than I do. But Dr. Thorndyke wants that barrow excavated and I want to do the excavation. And I may say that all the necessary preliminaries have been arranged. As the barrow is scheduled as an ancient monument, I have had to apply for, and have been granted by the Office of Works, a permit authorising me to excavate and examine the interior of the tumulus situated by the river Stour near Chilham in Kent and commonly known as 'Julliberrie's Grave'."

"Whose grave?" I demanded with suddenly-aroused interest, for as he pronounced the name there flashed instantly into my mind the words of Penrose's ridiculous entry: "*Moulin-a-vent, Julie: Polly*".

Elmhurst cast a quick, inquisitive glance at me and then proceeded to explain, "Julliberrie's. There is a local tradition that the mound is the burial-place of a more or less mythical person named Jul Laber, or Julaber, said to have been either a witch or a giant. If he was a giant we may be able to confirm that tradition, but I am afraid that a witch – in the fossil state – would defy diagnosis."

"And has this mound never been excavated, so far as you know?" I asked.

"It was excavated tentatively," he replied, "in 1702 by Heneage Finch, whose report is extant, but it appears that nothing was found beyond a few animal bones. Then an aerial photograph, taken only a week or two ago, shows signs of some more recent disturbance of the surface. Apparently someone has been doing a little unauthorised digging, which may account for this fragment of the doctor's. But still, we hope to find the burial chamber intact."

I reflected on the possible means by which Thorndyke had managed to locate this barrow and once more speculated on his inexplicable interest in this locality. And then suddenly I recalled Penrose's mysterious letter and the postmark on it.

"You say," said I, "that this mound is near Chilham. Isn't that somewhere in the Canterbury district?"

"Yes," he replied. "Quite near. Not more than half-a-dozen miles from Canterbury."

This began to be a little more understandable, though I was still unable to make out exactly what was in Thorndyke's mind. But I now had something like a clue which I could consider at my leisure, and meanwhile I returned to the subject of the excavation.

"I gather," said I, "that you are practically ready to begin operations. Is the date of the expedition fixed?"

"That is what we were discussing when you came in," replied Elmhurst. "Of course, there is no need for the doctor or you to attend the function. I can let you know if any pottery is found, and produce it for your inspection. But I hope you will both be able to come at least once while the work is in progress. One doesn't often get the chance of seeing a complete excavation of a virtually intact long barrow. If you can only make one visit, I would recommend you to wait until we are ready to expose the burial chamber. That is the most thrilling moment."

"It sounds like quite a big job," I remarked. "How long do you think it will take?"

"I should say from three to four weeks," he replied.

"My word!" I exclaimed. "Four weeks! Why, it will cost a small fortune. Of course, you will have to employ a gang of labourers."

"We shall want five men," said he, "in addition to the volunteers, and I reckon that sixty pounds will cover it easily."

I whistled. "I suspect, Thorndyke," said I, "that you will have to find that sixty pounds yourself. You won't get Brodribb to include archaeological researches in the costs. But do you tell me, Elmhurst, that this colossal work is necessary just to find out what sort of pottery there is in the barrow?"

"Perhaps not," he replied. "But, you see, the position is this: Julliberrie's Grave is scheduled as an Ancient Monument. No one may – lawfully – disturb it without a permit from the Office of Works. Now, they are perfectly willing to grant a permit to genuine archaeologists who are known to them as such, but subject to very rigorous conditions. They won't grant permits for mere casual digging. Their conditions are that, if you want to excavate, you must excavate completely and exhaustively so that the mound need never be touched again. All finds must be preserved and labelled and a detailed account of the excavation must be published, and when the work is finished, the barrow must be restored completely to its original condition. I explained all this to the doctor."

I must confess that I was staggered. The means seemed to be so disproportionate to the end. But Thorndyke seemed quite satisfied to pay sixty pounds for a few specimens of pottery and Elmhurst made no secret of his unholy joy at the prospect of a first-class "dig".

"Are you proposing to take part in this super-resurrection, Thorndyke?" I asked sourly.

"I am not proposing to join the diggers," he replied, "but I shall take the opportunity to see how a thorough excavation is done. I want to see the burial chamber opened, but I am also rather curious to see how the work is begun, and what the barrow looks like when the turf is removed and the mound exposed as it appeared when it was newly made. When do you reckon that you will have the barrow uncovered?"

"I expect," Elmhurst replied, "that we shall begin skinning off the turf on Thursday. We start operations, as I told you, on Tuesday morning, and there will be a full two days' work on the preliminaries –

pegging out the site, putting up an enclosing fence and preparing the dumps. I think, if you come down on Thursday – not too early – I can promise you that you will see the barrow as its builders saw it. I could, if you liked, meet you at Maidstone or Canterbury and personally conduct you to the scene of the operations."

"That isn't necessary," said Thorndyke. "We have the map, and you will want to be early at work. Moreover, I think I shall take the opportunity to do some prospecting on my way and I may be a little late in arriving at the barrow."

"That will be all to the good," said Elmhurst. "The later you arrive the more we shall have ready to show you."

This brought the discussion on ways and means to an end, and shortly afterwards our guest, having a train to catch, rose and took his leave.

During the week that intervened, very little was said either by Thorndyke or me on the subject of the expedition. Not that I was not keenly interested, for Thorndyke's reference to his "prospecting" intentions made it clear to me that he had something in his mind beyond the mere search for pottery. It seemed that now, for the first time, he was going to take some active measures to locate the elusive Penrose. But I asked no questions. I was going to take part in the prospecting operations and I hoped that their nature would throw some light on the methods by which Thorndyke proposed to attempt what looked like an impossibility.

One discovery I made, however, which was that Polton had in some way managed to attach himself to the expeditionary force. The fact was revealed to me when I found him in the act of pasting a couple of sheets of the six-inch ordnance map on thin mounting board. Observing that one of them included Chilham and our tumulus on Julliberrie Downs, I ventured to make inquiries.

"Why are you mounting them, Polton?" I asked. "You are not proposing to frame them and hang them on the wall?"

"No, sir," he replied. "When they are dry, I am going to cut them up into sections nine inches by six, that is four sections to a sheet. Then I shall number them and make a case to carry them in. You see, sir, a map is awkward to carry, even if you fold it, and most inconvenient to use out of doors if there is any wind. But by this method you can just take out the one or two sections that you are using, and the whole lot will go easily into my poacher's pocket, or The Doctor's either, for that matter. I'm getting them ready for our little trip next Thursday."

"Oh!" said I, "you are coming with us, are you?"

"Yes, sir," he replied, with a complacent crinkle. "The doctor mentioned to me that he was going down into Kent on some sort of exploring job, so I persuaded him to let me come and lend a hand. I understood him to say that they were going to dig up that old grave that is marked on the map – Julliberrie's Grave."

"That is quite correct, Polton," I assured him.

"Ah!" said he, with a crinkle of ghoulish satisfaction. "That will be very interesting. Do you happen to know when the party was buried?"

"I understand," I replied, "that the burial took place at some time from four- to ten-thousand years ago."

"Good gracious!" exclaimed Polton. "Ten-thousand years! Well, well! I should have thought that if he has been there as long as that they might have let him stay there. There can't be much of him left."

"That is what we are going to find out," said I, and with this I retired, leaving him to his pasting and his reflections.

Chapter XIII
The Track of
the Fugitive

In the course of my long association with Thorndyke, I had often been impressed by the number of things that he appeared to carry in his pockets. He reminded me somewhat of The White Knight. But there was this essential difference, that whereas that unstable equestrian was visibly encumbered with a raffle of things that he could never possibly want, Thorndyke was invisibly provided with the things that he did want. If the need arose for any instrument, appliance, or material, forthwith the desiderated object was produced from his pocket even as the parlour magician produces the required guinea-pig or goldfish. So, after all, the appearances may have been illusory – they may have been due, not to the gross quantity of things carried, but to an accurate prevision of the probable requirements.

The matter is recalled to my mind by the astonishing stowage capacity that Polton developed on the morning of our expedition to Chilham. Not only did the special outfit for the day's work – six-inch map, one-inch map, prismatic compass, telescope, surveyor's tape, and other oddments, laid out for Thorndyke's inspection – vanish into unsuspected pockets, leaving no trace but, as appeared later, his lading included a substantial meal, a big flask of sherry, and a nest of aluminium drinking cups. And even then he didn't bulge perceptibly.

Of the details of our travels on that day I have but a confused recollection. It was all very well for Thorndyke, who had apparently transferred the six-inch map bodily to his consciousness – he knew exactly where he was at any given moment. But to me, when once we had left the plain high road, all sense of direction was lost and I was aware only of a bewildering succession of abominably steep lanes, cart-tracks, and footpaths, which we scrambled up or stumbled down until we became finally and hopelessly submerged in a wood.

However, I will make an effort to give an intelligible account of this "prospecting" expedition, with apologies in advance for the somewhat nebulous topography. From Charing Cross we proceeded uneventfully to Ashford, where we got out of the train and took our places in a motor omnibus which was lurking in the vicinity and which was bound for Canterbury. Apparently it had been awaiting the arrival of the train, for as soon as we and one or two other train passengers had settled ourselves, the conductor, having taken a last fond look at the station, gave the signal to the driver, who thereupon started the vehicle with a triumphant hoot.

We rumbled along the main road for about six miles (as I afterwards ascertained) and then, shortly after crossing a small river, drew up at a village which the conductor announced as Godmersham. Here we got out and walked forward until we came to the cross-roads beyond the village, where Thorndyke turned to the right and led the way along the by-road. Presently we passed under a railway line and then, as the road made a sharp turn to the right, followed it along the bottom of a valley nearly parallel to the railway. About half-a-mile farther on, another by-road led off to the left and, as Thorndyke turned off into it, my sense of direction began to get somewhat confused. It was quite a good road and fairly level, but its windings made it difficult to keep a "dead reckoning", and when, half-a-mile along it, yet another by-road led off from it to the left at right angles – into which Thorndyke turned confidently – and then made a right-angle turn to the right, I abandoned all attempts to keep count of our direction.

Along this road we trudged for three-quarters-of-a-mile, still keeping fairly on the level, but then the ground began to rise sharply and the road zig-zagged more than ever. A mile or so farther on we passed through a village, and I found myself casting a slightly wistful glance at a couple of rustics who were seated on a bench outside the inn, sustaining themselves with beer and conversation. But Thorndyke plodded on relentlessly, and when, a few hundred yards beyond the village, we came to yet another cross-roads, he finished me off by taking the turning to the left.

"I suppose, Thorndyke," said I, when we had toiled up this road for about half-a-mile and he halted to look around, "you know where you are."

"Oh, yes," he replied. "That village that we passed through just now is Sole Street. I will show you on the map where we are. Let us have the six-inch, Polton."

The latter dived into the interior of his clothing, whence he produced the case of mounted sections and handed it to his principal.

"Here we are," said Thorndyke, when he had picked out the appropriate card. "That is the village at the bottom and this is the road we are on. You see that it peters out, more or less, when it enters the wood."

I compared the section of map with the visible objects and was able to identify a farm-house across the fields on our right and a considerable wood which we were approaching.

"Yes," I said, "it is clear enough so far, though it doesn't mean much to me. What is the significance of that pencilled cross by the roadside?"

"That," he replied, "marks the spot, as nearly as I could locate it from the evidence at the inquest, where the old woman was killed."

"Indeed!" I exclaimed. "So this is where the chapter of accidents began – or, at least, a few yards farther up. Then I may assume that the purpose of this prospecting expedition is to retrace the route of Penrose's car?"

"That is so," he admitted, "and presently we must begin to look for traces. At the moment, we don't need them, as there seems to be no doubt that the car came down this road. It was seen – or, at least, *a* car was seen – to come flying round the corner into the village and past the inn. Of course, it may not have been Penrose's car. But the time, the outrageous speed, and the wild manner in which it was being driven, all seem to connect it with the disaster."

"But," I objected, "even if it was the car that killed the woman, that is no evidence that it was Penrose's car. It seems to me that the argument against Penrose moves in a circle. Penrose is proved to have killed the old woman by the fact that he was on the road where she was killed, and he is proved to have been on that road by the fact that he killed the old woman. I respectfully suggest that my learned senior may probably be tracing, laboriously and with characteristic skill, the movements of a motor car in which we are not interested at all."

Thorndyke chuckled appreciatively. "Admirably argued, Jervis, and the point that you make is clearly realised by the police. There is very little doubt that it was Penrose's car, but there is no positive evidence that it was. And the police know, and we know, that you can't secure a conviction on mere probabilities. That is a further purpose of the prospecting expedition, not only to ascertain which way, and from whence, the car was travelling, but also, if possible, to establish what car it was."

As we continued to toil upwards towards the wood, I cogitated on this statement with considerable surprise. It seemed inconsistent with what I had supposed to be Thorndyke's object – and especially with his assurance to Kickweed – that no action was contemplated which might compromise Penrose or menace his safety. Yet here he was, by his own admission, industriously searching for the one missing item of evidence which could secure Penrose's conviction. Unless, indeed, he had any reason to believe that the wrong car had been identified, which his words did not in the least suggest. Incidentally, I was utterly unable to imagine how he proposed to identify a car which had passed down the road

333

months ago, or even pick up its tracks. The road was extraordinarily unfrequented. We had met not a single car, and only one farm cart, since we had passed under the railway. But still it was a metalled road, showing only slight traces of the carts and wagons that had passed over it, and obviously none of those traces had anything to tell us.

When we entered the wood, I noticed that Thorndyke kept a close watch on the borders of the road though he did not slacken his pace.

"I presume," said I, "that you are looking for the tracks of the car. But isn't that rather hopeless, seeing that it is about six months since Penrose passed down this road – if he ever did actually pass down it?"

"Of course," he replied, "it would be futile to look for tracks on the road, or even on the margins. But what I am looking for – though I don't expect to find it here – is some sign of a car having driven or backed off the road into the wood and along one of the footpaths. The marks made by a car entering the wood over the soft soil would be deep and they would remain visible for years. Moreover, they would be unique. They would not be confused with other tracks, as in the case of any kind of road."

"You have reasons, then, for believing that Penrose backed his car into the wood?"

"*We* have reasons, Jervis," he replied. "You saw the car and the dead leaves and earth on the wheels, and you will remember that the earth was of the same type as the surface soil here, a loam of the Thanet Sands type. Besides, there is the fact that, if Penrose was engaged, as the evidence suggests, in digging in the barrow, he must have left the car somewhere. But it appeared at the inquest that nobody had seen the car until it passed through Sole Street."

"There isn't much in that," said I. "We seem to have this tract of country all to ourselves. A car might remain parked by the side of this road for hours without being noticed."

He admitted the truth of this. "But," he added, "don't forget the state of the car, or the fact that Penrose was engaged in an unlawful act."

"And have you any idea," I asked, "where the car was probably left?"

"I have settled on a spot which seems likely," he replied. "But it is little more than a guess, and if I am wrong we shall have to give up the quest. We can't search the whole area of woodland."

Half-a-mile farther on, we came to a fork in the road, the left-hand branch being little more than a cart-track. Into this Thorndyke turned unhesitatingly, and by the care with which he scrutinised the margins, I judged that we were approaching the "likely spot". But the issue was rather confused by the fact that the rough, unmetalled road was fairly deeply rutted, having evidently been used by various carts and wagons. This road, however, after crossing a considerable open space, took a sharp, right-angle turn to the left opposite a pair of cottages, but its original direction was continued by a broad footpath. Thorndyke first followed the road in its new direction where it entered and crossed a narrow strip of wood but, after a careful examination of the ruts in the wood, he came back and explored the footpath. And here it was that we struck the first trace of what might have been a car-track.

The footpath passed along the front of the cottages, still in the open, but presently it skirted the edge of the wood. It was an old path, never disturbed by the plough, and its surface was trodden down hard by years of use. Moreover, its margins showed faint impressions of wheels, which had been nearly obliterated by the feet of the wayfarers who had walked over them.

"They don't look to me like the tracks of a car," I remarked as we all stooped to examine them.

"No," he agreed, taking a rough measurement with his stick. "The gauge is much too wide. Probably they are the tracks of some woodman's cart or timber-carriage. But a hard path like this would scarcely show an impression of a pneumatic tire excepting after heavy rain."

We continued our progress slowly for another hundred yards, keeping a close watch on the faint ruts beside the path. Then we all halted simultaneously, for here we could see the faint, but clearly distinguishable, tracks of some wheeled vehicle which had turned off the path on to the rough turf of the open field.

"This looks more likely," I remarked, and Polton supported me with the opinion that, "The Doctor's got him this time, as I knew he would."

Thorndyke made no comment but, producing from his pocket a steel tape, carefully measured the space between the wheel-marks.

"The measurement is correct," he announced, "but that is only an agreement. It would apply to thousands of other cars. However, we will see whither these tracks lead us."

We followed the tracks, not without difficulty, across the wide meadow until we readied another belt of woodland. Here the tracks entered the wood by a footpath and were easy enough to follow on the soft earth. The path continued for about a furlong and then emerged into the open, where it crossed a small grass-covered space and, following it, we were still able to distinguish the wheel-tracks by its sides. When it reached the edge of the wood, the footpath turned sharply to the right, keeping in the open. But here the tracks left the path and plunged straight into the wood, which was fairly free from undergrowth. Following the comparatively deep ruts which the wheels had made in the soft leaf-mould, we advanced by a rather tortuous route about a couple-of-hundred yards into the wood. And then, once more, we halted, for we had apparently come to the end of the tracks.

There seemed to be no doubt about it but, as the last year's leaves lay here more deeply, and the undergrowth had suddenly grown denser, I went on a few yards to make sure that the tracks did not reappear beyond the place where they had seemed to end. With difficulty I forced my way through the bushes and was further impeded by the brambles and spreading roots, and I had not gone more than a few yards when my foot was caught by some hard, angular object – obviously not a root or a bramble – whereby, after staggering forward a pace or two, I fell sprawling among the tangle of vegetation.

At the sound of the fall, and the accompanying pious ejaculations, Thorndyke hurried towards me to see what had happened. I picked myself up and, having wiped my hand, proceeded to search for the object which had tripped me up. Cautiously probing with my foot in a clump of nettles, I brought to light what looked like the haft of an axe but, when I seized it and drew it out, it proved to be a trenching tool.

It was at this moment, as I stood with it in my hand, trying to connect it with some vague stirring of memory, that Thorndyke appeared through the bushes.

"I hope you are not hurt, Jervis," he said, anxiously. "That would be a nasty thing to fall upon."

I assured him that I had come to no harm beyond a few scratches. "But," I added, "I am not quite clear about the significance of this thing. I have a vague idea that something was said by somebody about a trenching tool, but I can't remember what or who it was."

"The somebody," he replied, "was Kickweed. Don't you remember our interview in the garage when he told us, among other items, that he had a vague recollection of having seen a trenching tool there?"

"Yes, of course, I remember now. Then it is quite possible that this is the very tool he was speaking of?"

By way of answer, he took the tool from me and, having run his eye along the handle and turned it over, placed his finger on a spot near to the blade and held it out to me. Looking at it closely, I was able to make out in very faded lettering the name "D. Penrose," apparently printed with a rubber stamp.

I must confess that I was profoundly impressed. Once more Thorndyke had achieved what had seemed to me an impossibility. Not only had he traced the route that the car had followed, but he had clearly established the identity of the car. Moreover, he had settled the place from which the car started in a country which he had never seen, working by inference and aided only by the map. It was a remarkable performance – even for Thorndyke.

But here my reflections were interrupted by a hail from Polton in a tone of high excitement. For he, too, had been "prospecting", and as we returned to the end of the track, he met us, fairly bubbling with exultation and carrying his treasure trove in the form of a small spade and a leather case.

"Here is an astonishing thing, sir!" he exclaimed. "I found these in the bushes, and they've both got Mr. Penrose's name stamped on them. I could hardly believe my eyes. But there," he added, "I don't suppose, sir, that you are surprised at all. I expect you knew they were there before we started from home."

Thorndyke smilingly disclaimed the omniscience with which his admiring henchman credited him (though, in fact, Polton was not so very wide of the mark), and taking from him the spade and case, looked them over and verified the marks of ownership.

"You notice, Jervis," said he, "that these things correspond exactly with Kickweed's description: A small, light spade, pointed at the end, and a leather sheath or case to protect the point. The spade and the trenching tool appear to have been Penrose's equipment for his clandestine digging expeditions."

"Yes," I said, "and their presence here demonstrates that you were right in your inference as to the place where he parked his car. By the way, how did you arrive at it?"

"I can hardly say that I arrived at it," he replied. "As I said, it was little more than a guess. I started with the hypothesis – a very well-supported one – that Penrose went forth that day with the intention of digging in Julliberrie's Grave, and that he did dig there. If that were so, he would park his car as near to the place as possible, and the more so since he knew that he was committing an unlawful act and might have to clear out of the neighbourhood in a hurry. For the same reason, he would wish to leave his car where it would not be seen. But examination of the map showed this excellent place of concealment, less than half-a-mile from the barrow."

"Yes," I said, "it looks perfectly simple and obvious now that you have explained matters. But these tools, thrown away into the bushes, seem to suggest that the contingency that you mentioned did actually arise. Apparently, he did have to clear out of the neighbourhood in a hurry. Probably he was spotted in the act of digging and had to do a bolt, which would account for his having got rid of the incriminating tools. At

337

any rate, it looks as if the panic had started here and not after the accident."

"Exactly," Thorndyke agreed. "'The killing of the old woman was not the cause but the consequence of the panic. And now, as we have finished this part of our quest, we may as well move on and see how Elmhurst is progressing – unless there is anything more that you would like to see."

"There is," I replied with emphasis. "What I should like to see, above all other things in the world, is a good hospitable pub with oceans of beer and mountains of bread and cheese. As you seem to have memorised the whole neighbourhood, perhaps you know where one is to be found."

"I am afraid," said Thorndyke, "that there is nothing nearer than the Wool-pack at Chilham."

But here Polton, crinkling ecstatically, proceeded to unbutton his coat.

"No need for a pub, sir," said he. "We're provided. And we can do something better than bread and cheese and beer."

With this he fished out of his inexhaustible pockets a flat parcel – found to contain a veal-and-ham pie – a large flask of sherry, a nest of three aluminium drinking-cups, and a shoe-maker's knife in a leather sheath wherewith to carve the pie. There were no forks, but the need of them was not felt as the thickness of the flat pie had been thoughtfully adapted to the dimensions of a moderately-opened human mouth. Joyfully, we selected a place as free as possible from brambles and nettles and there seated ourselves on the ground, and while Polton, by his unerring craftsman's eye, divided the pie into three equal parts, Thorndyke and I filled our cups and toasted the giver of the feast.

When the banquet was finished and the empty flask, the cups and the knife had vanished into the receptacles whence they came, Polton thriftily utilised the wrapping-paper to disguise the naked form of the trenching tool. Then, with the aid of the compass, Thorndyke led the way through the wood and presently brought us out on to a stretch of rough pasture where, some three-hundred yards away, we could see the excavators at work.

338

Chapter XIV
Julliberrie's Grave

The scene on which I looked as we came out of the wood rather took me by surprise, though, to be sure, Elmhurst's lucid and detailed account of the proposed operations ought to have prepared me. But to an uninformed person like myself, excavation is just a matter of digging, and I had hardly taken in the elaborate preliminaries that exact scientific procedure demands.

Looking along the brow of the steep hill-side, one could see the barrow – a long, oval, grassy mound about fifty yards in length – standing out plainly against a background of trees that were just about to burst into leaf. Past it, to the left, down in the river valley, rose the tall white shape of Chilham Mill, while farther to the left and more distant was the town or village of Chilham. At ordinary times it must have been a rather desolate and solitary place, for no habitation was visible nearer than the distant mill, but now it was a scene of strenuous activity, peopled by busy workers.

The preparatory operations had apparently been nearly completed. The barrow was surrounded by a substantial spile fence – evidently new – which marked off a rectangular enclosure. Inside this, two rows of surveying pegs had been driven into the ground and a theodolite stand set up over one of them suggested a survey in progress. Outside the enclosure was a methodically spread dump of turf, and a trackway of planks was being laid to another spot, apparently the site of a dump for the chalk and earth which would be removed from the mound as the excavation proceeded. There was also a stack of half-a-dozen metal wheelbarrows and, hard by, a small shepherd's hut, in which a stoutly-built gentleman, apparently the surveyor, was at the moment depositing what looked like a theodolite case, which he did carefully with a proper respect for the instrument, and then, having shut the door of the hut, strode away briskly down the hill towards the village.

We seemed to have timed our arrival rather fortunately, for the work of uncovering the barrow had already commenced. Within the fenced enclosure two parties of workers were engaged, from opposite sides, in cutting out strips of turf and rolling them up like lengths of stair carpet. Of the two parties, one consisted of four labourers, who went about their work with the leisurely ease born of long experience, while the other party was, with the exception of one labourer, evidently composed of volunteers, among whom I distinguished, with some difficulty, our friend Elmhurst, transformed into the likeness of a coal-miner with leanings towards tennis.

We halted near the edge of the wood to observe the procedure without interrupting the work. Presently Elmhurst, having accumulated a goodly heap of turf-rolls, loaded them into a wheelbarrow, which was promptly seized by one of his two assistants – a fair-haired young Viking in a blue jersey and a pair of the most magnificent orange-red trousers of the kind known by fishermen as "fear-noughts" – who trundled it off through an opening in the fence and unloaded it neatly on to the turf dump on top of the already considerable stack that occupied it. Then he returned at a brisk trot and, having set down the empty wheel-barrow, picked up his spade and fell to work again on the cutting out of a fresh load.

It was at this moment that Elmhurst, happening to glance in our direction, not only observed our presence but evidently recognised us, for he laid down his spade and began to walk towards us, whereupon we hurried forward to meet him. As we approached, I noticed that he cast an inquisitive eye on the tools which Polton was carrying and, as soon as we had exchanged greetings, he inquired, "Are you proposing to take an active part in the proceedings? I see that you are provided with the necessary implements."

"The appearance is illusory," Thorndyke replied. "We did not bring these tools with us. They are the products of our prospecting activities in the wood hard by. And they are not going to be used on this occasion. It seems advisable to preserve them in the condition in which they were found."

Elmhurst regarded the tools with intelligent interest and, I thought, with some disfavour.

"I see," he said reflectively. "You connect those tools with the piece of pottery that you showed me?"

Thorndyke admitted that the connection seemed to be a reasonable one.

"Yes," said Elmhurst. "A pick and a spade do certainly seem to connect themselves with traces of unlawful digging in the neighbourhood. And they are quite workmanlike tools – especially the spade. I only hope that your friends have not been too workmanlike. In one respect they certainly have not. They have made a very poor job of replacing the turf."

"Then," said Thorndyke, "you have found evidence that the mound has really been dug into?"

"Yes," was the reply. "There is no doubt whatever. But they seem only to have made a short, irregular trench and, as they were nowhere near the burial chamber, I am still hopeful of finding that intact. But we shall see better how far they went when we get the turf off. As you see, we have got all the margin unturfed and we are just starting on the mound itself. We shall soon get that done with eight workers besides myself and, meanwhile, I can take you round and show you the arrangements for excavating a barrow."

"You mustn't let us waste your time," said Thorndyke, "and leave your colleagues to do all the work – though I must say, they seem to enjoy it."

"Yes, by Jove!" I agreed. "They are proper enthusiasts. I have been watching that sea rover in the decorative trousers and wondering what those labourers think of him. But perhaps they are not Union men."

Elmhurst smiled a cryptic smile but expressed complete satisfaction both with the labourers and his volunteer assistants. "I think," he added, "that my friends would like to make the acquaintance of the benefactor who has given us this very great pleasure."

Accordingly we proceeded towards the fenced enclosure and entered it by one of the openings left for the wheelbarrows to pass in and out.

"You notice," said Elmhurst, "that we have driven in a row of pegs all round the tumulus to define its edges. Those are for use in marking our plan and to guide us when we come to rebuild the mound. It has to be restored exactly to its original shape and size."

"You speak of rebuilding the mound," said I. "You don't mean that you are going to move the entire structure?"

"Certainly we are," he replied. "The essence of a complete excavation is in the thorough examination of every part of it. The whole of it will be moved, excepting a narrow longitudinal wall, or spine, along the middle, which has to be left to preserve the contour and serve as a guide to build up to. We shall move one-half at a time and the earth – or chalk rubble, as it will be in this case – that we take out will be carefully deposited in one of those dumps. Each dump will have a revetment of chalk blocks to prevent the piled earth from slipping away and getting scattered."

"Yes," said Thorndyke, "it is all very thorough and methodical, a very different thing from the slovenly methods of the casual digger. By the way, which side do you propose to begin with?"

"The right-hand side," replied Elmhurst. "That is the side on which your friends operated, and we are rather anxious to settle once for all what they really did in the way of excavation and how much damage

341

they have done. My colleagues are now beginning to peel off the turf from that side of the mound."

As he spoke, we rounded the end of the barrow and came in sight of the two volunteers and the labourer, all busily engaged in cutting lines in the turf with implements like cheese-cutters set on long handles. As we approached, the owner of the fear-noughts looked up and rather disconcerted me by disclosing an extremely comely feminine countenance, which accounted for Elmhurst's cryptic smile and caused me hurriedly to re-examine the other "gentleman", only to discover that the breeches which I had innocently accepted as diagnostic of masculinity appertained to a lady.

The introductions, effected by Elmhurst with a ceremonious bow and a grin of malicious satisfaction, informed us that the two ladies were, respectively, Miss Stirling – the wearer of the nautical garments – and Miss Bidborough, and that both were qualified and enthusiastic archaeologists (this was Elmhurst's statement, and neither denied it on behalf of the other), and that both were profoundly grateful to Thorndyke.

"It is the chance of a life-time," said Miss Stirling, "to carry out a complete excavation of a neolithic barrow, and such a famous one, too. I have often come here and looked at Julliberrie's Grave and thought how interesting it would be to turn it out thoroughly and see what it really contained. But we are in an awful twitter about those tomb-robbers who have been hacking at the mound. It will be a tragedy if they have reached the important part of the barrow."

"Yes," Miss Bidborough agreed, severely. "These clandestine diggers are the bane of scientific archaeology. They confuse all the issues by disturbing the stratification, they break or damage valuable relics and, worst of all, they sneak off secretly with things of priceless scientific value and never record what they have found. Do you happen to know who these people were, Dr. Thorndyke, who broke into this barrow?"

"The only person," replied Thorndyke, "known to me as being under suspicion is an amateur – a very amateur – collector of antiques."

"They usually are," said Elmhurst, gloomily, "and this fellow must have been worse than usual. Just look at the way he put the turf back!"

He pointed indignantly to an irregular area on the side of the mound in which even my inexpert eye could detect the ragged lines which marked the untidy replacement. From my knowledge of the man (and my distinct prejudice against him) it was just what I should have expected, and I was indiscreet enough to say so.

"By the way," said Miss Bidborough, addressing Elmhurst, "I am in hopes that we shall have a visit from Theophilus. He has to come down

342

to Canterbury to-day, and I think he intends to come on here and see how we are getting on with the work. I hope he will. I know he would like to meet Dr. Thorndyke."

Thorndyke looked inquiringly at Elmhurst. "Do I know Mr. Theophilus?" he asked.

"His name isn't really Theophilus," Elmhurst explained. "That is only a term of affection among his friends. He is actually Professor Templeton."

"Then I do know him, at least by repute," said Thorndyke. "And now I suggest that we move on and let these ladies proceed with their work and see what enormities the unauthorised diggers have committed."

With this we bowed to the fair excavators and, as they picked up their cheese-cutters to renew their assault on the turf, we resumed our personally conducted tour, passing round the head of the mound (where Elmhurst pointed out to us the probable position of the burial chamber) to inspect the works on the other side. As we came out on to the lower side, whence we could see the whole hill-side and the river valley below, we observed a figure in the distance striding up the steep ascent with a purposeful air suggesting a definite objective.

"Here is Theophilus, himself," remarked Elmhurst (whose power of recognising distant persons did credit to his spectacles). "We may as well go down and meet him and get the introductions over before we come to the scene of the operations."

Accordingly, we proceeded down the hill-side, but at a leisurely pace, as we had to come up again and, in due course, came within hail of the visitor, who viewed us with undisguised interest which, indeed, was mutual, for a man who gets called by an affectionate nickname by his juniors probably merits respectful consideration. And this gentleman – a tall, athletic, eminently good-looking man, very unlike the popular conception of a professor – made a definitely pleasant impression.

When we at length met, he shook hands cordially with Elmhurst and then looked at Thorndyke.

"I think," said he, "that I can diagnose the giver of this archaeological feast. You are Dr. Thorndyke, aren't you?"

Thorndyke admitted his identity, but protested, "I am really getting a great deal of undeserved credit for this excavation. Actually, I am greatly indebted to Elmhurst for all the trouble that he is taking, since I am hoping to get some useful information from the opening of the barrow."

Professor Templeton looked at him somewhat curiously.

"Of course," said he, "you know your own business – uncommonly well, as I understand – but I can't imagine what information you expect to get by the excavation that we couldn't have given you without it."

"Probably you are right," Thorndyke admitted, "at least in a scientific sense. But in legal practice, and in relation to a particular set of circumstances, an ascertained fact is usually of more weight than even the most authoritative opinion."

"Yes," said the professor, "I appreciate that. But when Elmhurst told me about the project, I wondered – and am still wondering – whether there might not be some – what shall we say? – some *arriere-pensee*, some expectation that the digging operations might yield some extra-archaeological facts. You see, your reputation has preceded you."

He smiled genially, and Thorndyke was evidently in no wise disconcerted by the implied suspicions, and I was just beginning to wonder, for my part, whether there might not be some justice in those suspicions when my colleague addressed Elmhurst.

"I think," said he, "your presence is required at the diggings. Some rather urgent signals are being made."

We all looked up towards the barrow, and there, sure enough, was a picturesque, red-trousered figure standing on the summit of the mound, beckoning excitedly and, even as we looked, a labourer came down the hill at a heavy trot and, when he had arrived within earshot, announced that Miss Stirling asked Mr. Elmhurst to return at once.

In compliance with this unmistakably urgent summons, Elmhurst immediately started up the hill at something between a walk and a trot, and we turned and followed at a more convenient pace.

"Those girls have apparently found something out of the common," the professor remarked. "I wonder what it can be. They can't have struck the burial chamber, for they have only begun peeling the turf off, and you don't look for anything important so near the surface."

We watched Elmhurst run round the end of the mound, where he disappeared for the moment. But in a very short time he reappeared, hurrying in our direction and as we thereupon quickened our pace, we met within a short distance of the mound.

"My colleagues," he announced in his usual sedate, self-contained manner, though a little breathlessly, "have found something, Doctor, which is rather more in your line than in ours. Apparently, there is someone buried just under the surface in the place where the unauthorised digging has been carried out."

"You say '*apparently*'," said Thorndyke. "Then I take it that you have not uncovered a body?"

344

"No," replied Elmhurst, as we turned to accompany him back. "What happened was this: Miss Stirling was rolling up a strip of turf when she saw what looked like the toe of a boot showing through the surface soil! So she scraped away some of the soil with her spade and I uncovered the greater part of a boot, and then the toe of a second boot came into view, whereupon she ran up the mound and signalled for me to come."

"You are sure that they are not just a pair of empty boots?" Thorndyke asked.

"Quite sure," was the reply. "I scraped away the earth enough to see the bottoms of a pair of trousers and then came on to report. But there is no doubt that there are feet in those boots."

Nothing more was said as we walked quickly up the hill, but I caught a significant glance from the professor's eye, and I noticed that Polton had developed a new and lively interest in the proceedings. As to Thorndyke, it was impossible to judge whether the discovery had occasioned him any surprise, but I suspected – and so, evidently did the professor – that the possibility had been in his mind. Indeed, I began to ask myself if this gruesome "find" did not represent the actual purpose of the excavation.

On arriving at the barrow, we passed round the foot end and came in sight of the scene of the discovery, where a broad patch of the chalky soil had been uncovered by the removal of the turf. The two ladies stood close by it, backed by the gang of labourers who had been attracted to the spot by the report of the discovery, and the eyes of them all were rivetted on a shallow depression at the bottom of which a pair of whitened boots projected through the chalk rubble.

"Would you like me to get the body out?" Thorndyke asked. "As you said, it is more in my line than yours."

"I didn't mean that," replied Elmhurst. "I'll dig it out. But, as I have had no experience of the exhumation of recent remains, you had better see that I go about it in the right way."

With this, he selected a suitable pick and spade and, having placed a wheelbarrow close by to receive the soil, fell to work.

We watched him cautiously and skilfully pick away the clammy chalk rubble in which the corpse was embedded and, as each new part became disclosed, attention and curiosity quickened. First the legs, looking almost as if modelled in chalk, then the skirt of a rain-coat, and one whitened, repulsive-looking hand. Then, partly covered by the body, an object was seen, the nature of which was not at first obvious, but when Elmhurst had carefully disengaged it from the soil and drawn it out, it appeared as the whitened and shapeless remains of a felt hat,

345

which was at once handed to Thorndyke, who restored it, as far as possible, to a recognisable shape, wiped its exterior with a bunch of turf, glanced into its interior, and then put it down on the side of the mound.

Gradually the corpse was uncovered and disengaged from its chalky bed until, at length, it lay revealed as the body of a stoutish man who, so far as could be judged, was on the shady side of middle age. Naturally, six months of burial in the clammy chalk had left uncomely traces and obscured the characteristics of the face, but when Thorndyke had gently cleaned the latter with a wisp of turf, the chalk-smeared, sodden features still retained enough of their original character to render identification possible by one who had known the man. In fact, it was not only possible – it was actually achieved. For, as Thorndyke stood up and threw away the wisp of turf, Polton, who had watched the procedure with fascinated eyes, suddenly stooped and gazed with the utmost astonishment into the dead man's face.

"Why!" he exclaimed, "it looks like Mr. Penrose!"

"You think it does?" said Thorndyke, without the slightest trace of surprise.

"Of course, sir," replied Polton, "I couldn't be positive. He's so very much changed. But he looks to me like Mr. Penrose, and I feel pretty certain that that is who he is."

"I have no doubt that you are right, Polton," said Thorndyke. "The hat is certainly his hat, and the fact that you recognised the body seems to settle the question of identity. And now another question arises: How is the body to be disposed of? The correct procedure would be to leave it where it is and notify the police. What do you say to that, Elmhurst?"

"You know best what the legal position is," was the reply. "But it won't be very comfortable carrying on the work with that gruesome object staring us in the face. Is there any legal objection to its being moved?"

"No, I think not," replied Thorndyke. "There are competent witnesses as to the circumstances of the discovery, and the soil is going to be thoroughly examined, so that any objects connected with the body are certain to be found."

"Quite certain," said Elmhurst. "The soil will not only be examined. That from this part will be sifted. And, of course, any objects found will be carefully preserved and reported. Still, we don't want to do anything irregular."

"I will take the responsibility for moving the body," said Thorndyke, "if you will find the means. But I think it would be as well to send a messenger in advance to the police so that they may be prepared."

"Very well," Elmhurst agreed. "Then I will send a man off at once and, if Mr. Polton will come and lend me a hand, we can rig up an extemporised stretcher from some of the spare fencing material."

With this he went off, accompanied by Polton, in search of the necessary material, the ladies migrated to the farther end of the mound, where they resumed their turf-cutting operations, and the labourers returned to their tasks.

When we were alone, the professor stood for a while looking thoughtfully at the ghastly figure, lying at the bottom of its trench. Presently he turned to Thorndyke and asked, "Has it occurred to you, Doctor – I expect it has – that the person who buried this poor creature showed very considerable foresight?"

"You mean in selecting a scheduled monument as a burial-place?"

"Yes – but I see that you have considered the point. It is rather subtle. According to ordinary probabilities, a scheduled tumulus should be the safest of all places in which to dispose of a dead body. It is actually secured by law against any disturbance of the soil. But for your intervention, this place might have remained untouched for a century."

"Very true," Thorndyke agreed, "but, of course, there is the converse aspect. If suspicion arises in respect of a given locality, the very security of a barrow from chance disturbance makes it the likeliest place for a suspected burial."

"I suppose," the professor ventured, "that an ordinary exhumation order would not have answered your purpose?"

"It would not have been practicable," Thorndyke replied. "I did not know that the body was here. I did not even know for certain that there was a dead body, and I don't suppose that either the Home Office or the Office of Works would have agreed to the excavation of a scheduled tumulus to search for corpse whose existence was purely hypothetical. The only practicable method was a regular excavation by competent archaeologists, which would not only settle the question whether the body was there or not but, in the event of a negative result, would not have raised any troublesome issues or disclosed any suspicions which might possibly turn out to be unfounded."

"Yes," the professor agreed. "I admire your tact and discretion. You have done valuable service to archaeology and you have managed very neatly to harness the unsuspecting Elmhurst to your legal chariot."

"I am not sure," said I, "that Elmhurst was quite so unsuspecting as you think. But he also is a discreet gentleman. He wanted to excavate the barrow and was willing to do it and ask no questions. But I fancy that he expected to find something more significant than neolithic pottery."

Here our discussion was brought to an end by the arrival of Elmhurst and Polton, bearing a sort of elongated hurdle formed very neatly by lashing together a number of stout rods. This they deposited opposite the place where the body was lying in readiness to receive its melancholy burden.

"I think, Jervis," said Thorndyke, "that the next proceeding devolves upon us. Will you lend us a hand, Polton? The body ought to be lifted as evenly as possible to avoid any disturbance of the joints."

Accordingly, we placed ourselves by the side of the trench, Thorndyke taking the head and shoulders, I taking the middle, while Polton supported the legs and feet. At the word from Thorndyke, we all very carefully lifted the limp, sagging figure and carried it to the hurdle on which we gently lowered it. As we rose and stood looking down at the poor shabby heap of mortality, Polton, who appeared to be deeply moved, moralised sadly.

"Dear, dear!" he exclaimed. "What a dreadful and grievous thing it is. To think that that miserable, dirty mass of rags and carrion is all that is left of a fine, jovial, happy gentleman, full of energy and enjoying every moment of his life. There is a heavy debt against somebody, and I hope, sir, that you will see that it is paid to the uttermost farthing."

"I hope so, too, Polton," said Thorndyke. "That, you know, is what we are here for. Can we find anything to cover the body? It is a rather gruesome object to carry down into the village."

As he spoke, the four labourers who had volunteered as bearers approached carrying a bundle of sacks, and with these, laid across the hurdle, the wretched, unseemly remains were decently covered up. Then the four men lifted the hurdle (which, with its wasted burden, must have been quite light) and moved away round the foot of the barrow, watched, not without evident relief, by Elmhurst and his two colleagues.

"I suppose," said Elmhurst, as we prepared to follow, "you won't be coming back here?"

"Not to-day," replied Thorndyke. "But we shall have to attend the inquest, either as witnesses or to watch the proceedings, so we shall have an opportunity to see your work in a more advanced stage. Don't think that our interest in it is extinct because we are no longer concerned with neolithic pottery."

With this we took leave of our friends and, starting off down the hill-side, soon overtook and passed the bearers and made our way to the foot-bridge over the river near the mill. A few yards farther on, we met our messenger returning in company with a police sergeant, and halted to give the latter the necessary particulars.

"I suppose," he remarked, "you ought, properly, to have left the body where it was and reported to us. Still, as you say, there's nothing in it as the witnesses are available. I'll just note your addresses and those of any other persons that you know of who may be wanted at the inquest."

We accordingly gave our own names and addresses (at which I noticed that the sergeant seemed to prick up his ears), and Thorndyke gave those of Brodribb, Horridge, and Kickweed. And this concluded the day's business. Of the spade and the trenching tool Thorndyke said nothing, evidently intending to examine them at his leisure before handing them over to the police.

I may say that the discovery had given me one of the greatest surprises of my life. The idea that Penrose might be dead had never occurred to me. And yet, as soon as the discovery had been made, I began to realise how all the facts that were known to us pointed in this direction, and I also began to see the drift of the many hints that Thorndyke had given me. But, although, over a very substantial tea at the Wool-pack Inn, we discussed the various and stirring events of the day, I did not think it expedient to enter into the details of the case in Polton's presence. Not that, in these days, we had many secrets from Polton. But there were certain other matters, as yet undisclosed, that it seemed better to reserve for discussion when we should be alone.

Chapter XV
What Befell at
the Wool-Pack

The inquest on the body of Daniel Penrose yielded nothing that was new to us. The coroner had been provided by Thorndyke with a brief synopsis of the known facts of the case (which my colleague had, apparently, prepared in advance) to serve as a guide in conducting the inquiry, but he was a discreet man who understood his business and avoided extending the proceedings beyond the proper scope of a coroner's inquest. Nor had we been able to increase our knowledge of the case, for neither the spade nor the trenching tool furnished any information whatever. All our attempts to develop finger-prints failed utterly, and the most minute examination of the tools for traces of hair or blood was equally fruitless – which was not surprising, for even if such traces had originally existed, six months exposure to the weather would naturally have dissipated them.

But if the coroner was not disposed to go beyond the facts connected with the discovery, there was another person who was. We had put up for the night at the Wool-pack in Chilham in order to be present at the *post mortem* (by the coroner's invitation), and were just finishing a leisurely breakfast when the coffee-room door opened to admit no less a person than Mr. Superintendent Miller. He had come down by an early train for the express purpose of getting an outline of the case from Thorndyke to assist him in following the proceedings at the inquest.

"Well, Doctor," he said, cheerfully, seating himself without ceremony at our table, "here we are, and both on the same errand, I take it."

"We are," Thorndyke replied, "if you have come to attend the inquest on poor Penrose."

"Exactly," rejoined Miller. "We have a common purpose – which isn't always the case. Lord, Doctor! What a pleasure it is to find myself, for once in a way, on the same side of the board with you, playing the same game against the same opponent! You won't mind if I ask you a few questions?"

"Not at all," replied Thorndyke. "But the first question is, have you had breakfast?"

"Well, I have, you know," said Miller, "but it was a long time ago. I think I could pick a morsel, since you mention the matter."

Accordingly, Thorndyke rang the bell and, having given an order for a morsel in the form of a gammon rasher and a pot of coffee, prepared himself for the superintendent's assault.

"Now, Doctor," the latter began, in his best cross-examining manner, "it is perfectly clear to me that you know all about this case."

"I wish it were as clear to me," said Thorndyke.

"There, now. Dr. Jervis," exclaimed Miller, "just listen to that. Isn't he an aggravating man? He has got all the facts of the case up his sleeve, as he usually has, and now he is going to pretend – as he usually does – that he doesn't know anything about it. But it won't do, Doctor. The facts speak for themselves. Here were our men trapesing up and down the country, looking for Daniel Penrose to execute a warrant on him, and all the time you knew perfectly well that he was safely tucked away in a barrow – though why the deuce they call the thing a barrow when it is obviously just a mound of earth, I can't imagine."

"That is a wild exaggeration, you know, Miller," Thorndyke protested. "After six months' study of the case, I came to the conclusion that Penrose was probably buried in this barrow. But I was so far from certainty that I had to take this roundabout way of settling the question whether I was or was not mistaken. It happened that my conclusion was correct."

"It usually does," said Miller. "And I expect you have formed some conclusions as to who planted that body in the barrow. And I expect those conclusions will happen to be right, too. And I should very much like to know what they are."

"Really, Miller," I exclaimed, "I am surprised at you. Have you known Thorndyke all these years without discovering that he never lets the cat out of the bag until he can let her right out? No protruding heads or tails for him. But, when everything is finished and the course is clear, out she comes."

"Yes, I know," said Miller, gloomily, "I know his beastly secret ways. I think that, in some previous state of existence, he must have been an oyster. Still, Doctor, you needn't be so close with an old friend."

"But my dear Miller," protested Thorndyke, "you are entirely mistaken. I am withholding nothing that could properly tell you. What Jervis has said, though crudely put, is the strict truth. If I knew who had committed this crime, of course I should tell you. But I don't know. And if I have any half-formed suspicions, I am going to keep them to myself until I am able to test them. In short, Miller, I will tell you all I *know*, but I tell nobody what I *think*. So now ask me any questions you please."

I must admit that it was not very encouraging for Miller. My experience of Thorndyke was fairly expressed in what he had just said. He would tell you all the facts (which you usually knew already and which were more or less common property) but the general truths which were implicit in those facts he would leave you to discover for yourself, which you never did until the final conclusions emerged, when it was surprising how obvious they were.

"Well, to begin with," said Miller. "There was that chappie at the hospital whom we all supposed to be Penrose. Have you any idea who he really was? You obviously spotted the fact that he was not Penrose."

"No," replied Thorndyke, "I have no idea who he was. My suspicion that he was not Penrose was based on his behaviour, especially on the fact that he appeared particularly anxious to avoid being seen or recognised by anyone who knew Penrose. As a matter of fact, he was not then recognisable at all, and nobody knows what he was really like. But I don't think that there is any utility in going into details of the case at that stage. Remember that my investigations were then concerned with the questions: Is Penrose alive or dead? And if he is dead, what has become of his body? Now, I have settled those questions and their solution has evolved the further questions: Was he murdered? And, if so who murdered him? The first question will be answered at the inquest – pretty certainly in the affirmative, and we shall then address ourselves to the second. And as you say, we have a common purpose and shall try to be mutually helpful.

"Now, I have given the coroner a synopsis of the case from the beginning, and I have a copy of it which I am going to hand to you. I suggest that you study it, and then, if anything occurs to you in connection with it, and you like to ask me any questions on matters of fact, I will give you all the information that I possess. How will that do for you?"

I suspected that it was not at all what Miller would have liked, but he saw clearly, as I did, that Thorndyke was not going to disclose any theories that he might have formed as to where we might look for the possible murderer. Accordingly, he accepted the position with as good a grace as he could and, when he had finished a very substantial breakfast, he demanded the synopsis, which Thorndyke fetched from his room and placed in his hands.

"Are you coming to watch the *post mortem*, Jervis?" my colleague asked.

"No," I replied. "I shall hear all about it at the inquest, so I think I shall improve the shining hour by taking a walk up to the barrow to see how the work is progressing."

352

"Ha!" said Miller. "Then perhaps you wouldn't mind my walking with you. I have never seen a barrow. Never heard of one until I read the report in the paper."

Of course, I had to agree – not unwillingly, in fact, for I liked our old friend. But I knew quite well what the proposal meant. As nothing was to be got out of Thorndyke, Miller intended to apply a gentle squeeze to me. And to this also I had no objection, for I was still in the dark as to how Thorndyke had reached his very definite conclusions and was quite willing to have my memories of the investigation stirred up.

The process began as soon as we were fairly outside the inn.

"Now, look here, Dr. Jervis," said the superintendent, "it's all very well for the doctor to pretend that he hasn't anything to go on, but there are certain obvious questions that arise when a well-to-do man like Penrose gets murdered. The first is: Who benefits by its death?"

"The answer to that," I replied, "is quite simple. Penrose made a will by which practically the whole of his property goes to a man named Horridge."

"Then," said Miller, "it will be worthwhile to give a little attention to Mr. Horridge. Do you know anything about him?"

"Not very much," I replied. "But I know this much, that he is about the most unlikely man in the world to have murdered Penrose."

"Why do you say that?" demanded Miller.

"Because if Penrose died when we believe he did, Horridge stands to lose something like a hundred and fifty thousand pounds by his death. Penrose was the principal heir of his father, who was quite a rich man. But when Penrose died – if he did die on the date which we are assuming – his father was alive and consequently the father's estate would not pass to him. But Horridge was Penrose's heir and would have inherited the father's property, as well as Penrose's, under the latter's will. So it didn't suit Horridge at all for Penrose to die when he did."

"And is the old man still alive?"

"No. He died quite recently."

"Ha!" said Miller. "Then somebody else benefits by Penrose's death. Do you happen to know who that will be?"

"No," I replied. "I understand, but do not know for certain, that the old man died intestate. In that case, the next of kin will benefit. They will benefit very considerably, as their expectations would have been quite small if Penrose had been alive when his father died. But I have no idea who they are."

"Well, we shall have to find that out," said Miller. "It seems that somebody had a perfectly understandable motive for getting rid of Penrose while the old man was still alive."

As Miller continued his interrogations, asking uncommonly shrewd questions and making equally shrewd comments, I began to feel an unwonted sympathy with Thorndyke in respect of his habitual reticence and secretiveness. For his approach to a criminal problem was quite different from Miller's, and there might easily arise some conflict between the two. Miller was evidently on the look-out for a suspect, and was considering the problem in terms of persons, whereas Thorndyke's practice was to watch, unseen and unsuspected, while he collected and sifted the evidence, and above all, to avoid alarming the suspected persons until he was ready to make the final move.

But our arrival at the top of Julliberrie Downs put an end, for the time being, to Miller's bombardment, for here we came in sight of the barrow, now stripped of its turf and presenting the smooth, white, rounded shape on which its builders had looked a couple-of-thousand years or more before the coming of the Romans. I explained its nature and its great antiquity to Miller, who was deeply impressed, but who, nevertheless, showed a strong inclination to "cut the cackle and get back to the case". But as we approached, the eagle-eyed Elmhurst observed us and came forward to do the honours of the excavation.

Under his guidance we went round to the farther side of the mound which was in the process of being cut away like a gigantic cheese, and the chalk rubble, stored in the dump, was mounting to the magnitude of a considerable hill. At this point, the superintendent's interest in the barrow awakened surprisingly, for an excavation was more or less in his line, and he took the opportunity to pick up a few technical tips. He was particularly impressed by a builder's sieve which had been set up at the dump.

"I see," he remarked to Elmhurst, "that you don't mean to miss anything. I shall bear your methods in mind the next time I have to direct a search. And speaking of a search, have you turned up anything that seems to be connected with the body that you found?"

"Yes," replied Elmhurst. "We found, near the place where the body was lying, quite an interesting thing and, I should say, decidedly connected with that body – a small bronze pestle, apparently belonging to an ancient drug-mortar. I'll show it to you. Miss Stirling, have you got that pestle?"

As the lady addressed turned round and greeted me with a friendly nod, the superintendent whispered to me in an awe-stricken tone, "Good gracious! That young person in the fisherman's trousers is a female! And I believe the other one is, too. Well, I never!"

354

"You would hardly expect them to wear evening dress for a job like this," I remarked, to which the superintendent assented, but continued to watch the ladies furtively and with fascinated eyes.

The pestle was presently produced from the shepherd's hut and offered for our inspection, a smallish pestle of bronze – now covered with a thick green patina – with a bulbous end and a rather elaborately decorated handle surmounted by a bearded head of the classical type which I assumed to represent Esculapius. Attached to it was a small tie-on label on which was written a note of its precise "find-spot" in the mound.

Miller took it in his hand and executed a warlike flourish with it, by way of testing its weight.

"It's of no great size," he remarked, "but it is quite a formidable weapon. Uncommonly handy, too, and as portable as a life-preserver. Perhaps I had better take charge of it."

He was about to slip it into his pocket when Elmhurst interposed firmly.

"I think I must keep it for the present. I am summoned to give evidence at the inquest and I shall have to produce this. Besides, I am personally responsible to the Office of Works for all objects found during the excavation."

With this he quietly resumed possession of the pestle, which Miller reluctantly surrendered, and as the latter had no further interest in the excavation, and made no secret of the fact, we presently took our leave and resumed our perambulations, with a running accompaniment of interrogation on the part of the superintendent which caused me to hail the luncheon hour with a certain sense of relief.

The superintendent, of course, lunched with us, and when at the table he continued his quest for knowledge, beginning, naturally, with inquiries as to the result of the *post mortem*.

"The cause of death is obvious enough," said Thorndyke. "There is a depressed fracture of the skull at the left side and towards the back, not very large, but deep, and suggesting a very violent blow. The shape of the depression – a fairly regular oval concavity – implies a blunt weapon of a smooth, rounded shape."

"Such as a pestle, for instance," Miller suggested.

"Yes," Thorndyke replied, "a pestle would agree with the conditions. But why do you suggest a pestle?"

"Because your excavating friends have found one – a bronze pestle, quite a handy little weapon, and portable enough to go quite easily into an ordinary pocket."

Here he gave a very excellent and concise description of the weapon, to which Thorndyke listened with deep interest.

"So you see," Miller concluded, "that it is a thing that ought to be quite easy to identify by anyone who had ever seen it. Dr. Jervis thinks that it would not be likely to be the property of a chemist or apothecary. What do you say to that?"

"I agree with him," Thorndyke replied. "That is to say, it does not definitely suggest an apothecary as would have been the case if it had been a Wedgwood pestle. Bronze mortars and pestles are not now in general use, and this is pretty evidently an ancient pestle."

"A sort of curio, in fact," said Miller, "and rather suggestive of a collector or curio monger?"

Thorndyke agreed that this was so, but he made no further comment, though the connection of a curio with the late Daniel Penrose was fairly significant. But my recent experiences of Miller's eager and persistent cross-examinations enabled me to understand the sort of defensive reticence that they tended to engender. Moreover, the connection, though significant, was not very clear as to its bearing. It would have been more obvious if Penrose had been the murderer.

The inquest was held in a large room at the inn, normally reserved for gatherings of a more festive character, and when we entered and took our places the preliminaries of swearing in the jury and viewing the body had already been disposed of. I looked round the room and noted that in the seats set apart for the witnesses, not only Elmhurst and his two coadjutors were present, but also Kickweed and Horridge. Both of the latter showed evident signs of distress, but more especially Horridge – which rather surprised me. The grief of the lugubrious, red-eyed Kickweed was understandable enough, for not only had he manifested a genuine affection and loyalty towards his dead master, but the death of Penrose was a very material loss to him. But I could not reconcile Horridge's condition with the callous selfishness that he had shown previously. It is true that the apparent date of the death put an end to his hopes of inheriting the fortune of the lately deceased Penrose senior but, on the other hand, he stood to gain forthwith the very respectable sum of fifty thousand pounds, for which he might reasonably have expected to wait for years. Nevertheless, he was obviously extremely upset, and it was evident from his pale, haggard face and his restless movements, that this sudden, unforeseen catastrophe had come on him as an overwhelming shock.

The first witness called was Miss Stirling, who gave a brief, matter-of-fact description of her discovery, to which the jury listened with absorbed interest. She was followed by Elmhurst, who amplified her

356

statement and described his disinterment of the body and the appearance and position of the latter. He also explained the methods of excavation and the procedure after the body had been removed.

"In the soil which was taken away after the removal of the body," the coroner inquired, "did you find any objects that seemed to be connected with it?"

"Yes," replied Elmhurst. "I found this pestle, which could certainly not have been among the original contents of the barrow."

Here he produced the pestle wrapped in a handkerchief and, having removed the latter, handed the "find" to the coroner, who inspected it curiously and then passed it on to the foreman of the jury.

"This," he remarked, "does not look like a modern pestle. As you are an authority on antiquities, Mr. Elmhurst, perhaps you can tell us something about it."

"I am not much of an authority on recent antiquities," Elmhurst disclaimed modestly, "but I should judge that this pestle belonged to a bronze drug-mortar of the kind that was in use in the seventeenth or early eighteenth century."

"You would not regard it as probably part of the outfit of a chemist's shop?"

"No," replied Elmhurst. "I understand that, since the introduction of grinding machinery, the practice of grinding hard drugs in metal mortars is quite extinct."

"Can you form any idea how long this object has been buried?"

"I could not judge the exact time but, assuming it to have been bright, or at least clean, when it was buried, I should say that it must have been lying in the ground for several months."

That concluded Elmhurst's evidence and, as he retired to his seat, the name of the medical witness was called.

"You have made an examination of the body of the deceased?" the coroner began, when the preliminaries had been disposed of. "Can you give any opinion as to how long the deceased has been dead?"

"My examination," the witness replied, "led me to the belief that he had been dead at least six months."

"Did you arrive at any conclusion as to the cause of death?"

"The cause of death was an injury to the brain occasioned by a heavy blow on the head. There is a small but deep depressed fracture of the skull on the left side just above and behind the ear, which appears to have been produced by a blunt, smooth weapon with a rounded end."

"Please look at this pestle, which you have heard was found near the place where the body had been lying. Could the injuries which you found have been produced by this?"

The doctor examined the pestle and gave it as his opinion that it corresponded completely with the shape of the fracture.

"I suppose that it is a mere formality to ask whether the injuries could have been self-inflicted or due to an accident?" the coroner suggested.

"They certainly could not have been self-inflicted," the witness replied. "As to an accident, one doesn't like to use the word impossible, but I cannot imagine my kind of accident which would have produced the injuries that were found."

This completed the medical evidence proper, but Thorndyke was called to give confirmatory testimony.

"You have heard the evidence of the doctor. Have you any observations to make on it?"

"No," replied Thorndyke. "I am in complete agreement with everything that my colleague has said."

"We may take it," said the coroner, "that you know more about this affair than anybody else. Can you throw any light on the actual circumstances in which the tragedy occurred?"

"No," Thorndyke replied. "My investigations have been concerned with the question whether Daniel Penrose was alive or dead and, if he was dead, when and where his death occurred. I can make no suggestion as to the identity of the person who killed him."

"As to the date of his death, have you arrived at any conclusion on that point?"

"Yes. I have no doubt that the deceased met his death at some time in the evening of the seventeenth of last October. I base that conclusion principally on the fact that his car was seen coming away from the neighbourhood of the place where his body was found, and that it was evidently being driven by some other person."

"And have you formed any opinion as to who that other person may have been?"

"I have not. At present I have no evidence pointing to any particular person."

"Well," said the coroner. "I hope you will now take up this further question, and that your efforts will be as successful in this as in the problem which you have solved in such a remarkable manner. Is there any question that any member of the jury would like to ask?"

Apparently there was not. Accordingly Thorndyke returned to his seat and the name of Francis Horridge was called. And, as he walked up to the table, I was once more impressed by his extraordinarily agitated and shaken condition. It was noticed also by the coroner, who, before beginning his examination, offered a few words of sympathy.

"This, Mr. Horridge," said he, "must be a very painful and distressing experience for you, as an intimate friend of the deceased."

"It is," replied Horridge. "I had not the faintest suspicion that my old friend was not alive and well. It has been a terrible shock."

"It must have been," the coroner agreed, "and I am sorry to have to trouble you with questions. But we have to solve this dreadful mystery if we can, or at least find out as much as possible about it. You have seen the body of the deceased. Could you identify it?"

"Yes. It is the body of Daniel Penrose."

"Yes," said the coroner, "there seems to be no doubt as to the identity of the body. Now, Mr. Horridge, the medical evidence makes it clear that the deceased met his death by the act of some unknown person. It is very necessary to discover, if possible, who that person is. You were an intimate friend of the deceased and must know a good deal about his personal affairs. Do you know of anything that might throw any light on the circumstances surrounding his death?"

"No," was the reply. "But I did not know so very much about his personal habits or his friends and acquaintances."

"I understand that the deceased had made a will. Do you know anything about that?"

"Yes. I am the executor of his will."

"Then you can tell us whether there was anything in connection with it which might give rise to trouble or enmity. In rough, general terms what are the provisions of the will?"

"They are quite simple. There is a handsome, but well-deserved legacy to his butler, Kickweed, amounting to two thousand pounds. Beyond that, the bulk of the property is devised and bequeathed to me."

"So you and Mr. Kickweed are the persons who benefit most in a pecuniary sense by the death of the deceased?"

"Yes, and I am sure we should both very gladly forgo the benefit to have our friend back again."

"I am sure you would," said the coroner. "But can you tell us if there are any other persons who would benefit materially in any way by the death of the deceased?"

"Yes, there are," replied Horridge. "Quite recently, the deceased's father died and left a considerable fortune. If the deceased had been alive at that time, the bulk of that fortune would have come to him. As it is, it will be distributed among his next of kin. Consequently, those persons will benefit very considerably by the deceased's death if that death occurred on the date given by Dr. Thorndyke. I do not know who they are and, of course, I do not suspect any of them of being concerned in this crime."

"Certainly not," the coroner agreed. "But one naturally looks round for some persons who might have had a motive for making away with the deceased. But you know of no such persons? You do not know of anyone with whom the deceased was on terms of enmity or who had any sort of grudge against him?"

"No. So far as I know, he had no enemies whatever. He was not likely to have any. He was a kindly man and on pleasant terms with every one with whom he came in contact."

"May the same be said of us all when our time comes," the coroner moralised. "But there is another motive that we ought to consider: That of robbery. Do you know whether the deceased was in the habit of carrying about with him – on his person I mean – property of any considerable value?"

"I have no idea," replied Horridge. "He must have done so at times, for he was a great collector and was in the habit of going about the country making purchases. I had supposed that his last journey was made with that object, and I am disposed to think so still. He used to come down to this neighbourhood to visit a dealer named Todd who has a shop at Canterbury."

"You say that he was a collector. What kind of things did he collect?"

"It was a very miscellaneous collection, but I have always believed that, in addition to the oddments that were displayed in the main gallery, he had a collection of jewels of much more considerable value which were kept in a small room. That room was always kept locked, and the deceased would never say definitely what it contained."

Here Horridge gave a description of the small room as we had seen it on the occasion of our visit of inspection, and he also gave an account of the supposed burglary, to which the coroner – and Superintendent Miller – listened with profound interest.

"This," said the former, "seems to be a matter of some importance. What is the precise date on which the supposed burglary took place?"

"The second of last January."

"That," said the coroner, "would be nearly three months after the death of the deceased, if Dr. Thorndyke is correct as to the date on which that death occurred. And you say that, if the cupboard was opened, it must have been opened with its own proper key, since the lock is unpickable and the cupboard had not been broken open. Is there any reason to believe that the cupboard was actually opened?"

"I think there is," replied Horridge. "It is certain that someone entered the room on that night, and it is practically certain that he entered the premises by the side gate, as there is no other way of approaching the

360

window. But that gate was always kept locked, and it was found to be locked on the morning after the supposed burglary. So it seems that the burglar must have had the key of the gate, at least."

"And who usually had possession of that key?"

"Mr. Penrose. It seems that he sometimes used that gate and he kept the key in his own possession. There was no duplicate."

"When you went to the mortuary to identify the body, did you look over the effects of the deceased which had been taken from the pockets?"

"No, but I asked the coroner's officer if any keys had been found and he told me that there had not."

The coroner nodded gravely and Miller remarked to me in a whisper that we were beginning to see daylight.

"It is unfortunate," the former observed, "that we have no clear evidence as to whether a burglary did or did not take place. However, that is really a matter for the police. But the question is highly significant in relation to the problem of the motive for killing the deceased. Do you know whether, apart from this burglary, there were any attempts to rob the deceased?"

"Yes," replied Horridge, "but I think it was only a chance affair. The deceased told me on one occasion that his car had been stopped on a rather solitary road by a gang of men who were armed with revolvers and who made him deliver up what money he had about him. But, apparently, his loss was only trifling as he had nothing of value with him at the time."

This concluded Horridge's evidence, and when the coroner's officer, who turned out to be the police sergeant whom I had met, had deposed to having examined the contents of the deceased's pockets and found no keys among them, the name of Edward Kickweed was called.

361

Chapter XVI
Mr. Kickweed
Surprises the Coroner

The evidence given by our friend, Horridge, had been listened to with keen interest, not only by the coroner and the jury, but especially by Superintendent Miller. For though it comprised nothing that we did not already know, it had elicited the important fact that the body of Penrose had apparently been rifled of his keys. But striking and significant as this fact was, it was left to Kickweed to contribute the really sensational item of evidence.

But this came later. The early part of his evidence seemed to be little more than a series of formalities, confirming what had already been proved. When he took his place at the table, his lugubrious aspect drew from the coroner a kindly expression of sympathy similar to that with which he had greeted Horridge, after which he proceeded with his examination.

"You have seen the body which is lying in the mortuary, Mr. Kickweed. Were you able to identify it?"

"Yes," groaned Kickweed. "It is the body of my esteemed and beloved employer, Mr. Daniel Penrose."

"How long had you known the deceased?"

"I have known him practically all his life. I was in his father's service and when he grew up and took a house of his own, he asked me to come to him as butler. So I came gladly, and have been with him ever since."

"Then you probably know a good deal about his manner of life and the people he knew. Can you tell us whether there was anyone who might have had any feelings of enmity towards him?"

"There was not," Kickweed replied confidently. "The deceased was a rather self-contained man, but he was a kind, courteous, and generous man, and I am sure that he had not an enemy in the world."

"You confirm Mr. Horridge's estimate," said the coroner, "and a very satisfactory one it is, and it seems to dispose of revenge or malice as the motive for killing him. By the way, it is not of much consequence, but do you recognise these objects?"

Here he took from behind his chair the spade and trenching tool which we had found in the wood and laid them on the table for Kickweed's inspection.

362

"Yes," said the witness, "they belonged to the deceased. He used to keep them in the garage. I am not quite sure what he used them for, but I know that he occasionally took them with him when he went out in the country in his car."

"Were you aware that he had taken them with him when he last left home?"

"I was not. But afterwards, when I saw that they were not in their usual place, I assumed that he had taken them with him."

The coroner entered this not very illuminating statement in the depositions, and then, noting that the witness's eyes were fixed on the pestle which lay on the table, he picked it up and, holding it towards him, said, "I suppose it is needless to ask you if you recognise this object?"

"I do," was the totally unexpected reply. "It belongs to a small bronze mortar which forms part of Mr. Penrose's collection."

"This is very extraordinary!" the coroner exclaimed. "You are sure that you recognise it?"

"Perfectly sure," replied Kickweed. "The pestle and mortar stood together on a shelf in the great gallery and I have often, when dusting the things in the collection, given this pestle and the mortar a rub with the cloth. I know it very well indeed."

"Well," the coroner exclaimed, "this is indeed a surprise! The weapon is actually the property of the deceased!"

There was a short interval of silence, in which I could hear Miller cursing softly under his breath.

"There," he muttered, "is another promising clue gone west!"

Then the coroner, recovering from his astonishment, resumed his examination of the witness.

"Can you explain by what extraordinary chance the deceased came to have this thing with him on the day when he was killed?"

"Yes. It was his usual custom, when he went out in his car and was likely to be on the road late, to slip the pestle in his pocket before he started. The custom arose after he had been stopped on the road by robbers, as Mr. Horridge has mentioned. I urged him to get a revolver or some other means of defending himself, but he had a great dislike of fire-arms, so I suggested a life-preserver. But then he happened to see me polishing this pestle, and it occurred to him that it would do as well as the life-preserver and, as he said, would be a more interesting thing to carry. So he used to take it with him, and he did on this occasion, as I discovered a few days after he had gone, when I saw the mortar on the shelf without the pestle."

363

"Well," said the coroner, "there is evidently no doubt that this pestle really belonged to the deceased, and that fact may have a rather important bearing on the case."

He paused and, having entered Kickweed's last statement in the depositions, turned to him once more.

"Apparently, Mr. Kickweed, of all the persons who knew the deceased, you are the one who last saw him alive. Can you recall the circumstances of his departure from his home?"

"Yes," the witness replied, "very clearly. At lunch-time on the seventeenth of last October, the deceased informed me that he should presently be starting for a run in the country in his car. He was not sure about the time when he would return, but he thought he might be rather late, and he directed that no one should sit up for him, and that a cold supper should be left for him in the dining room. He left the house a little before three to go to the garage and, about a quarter-of-an-hour later, I saw him drive past the house in his car. That would be about three o'clock."

"And after that, did you ever see him again?"

"I never saw him again. I sat up until past midnight but, of course, he never came home."

"Did you then suspect that any mischance had befallen him?"

"I was rather uneasy," Kickweed replied, "because he had apparently intended to come home. Otherwise, I should not have been, as he often stayed away from home without notice."

"When did you first learn that there was something wrong?"

"It was in the afternoon of the twentieth of October. Mr. Horridge had called to see him, and we were just discussing the possible reasons for his staying away when a police officer arrived, carrying the deceased's raincoat, and told us that the deceased had apparently absconded from the hospital at Gravesend. And that was all that I ever knew of the matter until I heard Dr. Thorndyke's evidence."

"Then," said the coroner, "to repeat, you saw him drive away on the seventeenth of October and you never saw him, or had any knowledge of him, again. Is that not so?"

"I never saw him again. But as to having any further knowledge of him, I am rather doubtful. I received a letter from him."

"You received a letter from him!" the coroner repeated in evident surprise. "When did you receive that letter?"

"It was delivered on the morning of the twenty-seventh of last March."

A murmur of astonishment arose from the jury and the coroner exclaimed in a tone of amazement, "Last March! Why, the man had been dead for months!"

"So it appears," Kickweed admitted, "and I am glad to believe that the letter was not really written by him."

"Why do you say that?"

"Because," Kickweed replied, "it was not a very creditable letter for a gentleman of Mr. Penrose's character. It was a foolish letter and not as polite as it should have been."

"Have you that letter about you?"

"No. I handed it to Dr. Thorndyke, and I believe he has it still. But I can remember the substance of its contents. It directed me to lock up the small room and deposit the key at Mr. Penrose's bank."

"And did you do so?"

"Certainly I did, though Dr. Thorndyke seemed rather opposed to my doing so. But at the time, I supposed it to be a genuine letter from my employer and, of course, I had no choice but to carry out his instructions."

"Have you formed any opinion as to who might have written that letter?"

"No, I have not the faintest idea. Until I heard Dr. Thorndyke's evidence, I still supposed it to be a genuine letter from the deceased."

"Well," said the coroner, "it is a most extraordinary affair. I, think we had better recall Dr. Thorndyke and hear what he can tell us about it."

Accordingly, as Kickweed had apparently given all the information that he had to give, and no one wished to ask him any questions, he was allowed to return to his seat and Thorndyke was recalled.

"Will you tell us what you know about this very remarkable letter that Mr. Kickweed received?" the coroner asked.

"I first heard of that letter when Mr. Kickweed called at my chambers late in the evening of the twenty-seventh of last March. He then informed me that he had received that letter and gave it to me to read. I read and examined it and at once came to the conclusion that it was a forgery. I took a photograph of it – of which I have a copy here – and carried the original to Mr. Brodribb, the deceased's solicitor, to whom I handed it for safe custody and to whom I stated my opinion that it was a forgery."

"You decided at once that the letter was a forgery. What led you to that decision?"

"My decision was based on the circumstances and on the character of the letter itself. As to the circumstances, I had by that time formed the very definite opinion that Daniel Penrose was dead and that he had died

365

on the seventeenth of the previous October. The letter itself presented several suspicious features. The matter of it was quite unreasonable and inadequate. The room was already locked up and the key was in the very safe custody of the deceased's trusted and responsible servant, and had been for months. The directions in the letter appeared to be merely a pretext for writing and suggested some ulterior purpose. Then the manner of the letter was quite out of character with that of the supposed writer – a gentleman addressing his confidential servant. It was written in a tone of coarse, jocular familiarity with a most ill-mannered caricature of Mr. Kickweed's name. It impressed me as a grotesque, overdone attempt to imitate the deceased's habitually facetious manner of speech. And on questioning Mr. Kickweed, who was obviously hurt and surprised by the rudeness of this letter, I learned that the deceased had always been in the habit of addressing him in a strictly correct and courteous fashion."

"Apart from these inferences, was there anything visible that marked this letter as a forgery?"

"I did not discover anything. Of the handwriting I could not judge as I was not familiar with the deceased's writing. But there were no signs of tracing or other gross indications of forgery. But I may say that Mr. Brodribb was of opinion that the writing did not look, to him, like that of the deceased."

"You say that the matter of this letter suggested to you that a mere pretext had been made for writing and that there was some ulterior purpose. Can you suggest what that ulterior purpose might have been?"

"I suggest that its purpose was to make it appear that the deceased was alive."

"That seems to imply that the unknown writer of the letter knew that he was dead, though no one but yourself had any suspicion that he was not still alive. There would seem to be no object in trying to prove that a man was alive when nobody supposed that he was dead. Don't you agree?"

"Yes," replied Thorndyke, "that seems to be the natural inference."

"I suppose you cannot offer any suggestion as to who the writer of the letter may have been?"

"I cannot. It seems clear that whoever he may have been, he must have been well acquainted with the deceased, for the phraseology of the letter, although greatly exaggerated, was a recognisable imitation of the deceased's rather odd manner of expressing himself. But I cannot give him a name."

"There was one matter that we overlooked when you were giving your evidence. You ascertained in some mysterious manner that the

366

deceased was buried in Julliberrie's Grave. But is that the place where he met his death, or was his body brought from some other place?"

"I should say that there is no doubt that he was killed close to the place where his body was found. The implements which we found in the wood and which have been identified as his property suggest very strongly that he came to Julliberrie's Grave of his own accord with the intention of searching for antiquities for his collection. Probably he had actually done some excavation in the mound and the cavity that he had dug offered the facilities for disposing of his body. And the finding of the weapon with which he was apparently killed, near to the body, supports this view."

"Yes," said the coroner, "I think you have made it clear that the death occurred in the neighbourhood of the barrow and that the body was not brought there from a distance. And that, I think, gives us all the evidence that we need."

He bowed to Thorndyke and, as the latter returned to his seat, he began a brief and very sensible summing up.

"The disappearance of Mr. Daniel Penrose involves a long and complicated story, but with that story we are not concerned. This is a coroner's inquest, and the function of such an inquiry is to answer certain questions relating to a dead body which has been found within our jurisdiction. Those questions are: Who is the dead person? And where, when and by what means did the deceased meet with his death? We are not concerned with the person, if any, who caused the death of the deceased, unless such person should be plainly and evidently in view. We have to decide whether or not a crime has been committed, but it is not our function to bring that crime home to any particular person. That duty appertains to the police.

"Now, in respect of those questions which I have mentioned, we have no difficulty. The evidence which we have heard enables us to answer them quite confidently. The body has been identified as that of a gentleman named Daniel Penrose, and it has been clearly proved that he met his death at a place called Julliberrie's Grave on the seventeenth of last October and that his death was caused by violence inflicted by some unknown person. These are matters of fact which have been proved, and the only question which you have to decide is that of the nature of the act by which the death was caused. The deceased was killed by a heavy blow on the head inflicted with a bronze pestle. The person who struck that blow killed the deceased and, therefore, undeniably committed an act of homicide. But there are many kinds of homicide, varying in their degree of culpability. A man may justifiably kill another in defence of his own life. Then there is no crime. Or he may kill another quite accidentally, when, again, there is no crime. Or he may kill another in the course of a struggle, by violence which was not intended to cause death. Here the act of homicide amounts only to manslaughter, and the degree of criminality will depend on the particular circumstances. Again, a man may kill another with the deliberate and considered intention of killing him – that is with what the law calls malice. Such deliberate and premeditated killing constitutes wilful murder.

"Now, in the present case, we have to consider the circumstances in which the death of the deceased occurred, and of those circumstances we have very imperfect knowledge. A striking fact is that the weapon with which the deceased was killed was his own property and must, apparently, have been brought to the place by himself. We have learned, also, that he habitually carried this weapon for the purpose of self-defence. There is thus the suggestion that he may have so used it on the occasion when he was killed. That is to say, there is a distinct suggestion of a struggle, and the actual possibility that the deceased may have been the aggressor, killed by the unknown in self-defence.

"On the other hand, the unknown, having killed the deceased, buried the body secretly and hurried away from the place – incidentally killing another person on his way – and has since given no information and made no sign, unless we assume that the very mysterious letter that Mr. Kickweed received emanated from him. And it is, perhaps, worthwhile to give that letter a brief consideration, as it seems to have some bearing on the question which we are trying to decide.

"Who was the writer of that letter and for what purpose was the letter written? From Dr. Thorndyke we learn that the writer must have been some person who was well acquainted with the deceased. That is an important matter, but we are not concerned with the actual identity of the writer. We are concerned with his connection with the death of the deceased, and that connection seems to be suggested by the purpose of the letter. That purpose seems to be indicated quite clearly by Dr. Thorndyke. It was to create the belief that the deceased was still alive. But nobody – excepting the doctor – had any doubt that he was alive. No suggestion had been made by anybody that he might be dead. Then why should the writer of this letter have sought to create a belief which was already universally held? The only possible answer seems to be that he, himself, knew that the deceased was dead and he wished, in the interests of his own safety, to forestall any suspicions that might arise that the deceased might be dead.

"Thus the consideration of this letter suggests to us, first, that the writer knew that the deceased was dead and, second, that he had reasons for desiring that the fact of the death should not become known or

368

suspected. But the fact of the death could have been known only to the person who killed the deceased, and his anxiety to conceal the fact suggests strongly that he had no reasonable defence if he should be charged with the murder of the deceased.

"That, I think, is all that I need say. The deceased was evidently killed by some unknown person, and it is for you to decide whether the circumstances, so far as they are known to us, suggest excusable homicide, accidental homicide, manslaughter, or wilful murder."

On the conclusion of the summing up, the jury consulted together for a few minutes. Then the foreman announced that they had agreed on their finding.

"And what decision have you arrived at?" the coroner asked.

"We find that the the deceased was murdered by some person unknown."

"Yes," said the coroner, "I think that it is the only reasonable conclusion at which you could have arrived. I will record a verdict of wilful murder by some person unknown, and we may hope that the police will presently be able to discover who that unknown person is and bring him to justice."

He entered the verdict in the depositions and this brought the proceedings to an end.

Chapter XVII
Thorndyke Retraces
the Trail

As the court rose and we all stood up, Miller turned on me fiercely.

"You never told me about that letter," he exclaimed, "and there was not a word about it in the synopsis that the doctor gave me."

"As to me," said I, "there is no question of reservations. I did not refer to it because I had not regarded it as having any particular bearing on the case."

"No bearing!" exclaimed Miller. "Why, it hits you in the face! But if you think it has no bearing, I'll warrant that is not the doctor's view."

"Naturally," I replied, "I don't know what his views are, but he is here and can answer for himself."

"Well," said Miller, "what about it, Doctor? You knew about that letter and you must know quite well who wrote it and why he wrote it."

"Now, Miller," said Thorndyke, "don't let us misuse words. We don't know who wrote that letter. We may have our opinions, and they may be right – or wrong. But in any case, they will be pretty difficult to turn into evidence."

"I suspect you have done that already," grumbled Miller, "and you are keeping that evidence to yourself."

"You are quite wrong," Thorndyke replied. "I have no evidence beyond the facts which are known to you. Actually, I have given very little attention to the letter. It threw no light on the problem which I was trying to solve – whether Penrose was alive or dead and, if he was dead, where we might look for his body."

"I should have thought it was highly relevant." Miller objected. "If it was good enough for someone to forge a letter to prove that Penrose was alive, when nobody supposed otherwise, that would suggest pretty strongly that the forger knew he was dead."

"So it would," Thorndyke agreed, "but that was of no use to me. I was not out for opinions or beliefs but for demonstrable facts."

"Well," said Miller, "you have produced your demonstrable facts all right, and you have solved your problem. And now, I suppose, you are going on to the next problem: Who murdered Daniel Penrose? And the solution of that problem is to be found in that letter, and as we are both working to the same end, I think you ought to put me in possession of any facts that are known to you."

"But, my dear Miller!" Thorndyke protested. "I have no facts respecting this letter that are not known to you. I will hand you the photograph, and you can have an enlargement if you want to employ handwriting experts, or you can have the original. That is all I can do for you."

He produced his letter-case and, taking the photograph of the forged letter from it, handed it to Miller, who slipped it into his wallet and buried the latter in the depths of an internal pocket. As he did so he looked round sharply and exclaimed, "What is the matter, Mr. Horridge? Are you not feeling well, sir?"

I looked at our friend, who seemed to be groping his way towards the door, and certainly the inquiry was justified. His aspect was ghastly. His face was blanched to a tallowy white, his hands trembled visibly, and he had the dazed, bewildered appearance suggestive of a severe mental shock.

"No," he replied unsteadily. "I am not feeling at all well. This awful affair has been too much for me. It was all so horrible and so unexpected."

"Yes," Miller agreed sympathetically. "I expect it has given you a bad shake-up. Better come along with me to the bar and have a good stiff whisky. Don't you think so, Doctor?"

"I think," replied Thorndyke, "that a hot meal and a glass of wine would be better, if Mr. Horridge is returning to town this evening."

"I am," said Horridge, "but I couldn't look at food just now. Besides, my train is due in less than half-an-hour."

"Well, then," urged Miller, "come along to the bar and have a good stiff drink. That will pick you up and fit you for the journey home. I happen to be going by that train, myself, so I can see you safely to Charing Cross, and into a cab if necessary."

I think Horridge would sooner have been without the proffered escort, but Miller left him no choice, and accordingly allowed himself passively to be led away in the direction of the bar.

Thorndyke watched the two men disapprovingly as they passed out, and when they had disappeared, he remarked, "I am afraid Miller is going to be a nuisance to us. His activity is premature."

"Yes," I agreed, "he is in full cry after Horridge and he thinks that he is on a hot trail. Obviously, he is convinced that Horridge wrote that letter, and I think he is right."

"I have no doubt that he is," said Thorndyke. "The obvious purpose of that letter was to create evidence that Penrose was alive after Oliver's death, and so would inherit his property. But it would be impossible to prove that Horridge wrote it."

"So it may be," said I. "But Miller has got him at a disadvantage, and he is going to push his opportunity for all that it is worth. If he lets on that he is a police officer, Horridge will probably collapse altogether. He is in a fearful state of panic."

"And well he may be," Thorndyke rejoined, "if he wrote that letter. For, quite apart from the suggestion of guilty knowledge that it offers, the mere writing and uttering of that letter is a serious crime. It is a forgery in the fullest sense. It was done with intent to deceive, and the purpose of the deception was grossly fraudulent. If Miller can frighten him into an admission of having written the letter, he will be absolutely certain of securing a conviction."

"On the charge of forgery," said I. "But that is not Miller's objective. You heard what he said. He is all out on the capital charge."

"Yes, I realise that," said Thorndyke. "Which is why I say that he is going to be a nuisance to us. Because he won't be able to prove his case and he will have set up a disturbance just at the moment when what is needed is a little masterly inactivity combined with careful observation. It is a pity that Miller will not trust us more. He will butt in when the case is not ready for police methods. However, I am glad he is not travelling up with us. His eagerness to acquire knowledge becomes rather fatiguing."

"We are not going up by that train, then?"

"No. We may as well have a little early dinner and take the motor omnibus to Canterbury."

We adopted this plan and, after a comfortable and restful meal, caught the omnibus and were duly deposited in the main street of Canterbury, not far from the cathedral. As we proceeded thence towards the station, we noticed an "antique" shop, the fascia of which bore the single word "Todd".

"This," I remarked, halting to glance at the antiquities – mostly of the prehistoric type – which were displayed in the window, "seems to be the shop that Horridge referred to as a favourite resort of poor Penrose. Probably some of the things that we saw in the collection came from here."

"One of them almost certainly did," said Thorndyke. "Don't you remember that Saxon brooch? The entry in the catalogue noted its origin as '*Sweeney's Resurrection*'."

"I remember the entry, now you mention it. Lockhart suggested that '*Sweeney*' probably meant Todd, and apparently he was right."

We went on our way, discussing the late Daniel Penrose and his harmless oddities, of which I had been so intolerant, and eventually reached the station in time to select our compartment at our leisure.

There were few passengers besides ourselves, so that we were able to secure a first-class smoking-compartment of which we were the sole occupants, a matter to which I attended with some anxiety, for the train ran through to Charing Cross without a stop, and the long, uninterrupted journey would afford an opportunity for certain explanations which I felt were now overdue. With this view Thorndyke apparently agreed for, when I presently opened my examination with a tentative question, he replied quite freely, without a sign of his customary reticence and evasiveness.

"Of course," I began, "when Penrose's body was found, I realised at once, in general terms, how I had managed to miss the essential points of the case. The possibility that Penrose might be dead never occurred to me, and it ought. It looks obvious enough now. But still I don't quite see how you contrived to establish the fact of his death – which you evidently did – and locate the place of his burial."

"It was all very hypothetical," he replied, "even up to the last stage. Until Elmhurst reported the discovery I was not certain that my theory of the course of events might not contain some fallacy that I had overlooked – hence my rather elaborate provisions to cover up a possible failure. But to come back to your own case, the initial mistake that you made was in disregarding the good old Spencerian principle that when certain facts are presented as proving a particular thesis, we should consider, not only that which is presented, but that, also, which is *not* presented. In other words, we should at once separate fact from inference.

"Now, when Brodribb gave us his narrative of the disappearance of Penrose, he honestly believed that his story was a recital of facts, whereas it was really a mixture of fact and inference. It had not occurred to him that the hospital patient might be some person other than Penrose, and he accordingly presented that patient as Penrose. And you accepted that presentation as a statement of fact, whereas it was only an inference. Hence you made a false start and got on the wrong track from the beginning.

"I was fortunate enough to avoid this pitfall, for even while Brodribb was telling us his story, I made a mental note that the identity of the patient had been taken for granted, and that it would have to be considered, before any action could be taken. But as soon as I began to consider the question, it became clear to me that the balance of probability was against the patient's being Penrose."

"Did it really?" I exclaimed. "Now, I should have said that all the known facts pointed to his being Penrose. And so it seems to me still."

"Then," said Thorndyke, "let us argue the question. We will take two hypotheses: *A*, that the patient was Penrose, and *B* – that he was some other person, and examine the evidence in support of each.

"Let us begin with Hypothesis *A*: What evidence was there that the patient was Daniel Penrose?

"There were five principal items of evidence. *1*. The car was certainly Penrose's car. *2*: The patient had been in possession of that car. *3*: The coat, which was undeniably the patient's coat, had Penrose's driving licence in its pocket. *4*: The initials on the patient's collar were Penrose's initials. *5*: A fragment of an ancient object was found in the pocket of the patient's coat. But Penrose was a collector of antiquities and there was reason to believe that he had gone out that day for the purpose of acquiring some such objects.

"Now, you will notice that the first three items are what we may call *extrinsic*. They afford no evidence of personal identity. They merely prove that the patient was in possession of Penrose's property, and they are thus of very little weight. The other two items we may call *intrinsic*. They are connected with the actual personality of the patient.

"Of these, the initials on the collar furnished by far the more weighty evidence of identity."

"I should have assumed them to be quite conclusive," said I.

"Then you would have been wrong," he replied, "for you would have been assuming that Penrose was the only man in the world whose initials were *D. P.* Still, the fact that the patient's initials were *D. P.* established a very high probability that he was Daniel Penrose."

"I should have put it higher than that," said I. "It would have seemed to me as nearly as possible a certainty. For if he were not Penrose the coincidence would be, as it was, such an amazing one."

"I think you exaggerate the abnormality," he rejoined. "It was a very remarkable coincidence, but there are two things that we should bear in mind. First, the adverse chances were not so enormous as you seem to imply. There are great numbers of men whose initials are *D. P.* And secondly, that the laws of probability relate to large numbers. They must be applied with great caution to particular cases. The tendency to assume that because a thing is improbable it will not happen is a mistake. Improbabilities and coincidences are constantly occurring, and we have to allow for that fact.

"Nevertheless, it had to be admitted that those initials made it, in a very high degree, probable that the patient was Daniel Penrose. But now let us take the alternative hypothesis and see what the probabilities were on the other side. And first, consider the conduct of the patient. Owing to his black eyes and contused face, he was completely unrecognisable.

374

Nobody could form any idea what he was like. But when his injuries cleared up he would have been recognisable, and the extraordinary and determined way in which he absconded from the hospital at a carefully-chosen time, is very suggestive. Evidently, during his simulated unconsciousness, he had been watching for an opportunity to get away at night when his odd appearance would be less observed. His behaviour was like that of a man who sought to escape before recognition should be possible.

"Then, there was the man's previous behaviour. Apparently he had abandoned his car. But a car which is abandoned is usually a stolen car. Again, the car which killed the old woman was being driven wildly and furiously. We knew then of no reason why Penrose should have been driving in that manner. But a stranger in unlawful possession of a car would probably have sufficient reasons, and in fact, persons who steal cars usually do drive furiously. Then, if Penrose had knocked down the old woman he would probably have stopped and reported the accident. He was a responsible, decent gentleman, and there was no reason why he should not have stopped. But a stranger, in possession of a stolen car – in effect, a fugitive – could not afford to stop and be interviewed.

"Furthermore, if this man had been in unlawful possession of a car, something must have happened to the owner of that car at some place. The stranger would have good reasons for getting away from that neighbourhood as quickly as possible. Thus, the furious driving both before and after the accident would be sufficiently explained.

"So, looking at the case as a whole, you will see that, on the assumption that the patient was Penrose, his conduct was utterly unreasonable and inexplicable, on the assumption that he was *not* Penrose, his behaviour was in every respect exactly what we should have expected it to be. For if he was not Penrose, he was under strong suspicion of having made away with Penrose, for the reasons *1*: That Penrose had unaccountably disappeared and, *2*: That the stranger was in possession of Penrose's car and his driving licence. Taking all the facts together, I came to the conclusion that, in spite of the initials, the balance of probability was against his being Penrose.

"Nevertheless, those initials presented a formidable objection to the view that I was disposed to adopt, and I decided that the question whether they were Penrose's initials or those of some other person must be settled before any further investigation would be worthwhile. It was not a difficult question to dispose of, and it turned out to be easier than I had expected. You remember how we obtained the answer?"

"Indeed, I don't," I replied. "I never knew that the question had been raised."

"You never followed this case very closely, for some reason," said Thorndyke, "but if you will recall our visit to the garage, you will remember that I was able, quite easily, to extract a statement from Kickweed which settled the question definitely.

"We learned from him that Penrose was in the habit of marking all his portable property, including his collars and handkerchiefs, with his name, *D. Penrose*, by means of a rubber stamp."

I grinned rather sheepishly. "I remember quite well now you mention it, but I am afraid that, at the time, I merely wondered, like a fool, why you were going into such trivialities at such length."

"Well," said Thorndyke, "you will now see that our conversation with Kickweed cleared up all our difficulties. Penrose's collars were marked '*D. Penrose*' with a rubber stamp, the patient's collar was marked '*D. P.*' with a marking-ink pencil. Therefore, the evidence of the collar supported all the other evidence, it went to prove that the patient was *not* Penrose.

"Then, at once, arose two other questions: If he was not Penrose, who was he? And what had become of Penrose? The first question had to be left until we had answered the second. Penrose had disappeared. What had happened to him? Was he alive or dead?

"Now, having regard to the strange and sinister circumstances: The disappearance of one man, the appearance of another man in possession of his property, and the anxiety of that other man to escape without being identified, there was only one reasonable conclusion that we could come to. The overwhelming probability was that Penrose was dead and that his body had been concealed by burial or otherwise.

"Adopting this view as I did, the next questions were: Where did Penrose meet his death? And where was his body concealed? The latter question was the more important, but the answer to both was probably the same. And both questions were contained in the further question: From what place did the car start on that wild journey home?

"Now in regard to this problem – the starting-point of the car's journey – we had two clues, and they were both very imperfect. The place where the woman was killed was in the Canterbury district, and the car was travelling via Maidstone towards Gravesend. But the speed at which it was travelling made it difficult to judge how far it might have come, especially as we had no exact information as to the time at which it started. All that we knew was that the car advanced towards the Canterbury-Ashford road from some place to the south and east.

"The other clue was the very distinctive pottery fragment. But this also was a very ambiguous clue. The pocket in which we found it was not Penrose's pocket, and we did not know how long it had been in that pocket. However, when we came to examine these difficulties, they did not appear insuperable. Thus, notwithstanding that the fragment was in another man's possession, I was disposed to associate it with Penrose for two reasons: First, that Penrose was a collector of antiquities and, second, that, when he started from home, he took with him – as we learned from Kickweed – two digging tools and was, apparently, intending to do some sort of excavation. As to the second difficulty, the earth in which the fragment was embedded was of the same kind as that which we scraped from the coat and that which we found later on the car. So it appeared practically certain that the fragment was the product of that day's digging.

"The next question was: Whence had that fragment come? That was a vitally important question, for there could be little doubt that the place where that fragment was dug up was the place where Penrose had met his death and where his body was concealed. But how was that question to be answered? It seemed that the only possible method was that which I had adopted in regard to the other questions, to form a working hypothesis and see whither it led. Now, the broken edges of the fragment showed fresh fractures. It had been broken off the pot at the time of the excavation, and as the digging had probably been done after dark, by a very imperfect light, the fragment had apparently been overlooked, the new fracture of the pot being mistaken for an ancient one. It followed that, somewhere, there was a broken pot with a space in it corresponding to this fragment, by which it could infallibly be recognised. If we could find that pot it would-probably be possible to ascertain where it had been dug up.

"But where were we to look for that pot? The only possible place known to us was Penrose's collection, and circumstances created an initial probability that it was there. But, further, I had a theory, as I mentioned to you, that the expedition on which Penrose had embarked that day possibly had the express purpose of recovering this fragment to make the imperfect pot complete. Accordingly, I took an opportunity of inspecting the collection, and I took with me my invaluable box of moulding wax.

"You know the result. The pot was there, easily recognisable at sight and conclusively identified by the wax squeeze. There was also a catalogue entry, presumably describing the piece and recording the source whence it had been obtained. But the wording of the entry was so obscure as to present a fresh puzzle. Nevertheless, it was a great advance, for the information was there, if we could only extract the meanings of the words.

"Those words were, you will remember: '*Moulin a vent, Julie, Polly*'. Now, the first term was obvious enough, the piece was a '*Windmill Hill*' pot. By the study of other entries in the catalogue, I reached the conclusion that '*Julie*' probably represented the locality, and '*Polly*' the person from whom the pot was obtained. Accordingly, the first thing to be done was to ascertain, if possible, the meaning of the word '*Julie*'.

"To this end, I procured and read various works dealing with neolithic pottery and, since our pot had almost certainly been dug out of a long barrow, I gave attention to those also. But the result, for a time, was very disappointing. I read through quite a large number of books and papers on barrows and pottery without meeting with any name resembling "*Julie*". At last, I struck the clue in Jessup's *Archeology of Kent*. There, in the chapter dealing with neolithic remains, I found a reference to a long barrow known as Julliberrie's Grave, in the neighbourhood of Chilham. Looking it up on the ordnance map, I saw at once that its situation fitted the circumstances exactly, for it was quite close to the known track of the car. Thereupon I decided that Julliberrie's Grave was almost certainly the place for which I had been searching, the starting-point of the car's wild career and the place in which the body of Daniel Penrose was probably reposing.

"The question then arose: What was to be done? I had not a particle of definite evidence to support my belief. My whole case was just a train of hypothetical reasoning – guess-work, if you will, and guess-work was not good enough either for the Home Office or the Office of Works. Besides, as you acutely observed, I didn't want to let the cat out of the bag prematurely. Yet it was impossible to get any further in the investigation until the barrow had been explored.

"There was only one thing to do – to organise a scientific excavation of the barrow by skilled and trained archaeologists. That would ensure an absolutely exhaustive exploration without injury to the barrow and without any disclosure of my suspicions if they should prove to be unfounded. Accordingly, I looked up our invaluable friend, Elmhurst and, to my great satisfaction, found that he had both the means and the will to carry out the excavation if I were prepared to finance the work.

"You know the rest. Everything went according to plan and the first stage of our investigation was brought to a triumphant conclusion. I only hope that the second stage will go as well. It ought to, for we have now a solid foundation of established fact to build on."

"Yes," I agreed. "We know that Penrose is dead and that somebody killed him. But I don't see much of a lead towards the conclusion as to who that somebody may have been. But I expect that you do. Perhaps the word '*Polly*' in that ridiculous catalogue entry, suggests something to you. Apparently, it refers to a person, though it is hardly safe to say even that. The only thing that is certain is that it doesn't mean Polly."

"The meaning of that word," he replied, "really belongs to the second stage of our inquiry, on which we are now embarking, the identification of the person whom we may call 'the murderer' – though the fact of murder is not established. Penrose was killed with his own weapon, which, as the coroner justly observed, suggests a struggle or conflict. But as to the identity of that person, I have not yet formed a definite opinion. There is one essential question that has to be settled before we begin to theorise. We have got to know whether the alleged burglary at Queen Square was an actual burglary, and whether the cupboard in the small room was actually opened."

"You mean," said I, "that, if the cupboard was opened, it must have been opened with Penrose's keys, as you have always maintained, and that, therefore, the person who opened it must have been the murderer."

"I would hardly go as far as that," he replied. "If some person did actually enter that room and open the cupboard, he must have opened it with Penrose's keys or with duplicates made from them. That would suggest that he was either the murderer or in league with the murderer. But even if he opened the cupboard, that would not be conclusive evidence that he stole the jewels. He might have found the cupboard empty. That is not probable, but it has to be borne in mind. And then we have to remember that the only evidence of the room's having been entered is the unsupported statement of one person."

"Yes," said I, "and not an entirely unsuspected person. Our friend, Horridge, seems to have had considerable misgivings as to the discreet and melancholy Kickweed, but I didn't think that you had any suspicions in that direction."

"I don't say that I have," replied Thorndyke, "or that I entertain seriously the various possibilities that I have mentioned. I am merely pointing out that we have got a good many eggs in our basket. A sensible man keeps in his mind all the possibilities, no matter how remote, but he also gives his special attention, in the first place, to those that are least remote. And, meanwhile, we have got to begin our quest by settling definitely whether that cupboard has or has not been opened. We have very little doubt as to what was in it when Penrose was alive, and Lockhart will now have to make an explicit statement. If the things are not there, we shall have a definite fact and can consider what follows from it, and if we find the collection intact – well, I shall be very much surprised."

379

Chapter XVIII
The Opening of
the Safe

On suitable occasions, Thorndyke could lie remarkably low and exhibit a most masterly inactivity.

But also on suitable occasions he could act with surprising promptitude, and the matter of the alleged burglary at Queen Square presented such an occasion. Armed with an authority from Mr. Brodribb as joint executor, he proceeded to call on Chubbs and make all necessary arrangements for the opening of the safe in the small room, and then, as I gathered, he had an interview with Lockhart. What passed at that interview I did not learn, but I suspect that there was some rather plain speaking. Not that it should have been necessary, for Lockhart was a lawyer and knew in what a very questionable position he stood. But whatever passed on that occasion, he was quite amenable. He frankly admitted that he had seen in the small room a collection of jewels which were almost certainly the Billington jewels, and he gave Thorndyke a written statement to that effect. Further, he wrote a letter to Miller, in somewhat ambiguous terms, referring him to Thorndyke for fuller particulars, and agreed to be present when the safe was opened.

Naturally, this letter brought Miller, hotfoot, to our chambers, and a preliminary discussion was unavoidable in spite of Thorndyke's efforts to stave it off.

"Now, Doctor," the superintendent began a little truculently, "this is the sort of thing that I was complaining of. You knew those jewels were there, but you didn't let on the faintest hint to me."

"I did not know," Thorndyke protested. "I only suspected, and I don't profess to communicate mere suspicions."

"Well," rejoined Miller, "there they were, at any rate, and we can take it as a certainty that they are not there now."

"I expect you are right," said Thorndyke, "but why not leave the discussion until we know?"

"For all practical purposes, we do know," replied Miller. "We can take it that there was either a real or a pretended burglary, and in either case the stuff is pretty certainly gone, and the question is, who lifted it?"

"You remember," said Thorndyke, "that the keys were stolen from Penrose's body. Presumably, they were taken for the purpose of being used, and they could have been used only by entering the premises.

380

Moreover, if the cupboard was opened, it could have been opened only with Penrose's keys."

"Yes, that's a fact," Miller agreed. "But suppose the murderer did enter the premises. How do we know that he found the stuff there? Or for that matter, how do we know that the place was ever entered? We have got only one man's word for it. And to an experienced eye, it looks a bit like an indoor job."

"I don't quite see what is in your mind," said Thorndyke. "You are not letting your thoughts run on Horridge?"

Miller grinned sourly. "No," he replied, "though I must admit that I did suspect him very considerably in connection with the murder. But I have squeezed him pretty dry – and I can tell you he didn't like being squeezed. But in the end, he was able to produce an undeniable alibi – a club dinner that he attended on the seventeenth of October at which all the members signed their names. So Horridge is now out of the picture."

"He was never in," said Thorndyke. "The proceedings at the inquest made that perfectly clear."

"What proceedings do you mean?" Miller demanded.

"I am referring to Kickweed's evidence," Thorndyke replied. "If you had not been so preoccupied with the forged letter, you would have seen that it excluded Horridge from any possible suspicion in regard to the murder. Kickweed deposed that on the twentieth of October, three days after the murder, and the very day after the flight of the presumed murderer from Gravesend Hospital, Horridge called at Queen Square to see Penrose, and the two of them, Horridge and Kickweed, interviewed a police officer who had come to bring the coat that was assumed to belong to Penrose. Now, if Horridge had been the murderer, he must also have been the hospital patient. But the patient had two very bad black eyes and a severe wound across his right eyebrow. Obviously, he would have been in no condition for paying calls, and you will remember that the police officer was looking for a man with two black eyes and a cut across his right eyebrow."

"Yes," Miller admitted, "I had overlooked that. But it did look as if Horridge had written that letter. Have you any idea who did write it? We have got to find that out."

"My dear Miller," Thorndyke said, a little impatiently, "you had better forget that letter. It is a criminal matter, but it has no bearing on the crime which we are investigating. But if you have dropped Horridge, what do you mean by suggesting that this burglary may have been an indoor job?"

"Well, you know," replied Miller, "this burglary rests on the story told by Mr. Kickweed, and Mr. Kickweed strikes me as a decidedly downy bird."

"He couldn't have been the murderer, you know," said Thorndyke. "But it was presumably the murderer who had the keys."

"I know," rejoined Miller. "But he was in the house, and there is such a thing as wax."

"You can take it," said Thorndyke, "that Penrose was not in the habit of leaving his keys about."

"No, probably not," Miller agreed, "but I suppose he had a bath sometimes, and I don't suppose he took his clothes into the bathroom with him."

Thorndyke smiled indulgently at the superintendent and admonished him in mock solemn tones. "Now, my dear Miller, let me urge you to beware of obsessions. At the inquest you allowed yourself to become letter-minded, and so you missed a vitally important item of evidence. And now you seem inclined to let yourself become Kickweed-minded. Why not leave Kickweed alone and address yourself to the more obvious lines of inquiry?"

"Still, you know, Doctor," Miller persisted, "somebody must have known that those jewels were there."

"There is not a particle of evidence that Kickweed did. You must remember that Penrose kept their existence absolutely secret from everybody excepting Lockhart, and he swore him to secrecy before he showed them. So far as we know, their existence was known only to two persons, Lockhart, and the man, whoever he was, who supplied them."

"Yes," said Miller, "the chappie who supplied them to Penrose certainly knew that they were there. It would be interesting, quite apart from the murder business, to know who he was. I wonder if it could have been Crabbe, after all."

"You needn't wonder, Miller," said Thorndyke. "It was Crabbe. I think there can be no doubt about that."

Miller sat up in his chair and turned a rather startled face to my colleague.

"Hallo, Doctor!" he exclaimed. "You seem to know a mighty lot about it. And how did you manage to dig up Mr. Crabbe? I've been wondering about that ever since that evening when you asked me about him."

"There was a document," replied Thorndyke, "a scrap of paper, apparently a descriptive label, which was found in the small room, on the morning after the alleged burglary. That was what enabled me to connect Crabbe with Penrose's collection."

382

"Then," Miller exclaimed excitedly, "we have got actual, tangible evidence against Crabbe. Who has got that scrap of paper?"

"Brodribb has the original, but I kept a copy. You shall see it." And with this, he rose and went to the cabinet in which the Penrose dossier was kept. Taking out from the collection of notes and papers the copy of Mr. Penrose's cryptogram, he brought it over and gravely handed it to Miller, who stared at it aghast while I watched him with unholy glee.

"I can't make anything of this!" the superintendent grumbled. "'*Lobster: hortus petasatus*'. It doesn't make sense. Besides, a lobster isn't a crab, and what in creation is a *hortus petasatus*?"

Thorndyke expounded the meaning of the inscription, explaining the late Mr. Penrose's peculiarities of speech, and Miller listened with incredulous astonishment.

"Well, Doctor," he commented. "I take off my hat to you. That thing would have conveyed nothing to me. It's like some damn' silly puzzle game. And you might have passed it all round the C.I.D. and no one would have been an atom the wiser. But I am afraid it wouldn't do as evidence in a court of law."

"Possibly not," Thorndyke admitted, "but I am not concerned with the robbery charge against Crabbe. I am investigating the murder of Daniel Penrose, and I am assuming that there was a burglary, that the burglar was in possession of Penrose's keys, and that he knew what the cupboard in the small room contained. Of course, if we find the jewels still in the cupboard, we shall know that those assumptions were wrong."

"Yes," Miller agreed, "but we shan't. Burglary or no burglary, those jewels have been pinched. I'd lay my bottom dollar to that. But you realise, Doctor, that, even if there was a burglary, the burglar couldn't have been Crabbe. He was in chokee at the time when it was supposed to have occurred."

"Yes," said Thorndyke, "I had noted that fact, so we shall have to look round for some other person who knew that the jewels were there. And no such person is actually known to us, if we except Lockhart, and I suppose we can hardly suspect him."

Miller grinned faintly at the suggestion and then became thoughtful. After a few moments of profound reflection he remarked. "Those locksmiths will make hay with poor old Penrose's safe. Are you going to be present to see how the job is done?"

I was instantly struck by this abrupt change of subject and I could see that it was also noticed by Thorndyke, who, however, followed the superintendent's lead.

"No," he replied. "I shall not turn up until they have had time to get the job finished. But Polton will be there to watch the proceedings and pick up a few tips on the correct method of opening a safe."

"Ah!" said Miller, "I shall have to keep an eye on Mr. Polton if he is going to qualify as an expert safe-breaker. He is mighty handy already in the matter of locks and skeleton keys and house-breaker's tools."

He pursued this facetious and quite irrelevant topic at considerable length and with no tendency whatever to revert to the subject of the Queen Square burglary. And then he pulled out his watch and, having bestowed on it a single startled glance, sprang up, declaring that, if he didn't look sharp, he would be late for an important appointment. And with this he took his departure hurriedly and with a distinctly purposive air.

"Miller has got a bright idea of some kind." I remarked when he had gone.

"Yes," Thorndyke agreed, "and he thinks he has got it all to himself. You noticed his sudden anxiety to switch the conversation off the subject of Mr. Crabbe. Well, it is all to the good if he doesn't get busy prematurely. I suppose you are coming to swell the multitude at Queen Square to-morrow?"

"If there is room," I replied, "I should like to see the fateful question decided. But it will be a bit of an anti-climax if the stuff is there after all, though I don't suppose Horridge will complain."

"He will have a bad disappointment," said Thorndyke, "if we find the jewels there and he is then told that they are stolen property. However, there is no use in speculating. To-morrow we shall know whether they were or were not stolen, and until we know that, neither Miller nor I can decide on the next move."

When, on the following morning, we arrived at the house in Queen Square and were admitted by Kickweed, we learned from him that the locksmiths had started their work on the safe about an hour previously and that the operations were still in progress. Our friend shook his head despondently as he showed us into the morning room and remarked that it was a dreadful business and very disturbing.

"Would you like to wait here until they are ready," he asked, "or will you join the – er – assembly in the great gallery?"

We elected to join the assembly, whereupon he ushered us into the gallery, announcing us with due solemnity as he threw open the door. The word "assembly" appeared to represent Mr. Kickweed's state of mind rather than the actual facts, for there were only three persons present: Lockhart, Miller, and Horridge, the latter very subdued, care-worn and decidedly gloomy. The cause of his depressed state was made

384

evident presently when he took us apart, leaving Lockhart and Miller amicably discussing the legal position of an accessory after the fact.

"This is a nice state of affairs," Horridge complained. "Do you know that this detective fellow actually accused me, in so many words, of having murdered poor old Pen? Me, his old and trusted friend and an executor of his will! And, if I hadn't had a conclusive alibi, I believe he would have run me in. And now he tells me that even if we find the jewels intact, it will be of no advantage to me because they are all stolen property, which I don't believe. I ask you, is it likely that a man of Pen's character would have been guilty of trafficking in stolen goods?"

"I should, say, certainly not," replied Thorndyke, "if he knew that the goods were stolen. But the point is hardly worth discussing if the goods in question have disappeared."

Here our conversation was interrupted by Polton, who entered to announce that the work on the lock was completed and that the safe door was free and ready to be opened. Thereupon we followed him into the small room where we found two very superior artificers standing on guard over the remains of a large iron safe, the massive door of which was disclosed by the opening of the wooden case. Miller's prognostications had certainly not over-stated the results of the locksmith's activities – to say nothing of the wooden door with its shattered detector lock, those artificers had undoubtedly "made hay with" the safe, itself.

"Now, Mr. Horridge," said Miller, "you, as executor, are the proper person to open the safe."

Horridge, however, deputed his functions to one of the workmen who accordingly took hold of the battered door and swung it wide open, disclosing a range of shallow drawers like those of an entomological cabinet.

"Are these drawers in the condition in which you saw them when Mr. Penrose showed you his collection?" Thorndyke asked.

"Yes, so far as I can see," Lockhart replied. "He took them out, one by one, in their proper order from above downwards, and carried each over to that table by the window so that we could see the contents better."

"Then," said Thorndyke, "we had better do the same."

But it was not necessary, for when the top drawer was pulled out it was seen to be undeniably empty. Horridge exhibited its vacant interior to the assembled company, turned it upside-down and shook it, and glumly returned it to its place. The case was the same with the second drawer and also with the third, excepting that when it was inverted some small object was heard to fall out on to the floor. Miller picked it up and exhibited it in the palm of his hand, when it was seen to be a small opal and was dropped back into the drawer. But that little opal was the solitary occupant of the cabinet. Apart from it and a plentiful covering of dust, the whole range of drawers from top to bottom was empty.

"That burglar," Lockhart commented as the last of the drawers was slid back into its place, "was pretty thorough in his methods. He made a clean sweep of the whole collection, not only the gems but the coins as well. And he must have been fairly heavily laden when he went away, for most of the coins were gold and I should say there were some hundreds of them."

"I don't fancy those coins were gold," said Miller. "I think I know where they came from and, if I am right, they were electros – copper, gilt. Still, even copper electros weigh something. But it's surprising what a lot of coins and jewellery you can stow away about your person if you have the right sort of pockets. And it's pretty certain that he had an overcoat as well."

"Do you remember, Lockhart," Thorndyke asked, "whether, when you saw the jewels, there were any labels attached to them?"

"Not attached," Lockhart replied. "There were no fixed labels, only slips of paper like those on the shelves of the gallery."

"Did you notice what was written on those slips of paper? Were they descriptive labels?"

Lockhart grinned. "You know what Penrose's descriptions were like," he replied, "and you have seen the catalogue. So far as I could make out, the descriptions on the labels were similar to those in the catalogue, apparently – unintelligible nonsense."

"You can't recall any of them?" Thorndyke asked.

"I remember one, because I tried to puzzle out what it could mean, and failed utterly. It was *'Decapod, jardin a chapeau'*. Does that convey anything to you?"

"It does to me, thanks to the Doctor's explanations," said Miller, who had been listening eagerly to the questions and answers. "I don't know what a 'decapod' is, but I've got enough French to infer that *jardin de chapeau* is much the same as *hortus petasatus*. And the Doctor can tell you what that means."

"What does it mean?" Lockhart demanded, and Thorndyke – not very willingly, I thought – gave the required explanation.

"Yes," Lockhart chuckled, "I see now, though I hadn't your ingenuity. Poor old Penrose! What nonsense he did write and speak! But I think I also see the point of your questions."

"And an uncommonly good point it is," said Miller. "That chappie was careful to take away the labels as well as the goods, and if he hadn't dropped one of them we should know a good deal less than we do. It's a very significant point, indeed."

"And now," said Thorndyke, "as we have done what we came to do, perhaps we had better leave Mr. Horridge to discuss the question of repairs. Are you walking in our direction, Miller?"

The superintendent was not. He was proposing, he said, to make a slight survey of the premises to elucidate the circumstances of the burglary, but I suspected that he was unwilling to run the risk of an interrogation by Thorndyke. So we left him to his survey and, having once more condoled with Horridge, we set forth in company with Lockhart, leaving Polton to spy on the superintendent and worm out any trifles in the way of technical tips and trade secrets that he could from the locksmiths.

Chapter XIX
Thorndyke's Dilemma

I have referred more than once to Thorndyke's habitual unwillingness to discuss uncompleted cases, excepting in relation to questions of fact, or to disclose any opinions or theories that he had built on the facts which were known to us both. I had come to accept this reticence as a condition of our friendship and usually refrained from any attempts to discover what lines his thoughts were pursuing or what inferences he had drawn. But when we met at our chambers in the evening after our visit to Queen Square, I found him in a mood of unwonted expansiveness, apparently ready to discuss our present case without any reservations.

The discussion opened with a question that I put tentatively, half-expecting the usual invitation to exercise my own admirable faculty of deduction.

"I noticed that you and Miller seemed to attach great importance to the circumstance that the burglar had carefully removed all the labels from the drawers. I don't quite see why. Would not a burglar ordinarily take away any labels that might furnish a clue to what had been stolen?"

"I don't see why he should," Thorndyke replied. "An ordinary burglar would assume that the contents of the drawers were known, so that the labels would give no additional information. But these were not ordinary descriptive labels. They gave very definite information as to the person who had supplied the jewels, and as those jewels were the proceeds of a robbery which was known to the police, the information would be very dangerous to the person named. But that would not concern an ordinary burglar. The labels would furnish no clue to his identity. Of course, we know that he was not an ordinary, casual burglar, since he had Penrose's keys. But the point is that, whoever he was, he seemed to consider it a matter of importance that the identity of the person who sold the jewels to Penrose should not become known."

"But the jewels were sold to Penrose by Crabbe."

"Yes."

"But Crabbe could not have been the burglar. He was in prison at the time."

"Exactly," Thorndyke rejoined. "That is the importance of the discovery. The labels implicated Crabbe. But Crabbe could not have been the burglar. It seems to follow that they implicated someone besides Crabbe, and as the burglar was in possession of Penrose's keys and

388

would thus appear to have been either the murderer or an accessory to the murder, it would be very interesting to know whom those labels could have implicated. I fancy that Miller has a very definite opinion on the subject, and I am disposed to think that he is right."

"The deuce you are!" I exclaimed. "Then it seems to me that you have got the investigation much farther advanced than I had imagined. I had supposed that the search for the murderer had still to be begun. But it seems that there is already a definite suspect. Is that so?"

He reflected for a few moments and then replied. "The word 'suspect' is perhaps a little too strong. My conclusions as to the possible identity of the murderer are at present on an entirely hypothetical plane. I have considered the whole complex of circumstances connected with the murder and have noted the persons who seem to have made any sort of contact with those circumstances, and I have considered each of those persons in relation to the questions whether he could possibly be the murderer and whether his known characteristics agree with those of the murderer."

"But," I demanded, "what do we know of the characteristics of the murderer?"

"Very little," he replied, "but still enough to enable us to apply at least a negative test in conjunction with the other considerations. Thus we can exclude Kickweed and Horridge because, although they make certain contacts, neither could have been present at the place and time of the murder. But let us take a glance at the positive aspects.

"We begin with the justifiable assumption that the hospital patient was the murderer. Now, what do we know about him? Of his personal characteristics we have no description whatever. All that we know is that his collar bore the letters D.P., which were presumably the initial letters of his name, and that he had a deep wound crossing his right eyebrow which must have left a rather conspicuous permanent scar. So you see that, little as we know, we have the means of excluding or accepting any given individual. If his characteristics agree with those of the patient, he is a possible suspect, if they do not agree, he is not possible."

"And do you know of any person whose characteristics do agree with those of the patient?"

"Up to a certain point," he replied. "The ascertainment of the scar would involve a personal examination. That will have to come later as a final test. For the present, we must be content with agreement so far as is known."

"But you have some such person in view?"

Again he reflected for a few moments. At length, he replied. "I am in a rather odd dilemma. I have two theoretically possible suspects, and I can make no sort of choice between them."

"And do the names of both of them begin with *D.P.?*" I asked, imagining that I was putting a poser.

"But," he exclaimed, "that is the extraordinary thing. They do. There is a coincidence for you if you like. It was a striking coincidence that the murderer should have the same initials as the victim. But this is more than striking. It is almost incredible."

"I suppose we name no names," I suggested humbly.

"I don't know why not," he replied. "We keep our own counsel until we can turn hypothesis into proof. Well, my two possible suspects are Deodatus Pettigrew and David Parrott."

"Parrott!" I exclaimed in astonishment. "I don't see where he comes into it, or Pettigrew either for that matter."

"It is just a question of the contacts that they make with the circumstances of the murder," he replied. "Let us take them separately and see what those contacts are. The odd and confusing thing is that their contacts are entirely separate and from different sides."

"Is it possible that they were both concerned in the murder?" I suggested, "that they may have been confederates?"

"I have considered that," he answered. "It is possible but, I think, unlikely. The crime has all the appearances of a one-man job. Moreover, I can find no evidence of any contact between these two men. So far as I know, they were strangers to each other and they persistently remain completely separate. So we will consider them separately.

"Now, as to Parrott. The hospital patient had in his pocket a fragment of pottery which almost certainly came from Julliberrie's Grave. That fragment had been broken off a pot which was in Penrose's museum and which had come from Julliberrie's Grave. The entry in the catalogue relating to that pot consisted of the usual three terms, the description of the piece – '*Moulin de vent*' – the place whence it came – '*Julie*' – and a third term – '*Polly*' – which presumably indicated the person who supplied it."

"Yes," I agreed, "that seems to have been Penrose's custom. So now the question is: Who is '*Polly*'? What is she? Have you found an answer to it?"

"I infer, having regard to Penrose's cryptic terminology, that '*Polly*' indicates Mr. Parrott."

"Of course," I exclaimed. "I ought to have spotted that. *Poll parrot. Pretty Polly*. But still, you know, Thorndyke, it is only a guess, after all."

"It is a little more than that," he objected. "Parrott is referred to frequently in the catalogue, and always by some allusive name, such as Perroquet, Psittacus, or Popinjay. Penrose may well have tried to find a new variant. But I admit your objection. This is not proof, it is only hypothesis. That is all I claim. At present we are only looking for someone whom it would be possible to suspect, as a guide to further investigation. Parrott is such a person, and so is Pettigrew, whose case is equally hypothetical. But you will note that Parrott agrees with the hospital patient in the initials of his name and that we have reason to believe that he knew Julliberrie's Grave and had actually dug into it.

"Now let us consider Pettigrew. He does not appear to be in any way connected with Julliberrie's Grave, or, so far as I know, with Penrose. But there are reasons for connecting him with the burglary. The burglar knew of the existence of the Billington jewels and apparently knew where they were kept. Moreover, he was at pains to take away the labels which contained evidence that the jewels had been supplied by Crabbe. Apparently, he was anxious that Crabbe's guilt should not be revealed. But why? He certainly was not Crabbe himself. What was his interest in the matter?

"You remember that Miller strongly suspected Crabbe of the Billington robbery. And it was not mere suspicion. He had enough evidence to make him consider seriously the possibility of a prosecution, though he decided that the evidence was not sufficient. The difficulty was that the jewels had disappeared and could not be traced. But now they have been traced and are known to have been sold to Penrose by Crabbe. So there is probably a complete case against the latter. But you will also remember that Miller's case against Crabbe included Pettigrew, for the reason – and no other – that Pettigrew was associated with Crabbe at the time of the robbery.

"Now, that robbery was committed by Crabbe, or by his agents – but almost certainly by Crabbe himself. Whether Pettigrew did or did not take part in the robbery, we don't know. But we do know that he was associated with Crabbe at the time, that that association put him under suspicion, and that if Crabbe should be proved guilty, he, Crabbe's associate, would certainly be implicated. You see, therefore, that Pettigrew agrees completely with the special characteristics that we have assigned to the burglar, and we know of no one else who does.

"But that burglar was in possession of Penrose's keys and was, therefore, either the murderer himself or a confederate of the murderer."

"Yes," I agreed, "it is a very complete case so far as it goes. But it is only a string of hypotheses, after all."

"Not entirely," he replied. "The association of Crabbe and Pettigrew is a fact, if we accept Miller's statement. There is really a definite case of suspicion against Pettigrew, at least that is my opinion, and it is certainly Miller's. If I am not greatly mistaken, the superintendent is in full cry after Deodatus. But you see the curious dilemma that we are in. Here are two men each of whom agrees in certain respects with the characters of the murderer. But the characters with which they agree are not the same. Parrott is connected with Julliberrie's Grave but seems to have no connection with the burglary. Pettigrew is connected with the burglary but seems to have no connection with Julliberrie's Grave. But the murderer must have been connected with both."

"It almost seems," said I, "that you will have to accept – at least provisionally – the idea of confederacy. The assumption that both men were concerned in the murder would release you from your dilemma."

"That is quite true," he replied. "But it would be a gratuitous assumption. There is nothing to support it. The two men are separate and there is no apparent connection between them, nothing to suggest that they were even acquainted. And again I must say that I have the strongest feeling that the murder was the work of one man absolutely alone."

"It certainly has that appearance," I admitted, "but still – "

I paused as the sound of footsteps on our landing caught my ear. A moment later, an old-fashioned flourish on the little brass knocker of our inner door at once announced the arrival of a visitor and declared his identity. I rose and, crossing the room, threw open the door, whereupon Mr. Brodribb bounced in, looking, with his glossy silk hat and his faultless morning dress, as if he had just bounced out of a band-box.

"Now," said he, holding up his hand, "don't let me create any disturbance. I am only a bird of passage. Off again in two or three minutes."

"But why?" said Thorndyke. "Polton will be bringing in our dinner by that time. Why not stay and season the feast with your illustrious presence?"

"Very good of you," replied Brodribb, "and very nicely put. I should love to. But I have got a confounded engagement. However, I will sit down for a minute or two and say what I have to say. It isn't very important."

He placed his hat tenderly on the table and then continued. "My principal object in calling, I don't mind admitting, is to bespeak the good offices of the incomparable Polton. I've got a fine old bracket clock – belonged to my grandfather, made for him by Earnshaw, and I set considerable store by it. Now, something has gone wrong with its strike and I don't like to trust it to a common clock-jobber, so I thought I would ask Polton to have a look at it. Probably he can do all that is necessary and, if he can't, he will be able to give me the name of one of his Clerkenwell friends who is equal to dealing with a fine bracket clock."

"Very well," said Thorndyke, "I will undertake the commission on his behalf. He will be delighted, I am sure, to do what he can for pure love of a good clock, to say nothing of his love of the owner."

"Does he love me?" asked Brodribb. "Well, I hope he does, for I have the greatest admiration and regard for him. Then that is settled. And now to the other matter. I thought you would be interested to know that I have got the intestacy proceedings *in re* Penrose well under way."

"You haven't lost much time," I remarked in some surprise.

"Oh, I don't mean that I have got it settled," said he. "That will be a work of months, at least. But I have got the essentials in train. As soon as I got your note informing me that Daniel Penrose was dead and that he died on the seventeenth of October, I set the machinery going. Seemed a bit callous, with the body still above ground, but I don't believe in wasting time. None of the law's delay for me if I can help it. So I put out the necessary advertisements at once. You see, it was pretty plain sailing as I had a copy of the Penrose pedigree. That told me at once who the principal next of kin were, though, of course, I didn't know where to find them. But I was able to give names and particulars which were likely to catch the attention of interested parties. And they did. As a matter of fact, there are only two persons who matter and I have got into touch with them both. They are descendants of a certain Elizabeth Penrose, an aunt of Oliver's, who married a man named John Pettigrew. What their exact relationship is to each other, I have forgotten, but they are both named Pettigrew. One of them is a young lady named Joan, a nice girl, poor as a church mouse but very independent and industrious. Works for her living and supports her mother – secretary to some professor fellow. And the mother is quite a nice lady. She had a job as manageress of some sort of antique shop, but the proprietor went bust and she lost the billet. It is pleasant to think of these two worthy ladies coming in for a bit of luck."

"You have seen them, apparently," said Thorndyke.

"Yes, they turned up two days after the advertisement appeared, and I liked the look of both of them. The girl, Joan, is very much on the spot and very modern – short skirts, head like a mop, you know the sort of thing. But I like her. She's a good girl and she has evidently been a good daughter."

"And the other person?" Thorndyke asked.

"The other is a man, Deodatus Pettigrew. Quaint name, isn't it? I hope he will justify it, but I have my doubts. Joan and her mother knew him, but they were mighty reticent about him. Rather evasive, in fact.

393

Made me suspect that he might be a sheep of the brunette type. But we shall see. In any case, his personal character is no concern of mine."

"You haven't met him yet?" Thorndyke suggested.

"No. He didn't seem keen on an interview. Joan and her mother turned up in person, but he just wrote and seemed to want to do the whole business by correspondence. Of course, I couldn't have that in the case of a big estate like this. Must know the people I am dealing with."

"What do you reckon these two persons are likely to receive?" Thorndyke asked.

"The whole estate is about a hundred-and-fifty-thousand pounds and, as there are practically no other claimants, they can hardly get less than fifty-thousand apiece."

"Fifty-thousand pounds," I remarked, "ought to be worth the trouble of an interview."

"So I told him," said Brodribb, "and, in effect, he agreed. So he is coming up to see me to-morrow."

"At what time?" Thorndyke asked.

"The appointment is for twelve o'clock, noon, sharp. But why do you ask that?"

"Because I rather want to see Mr. Pettigrew."

"Ho, ha!" said Brodribb. "So you know something about him."

"Not very much," replied Thorndyke. "I am interested. I should like to have a look at him in a good light to see if he agrees with a description that I had of a person of that name. Can you manage that?"

"I can and I will. Would you like an introduction?"

"No," replied Thorndyke. "I don't want to know him and I don't wish him to know who I am. I just want to have a good look at his face."

"Ha!" exclaimed Brodribb. "I scent a mystery. But I ask no questions. You will bear me out in that, Jervis. I ask no questions though I am bursting with curiosity. I just do what I am asked to do. I shall arrange for you to be shown into the waiting room – where, by the way, the clock is. Pettigrew will come to the clerk's office, but when he goes away I shall let him out through the waiting room. So if you sit or stand close to the outer door, which is by the window, you will have a good view of him in an excellent light. I wonder why the devil you want to see him. But I don't ask. No, not at all. I know my place."

Here Brodribb consulted a fat gold watch. Then, as he sprang up and seized his hat, he concluded. "Now I must really be off. To-morrow at noon, and don't forget to tell Polton about the clock."

When he had gone, I reopened our previous discussion with the inevitable comment.

"This communication of Brodribb's throws a fresh and lurid light on the case and lets you out of your dilemma. It looks as if Parrott might be dismissed from the role of suspect."

"It does," Thorndyke agreed. "But we mustn't exaggerate the significance of these new facts. Because a man stands to benefit by another man's death, it doesn't follow that he is prepared to murder that other man."

"True," I replied. "But that is not quite the position. It is not merely a case of a man standing to benefit by the death of another. The benefit was actually created by the murder. If Penrose had not been murdered, he would have taken practically the whole estate and the others would have received nothing. There is no blinking the fact that the murder of Daniel Penrose was worth fifty thousand pounds to Pettigrew, and that without the murder he would have got nothing. I should say that you might pretty safely forget Parrott."

"You may be right, Jervis," he rejoined. "You are, certainly, in regard to the reality of the motive. But that motive is no answer to the positive evidence that seems to implicate Parrott."

Here Polton stole silently into the room (having let himself in with his key), bearing the advance guard of the materials for dinner, and the discussion was necessarily suspended. Thorndyke lapsed into silence and, as his invaluable henchman laid the table in his quietly efficient fashion, he watched him thoughtfully, as if noting his noiseless, unhurried dexterity. As Polton retired to fetch a fresh consignment, he rose and, stepping over to the cabinet, pulled out a drawer and took from it the cardboard box in which the pottery fragment and its mould and the other objects from the pocket of the hospital patient had been deposited. From the box he picked out the cigarette-tube – the existence of which I had forgotten – turned it over in his fingers, looking at it curiously, and replaced the box in the drawer. Then he walked over to the table and, having laid the tube on the white cloth, went back to his chair.

I watched the proceeding with a good deal of curiosity but I made no comment. For the immediate purpose was plain enough and it remained only to await the further developments. And I had not long to wait. Presently Polton returned with the remainder of the materials for our meal on a tray. The latter he set down on the table and was about to begin unloading it when the cigarette-tube caught his eye. He looked at it very hard and with evident surprise for a few moments and then picked it up and turned it over as Thorndyke had done, examining every part of it with the minutest scrutiny.

"Well, Polton," said Thorndyke, "what do you think of it?"

Polton looked at him with a cunning and crinkly smile and replied comprehensively in a single word: "Tims?"

"Tims," I repeated. "What on earth are Tims?"

"Mr. Tims, sir," he explained, "now the deceased. Mr. Parrott's cabinet-maker."

"You think it once belonged to Mr. Tims?" Thorndyke suggested.

"I don't think," Polton replied. "I know. I saw him make it. The way it came about was this: There was a little cabinet of African ebony sent to the workshop for some repairs, and the owner of it sent with it a piece of the same wood that he had managed to get hold of – queer-looking stuff of a sort of brownish-black, rather like a lump of pitch, with a streak of grey sap-wood running through it.

"Well, Tims did the repairs and he was mighty economical with the wood because there was none too much of it. However, when the job was finished, there was a small bit left over, mostly sap-wood. But Tims cut most of that away and then put the piece in the lathe and turned up this tube, finishing the mouthpiece with a paring chisel, and he made these white dots by-drilling holes and driving little holly-wood dowels into them before he finished the turning. He was quite pleased with it when it was done."

"Did he keep it for his own use?" Thorndyke asked, "or did he sell it?"

"That I can't say, sir. But he would hardly have kept it, because he didn't smoke cigarettes. I supposed at the time that he had made it to give to Mr. Parrott, who smoked cigarettes a lot and always used a tube, and the one that he had was burned to a stump. Still, Tims may have given it or sold it to someone else. Might I ask, sir, how it came into your hands?"

"We found it," Thorndyke replied, "in the pocket of a raincoat that was left by the unknown man who was in possession of Mr. Penrose's car."

"Oh, dear!" said Polton. "Then I am afraid it has been in bad company."

He laid it down on the table and resumed the business of unloading the tray. Then, having removed the covers, he made a little bow to intimate that dinner was served and retired, apparently wrapped in profound thought.

"There, Jervis," said Thorndyke, picking up the tube and restoring it to its abiding-place, "you see how the evidence oscillates back and forth and still keeps a rough balance. Here we are, back in the old dilemma. First comes Brodribb and weights the balance heavily against Pettigrew, so heavily that you are disposed to drop Parrott overboard. But then comes Polton and weights the balance heavily against Parrott – and, by the way, I think he has his own suspicions of the Popinjay. He looked mighty thoughtful after I had answered his question."

"Yes," said I, "it seemed to me that your answer had given him something to think about. But with regard to this tube: There is not a particle of evidence that it was ever in Parrott's possession."

"Not of direct evidence," he admitted. "But just look at the *prima facie* appearances as a whole. Here was a man who was evidently intimately acquainted with Penrose, for they had been digging together in the barrow. He had in his pocket an object which had been dug up in that barrow and which was part of another object, dug up from the same barrow, and almost certainly dug up by Parrott and sold by him to Penrose. That, at least, suggests the possibility – even a probability – that the man was Parrott. Now we find in that same man's pocket an object that was certainly made in Parrott's workshop. That is a very striking fact. It makes, at least, another connection between Parrott and the hospital patient. And then there is the very strong probability that Tims made the thing as a gift to his employer, that it was actually Parrott's property. By the ordinary rules of circumstantial evidence, all these agreements create a very definite probability that the man was Parrott."

I had to admit the truth of this. "But," I objected, "this suspicion of Parrott is no answer to the positive evidence against Pettigrew. If you refuse to entertain the idea of a joint crime by two confederates – which still seems to me the only way out – you are left in a hopeless dilemma. You have got evidence suggesting that Tweedledum is the guilty party and evidence that Tweedledee committed the crime, and yet – on your one-man theory – they can't both be guilty. I don't quite see how you are going to resolve the puzzle."

"Don't forget, Jervis," said he, "that there are certain final tests which, if we can only apply them, will carry us out of the region of inference into that of demonstrable fact. If our inferences are correct, one of these men is pretty certainly in possession of the Billington jewels. And there are other confirmatory tests equally conclusive. The purpose of our hypothetical reasoning is to discover the persons to whom the tests may be applied."

Chapter XX
The Dilemma Resolved

It wanted some minutes to the appointed time when Thorndyke and I, accompanied by Polton and a burglarious-looking handbag, arrived at Mr. Brodribb's premises in New Square, Lincoln's Inn. The visitor, we learned from the chief clerk, had not yet made his appearance, and we were shown at once into the private office, where we found Brodribb seated at his writing-table sorting out a heap of letters and documents. He rose as we were announced and, taking off his spectacles, proceeded to the business on which we had come.

"You had better come out into the anteroom at once," said he, "as Pettigrew will come in through the clerks' office. I don't think you will have so very long to wait. The interview needn't be a very protracted affair as there isn't much to discuss. It is really only a matter of my making his acquaintance."

He opened a small, light door and ushered us through into the anteroom, a rather long, narrow chamber, lighted by a large window at one end which was close to the door of exit. A large office table occupied a good deal of the floor space and extended to the neighbourhood of the window, leaving a space just sufficient for a couple of chairs.

"There," said Brodribb, indicating the latter, "if you take those chairs you will be close to the window and the door. He will have to pass quite near to you and you will be able to inspect him in an excellent light. And I think this table will do for you, Polton. There is your patient on the mantelpiece. He is ticking away all right but, when he tries to strike, he makes a most ungodly noise."

Polton walked round to the mantelpiece and surveyed the clock with a friendly and appreciative crinkle.

"It's a noble old timepiece," said he. "They don't make clocks like that nowadays. Don't want 'em, I suppose, now that you can get the time by counting the hiccups from a loud-speaker."

He listened for a few moments with his ear close to the dial and then lifted the clock, cautiously and with loving care, on to the table. The keys were in the front and back doors and, when he had unlocked and opened them, he placed his bag on the table and began to discharge its cargo of tools and appliances. First he took out a roll of clean, white paper, which he spread on the table, weighting it with one or two tools and a couple of lignum-vitae bowls. Then he started the strike, which was accompanied by the most horrid asthmatical wheezing, and having listened critically to these abnormal sounds, he took off the pendulum and fell to work with a screwdriver to such effect that, in a jiffy, the clock was out of its case and lying on its back on the sheet of paper.

At this point a clerk appeared at the door of the private office and announced that Mr. Pettigrew had arrived, whereupon Mr. Brodribb directed him to show the visitor in and, after a last, anxious glance at the clock, went back into his office and shut the communicating door.

But the latter, as I have said, was by no means a massive structure and, in fact, hardly seemed to meet the requirements of a lawyer's office in the matter of privacy. Brodribb's voice, indeed, was hardly audible, but I heard quite distinctly the visitor's reply. "Yes, sir. I am Mr. Pettigrew."

But I was not the only person who heard that reply. As Pettigrew spoke, I noticed that Polton seemed to pause for an instant in his operations and listened with a rather odd expression of interest and attention. And so, as the interview proceeded, each time that Pettigrew spoke, Polton's movements were arrested and he sat with his mouth slightly open, listening, without any disguise, to the voice that penetrated the door.

It was a rather peculiar voice, resonant, penetrating and clear, and its quality was reinforced by the deliberate manner and distinct enunciation. The disjointed sentences that came through the door might have been spoken by an actor or by a man making a set speech. But I think that Brodribb must have done most of the talking, for the sounds that came through took the form, generally, of an indistinct rumble which certainly did not proceed from Pettigrew.

The interview was not a long one, but to me the inaction, coupled with an ill-defined expectancy, made the time pass slowly and tediously. Thorndyke relieved the tedium of waiting by following Polton's operations and discussing – almost in a whisper – the construction of the striking mechanism and the symptoms of its disorder. The latter did not appear to be very serious for, presently, Polton began to reassemble the dismembered parts of the movement, applying here and there, with a pointed style, a delicate touch of oil.

He had got the greater part of the striking movement together when the sound, from the private office, of a chair being drawn back seemed to herald the termination of the interview. Thereupon Thorndyke went back to his chair and Polton, softly laying down a pair of flat-nosed pliers, suddenly became immobile and watchful. Then the door opened an inch or two and Brodribb's voice became audible.

"Very well, Mr. Pettigrew," he said, "you shall not be troubled with unnecessary journeys. I shall let you know, from time to time, how matters are progressing and not ask for your personal attendance unless it is absolutely necessary."

With this he threw open the door and ushered his client into the anteroom, filling up the doorway with his own rather bulky person as if to prevent any retreat. I glanced with natural curiosity at Pettigrew and saw a rather large man, dark-complexioned and wearing a full beard and moustache, the latter turned up fiercely at the ends in a fashion slightly suggestive of wax. Apparently, he had supposed the room to be empty, for he looked round with quick, uneasy surprise. And then his glance fell on Polton, and I could see at once that he recognised him and was rather disconcerted by the recognition. But he made no sign after the first startled glance, walking straight up the room in the narrow space between the table and the fireplace, looking neither to the right nor left. But just as he had advanced midway, Polton rose suddenly and exclaimed, "Why, it's Mr. Parrott! Bless me, sir, I hardly knew you with that beard."

Pettigrew cast a malignant glance at the speaker and replied, gruffly, "My name is Pettigrew."

"Ah!" said Polton, "I suppose Parrott was the business name."

Pettigrew made no reply, but stalked up the room until he passed between our chairs and the table to reach the door. And then he suddenly clapped on his hat. But not soon enough. For I had already noted – and so certainly had Thorndyke – an irregular, rather recent, scar crossing his right eyebrow. And when I saw that, I realised what Thorndyke had meant by "the final tests".

As Pettigrew grasped the handle of the door, he cast a swift, apprehensive glance at my colleague. Then he opened the door quickly and, when he had passed out, shut it after him. Instantly, Thorndyke rose and followed him and, of course, I followed Thorndyke, and so we came out in a sort of procession into the Square.

As we emerged from the house, I became aware of a man loitering on the pavement at its northern end. He was a stranger to me, but I diagnosed him at once as a plain-clothes police officer. So perhaps had Pettigrew, for he turned in the other direction, towards the Searle Street gate. But that path also was guarded, and by no less a person than Superintendent Miller. When I first saw him, he was standing in the middle of the pavement, apparently studying a document. But as we turned in his direction, Thorndyke took off his hat, whereupon Miller hastily pocketed the paper and awaited the approach of his quarry.

400

It was evident that Pettigrew viewed the superintendent with suspicion for he turned and crossed the road to the railings of the garden, and when the superintendent also crossed the road, with the evident purpose of intercepting him, the position was unmistakable. Pettigrew paused for a moment irresolutely, thrusting his hand into his pocket. Then, as Miller rushed towards him, he drew out a revolver and fired at him nearly point blank. The superintendent staggered back a couple of paces but did not fall, and when Pettigrew, having fired his shot, dodged across to the pavement and broke into a run, he clapped his hand to his thigh and followed as well as he could.

The swift succession of events has left an indelible impression on my memory. Even now I can see vividly with my mind's eye that strange picture of hurry and confusion that disturbed the peace and repose of New Square – the terrified fugitive, racing furiously down the pavement with Thorndyke and me in hot pursuit, the plain-clothes man clattering noisily behind, and the superintendent hobbling after us with a blood-stained hand grasping his thigh.

But it was a short chase. For hardly had Pettigrew – running like a hare and gaining on us all – covered half the distance to the gate when suddenly he halted, flung away his revolver and sank to the ground, rolling over on to his back and then lying motionless. When we reached him and looked down at the prostrate figure, his aspect – wretch as he was – could not but evoke some feelings of pity and compunction. The ghastly face, the staring, terrified eyes, the retracted lips, and the hands, clutching at the breast, presented the typical picture of angina pectoris.

But this, too, was but a passing phase. Before any measures of relief could be thought of, it was over. The staring eyes relaxed, the mouth fell open, and the hands slipped from the breast and dropped limply to the ground.

The superintendent, hobbling up, still grasping his wounded thigh, looked down gloomily at his prisoner.

"Well," he commented, "he made a game try, and he has given us the slip, sure enough. It's a pity, but it's no one's fault. We couldn't have got him any sooner. Hadn't we better move him indoors before a crowd collects?"

It did seem desirable, for the pistol shot and the sounds of hurrying feet had brought startled faces to office windows and now began to bring curious spectators from office doorways.

"Do you mind if we carry him into your anteroom?" Thorndyke asked, turning to Brodribb, who had just come up with Polton.

"No, no," Brodribb replied. "Take the poor creature in, of course. Is he badly hurt?"

401

"He is dead," Thorndyke announced as I hastened with the assistance of the plain-clothes officer to lift the body.

"Dead!" exclaimed Brodribb, turning as pale as his complexion would permit. "Good God! What a shocking thing! Just as he was coming into a fortune too. How perfectly appalling!"

He followed the gruesome procession as the officer and I, now aided by Thorndyke, bore the corpse back along the pavement to the doorway from which we had emerged but a minute or two previously and finally laid it down on the anteroom floor, and he stole softly into the room and shrank away with a horrified glance at the ghastly figure. And his agitation was natural enough. There was something very dreadful in the suddenness of the catastrophe. I was sensible of it myself as I rose from laying down the corpse and my glance lighted on the clock and the litter of tools on the table, lying just as the dead man had seen them when he passed to the door.

"I think," said Thorndyke, "that we had better telephone for an ambulance to take away the body and convey the superintendent to the hospital. Where is he?" he added anxiously.

The question was answered by Miller in person, who limped into the room, his gory hand still grasping his wound and a trickle of blood running across his boot.

"My God, Miller!" exclaimed Brodribb, gazing at him in consternation, "you too! But aren't you going to do something for him, Thorndyke?"

"We had better see what the damage is," said I, "and at least control the bleeding."

"I don't think it is anything that matters," said Miller, "excepting to Mr. Brodribb's carpet. However, you may as well have a look at it."

I made a rapid examination of the wound and was relieved to find that his estimate was correct. The bullet had passed through the outer side of the thigh leaving an almost imperceptible entrance wound but a rather ragged wound of exit which was bleeding somewhat freely.

"You haven't any bandages or dressing material, I suppose?" said I.

"I have not," replied Brodribb, "but I can produce some clean handkerchiefs, if they will do. But bring him into my private office. I can't bear the sight of that poor creature lying on the floor."

We accordingly moved off to the private office where, with Brodribb's handkerchiefs, I contrived a temporary dressing which restrained the bleeding.

"There," said I, "that will serve until the ambulance comes. Someone has telephoned, I suppose?"

"Yes," replied Brodribb, "the police officer sent a message. And now tell me what it is all about. I heard a pistol shot. Who was it that fired?"

"Pettigrew," Thorndyke answered. "The position is this: The superintendent came here on my information to arrest Pettigrew and charge him with the murder of Daniel Penrose, and Pettigrew fired at Miller in the hope of getting away."

Brodribb was horrified. "You astound me, Thorndyke!" he exclaimed. "I have actually been conferring with poor Penrose's murderer. And not only that – I have been aiding and abetting him in getting possession of the plunder. But I don't understand how he comes to be dead. What killed him?"

"It was a heart attack," Thorndyke replied, "Angina, brought about by the excitement and the intense physical effort. But I think I hear the ambulance men in the anteroom. That sounded like a stretcher being put down."

He opened the door and we looked out. At the table Polton was seated, apparently engrossed in his work upon the clock and watched with grim amusement by the plain-clothes officer, while the ambulance men, having lifted the body on to the stretcher, were preparing to carry it away. I was about to help Miller to rise from his chair when Thorndyke interposed.

"Before you go, Miller," said he, "there is one little matter to be attended to. You had better get Pettigrew's address from Mr. Brodribb, and you had better lose no time in sending some capable officer there with a search warrant. You understand what I mean?"

"Perfectly," replied Miller. "But there isn't going to be any sending. I shall make that search myself, if I have to go down in an ambulance."

"Very well, Miller," Thorndyke rejoined. "But remember that you have got only two legs and that you can't afford to part with either of them."

With this warning he assisted the superintendent to rise, and when the latter had received and carefully pocketed the slip of paper on which Brodribb had written Pettigrew's address, we escorted him out to the ambulance and saw him duly dispatched en route for Charing Cross Hospital.

As we turned to re-enter the house, our ears were saluted by the cheerful striking of a clock, and passing into the anteroom, we found Polton, still seated at the table, surveying with an admiring and crinkly smile the venerable timepiece, now completely reconstructed and restored to its case.

"He's all right now, sir," he announced triumphantly. "Just listen to his strike." He moved the minute hand round and, having paused a moment for the "warning", set it at the hour and listened ecstatically as the hammer struck out six silvery notes.

"Clear as the day he was born," he remarked complacently, and forthwith moved the hand round to the next hour.

"You must stop that noise," exclaimed Brodribb. "I can't bear it. Have you no sense of decency, to be making that uproar in the house of death, you – you callous, indifferent little villain?"

Polton regarded him with a surprised and apologetic crinkle (and moved the hand round to the next hour).

"But, sir," he protested, "you can't set a striking clock to time any other way, unless you take the gong off. Shall I do that?"

"No, no," replied Brodribb. "I'll go outside until you've finished. And I apologise for calling you a villain. My nerves are rather upset."

We accompanied him out into the Square and walked up and down the pavement for a few minutes giving him some further explanations of the recent events. Presently Polton made his appearance, carrying his bag, and announced that the clock was now set to time and established in its place on the mantelpiece. Brodribb thanked him profusely and apologised still more profusely for his outburst.

"You must forgive me, Polton," he said. "My nerves are not equal to this sort of thing. You understand, don't you?"

"I understand, sir," replied Polton, "and I suppose I was callous. But he was a bad man, not worth troubling about, and the world is the better without him. I never liked him and I always suspected him of fleecing poor Mr. Penrose."

"Probably you were right," rejoined Brodribb, "but we must talk about that when I am more myself. And now I will get back to my business and try to forget these horrors."

He shook hands with us and retired into his entry while we turned away and set a course for the Temple.

"I suppose, Thorndyke," I said presently, "you were not surprised by our friend's recognition of Parrott. I am judging by the fact that you took the opportunity of having Polton with us."

"No," he replied, "I was not. The assumption that Parrott and Pettigrew were one and the same person seemed to offer the only way out of my dilemma if I rejected – as I certainly did – the idea of confederacy. There were the two men, making separate appearances. Each of them seemed, by the evidence, to be the murderer. But there was only one murderer. The only solution of the problem was the assumption

404

that they were the same man. That was a perfectly reasonable assumption and there was nothing against it."

"Nothing at all," I admitted. "In fact, it is rather obvious – when once it is suggested. But I have found this case rather confusing from the first, it has seemed to me a bewildering mass of disjointed facts."

"That is a mistake, Jervis," said he. "The facts form a perfectly coherent sequence. Some time, we will go over the ground again, and then I think you will see that your confusion was principally due to your having made a false start."

Chapter XXI
Afterthoughts

"It seems to me," Lockhart suggested, "that this case is, to a certain extent, left in the air. The essential facts, in a legal sense, are perfectly clear. But there is a lot that we don't know and, I suppose, never shall know."

The remark – which fairly expressed my own view – was made on the occasion of a little dinner-party at our chambers, arranged partly to celebrate the completion of the case, and partly to enable Lockhart – who had developed unexpected archaeological sympathies – to make the acquaintance of Elmhurst. The dinner was supplied by the staff of a neighbouring tavern, an arrangement which not only relieved Polton of culinary labours but included him in the festivities, for he was enabled thereby to entertain, in his own apartments adjacent to the laboratory, no less a person than Mr. Kickweed.

Both of our guests had been, in a sense, parties to the case, but each had made contact with it at only a single point. It was natural, then, that when the meal had reached its more leisurely and less manducatory stage, the desultory conversation should have subsided into a more definite discussion, with a demand from both for a complete exposition of the investigation. And it was then, when Thorndyke readily complied with the demand, that I was able, for the first time, to realise how clearly he had grasped the essentials of the problem from the very beginning and how steadily and directly he had proceeded, point by point, to unravel the tangle of false appearances.

I need not report his exposition. It contained nothing but what is recorded in the foregoing narrative of the events. It consisted, in fact, of a condensed summary of that narrative with the events presented in their actual sequence with a running accompaniment of argument demonstrating their logical connections. When he had come to the end of the story with an account of its tragic climax, he paused to push round the decanters and then proceeded reflectively to fill his pipe, and it was then that Lockhart made the observation which I have recorded above.

"That is quite true," Thorndyke agreed. "For legal purposes – for the purpose of framing an indictment and securing a conviction – the case was as complete as it could well be. But the death of Pettigrew has left us in the dark on a number of points on which we should probably have been enlightened if he had been brought to trial and had made a

406

statement in his defence. At present, the circumstances surrounding the murder – if it was a murder – and the motive – if there was a clear-cut motive – are more or less wrapped in mystery."

"Are they?" Elmhurst exclaimed in evident surprise. "To me it looks like a simple murder, deliberately planned in cold blood, for the plain purpose of getting possession of a very large sum of money. Fifty-thousand pounds would seem to furnish a very sufficient motive to a man of Pettigrew's type. But you don't take that view?"

"No," replied Thorndyke, "I do not. I am even inclined to doubt whether the money was a factor in the case at all. We must not lose sight of the conditions prevailing at the time. When Penrose left home, that is to say on the day of his death, his father was alive and well and the question of the disposition of his property had not arisen. At that time, the only persons who knew the state of affairs were Penrose, Horridge, and Brodribb, and even they knew it very imperfectly. Brodribb, himself, was not certain whether there was or was not a will. As to Pettigrew, there is no evidence, or any reason for believing, that he had any knowledge, or even suspicion, that Oliver's estate was not duly disposed of by a will."

"Penrose knew, more or less, how matters stood," said Lockhart, "and he may have 'let on' to Pettigrew."

"That is possible," Thorndyke admitted, "though it would be rather unlike the secretive Penrose to babble about his private affairs to a comparative stranger. For it seems pretty certain that he had no idea as to who Parrott was. Mrs. Pettigrew almost certainly knew who he was, but she must have been sworn to secrecy, and she kept the secret loyally. Still, we must admit the possibility of Penrose having made some unguarded statements to Parrott, unlikely as it seems."

"Then," said Lockhart, "if you reject the money as the impelling motive, what is there left? What other motive do you suggest?"

"I am not in a position to make any definite suggestion," replied Thorndyke, "but I have a vague feeling that there may have been a motive of another kind, a motive that would fit in better with the circumstances of the murder – or homicide – in so far as they are known to us."

"I am not sure that I quite follow you," said Lockhart.

"I mean," Thorndyke explained, "that the money theory of motive would imply a deliberate, planned, unconditional murder with carefully prepared means of execution, and the method would involve the necessary detail of taking the victim unaware and forestalling any possibility of resistance. But that is not what happened. The weapon with which Penrose was killed was not brought there by his assailant. It was

407

his own weapon. So that the method of homicide actually used must have been improvised. And Penrose must have been either on the defensive or offensive. There was an encounter. But it was a deadly encounter, as we can judge by the formidable weapon used, not a mere chance 'scrap'. And the deadliness of that encounter implies something more than a sudden disagreement. There is a suggestion of something involving a fierce and bitter enmity. Perhaps it is possible to imagine some cause of deadly strife between these two men. But I knew very little of either of them, and before I offer even a tentative suggestion, I would ask you, Lockhart, who at least knew them better than I did, if anything occurs to you."

"They were both practically strangers to me," said Lockhart. "I knew nothing of their relations except as buyer and seller. But could you put your question a little more definitely?"

"I will put it quite definitely," Thorndyke replied. "Looking back on your relations with these two men, and considering them by the light of what we now know, does it appear to you that there was anything that might have been the occasion of enmity between them or that might have caused one of them to go in fear of the other?"

Lockhart looked at Thorndyke in evident surprise, but he did not reply immediately. He appeared to be turning the question over in his mind and considering its bearing. And then a little frown appeared on his brow as if some new and rather surprising idea had occurred to him.

"I think I see what is in your mind, Thorndyke," he replied, at length, "and I am not sure that you aren't right. The idea had never occurred to me before, but now, looking back as you say, by the light of what we know, I am disposed to think that there may have been some occasion of enmity, and especially of fear. But you don't want my opinions. I had better relate the actual experiences that I am thinking of.

"I have told you about my visit to Penrose when he showed me his collection of jewels, which we now know to have been the stolen Billington collection."

"Do you think," Thorndyke asked, "that Penrose knew they were stolen property?"

"I can hardly think that," Lockhart replied, "or he would surely never have let me see them. But I do think that he had some uneasy suspicions that there may have been something a little fishy about them. I have told you how startled he seemed when I jocosely suggested that the Jacobite Jewel was a rather incriminating possession. My impression is that he may have got the collection comparatively cheap, on the condition that no questions were to be asked."

"Which," I remarked, "usually means that the goods are stolen property."

"Yes," Lockhart admitted, "that is so. But I am afraid that your really acquisitive collector is not always extremely scrupulous. However, there the things were, obviously property of considerable value, and I naturally raised the question of insurance. Penrose was quite alive to the desirability of insuring the jewels, but he was in a difficulty. Before they could be insured, they would have to be valued, and he had an apparently unaccountable objection to their being seen by a valuer. I put this down to his inveterate habit of secrecy. Now, of course, we know that he was doubtful of the safety of letting a stranger – and an expert stranger, too – see what they were. But he agreed in principle and promised to think over the problem of the valuer.

"Now, on the only occasion when I met Parrott in the flesh, it happened that Penrose was present. The meeting occurred in Parrott's workshop when I was waiting for a table that poor Tims had been repairing and Penrose was waiting for Mr. Polton. By way of making conversation, I rather foolishly asked Penrose what he was doing about the valuer. I saw instantly that I had made a *faux pas* in referring to the matter before Parrott, for Penrose – usually a most suave and amiable man – snapped out a very short answer and was obviously extremely annoyed.

"At the moment, Parrott made no comment and seemed not to have noticed what had passed. But as soon as Penrose had gone, he opened the subject of the insurance and the valuer, and as I, having been sworn to secrecy, was necessarily evasive in my answers, he pressed the matter more closely and went on to question me in the most searching and persistent fashion as to what I had seen and whether Penrose had shown me anything more than the contents of the large gallery. It was very awkward, as I could not give him a straight answer, and eventually I had to cut the interrogation short by making a hasty retreat.

"Looking back on this interview, I now see a new significance in it. Parrott was undoubtedly angry. He was quiet and restrained, but I detected an undercurrent of deep resentment, the occasion of which I entirely misunderstood, putting it down to mere pique on his part that Penrose should have contemplated employing a strange valuer when he, Parrott, could have managed the business quite competently. And I also misunderstood the drift of his questions, for I assumed that he knew nothing of the jewels and was merely curious as to whether Penrose had any things of value which had been obtained through some other dealer. Now I see that he suspected Penrose of having shown me the jewels and was trying to find out definitely whether he had or had not. And I think that my evasive answers must have convinced him I had seen the jewels."

"Yes," said Thorndyke, "I think you are right. And what do you infer from that?"

"Well," replied Lockhart, "by the light of what we now know, certain conclusions seem to emerge. The jewels were sold to Penrose by Crabbe, but I think we are agreed that Parrott – I will still call him Parrott as that is the name by which I knew him – was the go-between who actually negotiated the deal. Now, as these jewels were a complete collection, instantly identifiable by anyone who had seen them, and of which the police had a full description, I think it follows that they must have been sold to Penrose with the condition that he should maintain inviolable secrecy as to their being in his possession and that he should neither show them nor disclose their existence to anybody. Do you agree?"

"I do, certainly," Thorndyke replied. "It seems impossible that they could have been sold on any other conditions."

"Moreover," Lockhart continued, "there is nothing improbable in such a condition. Penrose wanted the things, not for display, but for the purpose of gloating over in secret. In consideration of a low price, he would be quite willing to accept the condition of secrecy. Very well, then, we are agreed that Penrose must have been bound by a promise of secrecy to Parrott, on the faithful performance of which Parrott's safety depended. Consequently, when it appeared to Parrott that Penrose had broken his promise by showing me the jewels and that he was actually contemplating their disclosure to a valuer (who would almost certainly recognise them), he would suddenly see himself placed in a position of great and imminent danger. Penrose's indiscretion threatened to send him to penal servitude. In your own phrase, Parrott must thenceforth have gone in fear of Penrose. But when a man of a criminal type like Parrott goes in fear of another, there has arisen a fairly adequate motive for the murder of that other. I think that answers your question."

"It does, very completely," said Thorndyke. "It brings into view exactly the kind of motive for which I have been looking. The money motive, even if Pettigrew had known about the intestacy, would have seemed hardly sufficient. Deliberate, planned murder for the purpose of pecuniary profit is rare. But murder planned and committed for the purpose of removing some person whose existence is a menace to the safety of the murderer is relatively common. The motive of fear is understandable and, in a sense, reasonable. It may even be, in certain circumstances, justifiable. But in any case, it is a strong and urgent motive, impelling to immediate action and making it worthwhile to take

410

risks. You don't remember the date of your interview with Parrott, I suppose?"

"I don't," replied Lockhart, "but it must have been quite a short time before Penrose's disappearance, for, when I came back to London, he had been absent for a month or two. It looks as if the murder had followed pretty closely on that interview."

"And now, Thorndyke," said I, "that you have heard Lockhart's story, what is your final conclusion? Apparently you exclude the money motive altogether."

"I would hardly say that," he replied, "because, after all, we have no certain knowledge. But I see no reason to suppose that Pettigrew knew anything about his position as next of kin until he saw Brodribb's advertisement. On the other hand, from the moment when he became a party to the sale of the jewels, he was at Penrose's mercy, and as soon as he formed the definite suspicion that Penrose was not keeping faith with him, he had a perfectly understandable motive for making away with Penrose."

"Then," said I, "you think it was a deliberate, premeditated murder?"

"I think that is the conclusion that we are driven to," he replied. "At any rate, we must conclude that Pettigrew lured Penrose to that place with the idea of murder in his mind. The intention may have been conditional on what happened there – on whether, for instance, Penrose could or would clear himself of the charge of bad faith. But the remarkable suitability of the time and place, both for the murder, itself, and for the secure disposal of the body, seems to imply a careful selection and a considered intention."

"What makes you suggest that the intention may have been conditional?" Lockhart asked.

"There are two facts," Thorndyke replied, "which seem to offer that suggestion. The piece of pottery that we found in Pettigrew's pocket shows clearly that an excavation was actually carried out by the two men. There would certainly have been no collecting of pottery after the murder. Then the fact that Penrose was killed with his own weapon suggests a quarrel, and a pretty violent one, for Penrose must, himself, have produced his weapon. But when Pettigrew had got possession of that weapon, his behaviour was unmistakable. He struck to kill. It was no mere tap on the head. It was a murderous blow into which the assailant put his whole strength.

"So, taking all the facts into account, I think our verdict must be wilful murder, not only in the legal sense – which it obviously was – but in the sense in which ordinary men use the words. But it is an impressive

411

and disturbing thought that only by a hair's-breadth did he miss escaping completely. He had abandoned and hidden the car and was sneaking off in the darkness to disappear forever, unknown and unsuspected. But for the incalculable chance of his being knocked down by that unknown car or lorry, he would have got away without leaving a trace, and we should still be looking for the missing Penrose."

There was a short interval of silence when Thorndyke had concluded. Then Elmhurst remarked, "It is rather a gruesome thought, that of the two men digging away amicably into the barrow when one of them must have known that the other was almost certainly digging his own grave."

"It is," I agreed. "But Thorndyke's interpretation of the facts suggests some other strange and gruesome pictures – that, for instance, of the murderer reading Brodribb's advertisement and realising that his murderous blow had been worth fifty-thousand pounds, and his visit to New Square to collect his earnings."

"Yes, indeed," moralised Elmhurst, "and he collected them truly enough. It is a satisfaction to think of that moment of disillusionment when he saw his ill-gotten fortune turn to dust and ashes and realised that, for him as for others, the wages of sin was death."

The End

U.S. Title: *Death at the Inn*
1937 Hodder & Stoughton, London Cover

Part I: The Gambler
Narrated by Robert Mortimer

Chapter I
The Man in the Porch

There is something almost uncanny in the transformation which falls upon the City of London when all the offices are closed and their denizens have departed to their suburban homes. Throughout the working hours of the working days, the streets resound with the roar of traffic and the pavements are packed with a seething, hurrying multitude. But when the evening closes in, a strange quiet descends upon the streets, and the silent, deserted by-ways take on the semblance of thoroughfares in some city of the dead.

The mention of by-ways reminds me of another characteristic of this part of London. Modern, commonplace, and dull as is the aspect of the main streets, in the areas behind and between them are hidden innumerable quaint and curious survivals from the past – antique taverns lurking in queer, crooked alleys, and little scraps of ancient churchyards, green with the grass that sprang up afresh amidst the ashes of the Great Fire.

With one of these curious "hinterlands" – an area bounded by Cornhill, Gracechurch Street, Lombard Street, and Birchin Lane, and intersected by a maze of courts and alleys – I became intimately acquainted, since I usually crossed it at least twice a day going to and from the branch of Perkins's Bank at which I was employed as a cashier. For the sake of change and interest, I varied my route from day to day – all the alleys communicated and one served as well as another – but the one that I favoured most was the very unfrequented passage which took me through the tiny churchyard of St. Michael's. I think the place appealed to me specially because somewhere under the turf reposes old Thomas Stow, grandfather of the famous John, laid here in the year 1527 according to his wish *"to be buried in the litell Grene Churchyard of the Parysshe Church of Seynt Myghel in Cornehyll, betwene the Crosse and the Church Wall, nigh the wall as may be"*. Many a time, as I passed along the paved walk, had I tried to locate his grave, but the Great Fire must have made an end of both Cross and wall.

I have referred thus particularly to this "haunt of ancient peace" because it was there, on an autumn even in the year 1929, that there befell the adventure that has set me to the writing of this narrative, an adventure which, for me, changed the scene in a moment from a haunt of peace to a place of gruesome and tragic memories.

It was close upon eight o'clock when I emerged from the bank and started rather wearily on my way homeward. It had been a long day, for there had been various arrears to dispose of which had kept us hard at work hours after the bank had closed its doors, and it had been a dull, depressing day, for the sky had been so densely overcast that no single gleam of sunlight had been able to break through, and we had perforce kept the lamps alight all day. Even now, as I came out and shut the door behind me, twilight seemed to have descended on the City, though the sun had barely set and it was not yet time for the streetlamps to be lit.

I stood for a moment looking up the gloomy, twilit street, hesitating as to which way to go. Our branch was in Gracechurch Street close to the corner of Lombard Street, and both thoroughfares were equally convenient. Eventually, I chose Gracechurch Street and, crossing to the west side, walked up it until I came to the little opening of Bell Yard. Turning into the dark entry, I trudged up the narrow passage, cogitating rather vaguely and wishing that I had provided something better than the scanty cold supper that I knew awaited me at my lodgings. But I was tired and chilly and empty, I had not had enough food during the day, owing to the pressure of work, so that the needs of the body tended to assert themselves to the exclusion of more elevated thoughts.

At the top of the yard I turned into the little tunnel-like covered passage that led through into Castle Court and brought me out by the railings of the churchyard. Skirting them, I went on to the entrance to the paved walk and passed in up a couple of steps and through the open gateway, noting that even "*the litell Grene Churchyard*" looked dull and drab under the lowering sky and that lights were twinkling in the office windows beyond the grass plot and in those of the tavern at the side.

At the end of the paved walk is a long flower-bed against the wall of St. Michael's Church and, just short of this, the arched entrance to another tunnel-like covered passage into which, near its middle, the deep south porch of the church opens. I was about to step down into the passage – which is below the level of the churchyard – when I noticed a hat lying on the flower-bed close up in the corner. It lay crown downwards with its silk lining exposed and, as it appeared to be in perfectly good condition, I picked it up to examine it. It was quite a good hat, a grey soft felt, nearly new, and the initials *A. W.* legibly written on the white lining, suggested that the owner had set some value on it. But where was the owner? And how on earth came this hat to be lying abandoned by the wayside? A man may drop a glove or a handkerchief or a tobacco pouch and be unaware of his loss, but surely the most absent-minded of men could hardly lose his hat without noticing the fact. And then the further question arose: What does one do with a derelict hat? Of course, I could have dropped it where I had found it, but from this my natural thriftiness and responsibility revolted. It was too good a hat to have been casually flung away by its owner and, since Fate had appointed me its custodian, the duty seemed to devolve on me to restore it.

I stood for a few moments holding the hat and looking through the dark passage at the shape of light at the farther end, but no one was in sight, and I now recalled that I had not met a soul since I entered Bell Yard from Gracechurch Street. Still wondering how I should set about discovering the owner of the hat, I stepped down into the passage and began to walk along it, but when I reached the middle and came opposite the church porch, my problem seemed to solve itself in a rather startling fashion for, glancing into the porch, I saw, dimly but quite distinctly in its shadowy depths, a man sitting on the lowest of the three steps that lead up to the church door. He was leaning back against the jamb limply and helplessly as if he were asleep or, more probably, drunk, the latter probability being rather confirmed by a stout walking-stick with a large ivory knob which had fallen beside him, and what looked like a rimless eyeglass which lay on the stone floor between his feet. But what was more to my present purpose was the fact that not only was he bare-headed, but that no hat was visible. This, then, was doubtless the owner of the derelict.

Holding the latter conspicuously, I stepped into the cavern-like porch and, addressing the man in a rather loud tone, enquired whether he had lost a hat. As he made no reply or any sign of having heard me, I was disposed to lay the hat down by his side and retire, when it occurred to me that he might possibly have had some kind of fit or seizure. On this I approached closer and, stooping over him, listened for the sound of his breathing. But I could hear nothing, nor could I make out any movement of his chest.

As he was sitting, or sprawling, with his legs spread out, his shoulders supported by the jamb of the door and his head drooping forward on his chest, his face was almost hidden from me. But I now knelt down beside him and, taking my petrol lighter from my pocket, held it close to his face. And then, as the gleam of the flame fell on him, I sprang up with a gasp of horror. The man's eyes were wide open, staring

419

before him with an intensity that was in hideous contrast to his limp and passive posture. And the face was unmistakably the face of a dead man.

Dropping the hat by his side, I ran through the passage into St. Michael's Alley and down this to Cornhill. At the entrance to the alley I stood for a moment looking up and down the street. In the distance, near the Royal Exchange, I could see a white-sleeved policeman directing the traffic, and I was about to start off towards him when, glancing eastward, I saw a constable approaching along the pavement. At once I hurried away in his direction and we met nearly opposite St. Peter's Church. A few words conveyed my information and secured his very complete attention. "A dead man, you say. Whereabouts did you see him?"

"He is lying in the south porch of St. Michael's Church, just up the alley."

"Well," said he, "you had better come along and show me." And without further parley he started forward with long, swinging strides that gave me some trouble to keep up with him. Back along Cornhill we went and up the alley until we came to the arched entrance to the passage, and here the constable produced his lantern and switched on the light. As we came opposite the porch and my companion threw a beam of light into it, the cave-like interior was rendered clearly visible with the dead man sitting, or reclining, just as I had left him.

"Yes," said the constable, "there don't seem to be much doubt about his being dead." Nevertheless, he put his ear close to the man's face, raising the head gently, and felt for the pulse at the wrist. Then he stood up and looked at me.

"I'd better get on the phone," said he, "and report to the station. They'll have to send an ambulance to take him to the mortuary. Will you stay here until I come back? I shan't be more than a minute or two."

Without waiting for an answer, he strode out of the passage and disappeared down the alley, leaving me to pace up and down in the gathering gloom or to stand and gaze out on the darkening churchyard. It was a dismal business, and very disturbing to the nerves I found it, for I am rather sensitive to horrors of any kind and, being now tired and physically exhausted, I was more than ordinarily susceptible. I had suffered a severe shock, and its effect was still with me as I kept my vigil, now glancing with horrid fascination at the shadowy figure in the dark porch, and now stealing away to the entrance to be out of sight of it. Once a man came in from the offices across the churchyard, but he hurried through into the alley, brushing past me and all unaware of that dim and ghostly presence.

After the lapse of two or three incredibly long minutes the constable reappeared and, almost at the moment of his arrival, the lights were switched on and a lamp in the vault of the passage exactly opposite the porch threw a bright light on the dead man.

"Ah!" the officer commented cheerfully, "that's better. Now we can see what we are about." He stepped up to the body and, stooping over it, cast the light from his lantern on the step behind it.

"There's something there on the stone step," he remarked, "some broken glass and some metal things. I can't quite see what they are, but we'd better not meddle with them until the people from the station arrive. But while we are waiting for the ambulance I'll just jot down a few particulars." He produced a large note-book and, taking an attentive look at me, added, "We'll begin with your name, address, and occupation."

I gave him these, and he then enquired how I came to discover the body. I had not much to tell but, such as my story was, he wrote it down verbatim in his notebook and made me show him the exact spot where I had found the hat, of which spot he entered a description in his book. When he had completed his notes, he read out to me what he had written, and on my confirming its correctness, he handed me his pencil and asked me to add my signature.

He had just returned the note-book to his pocket when an inspector appeared at the alley entrance of the passage, closely followed by two constables carrying a stretcher and one or two idlers who had probably been attracted by the ambulance. The inspector walked briskly up to the porch and, having cast a quick glance at the dead man, turned to the constable.

"I suppose," said he, "you have got all the particulars. Which is the man who discovered the body?"

"This is the gentlemen, sir," the constable replied, introducing me, "Mr. Robert Mortimer, and this is his statement."

He produced his note-book and presented it, open, to his superior, who stood under the lamp and ran his eye over the statement.

"Yes," he when he had finished reading and returned the book to its owner, "that's all right. Not much in it except the hat. Just show me where you found it."

I conducted him up into the churchyard and pointed out the corner of the flower-bed where the hat had been lying. He looked at it attentively and then glanced down the passage, remarking that the dead man had apparently come down from Castle Court. "By the way," he added, "I suppose you don't recognise him?"

"No," I replied, "he is a total stranger to me."

"Ah, well," said he, "I expect we shall be able to find out who he is in time for the inquest."

421

His reference to the inquest prompted mc to ask if I should be wanted to give evidence.

"Certainly," he replied. "You haven't much to tell, but the little that you have may be important."

We were now back at the porch, on the floor of which the stretcher had been placed. At a word from the inspector the two bearers lifted the corpse on to it and, having laid the hat on the body and covered it with a waterproof sheet, grasped the handles of the stretcher, stood up, and marched away with their burden, followed by the spectators.

The raising of the body had brought into view the objects which the constable had observed and which now appeared to be the fragments of a broken hypodermic syringe. These the inspector collected with scrupulous care, spreading his handkerchief on the upper step to receive them and picking up even the minute splinters of glass that had scattered when the syringe was dropped. When he had gathered up every particle that was visible, and taken up some drops of moisture with a piece of blotting-paper, he made his collection into a neat parcel and put it in his pocket. Then he cast a rapid but searching glance over the floor and walls of the porch and, apparently observing nothing worth noting, began to walk towards the alley.

"I wonder," he said as we turned into it and came in sight of the waiting ambulance, "how long that poor fellow had been lying there when you first saw him. Not very long, I should say. Couldn't have been. Somebody must have noticed him. However, I expect the doctor will be able to tell us how long he has been dead. And you had better note down all that you can remember of the circumstances so that you can be clear about it at the inquest."

Here we came out into Cornhill, where the ambulance had been drawn up opposite the church, and the inspector, having wished me "Good night", pushed his way through the considerable crowd that had collected and took his place in the ambulance beside the driver. Just as the vehicle was moving away and I was about to do the same, a voice from behind me enquired, "What's the excitement? Motor accident?"

I seemed to recognise the voice, which had a slight Scottish intonation, and when I turned to answer I recognised the speaker. He was a Mr. Gillum, one of the bank's customers with whom I had often done business.

"No," I replied, "I don't know what it was, but the dead man looked perfectly horrible. I can't get his face out of my mind."

"Oh, but that won't do," said Gillum. "It has given you a bad shake up, but you've got to try to forget it."

422

"I know," said I, "but just now I'm rather upset. This affair caught me at the wrong time, after a long, tiring day."

"Yes," he agreed, "you do look a bit pale and shaky. Better come along with me and have a drink. That will steady your nerves."

"I am rather afraid of drinks at the moment," said I. "You see, I have had a long day and not very much in the way of food."

"Ah!" said he, "there you are. Horrors on an empty stomach. That's all wrong, you know. Now I'm going to prescribe for you. You will just come and have a bit of dinner and a bottle of wine with me. That will set you up and will give me the great pleasure of your society."

Now I must admit that a bit of dinner and a bottle of wine sounded gratefully in my ears, but I was reluct ant to accept hospitality which my means did not admit conveniently of my returning. A somewhat extravagant taste in books absorbed the surplus of my modest income and left me rather short of pocket-money. However, Gillum would take no denial. Probably he grasped the position completely. At any rate, he brushed aside my half-hearted refusal without ceremony and, even while I was protesting, he hailed a prowling taxi, opened the door, and bundled me in. I heard him give the address of a restaurant in Old Compton Street. Then he got in beside me and slammed the door.

"Now," said he, as the taxi trundled off, "for 'the gay and festive scenes and halls of dazzling light', and oblivion to the demmed unpleasant body."

Chapter II
John Gillum

As the taxi pursued its unimpeded way westward through the half-populated streets, I reflected on the curious circumstances that had made me the guest of a man who was virtually a stranger to me, and I was disposed to consider what I knew of him. I use the word "disposed" advisedly for, in fact, my mind was principally occupied by my late experiences, and the considerations which I here set down for the reader's information are those that might have occurred to me rather than those that actually did.

I had now been acquainted with John Gillum for some six months – ever since, in fact, I had been transferred to the Gracechurch Street branch of the bank. But our acquaintance was of the slightest. He was one of the bank's customers and I was a cashier. His visits to the bank were rather more frequent than those of most of our customers, and on slack days he would linger to exchange a few words or even to chat for a while. Nevertheless, our relations hardly tended to grow in intimacy, for though he was a bright, gay, and rather humorous man, quite amusing to talk to, his conversation persistently concerned itself with racing matters and the odds on, or against, particular horses, a subject in which I was profoundly uninterested. In truth, despite our rather frequent meetings, his personality made so little impression on me that, if I had been asked to describe him, I could have said no more than that he was a tallish, rather good-looking man with black hair and beard which contrasted rather noticeably with his blue eyes, that he spoke with a slight Scotch accent and that two of his upper front teeth had been rather extensively filled with gold. This latter characteristic did, indeed, attract my notice rather unduly, for, though gold is a beautiful material (and one that a banker might be expected to regard with respectful appreciation), these golden teeth rather jarred on me and I found it difficult to avoid looking at them as we talked.

Yet even in those days I felt a certain interest in our customer, but it was a purely professional interest. As cashier, I naturally knew all about his account and his ways of dealing with his money, and on both, and especially his financial habits, I occasionally speculated with mild curiosity, for his habits were not quite normal, or at least were not like those of most other private customers. The latter usually make most of their payments by cheque, but Gillum seemed to make most of his in cash. It is true that he appeared to pay most of his tradespeople by cheque, but from time to time, and at pretty frequent intervals, he would present a "self" cheque for a really considerable sum – one-, or even two- or three-hundred pounds, and occasionally a bigger sum still – and take the whole of it away in pound notes.

It was rather remarkable, in fact very much so when I came to look over the ledger and note the fluctuations of his account. For at fairly regular intervals he paid in really large cheques – up to a thousand pounds – mostly drawn upon an Australian bank, which for a time swelled his account to very substantial proportions. But, by degrees, and not very small degrees, his balance dwindled until he seemed on the verge of an overdraft, and then another big cheque would be paid in and give him a fresh start.

Now there is nothing remarkable in the fluctuation of an account when the customer receives payment periodically in large sums and pays out steadily in the small amounts which represent the ordinary expenses of living. But when I came to cast up Gillum's account, it was evident that the great bulk of his expenditure was in the form of cash. And it seemed additional to the ordinary domestic payments, as I have said, and I found myself wondering what on earth he could be doing with his money. He could not be making investments, or even "operating" on the Stock Exchange, for those transactions would have been settled by cheque. Apparently he was making some sort of payments which had to be made in cash.

Of course it was no business of mine. Still, it was a curious and interesting problem. What sort of payments were these that he was making? Now when a man pays away at pretty regular intervals considerable sums in cash, the inference is that he is having some sort of dealings with someone who either will not accept a cheque or is not a safe person to be trusted with one. But a person who will not accept payment by an undoubtedly sound cheque is a person who is anxious to avoid evidence that a payment has been made. Such anxiety suggests a secret and probably unlawful transaction, and in practice, such a transaction is usually connected with the offence known as "demanding money with menaces". So, as I cast up the very large amounts that Gillum had drawn out in cash, I asked myself, "Is he a gambler, or has he fallen into the clutches of a blackmailer?" The probability of the latter explanation was suggested by certain large withdrawals at approximately quarterly periods, and also by the fact that Gillum not only took payment almost exclusively in pound notes, but also showed a marked preference for notes that had been in circulation as compared with new notes, of the serial numbers of which the bank would have a record. Still, the two possibilities were not mutually exclusive. A gambler is by no means an unlikely person to be the subject of blackmail.

Such, then, were the reflections that might have occupied my mind had it not been fully engaged with my recent adventure. As it was, the short journey was beguiled by brief spells of scrappy and disjointed conversation which lasted until the taxi drew up opposite the brilliantly lighted entrance of the restaurant and a majestic person in the uniform of a Liberian admiral hurried forward to open the door. We both stepped out, and when Gillum had paid the taxi-driver – extravagantly, as I gathered from the man's demeanour – we followed the admiral into a wide hail where we were transferred to the custody of other and less-gorgeous myrmidons.

Giamborini's Restaurant was an establishment of a kind that was beyond my experience, as it was certainly beyond my means. It oozed luxury and splendour at every pore. The basin of precious marble in which I purged myself of the by-products of the London atmosphere was of a magnificence that almost called for an apology for washing in it, the floor of delicate Florentine mosaic seemed too precious to stand upon in common boots, while as to the dining-saloon, I can recall it only as a bewildering vision of marble and gilding, of vast mirrors, fretted ceilings, and stately columns – apparently composed of gold and polished gorgonzola – and multitudinous chandeliers of a brilliancy that justified Dick Swiveller's description, lately quoted by Gillum. I found it a little oppressive and was disposed to compare it (not entirely to its advantage) with the homely Soho restaurants that I remembered in the far-off pre-war days.

A good many of the tables were unoccupied, though the company was larger than I should have expected, for the hour was rather late for dinner but not late enough for theatre suppers. Of the guests present, the men were mostly in evening dress, and so, I suppose, were the women, judging by the considerable areas of their persons that were uncovered by clothing. As to their social status I could form no definite opinion, but the general impression conveyed by their appearance was that they hardly represented the cream of the British aristocracy. But perhaps I was prejudiced by the prevailing magnificence.

"What are you going to have, Mortimer?" my host asked as we took our seats at the table to which we had been conducted. "Gin and It cocktail, or sherry? You prefer sherry. Good. So do I. It is wine that maketh glad the heart of man, not these chemical concoctions."

He selected from the wine list the particular brand of sherry that commended itself to him and then gave a few general directions which were duly noted. As the waiter was turning away, he added, "I suppose you haven't got such a thing as an evening paper about you?"

The waiter had not. But there was no difficulty. He would get one immediately. Was there any particular paper that would be preferred?

"No," replied Gillum, "any evening paper will do." Thereupon the waiter bustled away with the peculiar quick, mincing gait characteristic of his craft – a gait specially and admirably adapted to the rapid conveyance of loaded trays. In a minute or two he came skating back with a newspaper under his arm and a tray of hors-d'oeuvres and two brimming glasses of sherry miraculously balanced on his free hand. Gillum at once opened the paper, while I fixed a ravenous eye on the various and lurid contents of the tray. As I had expected, he turned immediately to the racing news, but he did not read the column. After a single brief glance, he folded up the paper and laid it aside with the remark, uttered quite impassively, "No luck."

"I hope you haven't dropped any money," said I, searching for the least inedible contents of the tray.

"Nothing to write home about," he replied. "Fifty."

"Fifty!" I repeated. "You don't mean fifty pounds?"

"Yes," he replied calmly. "Why not? You can't expect to bring it off every time."

"But fifty pounds!" I exclaimed, appalled by this horrid waste of money. "Why, it would furnish a small library!"

He laughed indulgently. "That's the bookworm's view of the case, but it isn't mine. I've had my little flutter and I'm not complaining, and let me tell you, Mortimer, that I have just barely missed winning a thousand pounds."

I was on the point of remarking that a miss is as good as a mile but, as that truth has been propounded on some previous occasions, I refrained and asked, "When you say that you have just barely missed winning a thousand pounds, what exactly do you mean? How do you know that you nearly won that amount?"

"It is perfectly simple, my dear fellow," said he. "I laid fifty pounds on the double event at twenty-to-one against. That is to say, I backed two particular horses to win two particular races. Now, one of my horses won his race all right. The other ought to have done the same. But he didn't. He came in second. So I lost. But you see how near a thing it was."

"Then," said I, "if you had backed the two horses separately, I suppose you would have won on the whole transaction?"

"I suppose I should," he admitted, "but there would have been nothing in it. The horse that won was the favourite. But the double event was a real sporting chance. Twenty-to-one against. And you see how near I was to bringing it off."

"Nevertheless," I objected, "you lost. And you went into the business with the knowledge, not only that you might lose, but that the chances that you would lose were estimated at twenty-to-one. I should have supposed that no sane man would have taken such a chance as that."

He looked at me with a broad smile that displayed his golden teeth to great disadvantage.

"Thus saith the banker," he commented. "But you are taking a perverted view of the transaction. You are considering it as an investor might, as a means of realising the greatest profit with the smallest risk. That is the purely commercial standpoint. But I am not engaged in commerce, I am engaged in sport – in gambling, if you prefer the expression. Now the essence of the sport of gambling is the possibility that you may lose. If you were certain to win every time, it might be highly profitable but it would be uncommonly poor fun. Believe me, Mortimer, the heart and soul of the game is the chance of losing."

He spoke quite gravely and earnestly and the statement put me, for the moment, rather at a loss for a reply. For, in its mad way, it was true, and yet, from a practical point of view, it was nonsense. Meanwhile, the waiter brought and placed before us a strangely sophisticated dish, based, I believe, on fish, and then proceeded to fill our glasses with champagne. It was, I think, quite good champagne, though I am no authority, my extreme dissipation, in the ordinary way, not going beyond the traditional "chop and a pint of claret". At any rate, it was highly stimulating, and when Gillum had raised his glass and, with a toast "to the next double event", emptied it and insisted on my doing likewise, the last traces of my depression vanished.

"I admit, Gillum," said I, resuming the discussion, "that there is a certain amount of truth in what you say. But we must try to keep some sense of proportion. Fifty pounds is a devil of a price for the fun of a little flutter. Surely you could have got your sport at a cheaper rate than that."

"But that is just what you can't do," said he. "What you don't seem to realise is that the intensity of the thrill is strictly proportionate to the amount of the possible loss and, of course, of the possible gain. I could have laid five shillings on the double event and been secure from appreciable loss. But then I should have stood to gain a mere flyer. No, my young friend, you can't get a respectable thrill for five bob. And there is another thing that you are over-looking. You speak as if I lost

428

every time. But I don't. Sometimes I win. If I never won, it would be a dull game and I expect I shouldn't go on."

"I think you would," said I. "You would always be hoping that at last you would get your money back."

"Perhaps you are right," he conceded. "It is certainly the fact that a genuine gambler is not put off by a succession of losses. The oftener he loses the more dogged he becomes."

"So I have always understood," said I. "But to come to your own case, you say that sometimes you win. How often do you win? Taking your betting transactions as a whole, how does the balance stand? Are you in pocket or out?"

"Out, of course," he replied promptly. "Everybody is, excepting the bookies. And they don't do it for sport, but just as a cold-blooded matter of business. They don't lose, in ordinary circumstances, and they don't win to a considerable extent. They just balance their books and make a comfortable living. But, of course, the fact that the bookies are in pocket by the transaction is clear proof that the backers, as a whole, must be out."

There seemed to me something very odd and rather abnormal in the reasonable and lucid way in which he discussed this absurdity. I had the sort of feeling that one might have had in discussing insane delusions with a lunatic. But I returned to the charge, futile as I knew the discussion to be.

"Very well," said I, "you agree that the balance of profit and loss is against you. How much, you know better than I do, but I suspect that your losses, from month to month, are pretty heavy." (Of course, I did not "suspect". I knew. The bank's books told the story.) "You must be paying very considerable sums for your little flutters and I put it to you, isn't it a most monstrous waste of money?"

He laughed cheerfully and refilled our glasses.

"I see," he replied, "that you are an incorrigible financier. You are taking a completely perverted view of the matter. You speak of waste of money. But what, after all, is money?"

"If you are asking me that as a banker," I replied, "I can only say that I don't know. I know what money was before the war, but now that the politicians and financial theorists have taken it over, it has become something quite different and I don't profess to understand it."

"That isn't quite what I meant," said he. "I was referring to money in general terms. What is it? It is simply a means of obtaining certain satisfactions or pleasures. No one wants money for itself, excepting a miser."

429

"You can rule out misers," said I. "They are an extinct race. A miser doesn't hoard paper vouchers which have only a conventional and temporary value."

"No, I suppose not," he agreed. "At any rate, I am not a miser – " (Which was most unquestionably true.) " – and I have no use for money excepting as a means of obtaining satisfactions. And that is the rational use of money. I put it to you, Mortimer, if a man has money and there are certain things that he desires and that money will buy, is it not obviously reasonable that he should exchange the thing that he doesn't want for the things that he does? You speak of waste of money. But is it wasted when it is being used for the very purpose for which it exists? Take, for instance, this bottle of champagne – which, by the way, is getting low and needs replacing. Now, I think we like champagne."

"I do, certainly," I admitted.

"I am glad you do. So do I. And we can get it in exchange for your despised paper vouchers. Accordingly, like sensible men, we make the exchange, and I submit that it is a reasonable and profitable transaction. For if, as you suggest, the money is a mere fleeting convention, the champagne for which we have exchanged it isn't. It is real champagne."

Seeing that we had already emptied one bottle, the cogency of this argument did not impress me. Probably I should have proceeded to rebut it, but at this point an interruption occurred and the discussion broke off.

When we had entered the room, I had noticed a party of three persons, two men and a woman, at a table in a corner. They had caught my attention because we had evidently caught theirs. But I don't think that Gillum observed them, and when we had seated ourselves, as his back was towards them, they were outside his range of vision, whereas I was nearly facing them, and throughout our meal I found myself from time to time looking in their direction, attracted as before by the occasional glances that they cast in ours. It seemed to me that they must be acquainted with Gillum, for there was otherwise nothing noticeable in our appearance. At any rate, they were obviously interested in us and I received the impression that we were being discussed.

They did not prepossess me favourably. I cannot say exactly why, but there was an indefinable something about them that jarred on me. The men did not look like gentlemen, and the woman, dressed in the extreme of an unbecoming fashion, was so heavily and coarsely made up as to extinguish any good looks that she might have had. Everything about her seemed to be artificial. Her hair was of an unnatural colour, her cheeks were visibly painted, and her lips were plastered with crude vermilion like the lips of a circus clown.

430

That these people were acquaintances of Gillum's became evident when they rose to depart, for they steered a course across the room which brought them opposite our table. And here they halted and, for the first time, Gillum became aware of their presence. His expression did not convey to me that he was overjoyed, but as the lady bestowed on him the kind of leer that is known as "giving the glad eye", he made shift to produce a responsive smile.

"Now, don't let us interrupt your dinner," said she, as he rose to shake hands. "But, as you cut us dead when you came in, we have just come across to say 'howdy' and let you know that we saw you. We are now off to the club. Shall you be coming along presently?"

Gillum was inclined to be evasive.

"I don't quite know what the programme is," he replied. "It depends on what my guest would like to do."

"Bring him along with you," said she, "and let him see the ball roll. I'm sure he'd enjoy it, wouldn't you?"

As she asked the question, she turned to me with the peculiar cat-like grin that one sees in newspaper portraits of young women, with a distinct tendency to the "glad eye", and I noticed that it seemed a rather tired eye and slightly puffy about the lower lids.

"I am not really an enthusiast in regard to billiards," I replied, "and I am no player. But it is interesting enough to look on at a good game."

Apparently I had said something funny, for the lady greeted my answer with a gay – and rather strident – laugh, and the two men, who had been looking on in silence, broke into sour grins. But Gillum, also smiling, evidently wished to get rid of his acquaintances for he interposed with the air of closing the conversation.

"Well, we shall see what we feel like when we have dined. I won't make any engagement now."

The lady took the hint graciously enough. "Very well, Jack," said she. "We will leave you in peace and hope to see you later." And with this and another smile which embraced us both, she moved off with her two companions, neither of whom seemed to take any notice of Gillum.

"What was the joke?" I asked when they had gone. "And what club was she referring to?"

"It isn't really a club," replied Gillum. "It is what, I suppose, you would call a gambling hell – a place where you can stake your money at *Trente et Quarante*, *Rouge et Noir*, *Chemin de Fer*, or any of the regular gambling games. The joke was that the ball she meant was not a billiard ball but the little ball that rolls round the roulette wheel. It is not a particularly amusing joke."

"No," I agreed. "And are these people connected with the club?"

"Very much so," he replied. "That tall chappie – the one with the squint – runs the place, and I should think he does fairly well out of it. He is a Frenchman of the name of Foucault."

"He doesn't look a particularly amiable person," I remarked, recalling the rather sulky way in which he had looked on at the interview.

Gillum laughed. "He is a silly ass," said he, "as jealous as the devil, and as Madame's manners are, as you saw, of the distinctly coquettish, slap-and-tickle order, there is pretty constant trouble. But he needn't worry. There is no harm in the fair Marie. Her engaging wiles are all in the way of business."

"Do you spend much time at the club?" I asked.

"I drop in there pretty frequently," he replied.

"And I suppose you drop a fair amount of money."

"I suppose I do. But not so much as you would think. You orthodox financiers seem to imagine that a gambler always loses, but that is quite a mistake. The luck isn't always on the one side. Sometimes I pick up a little windfall that pays my expenses for quite a long time."

"Still," said I, "the balance must be against you in the long run."

"I have already admitted," he replied, "that I lose on my gambling transactions as a whole, and probably I lose, in the long run, at the club, though it isn't so easy to keep accounts of what I do there. But supposing that the balance is against me. What about it? Foucault runs the club to make a profit. But he can only make a profit if the players make a loss. What they lose to the bank is, in effect, their payment to him for the entertainment that he supplies. Hang it all, Mortimer, you can't expect to get your fun for nothing."

"Some people do," said I. "The people, I mean, who have infallible systems. I gather that you don't use a system."

"Well," he replied cautiously, "I haven't managed yet to devise a system that really works, but I have given some thought to the matter. There ought to be some way of ascertaining how the Laws of Chance operate, and if one could discover that, one would have the means of circumventing them."

"You haven't tried the plan of doubling the stakes when you lose?"

"Yes, I have, and I must admit that, for sheer excitement there is nothing like it. Your real, rabid gambler loves it – and usually cleans himself out. But for a sane and sober gambler it is not practicable. There are too many snags. To begin with, at the best you only get your money back plus the amount of the lowest stake. Consequently, the first stake must be a fairly large one or there is nothing in it. But if you start with a substantial stake and the luck is against you, you are up in enormous figures before you know where you are. For instance, supposing you are

432

playing roulette and you lay a hundred pounds on *manque* or *impair* or any of the even chances. If you lose four times in succession, which would not be extraordinary, you have dropped fifteen-hundred pounds, and the danger is that you may empty your pocket before the winning coup comes round. Then you have lost the lot. But there is another snag. The bank won't let you go on doubling as long as you like. There is a limit set to each kind of bet, and when you reach that limit you are not allowed to double any more. If you go on playing you have got to go back to a flat stake, in which case it is impossible for you to win back what you have lost. So, regarded as a serious method of play, the doubling racket is no go."

"It seems astonishing," said I, "that anyone should practise it. But perhaps they don't."

"Oh, don't they?" said Gillum. "You must understand, Mortimer, that to the real, perfect gambler, the charm of the game is the risk of losing. The bigger the risk, the greater the thrill. Plenty of people at the club, particularly the roulette players, double the stakes when they lose, and there is a temptation, you know, when you have lost, to take another chance in the hope of getting your money back. But it is a bad plan, because you stand to lose so much more than you stand to gain."

"Don't some people double on their winnings?" I asked.

"Ah," said he, "but that is quite a different kind of affair. There is some sense in that because it is quite the opposite of the other method. If you win you win, you don't merely get your money back, and if you eventually lose, you have only lost your original stake – plus your winnings, of course. Supposing you take an even chance at roulette – say you put a hundred pounds on red and you win – and suppose that you leave the stake and the winnings – two-hundred pounds – on the table as a fresh stake. If the red turns up again you take up four-hundred, of which one-hundred is your original stake. You have won three-hundred. But if you lose, you have only lost a hundred, plus the three that you had won. From a gambler's point of view, it is quite a sound method."

"Yes," I agreed, "I see that, at least. You start with the knowledge of the amount that you stand to lose. But the whole thing is beyond my comprehension. I can't begin to understand the state of mind of a man who is prepared to risk his money in a transaction over which he has no control and in respect to which no judgement, calculation, or prevision is possible."

He laughed gaily and refilled our glasses. "You are a banker to the finger-tips, Mortimer," said he, "and, as you happen to be my banker, I am not disposed to quarrel with your eminently correct outlook. I suppose you have never seen a gambling den."

433

"Never," I replied, "and I am an absolute ignorant on the subject of gambling. I hardly know how to play the common card games."

"I think you ought to know what these shows are like," said he. "I can assure you that, as a mere spectacle, a regular gaming house is worth seeing. What do you say to strolling round to the club with me when we have had our coffee? It's too late to do anything else."

It was really too late to do anything but go home and to bed. But I could hardly, in the circumstances, suggest that course. Nor, in fact, was I particularly disposed to, for the excellent dinner and the equally excellent wine had produced a state of exhilaration that made me not-disinclined for adventure. In my normal state, nothing would have induced me to set loot in a gambling den. Now I fell in readily enough with Gillum's suggestion.

"But shan't I be expected to play?" I enquired. "Because I am not going to."

"That will be all right," he replied. "I shall explain to Madame, and she will see that you are left in peace. But you understand that this is an unregistered club and that you will keep your own counsel about your visit there. I shall have to guarantee your secrecy."

I gave the necessary undertaking and Gillum then held the wine bottle up to the light.

"There's half-a-bottle left," said he, making as if to refill my glass. "Won't you really? Not another half-glass? Well, I don't think I will, either. We will just have our coffee and a cognac and then toddle round to the club and see the ball roll."

Chapter III
The Gaming House

From Giamborini's we strolled forth into Wardour Street and, proceeding in a southerly direction, promptly turned into Gerrard Street. I knew the place slightly and on my occasional passage through it had found a certain bookish interest in contrasting its recent faded and shabby aspect with that which it must have presented in the days when Dryden was a resident and, later, when the Literary Club with Johnson, Reynolds, Goldsmith, and Gibbon, held its meetings here.

"Queer old street," Gillum commented, looking about him disparagingly. "Quite fashionable, I believe, at one time, but it is down on its luck nowadays. Very mixed population, too. All sorts of odd clubs, British and foreign, and tradesmen who seem to have survived from the Stone Age. There is a fellow some where along here who makes spurs. Think of it. Spurs! In the twentieth century. This is our show."

He halted at a doorway which, shabby and grimy as it was, yet preserved some vestiges of its former dignity, and having run his eye over an assortment of bell handles, put his finger on an electric button which surmounted them and pressed several times at irregular intervals.

"Are you ringing out a code message?" I asked.

"Well, yes, in a way," he replied. "There is a particular kind of ring that the regular members give just to let the people upstairs know that it isn't a stranger. There is always the possibility of a raid and our friends like to have time to make the necessary arrangements."

The idea of a police raid was not a pleasant one and the suggestion tended rather to damp my enthusiasm. I expressed the hope that this would not happen to be the occasion of one.

"No, indeed," said Gillum, "it would be unfortunate for you. Wouldn't increase your prestige at the bank. But you needn't worry. There has never been any trouble since I have known the place. I have sometimes suspected that Foucault has some sort of discreet understanding with the authorities, but in any case, I know there is a bolt hole through into the next house where an Italian club has its premises."

This did not sound very reassuring. I felt the exhilarating effects of the champagne evaporating rapidly, and when at length the door was opened, the aspect of the janitor did not produce a favourable impression. He was a big, powerful man, with a heavy jaw and beetling brows and a strong suggestion of the professional pugilist. He carried an electric

435

lamp, the light of which he cast on us while he inspected us critically. Then the truculent expression faded suddenly from his face and a cheerful Irish voice exclaimed, "Whoy, it's Mr. Gillum. Good evening, sorr. And the other gentleman, would he be a friend of yours?"

"Yes," replied Gillum, "it's all right, Cassidy. All's well and the lights are burning brightly, sir."

Mr. Cassidy chuckled as he let us in and shut the door. "Many's the time," said he, "as I've spoken them same wurrds in the days when I used the sea. What did ye say the gentleman's name was?"

"His name is Mortimer," replied Gillum.

"To be sure it is," said Cassidy, adding, as he threw his light downwards, "Kape your oyes on the stairs, sorr. There's a tread loose at the turn."

The stairs were, in fact, in somewhat indifferent repair, but I noticed as the light flickered over them that this had once been quite a handsome staircase though a trifle narrow, and even now the fine moulded handrail and the graceful twisted balusters redeemed its extreme shabbiness. At the top of the second flight we came to a bare landing with a door facing us. This Cassidy opened and, having admitted us, passed in himself, crossed the room, and disappeared through mother doorway, presumably to report our arrival and identity.

I looked round the room which we had entered and was conscious of a faint sense of anti-climax. It was so very ordinary and so very innocent, much like the interior of the cheaper kind of old-fashioned Soho restaurant. At the farther end of the room was a large sideboard, presided over by a man in a white coat and cap and piled with a variety of food, including a ham, a number of different types of sausage, a great stack of sandwiches, and long French loaves. On a shelf behind was a long row of bottles of mineral waters, but on the sideboard I noted several champagne bottles, a few of whisky, and some of absinthe and other liqueurs.

The room was moderately full of people, full enough to have given Mr. Cassidy considerable occupation if they had been admitted separately. Some of them were lounging about, talking. Others were seated at little tables, taking food rather hurriedly, and some were actually drinking ginger ale, though most of them were provided with wine, whisky, or Dutch gin. One or two of the tables were furnished with chess-boards and sets of dominoes, but none of them appeared to be in use. Apparently their function was purely psychological. They were part of the "make-up" of the establishment.

I had not much time to examine the company, but a rapid inspection conveyed to me the impression that they were all rather abnormal and slightly disreputable. There was an air of eagerness, anxiety, and excitement about them, mingled, in some cases, with a sort of wild hilarity. Those at the tables gobbled their food as if they were hastily stoking up and were anxious to get the business over. Particularly I noticed a group of four men standing by the sideboard devouring sandwiches wolfishly and gulping champagne from tumblers. But, as I said, I had little time to observe them for, after a brief pause and a curious glance round the room, Gillum conducted me to a door near the farther end from which Cassidy emerged as we approached.

There was certainly nothing innocent about the room that we now entered. A single glance convicted it. The roulette table alone furnished evidence to which there could be no answer, and the groups of haggard, intent men and women gathered round the card tables that filled most of the room, if less conclusive to a possible raider, were unmistakable, seen as I saw them.

From one of these tables the lady of the restaurant rose and, laying down her cards, came to meet us.

"So you have persuaded Mr. Mortimer to come," she said, bestowing a gracious smile on me and offering an extensive sample of teeth for my inspection. (Apparently she had got my name from Mr. Cassidy).

"Yes," replied Gillum, "but he has only come as a spectator. I have just brought him round to show him the ropes in case he may feel disposed for an evening's sport later on."

"That is very good of you, Jack," said she. "Of course, he can please himself as to whether he plays or not. Perhaps, when he has looked on for a while, he may feel inclined to try his luck. People who come to look on very often do."

"I have no doubt they do," said Gillum with a sly mile. "The complaint is catching and fools who come to scoff remain to play."

"I hope Mr. Mortimer hasn't come to scoff," said she, and when I had protested with more emphasis than sincerity she asked, "Where is your pupil going to take his first lesson?"

"Well," he replied, "as he knows practically nothing about card games, I think roulette will suit him best. Besides, it is the beginner's game and it is the most typical game of chance."

"That's true," Madame agreed, "though it seems to me a dull game, if you can call it a game at all. Let me find a couple of chairs so that you and your pupil can sit together, and then, when Mr. Mortimer is comfortably settled, I want to have a few words with you."

We secured two chairs and placed them in a vacant place at the end of the table by the compartment distinguished by a red lozenge on the green cloth. Then Madame introduced me to the croupier, whom she addressed as Hyman – his surname I found later to be Goldfarb – and when Gillum had placed his hat on his chair, she linked her arm with his and led him away among the multitude of card tables.

Left to myself, I first disposed of my hat and stick under my chair, as I noticed that several other men had done, though there was a large hat rack in the adjoining room. Then I proceeded to make my observations.

There was plenty to observe, and it was all strange and novel to me. There were, for instance, the various players, most of them seated at the table, though some preferred to stand and hover about behind the chairs, and there was the croupier, a pleasant faced Jew, calm, impassive and courteous, though obviously very much "on the spot", and there were the parties of players at the card tables, most of whom I could see from my position without appearing to spy on them.

I considered them one by one. My next neighbour was an elderly woman, whom I judged to be French, who sat like a graven image, silently and immovably intent on her game. She seemed to have the disease in a chronic form, for she played mechanically without a sign of satisfaction when she won or annoyance when she lost. At each spin of the wheel she laid a ten-shilling note on the space before which she sat – that marked with the red lozenge. If she won, she put the note that she had gained into a little hand bag and held the other in readiness for the next turn of the wheel, if she lost, she fished a note out of the bag for the next coup. So she went on as long as I observed her, always the same stake on the same spot. It looked deadly dull, and it was not gambling at all in any proper sense for, by the ordinary laws of chance, it was almost impossible for her either to win or lose to an appreciable extent. So fatuous her proceedings seemed that I almost felt more respect for her next-door neighbour, a small German who might, from his appearance, have been a waiter. He certainly took risks, for his formula was two numbers "a cheval" and he kept to the same two numbers. As the odds against him were seventeen to one, he naturally lost with great regularity, and when he lost cursed under his breath – not very far under – shook his head, and grimaced angrily. I think he must have been pretty near the end of his resources, for I saw him take out a wallet and look into it anxiously. But at this moment his magic number was announced, whereat he gave a yell of ecstasy, grabbed up his winnings, stuffed them into his wallet excepting one pound note, which he laid on the same spot as before and lost within a minute.

From the roulette table my attention wandered to the other occupants of the room and occasionally to Gillum and Madame, who walked slowly to-and-fro at the end of the room and conversing earnestly. Nor was I the only observer. Several of the card-players cast a glance from time to time at the pair, and the three occupants of the table from which Madame had risen made no secret of their interest. Two of these I could not see very well, but M. Foucault sat facing me, and never have I seen a more evil expression than that which his countenance bore as he watched them. He was not a pleasant-looking man at the best, and a slight squint did not improve matters, but now his aspect was positively villainous.

Not that his manifest anger was without provocation, for Madame's oglings and her caressing manner towards Gillum, regardless of the company, would have been offensive to the most tolerant of husbands. She might have been Gillum's lover – and not a very reticent lover at that. It is true that Gillum took it all very coolly with no sign of responsive demonstrations, but I felt that he was being more than indiscreet. Obviously, in his association with this woman, who seemed of set purpose to exasperate her husband, he was taking the risk of serious trouble.

Presently, to my relief they strolled over to Foucault's table and while Madame resumed her seat, Gillum drew up a spare chair and sat down facing her husband. Apparently the lady was giving some sort of explanation for she spoke volubly, leaning across the table to avoid raising her voice, while the others leaned forward to listen, and Foucault appeared to be gazing simultaneously at his wife and Gillum – an optical illusion, of course, due to his "swivel eye".

The discussion did not last long, and it was evidently quite an amicable affair, for when Gillum stood up, he shook hands with them all, including the grim-faced Foucault, before turning away to rejoin me, and I noted the leave-taking with considerable satisfaction, for it was getting alarmingly late and I began to feel that I had had enough of this not-very-thrilling form of entertainment.

"Yes," Gillum agreed, when I ventured on a hint to that effect, "time's getting on and you've to be at the bank as fresh as a lark to-morrow morning. But we must have one little flutter before we go. What shall it be? Shall we try an experiment with the doubling plan that we were discussing at dinner?"

Without waiting for an answer, he laid a pound note on the red beside the ten-shilling note that the elderly lady had just put down. I watched with unexpected interest as the revolving wheel was checked and the little white ball clattered round the dial, and was sensibly disappointed when it settled at last in compartment 21 – for 21 happened unfortunately to be black. But Gillum was as indifferent as the old lady, and while Mr. Goldfarb raked in the bank's winning's and paid out to the players who had won, he calmly selected two fresh notes from his bulging wallet.

Once more the wheel was spun, the ball was thrown out on to the revolving surface, then the croupier chanted "*Rien ne va plus*" and checked the wheel, Gillum laid down his two notes, and a dozen pairs of eyes anxiously followed the travels of the dancing ball. At length it dropped into compartment 32 – black again, and Gillum sorted out four pound notes from his wallet.

So it went on for a while. Regardless of the law of probability, the ball persisted in dropping into black compartments, and at each failure Gillum doubled his stake. I watched the proceedings with ridiculous anxiety. At the fourth losing coup when the croupier raked in eight of Gillum's pound notes, I noted mentally that my friend was already fifteen pounds out of pocket. If he lost the next coup, that fifteen would become thirty-one. It was positively harrowing to a thrifty man like myself, accustomed to keep a rigid account of every shilling that I spent.

However, he did not lose this time. My anxious eye following the ball, saw it eventually settle in compartment four which was red, and the croupier's rake, instead of sweeping away Gillum's sixteen pounds, added to them another sixteen.

"There, you see," said Gillum, "I am one pound to the good, and that is all I should have gained if I had gone on till doomsday. But I am a gainer to the extent that I have got back what I had lost."

He began to pick up the notes, counting them as he did so. Among them there had been four ten-shilling notes, but now there were only three, the explanation of which was that the old lady, when she had gathered up her two notes, had quietly added to them one of Gillum's. I saw her do it, and so did he, and he now ventured, with the utmost delicacy, to point out the little inadvertency. The lady gazed at him stonily, and I think was about to contest the matter, but at this moment a shout from the farther end of the room, followed by a crash and the sound of shattering glass, effectually diverted our attention.

I looked round quickly and saw two men, each grasping the other by the hair and both yelling like Bedlamites, one accusing the other – in Italian – of being a cheat and the other retorting – in French – that his accuser was a liar. A table and two chairs had been capsized, and very soon, as the combatants gyrated wildly and clawed at each other, more tables were capsized. Then the occupants of those tables joined in the fray with suitable vocal accompaniments and in a moment pandemonium reigned in the previously quiet room. As Foucault and his two friends sprang up and charged into the midst of the *mêlée*, the door burst open and Cassidy rushed in like an angry bull.

440

"We'd better clear out of this," said Gillum. "If they keep up this hullabaloo they'll bring the police up." As I agreed heartily, he grabbed up his winnings (but I observed that there were now only two ten-shilling notes) and we retrieved our hats from under the chairs and stole out as well as we could through the little crowd of spectators from the restaurant-room who had gathered round the door to look on at the battle. With the aid of my pocket lamp we made the perilous passage of the stairs – not forgetting the loose tread – and at last emerged safely into the street.

"My word!" exclaimed Gillum, as we crossed the road the more completely to sever our connection with the club, "how they do yell when they have a bit of a scrap. Just listen to them."

There was not much need to listen for the uproar was such that windows were opening and various night-birds were appearing from the doors of adjacent houses. Evidently, it was desirable for us to get out of the neighbourhood as quickly as possible, which we did, walking briskly but with no outward sign of undue hurry until we were safely out in Wardour Street, where we turned to the left and headed for Leicester Square. Here we had the good fortune to encounter prowling, nocturnal taxi, the driver of which Gillum hailed by voice and gesture. As the vehicle drew up to the kerb he turned to me and asked, "Whereabouts do you hang out, Mortimer?"

"I live at Highbury," I replied.

"Yes, but that's a trifle vague. What's the exact address?" I gave him my full postal address which he communicated to the driver. "And," he added, "you can drop me at Clifford's Inn Passage, opposite the Inner Temple Gate. Will that do for the whole journey?

"That" appeared to be a ten-shilling note and the driver replied that "it would do very well, thank you, sir," whereupon we got in and the cab trundled away towards the Strand. I made some ineffectual efforts to refund my share of the payment, but Gillum declared that the calculation was beyond his arithmetic and suggested that we should work it out on some more suitable occasion. We were still arguing the point when the cab stopped in the shadow of St. Dunstan's Church and Gillum got out.

"Well, good night, Mortimer," said he, "or good morning, to be more exact. I hope you have had a pleasant and instructive evening. You have certainly had a full one what with corpses, illegal gambling, and the battle."

He shut the door and waved his hand, and the taxi resumed its journey, turning up Fetter Lane and later heading for Gray's Inn Road. Now that I was alone, I felt a strong disposition to go to sleep, but by an effort I managed to keep awake and watch the familiar landmarks as they

441

slipped by until, in a surprisingly short time, the taxi drew up at the gate of the eligible suburban residence which enshrined the two rooms that served me as a home. The driver actually got out to open the door for me – possibly suspecting some temporary disability, or perhaps as a demonstration of his satisfaction with the fare. At any rate, he gave me a cheerful "Good night" and I inserted my latch-key with ease and precision as the clock of a neighbouring church was striking two.

Chapter IV
Abel Webb, Deceased

The events of the evening which I had spent with Gillum gave me a good deal to think about. There was no longer any mystery as to what he did with the large sums that he drew from the bank. He just gambled them away. As to how much it was possible for an inveterate gambler like Gillum to drop in any one transaction, I could form no guess. Apparently there was no limit excepting the total amount that the gambler possessed. I had heard and read of players who had lost thousands in a single game, but it had always seemed to me incredible. Now, however, judging by what I had seen, and still more by what Gillum had said, I felt that nothing could overstate the monstrous truth.

The reflection was a sad and depressing one. It made me quite unhappy, for Gillum was no longer a mere customer. He had become an acquaintance, almost a friend, and I had found him a pleasant, likeable man, and apparently a man of good intelligence – apart from his insane hobby. It really distressed me to think of a man with his brilliant opportunities frittering away the means of achievement in this puerile sport. And then, what of the future? If his source of supply was a permanent one he might go on indefinitely, simply flinging away his income as fast as he received it. But suppose it were not a stable, continuing income. Suppose it should dwindle or cease? What then? It was pretty certain that this relatively wealthy man would very soon be reduced to actual poverty.

But the mystery of Gillum's expenditure was not completely solved. Apart from the big drafts in cash at irregular intervals, there were those regular, periodic drafts which I had regarded with such suspicion. Had our evening's experiences thrown any light on them? I could not say positively that they had. And yet, there was at least a suggestion. The whole atmosphere of that sordid gaming house with its deeply shady frequenters – the sinister-looking proprietor – manifestly hostile to Gillum – the painted Jezebel, his wife, the ruffian Cassidy – obviously a paid bully – and finally, Gillum's long and mysterious conference with Madame – if these did not actually offer a suggestion of blackmail, they did at least suggest the very conditions in which blackmail is apt to occur.

From Gillum and his affairs my thoughts turned at intervals to the dead man who had been the means of our introduction. I had read a brief

443

notice of the discovery in the morning paper and had expected to receive on the same day a summons to attend the inquest. Actually, I did not receive it until the evening of the second day, when I found it awaiting me at my lodgings, requiring my attendance on the following day at two o'clock in the afternoon. Accordingly, on my arrival at the office in the morning, I showed it to our manager and, having received his authority to absent myself from the bank, duly presented myself at the time and place appointed.

The body had been identified as that of a man named Abel Webb, and that was all that was said about him in the first place. Further particulars were left to transpire in the evidence.

There is no need for me to describe the proceedings in detail apart from the essentials. The coroner opened with a concise statement of the matter which formed the subject of the inquiry, the jury were then conducted to the mortuary to view the body, and when they had returned and taken their places the coroner proceeded to deal with the evidence.

"I think," said he, "that we had better begin by calling Mr. Mortimer. His evidence is of no great importance, but it comes first in the order of time."

My name was accordingly called, and when I had given the necessary particulars concerning myself, the coroner said, "Now, Mr. Mortimer, just tell us how you came to be connected with the subject of this inquiry. We can ask any necessary questions later."

Thus directed, I gave a plain and rather bald account of my discovery of the body and the circumstances leading thereto, to which the jury listened with eager interest, naturally enough, since the coroner's statement had given but the barest indication of the nature of the case.

"We understand," said the coroner, "that you did not recognise the deceased as a person whom you had ever seen before?"

"That is so," I replied. "The man was a stranger to me."

"Would it have been possible for anyone passing along the alley as you did to fail to notice the body?"

"Yes," I replied, "and not only possible but rather probable. It was dark in the alley and still darker in the church porch. I am not sure that I should have seen the body myself but for the fact that I had found the hat and was on the look-out for the owner. Moreover, I was walking very slowly at the moment when I saw the body."

"You think, then, that a person walking at an ordinary pace and not closely observing his surroundings might have passed the porch without seeing the body?"

"I think it extremely likely," I answered. "In fact, while I was waiting for the constable, a man did actually pass through without

444

noticing the body. He was certainly in a great hurry, but I think if he had not been, he still might not have noticed anything."

"That," said the coroner, addressing the jury, "is, of course, only an opinion, but it agrees with the facts to which the witness has deposed, and the point may be of some importance. Does anything further occur to you, Mr. Mortimer, or do you think that you have told us all that you have to tell?"

"I think I have told you all I know about the matter," I replied, whereupon the coroner, having invited the jury to ask any questions that they wished to ask and receiving no response, the depositions were read and signed and the next witness called.

Constable Walter Allen of the City Police, having completed the preliminaries, deposed as follows: "I was on duty in Cornhill on the evening of Monday the ninth of September. At eight-two p.m. on that evening I was accosted by the last witness, Mr. Robert Mortimer, who informed me that he had seen the dead body of a man lying in the passage leading from St. Michael's Alley to the churchyard. I went with him at once to the place mentioned and there saw the body of the deceased in the church porch. The body was partly sitting and partly lying. It was seated on the lowest of the three steps and was leaning back in the corner against the church door. I examined the body sufficiently to assure myself that the man was really dead, and then I went away and telephoned to the station in Old Jewry, reporting the discovery, and returned to the passage to wait until I was relieved."

"You have heard what the last witness said about the darkness of the passage," said the coroner. "Do you agree that it would have been possible for anyone to pass through the passage without noticing the body?"

"Yes," the constable replied, "I do. It was growing dark out in the street, and in the passage, which is a sort of tunnel, the light was very dim, and in the porch, which is about eight feet deep, it was practically dark. A person might easily have passed through the covered passage without seeing the body in the porch."

This completed the constable's evidence, and as he retired, the name of Inspector Pryor was called, whereupon that officer came forward, and having been sworn, proceeded to give his testimony with professional conciseness and precision. Taking up the thread of the constable's story, he confirmed the description of the body and its position in the porch and agreed that it might have been lying there unnoticed for some time – perhaps as long as half-an-hour – before it was discovered.

"Were you able," the coroner asked, "to form any opinion as to how the deceased met with his death?"

"Yes. When the body had been put on the stretcher, I examined the place where it had been lying and there I found the pieces of a broken hypodermic syringe and some drops of liquid on the stone step. The fragments of the syringe gave off a smell rather like bitter almonds and so did the liquid, which I took up with a piece of clean blotting-paper. The fragments of the syringe are in this box but the blotting-paper was handed to the medical officer."

He handed a small cardboard box to the coroner who opened it, peered in, sniffed at it, and passed it on to the jury. Then he asked, "Were there any finger-prints on the fragments of the syringe?"

"Only a few smears that were quite undecipherable. I examined the button of the plunger very carefully, but even there I could find nothing but a smear."

"You were able to ascertain the identity of the deceased?"

"Yes, there were a number of letters in his pocket addressed to *Abel Webb, Esq.* which enabled us to make the necessary enquiries."

"Besides the syringe, did you find anything on the spot that could throw light on this mysterious affair? Any signs of a struggle, for instance?"

"Nothing whatever," was the reply. "But as to a struggle, seeing that the floor of the passage is paved and that of the porch tiled, there would hardly be any traces even if a struggle had occurred."

"No," said the coroner, "I suppose there would not." He reflected for a few moments, and then, as there was apparently nothing more to be got out of the inspector, he intimated that the examination was concluded, and when the depositions had been read and signed, the officer retired.

"I think," said the coroner, "that, as I see that Dr. Ripley is present, we had better take the medical evidence next so as not to detain the doctor unnecessarily."

The new witness, a small, very alert-looking gentleman, having been sworn and having stated his name and professional qualifications, looked enquiringly at the coroner who, after a brief glance at his notes, opened the examination.

"Perhaps, Doctor," said he, "it would save time if you were to give us your evidence in the form of a statement. You saw the body, I think, shortly after the discovery."

"Yes," replied the witness "On Monday evening, the ninth of September, at eight-fifty-six, I received a summons by telephone from the police to go to the mortuary to examine a body which had just been brought in. I went at once and arrived there at five minutes past nine. There I found the body of the deceased which had been undressed and

446

laid on the mortuary table. At the first glance I formed the provisional opinion that the deceased had died as a result of poisoning by hydrocyanic acid or some cyanide compound. The face, and especially the lips, were of a distinct violet colour. The eyes were wide open, set in a fixed stare. The jaws were firmly closed and there was slight stiffening of the muscles at the back of the neck. The hands were tightly clenched and the fingernails were blue. These are the usual appearances in cases of cyanide poisoning, but the froth on the lips, which nearly always occurs in such cases, was absent.

"I examined the body for bruises or other signs of violence, but there were none, excepting that on the left thigh, a couple of inches from the groin, was a very distinct puncture which looked as if it had been made with a hypodermic needle of unusually large size. I was shown a broken syringe which had been found close to the body. It was not an ordinary hypodermic syringe but a larger kind, what is known as a serum syringe, and the needle was not a regular serum needle, but a longer and stouter form with a larger bore, such as is used by veterinary surgeons. I produce for your inspection an exactly similar syringe, but fitted with an ordinary serum needle, which you can compare with the broken syringe that was handed to you by the inspector."

He laid the syringe on the table and paused while the coroner and the jury compared it with the fragments in the box. When they had made the comparison and put the two syringes aside, he resumed. "The broken syringe and the needle both contained minute quantities of a clear liquid, which I collected in a pipette for subsequent analysis. But, at the time, I could tell by the characteristic smell of bitter almonds that it was one of the cyanide compounds."

"So that, in effect," said the coroner, "you had then established the cause of death."

"Yes," was the reply, "there was practically no room for doubt. The body showed the distinctive appearances of cyanide poisoning. There was no froth on the lips, which suggested that the poison had not been swallowed. There was the mark of a hypodermic needle, and there was a syringe containing traces of a cyanide compound. It was all perfectly consistent."

"You subsequently made a *post mortem* examination?"

"Yes and, as it is very important in cases of poisoning by hydrocyanic acid or cyanide, I made the *post mortem* the same night, but first I analysed the liquid in the pipette, which I found to be a concentrated solution of potassium cyanide."

"Did the *post mortem* throw any fresh light on the case?"

447

"Not very much, but it converted the inference into an ascertained fact. I can say with certainty that the deceased died from the effects of a very large dose of potassium cyanide injected into the upper part of the thigh – the region which is known as Scarpa's Triangle. But one, possibly important, fact came to light, which was that the needle of the syringe entered the great vein of the thigh – the femoral vein."

"In what respect is that fact of importance?" the coroner asked.

"In its bearing on the rapidity with which the poison will have taken effect. Five grains of potassium cyanide will, if swallowed, produce death in about a quarter-of-an-hour. The same quantity injected hypodermically would cause death in a minute or two at the most, while if it were injected into one of the great veins, death would probably follow in a matter of seconds. Now, in the present case, a much larger quantity was discharged directly into this great vein, from which I infer that death must have occurred practically instantaneously."

"Is it possible to say how much was injected?"

"Not in exact terms. I made only a qualitative analysis. Anything like an exact estimate of quantity would have involved a long and complicated procedure and it would have served no useful purpose. But I can say confidently, that the amount of cyanide injected was at least ten grains."

"When you first saw the body, did you form any opinion as to how long the deceased had been dead?"

"Yes. Judging principally by the temperature of the body, I should say that he had been dead about an hour."

"You mentioned some stiffening of the muscles – apparently *rigor mortis*. Would that occur so soon after death?"

"The clenching of the jaws and hands was not due to *rigor mortis*. It was really cadaveric spasm and will have occurred at the moment of death. But the stiffening of the neck muscles did indicate the beginning of *rigor mortis* and was, of course, much earlier than in the average of cases. But there is nothing remarkable in this early onset. It very commonly occurs in cases of violent death and especially of suicide. I don't think the deceased had been dead more than about an hour."

The coroner wrote down this statement and appeared to scan the preceding evidence before putting the next question. At length he looked up and turned to the witness.

"You say that death was due to poison injected by means of a syringe. Could that injection have been administered by the deceased himself?"

"Yes. The site chosen was not a very convenient one for self-administration but it was well within reach, and self-administration would not have been difficult."

"So far as you could judge from your examination, was there anything that suggested either that the deceased had or had not administered the poison to himself?"

"In a medical sense and in terms of mere physical possibility, there was no evidence one way or the other."

The coroner looked at the witness critically, and then remarked, "I seem to detect a note of doubt and reservation in your answer. Is that not so?"

"Perhaps it is," the doctor replied. "But I am here as a medical witness and my evidence is properly restricted to what I know, or can reasonably infer from my examination of the body."

"That is a highly correct attitude, Doctor," said the coroner with a faint smile, "but I don't think we need be quite so particular. Have you any opinion, medical or other, as to whether the deceased did or did not administer the poison to himself?"

"I have," the witness replied promptly. "My opinion is that he did not administer the poison to himself."

"That is perfectly definite," said the coroner, "and I am sure the jury would like to hear your reasons for that opinion, as I should myself."

"My opinion," said Dr. Ripley, "is based upon the circumstances of the deceased's death. Either he killed himself or was killed by some other person. There is no question of accident or misadventure. It is either suicide or homicide. If we consider the theory of suicide, we are confronted by two anomalies.

"The first is the syringe. Why should the deceased have used a hypodermic syringe? There is no reason at all. In the case of morphia there would be a reason, for the poison acts comparatively slowly, and large doses, if swallowed, tend to cause vomiting and so defeat the suicide's ends. But cyanide poisons act very rapidly and tends to produce death before the stomach becomes disturbed. Suicide by means of potassium cyanide is not uncommon, but the usual method is to swallow one or more tablets, and this is quite efficient for the purpose. I have never before heard of a syringe being used for this poison.

"The conditions in the case of homicide are exactly the reverse. You can't compel a man to swallow a tablet or even a liquid poison. But you can stick a hypodermic needle into him, even if he has time to resist. And then the peculiarities of this particular syringe are adapted to homicide but not at all to suicide. The big veterinary needle would cause considerable pain in insertion. Its only advantage, its large bore, enabling

449

the syringe to be discharged rapidly, would be of no benefit to the suicide, but it would be of vital importance to a murderer, who would want to get the business over as quickly as possible and make off.

"The other anomaly is the place where the death occurred. Why should a suicide, having provided himself with the poison and the syringe, go forth to use them in a public thoroughfare when he could have done the business without disturbance in his own premises? And why, if he chose a public place, should he have selected a dark corner in an unfrequented passage? To a suicide, the solitude and obscurity of the place would offer no advantage. But to a murderer, those conditions would be essential, for he would want to get clear of the neighbourhood before the body was discovered. In short, the mode of death, the means used, and the place selected, were all unadapted to suicide, but perfectly adapted to homicide."

As the doctor concluded his exposition, a murmur of approval arose from the jury, and the coroner, who also appeared to be deeply impressed, commented, "Dr. Ripley has given us, in a very ingenious and cogent argument, his reasons for taking a particular view of this case, and I am sure that when we come to consider the evidence as a whole, we shall give them due weight. And now, as he is a busy man, I think we ought not to detain him any longer, unless any of you wish for further information."

He looked enquiringly at the jury, and the foreman, in response to the implied invitation, signified that he would like to put a question.

"The doctor," said he, "has referred to the solitude and obscurity of the place where the body was found. I should like to ask him if he has any personal acquaintance with that place."

"Yes," replied the witness, "I know it very well indeed. My practice is in the City of London and I am perfectly familiar with all the courts and alleys that form the short cuts from one main thoroughfare to others. As to St. Michael's Alley, I think that hardly a week passes in which I do not pass through it at least once."

"And if you pass through it," said the foreman, "I suppose other people do."

"Undoubtedly," the witness agreed, "and in the day a fair number of people pass up and down the alley, although after business hours, when the City has emptied, it is very little frequented. But the point is that when I go up the alley, I go straight up to Castle Court. I don't turn off through the covered passage. And other people do the same, and for the same reason, which is that the covered passage also leads to Castle Court but by a less direct route. The only people who habitually use the covered passage are those who are employed in the office building that

450

faces the churchyard. When they have gone, there are probably periods of half-an-hour or more during which not a soul passes through that passage."

The foreman expressed himself as quite satisfied with the explanation and thanked the witness, who was then released to go about his business. When he had departed, the name of Alfred Stowell was called and a middle-aged, gentlemanly man came forward and took his place at the table. Mr. Stowell, having been sworn, gave his particulars, describing himself as the manager of The Cope Refrigerating Company, of Gracechurch Street, London.

"You have viewed the body of the deceased," said the coroner. "Did you recognise it as that of anyone whom you knew?"

"Yes. It is the body of Mr. Abel Webb, lately my assistant manager."

"How long had he been with you?"

"Less than two months. He took up his duties with us on the twenty-second of last July."

"Do you know how he was employed before he came to you?"

"He was in the service of the Commonwealth and Dominion Steamship Company and had been for about ten years. He had served as purser on several of their ships, and it was on account of his experience in that capacity that my firm engaged him."

"I don't quite follow that. In what way is a purser's experience of value to you?"

"The ships of the Commonwealth Line are engaged in the frozen meat trade, and Mr. Webb had a rather special knowledge of refrigerating plant, as well as of the trade in general."

"What sort of person was the deceased – as to temperament, I mean? Did he strike you as a man who might possibly take his own life?"

"Most certainly not," the witness replied. "He was of a singularly cheerful and happy disposition and very pleased with his new occupation after the long years at sea."

"Have you any reason to suppose that he was in financial difficulties or in any way troubled about money?"

"No reason at all. Quite the contrary, in fact. I gathered from certain remarks that he let fall that he was in very comfortable circumstances. He was a bachelor without any dependants or responsibilities and had been steadily saving money all the time that he was at sea. That is what I understood from him. Of course, I have no first-hand knowledge of his affairs."

"So far as you know, had the deceased any enemies?"

451

"I am not aware that he had, and I have no reason to suppose that he had. In the excellent testimonial from his late employers he was described as an amiable and kindly man who was universally liked. I know no more than that."

"Do you know of anything that could throw light on the manner and circumstances of his death?"

"Nothing whatever," was the reply, and as this seemed to conclude the evidence, the coroner asked the jury the usual question, and when the depositions had been signed the witness was released.

For some time after he had retired, the coroner sat scanning his notes with a manifestly dissatisfied air. At length he confided his difficulties to the jury.

"There is no denying," said he, "that the evidence which we have heard has left this mysterious affair to a great extent unelucidated, and the question arises as to whether it is advisable to adjourn the inquiry and endeavour to obtain further evidence. On the whole, as the police have not succeeded in discovering any of the deceased's relatives, I am disposed to think that nothing would be gained by an adjournment. The further elucidation, if it is possible, seems to lie outside our province and within that of the police. Accordingly, I think it will be best for us to try to find a verdict on the evidence which is before us.

"It is unnecessary for me to recapitulate that evidence. It was all very clearly given and you have followed it closely and attentively. The question that you have to decide is: Who injected the poison? If the deceased injected it himself, it is obviously a case of suicide. If you decide that it was injected by some other person, you will have to find a verdict of wilful murder, since the injection could not have been given for any lawful purpose.

"The difficulty of deciding between suicide and murder is that there is no positive evidence of either. The medical evidence is to the effect that suicide was physically possible and that murder was physically possible. That is all that we have in the way of positive evidence. And in considering the medical evidence we must be careful to keep the facts separate from the opinions. The facts sworn to by the medical witness we can accept confidently, but the witness's opinions, weighty though they are, can be accepted only so far as your judgment confirms them. It is you who have to find the verdict, and that verdict must be based on the evidence which you have heard and on nothing else. That, I think, is all I need say, except to remind you that you are not in the position of a jury at a criminal trial, who are bound to decide yes or no, guilty or not guilty. If, having considered the evidence, you find it insufficient to enable you to decide between the alternatives of murder and suicide, you are at liberty to say so."

When the coroner had finished speaking, the members of the jury drew together and engaged in earnest and anxious consultation. It was a difficult question that they had to settle and they very properly took their time in debating it. At length the foreman announced that they had agreed on their verdict, and in reply to the coroner's question stated "We find that the deceased died from the effects of a poison injected into his body with a syringe, but whether the injection was administered by himself or by some other person there is no evidence to show."

"Yes," said the coroner, "I don't see that you could have found otherwise. I shall record an open verdict and any further inquiries that may be necessary or possible will be conducted by the police."

The proceedings having now come to an end, the audience and the witnesses rose and filed out into the street, and as I took my way back to the bank, I reflected a little uncomfortably on what I had heard. It was a horrible affair and profoundly mysterious. If I had been a member of the jury, my verdict would have been the same as that had been recorded, but it would not have expressed my inward convictions. The doctor's convincing exposition, which still rang in my ears, had but confirmed in my mind an already-formed belief.

The circumstance of the tragedy seemed to whisper "Murder", and as I entered Ball Court (instinctively avoiding the neighbourhood of the fatal passage) and threaded the maze of alleys into George Yard and Lombard Street, I looked about me with a shuddering interest, speculating on the way that poor Webb had gone to his death and wondering whether the callous murderer – with the charged syringe ready in his pocket – had walked at his side or had waylaid him in the covered passage.

Chapter V
Clifford's Inn

The events of the evening which I had spent with John Gillum, though they threw a good deal of light on his financial affairs, by no means diminished my interest in, or curiosity concerning, those affairs. On the contrary, having now clearly established the principal channel through which his money flowed – virtually into the gutter – I found myself the more concerned with the question whether that was the sole channel, or whether he might perchance be dropping money in ways even less desirable than gambling. I have mentioned that at intervals of about a month he was accustomed to present a "self" cheque for a considerable amount, never less, though usually more, than five-hundred pounds. It might be that this represented merely "the sinews of war" for the month's gambling, but to my eye it looked like something different, something suggesting a definite periodic payment, and this view was strengthened by the fact that other drafts, often for large sums, were presented at irregular intervals. These, from their irregularity in time and amount, seemed much more likely to represent his gaming losses.

The periodic cheque was usually drawn about the fourteenth day of the month (rather suggesting a payment on the fifteenth) and it was Gillum's custom to notify the bank a day in advance of the amount of cash that he intended to withdraw. Accordingly, as the day drew near, I awaited the notification with some expectancy, and sure enough, on the morning of the thirteenth – two days after the inquest – it was delivered at the bank and shown to me by the manager, as Gillum usually elected to transact his business with me. This time the amount was six-hundred-and-fifty pounds, and as Gillum had a preference for notes that had been in circulation, some sorting out of the stock was necessary.

On the morning of the fourteenth, soon after the hank had opened, he made his appearance, and coming straight over to my "pitch", laid his cheque on the counter.

"I'm afraid I'm the bane of your life, Mortimer." said he, "with my big cash drafts. You ought to have a note-counting machine – turn a handle, shoot 'em out by the dozen, and show the number on a dial."

"It would be a convenience," I admitted, "though I doubt whether a court of law would accept the reading of the machine as evidence. But it is no great trouble to count a few hundred notes, and at any rate, it is what I am here for."

I brought out the bundles of notes that I had prepared in readiness for the payment and, having re-counted them, passed the bundles across to him.

"You had better check them," said I as he picked them up and stuffed them into his pocket.

"No need," he replied. "I'll take them as read. I'm not equal to your lightning manipulation, and if we differed I should be sure to be wrong."

He paused to distribute the seven bundles more evenly and then, as there were no customers waiting at the moment, lingered to gossip. "I hope," said he, "you were none the worse for our little dissipation."

"Thank you, no," I replied. "A little sleepy the next morning, but I am quite convalescent now."

"Good," said he. "We must have another outing soon, not quite so boisterous. We might go and hear some music."

"That is quite a good idea," said I, "and it reminds me that an opportunity presents itself this very day. Do you care for organ music?"

"I like it in church," he replied, "not so much in a concert hall. The appropriate atmosphere seems to be lacking."

"Then," said I, "perhaps you would like to come with me this evening to St. Peter's, Cornhill. There is to be an organ recital from six to seven by Dr. Dyer. I am going, and if you can manage it, I can promise you a musical treat."

He considered for a few moments and then replied, "It sounds rather alluring and I've got the evening free. So I accept subject to conditions, which are that after the recital you come along to my chambers and join me in a little rough bachelor dinner. I can't do you in Giamborini's style but you won't starve. When we have fed, we can either smoke a pipe and yarn or go out somewhere. What do you say?"

I accepted promptly, for the proposed entertainment was much more to my taste than a restaurant dinner, and when we had made the necessary arrangements he took his leave and I reverted to my duties.

At half-past five he reappeared at the bank and found me waiting outside, and we strolled together up Gracechurch Street, looking in at Leadenhall Market on our way, and took our seats in the church at five minutes to the hour. The fame of the organist had drawn a surprisingly large number of men and women to the recital, and it was evident by the instant hush that fell as soon as the music began that Dr. Dyer had a genuinely appreciative audience.

And I was interested, and a little surprised, to note that Gillum not only enjoyed but – as I gathered from his whispered comments in the intervals – followed the rather austere and technical works that were played with manifest sympathy and understanding. One would hardly

455

have associated the gambling den and the racecourse with a refined taste for music, but Gillum was a rather queer mixture in many respects.

When the recital came to an end, we set forth on foot to stretch our legs and sharpen our appetites with the walk of a little over a mile from Cornhill to Clifford's Inn, beguiling the short journey with a discussion of the music that we had been listening to, and comments on objects of interest that we observed by the way. In Fleet Street, Gillum gave me another mild surprise by halting me opposite Anderton's Hotel and bidding me note the fine silhouette that St. Dunstan's Church and the Law Court made against the sunset sky.

"I always stop here to look at the view," said he, "and although the shapes are always the same, the picture is different every time I see it. There is a lot of fine scenery of a kind in the streets of London."

Once more, as we walked on, I reflected on the strange contradictions and inconsistencies of my companion's temperament. Somehow, he managed to combine a sensitiveness to the picturesque and beautiful with a singular tolerance of the sordid and unlovely.

A few yards farther on we turned up Fetter Lane and, crossing the road, made for an iron gate set in a row of railings and now standing wide open. Entering, we found ourselves in the precincts of Clifford's Inn and seemed in a moment to have passed out of the clamorous twentieth century into the quiet and dignified repose of a bygone age. I knew the place slightly from having occasionally ventured in to explore, and I now looked round with friendly recognition of the pleasant old red brick houses and the slightly faded grass and trees in the garden.

"This is my lair," said Gillum, indicating an arched doorway lighted by a hanging lantern and surmounted by a tablet bearing the inscription "*P.R.G. 1682*". Within the deep portal, a shadowy flight of stairs faded away into profound obscurity, and when Gillum led the way in and up the stairs, he too, faded into the darkness and became a mere black shape against the dim light from the landing above. I groped my way up after him (for the lamp at the entry was not yet lit) and presently emerged on to the landing where I found my host inserting a key into a massive iron-bound door above which was painted in black letters on a faded white ground, "*Mr. John Gillum*". The forbidding, gaol-like door swung open heavily disclosing a lighter inner door garnished with an ordinary handle and a small brass knocker. Gillum turned the handle and, throwing open the door, invited me to enter, and as soon as I was inside, he pulled to the outer door, which closed with the snap of a spring latch and a resounding clang suggestive of the door of a prison cell.

456

"Just as well to sport the oak," said Gillum. "Not that anyone ever comes after business hours, but it is more pleasant to feel that you can't be interrupted."

He switched on the light and I was instantly impressed by the contrast of the cheerful, cosy interior with the rather grim approach. A fire – well banked and enclosed by a guard – was burning in the grate, a couple of easy chairs faced each othier companionably, and the table, covered with a spotless white cloth, was laid with all the necessary appointments for a meal.

Gillum was a good host. This was a simple, informal "feed" and I was not a guest but a pal who had dropped in. He established the position at once by setting me to work at decanting the bottle of claret that had been stood on the mantel shelf to get the chill off, while he attended to the fire.

"May as well make a bit of a blaze," said he, "though it isn't a cold evening. But a fire is a companionable thing."

He tipped the remaining contents of the scuttle into the grate and then, after a hesitating glance at the empty receptacle, put it down.

"Where do you keep your coal?" I asked, with a view to replenishment.

"In the larder, or cellar or store-room," he replied. "It's that door across the landing, and a most excellent larder it makes – perfectly cool, even in the height of summer. And that reminds me that we shall want the butter and cheese and perhaps we might as well get out a bottle of Chablis to go with the lobster – and, by the way, the lobster is in there, too."

He went to the door and I followed to give assistance in carrying the goods. Not unnecessarily, as it turned out, for the door across the landing was fitted, not only with a night latch, but also with a rather strong spring, fixed to the inside of the door, as the latter opened outwards. I stood with my back against the open door and received the butter and the lobster, holding them until Gillum collected the cheese and the wine and came out, when I moved away and the door closed with a slam and a click of the lock.

"Now, Mortimer," said Gillum, when he had deposited our burdens on the table, "you are the wine waiter. Just open the chablis while I go into the kitchen and hot up the soup."

He retired through one of two small doorways which faced each other at the farther side of the room and I began operations on the capsule of the bottle. But at this moment the empty coal-scuttle caught my eye, and at the same time it occurred to me that we must have left the key in the larder door, since we had both come away with our hands full.

With the double purpose of retrieving the key and replenishing the scuttle, I picked up the latter and carried it out to the landing and, sure enough, there was the key in the door. I turned it, and bearing the spring in mind, when I had pulled the door open I set the scuttle against it while I went in and switched on the light. Then I took up the scuttle, carefully easing the door to, so that it remained unlatched (though there was a knob on the inside by which I could have let myself out), and proceeded to prospect. There was no difficulty in locating the coal, for a large bin or locker that extended right along the farther wall was so well filled that its lid gaped and displayed its contents.

I threw up the lid of the locker and, taking the scoop from the scuttle, began rapidly to shovel out the coal, my movements rather accelerated by the unpleasant cellar-like atmosphere, which struck an uncomfortable chill in contrast with the warm dining-room. I soon had the scuttle filled, but in my haste I let a few lumps of coal fall on the floor. Having put the scoop back in its socket, I stooped to pick up the stray lumps with my fingers, and at that moment I was conscious of a sudden feeling of giddiness and a loud ringing noise in my ears. Whether it was due to my position or to the abrupt change of temperature I cannot say, but as the place seemed to whirl around me and I felt myself swaying as if I were about to fall. I hastily grabbed the edge of the locker, pulled myself upright, and staggered out on to the landing.

As I emerged from the larder, letting the door slam behind me, Gillum appeared at the door of the living it and stared at me in dismay.

"Good God, Mortimer!" he exclaimed. "What on earth is the matter?"

Without waiting for an explanation, he hustled me into the living-room, threw up the window, and dragging a chair towards it, sat me down in the full draught.

"What was it?" he asked.

"I don't know," I replied. "I just stooped to pick up a lump of coal and then I suddenly turned giddy."

"Strange," said he, looking at me anxiously. "Have you ever had any attacks like this before?"

"Never," I answered, "and I can't imagine what brought it on now. I suppose it was the sudden stooping."

"But that won't do, Mortimer," said he. "You've no business to get giddy from stooping at your age. I don't believe you take proper care of yourself. You'd better let me get you a nip of whisky."

"No, thank you," said I. "The fresh air has done the business. I am all right now excepting a slight headache, and I expect that will go off in a few minutes. By the way, I left the light on in the larder."

"I'll go and switch off and get the coal-scuttle," said he, "and then we will have some grub. That will complete the cure, with a glass of wine."

He went out and presently returned with the scuttle, shutting the "oak" behind him. Then he fetched the soup from the kitchen and we drew our chairs up to the table and proceeded to business.

It was a pleasant little dinner, and not so very little, for when we had disposed of the lobster, the raising of a couple of covers revealed a cold roast fowl and a pile of sliced ham – the produce, as I learned, of an invaluable shop in Fetter Lane. Moreover, as the food was cold it lent itself to leisurely consumption and the free flow of conversation. And conversation with Gillum naturally tended to drift in the direction of betting and play.

"How is the infallible system progressing?" I asked.

"Slowly," he admitted, "but still, I think the thing is possible. I don't make much of it from the mathematical direction, so I am falling back on the excellent method of trial-and-error. I have got a miniature roulette box and I find it invaluable for trying out schemes of chances. I'll show it to you."

He produced a beautifully made little wooden box, and placing it on the table, affectionately twisted the ivory spindle.

"Yes," I agreed, "it is an excellent contraption, for you can play any odds you like against yourself and win in any event. I should advise you to stick to it. Do your gambling at home – and let the Foucaults have a rest."

He laughed, rather grimly I thought.

"Perhaps," said he, "it might rather be a question of their letting me have a rest. But your advice is futile, as you know perfectly well. Solo roulette is well enough for experimental purposes, but it isn't sport and it isn't gambling. You can't gamble if you don't stand to win or lose."

Of course, I knew this and his reply left me with nothing to say, so I reverted to the roast fowl and inwardly speculated on the possibility of a connection between the Foucaults and the morning's transaction at the bank. He had spoken as if they gave him more attention than he cared for, but obviously the subject was one that I could not even approach. When, searching for some new topic, I suddenly remembered the circumstances of our first meeting and their later developments, in which Gillum might probably be interested.

"I intended," said I, "to bring you a copy of *The Telegraph* which I kept for you. It contains a full report of the inquest on that poor fellow whose body I discovered. But perhaps you have seen it."

459

"I have," he replied. "I saw a pretty full account of it in an evening paper. Extraordinary affair. Rather horrible, too. I liked the way in which that doctor fellow let out. He knew his own mind."

"Yes, he was remarkably outspoken for a medical witness. But I certainly agreed with him, and so, I think, did the jury. If he hadn't been so downright, I suspect the verdict would have been suicide while temporarily insane."

"Very likely. But what was there to suggest insanity?"

"Nothing that I know of," I replied. "I was only repeating the usual formula. When a man commits suicide it is generally assumed that he was temporarily insane when he did it."

"I know," said Gillum. "But it is just a convention, and a silly convention which ought to be dropped. Really, it is a theological survival. The pretence of insanity is for the purpose of proving that the deceased was not aware of the nature of his act and that therefore he was not guilty of *felo de se* and did not die in a state of mortal sin. It was quite well meant, but it was always a false pretence, and now that we have outgrown theological crudities of that sort, the formula ought to be abolished, excepting in cases where there is actual evidence of insanity."

He spoke with an amount of feeling that rather surprised me, for it did not appear to me that the point was of any importance. Nor did I entirely agree with his view of the matter, and accordingly proceeded to contest it.

"I don't think that is quite the position, Gillum," I objected. "No doubt there is a theological factor, but the usual verdict is based on the assumption that the very act of suicide constitutes evidence of mental unsoundness, and I think it is quite a reasonable assumption."

"Why do you think so?" he demanded.

"Because," I replied, "the impulse of self-preservation – the preservation of one's own life – is so universal and so deep-seated as to amount to one of the fundamental instincts of intelligent living beings. But an act which is in opposition to a natural instinct is an abnormal act and affords evidence of an abnormal state of mind."

"I admit the instinct," he rejoined. "But man is a reasoning animal and is not completely dominated by his instincts. If in a particular case he is convinced that the following of those instincts is to his disadvantage, surely it will be reasonable for him to disregard them and adopt the action which he knows is to his advantage. Let us take an instance. Suppose a man to be suffering from a painful and incurable form of malignant disease. He knows that it is going to kill him within a measurable time. He knows that until death releases him he will suffer continual pain. Is he going to drag on a miserable existence, waiting for the inevitable death, or will he not, if he is a man, anticipate that death and cut short his sufferings?"

He had put his case with such cogency that I was rather at a loss. Nevertheless, I objected, somewhat weakly, "The instance you give is a very exceptional one. The conditions are quite abnormal."

"Exactly," he rejoined. "That is my point. The conditions being abnormal, the common rules of normal conduct do not apply. The conduct is adjusted to the conditions and consequently is rational, but that is true, I think, in a large proportion of suicides. If you consider them in detail with an open mind, you must come to the conclusion that the act is a reasonable response to the existing conditions."

"I doubt that," said I. "The case that you have cited I should be disposed to admit, but I can think of no other."

"The point is," said he, "whether the conduct is or is not adapted to the existing conditions. If it is, it is rational conduct, and a man is entitled to estimate those conditions for himself to decide whether they are or are not acceptable – whether, in those conditions, he would rather be alive or not. Whether, in short, life is or is not worth living. If he decides that it is not, then it is reasonable for him to bring it to an end."

"My point is," I rejoined, "that a normal man would always rather be alive than not."

"Then, Mortimer," said he, "I think you are mistaken. Let us take a concrete case. Suppose a man, like yourself, an employee of a bank, is tied down to a particular place. Suppose he has a quarrelsome wife who makes his life a misery and perhaps gets him into debt, and a family who are a constant trouble and disgrace to him. What is he to do? He can't escape because he is tied to his job. If he finds life intolerably unpleasant under these conditions, which he cannot alter, what could be more reasonable than for him to bring it to an end? Or again, take the case of a man who has inherited a fortune and has had a roaring good time enjoying all sorts of expensive pleasures. The natural result is that he steadily gets through his money. Now when he comes down to his last shilling what is the prospect before him? What is the natural thing for him to do?"

"The most reasonable thing," I replied, "would be to turn over a new leaf, to get a job, work hard at it, and live within his means."

Gillum shook his head. "No, Mortimer," said he. "That would not be possible to the type of man that I am describing. He couldn't do it, and he wouldn't try. If he was absolutely broke, he could try to live by sponging, by borrowing, by fraud, or by some other form of crime, but either method would bring him, sooner or later, to disaster, and almost certainly, in the end, to suicide. But I contend that the more reasonable

461

plan would be to anticipate and avoid all these troubles. When once his money was gone and the only kind of life that he cared for had become impossible, I say that the sane and sensible thing for him to do would be to recognise the facts and make his quietus – though not with a bare bodkin."

"But," I exclaimed, "do you mean to tell me seriously that is what you would do, as a considered act, in the circumstances that you mention?"

He laughed and shook a finger at me in mock reproof. "Now, Mortimer," said he, "you know that is quite an improper question. We are considering a hypothetical case, and in effect, a certain question of principle. But you immediately – and quite irrelevantly – turn it into a personal question. What I, personally, might do is beside the mark."

"I don't see that it is," I objected. "If you really mean what you say – I understand that if ever you should go stony-broke with no possible chance of recovery, you would proceed at once, as a matter of considered policy, to hang yourself or cut your throat."

"No, no, Mortimer," he protested, "I said nothing about hanging or throat-cutting. That would be temporary insanity with a vengeance. No, pray do me the justice of believing that, if the occasion arose, I should perform the coil-shuffling operation with decency, dignity, and the maximum of personal comfort. The rope and the carving knife are the wretched resources of the mere lunatic or moron. There is no excuse for such barbarities when, as we know, there are certain medicinal substances which are perfectly efficient for the purpose and which are not only painless, but rather agreeable in their operation."

To this I made no reply, for there had come on me a sudden dislike to the turn that the discussion had taken. He had spoken semi-facetiously, but yet there was an underlying seriousness that gave his words a rather gruesome quality. So I let the discussion drop and, after a short silence, directed our talk into a fresh channel.

After dinner, Gillum brewed a pot of excellent coffee, and we then adjourned to the easy chairs to smoke our pipes and talk, and as I listened to my host's comments and observations on the various topics that we discussed, I was surprised – having regard to the outrageous folly of his conduct – not only at the range of his knowledge and general information, but especially at the shrewdness and sanity of his outlook. Moreover, he was a man of some culture. I had already noticed his interest in the more serious forms of music and his lively appreciation of the fine grouping and skyline of the buildings of Fleet Street, and it now appeared that he shared my affection for the quaint nooks and corners and antique survivals of the older parts of London, and seemed to have a quite extensive acquaintance with them. Indeed, so pleasant and sympathetic was our gossip, and so agreeably did the time slip away, that I was quite taken aback when St. Dunstan's clock, reinforced by the more distant bells of St. Clement's, announced the hour of eleven and bade me set forth on my journey homewards.

"I will pilot you out as far as Fleet Street," said Gillum, as he helped me into my overcoat. "Next time you will know your way, and I hope the next will be quite soon."

"You have given me every inducement to repeat the offence," I replied. "It has been a jolly evening. Quite a red-letter day for me."

We sallied forth from the dark entry – but it was dark no longer now that the lamp was alight – and, crossing the courtyard, plunged into the tunnel which passes the Hall and, crossing the little courtyard, entered Clifford's Inn Passage. The main gate was shut and the night porter sat on a chair by the wicket, holding a newspaper and conversing with a spectacled gentleman who was formally arrayed in a frock coat and tall hat and supported himself on an umbrella.

"That is Mr. Weech," said Gillum, "the Inn porter. A queer old bird, quite a character in his way and a complete Victorian survival. I'll introduce you, as you like antiques."

As we approached, Mr. Weech opened the wicket for us and gave my companion "Good evening."

"Good evening, Mr. Weech," said Gillum. "Taking a last look round to see that we are all safe before you turn in?"

"That is so," replied Mr. Weech. "It is my custom to conclude the day's duty with a perambulation of the precincts to see that everything is in order."

"A very wise precaution," said Gillum. "It's of no use to have a locked gate if the doubtful characters are lurking inside. Let me introduce my friend, Mr. Mortimer, who has been spending the evening with me, so that you may know him in future as an accredited visitor. This is Mr. Weech, the custodian of the Inn and the faithful guardian of our security. As you see, he carries an umbrella as a symbol of his protective functions. Isn't that so, Mr. Weech? I notice that you are never without it."

Mr. Weech chuckled and glanced fondly at the symbol.

"I suppose I am not," he admitted. "When I put on my hat I take up the umbrella automatically. It has become a habit and I do it without thinking. *Consuetudo alterus naturum*, as the saying is."

"Well," said I, as I stepped through the wicket, "it is a wise habit in a fickle climate like ours. Good-night, Mr. Weech."

463

He raised his hat with an old-fashioned flourish as he returned my valediction, and Gillum and I walked slowly down the passage to Fleet Street.

"An odd fish is Mr. Weech," Gillum remarked. "Quite a good sort, but odd. I believe he takes that umbrella to bed with him. And he's a devil for Latin. I suspect he keeps a book of quotations and primes himself with them for conversation. Well, good night, Mortimer. Take care of yourself and come again soon."

As I made my way homewards to my lodgings, I turned over the events of the evening. It had been a pleasant experience and Gillum had been a most agreeable companion. Indeed, I had been rather surprised at the way in which he had improved on better acquaintance, and I was still puzzled by the contrast between his obvious intelligence and culture and the idiotic manner in which he was wasting his life and his substance. But as I recalled our conversation, there was one item that jarred on me badly. Gillum's defence of suicide may have been partly playful. Evidently, he rather inclined to the role of the Devil's Advocate and took a perverse pleasure in arguing and defending a paradox. But still, I had an unpleasant feeling that the views that he had expressed really represented his convictions. And what made the recollection of his argument especially disturbing to me was the fact that one of the cases that he had cited in illustration was alarmingly like what his own case might be. At present, it is true, his wild expenditure was balanced by his very ample income. He never overdrew, and as long as his income continued at its present rate, he would remain solvent and merely waste his possessions.

But suppose someday his source of income should dry up. Then he would soon be penniless and would quite possibly fall into debt. And if he did, the very conditions that he had postulated as justifying suicide would be brought into being. It was a profoundly disturbing thought, and though I tried to put it away, it recurred again and again, not only during my journey home, but at intervals in the days that followed.

Chapter VI
The Passing of John Gillum

Hitherto I have followed in rather close detail the circumstances of my association with John Gillum. This I have done advisedly, since the purpose of this narrative is to present as clear a picture as I am able of his personality and manner of life. But, having done this, I shall now pass more lightly over the events that occurred during the remainder of our association. That association, which extended over a period of about ten months, was fairly intimate and tended to become more so as the time ran on. Gillum was an entirely acceptable companion, cheerful, lively, humorous, and extremely well-informed. And, apparently, he liked my society, for he took every opportunity of cultivating it. The result was that we met as frequently as could be expected in the case of two rather self-contained men, each of whom had his own particular interests and occupations.

Sometimes he would call for me at the bank, but more commonly our rendezvous was Clifford's Inn, where we would take tea and then sally forth to spend the evening at a concert or a play or in a voyage of discovery into the lesser-known parts of the London in which we were both so much interested. Once, on an off day, I accompanied him to a race meeting, where he narrowly missed winning a considerable sum but actually – as I learned later – dropped about a hundred pounds. But this was the only occasion on which I came into contact with his gambling activities. He had, in his tactful, accommodating way, accepted the fact that betting and games of chance were outside the sphere of my interests and such evidence as came to me of his exploits at the tables or on the turf was in the nature of hearsay. But the books of the bank furnished direct evidence that, whatever those exploits may have been, the net result was displayed on the debit side of his account.

As the period of our friendship lengthened I began to be aware of a rather curious fact, which was that, intimate as we seemed to be, I really knew nothing about him. It was rather remarkable. In respect of his present mode of life and his daily doings he was – or, at least, appeared to be – open even to expansiveness. But of his past life or his antecedents, not a word was ever dropped. Gradually I came to realise that, under this appearance of free and frank confidence, lay a profound secretiveness. It was not a pleasing trait, and it occasioned a certain amount of reflection on my part. And when I came to consider it, I began to perceive that the secretiveness was not limited to the past, for, with all his expansiveness, he never made the slightest references to those periodical drafts on which I had looked – and still looked – with so much suspicion. In short, it began gradually to dawn on me that the confidences that he made with so much apparent openness were in fact limited to what I, in my capacity as his banker, already knew.

Of course, I asked no questions, but naturally, as I reflected on this secretive habit, amounting virtually to concealment, it aroused some curiosity. I am not in general an inquisitive person, but when I came to consider that this man, with whom I was on terms of daily intimacy, was an absolute stranger to me, that I knew nothing whatever of his past, of his relations, of the places where he had lived, of his profession or calling, if he had any, or of how he passed his time or whether he had any occupation other than gambling, it could not but appear very remarkable. And these reflections inevitably led to others. If his past life was never referred to, could there be any reason for this reticence? Was there anything in his past that made concealment necessary?

The question was not entirely without relevance. The periodical drafts, which had always seemed to me to suggest periodical payments, had raised a suspicion that he was being blackmailed and, as time went on, this suspicion tended to grow. But how should he come to be blackmailed? There is no smoke without fire. It is usually impossible to blackmail a man unless there is something in his life that he is unwilling to disclose. Could it be that his past was in some respects unpresentable? Or could it be that, even now, he was engaged in some activities that would not bear the light of day?

These questions presented themselves unsought and unwelcomed, for I liked the man and was unwilling to think ill of him or to harbour suspicions concerning him. Still, there were the facts, and I had to recognise them though the process of recognition cost me some mental discomfort. But presently I began to have anxieties of a different kind. I had always assumed that Gillum's income was derived from a permanent source. The large sums that he had paid in at approximately regular intervals had appeared to represent something in the nature of dividends or an annuity. But in the last month of my acquaintance with him this regularity had become suddenly disturbed. One or two large cheques – unusually large ones – had been paid in, but the balance created by them had begun immediately to melt away. I waited in expectation of the usual credit payment. But the time when it should have become due passed and no such payment was made, and Gillum's account began to show an uncomfortably small balance. It looked rather alarmingly like a failure of the source of supply.

466

Now, so long as his income was regular, his ridiculous expenditure merely kept him poor when he should have been rich. But with the failure of the supply and the continuance of the expenditure, a very different situation was created. As I scanned his account in our books and noted the growing tendency for the debit to overgrow the credit, I felt that – unless there were some change in the conditions – sooner or later, and probably sooner rather than later, some sort of crash was to be looked for and, knowing what his ideas were as to the way to meet a crash, I had already dimly envisaged the kind of disaster which actually occurred, and of which I shall now proceed to relate the circumstances.

It was in the early afternoon of a rather sultry day in July that a tall, sunburnt, athletic-looking man came to the bank and asked to see the manager, explaining that he had been sent by Mr. Penfield and that his business was connected with the affairs of our customer, Mr. John Gillum. On this I pricked up my ears, and when he had been ushered into the manager's room, I waited expectantly for the summons which seemed almost inevitable, having regard to my known intimacy with Gillum, and sure enough, in a few minutes, the bell rang and the clerk who went in to answer it returned to inform me that the manager wished to speak to me. Accordingly I went in and found the manager and the visitor seated on opposite sides of a small table.

"This," said the former, introducing me, "is Mr. Arthur Benson, a cousin of Mr. Gillum's, who has called to make some enquiries, and as you know Mr. Gillum personally as well as officially, you will probably be able to give him more information than I can. Mr. Mortimer is, I think I may say, a fairly intimate friend of your cousin's, Mr. Benson, and may be able to tell you what you want to know."

Mr. Benson shook hands heartily and proceeded at once with his enquiries.

"I am in rather a difficulty, Mr. Mortimer," said he, "and I may add, a little puzzled and worried by the way in which my cousin is behaving. But I had better begin by explaining the circumstances. I have just come from Australia, where I run a sheep farm in which my cousin, Gillum, is to some extent interested. I have been in regular correspondence with him about our affairs and have sent him cheques from time to time, which have been duly acknowledged. Now, as the business which has brought me to England arose quite unexpectedly, I wrote to him from Sydney telling him that I should be coming on by the next boat and asking him either to meet me at Tilbury, or to send a letter to the ship there telling me where and when I should find him. Well, he didn't meet me at Tilbury, but he sent a letter which was handed to me as soon as the ship brought up in the river. In this he asked me to come straight on to his chambers in Clifford's Inn.

"Accordingly, I did so, but when I called at his chambers, I could not get any answer to my knock. The place was all shut up, and though I hammered at the iron-bound door with my stick for some time, nothing happened. It was evident that he was not at home.

"This seemed a bit queer and not at all what I should have expected of him. However, I went off and got fixed up at an hotel, and then I came back to the Inn and made another attack on the door. But still there was no sign of life, so I gave it up for the time and went back to my hotel and spent the night there. Next day, I went to the Inn again and had another try. But still there was no result. The place was as still as the grave.

"It was really very extraordinary and I began to wonder whether there could be anything amiss. So I went on to Mr. Penfield, who acted for us in our business transactions, and asked him if he knew anything about Gillum's movements. But he knew nothing at all, not having seen my cousin for some months, but he recommended me to come along here and see whether you knew anything about him or could give me any advice. So here I am, and the question is, can you give me any sort of help or tell me where I may be likely to find him?"

The manager looked at me. "What do you say, Mortimer? You know Mr. Gillum's haunts pretty well, I think. Have you any idea where he is likely to be found?"

"Not the least," I replied. "I should have expected him to be at his chambers, especially as he had made an appointment with Mr. Benson. That is where he lives, and I had always supposed that he, at least, spent the night there."

"When did you see him last?" the manager asked.

"I haven't seen him for nearly a fortnight," I replied. "The last time that I saw him was when he came to the bank last Friday week to cash a cheque. I had a few words with him then but he did not say anything about his intended movements and, in fact, he could not have had any intention of going away as he had made this appointment with Mr. Benson."

The manager looked thoughtful and rather puzzled. "It really does seem a little odd," said he, "and I think we ought to try to help Mr. Benson as he is a stranger in London. What do you suggest, Mortimer?"

"I hardly know what what to suggest," I replied. "It is certainly an odd affair. Perhaps it might be worth while for me to run round with Mr. Benson to Clifford's Inn and try the door again, and if we still can't get any answer we might drop in at the lodge and see if we can get any information from Mr. Weech, the porter of the Inn. He might be able to tell us something."

"Yes," said the manager, "that seems about the best thing to do. At any rate, it is worth trying. So perhaps you will kindly take Mr. Benson in tow and see what you can do for him."

With this he stood up and shook hands with Benson, and the latter then accompanied me into the outer office, and when I had got my hat and stick we sallied forth together.

It is no great distance from Gracechurch Street to Clifford's Inn and we agreed to walk, Benson for the advantage of seeing the town and I for the opportunity to think things over and possibly get a little additional information. For, as I have hinted, I was more disturbed by the strange state of affairs than I had admitted either to the manager or to our visitor. I had not mentioned to them the amount of the cheque which had been cashed less than a fortnight ago, but it came to my mind now with a slightly ominous suggestiveness. The amount had been two-hundred pounds, which I had paid in one-pound notes, and that payment had not only cleared out the balance but had left the account a few pounds overrdrawn.

Reflecting on this, I ventured to make one or two discreet enquiries though avoiding direct questions.

"Your name is fairly familiar to me," I began as a cautious lead off.

"I suppose it is," he replied. "You must have had a good many of my cheques through your hands."

"Yes," said I. "They have come in at pretty regular intervals until just lately. But I don't think I have seen one for over three months. However, the last one was quite a big cheque, if I remember rightly."

"It was," said he, "eleven-hundred pounds. That was the final payment."

"Indeed!" said I, rather startled. "Then it was not a continuing transaction?"

"No," he replied. "The payments were instalments of purchase money. The sheep farm that I run originally belonged to Gillum. But he had a fancy to come to England and I was connected with a meat-exporting establishment, so he proposed that I should take over the farm and pay for it by instalments out of income while he should buy with the proceeds, or part of them, a partnership in a firm of meat importers in London. He thought that we could work things to our mutual advantage, and so did I. So I fixed up the deal with him and he came to England and arranged the partnership, and I paid off my debt as well as I could out of income. But after nearly two years I thought that it had gone on for long enough, so I raised a loan and paid off the final instalment in one sum."

469

"By the way," said I, "did it not occur to you to go 'round to his firm and ask if he had been there?"

"It did," he replied. "I went there before I went to Mr. Penfield. And then I got another surprise. It seemed that he didn't take to the meat-importing trade and about six months ago he sold his interest in the concern to the other partner and they have not seen anything of him since. It is curious that he should not have said anything about it to me in his letters."

"Very curious," I agreed. And it certainly was very remarkable. But it was not the oddity of his behaviour that principally impressed me. What instantly struck me with devastating force was the appalling fact that, at this moment, John Gillum must be absolutely penniless. Those big cheques had been paid into my knowledge and had produced a most impressive balance, but that balance had been dribbling away ever faster and faster as the "self" cheques were turned into cash to provide the means for his insane expenditure. And now, as I have said, he had not only drawn out the last penny of his balance but was actually in debt to the bank.

It was a terrible position, and when I reflected on it by the light of his expressed views on the appropriate way to meet a financial crash, the behaviour disclosed by Benson's experiences assumed an undeniably sinister aspect. I said nothing to my companion as to what was in my mind but, as we approached the neighbourhood of Clifford's Inn, my forebodings became so profound as to engender a very definite distaste for the errand on which I was bent.

We entered the Inn by the postern gate in Fetter Lane and, crossing the little quadrangle which I knew so well, made our way straight to the rather forbidding entry. As we plunged into the shadow which enclosed the staircase, I could hear the typewriters in the ground-floor office ticking away, conveying a sense of human life and activity which seemed to contrast almost uncannily with the silence and aloofness of the – presumably – empty room upstairs.

We groped our way up the dim staircase and came out on the rather sordid and ill-lighted landing where the empty dust-bin confirmed the suggestion of an absent tenant. But we did not stop to examine the landing. Walking up to the grim iron-bound door, above which the name of *Mr. J. Gillum* could be read on a painted label, now rather faded and dirt-stained, we listened for a few moments and then tapped on the massive oak panel. Perhaps the word "tapped" is inadequate, for Benson, who carried a stout stick of some hard and heavy wood, applied it in the manner of a battering-ram with such effect that the place resounded with the blows and I expected some protest from the office below.

"Well," said Benson, after banging away for a couple of minutes, "I think we may take it that there is no one at home. Shall we go round and hear what your porter man has got to tell us?"

"I think we had better," I replied, and forthwith led the way down the steep stairs, my state of mind by no means improved by the unpleasant fashion in which the noise of Benson's hammerings had echoed through the building. In fact, I found myself growing distinctly nervous and, as we made our way towards the passage in which the porter's lodge was situated, I began to consider what we had better do if we could get no more satisfactory tidings of the missing man. But I still had some hopes that the porter might be able to resolve the mystery, or at least give us a hint of some kind.

A hearty pull at the pendent handle outside the lodge door elicited a cheerful jangle from within, and in a few moments the door opened and Mr. Weech appeared, fully attired as usual in his long frock coat and tall silk hat. Whether he slept in that hat I cannot guess, but it seemed that he wore it constantly from the time when he arose in the morning until he retired at night. At least that was my impression, for I never saw him without it. He now regarded me benevolently through his spectacles and then cast an enquiring glance at my companion.

"We have called, Mr. Weech," said I, "to make one or two enquiries and see if you can help us. A rather unaccountable thing has happened. My friend, Mr. Gillum, seems to be absent from his chambers. We have hammered at his door and can't get any answer, and my friend here, Mr. Benson, tried yesterday and the day before, but he also could not make anybody hear."

Mr. Weech retired for a few moments, apparently to fetch an umbrella, for he reappeared with one in his hand, and thus fortified, he again inspected me, first through his spectacles and then over them and replied in a tone of mild protest, "But what about it, Mr. Mortimer? A gentleman is not bound to stay in his chambers if he doesn't want to. He isn't under any contract to be in residence excepting at his own convenience and by his own choice. Probably he has gone out of town for a few days. Gentlemen frequently do, and they are not under any obligation to give notice of their intentions. That is the advantage of living in chambers."

"Yes," I replied, "but that is not quite the position. Mr. Gillum had an appointment with Mr. Benson at his chambers and it was a rather special one, definitely made by letter. Mr. Gillum could hardly have gone away for a holiday and ignored this engagement."

Here I gave Mr. Weech a slight sketch of the circumstances to which he listened with interest and growing attention.

471

"M'yes," he agreed, when I had finished, "it does sound a little remarkable, the way you put it. Of course, he might have overlooked the matter, but that doesn't seem likely. Still, I certainly have not seen him about the Inn for the last day or two."

"When did you last see him?" Benson asked.

Mr. Weech considered for a few moments. "Now, let me see," said he. "I met him one evening just outside the Hall. He was coming down towards Fleet Street. Now, when would that be? I should say it would be about ten days ago." He reflected again and then confirmed his estimate with the definite statement: "Yes. Ten days ago it was. I can fix it by the fact that one of our tenants, who was a bit in arrears with his rent, came to the lodge to settle up. And very glad I was. The Court don't like rents to get behindhand."

"Very well, Mr. Weech," said I. "You haven't seen him for ten days. Now is that at all unusual?"

Mr. Weech, having duly considered the question, decided that it was slightly unusual. "You see," he explained, "I am pretty constantly up and down the Inn and I tend to run up against the resident tenants, particularly if they are fairly regular in their habits, as Mr. Gillum is. I should think I must have met him nearly every day since he came here. And he is a rather sociable man and likes to stop for a bit of a chat."

"Then," said I, "that seems to confirm our idea that there is something unusual about this affair. I suppose you don't happen to have a duplicate key of his chambers?"

Mr. Weech seemed to stiffen at my suggestion. "We don't usually keep duplicate keys of gentlemen's chambers," he replied. "The agreements stipulate that the tenants shall have full use and enjoyment of their premises, which would not be the case if we reserved either the right or the means of entry. But, as a matter of fact, I have a duplicate key of Mr. Gillum's chambers. I offered it to him, but he said that he had no use for a second key, and he thought that it might be as well for me to keep it in case he might lose his or in the event of some emergency arising. But why do you ask?"

"Well," I said a little diffidently, "it occurred to me that it might be as well, if you had a key, just to look in and see that all is as it should be."

Mr. Weech shook his head decidedly. "No, sir," said he, "I have no right to enter the chambers of any of our tenants without his express permission and authority."

I realised Mr. Weech's point of view and fully agreed as to its propriety. But, having ascertained that a key was available, I made up my mind quite definitely that those chambers had got to be entered.

472

"That is true enough in ordinary circumstances," said I. "But the circumstances are not ordinary. You must see that something unusual has happened, and I may say that Mr. Benson and I are extremely uneasy. Supposing Mr. Gillum should have been taken ill or had some sort of accident."

Mr. Weech was visibly impressed, though he made no reply, and I proceeded to press my advantage.

"What would people say if it should become known that he had been left in his chambers without help simply because of a mere scruple of official etiquette?"

"Yes," Mr. Weech admitted, "there is something in that. It would be very awkward for him, shut up there, *solus cum soli*, if he was seriously ill. But we don't know that he is."

"We don't," I agreed, "but we can easily find out. Come, now, Mr. Weech, don't stand on mere pedantic ceremony. Do the reasonable thing. Mr. Gillum may be, at this moment, lying in there, helpless, waiting for someone to succour him. We ought to go and see whether he is or not. And I am not suggesting anything irregular. Mr. Benson is his cousin and I am a responsible friend. I am only asking you to do what he would have expected you to do. You say that he left the key in your custody in case any emergency should arise. Well, an emergency has arisen, and you have got the key."

"I should hardly call it an emergency," Mr. Weech objected, "but still I don't want to be obstinate. You have shown cause why a visit of inspection might reasonably be made and, if you and Mr. Benson will take the responsibility, I will get the key and go 'round with you to the chambers. Then you will be able to see for yourselves whether there is or is not any foundation for your anxieties."

With this he went back into the lodge and presently returned carrying on his finger a couple of keys on a string loop to which was attached a wooden label.

Together we passed up the outer passage, across the small courtyard, through the covered way (not to call it a tunnel) on which the door of the Hall opened and, crossing the inner courtyard, approached Gillum's entry. Our previous visit with its very audible accompaniments had evidently not passed unnoticed, for, as we walked into the entry, the door of the typewriting office opened slightly and a face appertaining to an elderly woman appeared, surveying us with an interest that was not entirely benevolent.

On arriving at the landing, Mr. Weech transferred his umbrella from his right hand to the left, the better to manipulate the keys, the larger of which he inserted into the lock. It was not a very good fit but, after a few

473

tentative turns, he succeeded in shooting back the bolt, having done which, he drew the door outwards a couple of inches and sniffed audibly. Taking the key out of the door, he drew the latter wide open and was preparing to insert the key into the lock of the inner door when he observed that the latter was slightly ajar, whereupon he pushed it open and stepped into the room.

But he took only one two steps, and then, as he passed the open door, he stopped short, and ejaculating, "God save us!" hastily backed out. And, at the same moment, I became aware of a strange, musty, cadaverous odour.

With all my forebodings intensified and a feeling of extreme distaste, I nevertheless ventured to step in at the open door to see what it was that had given such a shock to Mr. Weech. But my stay was little longer than his, though in that instant my eyes took in a tableau that rises vividly before me as I write. As I cleared the edge of the door, I came into view of a couch drawn up by the window, whereon reclined a pyjama-clad figure whose aspect confirmed the worst of my fears.

It was a horrible spectacle, that motionless figure – half-strange and half-familiar, with its discoloured face and the open mouth from which the two gold teeth seemed to stare out as they gleamed in the bright afternoon sunlight. I stood, as I have said, gazing at it for but a few seconds and then, sick with the horror of the sight and the the effluvium that filled the room, I hurried out an joined Mr. Weech, who stood at the head of the stairs holding a handkerchief to his nose.

As I came out, Benson looked at me, but he asked no question. I suppose he guessed what we had seen, but his nerves were evidently stronger than ours for he strode into the room without hesitation and, pushing the door right back, opened the view into the room so far that I could see him stooping over that dreadful figure, regardless of the foul atmosphere and the obscene flies that buzzed around, He made a long and critical examination of the corpse and then turned to a small table that was placed beside the couch. This, I now noticed, bore a decanter, apparently containing whisky, a siphon, a tumbler, and a small corked bottle, and each of these objects Benson scrutinised minutely.

At length he came out, shutting the inner door after him, and looking very grim and solemn. Evidently he was deeply moved but, though he was a shade pale, he was quite calm and self-possessed, in striking contrast to Weech and me, whose nerves were quite unstrung by the horrid experience. He closed the outer door and, taking the key out of the lock, silently handed it to Mr. Weech.

"Well," he said, "what is to be done now?"

"I suppose," said Weech, "I had better communicate with the police. They have a telephone in the office below, and I dare say they will let me use it."

"Yes," Benson agreed, "that will be the best thing to do, and you had better ask the police how soon they can send someone up. We shall have to wait here and see them, as they will want some particulars and we may as well get the business over at once."

We went down to the ground floor and once more were the objects of interested scrutiny from the half-opened door. Then Mr. Weech made his request and was admitted forthwith while Benson and I went out into the quadrangle to wait for him. Presently he came out and joined us, with the information that an officer was being sent up and would be at the Inn in the course of a few minutes. Then he invited us to come to the lodge to await the officer's arrival, an offer which Benson promptly declined, explaining that he wanted to talk things over with me before the officer should arrive. Accordingly, Mr. Weech excused himself and went off in the direction of the lodge, and Benson and I turned into the quiet alley between a row of ancient houses and the garden railings.

"This is a very astounding affair, Mortimer," said Benson, when Mr. Weech was out of earshot. "Doesn't it seem so to you?"

I hesitated for a moment, but as there was no reason for secrecy, and as I should certainly have to make a statement to the police, or at the inquest, I replied, "It is a very dreadful business, but I can't say that I am so greatly surprised."

"Aren't you?" he exclaimed. "Now, I should have said that Jack Gillum was the very last person I should have expected to take his life. Why do you say that you are not surprised?"

"Well," I replied, "I have known a good deal about his way of living and the muddle that he has got his affairs into and, of course, I have certain special knowledge which it would not be permissible for me to refer to."

"If you mean knowledge that you have obtained in your capacity as an employee of his bank," said Benson, "there is nothing in it. He was your customer and you had to keep his affairs secret. But now that he is dead, his executor is your customer."

"He made a will, then?" said I, somewhat surprised.

"Yes, by special arrangement. Mr. Penfield is his executor and I am the sole beneficiary under the will. So I am, in effect, your customer and am entitled to know how his affairs stand."

I was not at all satisfied that this view was technically correct. But, as it was certain that poor Gillum's affairs would have to be more or less completely disclosed at the inquest, I felt it to be unreasonable to withhold the information from one who was so clearly entitled to know all the facts. Accordingly I replied, "I am not sure that you are right, but I am prepared to waive the strict letter of the law if you will promise to regard as absolutely confidential anything that I may tell you about Gillum's financial position."

"Certainly I will," said he. "But surely his financial position was perfectly satisfactory?"

"On the contrary," said I, "it was profoundly unsatisfactory. In fact, I don't think I am exaggerating if I say that he was absolutely penniless."

Benson stopped and gazed at me with a frown of astonishment. "Penniless!" he exclaimed. "But he should have been a rich man, comparatively speaking. When he came to England, he had his very substantial savings, which I know he sent to Mr. Penfield to be deposited in a bank – your bank, I suppose."

"Yes," said I. "Mr. Penfield opened the account in Gillum's name with a deposit of three-thousand pounds."

"Very well. Then he had payments from me from time to time, including the eleven-hundred pounds that I sent him a little over three months ago. And he must have got something from the business, to say nothing of the purchase price of his partnership, whatever that may have been. But, of course, you know all about that."

"Yes," said I. "All those big cheques have been paid in, and the amounts have gone out nearly as fast as they have come in, and the position now is that there is not only no balance, but the account is a pound or two overdrawn."

Benson continued to stare at me with the utmost amazement. "But," he exclaimed, "where the devil has the money gone? Do you suppose he has been playing the fool on the Stock Exchange?"

"I don't," I replied. "I know where the bulk of the money has gone. It has been frittered away in gambling, some of it on the turf and a good deal on cards and roulette and various other fooleries. I have sometimes suspected that there might be a blackmailer in the background, but I have no knowledge to that effect. I only know that the bulk of the money was drawn out in cash and that he usually asked to have his 'self' cheques cashed in notes of small denomination – preferably in Treasury notes. It looked as if he wanted to secure himself against the possibility of the notes being traced."

Benson reflected on this statement in silence for a few moments, still looking at me with an expression of angry incredulity. At length he rejoined, "We shall have to go into this in more detail later on. Obviously, as you are in possession of the actual facts, what you tell me must be true. But yet I find it beyond belief. The whole affair, including this suicide – for that is evidently what it is – is so utterly opposed to all that I know of Jack Gillum – and I have known him since he was a boy – that I can make nothing of it."

"Then," I suggested, "he was not always a gambler?"

"No," Benson replied, though without much emphasis. "No, I wouldn't call him a gambler. He liked a game of cards, and he liked to play rather higher than I cared about, and he had a way of betting in a small way and making wagers. But his play was never on a great scale, and his ordinary management of his financial affairs was perfectly reasonable. The amount that he had saved speaks for itself, and you can be sure that I should not have been willing to enter into the arrangements that existed between us if he had been a spendthrift and a wild gambler."

Benson's account of his cousin did not very greatly surprise me. It had been obvious to me that his habits could not always have been such as those that were known to me, or he would never have had any money at all. The gambling habit must have grown on him by frequent indulgence. So it appeared to me, and I answered to that effect.

"My acquaintance with your cousin," said I, "extends only to a short time, only about a year, or rather less. And when I first met him these new habits were already formed, so I never knew him otherwise. But even so, it has been a matter of surprise to me that a man, in other respects so sensible and capable, should have behaved in this idiotic manner. But what you have just told me makes it even more surprising. We can only suppose that the new surroundings, when he came to live in London, must have exerted some peculiar influence over him. And it may be that he fell into the society of people who had a bad effect on him. I happen to know that he was acquainted with some pretty shady characters, though how he came to know them I have no idea."

"There may be something in what you say," said Benson. "In fact, there must be. But the gambling alone doesn't seem to be a satisfactory explanation. I am inclined to suspect that you are right in your suggestion of a possible blackmailer. The way in which the money was drawn out in untraceable notes seems to support that view very strongly. There is no reason why a simple, straightforward gambler should take precautions against having his payments traced. However, we shall have to adjourn this discussion. That gentleman looks like the police officer."

As he spoke, Mr. Weech appeared emerging from the covered way in company with a tall, brisk-looking man in civilian clothes who carried a largish attaché case. The two men approached us and Mr. Weech effected a concise introduction.

"There is no need for you two gentlemen to come up with me," said the officer. "In fact it would be better for me to go alone so that I can make my observations undisturbed. But I will ask you to be good enough to wait here until I have seen what there is to see. I shall want to take a few particulars for the purposes of the inquest."

With this he departed under Mr. Weech's guidance in the direction of Gillum's entry, the approach of the pair closely observed from the window of the typewriting office. When they had gone, I rather expected Benson to resume our conversation. But apparently what had been said already gave him sufficient food for thought, for he paced up and down the alley at my side uttering no word and evidently deep in his own reflections, which, to judge by his stern, gloomy expression, were of a highly disagreeable kind.

The officer's observations took rather longer than I had expected. At each turn of our walk when we came to the end of the alley and in view of Gillum's chambers, I could see Mr. Weech at the open landing window, gazing out discontentedly across the quadrangle, and at the office window below watchful heads appeared from time to time over the wire blind. But the officer remained hidden from our sight.

At length, at about the twentieth turn, as we came to the corner of the alley, I observed that Mr. Weech had disappeared from his post at the window, and a moment later he came into view in the obscurity of the staircase and then emerged into the open, followed closely by the officer, whereupon Benson and I walked forward to meet them.

"Well, gentlemen," said the officer, "it seems quite a straightforward case from my point of view, but I may as well have a few particulars for the guidance of the coroner's officer in preparing the details of the inquest. I will begin by taking your names and addresses and your relations with the deceased."

He looked from one of us to the other, and Benson, as an actual relative, opened the proceedings by giving his name and address and stating his relationship.

"Ah!" said the officer, "you are the deceased's cousin. Then you will be the proper person to identify the body. Not that it is of any importance as there is no question as to who he is. But you have seen the body. Can you identify it positively?"

"Yes," replied Benson. "It is the body of my cousin, John Gillum."

"Exactly," said the officer. "Now, is there anything that you can tell us that would throw any light on the suicide – assuming it to be a suicide?"

"No," replied Benson. "I can't account for it at all. But I haven't seen the deceased for about two years, so I haven't any very recent information about him. This gentleman, Mr. Mortimer, knows a good deal more about his affairs than I do."

478

Thereupon the officer turned to me and asked me to give him any information that might guide him as to the kind of evidence that would be required at the inquest and the names of any witnesses who might have to be called. Accordingly I told him who I was, but pointed out that, as an employee of the deceased's bank, I was not at liberty to give any information as to his financial affairs.

"No," he agreed, "not in the ordinary way. But the customer's death releases the bank from its obligations of secrecy. However, I won't press you. Any information that the bank may be able to supply will have to be given at the inquest if it is relevant. Should you say that it would be relevant? I mean in relation to the motive for the suicide – assuming it to be a suicide?"

"Yes," I replied, "I think I may say that much. But perhaps you had better see the manager. He knows the ropes better than I do."

"Or Mr. Penfield," Benson suggested. "He is Gillum's executor and was his man of business and as he is a lawyer he will know exactly what information he ought to give."

The officer agreed to this and took down the addresses of the manager and Mr. Penfield. "And that," said he, "is all for the present. Now I must see about getting the body removed to the mortuary. I had better keep the keys until the inquest is over, as we don't want the rooms disturbed, and there may be some letters or papers which ought to be examined either by me or by Mr. Penfield. I will hear what he has to say about that. So I will wish you gentlemen good afternoon."

With this he bustled away, and Benson and Weech and I walked down to the lodge where, declining an invitation to go in and rest a few minutes, Benson and I left the porter and made our way out into Fleet Street. My companion was still silent and gloomy, uttering scarcely a word as we walked down towards Ludgate Circus. Only just before we parted at the corner did he make any observation on the tragedy.

Then, in a tone of almost passionate grief, he exclaimed, "It is a miserable business, and what makes it more awful to me is the feeling that I have been, in a manner, the cause of the disaster. It looks very much as if poor Gillum had funked meeting me."

I could not but admit that the same idea had occurred to me. It would certainly have been a very awkward meeting, involving some exceedingly uncomfortable explanations.

"But he needn't have funked it," said Benson. "Of course, I should have been pretty sick. But I shouldn't have reproached him and I should not have let him down. He could have come back with me and helped me to run the farm and got back to his natural way of life. However, it is no use thinking now of what might have been. Good-bye, Mortimer. You know where to find me if you should want me."

He shook my hand heartily and turned away down Farringdon Street and, as it was now too late to go back to the bank, I made my way towards my own place of abode.

Chapter VII
The Coroner's Inquest

If the facts which were disclosed by the evidence of witnesses at the inquest on the body of John Gillum were mostly new to me, only to the extent that they were facts, for most of them had already existed in my mind in the form of suspicions. Nevertheless, the grim proceedings had for me the melancholy interest that now, when all the contributory circumstances of the final catastrophe were assembled, I was able to realise the enormity of that catastrophe. It was really beyond belief. That a man who had seemed to have been the especial favourite of fortune should have mismanaged his affairs so unutterably as to bring himself to actual destitution and to a pauper suicide's grave, appeared, and was, an incredible instance of human folly and perversity. But I need not moralise on the tragedy, the facts deposed to in evidence tell their own tale.

The first witness was Mr. Weech, who gave a slightly verbose but very impressive description of the discovery. When he had finished and in answer to a question, had stated the date on which he had last seen the deceased alive, he was dismissed and his place taken by Arthur Benson.

"You were present with Mr. Weech when the body was discovered," said the coroner. "Were you able to identify the body?"

"Yes," was the reply, "it was the body of my cousin, John Gillum."

"The identity of the body is not in question," said the coroner, "but may we take it that you are certain that it was the body of your cousin?"

"I am quite certain," replied Benson. "The circumstances were so remarkable that I had at first some doubt whether it could really be John Gillum, so I examined it closely and carefully. There is no doubt whatever that it was John Gillum's body."

"Naturally," said the coroner, "you were greatly shocked at what had happened, but were you surprised?

"I was astounded," replied Benson. "John Gillum was the last man in the world whom I should have expected to have committed suicide. But I had not seen him for nearly two years, when he was leaving Australia to come to England. Up to that time he had been working on a sheep farm, and had seemed to be a happy, capable, well-balanced man. But I learn that since he came to this country his habits and even his character seem to have undergone a radical change. Of that, of course, I know nothing."

Here the coroner put one or two questions concerning Gillum's antecedents, to which Benson answered in much the same terms as those in which he had replied to mine, as recorded in the last chapter. And these details of Gillum's pecuniary position formed the remainder of his evidence.

The next witness was Detective-Sergeant Edmund Waters, who stepped up to the place appointed for witnesses and gave his evidence with professional readiness and precision.

"On Wednesday the eighteenth of July, I was informed that a telephone message had been received reporting the finding of the dead body of a man in a room at 64 Clifford's Inn. I proceeded there forthwith, going first to the porter's lodge where I met Mr. Weech, who had sent the message, Mr. Benson, and Mr. Mortimer. Mr. Weech conducted me to the room, which was in a set of chambers on the first floor, and unlocked the door to admit me.

"On entering the room, I saw the dead body of a man lying on a couch close to a window. From the appearance of the body and a very foul odour which pervaded the air of the room, I judged that the man had been dead several days. I inspected the body without disturbing it, but could see no injuries or any sign of violence or any indication of a struggle. The man was lying on the couch in an easy posture, as if he had fallen asleep there and nothing in the room appeared to be disturbed. By the side of the couch was a small table on which was a decanter containing whisky, a siphon of soda-water, a tumbler, and a small bottle labelled '*Tablets of morphine hydrochloride, gr. 1/2*' and containing a number of white tablets. The description on the label was written with a pen in block capital letters.

"I took possession of the bottle and then I examined the tumbler. There were quite a large number of finger-prints on it and most of them were perfectly distinct. There were also finger-prints on the bottle, but these were not so distinct and I had to develop some of them up, especially those on the label, before I could be sure of the pattern. As I had my finger-print apparatus with me, I proceeded very carefully to take a set of the finger-prints of the body to compare with those on the tumbler and the bottle. When I made the comparison, it became perfectly clear that all the prints on both vessels were made by the deceased. Those on the tumbler were prints of the fingers of the deceased's right hand and those on the bottle were principally prints of the left hand with one or two of the right."

"You are sure," said the coroner, "that there were no other finger-prints?"

"Quite sure," replied the sergeant. "The prints were all recognizable, and I compared each one separately with the prints that I had taken from the body."

"That is very important," said the coroner, "and it seems quite conclusive. Did you make any examination of the room?"

"Not a minute examination. I just looked round to see if there were any signs of anything unusual, but there were not. Everything looked perfectly normal."

"Have you made any further investigation since then?"

"Yes. I went to the chambers with Mr. Bateman, who was acting for the executors, to see if there were any papers or documents that might throw any light on the affair. We found the keys in the pockets of the deceased's clothes and with them we opened the drawers of the writing-table. In one of the drawers we found several letters in their envelopes tied up in a bundle. We read these letters and we both formed the opinion that they were blackmailer's letters. Mr. Bateman took possession of them, and I believe he has them still."

"Then," said the coroner, "as Mr. Bateman is here and will be giving evidence, we need not go into the question of the letters now. Is there anything else that you have to tell us?"

"No," replied the sergeant, "excepting that I notified the coroner – yourself – that I had the bottle of tablets and, in accordance with instructions, handed it to Dr. Sidney."

"Then," said the coroner, "we need not trouble you further unless any member of the jury wishes to ask any questions. No questions? Then we had better next take the medical evidence."

Accordingly, the medical witness, Dr. Thomas Winsford, was called and, having given his name and qualifications, deposed, in answer to the coroner's question, "I have made a careful examination of the body of the deceased. It is that of a man about forty years of age, well-developed and muscular and free from any signs of disease. I examined it in relation to the questions of the date of death and its cause. With regard to the first, there was a slight difficulty owing to the condition of the body, which was definitely in a state of incipient putrefaction. But, taking into account the temperature of the room in which it had been lying, I should say that the deceased had been dead from six to eight days."

"You speak of the heat of the room. Had you any personal knowledge of the conditions in that room?"

"Yes. I obtained the key of the chambers from Sergeant Waters and went there in the afternoon. The sun was shining in at the window and the room was very hot. I took the temperature with a thermometer and found it to be eighty-one degrees Fahrenheit. That would account for the rather advanced state of putrefaction in the time that I have mentioned, and I am inclined to the opinion that the deceased had not been dead more than six or seven days."

"Yes," the coroner remarked, "that seems to agree with what Mr. Weech has told us. He saw the deceased alive ten days before the discovery of the body. And what do you say as to the cause of death?"

"From the inspection of the body, it was difficult to assign any cause of death. There were no injuries or external marks of any kind or any abnormal appearances whatever. But I had been informed of the finding of the bottle of morphine tablets and I examined the body for signs of morphine poisoning."

"And did you find any such traces?"

"Morphine does not ordinarily leave very pronounced traces, and the condition of the body was not favourable for discovering the more minute signs. But I found a somewhat contracted state of the pupils, and this, with the absence of any other signs indicating death from any other cause, confirmed the suggestion that death was due to poisoning with morphine. But I can only say that all the appearances were consistent with morphine poisoning, and that I could not discover any other cause of death."

"Did you take any measure, to settle this question?"

"Yes. I removed from the body certain of the internal organs and put them in chemically clean jars which I closed and sealed and affixed to each a label on which I wrote the particulars and the date, and signed my name. These jars, in accordance with instructions, I handed personally to Dr. Walter Sidney for analysis."

This concluded the doctor's evidence. He was followed by Dr. Walter Sidney, who deposed that he was a pathologist and an analytical chemist, and that he had received from the preceding witness certain jars containing various organs from a human body which he was informed had been removed from the body of the deceased. He had also received from Sergeant Waters a bottle containing a number of white tablets and labelled with a written label: *Tablets of morphine hydrochloride, gr. 1/2*". He had analysed four of the tablets and found that they were composed of morphine hydrochloride and that each tablet contained half-a-grain of the drug. He had also made a chemical examination of the organs from the jars and had obtained from them a little over two-and-a-quarter grains of morphine. He estimated the amount of morphine present in the whole body at, at least, four grains, but probably more.

"What do you consider a poisonous dose of morphine?" the coroner asked.

"It varies considerably in different persons," the witness replied. "Half-a-grain has been known to cause death, but that is very unusual. One grain would be very likely to cause death in a person who was not accustomed to the drug, and two grains would ordinarily be a lethal dose."

"Then four grains is definitely a lethal dose?"

"Yes. It would almost certainly cause death in a person who was not in the habit of taking the drug."

"Did your examination enable you to form any opinion as to whether the deceased had been in the habit of taking morphine?"

"I should not like to give a very definite opinion. All the organs, including the liver, were quite healthy, which would hardly have been the case if the deceased had been in the habit of dosing himself with morphine. I can only say that I found no signs that suggested the habitual taking of the drug. And Dr. Winsford's evidence, in which he stated that the deceased appeared to be a strong, healthy man, is quite inconsistent with the idea that the deceased was a morphine addict."

"As a result of your examination, can you make any suggestion as to the cause of death?"

"Inasmuch as a lethal dose of morphine was found in the body, and as no other cause of death was discoverable, I should say that there is no doubt that the deceased died from poisoning by morphine."

"Thank you," said the coroner. "That is what we want to know, and I think that, if you have nothing more to tell us, we need not detain you any longer."

He glanced enquiringly at the jury and, as neither the jury nor the witness volunteered any remark, the latter withdrew to his seat.

The next witness was Mr. Alfred Bateman, a gentle man of typically legal aspect whose acquaintance I had already made. Having been sworn, he deposed that he was the managing clerk of Mr. Penfield, a solicitor and executor of the will of the deceased, for whom he also acted as man of business.

"Are you in possession of any facts that explain, or have any bearing on, the death of the deceased?" the coroner asked.

"I am in possession of certain facts which seem to me to be relevant to the subject of this inquiry," the witness replied. "In the first place, the deceased had, in less than two years, got through a fortune, and was, at the time of his death, so far as I can ascertain, absolutely penniless and in debt. In the second place, he was, at the time of his death, being harassed by blackmailers."

"Yes," said the coroner, "those facts certainly seem to be relevant to the subject of this inquiry. Perhaps you might give us a few particulars without going into unnecessary detail."

"As to the financial question," said Bateman, "the facts, in outline, are these: Nearly two years ago – on the sixteenth of April, 1928, to be exact – the deceased wrote to Mr. Penfield stating that he was coming to England to live, and remitting a sum of three-thousand pounds which he asked Mr. Penfield to deposit in a suitable bank in his, the deceased's, name, five-hundred to be placed to the current account and the remainder on deposit. I dealt with this matter myself, under Mr. Penfield's instructions, and placed the money in Perkins's Bank. Three months after the receipt of this letter, that is, on the eighteenth of September, the deceased called at our office to announce his arrival. There were certain business transactions connected with the purchase of a partnership which I think I need not describe in detail as they seem to have no bearing on recent events. When these were concluded, and the deceased had deposited his will with Mr. Penfield, I accompanied him to the bank and introduced him to the manager. Thereafter our contact with him practically ceased. He came to the office once or twice afterwards, and then, as we had finished with his affairs and he had kept the partnership deed in his own possession, we lost sight of him and, excepting that his address in Clifford's Inn was known to us – he having given Mr. Penfield as a reference when he applied for the chambers – we knew nothing of what he was doing or how he lived.

"He next came into view, so to speak, when his cousin, Mr. Benson, called at our office to ask if we could give him any information as to where he could find the deceased. That was on the seventeenth of this month. As we knew nothing, we referred him to the deceased's bank and, as he has deposed, he went there. On the evening of the eighteenth, Mr. Benson called at the office and informed me – as Mr. Penfield had already left – of the discovery of the body in the chambers. He also informed me that the keys of the chambers were in the possession of Sergeant Waters. Thereupon, as I knew that Mr. Penfield was the executor of the deceased's will, I thought it best to see the sergeant without delay and accordingly went forthwith to the police station where I was fortunate enough to find the sergeant. He suggested that we had better go to the chambers and see if there were any letters or papers which might throw any light on the motives for the assumed suicide.

"I agreed that it was desirable and we accordingly went together to the chambers and made the search. In a drawer in the writing-table we found a considerable number of letters and other documents, all neatly tied into bundles and docketed. There was one bundle tied with red tape

486

and labelled '*Horse-leech*', and this we examined first. It consisted of eleven letters, each enclosed in its envelope. They were all in a similar, and apparently disguised, handwriting. None of them bore any signature or contained any reference to any person by name, and none of them was dated, though the date could be inferred from the postmark on the envelope.

"On reading them, we came to the conclusion that they were undoubtedly from a blackmailer. Ten of them were quite short and were simply reminders that a payment was due. The other one, which appeared to be the first of the series, plainly demanded money with menaces. I produce the letters for your inspection."

Here the witness drew from his pocket a bundle of letters tied together with red tape and laid them on the table before the coroner.

"I think," said the latter, "that it would be better for you to read them to us, or, at least, the first letter and one of the others. The jury can inspect them afterwards if they wish to."

Accordingly, Mr. Bateman untied the bundle and, taking the two outside letters, opened one of them and read its contents aloud:

> *With reference to our little friendly talk last night, as you did not seem able to make up your mind, I will see if I can help you. To put the matter in a nutshell, I want £500 from you as a first instalment. The others we can arrange later, but I must have this at once, and I warn you that I am not going to stand any nonsense. If this is not handed over by Sunday night at the latest, the consequences which I mentioned to you will follow without further notice.*
>
> *The money is to be paid in pound notes (not new ones) and the parcel is to be handed personally either to me or to the party whom you know and whose name I mentioned to you.*
>
> *This is the final offer and I advise you to take it. You will be sorry if you don't.*

"I agree with you," said the coroner, "as to the character of that letter. It is a typical blackmailer's letter. What is the date on the envelope?"

"The postmark is dated the sixteenth of September, 1929. Shall I read the last letter?"

"If you please," the coroner replied, whereupon the witness drew the other letter from its envelope and, glancing at the latter, said, "This is dated by the post-mark the fourth of this present month of July and the contents are as follows:

In case you should forget to look at your calendar, as you did last time, I am sending you this little reminder. And don't forget that the notes must be old ones which have seen some service. There were several brand new notes in the last instalment which had to be kept for use on the turf. Don't let that happen again.

As he finished reading, Bateman laid the two letters on the table and the coroner, after glancing through them, passed them to the foreman of the jury.

"Beyond these blackmailing letters," said he, addressing the witness, "did you find anything that might throw light on what has happened?"

"Not in the way of letters," Bateman replied. "All the others were just normal business correspondence and letters from his cousin, Mr. Benson, sent from Australia. But we found also in that drawer the pass-book from the deceased's bank, and the entries in that were very significant. We began by looking up the entries corresponding to the dates of the blackmailing letters and, from what we could see, it appeared that the deceased had been paying out £500 every quarter, excepting the last. On the date corresponding to the last letter the amount drawn out was only £200. But when we looked through the entries other than those corresponding to the dates of the blackmailing letters, it was clear that a large number of sums of money had been drawn out in the form of cash, for what purpose we were, of course, unable to guess."

"You found no evidence of any other blackmailers?" the coroner asked.

"No evidence," Bateman replied, "but it looked highly suspicious. The 'self' cheques appeared at very frequent intervals and some of them were for considerable amounts. However, we could not make very much of the pass-book but, from what we could see, it looked as if the deceased had spent his money as fast as he received it, and the cheques that were entered to his credit were for quite large amounts.

"But it was on the following day, the nineteenth, that I learned the full enormity of the affair. On that day I accompanied Mr. Penfield to the bank, where we had an interview with the manager. He presented us with a statement of his transactions with the deceased and showed us how the account stood. I need not trouble you with details, but the position amounted to this: That the deceased had drawn out every penny that he

488

possessed and was actually in debt to the bank, though to only a small amount."

"You say that the deceased had received considerable sums of money. We don't want details but, roughly speaking, about how much had he spent and how long had he been in spending it?"

"The total amount that he had held to his credit, including the original deposit, was just over £13,000. And he had got through the whole of this between the end of September, 1928, and the middle of this present month, a period of one year and ten months."

"Did you learn at the bank whether he appeared to have been operating on the Stock Exchange?"

"I think we may definitely infer that he had not. Settlements on the Stock Exchange are made by cheque, and there were no records of any cheques payable to stockbrokers. The comparatively few cheques that appeared in the ledger were mostly small in amount and appeared to have been payable to tradesmen or other persons concerned with the ordinary, normal expenditure. What had exhausted the account was the large number of cheques payable to himself in cash."

"Well," said the coroner, addressing the jury, "there is no object in our enquiring further into the details of this astonishing instance of reckless prodigality. We have the material fact that in less than two years this unfortunate man flung away what most of us would have regarded as a fortune. We also know that, at the time of his death, he was penniless and in debt, and that he was the victim of a particularly rapacious set of blackmailers. I think Mr. Bateman has given us some most illuminating information and that we might now thank him for the clear and lucid way in which he has given his evidence and not detain him any longer. Unless any member of the jury wishes for any further information."

One member of the jury, apparently thrilled by the vast sums that had been mentioned, would have sought further details, but was politely suppressed by the coroner, whereupon Bateman was released and retired to his seat. There was a short interval during which the coroner glanced through the depositions, and then, as I had expected, my name was called.

"You have heard Mr. Bateman's evidence," said the coroner, when the preliminaries had been disposed of. "As a member of the staff of the bank, you will probably consider yourself prohibited from giving any particulars of the deceased's financial affairs. But can you tell us if you endorse what the last witness has stated?

"I endorse it completely," I replied. "I was present with the manager when the particulars were given to him. And I may say that I am fully authorised by the executor – in whom the account is now vested – and the manager, to give any information that may be required as to our late customer's dealings with the bank."

"Then," said the coroner, "as you, in your capacity of cashier, knew exactly what monies the deceased received and what he drew out, and in what form, perhaps you can tell us what opinions you held as to his very unusual manner of conducting his affairs. Did you ever suspect that he was being blackmailed?"

"I did."

"What circumstances in particular led you to form that suspicion?

"In the first place, there were the very large sums which he drew out in cash. It is very unusual for customers to draw out in cash more than quite modest amounts, and these large drafts in cash were, in themselves, rather suggestive of some slightly irregular transactions. But what specially tended to arouse my suspicions was the fact that the deceased usually asked expressly for old notes – notes that had been in circulation and were more or less soiled."

"What did you infer from that?"

"As the only possible advantage of a note that has been used is that it cannot be traced, I inferred that the notes were to be used for making payments of a secret, and possibly unlawful, character."

"Is it unusual for customers to ask for used notes?"

"It is rather unusual, though some customers prefer the used notes because they are less liable to stick together than the new. But usually, customers express a marked preference for new, clean notes."

"But the new notes are more easy to trace?"

"They are quite easy to trace. Usually, when a customer presents a bearer cheque for a considerable amount, he is paid in notes which have been newly issued and supplied direct to the bank. Such an issue is in the form of a series of notes of which the numbers are consecutive, and the numbers of the series are entered, not only in our own books but in the books of the bank of issue. Moreover, the numbers of the notes paid to the customer are also recorded, so that, if any question arises, it is possible to say with certainty that a particular note was paid to a particular person on a known date."

"You inferred, then, that these notes were being used to make payments of a questionable kind? What led you to suspect blackmail in particular?"

"It is common knowledge that blackmailers always refuse cheques and insist on being paid in cash, and their objection to cheques would equally apply to a series of newly issued notes. The only other kind of persons known to me who demand payment in untraceable cash are either thieves or receivers of stolen goods. But in the case of the

490

deceased, blackmailers were more probable than thieves or receivers. And there was another circumstance that strongly suggested a blackmailer. In addition to the smaller drafts which were presented at irregular intervals, there were certain larger drafts which were presented periodically and pretty regularly at intervals of three months. This suggested that someone was being paid a quarterly allowance and, having regard to the mode of payment, I felt very little doubt that that person was a blackmailer."

"You speak of a blackmailer. It has been suggested that there may have been more than one. What do you say to that?"

"I can only say that I think it highly probable. I have always, from the first, suspected a blackmailer in the background, simply by reason of the large cash withdrawals, but I had nothing more definite than that to go on until the large periodical drafts began last September. If there were any other blackmailers they must have been paid at irregular intervals and, I should say, in smaller amounts. But it is possible that the irregular cash drafts merely represented what the deceased spent on gambling. I know that his expenditure on betting and play was very large."

"But would he have needed used notes for that purpose? Gambling is a foolish pursuit, but it is not usually unlawful."

"No, but it may be associated with other acts which are unlawful. This was certainly the case in the one instance in which I accompanied him to one of his gambling resorts. It was a most disreputable place and the persons present seemed to me to be of the shadiest type. And drink was being sold freely on unlicensed premises and during prohibited hours. The place might have been, at any moment, raided by the police and, in that case, the deceased would not have wished that any evidence should exist that he had been associated with it, if he had happened not to be there at the time of the raid."

"Is it actually known to you that the deceased gambled to a really serious extent?"

"Yes. I was present on two occasions, the one that I have mentioned and another at a horse-race. On the first occasion he played very little as he was merely showing me the place and the people. But at the race he plunged rather heavily and lost – as he informed me – about a hundred pounds. But he was quite unconcerned about it. He seemed to consider the dropping of a hundred pounds as quite a negligible loss."

"Did he know that you were aware of the extent to which he gambled?"

"Oh, yes. He made no secret of it. I spoke to him very seriously on several occasions and pointed out to him how his capital was wasting. But he was incorrigible. He took my lectures quite amiably, but he would promise no reform. He was quite confident that he would get all his losses back presently."

The coroner reflected for a few moments on this statement. Then, in a grave and emphatic tone, he said, "As you were a friend of the deceased's, and the only person who appears to know much of his affairs, I am going to ask you two questions. The first is: Have you any inkling as to the identity of the person who was blackmailing him?"

Now I had expected this question and had carefully considered the reply that I ought to make. I had a very definite suspicion as to who the blackmailer was, but it was only a guess, and a guess is not an inkling in the sense intended. I was prepared to communicate my suspicions to the police, but I had no intention of making guesses in sworn testimony with the certainty of publicity. Accordingly, I replied with strict truth: "I have no knowledge whatsoever. The deceased made no confidences to me, and I never hinted to him what I suspected."

The coroner, whatever he may have thought, accepted this answer without comment and wrote it down. Then he put his second question.

"Had you ever any reason to think it possible that the deceased might take his life?"

"Yes," I replied, "I have had that possibility in mind for some time and, as soon as I heard that he was missing, I suspected what had happened."

"What led you to that belief?"

"It was something that the deceased himself had said. On a certain occasion we happened to be speaking of suicide and I remarked that, to me, it seemed that the fact of suicide was in itself evidence of an unsound state of mind. With this he disagreed emphatically. He contended that suicide was a perfectly rational proceeding in appropriate circumstances, and when I asked him what he considered appropriate circumstances, he mentioned as an example, total and irremediable financial ruin. From that time, since his affairs were obviously tending in that direction, I have always had an uneasy expectation that, when the crash came, he would take that course for solving his difficulties."

"You had that expectation," said the coroner, "but was it based on the mere opinion that he had expressed, or on some more definite indication of intention? I mean, did he ever convey to you that he actually contemplated suicide as an act possible to himself?"

"He conveyed to me quite definitely the view that, if he were reduced to abject poverty, life would not be worth living, and that he would take measures to bring it to an end. He seemed to consider that it was the natural and reasonable thing to do."

492

The coroner pondered this statement for a while. Then he looked towards the jury.

"Are there any further questions that you would like to ask this witness?" he enquired. "It seems to me that he has given us all the material facts."

That was apparently the view of the jury, for no further questions were suggested. Accordingly, when the depositions had been completed, I was released and returned to my seat and, as there were no other witnesses, the coroner proceeded to sum up briefly but quite adequately.

"You have now heard all the evidence," he began, "and you will have noticed that it all seems to establish a single conclusion. The medical evidence is quite clear. The deceased died from the effects of a large dose of morphine, or morphia, as it is more commonly called. On the question whether the poison was administered by himself or some other person, we have the evidence of the sergeant that the finger-prints on the drinking-vessel and on the poison bottle were those of the deceased himself, and that there were no signs of the presence of any other person. Then we have the clear evidence of Mr. Mortimer that the deceased had contemplated suicide as a means of escape from the consequences of financial ruin, and we have the evidence of both Mr. Bateman and Mr. Mortimer that financial ruin had actually occurred on a scale that almost takes one's breath away. So you see that the drift of the evidence is all in the same direction, and I will leave you to consider it with the feeling that you will have no difficulty in finding your verdict."

Apparently the coroner's feeling was a just one, for the jury, after a very brief consultation, communicated their verdict through the foreman. It was to the effect that the deceased died from the effects of a large dose of morphine, administered by himself.

"That," said the coroner, "is a verdict of suicide. What do you say as to the state of the deceased's mind at the time of the act?"

The decision of the jury, in direct contradiction of poor Gillum's own view, was that he was insane at the time when the act was committed. And when this finding had been recorded, the proceedings came to an end.

I lingered after the court had risen to exchange a few words with Benson, to whom I had taken a rather strong liking, and presently we were joined by Mr. Bateman, who apparently wanted to learn how his client had been affected by the incidents of the inquiry.

"A most amazing story," he commented, "the evidence in this case has brought to light. I have never heard anything more astonishing. The finding of the jury as to the state of mind of the deceased at the time of the act might fairly be extended to all his other acts. The conduct that the

493

evidence has disclosed is the conduct of a sheer lunatic. Don't you agree with me, Mr. Benson?"

"I do indeed," Benson admitted gloomily.

"And I think," pursued Bateman, "that you will also agree that, however incomprehensible poor Gillum's conduct may seem to a sane man, the fact that he did act in that insane manner has been established beyond any possible doubt. A consistent story has been elicited and established on an undeniable basis of ascertained fact."

He looked a little anxiously, as I thought, at Benson, who reflected a few moments before replying but, at length, gave a qualified assent to Bateman's proposition.

"As to the facts which were proved in evidence," said he, "they seem to admit of no doubt or denial. But I still have the feeling that there is something behind all this that I don't understand. The whole affair is too abnormal."

"As to its abnormality," said Bateman, "I am entirely with you. But, abnormal as it is, I think we have got to accept it as a sequence of events that actually happened. Surprise is natural enough, but doubt would seem to be unreasonable."

He paused and looked questioningly at Benson and, as the latter did not reply immediately, he asked, "You are not contemplating any further action in the matter, are you? Any sort of private or unofficial inquiry? I hope not, for I feel that nothing could come of it – nothing, that is to say, but the dredging up of a quantity of unprofitable and unsavoury details. And inquiries of this kind are apt to prove costly out of all proportion to their value."

"It would certainly be proper," Benson replied, "for me to give very respectful consideration to your advice, seeing that your experience is so much greater than mine. But I must confess that I am not satisfied. Still, I will not take any decision without earnest consideration of what you have said. I will think things over for a day or two, and I will let you know whether I decide to accept this mysterious affair at its face value or to see if any sort of unravelment is possible."

"Very well," rejoined Bateman. "We will leave it at that. If, in the end, you decide to open the matter further, we have the material. Mr. Penfield has carried out your instructions. We had, as you may have noticed, our Mr. James – a very skilful shorthand reporter – in court to-day to make a complete verbatim report of everything that was said, in evidence or otherwise, so that we are independent of the newspaper reports and we shall have no need to ask for access to the depositions. But I hope that neither will be required."

With this, Mr. Bateman took his leave and bustled away and, as Benson appeared more disposed for reflection than conversation, and I had my own business to attend to, I parted from him at the entrance to the building and we went our respective ways.

And here my narrative comes to its natural end. Its purpose was to give an account of my association with John Gillum, and this I have done, and if my story is not without an epilogue, that epilogue will issue from a pen other than mine.

Part II – The Case of John Gillum, Deceased
Narrated by Christopher Jervis, M.D.

Chapter VIII
Is There a Case?

The George and Vulture Inn has always been I associated in my mind with the historic case of Bardell and Pickwick and those extremely astute gentlemen, Messrs. Dodson and Fogg of Freeman's Court hard by. But nowadays that venerable tavern associates itself more especially with the very queer case of John Gillum, deceased, and a less famous but much more respectable practitioner of the law. For it was at the George and Vulture that I – together with my colleague, John Thorndyke – became introduced to the queer case aforesaid, and the introducer was no less a person than Mr. Joseph Penfield.

There was nothing surprising in our encounter there at lunch-time with Mr. Penfield, for his office in George Yard was but a few doors from the tavern. Probably it was his daily resort, at any rate, as we entered the grill-room, there he was, seated at a table gravely contemplating a grilled chop which the waiter had just set before him. He observed us as we entered and immediately indicated a couple of vacant chairs at his table.

"This is an unexpected pleasure," said he as we took possession of the chairs. "Isn't the City of London rather outside your radius?"

"No place is outside our radius," replied Thorndyke. "But we have just come from the Griffin Life Office where we have been conferring with our old friend, Mr. Stalker. The Griffin retains me permanently."

"As medical referee, I suppose?" Mr. Penfield ventured.

"No," replied Thorndyke. "As medico-legal adviser, I might almost say as adviser in doubtful cases of suicide, for that is the kind of problem that is usually submitted to me."

"Ha!" said Penfield. "And I presume that Mr. Stalker's bias is usually towards an affirmative view."

"Naturally," Thorndyke agreed, "but he doesn't expect me to share that bias. On the contrary, my usual function is rather to shatter his hopes and to convince him of all the things that he doesn't want to believe."

"Yes," said Penfield, "and a very useful function, too. If more people would seek the services of an expert destructive critic, there would be a good deal less litigation."

With this he returned to the consideration of his lunch while I, having secured the waiter's attention, communicated to him our joint requirements. Meanwhile, Mr. Penfield proceeded methodically with his meal, dropping an occasional remark but chiefly leaving the conversational initiative to Thorndyke and me. But as I watched him skilfully dissecting his chop and noted his reflective expression, I had the feeling that he was cogitating some matter arising out of Thorndyke's explanation and his own rejoinder, and I waited expectantly for it to rise to the surface. And at length (as Pepys would have expressed it) "Out it come."

"Your description," said he, "of your connection with the Griffin has brought to my mind a matter that is causing me some embarrassment. In short, to be quite honest, it has raised the hope that I may be able to transfer the burden of it from my shoulders to yours. You may consider the case as being within your province. It certainly isn't within mine."

"That suggests to me," said Thorndyke, "that it is a criminal case."

"Yes," replied Penfield, "it is. Highly criminal. A nasty, unsavoury, disreputable affair and, legally, quite impossible at that. I will just indicate its nature, though I expect you know something of it already from the newspapers. Probably you heard of a case of suicide that occurred in Clifford's Inn about a month ago."

"I remember it quite well," said Thorndyke, "and I recall that you were the dead man's solicitor."

"Then," said Penfield, "you will remember that the dead man, John Gillum by name, having wasted his substance in riotous living, to wit, in gambling, and having – presumably by his own folly – become the victim of blackmailers, proceeded to overdraw his accounts at the bank and then to commit suicide."

"Yes," said Thorndyke, "I remember that."

"Very well," said Penfield. "Now the deceased had a cousin who was much too good for him, a most estimable Australian gentleman named Benson. I speak of him with sympathy and respect, although he is now the bane of my life. He was present when Gillum's body was discovered and he at once formed the opinion that there was something abnormal about the affair, something more than met the eye. And so there may have been. However, he asked me to send a shorthand writer to attend the inquest and make a verbatim report of the proceedings, which I did, and I can let you have a transcript of that report if it is of any use. But I must admit that, on reading it, I was utterly unable to see anything in the case that was not perfectly normal, the circumstances being what they were. And that is still my position, and I have tried to impart that view to Benson, but he is still unsatisfied and he continues to stir me up from time to time with demands that some kind of action shall be taken."

"What does he want you to do?" Thorndyke asked.

"To tell you the truth," replied Penfield, "I am not quite clear. But, primarily, he wants the blood of those blackmailers."

"Naturally," said Thorndyke, "and very properly. But is there any clue to their identity?"

"Not the slightest," replied Penfield. "He expects me, in some mysteric manner, by employing private detectives or other agents, to discover who the blackmailers are and to drag them forth from their lairs and bring them to justice."

"You say that he has nothing to go on. Nothing at all?"

"Nothing," replied Penfield, "but a few letters in a disguised hand, dated only by the postmarks, unsigned, of course, and mentioning nobody by name nor hinting at any locality."

"And have you no letters or documents that might be of assistance?"

"I have Gillum's will. Benson is the sole beneficiary, and the sole benefit that he has enjoyed has been a small debt to the bank, which he has insisted on paying. I have also one or two of Gillum's letters to me, but they are simple business letters making no reference to his private affairs."

"And what do you want me to do?" Thorndyke asked.

"I should like," replied Penfield, "to bring him to you and let him state his case and say what he wants. If you think that it is possible to do anything for him, well and good, and if you think otherwise, I should suggest that you give him some of the medicine that you tell me you administer to Mr. Stalker for the cure of unreasonable optimism."

Thorndyke did not reply immediately, but I could see that the case, unpromising as it looked, was not without its attractions for him, for, unlike Penfield, he was stimulated rather than discouraged by apparent difficulties. Still, even Thorndyke could not embark on a case without data of some sort. Eventually, he replied without committing himself to any definite course of action. "I think it would be worthwhile to hear what Mr. Benson has to say. He may know more than he is aware of, and I recall that at the inquest a friend of Gillum's gave evidence, a man named Mortimer. He seemed to know more about the deceased's affairs than anybody else. Perhaps we might get some information from him."

"Excellent!" exclaimed Penfield, obviously delighted at the prospect of shifting his burden on to Thorndyke's shoulders. "Excellent. I can put you into touch with Mr. Mortimer, and I am sure he will give you any assistance that he can. And now, as we seem to have finished our lunch, perhaps you will walk down to my office with me and I will hand you the report. It contains all the positive information that I think you are likely to get."

Accordingly, when we had settled our score, we set forth from the tavern down George Yard to Mr. Penfield's office. There we observed a rack of deed-boxes, the lids of which were decorated, rather like coffin-plates, with the names of Mr. Penfield's clients. One of these, bearing the name of "*John Gillum Esq.*", our friend let down, when he had unlocked the box, displaying a small collection of documents within. From these he selected a large envelope, and having opened it and verified its contents, handed it to Thorndyke.

"That," said he, "is the report. If you decide to undertake the case, I shall, if you wish it and Mr. Benson agrees, transfer the deed-box with its contents to you. And now, perhaps we can make an appointment for your meeting with Mr. Benson. Will you come here, or shall I bring him to your chambers?"

"I don't see why you should bring him," said Thorndyke, "unless you would prefer to. I suggest that he calls on me one evening by appointment for an informal talk, and if he can bring Mr. Mortimer with him, we shall be able to see exactly how we stand."

"Thank you," said Mr. Penfield. "It will suit me much better to send him than to bring him, so, if you will give me a date, I will make the appointment."

"I will give you two dates," said Thorndyke, "and you can notify me when to expect the visit. One will be the day after to-morrow at eight o'clock in the evening, if that will suit you, Jervis, and the other two days later."

"Both these dates will do for me," said I, on which Mr. Penfield entered them in his book with undissembled satisfaction.

"I must thank you again," said he, accompanying us out into George Yard. "You have really rendered me a great service."

He shook hands cordially with us both and even stood watching us as we walked away up the court towards Cornhill. And thus was set rolling the ball whose evolutions I was to watch with so much interest during the next few months. None of Thorndyke's cases ever started less hopefully, and few developed in a more surprising fashion.

Mr. Benson chose the earlier of the two dates and arrived at our chambers punctually at eight in the evening thereof, so punctually that the Temple clock was actually striking the hour as the knock on our door was heard. He was accompanied by another gentleman, and when I let him in, mutual introductions were effected and followed by mutual inspection. Like Mr. Penfield, we were pleasantly impressed by our visitor – indeed by both our visitors. Benson was a typical Australian: Tall, well set up, and athletic looking, with a fresh, weather-beaten face and a frank, agreeable manner. His companion, Mr. Mortimer, was of a quite different type, a quiet, sedate man with something rather studious and bookish in his appearance.

"I suppose," said Benson, when the conversational preliminaries had been disposed of, "Mr Penfield has given you a general outline of the business?"

"He has given me the report of the inquest," replied Thorndyke, "and I and my colleague, Dr. Jervis, have read it most carefully. So now we probably know as much as to the facts of the case as you do, and are in a position to discuss them. Mr. Penfield informs me that you wish some action to be taken, and the first question is what kind of action you contemplate."

This very definite question seemed rather to disconcert Benson, for he answered in a somewhat hesitating manner. "Well, you see, I have had all along the feeling that this dreadful affair was perfectly unnatural and that there was something behind it that was never brought out by the inquest. In the first place, my cousin, Gillum, was the very last person whom I should have expected to commit suicide."

"That," said Thorndyke, "is frequently said by witnesses at inquests and probably quite truly. But let us be definite. There are only two possibilities in the case of your cousin's death. Either he committed suicide, or he was murdered. The jury decided that he killed himself. Do you contest the fact of the suicide?"

"Well, no," replied Benson. "I don't see how I can. I heard all the evidence and, unwilling as I am to believe that he killed himself, I don't see that there is any escape from the facts."

"No," Thorndyke agreed, "that is how it appears to me. Then, if we accept, as we seem bound to do, the fact that John Gillum died by his own hand, we can pass on to the next point. What is the further question that you want to raise?"

"The further question," replied Benson, "is, why did he commit suicide? Mortimer thinks that he killed himself because he had gambled away all his money, but I don't believe that. It isn't a sufficient reason. And we know that he was being harassed by blackmailers. Now, my feeling is that it was not the loss of his money that drove him to suicide, but the agony of mind that he was suffering on account of these blackmailing devils."

"That," said Thorndyke, "is a perfectly reasonable view, and I am inclined to agree with you. But what practical effect do you propose to give to your belief?"

"If John Gillum was driven to his death by these wretches," Benson replied with some heat, "they are virtually his murderers. I know that, in law, they are not chargeable with murder. But, even legally, they are guilty of a very serious crime, and I want them found and brought to justice."

"That, again," said Thorndyke, "is a perfectly reasonable position, and I view your desire very sympathetically. But there are two points that I think it necessary to put to you. The first is that what you propose is as nearly as may be an impossibility. So far as I know at present, there is no clue whatever to the identity of these people, nor – so far as I am aware – is anything known as to the circumstances in which the payments were made."

"I think," said Benson, "Mortimer can tell us something about that, and I believe he has some suspicions as to who these people are."

"We will hear what Mr. Mortimer has to tell us presently," said Thorndyke. "Meanwhile let us consider the second point. That raises the question whether it is, in fact, expedient to take any action, even with a chance of success."

"Expedient?" Benson repeated. "Is there anything against it besides the difficulty?"

"I think," said Thorndyke, "that if we consider the circumstances as they are known to us, we shall see certain objections to taking the kind of action that you contemplate. May I ask whether your cousin was at all a nervous or timorous man? A man easily intimidated?"

"Most certainly not," replied Benson. "He was a decidedly bold, self-reliant man."

"Very well," said Thorndyke, "then consider his position at the time of his death. He was being blackmailed by at least one person, and that at the value of two-thousand pounds a year. Now, you know, Mr. Benson, it is not usually possible to levy blackmail on a person who has nothing to conceal unless that person is more than ordinarily easily frightened. But your cousin was not easily frightened, and yet he was paying this enormous amount. Moreover, as you believe, he was so distressed by his position that he took his life to escape from the persecution. What are we to infer from this? Is it possible to resist the inference that there was something in his life that he was compelled to conceal at any price?"

Benson was evidently a good deal taken aback by Thorndyke's blunt statement of the case. He remained silent for some moments. Then he replied, "It had occurred to me that some mud might be stirred up if we were to bring the blackmailers to justice, but I hadn't put it as strongly as you have."

"It is necessary to face the facts squarely," said Thorndyke, "and those facts suggest very strongly that your cousin was concealing something highly discreditable, and it could have been no trivial scandal. In that case he could have appealed to the police and would have been given ample protection without any inquisition. The amount which he paid suggests something of extreme gravity, something which he dared not allow to come to light. Therefore, I ask you again: Would it not be wiser to let sleeping dogs lie?"

Once more Benson reflected before replying, but he was not long in coming to a decision. "It might be wiser," he admitted, "but it would be against justice and common morality. As to the scandal, poor old Jack is dead, so it won't affect him. And I don't suppose it was anything that would lessen my respect for him. At any rate, I feel strongly that those devils who drove him to a miserable death ought to be dragged out into the light of day and made to pay their debt."

"Yes," Thorndyke agreed, "I think you are right in principle. But I must finally remind you of the difficulties of the case. Remember that, not only are we without any clue as to who these people were – unless Mr. Mortimer can supply one – but, even if we could discover them, the principal witness – the vital witness, in fact – is dead, and it might easily turn out to be impossible to make out a case against them, or, at any rate, to prove it. Furthermore, the proceedings, involving the employment of private enquiry agents, might prove to be extremely costly, and in the very probable event of total failure, a vast amount of money would have been wasted."

"I know," said Benson, "and it is very good of you to put the matter so clearly. But my mind is made up. Whatever it costs, if you are prepared to undertake the case, I should like you to get on with it. I am a man of ample means, and I am a bachelor, and if I spend every penny that I have, and even if we fail after all, I shall feel that the money was well spent in trying to bring Jack Gillum's murderers to the punishment that they deserve."

I could see that Benson's attitude had secured Thorndyke's warm sympathy as, indeed, it had secured mine. But I think both of us rather regretted that he should have embarked on an enterprise that was almost certain to end in disappointment.

"Well, Benson," my colleague said cordially, "I congratulate you on your courage and your very proper desire for justice. I will certainly do what I can to get you satisfaction, but I warn you that, if the case turns

502

out to be quite impossible, I shall not waste my time and your money in pursuing a will-o'-the-wisp."

"Thank you," replied Benson. "I put myself entirely in your hands, and I promise you to abide loyally by your decision."

"Then," said Thorndyke, "as we are agreed on the conditions, we may as well make a start and see exactly what our position is. You said that Mr. Mortimer could give us some useful information. Perhaps we had better begin with that."

He looked enquiringly at Mortimer, who, in his turn, looked a little sheepish.

"I am afraid," said he, "that I haven't much to tell. It is only a matter of suspicion."

"Suspicions," remarked Thorndyke, "are of no use as evidence, but they may be quite useful as indicating a line of enquiry. At any rate, let us have them."

"They relate," said Mortimer, "to some people named Foucault who run a gaming house in Gerrard Street. I went there with Gillum on one occasion – on the very night, in fact, when I first made his acquaintance in a social sense. They were an obviously shady lot, but what specially struck me was that Madame Foucault made a dead set at Gillum – flirted with him, or made a show of doing so, in the most ostentatious, almost indecent, manner before the whole roomful of gamesters."

"And was Gillum responsive?" Thorndyke asked.

"Not in the least," replied Mortimer. "But Monsieur Foucault was. He watched them closely the whole of the time that they were together, and his expression as he looked at Gillum was positively murderous. And I gathered that there had been some trouble on previous occasions, for Gillum remarked to me on Foucault's jealousy and made rather a joke of it. And there was no mistaking Foucault's hostility to Gillum. I noticed it when we met in the restaurant before we followed them to the gambling den."

"Have you any further knowledge of these people?" Thorndyke asked.

"No," Mortimer answered. "That was the only occasion on which I met them, and I know nothing more than what I have told you. I must confess that there doesn't seem to be very much in it."

"I am inclined to agree with you," said Thorndyke. "A little made-up scandal of the kind that you suggest might account for an attempt at blackmail on a modest scale. But the one which we are considering seems to have been something much more formidable. Still, I will get you to let me have the names and address of these people so that we may make a few enquiries. And now, as we have squeezed Mr. Mortimer dry, let us hear what Mr. Benson has to tell us."

"I am afraid," said Benson, "that I have nothing at all to tell. You see, it is two years since Gillum left Australia and I know nothing about his doings or way of living since he came to England."

"No," said Thorndyke, "we have to depend on Mr. Mortimer for that. But there is his life in Australia. I want you to review that. Blackmail is usually related to the past, and often to a rather remote past. I ask you to try to recall the circumstances of Gillum's life in Australia and consider whether there may not have been some incident which could have been the subject of blackmail."

"I will think that question over," said Benson, "but, at the moment, I can recall nothing that could possibly have been used against him to extort money. He had no enemies. He never, to my knowledge, had any troubles with women, and I never heard of any sort of scandal."

"Well," said Thorndyke, "turn the question over at your leisure. Now, as we seem to have drawn a blank in Australia, let us take the next stage, his voyage to England. Do you know anything of the incidents of that voyage?"

"Not in much detail," replied Benson, "but I came to England in the same ship, and I had some talk about him with the captain and the first officer."

"Then," said Thorndyke, "try to recall what you learned from them and consider whether there was anything – in his relations with the other passengers, for instance – that might be worth enquiring into."

"I don't think he had much to do with the other passengers. There were only a few of them – the ship was chiefly a cargo ship – and they were mostly men in the meat trade. I gathered that Gillum spent most of his time playing cards with the doctor and the purser in their cabins, particularly in the purser's room. Those two men were his special cronies and, by all accounts, he struck up a very close friendship with them both."

"Then," said Thorndyke, "they ought to be able to tell us all about the voyage and who the other passengers were."

"Why do you suppose anything happened on the ship?" Benson asked.

"I am merely considering it as a possibility," Thorndyke replied. "Remember, Benson, that something happened somewhere. That blackmail was not paid for nothing, and as we have not yet found a starting-point for an inquiry, we must trace Gillum's doings and his contacts with other persons as well as we can. Probably these two men are at present not available for inquiries. I suppose the ship is now outward bound?"

"Yes," replied Benson, "but neither of those men is on board. Both of them left the ship and the service at the end of the voyage. I learned that when I was on board."

"You mean that they both left the ship at the same time as Gillum?" Thorndyke asked.

"Not actually at the same time," Benson replied. "Gillum went ashore at Marseilles and travelled overland, making a leisurely journey across France so as to see something of the country. I think he arrived in England about six weeks or two months after the others. But I know that the doctor and the purser both left the service at the end of the voyage, when they had settled their business with the owners."

"Then," said Thorndyke, "it is possible that their relations with Gillum may have continued during the time of his residence in England – in fact, it is rather likely. You don't, I suppose, know where it would be possible to find them?

"I asked about them at the shipping office," replied Benson. "As to the doctor, they knew nothing but that he had some idea of going into practice or else getting a job on a different line. But the purser is certainly beyond our reach. He is dead. They told me about him when I called at the office. It seems that he died under rather mysterious circumstances, for there was some uncertainty as to whether he had committed suicide or had been murdered. But I don't know any of the details. As the man was a stranger to me, I didn't go into the matter."

"No," said Thorndyke, "but I think we shall have find out what the circumstances were. A suicide, and still more a murder, seems to demand investigation. Do you remember the purser's name?"

"Yes," replied Benson, "his name was Abel Webb."

"Abel Webb!" Mortimer exclaimed in a tone of the utmost astonishment. "Why, that was the name of the man whose body I discovered in the porch of St. Michael's Church. It is a most astonishing coincidence. And what makes it still more so is the fact that the finding of that body was the occasion of my making Gillum's acquaintance."

"You had better tell us about that," said Thorndyke. "I mean as to Gillum's connection with your discovery. The case itself I remember quite clearly."

"It happened this way," said Mortimer. "I had seen the police carry the body down to the ambulance and was standing there in the crowd waiting to see it move off when someone came up and asked me what the excitement was about and whether it was a motor accident. I turned round to answer, and then I recognised the questioner as one of the

505

bank's customers, Mr. Gillum. I told him what had happened, and I also told him, and he could see for himself, that I was a good deal upset by the affair. He was extremely kind and sympathetic and eventually insisted on taking me off in a taxi to dine with him at a restaurant. And it was that same evening after dinner that I went with him to the gaming house that I told you about."

"I take it," said Thorndyke, "that you did not know at the time who the dead man was."

"No," answered Mortimer. "I learned that first at the inquest."

"Did Gillum come forward to give any evidence as to the deceased at the inquest or afterwards?"

"He couldn't have come forward before the inquest because the identity of the deceased had not been disclosed. But I should say that he never did."

"Do you know whether Gillum ever learned who the dead man was?"

"I know he did, for I discussed the case with him. He had read a very full report of the inquest and seemed to remember all about the evidence. And the report contained not only the name of the deceased but his description as a former purser of one of the Dominion Line ships."

"Did he tell you much about his relations with Webb?"

"No," replied Mortimer, "the astonishing thing is that he never let drop the faintest hint that he had ever heard of the man before. In our talk about the inquest, he spoke of the dead man as if he had been a complete stranger."

"That is very extraordinary," exclaimed Benson.

"It is," Mortimer agreed, "though Gillum's reticence in this case is less remarkable than another man's would have been, for he was reticent about everything, I might almost say, secretive. He never told me anything about himself – excepting his gambling exploits. He was confidential enough about those. But he was extraordinarily close respecting his private affairs. You will hardly believe it, but until after his death I never knew that he had been in Australia."

When Mortimer had finished speaking, a rather curious silence fell on us all. Benson looked puzzled, but he made no remark and put no question to Mortimer. But I could see that the latter's statement had made a deep impression on Thorndyke, as it had on me, and when the discussion was resumed, the drift of his questions made it clear to me that what had struck me had also struck him.

"I think," said he, "that Webb's death occurred about a year ago. Do you happen to remember the approximate date, Mortimer?"

"I remember the exact date," was the reply. "It was the ninth of last September."

Thorndyke made a note of the date and then remarked, "The fact that Abel Webb met a violent death makes it necessary to look rather more closely into the incidents of the voyage to England. Of course, there may be no connection, but it is an abnormal circumstance and we are bound to take note of it. And as Abel Webb has gone out of our ken, the only person left from whom we could get any in is the doctor. Benson can't tell us where he is to be found, but a doctor is usually easy to trace, as he is bound to keep the Registrar informed as to changes of address. What was his name?"

"His name was Peck," replied Benson. "Augustus Peck."

"I will look him up in the directory," said Thorndyke "or at the Registrar's office and see if we can get into touch with him. And now, Mortimer, to return to the evidences of blackmail. Apart from the large drafts that you have mentioned, evidently connected with the letters that were found, is there any positive suggestion of other payments, earlier in date? It is important that we should fix, if possible, the time when the blackmailing began. Can you tell us anything definite about that?"

"Yes," replied Mortimer, "I think I can. Quite recently I have gone into the question afresh. Benson has kindly lent me Gillum's pass-book so that I could study it at home. I have gone through it very carefully, and it occurred to me that if I made a graph of the dates and amounts, any small periodic fluctuations would be made visible."

"Excellent," said Thorndyke. "And what did your graph show?"

"It showed a small periodic rise corresponding roughly with the ordinary quarter-days. This began quite early, within a month of the opening of the account, and it went on until the big drafts began."

"Do you say," Thorndyke asked, "that the small rises ceased when the large drafts began, or were you unable to ascertain that?"

"I am disposed to think that the small rises ceased when the large quarterly payments began, though they might have become merged in higher rises of the curve due to the big payments. But, allowing for the possibility of this confusion, the smaller payments ceased and were replaced by the larger."

"What were the amounts of the smaller payments?"

"So far as I could judge, the excess above the ordinary withdrawals would be about two-hundred-pounds-a-quarter."

"What did you infer from this? Did it seem to you to suggest that there was more than one blackmailer?"

"No," replied Mortimer. "My reading of it was that there was only one, that for about a year he had been satisfied with a payment of something like eight-hundred-a-year, and that he had then suddenly raised his demands. That would account for the smaller payments ceasing when the larger ones began."

"Yes," Thorndyke agreed, "that appears to be a reasonable inference, but it is difficult to judge. We really want to know more about Gillum's private life and habits, but I don't see where we are to gain the knowledge."

"I think," said Benson, "that Mortimer may be able to help you in that. He is writing some sort of account of his connection with my cousin. How are you getting on with it, Mortimer?"

"I have finished it," Mortimer replied, "but I don't think it would be of much use to Dr. Thorndyke. You see," he continued in response to an enquiring glance from my colleague, "it occurred to me after the inquest that it would be rather interesting to put on record, while the facts were still fresh in my memory, the whole incident of my acquaintance with John Gillum, and I have found it quite interesting to write, but I don't think it would be very thrilling to read. And I doubt whether it would be of any use to you, for I wrote it without any thought of an inquiry such as you are engaged in."

"But my dear fellow," said Thorndyke, "that is precisely its most valuable quality. A man writing an account with the conscious intention of throwing light on some question tends unconsciously to select the facts which appear to him to be important and to ignore other facts which seem to have no bearing. But his selection may be all wrong. He may omit something of vital importance through having failed to realise its significance, whereas your little history gives the facts impartially without selection. Would it be possible for us to have the privilege of reading it?"

Mortimer smiled rather shyly. "It is a poor performance in a literary sense," said he, "but, of course, you can see it if you wish to. I rattled it off on the typewriter and, as I did it in duplicate, you can have one copy to keep as long as you like. I will post it off to you to-night."

"Thank you," said Thorndyke. "I shall read it with interest, even if it throws no further light on the case. And there are two other matters that may be mentioned before we adjourn this meeting. Who has the blackmailer's letters?"

"They are in Penfield's custody at present," replied Benson. "He has all the documents."

"The other matter," said Thorndyke, "refers to Gillum's chambers. Who has possession of them? You, I suppose, are the nominal tenant."

"Yes, I am the tenant until Michaelmas or until they are let. Why do you ask?"

"I merely wanted to know whether they would be available if it should seem desirable to make an inspection."

"What use would an inspection be?" Benson asked.

"It is impossible to say," replied Thorndyke. "Probably none. But some point may arise from the reading of Mortimer's manuscript which may be elucidated by looking over the premises."

"Well, you know best," said Benson. "At any rate, I will send you the keys in case you should want them. And I think that finishes our business for the present. It is very good of you to have given us so much of your time but, before we go, there is one question that I should like to ask. You have gone very patiently into the case to-night. From what you have learned from us, do you think you will be disposed to do what I am hoping you will – to prosecute a search for those wretches who are responsible for poor Jack Gillum's death?"

"I am prepared to look into the case," Thorndyke replied. "If I find that we come to an absolute dead end, I shall advise you to abandon the inquiry. But if I see any prospect whatever of bringing it to a successful conclusion, I shall place my services unreservedly at your disposal. Will that satisfy you?"

"It will more than satisfy me," replied Benson, "and, for my part, I promise to be guided by your advice, whatever you may decide."

With this, the two men rose and, when we had escorted them to the landing and seen them safely launched on the stairs, we wished them good-night and re-entered our chambers.

Chapter IX
The Empty Nest

"Well, Thorndyke," I said when we had re-entered and closed the door, "this has been quite an entertaining interview. I fancy that your drag net brought up rather more than you expected. A mighty queer catch, in fact."

"Yes," he agreed, as he dug out his pipe with a thoughtful air, "a decidedly queer catch. And it will need some sorting out. What do you make of it?"

"It seems to me," I replied, "that we have identified one of the blackmailers and accounted for the other."

"That is the result in a nutshell," said he. "But I should like to hear how you arrived at it."

"The argument," I replied, "consists in stating the facts in their natural sequence. To begin with Abel Webb. I remember the case quite clearly. It was that cyanide injection case, and when we discussed it, we agreed that suicide could not be entertained. It was a blatant case of murder."

"Yes," Thorndyke agreed. "I accept that."

"Then we agree that Abel Webb was murdered. He was murdered on the ninth of September. At that time Gillum was being blackmailed at the rate of eight-hundred a year. But exactly a week after the murder, on the sixteenth of September, the blackmail suddenly jumped up to the rate of two-thousand a year.

"At, or about, the time of the murder, Gillum is known to have been in the neighbourhood, within a few yards of the place where it was committed and, after the murder, although he and Mortimer discussed it in detail, he concealed from Mortimer the fact that he had been acquainted with Webb. You agree to that?

"Yes," Thorndyke replied. "Mortimer referred to it as reticence, but reticence to that extent amounts to concealment."

"Those, then," said I, "are the facts, and my interpretation of them is this: Abel Webb was blackmailing Gillum to the tune of eight-hundred a year. Possibly he was also becoming troublesome. At any rate, Gillum got tired of it and took an opportunity to kill Abel Webb. For that I don't blame him, although his methods were not pretty. But then Gillum had bad luck. Somebody knew more than he was aware of and promptly put on the screw, and put it on so forcibly that when Gillum came to the end

510

of his resources, he committed suicide rather than face the consequences of not being able to pay. That is my reading of the case, and I rather think it is yours too."

"Yes," Thorndyke agreed, "that is what the facts seem to suggest, and I am prepared to accept your theory as a working hypothesis. Without prejudice, however, as our friend Penfield would say. I mean that, while adopting it as a working hypothesis, we must not lose sight of its hypothetical nature. Fresh facts may lead us to modify our views."

"Yes, that is true," I admitted, "but you speak of a working hypothesis. But how does it work? The problem is to find the principal blackmailer. But I don't see that what we have learned gets us any more forward on that quest."

"There," said Thorndyke, "I disagree entirely. Assuming your interpretation of the facts to be correct, we have a most important clue to the identity of the chief blackmailer. You have said it yourself: 'Somebody knew more than he was aware of.' But what did that somebody know? He must have known, not only of the connection between Gillum and Webb, but that Webb was blackmailing Gillum. That implies that the blackmailer must have known Webb pretty intimately, but if Webb was really a blackmailer, the suggestion is that the matter which supported the blackmail was something connected with the voyage from Australia to England. But that, in its turn, seems to connect the unknown blackmailer with the voyage, and if we are right in inferring such a connection, we have a very valuable hint as to where to look for further information."

"You mean the ship's doctor?"

"Yes. If the blackmail arose out of any incident that occurred on board ship, and still more if the blackmailer should have been one of the other passengers, the doctor could hardly fail to have some knowledge of the matter, or some knowledge of the circumstances out of which the blackmail arose. Even if he had no suspicion of the blackmailing transaction, he must know what the general conditions were on the voyage. There isn't much privacy on board ship, especially on a long voyage."

"Yes," I agreed, "the doctor should be a useful witness. Benson's knowledge of the matter is based on hearsay, but Dr. Peck's is first-hand, so that we could cross-examine him in detail. But the question is, how are we to get into touch with him? He may be in India or China by this time."

"That is a possibility," said Thorndyke, "but we had better begin by finding out his permanent address from the *Medical Directory*."

He went into the office and returned with the volume in his hand. Laying it down on the table, he turned over the leaves until he found the entry, which he read out:

"*Augustus Peck, M.R.C.S., L.R.C.P., L.D.S., Surgeon, Commonwealth and Dominions Line. Permanent Address: 87 Staple Inn.*"

"Staple Inn," I repeated. "It is rather odd that this case should be connected with the only two remaining inns of Chancery. And I notice that he has the dental as well as the medical qualification."

"Yes," said Thorndyke, "and quite a useful combination for a ship's surgeon. I suppose our next move must be to call at Staple Inn and see if we can discover his present whereabouts. But there is no hurry. We shall have Mortimer's manuscript in the morning and it may be that we shall pick up some hint from that."

This ended our discussion for the time being, and if it had not carried us far, it, and the preceding interview, had yielded more matter for investigation than Penfield's dismal account of the case had led us to expect.

On the following morning, Mortimer's manuscript arrived, and the same post brought a package from Benson containing two keys tied together and bearing a parchment label inscribed, "*64 Clifford's Inn, 1ˢᵗ Floor*". As Thorndyke was occupied during the morning and I was free, I took possession of the manuscript and read through the seven chapters of which it consisted with close attention and growing disappointment. For I had expected that Mortimer's story would furnish us with some new facts, whereas it seemed to me merely to repeat at greater length what he had already told us or what we had gathered from the report of the inquest.

But in this, as appeared later, I was mistaken, and as Mortimer's history contained practically all that we ever knew of the period that it described, I have attached it as a preface to this record and shall hence forth assume that the reader is fully acquainted with its contents. And it may be that he, or she, more discerning than I, will already have noted certain points the significance of which I failed to appreciate.

Certain suspicions did, indeed, cross my mind on the subject, especially when I noted the deep interest and attention with which Thorndyke studied the document. But then my colleague was a man who habitually gave his whole attention to even the simplest matters, and I could see that this case, with all its obscurities and ambiguities, had taken a strong hold on him. It was the kind of puzzle that he really enjoyed, and he was going to spare no pains in seeking out the solution.

About a week after the arrival of the manuscript I ventured to ask his views on it, with the above suspicions in mind.

"What do you make of Mortimer's history?" said I. "To me it seems rather barren of matter. I have not extracted from it anything that I did not already know."

"Nor have I," he replied, "in the sense of new facts of a fundamental order. I hardly expected to. But the story has its value in that it gives us a lively picture of the man, Gillum. It shows us a shrewd, ingenious, rather subtle man, with a distinctly casuistical type of mind, and it enables us to contrast his apparent intelligence with his amazingly foolish conduct."

"But we were able to do that already," I objected, "and as to the main problem, the identity of the principal blackmailer, it gives us not the faintest hint."

"That is true," said Thorndyke. "But perhaps the immediate problem is rather the occasion of the blackmail, what it was that Gillum had done to render him susceptible to blackmail. Mortimer throws no light on that question either. Whatever we are to learn from his story must be gathered by reading between the lines and considering the possible significance of apparently trivial things and events."

"You mean, in relation to our working hypothesis?" I suggested.

"Yes," he replied. "But let us not be obsessed by our hypothesis. It may be entirely erroneous, and while we are using it as the only instrument of investigation which we possess, we should scrutinise every new fact, as well as the old ones, to see whether any alternative hypothesis is suggested. Read Mortimer's history again, Jervis, and ask yourself in respect of Gillum's sayings and doings and the little trivial occurrences which Mortimer chronicles, whether they support our hypothesis or whether they seem to be consistent with some different meaning."

As this implied that Thorndyke had already taken his own prescription, I decided to study the manuscript afresh. Meanwhile, by way of "getting some of my own back", I remarked with a grin, "There is one thing that I have been expecting ever since Mortimer's document turned up, and I'm still expecting it."

"What is that?" he asked, regarding me suspiciously.

"I have been expecting that you would want to go across to Clifford's Inn and nose round the empty chambers."

"And why not?" said he. "I think it is an excellent suggestion. It would be quite interesting to fill in Mortimer's picture with its appropriate background, and as we have the afternoon free, I propose that we put your idea into execution forth with. We will go over as soon as we have had lunch."

Of course, I agreed (noting that Thorndyke, according to his habit, had planted his "idea" on me) and, when we had dispatched our meal, and Thorndyke had provided himself with his invaluable research-case and his graduated walking-stick, we went forth, and passing out of the Inner Temple gate, crossed Fleet Street, and walking up Clifford's Inn Passage, came out into the courtyard by the garden.

"*Sic transit*," Thorndyke remarked, regretfully, as he cast a disparaging eye on the garish new buildings that were beginning to replace the pleasant old houses. "John Penhallow's chambers have gone and soon all the others will follow, and then all that will remain to show posterity the quiet sumptuousness and dignity of London chambers in the seventeenth century will be Penhallow's rooms in the Victoria and Albert Museum."

He stood for a few moments running a reflective eye over the exterior of Number 64, observed by a pair of inquisitive eyes from the window of the typewriting office on the ground floor. Then he plunged into the dim entry and I followed him up the stairs until we emerged into the daylight of the first-floor landing.

"This is rather gruesome," said I, as we threw open the inner door and looked into the room. "With the exception of the corpse, the place is just the same as it appeared to Mortimer when he and Benson and Weech discovered the body. Nothing seems to have been moved."

"No," Thorndyke agreed. "We have only to imagine the body lying on the couch and we have the tableau that Mortimer described."

We went in and looked curiously at the couch, the pillow of which still bore the impression of the dead man's head, and the little table by its side with the siphon, the tumbler, and the decanter, all bearing the very distinct prints of the dead man's fingers.

"We may as well preserve these," said Thorndyke, slipping on a pair of loose gloves. "They are not likely to help us, but you never know. It is a good rule never to destroy evidence."

"I don't see what evidence they could furnish," said I, "seeing that they were proved to be Gillum's own finger-prints."

"But that is evidence," he replied. "Prints like these are Gillum's, and prints unlike them are those of somebody else. As we are seeking an unknown person, that kind of evidence may be quite material. And you notice that there is a nearly complete set of both hands."

He looked about the room, and observing a built-in cupboard by the fireplace, turned the key which was in the lock, and opened the door. One of the shelves was nearly empty, and as the height was sufficient to take the siphon, he transferred that and the tumbler and the smooth,

514

patternless decanter from the table to the vacant space and closed the door.

"We will lock the cupboard and take the key when we go," said he. "Meanwhile, we may find some other things which we may think fit to put in it."

He went back to the couch and ran his eye over the cushions and the pillow, stooping over the latter and examining it more closely.

"This is worth noticing," said he. "The man's head could have rested on this pillow only a few hours while he was alive and capable of movement, but yet there are no less than three hairs sticking to the fabric."

"He may have used the pillow on other occasions," I suggested, to which Thorndyke assented.

"At any rate," he added, "we may as well collect these hairs, as we can assume them to be authentic samples of Gillum's hair."

"I suppose so," I agreed, though without enthusiasm, for it would have been more to the point if they had been authentic samples of the blackmailer's hair. Thorndyke noted the tone of my remark and smiled as he opened his research case, which he had deposited on the table.

"You think," said he, "that we are collecting all the things that don't matter. Probably you are right, but it is better to provide yourself with useless material than to throw away things that may later be badly needed."

He took out of the case a pair of forceps and one of his invaluable seed envelopes, and with the former picked out the three hairs – two black and one white – and transferred them to the envelope, on which he wrote a brief description, before returning it to the case. Then he began a leisurely perambulation of the room, inspecting its various contents and making occasional remarks on them. The bookcase seemed to interest him, for he stood before it running his eye along the rows of volumes and apparently reading their titles.

"In general," said he, "the books seem to confirm Mortimer's estimate of Gillum's character and tastes. There are six works on London topography, catalogues of the National Gallery, the Tate, and the Wallace Collection, a book on games of chance, and one on the theory of probability. Those are according to expectation and so is the book on *Modern Organ Music*, but Staunton's *Chess* is not. I don't think that chess-players are usually interested in games of chance."

He turned away from the bookcase and resumed his travels round the room, halting presently before a rather elegantly turned roulette box.

"This," said he, "is the box that Mortimer speaks of. Apparently, Gillum used it for experiments in connection with his projected system, but it is possible that he may have used it for actual play with some of his visitors. Perhaps it would be as well to put it away with the other specimens."

He took it up in his gloved hands and carried it over to the cupboard, where he placed it on the shelf with the objects from the table. Then, having exhausted the interest of the living-room, he passed through into the bedroom.

It was a small room, simply and rather barely furnished, but clean and orderly with the tidiness of a ship's cabin, a fact which attracted Thorndyke's attention as well as mine, for he remarked, "The late Gillum seems to have been a tidy, methodical man. You noticed evidences of that in the living-room, and it is still more striking here. The bed, you observe, has been carefully made, and he made it himself, though he must have known that he was never going to sleep in it. And no cast-off clothes lying about or even hanging on the pegs. I suppose, when he undressed, he put them into the wardrobe."

He verified the surmise by opening the doors of the wardrobe, which showed, in the one division, the clothes that Gillum must have taken off hanging on the side pegs, while, in the other division, which was fitted with shelves, were stored clean shirts, collars, handkerchiefs, several pairs of shoes, and three hats. These things he considered attentively, and especially the cast-off clothes, which he took down from the pegs and, having looked them over, turned out the pockets, returning the contents of each after having examined them. But Gillum seemed to have carried few things in his pockets, and of those which we found none appeared to be of any interest. A bank-note case – empty – a handful of silver and bronze coins, a pocket-knife, and a set of well-worn dice formed the principal items.

"Not much to be learned from those," Thorndyke remarked as he closed the wardrobe, "excepting that he respected his clothes and avoided bulging pockets."

He walked across the room to the large chest of drawers that stood in the corner near the bed, lifting the valance of the latter and revealing a sponge bath underneath. As we reached the chest, I observed in the dark corner between it and the wall a good sized cylindrical basket which had apparently served as a rubbish dump, and drew Thorndyke's attention to it as a possible mine of evidential wealth. He ignored the irony of my tone and, promptly adopting my suggestion, picked up the basket and turned out its contents on to the bed. It was certainly a very miscellaneous collection and as I regarded it with a faint grin I wondered what Mr. Penfield would have thought if he could have seen my colleague systematically sorting it out and placing each article after inspection at the foot of the bed. Over some of these, such as three obviously superannuated socks and a couple of slightly frayed collars, he passed lightly with a single glance, but most of the things he inspected attentively, little as they seemed to merit his attention, evidently considering what inferences they suggested. I watched him curiously, my tendency to be amused by the apparent triviality of the proceedings restrained by the recollection of the surprising results of similar examinations in the past and, as I looked on, I made a mental inventory of the collection with a view to possible results in the future.

Besides the socks and collars, a pair of worn fabric gloves and a broken shoe-lace, the "find" included an empty tin which had once contained an antiseptic tooth powder, which Thorndyke opened, and sniffed at the pinch of powder which still clung to the box, two empty *"Milk of Magnesia"* bottles, a worn-out toothbrush (which Thorndyke examined closely and also smelt), an empty bottle labelled *"Bromidia"*, which seemed to suggest that Gilum had suffered from insomnia, another empty bottle labelled *"Cawley's Cleansing Fluid"*, from which Thorndyke drew out the cork in order to smell at what remained of the contents, several crumpled-up tradesmen's bills, and a small, heavy object wrapped up in a sheet of writing-paper. This Thorndyke took up and carefully opening out the paper displayed a small bolt with a fly nut attached.

"Now," said he, "I wonder what that might have belonged to. A one-inch, square-headed eighth-inch bolt with what looks like a Whitworth thread and a fly nut. Apparently part of some mechanism, but we have not come across any mechanism to which it corresponds."

He smoothed out the paper and examined it on both sides, but there was no writing on it to give any clue to the use of the bolt. Finally he wrapped the latter up again in its paper and dropped it into his pocket, presumably for further consideration at his leisure. And having thus exhausted the material from the basket, he gathered the derelicts together and returned them to their receptacle.

The chest of drawers had apparently served the purpose of a dressing-table in conjunction with a good-sized looking-glass which hung on the wall beside the window. Like the rest of the room, it was quite tidy though now covered with dust, and the objects set out on it represented the bare necessaries for the toilet, On a china tray were two toothbrushes and a small tin of *"Odonto"* dentifrice, and beside the tray were a pair of nail scissors, a button-hook, and a turned wooden box containing spare collar-studs – one gold and several ivory – and a pair of cheap rolled gold links. There was also an earthenware bowl and a pair of hairbrushes. The latter Thorndyke took up and, separating them,

517

looked them over in his queer, inquisitive way. They were good brushes, though old and much worn as to the bristles, with ebony backs in which the initials "*J.G.*" had been inlaid in silver, but they appeared not to have been cleaned very lately, for the bristles held a considerable quantity of hair.

"I think," said Thorndyke, "we will take these and sort out the hairs. Probably they are all Gillum's, but it is possible that the brushes may have been used by some of his visitors, if he ever had any, and we may learn something about them."

He put the brushes in his coat pocket and then took up the bowl, which was of red earthenware, fitted with a cover bearing a highly-coloured label with the inscription: "*Dux Super-fatted Shaving Soap*".

"Rather a nice bowl," said Thorndyke, holding it out at arm's length to view it. "A pleasant shape and very suitable to the plain earthen body. But I am surprised that Gillum didn't soak off that label."

He lifted the lid of the bowl and, finding it empty save for a few drops of moisture at the bottom, sniffed at it and passed it to me.

"It smells to me," said I, "like chlorine, or perhaps chlorinated soda – some lotion of the Eusol type."

"Yes," he agreed, "something of that kind. Apparently it came from the bottle of antiseptic cleansing solution that we found in the tidy."

He put the bowl back in its place and then pulled out the drawers of the chest in succession. All of them seemed to be filled with articles of clothing, neatly folded and smelling slightly of camphor. These he glanced at but without disturbing them and, when he had pushed in the last of the drawers, he turned away and stood a while, looking thoughtfully around the room, apparently memorising its contents and their arrangement. There was not very much to see. The mantelpiece was bare save for a couple of candlesticks carrying rather large stearine candles. There remained only the large porcelain sink in the corner – a deep, rectangular sink of the kind used in chemical laboratories, but which here seemed, by the bracket over it bearing a soap dish, a nailbrush, and a bath sponge, to have served the purpose of a lavatory basin as well as a means of emptying the bath.

When we had inspected the sink, Thorndyke drew my attention to a mouse-hole in the corner beneath it which had been very neatly and effectively filled with Portland cement.

"That," said he, "suggests a man with a practical and efficient mind. Some people will go on forever setting traps, regardless of the rate at which rodents increase. But in old buildings the only effective method is to stop the holes with Portland cement, preferably mixed with an 'aggregate' of sand or powdered glass. That is Polton's plan, and it keeps our chambers practically free from mice."

From the bedroom we passed through a narrow doorway into the kitchen, and here we noticed the same appearance of order and tidiness as in the other rooms. It was a small place, but very completely equipped. There was a little gas cooker mounted on a stand and bearing a large aluminium kettle, a range of shelves on which the china was neatly disposed, the plates on edge and the cups inverted and all spotlessly clean. Another shelf bore a row of covered jars and tins, each labelled with the name of its contents. Several dish-covers of wire gauze or aluminium hung from nails on the wall with a frying-pan and a couple of small saucepans, and a carpet-sweeper in the corner accounted for the conspicuous cleanness of the floor. And here, too, I noticed a couple of neatly stopped mouse-holes.

The kitchen communicated with another room by a narrow doorway. The door was locked, but as the key was in the lock we were able to open it and pass through into the adjoining room, which I recognised as the larder that Mortimer had described.

It was smaller even than the kitchen, being only about eight-feet-by-six, and this small space was further reduced by the great coal-bin, which occupied the whole of the longer side of the room. But like the kitchen it was admirably arranged. There were two shelves on one of which lay three bottles of claret and one of sauterne, while the other was occupied by one or two dishes protected by wire covers through which could be seen – and smelt – some mouldy remains of food. In addition to the open shelves there was a tall, narrow, meat-safe through the wire gauze panels of which a mouldy, cadaverous odour exhaled. I opened the door and looked in, but as the odour then became more pronounced, I was about to shut it when Thorndyke stooped to examine the bottom shelf and then, reaching in, brought out from the back of the shelf a basin which was thickly encrusted with Portland cement and in which a rough bone spatula still stuck.

"I see," said Thorndyke, "that he used the same 'aggregate' that Polton favours – powdered glass. It is more effective than sand."

"Yes," said I, "and I notice that he has infringed another of Polton's copyrights – the utilisation of worn-out toothbrushes by shaving off the bristles."

I broke the spatula off the cement and scraped it clean with my pocket-knife, when it revealed itself as a bone handled dental-plate brush from which the bristles had been cleanly shaved off leaving a broad, blunt blade perfectly suited for the purpose for which it had been used.

"It is really remarkable," I commented, "that a man of so much common sense and capacity in small things should have been such a fool in the things that seriously matter."

"It is," he agreed, "but Gillum's case is by no means unique in that respect."

He turned away from the safe and transferred his attention to the coal-bin.

"I think," he remarked, "that this is the largest bin that I have ever seen in a set of chambers. Coal storage is not usually their strong point."

He measured the principal dimensions roughly with his graduated stick and then continued. "Eight feet long by thirty inches wide and twenty-nine inches deep – roughly fifty cubic feet. I don't know what that represents in coal, but it would seem to be a fairly liberal allowance for a man living alone and cooking by gas."

"Yes," I agreed. "Nearly a year's supply, I should think. And it seems," I added, as I lifted the lid and found the bin nearly full, "as if he had replenished his stock shortly before his death. Which appears an odd proceeding when we remember what the weather was like at that time. But perhaps he took advantage of the low summer prices to lay in his year's supply."

"Possibly," Thorndyke agreed. "That is to say, if it is really all coal. The quantity seems rather incredible."

He thrust his stick down into the loose coal, and at a few inches of depth found it stopped by an obviously solid obstruction.

"There seems to be a false bottom," I remarked. "Convenient enough for keeping the coal within easy reach, but rather a waste of space."

"Perhaps he didn't waste the space," said Thorndyke. "Let us see."

With the scoop that lay on top of the coal, he began to shovel the latter away from the right-hand end, piling it in a heap at the left end. This soon brought the false bottom into view, and with it an iron ring sunk into the board near the right-hand end. Further shovelling disclosed a crack across the bottom near the middle that divided it into two halves. Taking down a brush that hung from a nail on the wall, and that had manifest traces of coal dust on its hair, Thorndyke proceeded to brush away the small coal and dust until the surface of the false bottom was comparatively clean. Then he slipped his finger through the ring and lifted the right half of the bottom out bodily.

"The space wasn't wasted, you see," he said. "It seems to have been used as a store for things that were only occasionally wanted."

As he spoke, he threw the light of his pocket-lamp into the dark cavity, revealing a number of tins of various sizes, apparently containing

520

tongue and other preserved foods, and seven or eight bottles of port and sherry.

"There was a good deal of space wasted nevertheless," said I. "The cavity looks about eighteen-inches deep, and only four or five have been used."

Thorndyke dipped his stick into the cavity and read off the measurement. "Nineteen inches from the top of the supporting blocks to the floor. It would have held a good deal more than he put into it, but it was not a very handy container, as the coal had to be moved every time it was opened. But it looks as if the contrivance had been put in by Gillum, himself. The bin is obviously old, perhaps as old as the house, but the false bottom and the blocks that support it look quite fresh and new. Evidently, they were a recent addition."

He put the false bottom back in its place and then, taking a last look round, stepped up to the window. Apparently, a sash cord had broken and not been repaired, for the lower half of the sash was held up as far as it would go by a piece of wood on either side, which had been jammed into the groove and fixed with screws. It looked a makeshift arrangement, but as Thorndyke pointed out, it had been adopted deliberately, for the little wooden props had been neatly planed and fitted their place exactly, and the holes for the screws had been properly countersunk.

"I think," he said, "that there is no need to assume a broken sash line. It looks like an arrangement to fix the window open permanently so as to make sure of constant ventilation. You notice the row of holes at the foot of the door, evidently bored for the same purpose, and apparently by Gillum, himself to judge by the fresh, unstained wood inside them."

We let ourselves out by the door which opened on to the landing and which, presumably for that reason, had been fitted with a Yale night-latch and a spring. When we had come out and closed the door, Thorndyke stood for a few moments hesitating.

"I suppose," he said, "that is all, excepting the key of the cupboard." He unlocked the living-room door and re-entered, and when he had locked the cupboard and pocketed the key, looked about the room to see if there was anything that we had omitted to examine.

"What about the writing-table?" said I. "Oughtn't we to see what is in the drawers?"

"I expect Bateman took away all the papers," he replied. "Still, we may as well take a glance at them."

We went over to the table and tried the drawers, but they were all locked, excepting the top one, and we had no key, and the top drawer contained nothing but Gillum's stock of note-paper and envelopes, of each of which Thorndyke took a sample before closing the drawer.

"And that," said he as he folded the paper neatly and slipped it into the envelope, "I think completes the inspection – for the time being, at any rate, unless you can suggest anything further."

"I can suggest lots of things," I replied with a grin. "For instance, you might take the legs off the tables and chairs as the police did in Poe's story of 'The Purloined Letter', and you might go over the walls and furniture for finger-prints. And then there is the floor. You might set Polton to work on it with a vacuum cleaner and examine with the microscope the dust that he collected. This has been quite a superficial inspection."

He smiled indulgently at my rather feeble joke, but the result of it was not quite what I had expected.

"I think," he replied, "that we will leave the furniture intact and reserve the finger-print hunt for some future occasion. But, really, your suggestion of the vacuum cleaner is an excellent one, though Gillum's sweeper may have left us a rather meagre gleaning. I will get Polton to go over the floors, and hope that Gillum was not too thorough in his use of the sweeper."

This reply to my facetious suggestion took me aback completely, for my knowledge of Thorndyke told me that he was, according to a playful habit of his, crediting me with an idea which was already in his own mind. He had certainly intended to collect the dust from those floors for examination. But I could not imagine why. Considering the nature of our problem, the proceeding seemed to be completely futile and purposeless. Yet I knew that it could not be. And so the old familiar feeling came over me, the feeling that he had seen farther into this case than I had, that he had already some theory and was not groping in the dark as I was, but was even now seeking an answer to some definite question.

Chapter X
Mr. Weech Disapproves

As we came out of the entry into the courtyard, we became aware of our old acquaintance, Mr. Weech, the porter of the Inn, hovering in the background, whence he had probably observed us at the landing window. Mr. Weech had always interested me. He was a complete and unabridged survival from the Victorian age, alike in his dress, his habits, and in a certain subtle combination of dignity and deference in this bearing towards his social superiors. His costume invariably included a tall silk hat and a formal frock coat. Formerly, perchance, but not in my time, the hat may have borne a gold-laced band, and the coat have been embellished with gilt buttons. But nowadays the hat and coat were distinctive enough in themselves, and even the umbrella which was his constant companion, his sceptre and staff of office, seemed not quite like modern umbrellas.

In speech he was singularly precise and careful in his choice of words, though, unfortunately, his judgement was not always equal to his care, for he loved to interlard his sentences with Latin tags and, as he obviously had no acquaintance with that language, the results were sometimes a little startling.

As we came into view, then, Mr. Weech quickened his pace and advanced towards us with the peculiar splay-footed gait characteristic of men who stand much and walk little, and peering at us inquisitively through his spectacles, essayed cautiously to ascertain what our business was.

"I am afraid," said he, "that you will have found poor Mr. Gillum's chambers locked up – if it was his chambers that you wanted."

"Thank you, Mr. Weech," Thorndyke replied, "but we have the keys. Mr. Benson has lent them to us."

"Oh, indeed," said Mr. Weech, in a tone of mild surprise and still milder disapproval.

"We just wanted to look over the chambers," Thorndyke explained.

"Did you indeed, sir?" said Mr. Weech with rather more definite disapproval. "Not, I venture to hope, for professional reasons?"

"I am sorry, Mr. Weech," Thorndyke replied suavely, "but it must be admitted that our interest in the chambers has a slight professional taint. The fact is that Mr. Benson has asked me to make certain enquiries concerning his late cousin."

"Oh, dear!" exclaimed Weech, now undisguisedly disapproving. "Has it come to that? I had hoped that we had heard the last of that dreadful business. Don't tell me that these quiet, respectable precincts are to be involved in another scandal."

"I'll tell you all about it," said Thorndyke. "There is no need to be evasive with an old friend like you, and I know that I can trust to your discretion."

"Undoubtedly you can," replied Mr. Weech, evidently mollified by Thorndyke's candour. (He didn't know my colleague as well as I did.)

"Well," said Thorndyke, "the position is this: The evidence at the inquest disclosed the existence of certain blackmailers who had been preying on Mr. Gillum. Now, Mr. Benson holds those blackmailers accountable for his cousin's death, and he wants them identified and, if possible, brought to justice."

"M'yes," said Mr. Weech, clearly sceptical and unsympathetic. "I don't see why. What's the use, even if it were possible? Poor Mr. Gillum is beyond their reach now. Your protection of him has come – or would come, if it came at all – too late. It's a case of *post bellum auxilium.*"

"I am inclined to agree with you, Mr. Weech," Thorndyke replied, "but it is not my choice. Mr. Benson wants these rascals found and prosecuted, and he has engaged my professional services to that end, and it is my duty to render those services to the best of my ability."

"Certainly, sir," Mr. Weech agreed, "and I don't say that I would not be glad to hear that those wretches had been brought to justice, if it were possible – which I don't believe it is."

"And I am sure," said Thorndyke, "that you would give me any help that you could, as a matter of public policy."

"I would for old acquaintance sake," replied Weech, "though I can't pretend that I am anxious for you to succeed, seeing what a rumpus there would be if you did. And I really don't see how I can help you."

"I think," said Thorndyke, "that you could help me by supplying certain information that I should like to have. For instance, as a rather important point, you could tell me what visitors Mr. Gillum received."

"But I don't know," Weech protested. "How should I? Both gates are open all day and strangers pass in and out unquestioned. My impression is that he had very few visitors, but that is only a guess. As far as actual knowledge goes, I can recall only two. One was a Mr. Mortimer, who, I think, came to him several times – "

"We know Mr. Mortimer," interrupted Thorndyke. "Who was the other?"

"I have no idea," replied Weech. "I know about him because he spoke to me when I was standing at the gate by the lodge. That would be about the beginning of last September. He asked me if a Mr. John Gillum lived in the Inn. I replied 'Yes,' and gave him the number of the chambers, whereupon he bustled off. I didn't go with him, as he couldn't make any mistake, there being only the one set of chambers in that building."

"Can you describe him?" Thorndyke asked.

"Yes," was the reply. "Curiously enough, I remember him quite well, perhaps because he was little out of the ordinary. He was a short, stocky man with a sallow face, a small moustache, waxed at the ends, and bushy black eyebrows. He wore a rather queer kind of single eyeglass. It had no rim and no cord, it was just a plain glass, stuck in his eye with no kind of support. How he kept it there I can't imagine. Then, as he walked off up the passage, I noticed that he had a slight limp and that he used a stick to help himself along, and a most uncommonly fine stick it was, a thick malacca with a silver band and a big ivory knob."

Thorndyke jotted down in his note-book the points of this excellent description and then asked, "Do you know how long he stayed with Mr. Gillum?"

"I don't. I never saw him again, but he might have gone out by the Fetter Lane gate. It couldn't have been a long interview because, about a quarter-of-an-hour later, I saw Mr. Gillum come out of his chambers alone, and I thought he looked a little annoyed and upset."

"By the way," said Thorndyke, "you mentioned just now that there is only one set of chambers in that building. But there is a second floor."

"Yes," Mr. Weech explained, "but it is not suitable for chambers. We use it as a general lumber room for the Inn, and it is always kept locked."

As the conversation had developed, we had moved away from the window of the typewriting office on the ground floor and began slowly to pace up and down the courtyard, but I noticed that every time that we re-passed the window there happened to be some person looking out of it. Apparently we were being kept under observation.

"I am wondering," Thorndyke said after a pause, "by what chance Mr. Gillum, an Australian, strange to England, should have happened to discover such a retired backwater as Clifford's Inn. Did he ever tell you?"

"He did not, because, in fact, he did not discover it. Being a stranger, he very wisely employed an agent to find him rooms."

"Do you mean a regular house-agent?"

"I don't know what he was, but I had an idea that he was a personal friend of Mr. Gillum's. At any rate, he not only carried out all the negotiations, but he furnished the chambers and got them ready for the tenant by the time he wanted them."

"I wonder," said Thorndyke, "whether you would mind giving us a more circumstantial account of this transaction."

"Well," Mr. Weech replied, "let me see. It happened, so far as I can remember, somewhat like this. One morning, towards the end of August, 1928, a man came to the lodge to enquire about some chambers that we had to let at that time. He seemed to think that Number 64, which was empty, might suit him, so I gave him the keys and he went off to have a look at them. Presently he came back and said that they would suit him perfectly and that he would like to take a lease of them. But then he explained that they were not for himself but that he was acting as agent for a gentleman of means, and that he was fully authorised to execute an agreement and to furnish references and to pay whatever deposit I might think necessary. I would rather have dealt direct with the prospective tenant, but he produced a written authority from his principal, Mr. Gillum, who, he assured me, was a gentleman of good position and ample means, and he referred me to Mr. Gillum's solicitor and his bank, but he did suggest that it would be better not to take up the references until the tenant came and entered into residence."

"Did he give any reason for that suggestion?"

"Yes, and quite a sound one. He said that Mr. Gillum had lived abroad for some years and was still abroad and that his relations with both his solicitor and his bank had been conducted by correspondence and that neither of them knew him personally. Well, he was willing to pay half-a-year's rent in advance and to sign a provisional agreement *per procurationem*, I closed with him. He paid the money – twenty-five pounds – signed the agreement, and I handed him the keys. He wanted them because Mr. Gillum had asked him to get the rooms furnished so far as to be ready for immediate occupation. And that, in fact, is what he did. He took possession and had the chambers furbished up and some odd jobs done, and he ordered in enough furniture to enable Mr. Gillum to go into residence at once."

"I am rather surprised that you agreed to the deal," said I.

"I don't see why," he retorted. "It was a slightly unusual transaction, but it was quite straightforward. The man couldn't run away with the chambers. What possible danger of injury was there? *Ad quod damnum*, as the lawyers would say." (He pronounced the last word "*damn 'em*".) "At any rate, the transaction turned out all right, so my action was justified by the results."

"Yes," I replied, "that has to be admitted. *Finis coronat opus*."

"Exactly," he rejoined eagerly (and, I suspect, make a mental note of the tag with a view to future use). "The proof of the pudding is in the eating, as the vulgar saying has it."

"When Mr. Gillum arrived," said Thorndyke, "was he introduced to you by the agent?"

"No," replied Weech. "As I understood from the night porter, the two gentlemen came to the Inn together at night between nine and ten. He mentioned the matter to me the next morning, because the agent had asked him to. When they knocked at the wicket, he opened it and, as he knew the agent by sight, having seen him once before, he let them pass through, and they went up the passage. Presently the agent came back alone and said, 'By the way, that gentleman is Mr. Gillum, the new tenant of Number 64. You might mention to Mr. Weech that he has come to take possession.' Which, as I have told you, he did."

"Did he mention to you how long the agent stayed that night?"

"No. But, you see, that was no business of mine."

"And when did you first meet Mr. Gillum?"

"The very next morning. I made it my business to. I looked in at the chambers about eleven in the forenoon, and the door was opened by Mr. Gillum himself. I told him who I was and asked him if he acknowledged the agreement signed by his agent. He said 'Yes,' but that he would rather have a new agreement signed by himself to put things on a regular basis. I thought he was quite right and, as I had the agreement with me and some forms in my pocket, we filled in a new form and, when he had signed it, we tore up the old one. Then he gave me his references and that finished the business."

"By the way," said Thorndyke, "you didn't mention the agent's name."

"I'm not sure that I remember it," replied Weech. "But does it matter?"

"It might matter," Thorndyke replied, "if it should seem desirable to get into touch with him, as I think it may be."

"Well," said Weech, "I seem to remember that it was something like Baker or Barber, or it may have been Barker – something of, that sort."

"Of that sort!" I protested. "But there is all the difference in the world between a man who bakes your bread and one who shaves you or barks at you."

Mr. W. smiled deprecatingly. "I was referring to the sound," said he. "They are a good deal alike. And really, his name did not arise, excepting when he signed the agreement, and his signature was not very distinct."

"But," objected Thorndyke, "there was the cheque and the receipt that you gave him."

"There was no cheque," replied Weech. "He paid in five five-pound notes. And the receipt was made out, at his request, to Mr. John Gillum. So, you see, his name was never mentioned, and I only saw it once in writing."

"Perhaps," Thorndyke suggested persuasively, "you might give us some idea as to what this gentleman was like. I am rather interested in him, because he must know more about Mr. Gillum than most of my informants seem to."

"Well," Weech replied musingly, "I don't remember much about him. He was a tallish man – about my height – and he was a fair man, with a light-brown, tawny beard and moustache and blue eyes. He was quite a gentlemanly man with a pleasant, persuasive manner – not to say plausible. And that is really all that I can remember about him. You see, I only saw him once to speak to, and only once or twice at a distance when he was furnishing the chambers, and I have never seen him since. He may have been here to see Mr. Gillum on some occasions but, if so, I never happened to see him."

Thorndyke reflected on this statement for a few moments. Then he asked, apparently apropos of nothing in particular, "I noticed that some carpenter's work had been done in the rooms at Number 64, some alterations to the coal-bin and the larder door. Do you happen to know whether they were done by Mr. Gillum or by the agent?"

"They were done by the agent – Mr. Barker, we'll call him. I only heard of it afterwards from Mr. Wing, the carpenter, of Fetter Lane, who does most of the odd jobs about the Inn. He ought really to have got permission to have the alterations made, though there isn't much in it. The false bottom to the coal-bin was a distinct improvement, but I did think the holes in the larder door a trifle *ultra vires*." (Mr. Weech made "*vires*" rhyme with '*fires*', but we knew what he meant.)

Then there was a brief pause and, as we passed the window of the typewriting office, I observed a lady in a hat, putting on her gloves. Then Thorndyke resumed the conversation with the question: "Did you find Mr. Gillum a satisfactory tenant?"

"Very," Mr. Weech replied. "A model tenant. Paid his rent promptly on quarter-day, kept his chambers clean and tidy, and gave no trouble in any way. I greatly regret his loss, and so, I am sure, does Miss Darby, the lady who has the ground floor."

"Why?" I asked, scenting a romance.

"Well, you see," he replied, "the gentleman who had Mr. Gillum's chambers before him was terribly untidy, particularly in the matter of food, which is what matters in chambers. He used to leave food uncovered on his table and even in the larder, and the crumbs from his meals all over the floor. The natural consequence was that the place was overrun with mice and, of course, they overflowed into the ground floor and kept the lady's nerves fairly on edge. But when Mr. Gillum took over, the nuisance stopped at once. The mice disappeared like magic. Of course, it was quite simple. Mr. Gillum used to sweep up his crumbs after each meal and keep all food in the larder under covers or in tins or jars with lids. There was nothing for the mice to feed on. And what is more, he stopped up all the mouse-holes. Here is Miss Darby, and I am sure she will bear out what I have said."

At this point the lady whom I had seen at the window emerged from her entry and met us on our return march. Mr. Weech raised his hat with the kind of flourish which is possible only with a "topper" and accosted her. "We were just speaking of the way poor Mr. Gillum cleared the mice out of his chambers. You remember, I dare say."

"Indeed I do," she replied emphatically. "Before he came, my rooms simply swarmed with the nasty little creatures. The man on the first floor must have lived like a pig – kept a regular restaurant for mice. It was awful. I had great difficulty in getting the young ladies to stay with me. But when Mr. Gillum came, the little beasts disappeared completely. We never saw a mouse. I can't tell you how grateful we were."

"Very naturally," said Thorndyke. "Mice are pretty little animals, but they are most unpleasant in their habits. However, I hope that your mice have gone for good. I suppose you are still clear of them?"

"Well, you know," Miss Darby replied with a slight frown, "the rather curious thing is that we are not. Just lately, one or two have made their appearance again. I can't understand it. Of course, we have our teas in the office, and sometimes our lunches. But we used to do that before. And we are most careful to sweep up all crumbs and to leave no food about. It is really rather strange."

"It is," Thorndyke agreed. "But perhaps you would get rid of your uninvited guests if you were to adopt Mr. Gillum's plan, stop up the holes with Portland cement mixed with powdered glass. I strongly recommend you to try that remedy."

Miss Darby thanked him for the advice and then, with a smile and a little bow, bustled away and disappeared into the tunnel-like passage that ran past the hall door. And thither we shortly followed her, as it appeared that Thorndyke had squeezed his informant dry – with mighty little result, as it seemed to me. But then you could never tell what was in Thorndyke's mind or what might be the significance to him of trivial facts that seemed to have no significance at all.

Mr. Weech walked with us down the passage to Fleet Street and finally dismissed us with another impressive flourish of his hat, which we returned punctiliously and then crossed the road to the Inner Temple gate.

As we walked down the lane past the church I reflected on what we had heard and seen. Presently I remarked "Weech's description of the unknown visitor at the Inn seemed to me to correspond pretty closely with that of Abel Webb."

"So I thought," replied Thorndyke, "and, for the present, I am assuming that he was Abel Webb, though we shall have to get confirmation if possible."

"I don't quite see how," said I. "But assuming him to have been Webb, how does that square with what we have been inferring about the relations between him and Gillum? It seems to me to be rather a misfit. If the man was Webb, that must have been his first visit to Gillum, as he had to inquire of Weech and was not sure of the address or that Gillum did actually live there. Now that visit was made only a few days before his death. But we inferred – at least, I did – that Webb had been blackmailing Gillum for the best part of a year. There seems to be a radical disagreement. You can hardly blackmail a man whose address you do not know."

"It is not actually impossible," said Thorndyke, "but I agree with you that it is extremely difficult to see how it could be done. However, we are not certain that this man was Webb and, before we make any further inferences, we must get more evidence. The whole question of the relations of these two men needs to be elucidated, for if we were wrong in our original inferences we may have to recast our theory of the circumstances of Webb's death. Obviously the first thing to do is to ascertain, if possible, whether the man who came to the inn was really Abel Webb."

Chapter XI
A Fresh Puzzle

M_y colleague's remark that it would be necessary to test our belief as to the identity of the visitor to Gillum's chambers rather puzzled me for, apparently, Mr. Weech was the only person who had seen that visitor, and he had told us all that he had to tell, and I could not think of any means by which we could check his description. But on the very next day, Thorndyke reopened the subject and disposed of my difficulties. "I think," said he, "that it is desirable that we should confirm or disprove our assumptions as to the identity of Gillum's visitor at the Inn. At present our belief is founded entirely on Mortimer's not-very-precise description of the stick and the eye glass. That is not enough. The question whether Abel Webb did or did not go to Gillum's chambers is a very important one, and we ought to settle it more definitely. Indeed, the whole of the Abel Webb incident requires clearing up."

"And how do you propose to set about it?" I asked.

"I propose," he replied, "to go to the place where Webb was employed and get a description of his person. We have an excellent one from Weech with which to compare it. And perhaps, if we are fortunate, we may pick up some additional information. We want it badly enough."

"Yes," I agreed, "the Abel Webb business is rather in the air."

"Very much so," said he. "We have adopted the provisional theory that John Gillum, a most respectable gentleman, murdered Webb. That is a theory that wants clearing up, one way or the other. So, as the matter is of some urgency, I am proposing to devote the afternoon to it, as we are both free and I hope that the expedition will interest you. What do you say?"

Of course I agreed, with some enthusiasm and, as there were no preparations to make, we set forth within a few minutes.

It was characteristic of Thorndyke that, in making his way to Webb's place of business, he should choose the route that carried us over the scene of the tragedy. Leaving, the Temple by the Tudor Street gate, we made for the Temple Station and travelled to the bank, whence we started along the south side of Cornhill until we reached the Church of St. Michael. Here we turned up the alley and, in a few paces, came to the arched entrance to the covered passage that Mortimer had described. A few steps along this brought us to the cavern-like south porch of the church, and here we both halted to reconstitute the picture that Mortimer

531

had drawn so vividly, though the appearance of the place, in the bright afternoon light, was not easily reconciled with his description.

"It is an astounding affair," said Thorndyke, as he gazed into the now well-lighted porch. "By whomsoever that murder was committed, it was a remarkable exploit, and the murderer must have been a remarkable man – a man of iron nerve who combined the utmost audacity with caution and sound judgment. Not a man in ten-thousand would have dared to take the risk, but yet, apart from that momentary risk, the crime was absolutely safe from detection. The actual murder can have been but a matter of seconds, and the instant the blow was struck the murderer could slip out into the alley, quietly walk down into Cornhill, and there instantly become merged into the indistinguishable population of the street. For a premeditated murder, which it must have been, it was the boldest and the most skilfully managed crime that I have ever known."

"I don't know," said I, "that I am so much impressed with his judgment. It was a terrific gamble and he took a frightful risk. It doesn't seem to me that he made such a very good choice of the place."

"I am rather assuming," Thorndyke replied, "that he had not much choice. The suggestion to me is that of a desperate man who felt an immediate need to dispose of Webb, who had no time to make suitable arrangements but had to seize the one opportunity that presented itself. It was an opportunity, and he took it, and the result justified him in accepting the risk."

I was disposed to smile at Thorndyke's ultra-professional view of this murder, which he was evidently considering purely in terms of efficiency, putting himself, in his queer way, in the murderer's shoes and debating the appropriate technique. But I suppressed my amusement and, following his own train of thought, asked, "How do you suppose the murder was actually carried out?"

"I should assume," he replied, "that the murderer knew that Webb would pass through this passage at a certain time and that – greatly favoured by the unusual darkness of the evening – he lurked here, keeping a look-out from either end for possible wayfarers who might be approaching. Then, when Webb appeared at the entrance – the coast being clear at the moment – he made his attack. Probably Webb saw him, and there was a brief struggle, as suggested by the hat in the churchyard. But when they came opposite the porch the murderer thrust in the syringe, pushed his victim down on the steps, and walked away down St. Michael's Alley. But the point of interest to us is that the murderer seems to have been familiar with Webb's habits. Perhaps we may get some further light on that point from our enquiries at Cope's."

With this we turned away from the porch and, stepping up into the churchyard, took our way along the paved walk, out into Castle Court, and through the little covered passage into Bell Yard. At the entrance of the yard into Gracechurch Street, Thorndyke paused and ran his eye along the houses on the south side of the street until it rested on a building which bore in large gilded letters the inscription, *"The Cope Refrigerating Company"*, when we crossed the road and bore down on it.

On entering by the main doorway, we found ourselves in a large showroom filled with a bewildering assortment of various types of refrigerators, and were confronted by a member of the staff.

"I think," said Thorndyke, addressing him, "that the late Mr. Abel Webb was employed here."

"Yes," was the reply, "but not in this department. We deal here with refrigerating apparatus and plant. Mr. Webb was in the solid carbonic acid department. That is next door. You turn to the right as you go on."

Following this direction we entered a small doorway adjoining the main entrance and came into a long, narrow shop or warehouse fitted with a counter which ran from end to end. Behind this were two men, one at the farther end, who was delivering one or two large and heavy packages to a carman, and the other, nearer to us, who appeared to be disengaged. To the latter Thorndyke repeated his former question, and thereby immediately captured his attention.

"Yes," he replied, "poor Mr. Webb was employed here. He was assistant manager. Most of his time was spent in the manufacturing section, which adjoins this warehouse, and it was there that I knew him. I only came out into the retail department a short time before his death."

"Then," said Thorndyke, "as you knew him fairly well, perhaps you could tell us what sort of a man he was to look at. Would you mind?"

"Certainly not," was the cordial reply. "But may I ask, if it is not an impertinence, whether you two gentlemen are connected with the police?"

"We are not," Thorndyke replied. "My friend and I are lawyers, but I may say that our interest in Mr. Webb is a professional interest. We are trying to get some fresh light on the circumstances of his death."

"I am glad to hear that," said the assistant. "It's time someone did. The police came here once or twice after the inquest but, of course, we couldn't tell them much, and they didn't seem particularly keen. But I don't think the affair ought to have been let drop in the way that it was. Now, as to what Mr. Webb was like: He was rather a noticeable man, though short. He was a bit of a dandy, always well-dressed and smartly turned out. Waxed the ends of his moustache and wore a single eye-glass. Quite a nut in his way."

"Yes," said Thorndyke, "and to come to particulars, was he dark or fair, fat or thin?"

"He was dark. Sallow face, black moustache, and eyebrows – bushy eyebrows like young moustaches, and I wouldn't call him fat. He was just stoutly built, and looked stouter because of his shortness."

"You spoke of an eyeglass. What was that like?"

"It was just an eyeglass. No rim or frame, no cord or ribbon. Just a plain glass. He used to carry it in his waistcoat pocket and, when he wanted it, he would take it out and fix it in his eye, and there it stuck as if it were glued in."

"When he was out of doors, did he carry an umbrella or a stick?"

"A stick, always. He had just a slight limp – I think one leg was a little shorter than the other. That was why he gave up the sea. Found it a trifle inconvenient on board ship. So he used a stick for a bit of extra support. And a rare fine stick it was, a very thick malacca with a silver band and an ivory knob like a young billiard ball. And that, I think, is all that I can tell you about Mr. Webb."

"Thank you," said Thorndyke, "you have given us a very admirable and complete description." He paused for a few moments and appeared to be reflecting. Then he opened a new topic. "I notice that you seem to reject the idea that Mr. Webb committed suicide."

"That I certainly do," was the reply. "Webb was not the man to commit any foolishness of that kind. Besides, it was a plain case of murder. Anyone could see that from the way it was done – and the place, too, for that matter."

"What is the significance of the place?" Thorndyke asked.

"The significance is that anyone waiting at that place at the right time would have been sure of meeting him. He used to get on his bus at the Royal Exchange and he always walked there by the same route, through Bell Yard, Castle Court and the churchyard and out into Cornhill by St. Michael's Alley. Always the same way, he told me so, himself, one day when I walked that way with him. He that he liked the walk through the churchyard. And he was wonderfully punctual, too. He would stay on here finishing up the day's work after the rest of the staff had gone, but at seven-thirty, sharp, he would take his stick and hat and off he would go. Anyone waiting for him in that dark passage could have been certain of him to half-a-minute. It would have been perfectly easy if there happened to be nobody about."

"Yes," Thorndyke agreed, "that is quite an important point. But you see that the idea of some person lying in wait there suggests the further idea someone who had an intimate knowledge of Mr. Webb's habits. Can you think of any persons who had that knowledge?"

"No. I don't know that anyone besides myself knew what his habits were, and even if any of our people knew, there is none of them that I could possibly suspect."

Thorndyke agreed cordially with the latter statement and again paused with a reflective air, and I got the impression that he was feeling about for a new opening. Apparently he found one, for he proceeded to put a fresh case. "Looking back on that time – the time just before Mr. Webb's death – can you recall any incident that could possibly be, in any way, regarded as suspicious?"

Our friend weighed the question seriously for some seconds but finally concluded that he really did not think that he could. But yet I seemed to detect a certain hesitancy in his reply as if he did not absolutely reject the suggestion. And this was evidently perceived also by Thorndyke, for he returned to the attack with his customary persistence, tempered by suavity.

"You must forgive me for pressing you, Mr. – "

"My name is Small."

"Mr. Small. But, looking back by the light of what happened, can you think of any incident – we won't say actually suspicious – perhaps quite trivial and commonplace, but which, considered retrospectively, might conceivably have had some connection with the tragedy. Any strangers, for instance, who might have called to see Mr. Webb, or who might have met him by chance. Now, what do you say?"

Mr. Small was still hesitant and slightly evasive.

"You see," said he, "when an awful thing like that has happened, it tends to upset your judgment and sense of proportion. You look back on what went before and you are apt to magnify every little simple thing that occurred and think that it might have had something to do with the disaster."

"Exactly," said Thorndyke. "And so it might have had. Don't forget that. It is by the close scrutiny of little simple things that we sometimes get a valuable hint. Now, Mr. Small, I can see that there is something in your mind that you have given some thought to, but that you are shy of mentioning because of its apparent triviality. Let us have it. Perhaps it may not appear so trivial to me, and if it does, there will be no harm done."

"Well," Mr. Small replied with some reluctance, "it is really a very trivial incident, but yet I have thought it rather odd. It just amounts to this: One evening, not very long before closing time, a man – a gentleman, I might call him – came here to buy some four-pound blocks of snow – solid carbonic acid, you know – and he had brought a sort of suit-case to carry it away in. Now, I had got the blocks, wrapped in a

535

rough insulated packing, and was just handing them to him when Mr. Webb came in through that door and stopped to look up at the shelves, standing about where the other assistant is standing now. Well, what attracted my notice was this: As Mr. Webb came through the doorway, the customer glanced at him, and then he looked again very hard with an expression as if he was surprised or startled. And at that moment Mr. Webb noticed him, and *he* looked very hard at him. But he couldn't get a very good view of him, for the customer turned away so that his back was towards Mr. Webb while he was packing the blocks in his vase. And when he had got them in, as he had already paid for them, he said 'Good evening' and walked out. When he had gone Mr. Webb asked me if I knew who the customer was, and I said I didn't. 'Well,' he said, 'the next time that he comes, find out his name if you can,' and I said I would."

"And did you?" Thorndyke asked.

"No," replied Small, "because he never came again, and I have never seen him since."

"Do you remember, roughly, the date on which this incident occurred?"

"I should say that it was from ten days to a fortnight before Mr. Webb's death, and that happened on the ninth of September. That is what has made it stick in my memory. I have often wondered whether it could have had any connection with that dreadful affair."

"Naturally," said Thorndyke, "and it does not appear so very improbable that it had. It might be useful to have a description of that customer if you could remember what he was like."

"I can't remember much about him," said Small, "though I should know him if I met him but, of course, I didn't notice him particularly. I know that he was a rather tall man, say about five-foot-ten, and dark, black hair and a smallish black beard with a close-clipped moustache, and that is about all that I do remember."

"You didn't by any chance notice what his teeth were like?"

Mr. Small seemed to start, and gazed at Thorndyke in evident surprise. "Well, now," he exclaimed, "that's curious, because, now that you come to mention it, I did notice his teeth, when he smiled at something that I said. His upper front teeth had been stopped with gold – pretty extensively, too – and those stoppings were no ornament. I wonder he let the dentist disfigure him in that way. But you seemed to know the man, to judge by your question."

"It was only a shot," replied Thorndyke. "I remembered a man who might have been surprised at seeing Mr. Webb here. But, as that man is now dead, there isn't much in it."

As Thorndyke seemed to have elicited the information that he had come for, I ventured to seek a little on my own account.

"What sort of people use those blocks that you were speaking of," I asked, "and what do they use them for?"

"All sorts of people use the solid carbonic acid," replied Small. "The standard twenty-five-pound blocks are mostly used by brewers and mineral water manufacturers. The small four-pound blocks were made in the first place principally for the convenience of the ice-cream tricycles, to keep their stuff cold, but nowadays those blocks are used for a number of purposes. Doctors use them for freezing warts and moles, and engineers and motor repair men use them quite a lot."

"What on earth do engineers want carbonic acid now for?" I asked.

"Principally," he replied, "for shrinking metal. Say you have got a bush that is just too big to drive into its hole. Well, you can get it in either by expanding the piece with the hole in it by making it hot, which may be a big job, or you can shrink the bush by freezing it with the dioxide snow, which is much more convenient."

Hitherto, fortunately for us, the warehouse had been so nearly empty that the other assistant had been able to deal with the business. But now several customers came in, and their arrival brought our conversation to an end. Mr. Small apologised for having to leave us in order to attend to them, and accordingly, when we had thanked him for having given us so much of his time, we wished him good afternoon and retired.

We took our way back by the way we had come, through Bell Yard and the paved walk beside the little grass plot, lingering a while in the quiet and seclusion of the churchyard to discuss the results of the expedition.

"That was a bold shot of yours," I remarked, "with respect to the teeth. What made you think that the man might be Gillum – for there can be no doubt that it was he?"

"Practically none," he replied. "But the reasons that made me chance the suggestion were, first, that the circumstances seemed to make it probable that the man was Gillum and, second, the description that Small gave fitted Gillum perfectly, as far as it went."

"I don't quite see the probability that you mention," said I, "in fact, I find these new developments rather bewildering. I can't fit them into our scheme. Small's description almost suggests an unexpected meeting, which might be natural enough on Webb's part, but hardly on Gillum's, for, as he was neither an ice-cream vendor nor a doctor nor an engineer, it would seem that the purchase of the blocks was merely a pretext for going to Webb's place of business and getting into touch with him. But that doesn't seem to fit in with our theory at all, and neither does Webb's visit to Clifford's Inn – for that visitor certainly was Webb."

"Yes," Thorndyke agreed, "Small's description corresponds exactly with Weech's. But you are quite right, Jervis. These new facts do not fit our theory in its original form. We shall have to modify it. But you notice that our new discoveries, so far from exonerating Gillum, tend to confirm our suspicion that he was responsible for Webb's death. What we shall have to reconsider is the possible motive for the murder. We assumed that Webb was a blackmailer. We may have been right, but these two meetings, as you say, do not fit comfortably into the group of events that we assumed. We must have another try. But what will be much better than speculating on the possible alternatives, will be the collection of some further data. There are still some unexplored territories in which we may possibly make new discoveries."

"Yes," I agreed, "there is, for instance, Dr. Peck. He might be able to give us some useful information. But the question is: Where is he? He may be in the middle of the Pacific."

"True," Thorndyke admitted, "but, on the other hand, he may not. I think that your question has to be answered, and I propose that we seek the answer without delay."

Chapter XII
The Pursuit of Dr. Peck

Thorndyke's decision that an immediate answer must be found to my question, "Where is Dr. Peck?" was given effect on the very following morning, when, as our engagements permitted, we set forth together for the pleasant old precinct of Staple Inn. As our business was with the porter, and he was most likely to be found in his lodge by the main gate, we took our way up Fetter Lane and along Holborn until we reached the arched entrance in the ancient timber houses through which the wayfarer in the busy street can get a glimpse of the quiet, secluded quadrangle. And here, passing under the archway, we found the lodge door open and the porter plainly visible within.

Observing that we had halted with an air of business, he came to the door and asked, civilly, what he could do for us.

"I want," said Thorndyke, "to get into communication with one of your tenants, a certain Dr. Peck."

"Ah!" the official replied, "then you have made a bull's eye at the first shot, though he is not one of our tenants now. But I can give you his address."

This he proceeded to do, writing it down on a slip of paper which my colleague offered for the purpose. And, with this, it seemed to me that our business had come to an unexpectedly swift conclusion, and that we might forthwith go about "getting into communication" with our quarry. But this was evidently not Thorndyke's view, for, having put the slip of paper in his pocket-book, he developed an unmistakeable tendency to open a conversation and to start the porter talking, from which I inferred that he hoped to gather up a few unconsidered trifles of a biographical nature which might be dropped in the course of a properly directed gossip.

"I came here," said he, "because this was given as his address in the *Medical Directory*, though I hadn't much hope of finding him, as he spends most of his time at sea."

"No," replied the porter, "and if you had come a little earlier you wouldn't have found him or got any news of him either. He seems to have been all over the world this last trip, not on an ordinary voyage out and home, but changing about from one ship to another and going into all sorts of unheard-of places."

"But I suppose," said Thorndyke, "he kept in touch with you so that you could send on his letters?"

"Not a bit," was the reply. "He couldn't. He never knew where he was going to next, and he never stayed long in any place. He meant this to be his last trip at sea, and he was determined to see as much of the world as he could before he settled down ashore. And he did. It must have been a regular Captain Cook's voyage."

"And he never gave you any place to send his letters to all the time that he was away? There must have been a pretty considerable accumulation when he came home."

"I expect there was. But I never collected them from his chambers, as I had no place to send them to. In fact, he told me to leave them where they dropped through the letter slit."

"I suppose you heard from him from time to time – when the rent became due, for instance?"

"No, he never wrote. There was nothing to write about. He had always left an order with his banker to pay his rent as it became due when he was away at sea, and he did the same this time."

"It seems a wasteful arrangement," said Thorndyke, "to have kept a set of chambers empty, month after month, while the tenant was wandering about the earth. Don't you think so?"

"I do, and I told him so. But he said that a doctor has to have a permanent address to keep his name on the register, and he liked to have a place to come to when he returned from a voyage. But this last trip did really seem to me out of all reason. He was away close upon two years, and all that time there were the chambers lying empty and the rent going on just the same as if he had been living in them. It happened to be a low rent, because he was an old tenant. He came here years ago when he was a medical student. We used to have a lot of students in those days, mostly from Barts, and when one qualified and gave up his chambers, he was allowed to hand them on to a new student. So Dr. Peck had been living here more years than I can remember, and I suppose he didn't like the idea of giving up his old chambers. But still, as you said, two years' rent for unoccupied chambers does seem a wicked waste."

"Perhaps," Thorndyke suggested, "he didn't expect to be away so long."

"Oh yes, he did. He told me that he might be away for as much as a couple of years. He meant to go overland to Marseilles and there pick up some kind of foreign tramp and go with her wherever she might be going, and after a time, change over to another ship and make a voyage somewhere else. And he made mighty preparations so that he should be as comfortable as possible. He got a brand new cabin trunk, in addition

540

to his old ones, and he had a couple of portable bookcases made so that he could have his library with him."

"He must have reckoned that those tramps would have pretty liberal cabin space," I remarked. "You couldn't get many bookcases into an ordinary tramp's cabin, so far as my experience goes."

"Oh, but these were quite small things," the porter explained. "Only about three foot high by a couple of foot wide. And uncommonly cleverly they were planned, too – at least, so I thought. You see, they were intended to travel with the books in them. They had moveable fronts fixed on with a dozen long screws, well greased so that they would come out easily, and lying flush so that there was nothing projecting to catch when they were travelling. And when you had got them into your cabin, all you had to do was to take out the screws and the front was free. You could just take it off and slip it behind the case out of the way, and there was your bookcase with all your books properly arranged and ready for use. I thought it a mighty neat idea."

"So it was," Thorndyke agreed. "Extremely convenient, not only for use on board ship, but for travelling on land. Did you see the cases?"

"Yes," was the reply, "I saw them in Mr. Crow's workshop just before he delivered them, and I complimented him on having made such a good job of them. He had got them stained and varnished so that they looked quite smart, although they were only made of deal, you understand."

"Mr. Crow, I take it," said Thorndyke, "is a local craftsman."

"Yes, he lives close by in Baldwin's Gardens, so we give him all the jobs that we want done about the Inn. And a real good tradesman he is. I always recommend him whenever I can. It's a kindness to him and to the customer, too."

"It is, indeed," said Thorndyke, "especially to the customer. Really skilful and dependable tradesmen are getting scarce, and it is no small advantage to know where one can find such a man on occasion. I shall make a note of Mr. Crow's address, and perhaps call on him. I am quite impressed by your description of those bookcases."

"Well, I think you would find them handy if you travel much," said the porter, apparently much gratified by the impression he had made. "Dr. Peck did, as he told me, and they took the fancy of the captain of his last ship to such an extent that when the doctor left the ship at Marseilles to come home overland, the skipper insisted on buying the cases, books and all."

"Then you have seen Dr. Peck since he came home?"

"Lord, yes," the porter chuckled, "and I didn't recognise him at first. You see, he had shaved off his beard, and when a beaver does a clean shave, the results are apt to be surprising. But he was quite right. A beard is the thing on board ship, where shaving isn't very convenient and not at all necessary but, as he said very truly, when a man is in practice as a doctor, he doesn't want a bunch of hair on his chin to stick in his patient's face. Yes, he came here to give notice and settle up, and to move his things out of the chambers."

"When did he arrive in England?"

"Ah!" was the reply, "that I can't say, exactly. I didn't know that he was back until he turned up here, as I have told you. That was about three weeks ago. But he must have been in England some time before that, seeing that he had taken a house, and perhaps a doctor's business as well."

"Then he never came back here to live?"

"No. Which makes the waste of money seem worse than ever. He appears to have taken his new premises, furniture and all, and settled there at once. So I understood."

"And he is now engaged in medical practice at the address you gave me just now?"

"Well," the porter replied with a faint grin, "That's as may be. If he bought a going concern, I suppose he is. But if he just took the premises without any goodwill, he is probably squatting there and waiting for business to turn up. However, in either case, he has got a brass plate at the address I gave you, and there you'll find him, and he will able to give you the particulars about himself better than I am."

I seemed to detect in the final sentence a subtle hint that our friend thought that he had asked questions, and so, apparently, did Thorndyke, for he accepted the hint – the more readily, I suspect, because he had no further questions to ask – and brought the interview to an end by thanking our friend for the address and wishing him good morning.

As this dialogue had proceeded, I had become and more puzzled, for I had supposed mission had the simple purpose of finding out, if possible, the whereabouts of Dr. Peck, and I had imagined that our business with Peck was to elicit from him whatever he might be able to tell us about the incidents of the voyage from Australia as affecting John Gillum. But it seemed that neither of these suppositions was true. Thorndyke was not interested only in what Peck might be able and willing to tell us – he was interested in Peck, himself. The apparently trivial conversation to which I had listened was, I felt sure, a carefully conducted examination designed to elicit certain facts. But what facts? I had listened attentively and even curiously, but not a single fact of any apparent significance seemed to have transpired. Yet something had transpired, unperceived by me. Thorndyke's behaviour had convinced

542

me of that. The way in which he had, almost abruptly, closed the conversation told me that, whatever might be the item of information which he had been seeking, that item was now in his possession. But I could not form the vaguest guess as to what it could be.

My confusion of thought was rather increased by Thorndyke's conduct when we emerged from the Inn, for, halting at the edge of the pavement and looking across the road, he said meditatively, "Baldwin's Gardens. I think that turns out of the Gray's Inn Road a little way down on the right, doesn't it?"

"Yes," I replied. "About the third turning. Were you thinking of paying a visit to the ingenious Mr. Crow?"

"Why not?" said he. "We may as well look him up now, as we are so near."

"But," I protested, "why look him up at all? Those bookcases were very ingenious and handy for the purpose for which they were made, but you have no use for such things. You don't make sea voyages or even prolonged journeys away from home, and if you did, you would hardly want to take your library with you."

"But they would be useful for carrying other things besides books," he replied. "Apparatus and reagents, for instance. At any rate, I should like to get particulars of construction and dimensions."

"With a view," said I, "to pinching Mr. Crow's copyright and having a pirated edition turned out by Polton."

"Not at all," he retorted. "If I decided to have one, or a pair, made, I should certainly commission Mr. Crow to make them."

As he had evidently got some kind of unreasonable fancy for those bookcases, I said no more. We crossed the road and in two or three minutes found ourselves at the corner of Baldwin's Gardens, whence we began a perambulation of the street. It was some time before we were able to locate Mr. Crow's premises, but eventually we discovered, at the corner of a side passage, a painted board inscribed with the name of *"William Crow, Carpenter and Joiner"* and the intimation that his workshop would be found on the right up the passage. We accordingly followed the direction and, coming to a door on which the description was repeated, pushed it open and entered a spacious, well-lighted workshop in which a tall, elderly man was engaged in planing up the edge of a board. At the sound of our entry, he turned and looked at us over the tops of his spectacles, and then, laying his plane down on the bench, enquired politely what he could do for us.

Thorndyke briefly stated the purpose of our visit, whereupon Mr. Crow took off his spectacles to get a better view of us and appeared to meditate on what my colleague had said.

"A pair of bookcases, you say, sir, made for a gentleman in Staple Inn of the name of Peck. Yes, I seem to remember a-making of them, but I can't rightly recollect exactly what they were like. Small cases, I think you said?"

"Yes, about three-feet-by-two."

"Well, sir – " said Mr. Crow, very reasonably, I thought, " – if you will tell me just what you want, I can take down the particulars and make the articles without troubling about those other ones."

But this simple plan apparently did not commend itself to Thorndyke, for he objected, "I am not sure that I have got the full particulars and I rather wanted to see the construction and dimensions of those that you made for Dr. Peck. Don't you keep an account in your books of work that you have in hand?"

"Oh, yes," replied Crow, "I've got the particulars all right, if I only knew where to look for them. But you see, it's a longish time ago and my memory ain't what it was. I suppose. Now, you couldn't tell me about when those cases were made?"

"I can't give you the exact date," said Thorndyke, "but I should say that it would have been some time in September, 1928, probably the early part of the month. Or it might have been the latter part of August. What do you say, Jervis?"

"I expect you are right," I replied, "though I don't quite see how you arrived at the date."

But however he had arrived at it, the date turned out to be correct, for when Mr. Crow, having resumed his spectacles, had picked out from a row of trade books a shabby-looking folio volume and opened it on the bench, the required entry came into view almost at once.

"Ah!" said Crow, "here we are. Twenty-eighth of August, 1928. I see the order is marked '*Urgent*'. Things wanted as soon as possible. They usually are. So I treated it as urgent and delivered the goods at the Inn on the thirty-first, in the evening, as soon as I had got them finished."

"That was a fairly quick piece of work," I remarked.

"Yes," he replied. "I got a move on with 'em. But there was not a lot of work in 'em, as you can see by the drawings. No dovetails and no gluing up except for the backs. They were just screwed together and stained and brush-varnished. It wasn't a job to take up much time. I have written the dimensions on the drawings, so you can see exactly what the cases were like."

We looked over the drawings, which were quite neatly executed, though rapidly sketched in, with the dimensions marked on them in clear legible figures notwithstanding which, Mr. Crow proceeded to expound them and the details of construction.

544

"The cases," said he, "were of yellow deal, stained and varnished, three-foot-three-high by twenty-inches-wide and fourteen-inches-deep, all outside measurements, and as the stuff was full one-inch board, the inside measurements would be two inches less in height and width and one inch less in depth. There were three shelves in each case, equal distances apart, so you have got four spaces of a little under nine inches each, as the shelves were only half-inch stuff. All the parts were fastened together with screws, excepting the shelves, and they slid freely in grooves. The fronts were the same size as the backs, and they were just laid on and fixed in position by twelve two-and-a-half-inch number eight screws, which had to be well greased with tallow so that they would come out easily. It was quite a handy arrangement for, you see, you just filled the case up with books and then you put on the front and ran in the screws and you'd got a thoroughly secure packing-case with no hinges or other projections to get in the way when it was being stowed. Then, when you had got it in the place where it was to be, such as the cabin, all you had got to do was to draw out the screws, take off the front, and slip it behind the case, and there you were with all your books ready to hand."

"Wouldn't it have been stronger," I suggested, "if the top and bottom had been dovetailed to the sides?"

"Yes, it would," he agreed, "and that is what I wanted to do. But he wouldn't have it. He said that all the parts were to be screwed together with greased screws so that it could be taken to pieces if necessary for stowage or storing."

"I don't see much utility in that," I remarked.

"There isn't," he agreed, "excepting that, if the cases should be out of use at any time, they could be taken apart, and then the pieces would lie flat and take up less room than the assembled cases."

"I certainly think it a good method of construction," said Thorndyke. "The case would be strongly bound together by the back and front when it was travelling, and when it was not travelling, the extra strength would not be wanted."

"Then," said Crow, "you'd like yours made the same way, I suppose. Did you wish me to make one case or two?"

"You may as well make two while you are about it," answered Thorndyke, "and I think you had better make them in every way similar to those that you have in your day book and of the same dimensions. They are quite suitable and I don't think they could be improved on. But I may say that this order is not urgent. You can take your own time over them."

Mr. Crow thanked him for his consideration, and when he had booked the order in the current book and taken Thorndyke's name and address, we took our leave and made our way homeward. During our walk along Holborn and down Fetter Lane very little was said by either of us. Thorndyke appeared to be cogitating on the morning's experiences, and my own reflections were principally concerned with speculations on the nature of his. For, as far as I could see, the only tangible result of the expedition was that we had got Peck's address and had secured two bookcases which we did not want. In addition, we had picked up a number of rather trivial personal particulars relating to Peck and his comings and goings, none of which seemed to have the slightest bearing on the problem which we were endeavouring to solve. But I suspected that there was more in it than this, and that out of the porter's trifling reminiscences, Thorndyke had gathered something, the significance of which was evident to him although it had, for the present, escaped me.

We entered the Temple by Mitre Court and, as we emerged into the upper end of King's Bench Walk, we observed a figure advancing up the pavement from the direction of our chambers, which, as we drew nearer, resolved itself into that of our friend Benson. He recognised us at the same moment and quickened his pace to meet us.

"I have taken the liberty," said he, when he had shaken hands heartily, "to drop in at your rooms, as I was in the neighbourhood, not to detain you and waste your time, but just to ask if there were any news of our case."

"There is nothing definite to report," replied Thorndyke. "I am making various enquiries and picking up such facts as I can but, so far, the result is a rather miscellaneous collection which will want a good deal of sorting out and collation. But I am by no means hopeless. Won't you come back and have a bit of lunch with us? There are one or two questions that I wanted to ask you, and we might discuss them over the lunch table."

Benson looked at his watch. "I should like to," said he, "but I think I had better not. I have an appointment at half-past-two, and I mustn't be late. Could I answer your questions now?"

"I think so," replied Thorndyke. "It is just a matter of personal description. You see, as I never saw John Gillum and have only the vaguest idea as to what he was like, I shall be rather at a loss if I have occasion to trace his movements. I can give no description of him. Could you sketch out a few personal characteristics by which he could be described or identified?"

Benson reflected as we turned to walk slowly down the pavement.

"Let me see," said he. "Now, what do you call personal characteristics? There is his height. He was rather a tall man, about five-feet-ten. In colour he was a mixture – dark and fair. His hair and beard were black, but his skin was fair and his eyes were blue – you know the type of black-haired blond. But probably the most striking and distinctive characteristic, and the most useful for identification, would be the peculiarity of his teeth. You have heard, I think, that his upper front teeth were extensively filled with gold and as they showed a good deal, they were a very serious disfigurement."

"Yes, I have heard of those teeth," said Thorndyke, "and I have rather wondered why a fairly good-looking man, as I understood him to be, should have allowed himself to be disfigured in that way. Were his other teeth filled extensively in the same way?"

"No," replied Benson, "that was the exasperating feature of the case. He had an exceptionally fine, sound set of teeth, not a stopping among the whole lot, I believe. It was bad luck that the only unsound ones should have happened to be those that were constantly on view. And I have an impression that they were really sound, and that the spots of decay on them were started by some kind of blow or injury. But I think the dentist might have done something better for him."

"Yes," I agreed. "A competent man would not have used a gold filling at all. He would have put in a porcelain inlay."

"To return to the hair," said Thorndyke. "You described it as black. Do you mean actually black, or very dark brown?"

"I mean black. There was no tinge of brown in it, to the best of my belief. It seemed to be dead black, with just a tiny sprinkling of grey. But the grey was hardly noticeable, except, perhaps, on the temples above the ears. Otherwise, there was only a white hair here and there, single hairs that you would scarcely notice and that did not interfere with the general effect of black hair."

"Thank you," said Thorndyke, "Your description is quite helpful. But what would be still more helpful would be a portrait. If you can show a portrait and say, 'Is this the man whom you saw?' the identification is much more definite. I suppose you don't happen to have a photograph of your cousin?"

"Not here," Benson answered, and then, as with a sudden afterthought, he said, "Wait, though. I have got something that will possibly answer your purpose. You must know that I am an amateur in a small way. I run a pocket camera, and I have a sort of a book file for the film negatives. That file I have brought with me and it is in one of my trunks. Among the old films are one or two of Gillum, mostly in groups, but I don't suppose that will matter. They are not very good portraits –

you know what snapshot portraits are like – and of course, they are rather small. But they could be enlarged. Do you think they would be of any use to you?"

"They would be of the greatest use," Thorndyke replied. "They could not only be enlarged, but they could be retouched to get rid of the exaggerated shadows, which are the principal cause of the bad likeness in outdoor snapshots. Will you let me have one or two of them?"

"Certainly," said Benson. "I will look them over and pick out a few of the best and clearest and send them to you. And I have got a photograph that the first officer gave me, which he took on the former voyage. It is a group of officers and passengers, including a fairly good portrait of Gillum. I will send that too. And now," he added, once more glancing at his watch, "I think I must really be running away. There wasn't anything more that you wanted to ask me, was there?"

"No," replied Thorndyke, "I think that was all. If you send me the photographs and they are reasonably good ones, my difficulties in the matter of identification will be disposed of."

With this we both shook hands with him and stood awhile, watching him as he strode away towards Crown Office Row, the picture of health and strength and energy. Then, as our fancies lightly turned to thoughts of lunch, we walked back to our entry and ascended to our chambers where we found the table already laid and Polton on the look-out for our arrival.

Chapter XIII
Dr. Augustus Peck

Of certain men we are apt to say that once seen they are never forgotten. They are not mere samples of the human race, turned out from the common mould, but executed individually as special orders and never repeated. Such were Paganini and the great Duke of Wellington, recognisable by us all from their mere counterfeit presentments after the lapse of a century.

Now Mr. Ethelbert Snuper was exactly the reverse. He might have been seen a thousand times and never remembered. So exactly was he like every other ordinary person that he might have come straight out of a text-book of *The Dismal Science – the Economic Man, Now for the First and Only Time Enjoying a Concrete Existence!* Often as I met him, I recognised him with doubt. And the worst of it was that when at last I thought that I had committed his impersonality to memory, behold! The very next time I met him he was somebody else. It was quite confusing. There was a sort of unreality about the man. His very name was incredible, so exactly did it define his status and his "place in Nature". (But one meets with these coincidences in real life. I once knew a ritualist clergyman named Mummery).

For Mr. Snuper was a private inquiry agent and, especially, a professed and expert shadower, a vocation to which his personal peculiarities (or should I say, his impersonal unpeculiarities?) adapted him with a degree of perfection usually met with only in the lower creation. Even as the cylindrical body of the mole answers to the form of his burrow, and the flatness of *Cimex lectularius* (Norfolk Howard) favours unostentatious movements beneath a wallpaper, so Mr. Snuper's total lack of individual character enabled him to walk the streets a mere unnoticed unit of the population.

I had often met him about our premises, for Thorndyke had employed him from time to time to make such enquiries and observations as were obviously impossible to either of us, and now, the day after our visit to Staple Inn, I met him once more, descending our stairs, and should certainly have passed him if he had not stopped to wish me "Good afternoon." As he had evidently just come from our chambers, I assumed that there was something afoot and was a little curious as to what it might be, and the more so as we had no case on hand which seemed to need Mr. Snuper's services.

549

Of course, I could not put any questions to the gentleman himself, but I had no such delicacy with Thorndyke. As soon as I entered our chambers I proceeded to make a few private enquiries on my own account.

"I met Snuper on the stairs," said I. "Is there anything doing in his line?"

"It is just a matter of one or two enquiries," Thorndyke replied. "I have set him to collect a few data concerning Peck."

"What sort of data?" I asked.

"Oh, quite simple data," he replied. "What sort of practice he has, whether he lives on the premises, how he spends his time, what bank he patronises, and so on. You see, Jervis, we know nothing about Peck, and it would be useful to have a few facts in our possession when we call on him."

"I don't see that the kind of facts that you mention have much relevance to our inquiry," I objected.

He admitted the objection. "But," he added, "your experience in cross-examination will have taught you that an irrelevant question, to which you know the answer, may be a valuable means of testing the general truth of a witness's statements."

To this I had to assent, but I was not satisfied. Such extremely vague enquiries would have suggested that Thorndyke was at a loose end, which I did not believe he was.

"You are not connecting Peck with the blackmailing business, are you?" I asked.

"Why not?" he demanded.

"But the thing is impossible," I exclaimed. "The man was absent from England during the whole of the material time."

"Which is a fact worth noting," said he. "But what do you call the material time? When we were discussing Abel Webb, we agreed that the clue to this business was to be sought in the events of the voyage from Australia. Peck was present then."

"But he was on the other side of the world when the great blackmailing took place, after Abel Webb's death and apparently connected with it. However," I concluded, "it is of no use discussing the matter. I expect you have perfectly good reasons for what you are doing and are keeping them to yourself."

He smiled blandly at this suggestion and the subject dropped, and as we had several court cases which kept us employed during the fortnight which followed, the Gillum mystery fell into abeyance – or, at least, appeared to. Mr. Snuper made no further appearances (but then he never did in the course of an inquiry, reports by post being more safe from observation), and the case had nearly faded out of my mind when my interest in it was suddenly revived by Thorndyke's announcement that he proposed to call on Dr. Peck on the following day shortly before noon.

"By the way," said I, "where is he carrying on his practice?

"His premises are in Whitechapel High Street," Thorndyke replied.

"Whitechapel High Street!" I repeated in astonishment. "What an extraordinary place to have pitched upon."

"It does seem a little odd," he admitted, "but somebody must practise in Whitechapel, and there are some advantages in a poor neighbourhood. At any rate, that is where he is, and I hope we shan't find him too busy for an interview. I don't much think we shall, judging from Snuper's reports of the practice."

How far Mr. Snuper's estimate was correct I was unable to judge when we arrived at the premises on the following morning. From a brass plate on a jamb of the side door of a tailor's trimming warehouse I learned that *Augustus Peck, Physician and Surgeon* had consulting-rooms on the first floor and was to be found in them between the hours of 10:30 a.m. and one, and in the afternoon from two to six p.m. Accordingly, it being then about 11:30 a.m., we entered the doorway and ascended a flight of rather shabby stairs to a landing on which two doors opened, one of which bore the doctor's name in painted lettering with the instruction: "*Ring and Enter*" – which we did – and found ourselves in a large room covered with floor-cloth and provided with a considerable number of chairs, but otherwise almost unfurnished. However, we had no time to inspect this apartment – of which we were the sole occupants – for, almost as we entered, a communicating door opened and a rather tall, well-dressed man invited us to come through into the consulting-room. We followed him into the sanctuary and, when he had shut the door and placed a couple of chairs for us, he seated himself at his writing-table and, having bestowed on us a look of more than ordinary attention, asked, "Which of you is the patient?"

Thorndyke smiled apologetically as he replied, "Neither of us is. We have not come for medical advice, but in the hope – rather a forlorn hope, I fear – that you may be able and willing to assist us in some inquiries that we have in hand."

Dr. Peck smiled. "I was afraid," said he, "that you were too good to be true. My practice doesn't include many members of the aristocracy. But what kind of inquiries are you referring to? And, if you will pardon me, whom have I the honour of addressing?"

Thorndyke took out his card-case and, extracting a card, said, as he handed the latter to Peck. "This will introduce me. My friend is Dr. Jervis, who is collaborating with me."

Dr. Peck took the card from him and glanced at it, at first rather casually, but then he looked at it again with such evidently awakened interest that I felt sure that he had recognised the name. Indeed, he said so when he had pondered over it a while, for, as I offered him my card and he took it from me, laying Thorndyke's down on the table, he asked, "Are you the Dr. Thorndyke who used to lecture at St. Margaret's on medical jurisprudence?"

Thorndyke admitted that he was the person referred to. "But," he added, "I don't remember you. Were you ever at St. Margaret's?"

"No," replied Peck, "I am a Barts man. But I remember your name, as our lecturer used to quote you rather freely. And that brings us back to the question of your inquiry. What is its nature, and how do you think I can help you?"

"Our inquiry," said Thorndyke, "is concerned with a man named John Gillum who came from Australia to England about two years ago. Do you remember him?

"Oh, yes," replied Peck, "I remember him quite well. He was a passenger on the *Port Badmington*, of the Commonwealth and Dominions Line, of which I was medical officer. He came on board, I think, at Perth, and travelled with us to Marseilles. What about him?"

"Did you know that he is dead?"

"Dead!" exclaimed Peck. "Good Lord, no. When did he die?"

"He was found dead in his chambers in Clifford's Inn nearly three months ago. Apparently, he had committed suicide – at least, that was the verdict of the coroner's jury."

"Dear, dear!" Peck exclaimed in a tone of deep concern. "What a dreadful affair! Poor old Gillum! A most shocking affair, and surprising, too. I can hardly believe it. He was such a cheerful soul, so gay and happy and so full of the high old times that he was going to have when he got to England. I suppose there is no doubt that he really did make away with himself?"

"There seemed to be no doubt whatever," replied Thorndyke, "but I can speak only from hearsay. I had no connection with the case at the time."

"And now that you are connected with the case," said Peck, "what is the nature of your inquiry? What do you want to know?"

"The answer to that question," said Thorndyke, "involves a few explanations. From what transpired at the inquest, it appeared that Gillum had been driven to suicide by the loss of his entire fortune. It was only a modest fortune – about thirteen-thousand pounds – but he had got through every penny of it. Part of it he had wasted by betting and other forms of gambling, but a quite considerable portion of what had been lost appeared to have been paid away to blackmailers."

"Blackmailers!" Peck repeated in a tone of the utmost astonishment. "It seems incredible. The gambling I can understand to some extent, though that surprises me. For, though he certainly did like a little flutter at cards, I should hardly have called him a gambler. But blackmail! I can't believe it. Who on earth could have blackmailed Gillum? And what possible chance could he have given them to do it?"

"Precisely," said Thorndyke. "That is our problem. Gillum's relatives are convinced that it was the blackmail, and not the mere gambling losses, that was the determining cause of the suicide, and they have commissioned me to make such inquiries as may establish the identity of the blackmailers and bring them within reach of the law."

"Very proper, too," said Peck, "but it doesn't look a very hopeful job. Have you anything to go on?"

"Not very much," Thorndyke replied. "There is this and there are some other letters but, as you will see, they are not very helpful."

As he spoke he took from his pocket a little portfolio, from which he drew out a single sheet of paper and handed it to Peck, who read its contents slowly and with deep attention and then asked, "Is this the original letter?"

"No," Thorndyke replied. "One doesn't hawk original documents about, which may have to be produced in court. This is a copy, but it is certified correct. The attestation is on the back."

Peck turned the sheet over and glanced at the certificate, then he turned it back and once more read through the letter.

"It's an astonishing thing," said he. "The blackmail works out at two-thousand a year. Gillum must have had some pretty hefty secrets if he was prepared to pay that. But I don't quite see where I come in."

"You come in," said Thorndyke, "at precisely the point which you, yourself have indicated: The identity of the blackmailer and the subject of the blackmail."

Peck looked at him in astonishment. "I don't understand what you mean," said he. "This man, Gillum, travelled on my ship from Australia to Europe. He came on board a complete stranger to me, he went ashore at Marseilles, and I never saw him again. Moreover, I have been abroad for nearly two years, and I came back only a couple of months ago. How could I know anything about Gillum or his blackmailers?"

"It had occurred to me," Thorndyke replied, "that the blackmailers might have been some of his fellow passengers on that voyage, and that the blackmail might have been based on some incidents that had occurred on board. What do you say to that?"

"It is quite possible," replied Peck, "but I know of nothing to support the idea. Gillum seemed to be on good terms with everybody and, as to the other passengers, I knew very little about them. A much more likely source of information would be the purser, if you could get into touch with him. He knew Gillum better than I did, and he knew more about the passengers. Get hold of him if you can. His name is Webb. Abel Webb."

"Abel Webb is dead," said Thorndyke. "He was found dead about a week after the date of that letter."

Dr. Peck stared at Thorndyke, round-eyed and open-mouthed. "Good God!" he exclaimed. "Found dead! Don't tell me that he committed suicide, too."

"It was suggested that he did," Thorndyke replied, "but it is more probable that he was murdered. The jury returned an open verdict."

For some seconds Peck sat motionless and silent, his wide-open blue eyes fixed, with an expression of horror, on Thorndyke's face. At length he said in a low tone, as if deeply moved. "You are making my flesh creep, Doctor. Two of the ship's company cut off by violence in a few months! I almost ask myself if it will be my turn next."

There was a long pause, during which Peck and Thorndyke looked at each other in silence and I continued my observation of the former. He was a rather good-looking man, clean-shaved and well groomed, with close-cropped light-brown hair and clear blue eyes. His manners were easy and pleasant, and he had an undeniably engaging personality. And yet, somehow, I did not very much like him, and I liked him least when he smiled and exposed an unpleasing array of false teeth, mingled with one or two rather discoloured "aboriginals." He had better have kept his moustache.

"Well, Doctor," he said, suddenly recovering himself and handing the letter back to Thorndyke – who replaced it in the portfolio, "you see what my position is. I should have liked to help you, but I really have no connection with the business at all."

"No," Thorndyke agreed, "that appears to be the case. But I am not greatly disappointed. It was, as I said, only a forlorn hope. Nevertheless," he added, as he rose and pocketed the portfolio, "I am greatly obliged to you for having received us so kindly and given us so much of your time."

"Not at all," Peck replied, opening the side door, which gave access to the landing, "I am only sorry that your time has been occupied to so little purpose. Good morning, Doctor. Good morning, Dr. Jervis." He bowed and dismissed us with a genial smile, and we retreated down the shabby stairs and out into the busy High Street.

Chapter XIV
Further Explorations

The advantages of modern transport do not include facilities for conversation. The fact was recognised by us both as we sat in the motor omnibus which bore us at lightning speed – when it was not held up by an immovable jam of other lightning speeders – from the cosmopolitan region in which Dr. Peck had pitched his tent towards the less picturesque but more respectable west. But even in a motor-bus thought is possible, and thus I was able to beguile the – intermittently – swift journey by cogitating upon our recent interview.

As to the results achieved, they were, so far as I was concerned, exactly what I had expected. The man had been absent from England during the whole of the blackmailing period and had nothing whatever to tell. And if Thorndyke had learned anything of his personality – which I had not – the knowledge could be only curious and irrelevant. For the one fact that had emerged was that, for the purposes of our inquiry, Dr. Peck was completely outside the picture.

When the bus delivered us at Holborn Circus and we strode away along the broad pavement, I ventured to present my views as aforesaid, adding, "It doesn't seem to me that Snuper's inquiries have helped us very much but, of course, I don't know what discoveries he made."

"They were not very sensational," Thorndyke replied, "and mainly they agree with our own. Peck has just squatted in Whitechapel. His practice consists, at present, of a brass plate and an empty waiting-room, and his arrangements dispense with the inconveniences of a night-bell."

"He doesn't live there, then?"

"No. He lives at Loughton, on the skirts of Epping Forest, quite accessible to East London, and very delightful in the summer but rather bleak and muddy in the winter."

"It is not very obvious why he gave up his chambers," said I. "Staple Inn is nearer to Whitechapel than Loughton. What else did Snuper find out about him?"

"Very little. He ascertained that Peck seems to be a solitary man with no discoverable friends or acquaintances, that he spends his spare time in wandering about the far east of London or in long walks in the forest, and also – which is the most curious discovery – that he, apparently, has three banks, and that he visits each of them regularly twice a week."

"That really is odd," said I. "What on earth can he want with three banks? And for what purpose can he make these regular visits? If he has no practice there can be no cash to pay in, and he can't draw out twice a week, and from three banks, too."

Thorndyke smiled in his exasperating way. "There, Jervis," said he, "is quite a pretty little problem for you to excogitate. Why should a man who has no visible cash income pay into three banks at once, or, alternatively, why should a man whose visible expenditure is negligible draw out twice a week from three banks?"

"Is there any answer to it?" I asked dismally as we turned into Fetter Lane.

"There must be," he replied. "Probably several, and one of them will be the right one. I strongly recommend the problem for your consideration. Attack it constructively. Think of all possible explanations, and then consider which of them is applicable to the present case. And meanwhile, I suggest that we drop in at Clifford's Inn and see how Polton is progressing."

"What is Polton doing at Clifford's Inn?" I asked.

"My dear fellow," he replied, "he is carrying out your own suggestion: Collecting dust for microscopical examination."

I smiled acidly at this outrageous fiction for, of course, my suggestion had been made ironically as an example of superlative futility. The idea had been Thorndyke's own, and since there must have been some reasonable purpose behind it, I was now all agog to discover what that purpose was. It was not discoverable, however, from Polton's activities, for they exhibited only the method of procedure, which was, characteristically, orderly and systematic. The vacuum cleaner that he was using consisted of a sort of steel jar, into which the suction tube opened, the latter having a nozzle on which a gauze bag could be fastened. Thus, when the air-tight lid was on the jar and the machine was set working, a stream of dust-laden air was discharged into the bag, which detained the dust and let the air escape through its pores. Polton had provided himself with half-a-dozen or so of these bags and, by the time when we arrived – letting ourselves in with a duplicate key of his manufacture – most of them had been filled and now stood in a row on the mantelpiece, each fitted with a label describing the source of its contents and referring to a sketch plan of the premises.

"You see, sir, I have nearly finished," said Polton, as Thorndyke glanced along the row of bags and scanned the labels. "I've done the bedroom, the kitchen, and the larder, and now I am going over this room in sections. But," he added gloomily, "I'm afraid it will be a poor harvest. The floors are terribly clean. That carpet-sweeper must have taken off the cream of the really valuable dust, and they seem to have used it to a most unnecessary extent. However," he concluded, "I've got what I could out of that sweeper. I've combed the brushes and vacuumed the inside thoroughly."

"That was a capital idea," said Thorndyke. "The sweeper is probably quite a storehouse of ancient dust, and of the most useful kind for our purpose. By the way, did you have time to make that key?"

"Yes, sir," replied Polton. "I've got it here. It's only a skeleton. There was no use in fiddling about with wards, so I just cut the middle of the bit right out. But it opens the lock all right. I've tried it."

With this, he produced from his pocket a monstrous skeleton key, such as might have been fabricated by Jack Sheppard to open the gates of Newgate, and handed it to Thorndyke, who remarked as he took it that, "They liked good, substantial keys in the days when these houses were built."

"What key is it?" I asked.

"It belongs to – or rather, it opens – the door on the landing, which I have assumed to be that of the staircase leading up to the lumber-room above which you heard Mr. Weech refer to. I hope there isn't another locked door at the top. Shall we go and see?"

I assented and followed him out to the landing, speculating on his object – if he had one – in surveying the lumber-room. But I asked no question and made no comment. His proceedings in this case were getting out of my depth.

The big key seemed to fit the lock snugly and shot the bolt back with unexpected ease, but the ancient hinges groaned when Thorndyke pulled the door open and exposed the bottom of a flight of rude steps, a sort of compromise between stairs and a ladder. Only the lower steps were visible, for they rapidly faded upward into the total darkness of the chimney-like cavity, but we both noticed that they bore distinct footprints on their dusty treads. Thorndyke went first, lighting our way with the little electric lamp that he always carried, until we were near the top, when a faint glimmer from above mitigated the darkness, and increased as we ascended.

There was no landing at the top, but just a space cut out of the floor to accommodate the steps, so that we came up into the room like a couple of stage demons rising through a trap. When he reached the floor level Thorndyke stepped sideways, clear of the well, and stood motionless, peering into the dim interior. I followed him in the same way, to avoid having the dangerous staircase well behind me, and stood beside him, looking about me with mild curiosity.

It was a rather eerie place, a great, bare room, little lighter than the staircase. For, though there were three large windows, they were all closely shuttered, and what vestiges of light there were filtered in through the cracks and joints at the hinges and folds. But to our accustomed eyes the general features of the place were visible in the dim twilight: The disorderly piles of "junk" ranged along the sides of the room, shadowy forms of chairs, cupboards, baths, tables, rejected and forgotten and probably ruinous, chandeliers, lengths of water-pipe, and multitudinous indistinguishable objects – the accumulations, it might be, of a century or more. But it was not the "junk" that had attracted Thorndyke's attention. Along the clear space in the middle of the room a double row of footprints could be seen, extending from the head of the staircase and fading away into the darkness at the farther end.

"Someone has been up here comparatively recently," said he, "and went directly to the farther end either to fetch or to deposit something. Perhaps we shall be able to judge which. But before we disturb anything I think we had better take a record of these footprints. Polton has the small camera downstairs as there were one or two photographs to take. I'll just go and fetch him up. And, meanwhile, you might open one set of shutters, if you can get at the window."

He handed me his lamp and, when I had seen him safely on to the steps, I approached the only accessible window and investigated the fastenings of the shutters. They were simple enough, consisting of a thick wooden bar resting in wooden sockets and requiring merely to be lifted out, and when I had done this I was able to pull back the shutters and let in the light of day. And now I could see how the footprints had come to be so surprisingly distinct on the bare floor. In the years during which this room had lain undisturbed, the dust had been settling continuously until it now formed a thick grey mantle on every horizontal surface and the footprints were almost as clear as if they had been in snow or on a sandy shore. In some the very brads in the soles and heels could be seen.

I was still examining them and speculating on Thorndyke's unaccountable interest in them when the staircase became brightly illuminated and my colleague appeared carrying an inspection lamp and followed by Polton with the camera slung over his shoulder and the tripod under his arm. Apparently he had his instructions, for he proceeded at once to walk along parallel to the tracks, minutely examining each footprint until he found one that satisfied him. Then he opened the tripod, fixed the camera to the attachment specially designed for the purpose, laid a footrule down beside the print, and proceeded to focus them both.

When he had made the exposure – carefully timed by his watch – and changed the film, he picked up the rule and moved along a few paces, when he halted by a specially clear impression of a left foot and, having drawn Thorndyke's attention to its remarkable sharpness, fetched the camera and repeated his former procedure.

"And now," said Thorndyke, as Polton carefully re-packed his apparatus, "let us see if we can find out what was the object of this visit, to take something away or to get rid of some unwanted article. The latter seems the more probable."

He followed the double line of footprints to a dark corner at the farther end of the room, where they became confused with various large objects – including a big copper bath – which had evidently been moved, as we could see by the marks on the dusty floor. Behind these, and close to the wall, was a pile of dismembered remains – a small cupboard door, a broken table-top, some odd shelves, pieces of board, and fragments of some kind of box or case. A glance at the pile made it evident that the collection had been disturbed, for there were traces of finger-marks on some of the fragments and others seemed to have been wiped, while the heap, as a whole, was free from the thick mantle of dust which shrouded all the untouched objects in the room. Apparently this pile had been the object of the unknown visitor's activities.

"It is evident," said Thorndyke, "that all these things have been moved, and that they were piled up as we see them, by the person who made the footprints. Now, the question is: Did he take something away or did he add something to the pile? And if he added something, what is it that he added?"

"It is impossible to say," I replied, "whether he took anything away, but some of those pieces of wood at the bottom look newer than the rest and, if they are, they are probably what he added, though it is curious that they should be at the bottom. What do you say, Polton, as a practical wood-worker?"

"If you mean those bits of a chest or case," he replied, "I should say they are not more than six months old, and the broken edges are quite fresh. Shall I get them out?"

Without waiting for an answer he scrambled over the obstructions and proceeded to lift off the upper members of the pile, handing them to Thorndyke and me as he removed them, until he came down to six pieces of board, the clean surfaces of which contrasted noticeably with the ancient grime of the objects that had been removed. When he had handed these out he scrambled back, and he and Thorndyke began a systematic examination of the fragments – rather to my surprise, for there was nothing remarkable in their appearance. They seemed to be just the remains of a broken box or case of some kind.

"What puzzles me," said Polton, who was keenly interested because he saw that Thorndyke was, "is how these pieces got broken. Sound one-inch board like this takes some breaking. It couldn't have been an accident, yet why should anyone want to, break up a good piece of board?"

"What do you suppose it was, originally?" I asked. "Was it some sort of packing-case?"

"No, sir," he replied, "it couldn't have been that. The stuff is too good – prime yellow deal, excepting that bit of American white wood – and so is the workmanship. You see that there are three glued joints and they have all held. It was the wood that broke, not the joints, which means that whoever made it was a proper tradesman who could plane a joint true. Besides, all these pieces were stained on both sides and varnished on one, which must have been the outside. I should say it was a permanent case made to carry some particular thing. You see, there are three grooves in the side piece, so there were three partitions. But whatever it was meant to carry must have been pretty heavy to require one inch board throughout. And just look at the screw-holes. Number eight screws they will have been, and plenty of them, too."

"I suppose they are all parts of the same thing?" said I.

"They seem to be," he replied, running his footrule along one piece and then resting them upright on the floor. "They are all one length – thirty-nine inches – and these three broken pieces fit together to make a complete top or bottom twenty inches wide, while the other two broken ones seem to make two-thirds of a similar top or bottom, and the screw-holes in them correspond to those in what must have been one of the long sides. That's what I make of them, sir."

As he concluded, he looked enquiringly at Thorndyke, who agreed that the reconstruction appeared to be correct. "But," he added, "I think we might consider them more conveniently in our own premises. I suppose you have a bit of string about you, Polton?"

"Do you propose to annex them, then?" I asked as Polton produced the inevitable hank of string and proceeded to lash the pieces of board together.

"Yes," Thorndyke replied. "It is a little irregular, but I shall call on Weech and explain matters."

But the explanatory call proved unnecessary for, almost as Thorndyke was speaking, we became aware of sounds from the staircase as of someone ascending the steps, slowly and by no means easily. As the sounds drew nearer we turned to see who the intruder might be, and presently there arose out of the well, first a chimney-pot hat, then a pair of spectacles, and finally the entire person of Mr. Weech, complete with umbrella. When he reached the floor level he stood for a few moments gazing at us, steadily. Then he advanced towards us with an expression of something less than his usual cordiality.

"I happened to notice," he said, rather dryly, "as I passed, that the shutters of one window were open, and as the only key of these premises is at this moment hanging on the key-board in the lodge, I concluded that some person, or persons, had obtained access to the said premises without authority and by some irregular means. Apparently I was right."

"You were perfectly right, Mr. Weech," said Thorndyke, "as you always are. We are entirely unauthorised intruders. I ought to have applied to you for authority to inspect this room, but as I happened to have a key that fitted the lock, and as I merely wanted to look round, I – well, I waived the formality, thinking that I would mention the matter the next time we met."

"Yes," said Mr. Weech, fixing a stony gaze on the pieces of board under Polton's arm. "Quite so. Perhaps it would have been more regular to obtain the authority before the event rather than after. May I ask why you wished to inspect this room?"

Now this was precisely the question that I had been asking myself, but I had not the slightest hope of enlightenment. My learned senior was not in the least addicted to disclosing his motives. Nevertheless, I was curious to see how he would avoid this rather awkward question.

"I wished," he replied, "for certain reasons connected with my inquiries, to ascertain whether this apparently disused room is, in fact, really disused, or whether it is ever visited or made use of."

"I could have told you that if you had asked me," said Weech. "It is not. I could have told you that nobody has entered this room for several years."

"Then, Mr. Weech," Thorndyke retorted, "you would have told me what is not true. For I have just ascertained that it has been entered within the last six months, and that it was entered, apparently, for the purpose of depositing these remains of an obviously new box or case."

"Which," said Weech, with a sly smile, "I see you have taken possession of and are carrying away without authority. However," he concluded with a return to his usual geniality, "I raise no objection. The things are of no value, and *de minimus non curat lex*. I don't understand what you want them for, but that is your affair. Have you finished your explorations?"

561

"Yes," replied Thorndyke, "we were just about to retire, and you had better let me hand you your umbrella when you are safely at the bottom of the steps."

Mr. Weech gratefully accepted this offer and, when he had closed the shutters, he embarked on the perilous descent and we followed. He lingered on the landing to wait for us and, when Polton had let himself into the chambers, he strolled in and looked round.

"I see you are having a spring clean," said he, glancing at the vacuum cleaner. "Not very necessary, I should think, but perhaps just as well after what has happened."

He wandered through the rooms while Thorndyke retired to the bedroom – where I caught a glimpse of him making a survey of the late John Gillum's shoes – and eventually accompanied us down to the court yard, when we departed for home and a rather belated lunch, attended by Polton with the camera and the purloined wood. We paused for a minute or so outside the entry to exchange a few final words with Mr. Weech, and it was at this moment that a rather curious thing happened.

As we were standing there, almost facing the covered passage that connected the two courtyards, I saw a man come through it and appear at the arched entrance. And there he halted. But only for a moment. For, having taken a single quick glance at us, he turned about, looked at his watch, and hurried away back through the passage. It was but an instantaneous glimpse that I had of him, but yet, in that instant, it seemed to me that the man was extraordinarily like Dr. Peck. Obviously it could be no more than a chance resemblance, for we had left that gentleman established in his consulting-room waiting for the arrival of patients. But yet his was a face that one would remember, and the resemblance had certainly been rather remarkable.

I was still reflecting on the coincidence when another man came up the passage and emerged from the arch. Preoccupied as I was with the first man, I hardly noticed him for, unlike the other, he was quite, undistinctive – he might have been a solicitor's clerk or a superior type of traveller. Subconsciously, I was aware that he wore horn-rimmed spectacles, that he carried a small bag and an umbrella and that he walked with a slight limp. Only as he passed close to us on his way to the Fetter Lane gate did I become conscious of a feeling that I had seen him somewhere before, and that feeling might have been due to the fact that, as he passed us, he gave a quick look at Thorndyke, who seemed to return an instantaneous glance of recognition.

When we had shaken off Mr. Weech at the door of the lodge, I raised the question. "Did you recognise that man who passed us in the Inn?"

"Hardly," Thorndyke replied with a laugh. "Not until he looked at me. Did you?"

"I seemed to have seen him before, but I can't give him a name."

"You weren't meant to," Thorndyke chuckled. "That was our invaluable and Protean friend, Mr. Snuper."

"Of course!" I exclaimed. "But I never can spot that fellow. He looks different every time I see him. But there was another man who came up the passage and who produced exactly the opposite effect. I thought I recognised him though I must have been mistaken. Did you notice him?"

"Yes," he replied. "What was your impression of him?"

"I thought he was extraordinarily like Dr. Peck."

"So I thought," said Thorndyke.

"Then it was a real resemblance and not a mere illusion. But it is a queer coincidence for, of course, the man couldn't have been Peck. The thing is impossible."

"It isn't impossible," he replied. "Only wildly improbable. He had no apparent reason for following us as he had our cards and knew where we lived. But if he had wanted to follow us, it was actually possible for him to have done it. Snuper did."

"Snuper!" I exclaimed. "You say that Snuper followed us! How do you know that he did?"

"I saw him in Whitechapel High Street as we came away from Peck's."

Chapter XV
Sermons in Dust

The appearance of the party that gathered that same evening round the table in our sitting-room to examine Polton's gleanings from John Gillum's chambers struck me at the time as slightly ludicrous. And that is still my impression when I recall the scene. In the middle of the table was a collection of the labelled bags, containing the floor-sweepings, or vacuum-cleanings, from the respective rooms. Before each of the three investigators was a microscope with triple nose-piece, flanked by a large photographic dish, a jar for waste, and a small covered glass pot for "reserved specimens", and the appointed procedure consisted in scanning the material with a very low magnifying power, examining objects of interest with the higher powers, and the preservation of special "finds" for subsequent consideration.

We began by each taking a bag and turning out its contents on to the dish, the said contents forming an unsavoury heap of the material known to housewives as "flue" – the sort of stuff that you can rake out from under a chest of drawers or a neglected bedstead. From the heap a pinch was taken up with forceps, spread out on the glass plate and rapidly inspected through the microscope. If it contained nothing of interest, it was cast into the waste jar and a fresh pinch taken.

"Are we looking for anything in particular?" I asked as I turned out my mass of flue into the dish, "or do we report everything?"

"You know what is likely to turn up in a floor sweeping," Thorndyke replied. "We can ignore the inevitable wool fibres from the carpet, and cotton and linen fibres. Everything else had better be noted."

With this we all fell to work, stimulated at first by the hope of turning up something interesting or curious. But as the things which we were to ignore appeared to be the only things discoverable, the occupation began presently to pall, and I don't mind admitting that I found it rather tedious. By the time that my heap was reduced to a mere handful, I had observed – apart from the ubiquitous fibres – nothing more thrilling than a few minute particles of what looked like broken glass.

"Yes," said Thorndyke, when I mentioned my discovery, "I have found some, too. It isn't quite obvious what they are, but we had better keep them. Possibly we may come on a larger fragment with a more definite character."

Accordingly, I picked out the grains with fine forceps, aided by a pointed sable brush, moistened at the tip, and deposited them in the glass pot. Having done this, I was about to reach for a second bag when Polton announced a discovery.

"I've found a hair," said he. "It looks like a moustache hair, but it must have been a funny sort of moustache. It seems to have been dyed. Must have been. But did you ever see a man with a violet moustache?"

He passed the slide to Thorndyke, who confirmed the discovery.

"Yes," said he, "it is a moustache hair – a rather fair one – dyed black."

"But," protested Polton, "it's violet."

"Hardly violet," said Thorndyke. "A dull, bluish purple, I should call it. That is the appearance of a single hair, seen under the microscope by a strong transmitted light. Seen in a mass by the naked eye and by reflected light, it would appear jet black."

"Would it, now," said Polton. "Think of that. The microscope is a wonderful instrument, but you mustn't believe all that it tells you."

He took back his slide, and picking the hair out daintily with his forceps, deposited it in the glass pot, while I, encouraged by his success, began an attack on a fresh bagful of flue.

This time, I had considerably better luck. At the first cast I struck an object which looked like a coarse and rather irregular thread of glass and, as I could make nothing more of it than that, I passed the slide to Thorndyke for a "further opinion."

"Ha!" said he, when he had taken a look at it, "now we know what those other particles were. This is undoubtedly a fibre of silicate wool, or slag-wool, as it is sometimes called. It is made from the slag from the smelting furnaces, which is really a kind of crude glass."

"And what is it used for?"

"For a variety of purposes. As it is cheap and incombustible, is unaffected by acids – excepting hydrofluoric acid – or by moisture, and is a bad conductor of heat, it is useful for packing, and especially for packing hot or cold substances."

"I wonder what Gillum used it for," said I.

"We had better defer speculations and inferences," Thorndyke replied, "until we have examined the whole of the material." And with this he took a fresh bag and resumed his observations.

My good fortune did not stop at the slag-wool fibre. Presently there came into the field of the microscope a hair, obviously a scalp hair and probably from a man's head, though the sex is not so easy to decide in these days of shingling and Eton cropping. At any rate, it was a short hair and had been recently cut, and as it had been dyed the same dull purple colour as Polton's moustache hair, it was reasonable to infer that it came from the same person. Accordingly, I considered it attentively in its bearing on that person's natural characteristics. The dye did not, of course, extend to the root. There was a space of perhaps, a twelfth of an inch above the neck of the bulb – representing the growth since the last application of the dye – which was of the natural colour, and from this I was able to infer that the man was of a medium complexion, inclining to be fair rather than dark, that the hair had been originally of a somewhat light brown tint. This was also Thorndyke's opinion, based on an inspection of my "find" and of another scalp hair which he had found in his own material.

"So," he concluded, "we now know that this was a rather blond man who wore a moustache. What we don't know is whether he shaved his chin or wore a beard."

"Begging your pardon, sir," Polton interposed, "I think we do. I have just found another hair – a thick, rather wavy one. It isn't a moustache hair and it doesn't look like a hair of the head. I think it must be a beard hair. Will you just take a look at it, sir?"

Thorndyke took the slide from him and, having made a brief examination of the specimen, decided that it was undoubtedly a beard hair, a decision that I confirmed when the slide had been submitted to me.

"So," said I, "we now have a fairly complete picture of this man, and the question is: Who can he have been? Do you think it possible that Benson could have been mistaken? That what he took for natural black hair was really dyed hair?"

"No," Thorndyke replied, decidedly. "That is impossible for two reasons. First, Benson had known Gillum since his boyhood – practically the whole of his life. But the second reason is absolutely conclusive. You remember that Benson described Gillum's hair as being slightly streaked with grey – that is to say, there was a slight sprinkling of white hairs among the black. And he expressly stated that he had examined the hair of the corpse to see whether the proportion of white hairs had increased, and that he found them apparently unchanged. Moreover, there are the hairbrushes that we found in the chambers – apparently Gillum's brushes. I have examined some of the hairs from those brushes and found them to be natural black hairs with a very few white ones. So these dyed hairs are not Gillum's, but those of some other person who had frequented those chambers."

"Yes," I agreed, "that is perfectly clear. I wonder who he can have been. Is it possible that we have struck the actual villain – the blackmailer, himself?"

"It seems quite possible," Thorndyke replied, "but we had better get on with our search and see what the other bags have to tell us."

We worked on steadily for another hour, making no further comments but transferring all new finds to the glass pots. By this time we had dealt with all the bags excepting the two small ones containing the material from the sweeper and the coal-bin, and the net result was, five more dyed hairs, one natural black hair, and seven fibres of slag-wool. Of the two small bags, I took the one labelled "*Coal-Bin*", while the other was divided between Polton and Thorndyke, the latter taking the extracted dust while Polton was awarded the fibrous mass that he had so industriously combed from the sweeper's brushes.

As for my material, I approached it with no expectation of any discovery, whatever. In a coal-bin one may reasonably anticipate the presence of coal. And coal there certainly was. When I turned the bag out into my dish, the contents presented an undeniable heap of coal-dust, a trial sample of which I took up with the blade of my pocket-knife and sprinkled over the glass plate. But when I applied my eye to the microscope, the appearance of that sprinkling came as a considerable surprise. Undoubtedly there was coal galore, a scattered mass of black, opaque, characterless fragments. But everywhere in the spaces between the particles of coal, the glass surface was covered with a multitude of slag-wool fragments of all sizes from quite considerable lengths of thread down to mere grains of glassy dust. I announced my discovery to Thorndyke and passed the slide to him, but when he had examined it, with evident interest, he handed it back to me with no comment beyond the suggestion that it seemed desirable to preserve the whole of the material from the bin.

His own portion of sweeper dust yielded nothing but a single dyed hair and a few particles of slag-wool, but Polton's combings from the sweeper-brushes were quite rich in material so far as quantity went. But they contained nothing new. There were no less than seven hairs, all dyed, one or two threads of slag-wool, and a number of particles of no interest such as crumbs of bread or biscuit, tobacco ash, a piece of cotton thread, and some shavings from a lead pencil. The combings were, in fact, but a sort of condensed epitome of the general "floor-sweep".

"Well, Thorndyke," I said, as I rose and stretched myself, "I think my brilliant and original idea has justified itself by the results. But I'm hanged if I understand them. The gent with the purple hair has deposited well over a dozen samples in different parts of the premises, including the sweeper, whereas John Gillum has dropped only one. But Gillum was the resident. The other fellow could only have been a visitor, even if

Gillum put him up. It seems quite inconsistent, unless we assume that the purple chappie was moulting, which I am not prepared to do."

"No," Thorndyke agreed, "we shall have to find some explanation more plausible than that. And now, if you and Polton will clear away the remains while I jot down a few particulars of the evening's work, we shall all be ready for supper. I presume," he added, addressing Polton, "that the contingency has been foreseen."

It had. There could be no doubt of that, though Polton's only reply was a smile which converted his countenance into the likeness of one of good Abbot Mendel's famous wrinkled peas. But even that smile understated the gorgeous reality. A cold boiled fowl and a ham were mere incidents in the Sybaritic menu. As Polton deposited "the goods" on the table with another smile – which left the Mendelian pea nowhere – I was once more impressed by the queer contradictions in his character. For Polton, himself a spare-living, almost ascetic little man, was apt, when Thorndyke was concerned, to manifest his devotion by developing a sort of vicarious gluttony. He would contemplate Thorndyke's robust appreciation of good food and wine with the sympathetic joy of a fond mother administering delicacies to a beloved child.

Of course, we made him join us at the feast. He could not be allowed to go away and feed in the laboratory, as he had proposed, and when he had taken his place at the table and I had filled his glass with Chambertin (I believe he would rather have had ginger beer), the cup of his happiness was literally full. It was a glorious ending to what had been, for him, a red-letter day.

When the banquet had passed through its final stages and Polton had retired triumphant to his own dominions, Thorndyke and I drew up our chairs to a rather premature but highly acceptable fire and filled our pipes. And, naturally, my thoughts reverted to the evening's researches and their rather surprising results. My colleague had seemed unwilling to discuss them at the time, though we had few secrets from Polton in these days, but now that we were alone, I thought he might be less reticent, and accordingly I ventured to reopen the topic.

"The presence in Gillum's chambers," I began, "of that mysterious stranger with the dyed hair seems to be a new discovery. At least, it is new to me. Have you any idea who he was?"

"Yes," Thorndyke replied. "I think that the facts in our possession enable us to form a fairly definite opinion as to his identity."

"You say 'the facts in our possession'. Shouldn't you rather say 'in your possession'?"

"Not at all," he replied. "Whatever is known to me is known also to you. As to the actual observed facts, we are on an equal footing. Any difference between us is in their interpretation."

This was so manifestly true that it left me nothing to say. It was the old story. I lacked that peculiar gift that Thorndyke had by virtue of which he was able to perceive, almost at a glance, the relations of facts which appeared to be totally unrelated. For some time I smoked my pipe in silence, reflecting on this unsatisfactory difference between us. Presently I remarked, "You have put in a good deal of work on this case. Does it seem to you that you have made any real progress?

"Yes," he replied. "I am quite satisfied."

"And have you marked out any further line of investigation?

"No," he answered. "I am making no further investigations. I have finished. The details can be filled in by the police."

I looked at him in amazement. "Finished!" I exclaimed. "Why, I imagined that you had hardly begun. Do you mean to say that you have identified the blackmailer?"

"I believe so," he replied. "Indeed, I may say that I have no doubt. But there is one point at which I have an advantage over you which must be redressed at once."

He rose and, opening the cabinet in which the "exhibits" connected with the case were kept, took out two sheets of paper, which he laid on the table.

"Now," said he, "here is the blackmailer's letter, which you have seen, and here is a sheet of paper which you have also seen. We found it in the tidy in Gillum's bedroom with a little bolt and nut wrapped in it. Do you remember?"

"I remember. But I thought it was the bolt and nut that were the objects of interest."

"So they were at the time," said he. "But I had a look at the paper, too, and then that became the object of interest. I have flattened it out in the press to get rid of the creases, so that it is now easy to compare it with the letter. See what you think of it."

I took up the two sheets and compared them. It was at once obvious that they were very similar. Both had been torn off a writing-pad, they appeared to be of the same size, the paper seemed to be the same in both – a thin, rather low-quality paper, ruled, with very faint lines. When I held them up to the light, I could see in each a portion of what was evidently the same watermark, and the ruled lines were exactly the same distance apart in both.

"Your point," said I, "is that these two pieces of paper are identically similar. I agree to that. But is the similarity of any great

569

significance? Writing-pads such as these sheets were torn from are made by the thousand. There must have been thousands of persons using pads indistinguishably similar to these at the time when this letter was written."

"That is perfectly true," Thorndyke agreed. "But now make another comparison. I put the two sheets of paper together, thus, both face upwards, as we can tell by the watermark. Now, see if all four of their edges coincide."

"So far as I can see, they all coincide perfectly."

"Very well. Now I turn one sheet over face downwards and again put the two together. Can you still make all four edges coincide?"

I tried, but found it impossible. "No," I replied. "They agree everywhere but at the bottom. One of them must be a little out of the square."

"Not one of them, Jervis," he corrected. "They must be both equally out of the square since all four edges coincided when they were both face upwards. And in fact they are. Test each of them with this set-square. You see that, in each, the bottom edge is out of the square with the sides, and in both to the same amount. I measured them with a protractor and found the deviation in both to be just under one degree. The reasonable inference is that they are both from the same pad."

"Reasonable," I agreed, "but not conclusive. The whole batch of pads must have presented the same peculiarity of shape."

"True," he admitted. "But consider the probabilities. Either these two sheets were from the same pad, or they were from two different pads in the possession of two different persons. Now, which is the more probable?"

"Oh, obviously, as a mere question of probability, they would appear to be from the same pad. But you seem to be suggesting that the blackmailer was Gillum himself, which is so improbable that it cancels the other probabilities. I shouldn't admit that the coincidence in the shape of these sheets is enough to support such an extraordinary conclusion."

"I agree with you, Jervis," he rejoined. "The coincidence alone would not justify that conclusion. But it is not alone. From facts known to us both I had already concluded that the blackmailing letters had been written by Gillum himself. The evidence of these two sheets is merely corroborative. But, as corroboration, it is enormously weighty."

"When you speak of facts known to us both," I said hopelessly, "you leave me stranded. I know of no such facts. But apparently you have worked out a complete case. What is your next move?"

"I am sending Miller the report of the inquest on Gillum's body and informing him that I propose handing the case over to him. That will probably bring him here by to-morrow evening at the latest to get the particulars. Then I shall, in effect, lay a sworn information."

"An information!" I exclaimed. "But against whom? You say that the blackmailer is a myth – that Gillum pretended to blackmail himself. But Gillum is dead, and if he were not, he would have committed no legal offence. It was a pretence, according to your assertion, but it was not, in a legal sense, a fraud."

"Now, Jervis," said he, "to-morrow evening I shall show you the suggested indictment before Miller sees it. But I should like you, in the interval, to make a final effort to work this case out for yourself. You have all the facts. Turn them over in your mind without reference to any preconceived theory, and read Mortimer's narrative once again. If you do that, I think you will be forced to the conclusion that I shall propound to Miller."

I could do no less than agree to this. But I foresaw the inevitable result. Doubtless, I had all the facts. But alas! I had not Thorndyke's unique power of inference and synthetic reasoning.

Chapter XVI
The Disclosure

A telephone call shortly before midday making an appointment for eight o'clock in the evening, informed us that Mr. Superintendent Miller had "caught on". Indeed, he was distinctly curious and would have liked a few particulars in advance, but as his call was answered by Polton, in Thorndyke's absence, these were not available. I sympathised with Miller and should have "liked a few particulars" myself, for I had re-read Mortimer's narrative before going to bed and cogitated on the case all the morning, and was as much in the dark as ever.

I saw little of Thorndyke during the day, for he went abroad alone, and even seemed to make a point of doing so. But we went out together in the evening for a rather early dinner at a tavern in Devereux Court, and it was on our way home that I had the unique experience of recognising Mr. Snuper. We were just about to enter through the little iron gate that leads from Devereux Court into New Court when a man emerged from a doorway in the former and came along at a quick pace behind us. He followed us into New Court and there overtook us, and as he passed ahead, I observed him, though with no particular attention – noting, in fact, no more than that he was a nondescript sort of person and that he carried a large parcel.

It was this parcel that brought him to my notice, for, when he had got some little distance ahead, he seemed to get into difficulties with it and nearly dropped it, whereupon he halted to make some readjustments, allowing us to pass him. And it was at this moment, when he turned his face towards us and the light from a lamp fell on him, that I suddenly realised who he was.

Almost at the instant of the recognition Thorndyke seemed to change his direction. He had appeared to be heading for the passage that leads through into Essex Court, but now he turned sharply to the right and led the way down into Fountain Court, which he crossed to the left into Middle Temple Lane, following the Lane down as far as Crown Office Row and passing along the latter until we emerged into King's Bench Walk. And all the way I could hear the footsteps of Mr. Snuper padding along behind us, and still, to judge by the occasional stoppages, wrestling with his parcel. When we came out into King's Bench Walk he passed us once more and, turning to the right, made for the pavement at the lower end, where presently he vanished into one of the entries.

It was a mysterious affair for the man appeared to be shadowing us, which was a manifest absurdity. I was about to seek enlightenment from Thorndyke when he forestalled my enquiries by producing from his pocket a small folded paper which he handed to me.

"That," said he, "is a copy of the statement that I am going to hand to Miller. You had better look through it before the interview so that you may be in a position to join in the discussion."

I took the little document very gladly, for it would have been rather humiliating if I had had to expose my ignorance to Miller. And it was none too soon, for even as we passed in at our entry, fully five minutes before our time, I caught a glimpse of the superintendent bearing down on us from the direction of Tanfield Court.

I hurried up the stairs to my bedroom and eagerly took out the paper, all agog to learn what Thorndyke's conclusions were. My expectations had been of the vaguest, but whatever they may have been, a glance at the little document blew them to the winds. I read it through again and again, hardly able to believe my eyes. For what it affirmed was not only astounding, it was bewildering and incredible. If the statement that it set forth was true, I had never even begun to understand the nature of the problem.

Slipping the paper back into my pocket, I ran down to the sitting-room where I found Miller already established in an easy chair with a big whisky-and-soda at his side and a cigar of corresponding size between his fingers. He greeted me with an affable smile as I entered and struck a match by way of getting the cigar going.

"Well, Doctors both," said he, "here we are again with another prime mystery in the offing. But I can't imagine what it may be."

"You have read the report of the inquest on John Gillum?" Thorndyke asked.

"Yes," replied Miller. "I haven't had time to read Mortimer's screed, but I have gone through the inquest carefully, and I have come to the same conclusion as the jury – a perfectly straightforward and obvious case of suicide. And I suppose I am wrong. Isn't that the position?

"Yes," Thorndyke replied, "at least, that is my position."

"You are not suggesting that it was a case of murder?"

"I am not suggesting anything," replied Thorndyke, producing a small sheet of paper from his wallet. "I am making a perfectly definite statement. This is what I say, and what I am prepared to prove, and you can have it in the form of a sworn information if you like."

With this he handed the paper to Miller, who took it, opened it, and read through the short statement. Then he read it through again, with deep attention and much wrinkling of the brow. Finally, he laid down his cigar and faced Thorndyke with an air of perplexity.

"I don't quite understand this," said he. "Of course the dates are all wrong. Clerical error, I suppose."

"The dates are perfectly correct," Thorndyke assured him.

"But they can't be," the superintendent protested. "It's an absurdity. What you say is that you accuse Augustus Peck, a registered medical practitioner, that he did, on the night of the 17th of September, 1928, at 64, Clifford's Inn, London, maliciously and feloniously kill and murder one John Gillum. Do you say that you really mean that?"

"Certainly, I do," replied Thorndyke.

"But, my dear doctor," Miller protested, plaintively, "the thing that you are alleging is an impossibility. Gillum's body was discovered on the 18th of July, 1930. That is nearly two years after the date which you give as that of the murder. You admit that?"

"Of course I do," Thorndyke replied. "It is the simple fact."

"But the thing is impossible," persisted Miller. "You are alleging, in effect, that the body which was discovered had been dead nearly two years."

"Not only in effect," said Thorndyke. "That is my definite statement."

The superintendent groaned. "But, Doctor," he urged, "that statement is not reasonable, and what is more, it isn't true. It is contrary to all the known facts. That body was examined by a very competent medic witness who deposed at the inquest that it had been dead from six to eight days."

"'Appeared' to have been dead from six to eight days," Thorndyke corrected. "That is what he said, and I agree to the appearance."

"Very well," said Miller. "Appeared if you like. But the time he stated was about correct, for the man had been seen alive only ten days previously by Mr. Weech, and Mortimer had seen him alive only a few days before that."

"My position is," said Thorndyke, "that neither Weech nor Mortimer had ever set eyes on John Gillum."

"Never set eyes on him!" exclaimed Miller. "Why, they both knew him intimately, and had known him for – " He paused suddenly. Then, directing an intent look at Thorndyke, he added, slowly, "Unless you mean – "

"Exactly," said Thorndyke. "That is what I do mean. Weech and Mortimer and Penfield knew a certain man by the name of John Gillum. But he was *not* John Gillum. He was Augustus Peck, made up so far as was necessary to play the part. And he played the part successfully as long as it was possible, and when it became impossible, he quietly disappeared leaving John Gillum's body to carry on the illusion."

Miller was profoundly impressed, but he was evidently not convinced, for he returned to the charge with further objections.

"You say he left the body on view when he disappeared. Then he must have had it in his possession. Where was it all that time?"

"It was lying hidden in a large coal-bin in the chambers at Clifford's Inn."

"But how was it that it didn't – well, you know, a dead body tends to undergo a good deal of change in two years. But the doctor said that it looked as if it had been dead not more than eight days. How do you account for that?"

"My dear Miller," said Thorndyke, "we live in a scientific age, an age in which natural processes are largely under our control. We can, if we please, prevent dead bodies from decomposing. And we do. In the Paris Morgue, bodies which have not been identified are now put into storage and kept, in a perfectly fresh state, ready for further inspections. I don't know how long they are kept but, physically, there is no limit to the possible time."

"Yes," said Miller, "I see. Of course, you have got an answer to every objection. You would have. I might have known that you wouldn't propose an impossible case. But now, Doctor, let us come down to the immediate business. As I mentioned when I phoned, I am not free to-night. In fact," he added, looking at his watch, "I must be off in a few minutes, but I should like to fix things up before I go. You have given me the substance of the case, a sort of sketch of an indictment. Now, I needn't tell you that that's no use even if you swore to it and signed it. Before I can make an arrest, I must have enough evidence to establish a *prima facie* case. When can I have that evidence? The sooner the better, if we are not to risk a misfire."

"I agree with you as to the of the matter," said Thorndyke, "for I suspect that our friend, Peck, has smelt a rat. I have him under close observation, but I fancy he has me under observation, too."

"The devil he has!" exclaimed Miller. "I don't like that. What do you mean by having him under close observation?"

"I have got Snuper and a couple of assistants watching him night and day. You know Snuper?"

"Yes," replied Miller. "A capital fellow. A genius in his own line. But he doesn't meet the present case. He has no *locus standi*. He couldn't make an arrest unless he caught Peck committing some overt criminal act. And we don't want that. You had better give me his address and then I can detail one or two of our men to take over or act with him."

Thorndyke wrote the address on a slip of paper and handed it to the superintendent, who put it into his note-case and then resumed. "We mustn't let the grass grow, Doctor. Watching is all very well, but we ought to get that gentleman under lock and key. If your statement is true he must be a pretty slippery customer. When can I have that evidence?"

"Can you come in to-morrow evening?" Thorndyke asked.

"Yes," was the reply. "I've got the whole evening free."

"Then," said Thorndyke, "what I propose is this: I ask you to arrange, if you can, for Anstey to lead for the prosecution, as he is used to working with me."

"The choice of counsel doesn't rest with us," replied Miller. "The Director of Public Prosecutions decides that, subject to the Attorney General. But I expect the Director will be willing to appoint Mr. Anstey as you will be the principal witness. What then?"

"I shall assume that Anstey will be appointed and I shall get him to meet you here to-morrow night. I know that he will be able to. Then I shall lay before you a complete scheme of the evidence. How will that do?"

"It will do perfectly," replied Miller.

"I should like, also, if you agree," said Thorndyke, "to have Benson and Mortimer here. We can rely on their secrecy and discretion."

The superintendent was inclined to demur to this proposal. "It doesn't seem to be quite in order," he objected. "They will both be witnesses."

"They are not witnesses yet," retorted Thorndyke. "And you want to know what yours are prepared to say and swear to. But apart from that, I think they may be able to give us some valuable help by answering questions on matters of fact."

"Very well," Miller agreed. "I don't much like it, but it's your funeral."

With this, he finished his whisky and, having been provided with a fresh cigar, rose to take his leave.

"And, look here, Doctor," he said, as he shook hands, "don't you go taking too much outdoor exercise. If this fellow has rumbled you, it's a case for minding your eye and seeing that you don't make a target of the principal witness for the prosecution. We shall want you when the day comes, and for that matter, I expect you'll want yourself. Keep an eye on him, Dr. Jervis, and by the same token, keep an eye on his invaluable coadjutor."

He shook hands again and, having lit the new cigar, bustled away. And as his footsteps receded down the stairs, we heard him apparently trying to whistle and smoke at same time.

Chapter XVII
A Symposium

The instinctive sense of simple hospitality which was the gift alike of Thorndyke and his devoted follower Polton tended to impart a pleasant informality to what were essentially professional conferences. I noted it, not for the first time, when, on the evening following Miller's visit, we gathered round a cheerful fire to "hearken to the evidence" that my colleague had promised to expound to us. To an onlooker we should have seemed more like a party of cronies who had assembled for gossip and the exchange of "yarns" than a gathering of lawyers and police concerned with the detection and punishment of a capital crime.

Nevertheless, the attention of us all was concentrated on the business of the evening, and when Polton had provided for the comforts of all the guests and, having placed on the table three wooden objects, one resembling an elongated brush-box and two shorter, upright boxes, had retired to the adjoining office (leaving the communicating door ajar) and the social preliminaries appeared to be getting unduly prolonged, Miller interposed with the blunt suggestion that Thorndyke "had better get on with it", whereupon my colleague began his exposition without further preamble.

"I have considered," said he, "the most suitable way in which to present the scheme of evidence in this case and it has seemed to me that the best plan will be to follow the line of my own investigation, to produce to you the items of evidence in the order in which they became apparent to me. Do you agree to that, Anstey?"

"Undoubtedly I do," replied Anstey, "as that will be the order in which they will be best presented to the jury in the opening address."

"Very well," said Thorndyke, "then I will proceed on those lines. You have all read the report of the inquest on John Gillum's body and Mortimer's narrative of his relations with Gillum, and as those documents contain all the facts with which I started, I can refer to those facts as matters known to you all.

"The original inquiry was concerned with the identity of the persons who had blackmailed Gillum. That was the problem that Benson submitted to me. But though he did not contest the suicide – which seemed to have been conclusively proved – I could see that, at the back of his mind, there was a feeling that things were not as they appeared –

that behind the apparent facts of the case, there was something that had never come to light.

"Now, as soon as I began to look into the case, I had precisely the same feeling. The whole affair had a curiously abnormal appearance, so much so that it at once suggested to me the question whether the ostensible facts might not cover something of an entirely different nature. There were unexplained discrepancies. For instance, of the large sum of money that had been thrown away, no less than three-thousand pounds had been money saved by Gillum in the course of his business in Australia. One naturally asked oneself how such a man ever came to have any savings at all. The result of these reflections was that I postponed the blackmailing problem and proceeded to a critical consideration of the case as a whole."

"Now, the outstanding fact of the case was that a sum of about thirteen-thousand pounds had disappeared in less than two years. It had been drawn out of the bank in cash – in currency notes and, by special request, in notes which had been circulated and of which the serial numbers were unrecorded, and which it was, therefore, impossible to trace. The explanation offered for this procedure was that this untraceable money was to be used for payments to blackmailers and for discharging gambling debts.

"So far as the blackmail was concerned, this explanation was reasonable enough, but not in connection with gambling. Why should a man take such elaborate precautions to make it impossible to trace the money with which he had paid his gambling debts? There was no reason at all. Gambling debts can be, and usually are, paid by cheque. Why not? Such payments are not unlawful and there is no valid reason for secrecy. Therefore I decided that the explanation offered was not adequate. It was really no explanation at all. But if one rejected the explanation, the original problem reappeared. Thirteen-thousand pounds had disappeared, leaving no trace. Of that sum, about two-thousand could be accounted for by blackmail. But what of the remaining ten- or eleven-thousand? Had it really been gambled away, or was it possible that the gambling was a mere pretext, covering the disposal of the money in some other way? Having regard to the inadequacy of the explanation, I was disposed to suspect that this might be the case, and this suspicion was strengthened by the fact that Mortimer – the only witness as to the gambling – had no first-hand knowledge of the matter at all. His belief on the subject was based on what Gillum had told him, and in reading his narrative I could not but be struck by the way in which Gillum had posed as a reckless and desperate gambler and the pains that he had taken to impress that view of himself on Mortimer.

"From this it appeared that there was really no evidence that any gambling – on a considerable scale – had ever occurred, and there was a reasonable suspicion that it was a myth invented and maintained to cover some other kind of activity. But what kind of activity? The entertainment of that suspicion raised a new problem. What reason – apart from blackmail – could a man have for drawing large sums of money out of his bank in such a form that it could never be traced? I turned this question over in my mind and I could think of only one case in which a man might behave in this way: It was that of a man who had got temporary control of another man's banking account. Such a man – obviously a dishonest man – would naturally seek to get permanent possession of the money under his temporary control. But how could he do this? He could not simply draw cheques in his own favour and pay them into another bank, for those cheques could be traced and the money recovered. And the same would be true of bank notes of which the serial numbers were known. The only plan possible to him would be that adopted by Gillum. He would have to draw the money out in untraceable cash. That cash he could pay into another bank or store for future disposal.

"That was the only alternative that I could think of to the gambling theory, and it appeared to be totally inapplicable to the present case, for the banking account was Gillum's own banking account and the money in the bank was his own money which he had himself paid in. What object could he have had in transferring that money to another bank, or hoarding it? I could imagine none.

"Nevertheless, I did not immediately abandon the idea, for the alternative – the gambling theory – was almost as difficult to accept, and there was a general queerness and abnormality about the case that disposed one to consider unlikely explanations. There was the suicide, for instance. Apparently it was a genuine suicide, but there had been no positive proof that it was. Actually, it was possible that it might have been a skilfully arranged murder. Accordingly, I decided to consider this imaginary case in detail and see whether it was as completely inapplicable as it seemed.

"First, I asked myself the question, how would it be possible for a man to get control of another person's banking account? Apparently, the only possible method would be that of personating the real owner. The case, then, which I had imagined involved, necessarily, the idea of personation. Accordingly, I set up the working hypothesis of personation and proceeded to apply it to the case of John Gillum to see how it fitted and whither it led.

579

"Now, when one sets up a hypothesis and proceeds to test it and deduce consequences from it, if the hypothesis is untrue it very soon comes into conflict with known facts and leads to manifestly false conclusions. But when I began to apply the personation hypothesis to the Gillum case, instead of conflicting with known facts it developed unexpected agreements with them, instead of evoking fresh difficulties, it tended to dispose of the difficulties that had at first appeared.

"The theory of personation involved the idea of two separate individuals, the personator and the personated. It was thus necessary, for the purposes of the argument, to decompose the person, John Gillum, into two hypothetical individuals: John Gillum of Australia and John Gillum, the tenant of Clifford's Inn. They had been assumed to be one and the same person. We had now to see what evidence there was to support that assumption.

"But the first glance showed that there was no evidence at all. The identification had been illusory. In effect, there had been no identification. Benson had identified the body as that of Gillum of Australia – whom we will call simply Gillum – but he had not identified it as that of the tenant of the Inn – hereinafter called the Tenant. And Weech and Mortimer and Bateman gave evidence referring to the Tenant, but their evidence furnished no proof that the body was the Tenant's body. There were really two sets of witnesses. There was Benson, who knew Gillum but had never seen the Tenant, and there were Weech, Mortimer, Bateman and Penfield, who knew the Tenant but had never seen Gillum.

"Thus the personation hypothesis did not conflict with the known facts. No evidence had been produced to prove that Gillum of Australia and Gillum the Tenant were one and the same person. Therefore, it was possible that they were different persons. But as soon as this possibility was established, two rather striking agreements with it came into view. Let us consider them.

"First there was the time of Benson's arrival in England. He arrived immediately after the suicide, or, to put it the other way round, the suicide occurred immediately before his arrival. But not only was it known that he was coming, the actual date on which he would arrive was known. Now, on the personation theory, the Tenant of the Inn was some unknown stranger who was falsely personating John Gillum. He could not possibly have confronted Benson, for the fraud would then have been instantly detected. He would have had to clear out. But if he had simply disappeared, suspicion would have been aroused, whereas the presence of the body and the apparent suicide continued the illusion of the personation. Indeed, it did much more. For when Benson had identified the body as that of John Gillum, and that body had been accepted by Mortimer and Weech as that of the Tenant of the Inn, the personation seemed to be covered up forever beyond any possibility of discovery.

"The second striking agreement is the state of the Tenant's finances. At the inquest it transpired that the deceased was absolutely penniless and that he had no expectations whatever. The last payment of the purchase money for the sheep farm had been paid into the bank and drawn out. All the money was gone and there was no more to come.

"Now see how perfectly this agrees with the personation theory. What could have been the object of the personation? Obviously, to obtain possession of the ten-thousand pounds paid for the sheep farm and the three-thousand forming Gillum's savings. Well, at the time of the suicide this had been done. The whole sum of thirteen-thousand pounds had been drawn out. There was not a penny left in the bank and there were no more payments to come. Then the personator's object had been achieved and there was no occasion to continue the personation any longer. It was time for the personator to disappear, and disappear he did. Benson's arrival simply accelerated matters and fixed the date of the disappearance.

"So far, then, the results seemed to be positive. The more the personation theory was examined, the more did it appear to agree with the known facts. But there were other difficulties, and the most formidable of them was the body. If there had been personation, it must have begun immediately on Gillum's arrival in England and it had been maintained for nearly two years. But where was Gillum all this time? He could hardly have been alive, but if he was dead his body must have been preserved and kept somewhere ready to be produced at the psychological moment – for the pretended suicide must be assumed to have been an essential feature of the scheme.

"Of course, there was no physical difficulty. It is quite easy to preserve a dead body indefinitely, given the suitable means and appliances. The problem was how it could have been done in the circumstances of this particular case. But even while I was puzzling over this difficulty I received sudden enlightenment from Mortimer's narrative. You will remember that, on the occasion of his first visit to Clifford's Inn, he had a very remarkable seizure. From his admirable description it is evident that his symptoms were exactly those of rather acute carbonic acid poisoning, and he notes that the room – the larder, or storeroom – in which the attack occurred was noticeably cold. Further, he mentions that, just before the attack, he had been shovelling up coal from a bin which he describes as occupying the whole of one side of the room.

"Now this combination of low temperature with a considerable concentration of carbonic acid gas was very impressive. It immediately suggested the presence, somewhere in the room, of a substantial quantity of solid carbonic acid, and as the gas appeared to issue from the coal-bin, it seemed probable that the solid acid was contained in the bin. But if that bin was of the size that Mortimer's description conveyed, it would be easily large enough to contain a dead body."

"But Mortimer says that it was full of coal," Anstey objected.

"It appeared to be," Thorndyke corrected. "But there might be room for a false bottom under the coal, and still room for the body under that. A false bottom would be a necessary feature of the arrangement."

"I think," said Anstey, "that we had better be clear about this solid carbonic acid. You know all about it, but we don't. Could you just give us a few particulars as to what it is like and what is its bearing on the case?"

"A very few particulars will be enough for our purposes," replied Thorndyke. "I need not go into the method of production. The substance, itself, is a white solid, rather like block table salt. It is simply frozen carbonic acid, just as ice is frozen water. And as ice has a maximum temperature of 0 degrees Centigrade – commonly known as freezing point – and becomes a liquid if it is raised above that temperature, so solid carbonic acid – sometimes called carbonic acid snow, from its resemblance to ordinary snow – has a temperature of minus 79 degrees Centigrade, that is, 79 degrees Centigrade below the freezing point of water. But unlike ice, it doesn't melt into liquid when its temperature is raised. It changes directly into gas, intensely cold gas, which hangs round it and protects it from contact with warm air. If we were to place a block of it on the table, it would simply dwindle in size until it disappeared altogether, but it would not leave the slightest trace of moisture. And it would dwindle remarkably slowly, for the gas into which the solid snow changes is a very heavy gas and a specially bad conductor of heat."

"Thank you," said Anstey. "That is quite clear. There is only one other question. Is carbonic acid snow obtainable without any great difficulty?"

"It is quite easy to obtain," replied Thorndyke. "The snow is now manufactured on a considerable scale, as it is used for a variety of purposes. It is sold in two forms, the standard twenty-five-pound blocks, which are the most commonly used, and smaller, four-pound blocks, made principally for use in ice-cream tricycles to keep the cream frozen. You can buy the blocks, retail, without any difficulty, and they will probably be delivered in packages enclosed in insulating material such as silicate wool, or slag-wool. Is that clear?"

"Perfectly clear," replied Anstey. "Now we can return to the argument."

"Well," Thorndyke resumed, "you will now see the significance of the presence in this very cold room of free carbonic acid gas in conjunction with a very large coal-bin. It suggested a perfectly simple and efficient method of preserving a dead body for a practically unlimited time, and it thus disposed of what had been my principal difficulty. I was so much impressed by this new agreement that I abandoned the rather academic attitude in which I had considered the personation theory. For that theory was no longer a merely tenable hypothesis. It agreed with the facts much more closely than did the gambling theory. Indeed, it offered a perfectly reasonable explanation of those facts, which the gambling theory did not, and I began to feel that it was probably the true explanation of those facts.

"But there were still some difficulties – not very formidable ones, but still they had to be disposed of before the personation theory could be definitely accepted. There was, for instance, the question of resemblance and disguise. How far was it necessary for the personator to resemble John Gillum, and what amount and kind of disguise would be required to secure the resemblance? Now, it is important to realise that no very exact likeness was necessary. However much the personator had been like the personated and however skilfully he had been disguised, it would have been impossible for him to deceive any person who had really known John Gillum. On the other hand, in the case of persons like Penfield, Mortimer and Weech, who had never seen John Gillum, no resemblance at all was necessary.

"Yet, for other reasons, the personator would have had to bear a general likeness to the man whom he personated. The production of the body, for instance, must have been an essential part of the scheme, and its production involved the idea of its identification as the body of the Tenant. Therefore, the Tenant must have been so far like John Gillum that the body of the one could be mistaken for the body of the other. But for this purpose it would be sufficient for the two men to be alike in their salient characteristics.

"Now what were the salient characteristics of John Gillum? He was a tallish man – about five-feet-ten – with blue eyes, black hair and beard, and upper front teeth which were very conspicuously filled with gold. He also, apparently, spoke with a slight Scotch accent. In all these respects, as we know from Mortimer's narrative, the Tenant resembled John Gillum, and as the body presented the salient physical features common to the two men, it was naturally recognised by Mortimer and Weech as the Tenant's body in the single hasty glance that they took.

"But how many of those characteristics must have been natural to the personator? Evidently, the stature and the eye-colour must have been real. The personator would have to be a rather tall man with blue eyes. But the other characteristics could have been produced artificially. Whatever might have been the natural colour of the hair and beard, they could easily have been dyed black. The only real difficulty would have been the teeth. But, even in their case, there would be no physical difficulty. It would be perfectly easy for the personator to have his front teeth filled with gold, or, preferably, covered with a removable gold plating, while, if he should happen to have false teeth, there would be no difficulty at all. He would simply have a duplicate plate made with gold-filled teeth in front. But either of these methods would require the services of a skilled dentist, and that was the fatal objection to them. They would involve an accomplice. But, since the personation would not only be a serious crime in itself, but would seem inevitably to involve a previous murder, the existence of an accomplice would constitute an appalling danger.

"However, as I have said, there was no physical impossibility or even any difficulty and, accordingly, I accepted it provisionally as a practicable method, reserving further consideration of it until more facts were available.

"The next question was, assuming personation to have occurred, who could have been the personator? On this point, neither the report nor Mortimer's narrative gave any help beyond furnishing certain dates. But one saw at a glance that the personation would have had to begin almost on the very day of Gillum's arrival in England, for, immediately afterwards, the Tenant appeared in the Inn and at Penfield's office. From this it seemed to follow that, since Gillum knew nobody in England, the personator must be somebody who had travelled with him from Australia to England. Of such persons, only two were known to me. I learned from Benson that Gillum had had two cronies on board the ship. The purser, Abel Webb, and the ship's surgeon, Dr. Peck, and as both these men had left the ship on its arrival in England, either of them might possibly have been the personator. There was no positive reason for suspecting either, but both fulfilled what appeared to be the necessary conditions. They had been Gillum's shipmates during the voyage, and both had left the ship for good at about the same time as Gillum.

"Of these two, poor Abel Webb was clearly out of the picture, and even if he had not died, he would still have been impossible as the personator. He was the wrong size, the wrong shape, and the wrong colour. There remained, then, Dr. Peck, the only person known to us whom we could possibly suspect, and it was desirable to get into touch

584

with him for two reasons: First, to ascertain whether his size, form, and colour were such as to render the personation possible, and second, to get some information from him respecting the passengers and personnel of the ship.

"This brings us to the end of what I may call the first stage of the inquiry. Up to this point I had been concerned with the original sources of information, with a critical examination of the report of the inquest, of Mortimer's narrative, and of the information supplied by Benson. The inquiry had started as a search for a hypothetical blackmailer. But examination of the material had brought into view a problem of an entirely different character, and the result of the first stage of the inquiry was the establishment of a *prima facie* suspicion of false personation against some person unknown. We now enter on the second stage, that of investigation proper, the search for new facts which might either confirm or rebut that suspicion."

Chapter XVIII
Circumstantial Evidence

"Hitherto," Thorndyke resumed after a brief interval, "I have followed the enquiry in the chronological order of events. But now, as we are dealing with an investigation *ad hoc*, it will be more convenient to consider it in terms of the particular items of evidence brought to light, maintaining the chronological sequence only so far as is practicable. The first stage of the inquiry had left us with certain matters of fact which required verification and certain others which had to be ascertained. Among the former was Mortimer's description of the coal-bin. From it I gathered that the bin was amply large enough to contain a human body, and I assumed that it probably had a false bottom to preserve an empty space under the coal. These were matters of vital importance, for if the bin should prove to be too small, or to have been kept completely filled with coal, my theory as to the disposal and preservation of the body would fall to the ground.

"Accordingly, my first proceeding was to get the keys of Gillum's chambers from Benson. Then Jervis and I went across to the Inn and made a preliminary tour of inspection. To come at once to the bin, we found it, as Mortimer had said, to occupy the whole length of the wall and, on measurement, it proved to be of these dimensions: Eight feet long, thirty inches from back to front and twenty-nine inches deep. It appeared to be brimful of coal, but when I took soundings through the coal with my stick, I came to a firm bottom nine inches from the top. Thereupon, we shovelled the coal away to one end, when there was brought into view a tray, or false bottom, of stout board, which we ascertained to be of the full length and width of the bin. A transverse crack showed it to be divided into two equal parts, and each half was furnished with a sunk iron ring. We brushed away the coal dust with a brush that hung close by – apparently for this purpose, as its hair was full of coal dust – and then lifted one half by means of the ring, when we found that the tray was of comparatively new wood, that it was supported by small wooden blocks which had been screwed on to the sides of the bin, and that its removal disclosed a cavity underneath nineteen inches deep and of the full length and width of the bin.

"Here, then, was a receptacle with a capacity amply sufficient to accommodate, not only a body, but also the mass of insulating material that would be necessary if that body was to be kept in a frozen state. The

586

question of possibility was disposed of. It remained to ascertain whether there was any positive evidence that a body had actually been preserved in the manner which I have suggested.

"Having finished with the bin, we examined the little room in which it was situated. It had evidently been intended for a larder or storeroom and it had no fireplace or other outlet and only one window, which was about two-feet-six-inches high by eighteen-inches-wide. But this window was fixed permanently as wide open as possible. The lower sash was pushed right up and secured in position by two wooden supports screwed to the jambs. Further, we found that a row of holes, each one inch in diameter, had been bored in the foot of the door, which, together with the permanently opened window, must have maintained a very free draught of air through this small room. And I may say that we learned from Mr. Weech that the holes had been made and the window supports and the false bottom of the bin added by the Tenant – or rather by the Tenant's agent – at the beginning of the tenancy."

"The Tenant's agent!" exclaimed Miller. "Who was he?"

"Ah!" replied Thorndyke, "who was he? That is a very curious and interesting question. But the answer to it does not belong to this part of the story. We shall go into that at a later stage. At present we are considering the evidence bearing on the subject of refrigeration by means of solid carbonic acid.

"To resume: In the course of our survey of the chambers we found several mouse-holes which had been most carefully and efficiently stopped with Portland cement. There appeared nothing remarkable in this, as the Tenant had evidently taken pains to keep all food in metal or earthenware containers so as to avoid harbouring mice. But later, in conversation with Mr. Weech, we got quite a new light on the matter. It seemed that he had learned from the lady who conducts the typewriting establishment on the ground floor that, up to the time when Mr. Gillum came to the Inn, the house swarmed with mice to such an extent that she had seriously considered giving up her premises. But, as soon as Mr. Gillum's tenancy began, the mice suddenly disappeared, and disappeared so completely that not a single mouse was ever to be seen. While we were talking, the lady herself came out of her office and fully corroborated Mr. Weech's statement. Then it occurred to me to ask her whether her premises were still free from mice, to which she answered with natural surprise that they were not. Since Mr. Gillum's death they had begun to reappear.

"This was a very remarkable fact. The disappearance of the mice might reasonably have been assumed to be due to the Tenant's care to keep all food covered, and especially to the very thorough stopping of all mouse-holes. But their reappearance after Gillum's death made it clear that there must be some other explanation, for the holes were still stopped and all the conditions were precisely the same. The disappearance had evidently been due to something connected with the Tenant himself."

"Yes," Anstey agreed, "that seems to be so. What do you wish us to infer from this fact?"

"I suggest that the behaviour of the mice is exactly what we should expect in the conditions which I have postulated. Let us see what those conditions would be. I assume that the bin contained a dead body kept frozen by means of solid carbonic acid. New supplies of the snow would be constantly fed into it, and this snow would be slowly but continually converted into the gas. Thus the bin would be filled with the icy gas which would be constantly increasing in quantity and finding its way out. Now, carbonic acid gas is an extremely heavy gas. It behaves almost like a liquid. You can fill a tumbler with it and you can pour it from one tumbler to another as if it were water. Like all gases, it diffuses upwards into the air, but while it is pure, it falls by its own weight.

"Thus, as the bin filled up with the gas, this would be constantly overflowing on to the floor and would tend to pour down through the cracks between the boards and especially to trickle down through the mouse-holes into the burrows, so that these and the spaces between the joists would be full of the gas. In such conditions, it would be impossible for mice to exist. They would all be either killed or driven away.

"My conclusion is, therefore, that these facts are completely consistent with the presence of solid carbonic acid in the bin and that there seems to be no other explanation."

"Yes," said Anstey, "I am prepared to admit that. What do you say, superintendent?"

"I agree," replied Miller, "that it seems to establish the point, subject to the condition that the theory is supported by other evidence."

"That is all I ask," rejoined Thorndyke. "This is only a single point. The charge against Peck rests on the whole body of evidence. But I have not completed the case for the carbonic acid snow. While we are on the subject, I may as well produce the rest of the evidence.

"Shortly after our visit to the Inn, Jervis and I made a call at the premises of the Cope Refrigerating Company. My object was twofold. First, I wanted to verify a description of Abel Webb, which, I may say, I did. But we will leave the case of Webb for consideration later. The other object was to ascertain whether the man known as John Gillum had ever had any dealings with Copes. I had reason to believe that he had obtained at least a part of his supplies from them and in this it turned out that I was right. For when I interviewed a very intelligent gentleman named Small, I learned, among other interesting matters, that a man corresponding to the description of the Tenant had, on at least one occasion, purchased from him some four-pound blocks of solid carbonic acid, which, I also learned, were delivered in parcels roughly packed in insulating material. I ask you to note the insulated packing since the material used for that purpose is almost invariably silicate wool, or, as it is sometimes called, slag-wool.

"With regard to the identification, I may say that it does not seem to admit of any doubt. The man whom Mr. Small served resembled the Tenant, as Mortimer has described him, not only in size and general appearance but even in respect of his teeth. Mr. Small particularly noticed the extensive filling of the front teeth with gold and commented on the disfigurement that it caused.

"This completes the case for the carbonic acid snow, and you see that it is based on a remarkable body of evidence. There is the illness of Mortimer, exactly resembling carbonic-acid poisoning, occurring in a very cold room and close to the bin, the mysterious affair of the mice, and the direct evidence of the purchase by the Tenant of carbonic acid snow in blocks of a size exactly suitable for use in the manner that I have suggested. I submit that it constitutes conclusive proof that the Tenant had something in that bin which he was preserving by means of carbonic acid snow."

Both Anstey and Miller appeared to be profoundly impressed by this demonstration and the latter expressed the hope that the rest of the evidence would be equally convincing.

"Perhaps," said Anstey, "one might hesitate to use the word 'conclusive', but even if one should not put it quite as high as that, still, it is difficult to imagine any alternative explanation. And I take it that the refrigeration theory is supported by other evidence."

"It is amply supported," Thorndyke replied, "and I shall now proceed to the consideration of some of the other evidence. To return to the chambers. My primary object in visiting them was to verify the dimensions of the bin. But there was another question to which I was anxious to find an answer, but had very little expectation of finding it. That question was whether or not the Tenant had artificial teeth. It was an important question, for there would obviously be great difficulty in fixing a false gold filling to natural teeth, though it would not be impossible. But with a dental plate there would be no physical difficulty at all. The only difficulty would be that the making of such a plate – obviously for the purpose of disguise – would involve the very dangerous complicity of a dentist. But that danger would exist equally in the case of 'faked' natural teeth.

"However, I had better luck than I had expected. In a rubbish basket I found an empty bottle labelled '*Cawley's Cleansing Fluid*', which is a sort of detergent lotion, principally used for filling the bowls in which wearers of false teeth put their dental plates at night so that they may be clean by the morning. Then, on the chest of drawers which served as a dressing-table, I found an earthenware bowl labelled '*Super-fatted Shaving Soap*'. But, as the Tenant, whoever he was, wore a beard, he evidently had no use for shaving soap. And, in fact, the bowl was empty. But there were in it traces of the cleansing fluid, plainly recognisable by the smell. Apparently, the bowl had been used as a receptacle for a dental plate during the night and, in confirmation of this, we found in the larder the handle of a dental plate brush, which had been used as a spatula for mixing Portland cement.

"Here, again, you will probably demur to the use of the word 'conclusive', but the fluid, the bowl, and the brush, taken together, furnish very convincing evidence that the Tenant wore a dental plate. But if he did, he could not have been John Gillum, since it is known that Gillum had a full set of natural teeth and certainly did not wear a denture. I may add that we found a worn-out toothbrush of the ordinary kind and a small tin which had contained a toothpowder, as is used for cleaning natural teeth. So that, judging by these observations, it would appear that the occupant of these chambers was a man who had some natural teeth but also wore a dental plate. And I repeat, that man could not have been John Gillum.

"We made some other discoveries which I shall not deal with now. Among them was a piece of paper which was so exactly like the paper on which the blackmailer's letter was written that it was nearly certain that it was derived from the same writing-pad. But I leave that for your consideration later with the other letters and documents. You will probably decide to have these examined by an expert and, at any rate, they form no part of my present case.

"The next stage of the investigation deals with the identity of the personator. I have already explained that Dr. Peck was the only person known to me who could possibly have personated John Gillum. There was no positive reason for suspecting him, but he fulfilled the conditions that made the personation possible, and it was necessary that some enquiries should be made concerning him. Accordingly, I began by looking him up in the Medical Directory, and then the interesting fact emerged that he was not only a qualified medical practitioner, but also a fully qualified dentist. So that, in his case, the difficulty of getting the counterfeit gold teeth made did not exist. He could do whatever was necessary himself. This was, of course, no evidence against him, but it was another rather striking agreement.

"Dr. Peck's permanent address was given as Staple Inn, and thither Jervis and I went to pursue our enquiries. We were fortunate enough to find the porter of the Inn a rather talkative person, so that a few discreet questions, just to help his conversational powers, soon put us in possession of all the facts that we wanted. And very striking facts some of them were. I need not reconstitute the conversation but will give you the substance of what we elicited.

"In the first place, we were glad to learn that Dr. Peck was in England. He had just returned from a long voyage, a very long voyage, for it had taken him close upon two years. And what instantly struck me when I made a rough estimate of the dates was that he appeared to have started on his voyage just about the time when John Gillum's tenancy at Clifford's Inn began and that he had returned a short time after John Gillum's death. This must be admitted to be a very remarkable coincidence. And there were certain other circumstances that were at least rather singular. For instance, he went away with a full beard and moustache and came back clean-shaved, and he had not come back to Staple Inn although he had chambers there ready to receive him, and which he had always kept so that he should have some place to come to when he returned from a voyage. Instead of this, he had gone straight, as soon as he had landed, to some premises in Whitechapel where he had put up a brass plate and started in practice.

"All this was rather odd but, of the facts disclosed by the porter's rambling discourse, I was most interested in certain preparations which Dr. Peck had made before he had started on his voyage. These included a pair of portable bookcases in which he proposed to carry his travelling library, packed for transport and yet instantly available for use. Of these, the porter was able to give us fairly exact particulars and, as he gave us the name and address of the man who had made them, I had – and took – the opportunity to fill in the precise details. And, as those details are highly material to the subject of our inquiry, I ask you to give very particular attention to them, both in regard to dimensions and construction.

"These bookcases were very ingeniously planned. The idea was that they could be filled with books in their proper order on the shelves and could then be closed by simply screwing on the fronts, when they would be ready for transport either by rail or sea. On arrival at their destination, they could be stowed in the doctor's cabin and the fronts removed, and they would be ready for immediate use. Furthermore, they could, if

591

necessary, be quite easily taken apart for storage. There were no dovetails or other permanent joints. The parts were simply screwed together with well-greased screws, and when these had been withdrawn, the cases could be resolved into a collection of boards which would lie flat for stowage and take up a minimum of space.

"Now, as to the alleged disposal of these cases. They were delivered by the maker, Mr. Crow, of Baldwin's Gardens, at Peck's chambers in Staple Inn and, so far as I could learn, were never seen again. The statement is that Peck took them with him when he started on his voyage – he is said to have travelled overland to Marseilles and embarked there on a foreign ship – to have had them in use throughout that voyage, and finally to have sold them, with the books that they contained, to the captain of the ship from which he landed at Marseilles.

"That is the story. Now we return to the cases. They were made throughout of one-inch board, excepting the three equi-distant shelves, which were of half-inch stuff and slid freely in grooves. Each case was three-feet-three-inches-high, twenty-inches-wide and fourteen-inches-deep. The depth, you notice, was inconveniently great, as the books which would stand in the nine-inch spaces between the shelves would not be more than six or seven inches deep. But the dimensions as a whole interested me profoundly. I wonder whether you notice anything significant in them."

"I certainly do not," said Anstey, glancing enquiringly at Miller, who shook his head with a hopeless expression, "in fact, I cannot imagine what possible bearing these cases can have on the matter that we are considering."

"Their significance," Thorndyke explained, "lies in the possibility of their conversion into something totally different. Each is three feet three inches high, the two placed end to end with the shelves and the adjoining ends removed, would form a long case with an interior capacity of six feet four inches by eighteen inches by thirteen inches. Such a case would hold quite conveniently the body of a tall man, and it would go into the coal-bin with eighteen inches to spare in the length, ten inches in the width and fifteen inches in the depth, of which ten inches must be subtracted for the false bottom, leaving a space of five inches. The two halves of the case could be secured together firmly enough for practical purposes by screwing to each side a short board such as one of the shelves."

Anstey looked at me with a somewhat wry smile. "This is ingenuity with a vengeance," said he. "It almost looks like perverted ingenuity, for even The Great Unraveller must admit that there are plenty of quite innocent containers which would accommodate a human body perfectly well. The mere suitability is of no evidential value excepting as corroboration of evidence showing that it was in fact so used."

"Exactly," Thorndyke agreed. "But at present I am merely proving that such a container existed. The other evidence comes later."

"But," Anstey objected, "the container appears to have been disposed of at Marseilles and to be, at present, somewhere on the high seas."

"My thesis," Thorndyke rejoined, "is that Peck's voyage was a myth, that the cases never went to sea at all, but were simply dismantled and conveyed piecemeal to Clifford's Inn. But may I suggest that my learned friend should allow me to produce my evidence in the appointed order and to defer argument until the facts have been presented?"

"I am sat upon," said Anstey. "Deservedly. I admit it. Let the demonstration proceed."

"I think," said Thorndyke, "that you hardly appreciate the extraordinary suitability of these cases for the use that I suggest. I thought it might be so, and I have accordingly asked Polton to make a set of scale models – two inches to the foot – to help your imaginations and, if necessary, to produce in court. The models are on the table, but we shall have to find Polton to demonstrate the method of conversion."

The necessity of finding Polton, however, did not arise, for even as Thorndyke spoke, he emerged unblushingly from the office and enquired if anything was wanted. Miller greeted his arrival with a broad grin and bluntly accused him of eavesdropping, to which Polton made no reply beyond a bland and crinkly smile but, producing from his pocket a pair of forceps and a watchmaker's screwdriver, bore down on the models.

"We will begin with the coal-bin," said Thorndyke, picking up the long, narrow box and handing it to Polton, "and I shall refer to the real dimensions, of which all these models are exactly one-sixth – two inches to the foot. This bin is eight-feet-long by thirty-inches-wide and twenty-nine-inches-deep. On opening the lid, you see the false bottom with a cavity above it nine-inches-deep – deep enough to accommodate a good supply of coal. But I need not continue the description. You can see the details for yourselves."

Our friends watched with profound interest while Polton picked up with his forceps the little sunk rings in the false bottom and lifted the latter out in its two halves, displaying in the cavity underneath a number of flat pads of cotton wool, which he picked out and laid on the table.

"What are those little pads?" Anstey asked.

"They represent the pads of insulating material," Thorndyke replied. "You will see their use presently. The actual pads were almost certainly made of silicate wool."

Having passed the bin round, Polton took up one of the model bookcases, and with his screwdriver extracted the little screws from the front, when the latter came off, displaying the interior with its three shelves. When he had repeated the operation on the other one, and passed both round for inspection, Thorndyke replaced them on the table.

"You have seen these cases," said he, "in their ostensible character as bookcases, and you will agree that their appearance is quite convincing. Now we shall see the transformation."

It was very interesting to observe how complete the transformation was. Polton began by drawing out the shelves, which slid freely in their grooves. Then, having extracted the lower screws, he let the bottom of each fall out. Next, laying the two cases on their backs, he brought the two open ends together, when they formed a long, narrow box, similar in shape to, but smaller than, the bin. Then he took two of the shelves, each of which was perforated by six holes, and laying them on either side of the long box across the junction of the two halves, fixed them in position with screws. Lifting the box, he demonstrated that the two cases had now become united to form a single structure with a continuous cavity.

When this had been passed round and examined, he took up one or two of the pads and laid them on the floor of the bin. Then he placed the box inside the bin, packed some more of the pads at the ends and sides, put the fronts on, laid the rest of the pads over them, and finally replaced the false bottom, which dropped comfortably into its place on top of the pads.

"You now see for yourselves," said Thorndyke, "how perfectly these cases are adapted to the purpose that I have suggested. The adaptability seems too perfect to be accidental. Not only is the long case exactly the right size and shape to accommodate the body of a tall man, it is also exactly the right size and shape to lie in the bin with enough space around it for the insulating pads and still room enough for the false bottom. There is not an inch to spare in any direction. Those cases have the appearance of having been carefully designed for this very purpose. And I submit that they were."

We were all deeply impressed by the demonstration, and Anstey expressed the sentiments of us all when he remarked, "You were wise, Thorndyke, to have these models made. Seeing is not only believing, it is understanding. No amount of verbal description could have conveyed the extraordinary fitness of these cases for the purpose that you suggest. I take off my hat to you and Polton. I am even prepared to take off my wig, but I will defer that until you have produced the rest of the evidence."

The demonstration completed, Polton made as if to retire to the office, but before he could escape, Miller grabbed him and pulled him into a chair. "What's the use of pretending, Mr. Polton?" said he. "You know you have been listening all the time. Better sit here and listen in comfort!" – Which view, being endorsed by Thorndyke, was duly carried into effect.

"The fact that we have established," said Thorndyke, "is that these bookcases were capable of being converted into a receptacle which would hold the body of a tall man and which would fit the interior of the coal-bin. The objection to the suggestion that they were so used is that they are said to have been taken overseas and never brought back. I now proceed to deal with that objection.

"On the floor above Gillum's chambers at Clifford's Inn is a large lumber-room which has been used by the authorities of the Inn for storing old furniture and other bulky rubbish left by outgoing tenants in their chambers, but I learn that it has been out of use and undisturbed for some years. Now, it occurred to me, as a bare possibility, that the Tenant might, at the end of his tenancy when his proceedings would necessarily be somewhat hurried, find himself burdened with some objects which he would not wish to leave in the chambers but which he had no opportunity to take away or destroy and, in fact, I had these very cases in mind. Accordingly, I decided to take a look round the lumber-room and see if anything appeared to have been deposited there, and did so, assisted by Jervis and Polton."

"Wasn't the room locked?" asked Miller.

"It was," Thorndyke replied. "A common builder's lock which could have been turned with a stiff wire. We actually used a provisional key."

Miller chuckled delightedly. "A 'provisional key'," he repeated. "I must remember that expression. Sounds so much better than 'skeleton key'. Yes, Doctor and, of course, you did find something."

"We did," Thorndyke replied. "Perhaps Polton will be so good as to produce our gleanings for your inspection."

Thereupon Polton retired to the office and immediately returned bearing a bundle of pieces of board which he laid out in order on the table.

"These," said Thorndyke, "we found hidden under a pile of much older lumber. The wood is obviously comparatively new and the broken edges quite fresh. Let us fit those broken edges together and see what results. Here, for instance, are three pieces which fit together perfectly and form a rectangle with finished edges. It is three-feet-three-inches long by twenty-inches-wide, the exact dimensions of the front or back of

595

Peck's bookcases. Moreover, there are twelve countersunk screw-holes, each of which fits a number eight screw, and those screws are not only the same size as those in Peck's cases, but have the same distribution – namely, four equidistant holes on each side and two at either end.

"Then, here are two pieces which evidently formed part of a similar structure. They fit together exactly and their screw-holes are the same size and have the same distribution. Finally, here is a complete piece which corresponds completely with the sides of Peck's cases. It is three-feet-three-inches long, thirteen-inches-wide, it has three equidistant half-inch grooves, and the screw-holes in the edges correspond exactly in size and position with those on the back and the front. But there is in addition an extremely interesting feature. At one end of this side are three holes which have been made by screws, showing that something, not part of the original structure, had been screwed on to the outside. Now, if you will look at Polton's model of the long case, you will see that the two halves are secured together by screwing on one of the shelves on either side, forming a sort of fish-plate, and I submit that these screw-holes afford evidence that a precisely similar procedure had been followed in the cases of which these fragments are part."

Miller and Anstey were both greatly impressed. Nevertheless, the latter objected. "What you have proved, Thorndyke – and proved most conclusively – is that these fragments are parts of some structure which was exactly like one of Peck's bookcases. But you haven't proved that it actually *was* one of his cases."

"No," Thorndyke agreed, "I admit the objection, and I shall now proceed to dispose of it. I sent Polton with the complete back to show it to Mr. Crow, who made Peck's cases. He shall tell you what Mr. Crow said."

"I went to Mr. Crow," said Polton, "and showed him the three pieces and we put them together on his bench. Then he looked up his book and compared the dimensions and the size and position of the screw-holes, and he said that the three pieces made up something that was exactly like the back or front of one of the cases that he had made for Dr. Peck. I told him that we knew that, and I asked him if he couldn't be more definite. So he took another look at the pieces, and then he noticed this bit of American white wood," – here Polton pointed out the strip of foreign wood – "and that brought the job back to his memory. He remembered that he had then had a small piece of good American white wood left over from another job, and as the case was going to be stained, he thought he might as well use it up. So he did, and by that piece of white wood he was able to swear, and he was prepared to swear, that these pieces were actually the back of one of the cases that he had made for Dr. Peck."

"I think that is good enough," said Miller and, as Anstey agreed, the evidence as to the cases was accepted as complete, so far as it went.

"We are agreed, then," said Thorndyke, "as to the identity of the cases, and that somebody brought them from Staple Inn to Clifford's Inn. The next question that we have to settle is: Who brought them? Fortunately, we have some fairly conclusive evidence on that point. I have mentioned that the lumber-room had not been disturbed, or even entered, for at least several years. Apart from Weech's statement, this was evident from the appearance of the place. Everything in it, including the floor and the steps leading up to it, was covered with a thick, even coating of dust, almost like a thin covering of snow. Now, when we started to ascend the steps, we could see on them the very distinct footprints of some person who had gone up a short time previously, and when we reached the room, we could see a double line of footprints extending from the head of the steps to the farther end of the room – actually, as we found later, to the pile of lumber under which the fragments of the cases were hidden.

"As the dust must have been something like an eighth-of-an-inch thick, these footprints were extraordinarily distinct. Like footprints in the snow, they were actual impressions, having a sensible depth and showing some detailed characters of the feet that made them, and their distinctness emphasised the fact that there was no trace whatever of any other footprints. As it happened that Polton had a camera with him in the chambers below, I asked him to photograph two of the footprints, a right and a left, selecting those which showed the most detail.

"This he did, laying a footrule beside each print to give a measuring standard and including the rule in the photograph. I produce here enlargements of the two photographs of the footprints, and I also produce photographs to the same scale, likewise including a footrule, of a pair of house-shoes which I found in the bedroom of the chambers and which seemed to correspond to the footprints. If you examine the two sets of photographs, you will see that the correspondence is quite unmistakable, even to the position of the brads in the soles and heels, which, as well as the various dimensions, you can verify with a pair of dividers and the footrule. I have done this, and I am prepared to swear, and to prove, that the footprints were made by these shoes. Whence it follows – since there were no other footprints, and the cases must have been deposited after the last previous visit to the room – that the fragments of the cases must have been put where we found them by the Tenant, whomever he may have been. Do you agree to that?"

"It is impossible not to agree," replied Anstey. "The proof is absolutely conclusive."

"Then," said Thorndyke, "we will consider the cases as disposed of, and I shall now pass on to another investigation which yielded evidence on two separate aspects of our inquiry. On Jervis's suggestion, I decided to make a systematic collection of dust from the floor of Gillum's chambers. The collection was carried out by Polton with a vacuum cleaner, and he not only kept the dust from the different areas separate but, finding that the Tenant had used a carpet-sweeper, he extracted the dust from that and also carefully combed out its brushes. The same evening, we formed a sort of committee, with three microscopes, and went through the entire collection of dust. I need not trouble you with details of the procedure. Of the objects brought to light by our microscopes, there were only two kinds that are of interest to us, human hairs and particles of silicate wool."

"Silicate wool!" exclaimed Miller. "That sounds rather significant."

"It does," Thorndyke agreed, "but the hairs are, perhaps, even more illuminating, so we will deal with them first. We found, in all, nineteen hairs, of which seventeen were from the scalp, one a moustache hair and one a hair from a beard. Three of the hairs were taken by me from the pillow on which the head of Gillum's corpse had rested. Two of these were natural black hairs and one was white. We found, in the dust from the sitting-room floor, one other natural black hair. Of the other fifteen hairs, all were rather fair hairs dyed black."

"My eye!" exclaimed Miller. "Fifteen dyed hairs out of a total of nineteen! I suppose it isn't possible that they could have been Gillum's?"

"It is quite impossible," replied Thorndyke. "Not only were the black hairs from the pillow natural black, but one of them was white. And Benson will tell you that John Gillum's hair, both during life and after death, was black streaked with white. I need not point out to you that the presence of white hairs is incontestable evidence that the hair is not dyed.

"Let us, then, consider what we are compelled to infer from these dyed hairs. And first as to their number. Of the four natural hairs, three were from the pillow and had evidently come from the head of the corpse, while the fourth came from the floor of the same room. It had probably been detached when the corpse was moved either to or from the couch. At any rate, it was only a single hair. But there were fifteen dyed hairs collected from a fairly clean and habitually well-swept room. The unavoidable inference is that the owner of those dyed hairs was the person who occupied those chambers. Of Gillum himself there is no trace excepting four hairs, three of which certainly, and the fourth most probably, came from the corpse. But there are abundant traces of a rather fair man with hair, moustache, and beard dyed black. In other words, of a man who was not Gillum, but who was disguised so as to resemble Gillum."

"Amazing!" said Anstey, "and all this impressive evidence from a few handfuls of dust!"

"Yes," said Thorndyke, "but we have not finished with the dust. Besides the hairs, we found, as I told you, particles of silicate wool. In the living-room they were few in number and mostly broken quite small by having been repeatedly trodden on. But Polton made a separate operation of the coal-bin, and when we came to examine the dust from that, we found it to consist entirely of coal and silicate wool. And the wool was not only present in large quantities, it consisted to a considerable extent of recognisable lengths of fibre."

"I need hardly ask," said Anstey, "whether you have preserved these tell-tale dust particles for production in evidence?"

"They have all been kept intact," replied Thorndyke, "so that they can be shown direct as well as by enlarged photographs – indeed, all possible exhibits have been carefully preserved. And now, you will be relieved to hear, I am getting near to the completion of my case. Only two more points of evidence remain to be considered, and I will take first that relating to the beginning of the tenancy at Clifford's Inn. I had the particulars from Mr. Weech, and this is what he told me.

"One morning, towards the end of August 1928, a man came to the lodge to enquire about some chambers that were to let. He thought that Number 64, which was empty, might suit him, so he was given the keys, and presently he returned and announced that the chambers would suit him and that he would like to take a lease of them. But he then explained that he was not taking them for himself but that he was acting as agent for a gentleman of means who was, at the moment, abroad, but wanted a set of chambers made ready for him to come home to. He was fully authorised to execute an agreement, to furnish references, and to pay whatever deposit might be thought necessary.

"As he produced a written authority from his principal, Mr. John Gillum, and referred Weech to Mr. Gillum's solicitor and banker, and was willing to pay a half-year's rent in advance, Weech accepted the tenancy. A provisional agreement was signed, the money paid, the keys handed to the agent to enable him to proceed with the furnishing and repairs, and the transaction was closed with one exception. The agent suggested that the references should not be taken up until Mr. Gillum came into residence."

"Why did he stipulate that?" asked Anstey.

"His explanation – quite a reasonable one – was that Mr. Gillum had lived abroad for some years and had done all his business with his solicitor and banker by correspondence and that neither of them knew him personally. This satisfied Weech, and the agent was allowed to take possession of the chambers and get on with the furnishing and the repairs. And it is interesting to note that those repair included the false bottom to the coal-bin, the fixed window in the larder, and the holes in the larder door."

"What was the agent's name?" Miller asked.

"Weech is a little obscure on that point. He thinks it was either Baker or Barker or Barber."

"But," said Anstey, "there is the agreement with his signature."

"That agreement was destroyed when Gillum arrived and a new one executed."

"Then," said Anstey, "there was the agent's cheque. That ought to be traceable."

"There was no cheque," replied Thorndyke. "The money – twenty-five pounds – was paid in five five-pound notes."

"Then there must have been a receipt."

"There was, but it was made out to John Gillum. Mr. Baker, as we will call him, left no trace whatever. But let us finish with Mr. Weech's story.

"About three weeks after the signing of the agreement – on the seventeenth of September, to be exact – John Gillum came to the Inn, and the circumstances of his arrival were these, as related to Weech by the night porter: That night, between nine and ten, someone knocked at the gate, and when he had opened the wicket, he saw two gentlemen, one of whom was Mr. Baker, whom he had seen once before. Accordingly he let them pass through and they went up the passage. Presently Mr. Baker came back alone and said, 'By the way, that gentleman is Mr. Gillum, the new tenant of Number 64. You might mention to Mr. Weech that he has come."

"The porter did so in the morning, and Mr. Weech then called at the chambers. The door was opened by the man thereafter known as John Gillum. Mr. Weech introduced himself and a new agreement was then executed and, the old one torn up. So the tenancy began, and the mysterious Mr. Baker was seen no more."

"How long did he stay that night?" asked Miller.

"There is no answer to that question. The night porter saw him go back into the Inn, and so far as I can learn he was never seen again."

"Did you get any description of him?" Miller asked.

"Yes," replied Thorndyke. "Weech described him as a tallish man, about his own height – that is, about five-feet-ten – fair complexioned, with light-brown hair, a tawny beard and moustache, and blue eyes – apparently a gentleman with a pleasant, persuasive manner and a rather engaging personality. You notice that if his fair hair and beard had been dyed black, he would have seemed to correspond completely to Mortimer's description of the man whom he knew as John Gillum.

"I now come to the last stage of the investigation, and I must admit that I approached it with some anxiety, for if the result should not be what I expected, I should be left with the greater part of the inquiry to be begun afresh with no data to work from. I had assumed that Dr. Augustus Peck was the personator of John Gillum, and that Mr. Baker and Dr. Peck were one and the same person. If these propositions were true, it followed that Dr. Peck must be a man of about five-feet-ten-inches in height, of blond complexion with blue eyes and light-brown hair. Further more, I should expect him to have some false upper front teeth. If he did not agree with this description, then he could not be the man, and I should have to look for another person to fill the role of personator.

"I need not describe our interview with him at length. When Jervis and I called on him, we were confronted by a rather spare man about five-feet-ten-inches in height with light-brown hair and blue eyes. As he was clean-shaved, the colour of his beard was not ascertainable, but it could reasonably be assumed to agree with that of his hair. While we were conversing I was able to observe his teeth, as he had a short upper lip and showed them a good deal, and it was quite easy to see that there were several false teeth in the upper jaw and that these included the four upper incisors – the very teeth that had contained the gold fillings.

"Thus, you see, Dr. Peck's physical characteristics agreed in every respect with those of the Tenant of the Inn, of the man whom Mortimer knew as John Gillum, and of the mysterious Mr. Baker, and I affirm his actual identity with those persons. And I further affirm that, in view of that identity and of the body of evidence which I have presented, I have proved that Augustus Peck is the man who, on the night of the seventeenth of September, murdered John Gillum and thereafter falsely personated him at the Inn and elsewhere.

"And, as we say in court: That is my case."

Chapter XIX
Re-Enter Mr. Snuper

For some time after Thorndyke had finished speaking, a profound silence prevailed in the room. We were all deeply impressed by the ingenuity with which the complicated train of evidence had been constructed and presented. And yet, there was probably the same thought in the minds of us all. Despite the completeness and conclusiveness of the demonstration, the case seemed to be pervaded by a certain unreality. Something seemed to be lacking.

It was Anstey who broke the silence and put our thoughts into words.

"You have presented us, Thorndyke," said he, "with a most remarkable scheme of circumstantial evidence. I have never heard anything finer of its kind. The proof of your thesis appears to be absolutely conclusive, and it would seem almost ungracious for me to offer any criticisms. But, after all, the superintendent and I are practical men who have to deal with realities. It will fall to us to translate this scheme of evidence into action. And we are at once confronted with a serious practical difficulty. I dare say you realise what it is."

"Your difficulty, I presume," replied Thorndyke, "is that the whole case, from beginning to end, rests on circumstantial evidence."

"Exactly," said Anstey. "If we arrest this man and charge him with the murder, we have not a particle of direct evidence to produce against him. Now, the late Lord Darling once said that circumstantial evidence is more conclusive than direct evidence. But juries don't take that view, and I think the juries are right. If we bring this man to trial on the evidence that you have given us, we may easily fail to get a conviction, and there is even the possibility that some fact might be produced by the defence which would upset our case completely. You see the difficulty?"

"I do," replied Thorndyke. "I have seen it all along, and I have provided the means to meet it. Hitherto, I have dealt exclusively with the train of circumstantial evidence because that is really what the case rests upon. But I have borne in mind the need for some direct evidence to impart a quality of concrete reality to the other evidence, and I am able to produce two items which I think will satisfy you and Miller. The first is a set of photographs which Polton has prepared and which I will ask him to hand to me that I may show them to you."

Here Polton paid another visit to the office and came back carrying a small portfolio which he delivered to Thorndyke, who took from it two ten-by-eight mounted photographs and resumed. "These two photographs are enlargements from small originals lent to me by Mr. Benson. The first is a group taken by Mr. Benson, himself, in Australia, and enlarged from the negative. I chose it because it had been taken in the shadow of a building and the faces were quite well lighted. What do you think of it, Benson? Is the likeness fairly good?"

Benson took the photograph from him, and having looked at it, replied, "It is an excellent likeness. The enlargement has brought it out wonderfully."

"Then," said Thorndyke, "pass it to Mortimer."

"Has Mortimer seen it before?" asked Anstey.

"No," Thorndyke replied. "I thought it best that you should see the actual trial."

"You are pretty confident," said Anstey, and the the thought had occurred to me. But apparently his confidence was justified, for, after a prolonged and careful examination of the photograph, Mortimer announced, "There is nobody that I know in this group."

"The man with the beard is John Gillum," said Benson.

"So I had supposed," replied Mortimer. "But I don't recognise him. He appears to be a complete stranger to me."

"Then," said Thorndyke, "we come to the second photograph. That is an enlargement from a small print and is not quite so clear as the other. It was taken by the first officer of the ship and shows a group of four men, one of whom is John Gillum. Look at the group carefully, Mortimer, and see if you can recognise Gillum this time."

Mortimer took the photograph and examined it attentively, and as he did so he appeared to become more and more surprised.

"This is really very curious," said he. "I recognised him at a glance. I suppose this must be a better likeness than the other."

"Show Benson which is John Gillum," said Thorndyke.

Mortimer turned to Benson, holding out the photograph and pointing to one of the figures.

"I say that this is Gillum," said he.

"Then," replied Benson, "you are wrong. That is the ship's surgeon, Dr. Peck. The man standing next him is Jack Gillum."

Mortimer looked at him in astonishment – though I didn't quite see why, after what we had heard. Then, after another look at the photograph, he exclaimed, "So that man is Dr. Peck! Then the man I knew as John Gillum must have been Dr. Peck, for the likeness is quite unmistakable. It is rather an appalling thought, though, considering the sort of terms we were on."

Miller rubbed his hands. "Now," said he, "we are getting down to brass tacks." (apparently he regarded the circumstantial tacks as being of an entirely different metal). "Mr. Mortimer's evidence seems pretty convincing, but I think you said, Doctor, that you had another item up your sleeve."

"I have," replied Thorndyke, "and I think it will be particularly acceptable to you."

He rose and, stepping across to a cabinet, opened it and took out an object which I recognised as the little roulette box that I had seen in Gillum's chambers. Having briefly explained its nature and origin, he continued. "I have fixed it to this board with a spot of glue so that it can be handled without being touched. You will see that it is marked all over with a multitude of finger-prints, many of them superimposed and most of them undecipherable. The grey powder with which I developed them doesn't show up at all well to the eye, but it photographs admirably, so I suggest that you give your attention to the excellent photographs which Polton has made of this box, which show the prints much more distinctly than they appear in the original."

He took from the portfolio a number of prints on glossy bromide paper and passed them to Miller, who examined them with eager interest.

"But these are not so bad, Doctor," he said, when he had looked them over. "I can pick out at least half-a-dozen which our experts could identify quite easily. But what is the point about them? What do they prove?"

"The point is," Thorndyke replied, "that they are the prints of someone who had handled this box. But the box was the property of the Tenant of the Inn and the prints are presumably the prints of his fingers. At any rate, they were made by somebody who had been in those chambers, and Mortimer actually saw the Tenant handling this box. They furnish evidence, therefore, that the person who made them must, at some time, have been in John Gillum's chambers. And now cast your eye over this other collection."

As he spoke, he took out of the portfolio a sheet of paper on which there were two groups of finger-prints, apparently made with printing ink and accompanied by a signature of the same intense black. Miller took the paper and, after a careful scrutiny, compared the prints on it with those shown in the photographs.

"There is no doubt," said he, "that these finger-prints are the same as those that came from the box. But whose are they, and what are they?

I should have taken them for lithographs. And what is this signature? That looks like a lithograph, too."

"It is a lithograph," replied Thorndyke, taking yet another paper from the portfolio. "I will explain how it was made. Here, you see, is a copy of the famous blackmailer's letter. I wrote it out myself on a carefully prepared sheet of lithographic transfer paper. When we called on Dr. Peck, I gave it to him to read. When he had read it, I drew his attention to the attestation on the back, whereupon he turned it over, read the attestation, and turned it back. Thus his fingers and thumbs touched the paper at three different points, all of which I carefully avoided when I took the letter from him.

"Later, I called on a very skilful lithographer and got him to transfer both sides of the letter to the one and take off a few proofs. But first I asked him to write his signature on the letter with lithographic chalk so that it would link up with the finger-prints and enable him to swear to the proofs."

"Then," said Miller, "these are Peck's finger-prints, excepting those at the upper corners, which I presume are your own, and it follows that the prints on the box are his, too. But that seems to put the coping-stone on your case, Doctor, though, as this is a murder case, we could still do with a bit more evidence."

"You will find plenty of further evidence," said Thorndyke, "when you get to work with regular enquiries, evidence from the banks, from Copes, and from various other sources. But you now have enough to enable you to arrest Peck. These finger-prints prove that he was in Gillum's chambers at the very time when, according to his own story, he was on the high seas at the other side of the world. Are you satisfied, Anstey?"

"Perfectly," he replied. "I should go into court confidently on what we have now, without depending on the further evidence that the police will be able to rake together. I see the shadow of the rope already."

It was at this point that Mortimer interposed a question.

"I have been expecting," said he, "to hear some reference to poor Abel Webb. Doesn't he come into the scheme of evidence?"

"He did," Thorndyke replied, "for the purposes of my investigation, but he does not for the purposes of the prosecution. I have not the slightest doubt that Peck murdered him. But I can't prove it, and without proof it would be useless to introduce any reference to the murder."

"Can you form any guess as to why Peck should have murdered him?"

"My dear fellow," exclaimed Thorndyke, "it is not a matter of guessing. It is obvious. Abel Webb was intimately acquainted with both

John Gillum and Augustus Peck. Now, it happened that he saw Peck at his place of business, and he must have recognised him and have noticed that his hair was dyed black – that, in fact, he was disguised so as to resemble Gillum. He seems to have got Gillum's address – probably from the shipping office – and he certainly called at Gillum's chambers, apparently to make enquiries. There he met Peck, disguised and obviously impersonating Gillum. Then the murder was out. Peck had the choice of two alternatives, either to kill Webb or to abandon his scheme and disappear. Naturally, being Peck, he elected to murder Webb and, accordingly, Webb was murdered immediately after his visit to the Inn – apparently on the very same day."

"While we are on the subject of explanations," said Benson, "could you give us just an outline of the actual events? A sort of condensed narrative of Peck's proceedings? I am not perfectly clear as to how the crime was carried out."

"To put it very briefly," Thorndyke replied, "I take it that the sequence of events was this: During the voyage, Peck learned a good deal about Gillum's affairs and, among other matters, two very important facts. First, that Gillum was coming into a large sum of money, accruing in instalments, and second, that he was a total stranger to England, that he knew nobody there and that nobody knew him. These two circumstances suggested to him the possibility of making away with Gillum, personating him while the instalments were being paid, and getting the money into his own possession.

"During the rest of the voyage, he must have devoted himself to finding out everything that he could about Gillum and his affairs and establishing himself as Gillum's intimate friend. Perhaps Gillum may have commissioned him to find a residence for him in London. At any rate, when Gillum went ashore at Marseilles, the friendship was already established and the two men must have been in communication while Gillum was travelling in France. That is clear from the fact that Peck knew when he would arrive in England and was able to meet him and bring him to the Inn, either as a guest or as the actual tenant of the chambers.

"As soon as Peck arrived in England, he set about the preparations to carry out his scheme, and he had the extraordinary good luck to find a set of chambers which contained an enormous coal-bin in an isolated room. When he had secured those chambers, his difficulties were practically over. He had merely to execute the necessary details, to have the bin made suitable for his purpose, to get a container to hold the body with the refrigerating material, to lay in a supply of slag-wool and solid carbon dioxide, to prepare the denture with the gold-filled teeth, and to obtain a suitable hair dye. All this he was able to do without committing himself in any way. If the scheme should prove impossible, he could simply call it off. He had done nothing unlawful or even irregular.

"Then, when Gillum arrived, everything was ready, even to the refrigerating chamber lying on its bed of slag-wool, enclosed in the insulating material, and already charged with carbonic acid snow. The unsuspecting victim was led into the chambers, the oak was shut, and Peck proceeded quietly to convert the living man into a corpse. Probably he gave him food and as much liquor as he would take, with a moderate dose of morphia mixed in with it, and when this had taken effect and Gillum had fallen asleep, he administered the lethal dose with a hypodermic syringe."

"No marks of an injection were found at the *post mortem*," Anstey remarked.

"They were not looked for," replied Thorndyke. "But it would be easy for a doctor to give an injection to a sleeping man so that the marks would not be discovered. However, the point is not material. The poison was administered, and when this had been done, Gillum was, in effect, a dead man. Peck was now irrevocably committed. He had burned his boats, and the instant, pressing necessity, was to get rid of the corpse. For if he should be found there with the dead man, he was lost. Probably he proceeded with the disposal as soon as Gillum was quite unconscious, he stripped the body, put it into the container with the carbonic acid snow, closed the lid, covered it with the slag-wool pads, fitted the false bottom over it, and emptied a scuttle or two of coal on to the false bottom."

"Do you mean to suggest," Anstey exclaimed, "that he put the living man into the refrigerator?"

"He wouldn't be a living man very long," replied Thorndyke, "in an atmosphere some fifty degrees below freezing-point. But that is what he must have done. As long as the dead body was visible in the chambers, he was in deadly peril, but as soon as it was put out of sight and covered up, he was safe. He could spend the rest of the night dyeing his hair and completing his arrangements for the morning. And when his hair was dry and his dental plate with the gold teeth substituted for the one that he had been wearing, he was ready to begin the personation and to carry it on as long as should be necessary in perfect safety, provided that he should never meet any person who knew Dr. Peck or John Gillum – or, still worse, both of them.

"Moreover, you will note the completeness of his arrangements. Sooner or later, he would have to bring the personation to an end. What was he to do then? A simple disappearance would not answer at all. It would give rise to enquiries. But no disappearance would be necessary.

607

At the appointed time, he could simply produce the body, properly staged for a suicide, and the exit of John Gillum would be perfectly natural. But he did not leave it even at that. He created in advance the expectation of suicide so as to forestall enquiries, and he prepared the blackmailing letters with such skill and foresight that they not only agreed with his drafts on the bank but, if any suspicion should have arisen as to his connection with the murder of Abel Webb, they agreed with that, too. Actually, Jervis and I did, at first, connect the blackmail with that murder.

"Then, finally, observe the forethought displayed in the production of the body. As it was managed, it was practically certain that the corpse would lie undiscovered for several days at the least. But in that time it would undergo such changes as would effectually cover up any traces of either the murder or the refrigeration. Looking at the case as a whole, one has to admit that it was a most masterly crime, amazingly ingenious in design and conception and still more astonishing in the forethought, the care and caution, combined with daring and resolution displayed in its execution."

"That is true," said Anstey, "but what strikes me more is the callous villainy of the scheme and the way it was carried out. I am glad you told us the story, Thorndyke, because it has brought home to me what an inhuman monster we have to deal with. If he escapes the rope, it will not be from any lack of effort on my part."

We continued for some time rather discursively to debate the various features of this extraordinarily villainous crime. At length, Miller, having looked at our clock and then at his watch, remarked that "time was getting on" and stood up, and the others, taking this as an indication that the proceedings were adjourned, rose also.

"We will see you safely out of the precincts," said Thorndyke. "It has been a long sitting and we shall all be the better for a breath of fresh air."

Accordingly we set forth together, and having discharged Anstey at his chambers, sauntered by way of Tanfield Court to the Inner Temple Gate, where we took leave of our guests. As we turned to retrace our steps, I noticed two men whom I had previously observed loitering opposite our chambers in the shade of Paper Buildings. Apparently they had followed us and seemed to be doing so still, for as we turned, they retired, and slipping round the corner of Goldsmith Building, moved away along the walk towards the cemetery. I drew Thorndyke's attention to them but, of course, he had already noticed them.

"I wonder," said I, "whether that will be Snuper and one of his myrmidons."

"It is quite possible," he replied. "I know that Snuper is keeping an eye on me. He divides his attention between me and Peck. But they may be a couple of Miller's men. The Superintendent is nearly as anxious about me as Snuper is."

He had hardly finished speaking when two shots rang out – sharp, high-pitched reports, suggesting an automatic pistol. At the moment we were crossing Tanfield Court and the sound seemed to come from the direction of the covered passage that leads through to the Terrace.

"That will be Peck," Thorndyke remarked quietly, and forthwith started off at a run towards the passage. It was extremely uncomfortable, for, though I would have much preferred to take cover and raise an alarm there was nothing for it but to keep close to Thorndyke. As we raced down the echoing passage, I caught, faintly, the sound of quick footsteps ahead, and almost at the same moment, similar but louder sounds from our rear, punctuated by the shrieks of a police whistle.

At the moment when we emerged from the passage on to the Terrace, I had a fleeting glimpse of a man running furiously, but even as I looked, he shot round the corner into Fig Tree Court and was lost to view. Here I would very willingly have called a halt to discuss tactics, for Fig Tree Court, with its two covered passages, both leading into Elm Court, afforded perfect opportunities for an ambush. It was about as dangerous a place as could be imagined for the pursuit of a man armed with an automatic and evidently bent on murder. But there was no choice. Thorndyke was leading, and when another shot sounded from ahead, accompanied by the shattering of glass, he merely noted the direction and bore down straight on the left-hand passage.

It was in Elm Court that the pursuit came to a sudden end. As we rushed out of the passage we saw two men sprawling on the pavement, engaged in a fierce and deadly struggle. One of them grasped a pistol and was trying to turn its muzzle towards his adversary, who, clinging tenaciously with both hands to the wrist that controlled the pistol, concentrated his attention on the weapon. But it was an unequal contest, for, even as we emerged, the man with the pistol was groping with his free hand under the skirt of his coat.

Thorndyke went straight for the pistol, and seizing it with both hands, wrenched it out of the holder's grasp, while I gripped the free arm at wrist and elbow and pinned it to the ground. And none too soon, for, as I straightened out the arm, I saw that the handheld one of those deadly, double-edged surgical knives known as Catlins.

But the struggle was by no means over, for our prisoner seemed to have the strength of twenty men and the ferocity of a hundred. He writhed and twisted and kicked and even tried to bite. As I looked at his mouthing, distorted face in the dim lamplight – the face, it seemed, of a maniac or a wild beast – I found it difficult to connect it with the calm and dignified Dr. Peck of our Whitechapel interview, but easy enough to recognise the murderer of Abel Webb and poor, confiding John Gillum.

The struggle ended as suddenly as the pursuit. It was only a matter of seconds, though it seemed an hour, before our two followers came flying out of the passage and instantly fell upon the prisoner. As one of them helped Thorndyke and me to drag the hands together – with an anxious eye upon the knife – the other produced a pair of handcuffs and expertly snapped them on to the wrists.

"There," said he in a soothing, persuasive tone, "that's fixed you up. It's no use wriggling, and you'd better let me have that knife," which, in fact, he took possession of by a method which caused the prisoner suddenly to drop it.

Apparently Peck realised the futility of further resistance, for he allowed his captors to raise him to his feet, when he stood glowering sullenly at Thorndyke, breathing hard but uttering not a word, while his original antagonist, who had risen unaided, regarded him with mild satisfaction and cast an occasional pensive glance at a ragged hole in his own sleeve through which issued a little oozing of blood. Noticing this, I exclaimed anxiously, "I hope you are not seriously hurt."

"Oh, no," he replied, turning to me with a smile, "it's just a matter of sticking-plaster and a tailor" and as he spoke and looked at me, I suddenly realised who he was. It was Mr. Snuper.

We accompanied the two officers and their prisoner up to the Inner Temple Gate and stood by until a police car arrived in response to a telephone call. Then as the door slammed and the car moved away, we turned back once more towards our chambers. Mr. Snuper would have said goodnight and faded away in his usual inscrutable fashion, but Thorndyke would have none of this.

"No, no, Snuper," said he. "You come back with us. We owe it to you that we are still alive and you were very near to giving your own life for ours. Neither of us is likely to forget your courage and devotion. But now you have got to come and undergo the necessary repairs."

The repairs were executed by me and assisted by Polton (who positively grovelled at Snuper's feet when he heard the story) while Thorndyke attended to the hospitality and, speaking as a surgeon, I am not sure that his methods were quite orthodox, even though it really was little more than a matter of sticking-plaster.

Chapter XX
Epilogue

The trial of Augustus Peck lies outside the scope of this narrative. To follow it in detail would be merely to repeat what the reader has already been told. For there was practically no defence, ingenious and convincing as the scheme of the crime had been, directly the alleged and presumed facts were challenged the whole edifice of deception collapsed. So overwhelming was the evidence for the prosecution that the jury agreed on their verdict of "Guilty" after less than ten minutes' deliberation.

The case for the Crown was based mainly, as Thorndyke had predicted, on the complete train of circumstantial evidence. But his prediction turned out to be correct in another respect. No sooner had systematic enquiries been set afoot by the police than an imposing mass of confirmatory evidence was brought into view. Inquiries, for instance, at Copes and other manufacturers of refrigerating material elicited the fact that Peck had kept himself regularly supplied with blocks of solid carbon dioxide. And an examination by experts of the various documents, including Gillum's holograph will, showed that the will and the letters received from Australia were clearly distinguishable from the skilfully forged documents executed by Peck, and this examination (together with Thorndyke's sheet of blank paper) enabled the experts to testify that the blackmailer's letters had undoubtedly been written by Peck, himself.

But perhaps the most striking corroborative evidence came from the three banks at which Peck had kept accounts. When Miller, armed with an order of the Court, called on them to make enquiries, it was revealed that Peck had been in the habit of paying into each bank some thirty pounds a week in cash – mostly old one-pound notes – ostensibly the receipts from his Whitechapel practice, though, in fact, it was proved that the said practice was a pure fiction. As the money accumulated at the banks, it was promptly converted into gilt-edged securities, which Peck retained in his own possession and which were found locked up in his writing-table at Whitechapel.

But even more striking were the discoveries which were made in the strong-rooms of those banks, which included three large dispatch boxes, each crammed with old one-pound notes, evidently forced in under heavy pressure and forming a solid, compact mass. On counting them, the total amount contained in them was found to be just over ten-thousand pounds, which, together with the securities and the combined credit balance, came near to accounting for the whole sum of thirteen-thousand pounds which had been withdrawn from Gillum's bank.

"If one were disposed to moralise," said Thorndyke, as he laid down the newspaper in which an account of Peck's execution was printed, "one would lament the misuse of the remarkable gifts with which Augustus Peck was undeniably endowed. He was a very unusual type of criminal. I do not recall any other quite like him. He was clearly a man of some culture. He was gifted with a constructive imagination of a high order, and with inexhaustible ingenuity and resourcefulness. He avoided risks whenever they could be avoided, and when they could not be, he took them with a courage and resolution that would be admirable in any other circumstances. Consider his murder of Abel Webb: The risk of committing a murder in a public thoroughfare was enormous. But yet, as a matter of mere policy, the risk was justified, for when he had taken the immediate risk and escaped, the very publicity of the crime was a safeguard so complete that though we were certain that he had committed the crime, we could never have brought it home to him. And Abel Webb was silenced forever.

"Nevertheless, he suffered from the inherent folly that is characteristic of all criminals. The paltry thirteen-thousand pounds was not worth the risk that he took, and his ridiculous attempt to murder you and me – when, I suppose, he had to some extent lost his nerve – was sheer imbecility, for he still had a sporting chance of escape.

"But, at any rate, the world is better without him, and I am not dissatisfied to have been the means of his elimination."

"No," I agreed. "You have done a brilliant piece of work, and as to the result of your labours, as Mr. Weech would express it: *Finis coronat opus.*"

The End

About the Author

Richard Austin Freeman was born on April 11th, 1862 in the Soho district of London. He was the son of a skilled tailor and the youngest of five children. As he grew, it was expected that he would become a tailor as well, but instead he had an interest in natural history and medicine, and so he obtained employment in a pharmacist's shop. While there, he qualified as an apothecary and could have gone on to manage the shop, but instead he began to study medicine at Middlesex Hospital.

Austin Freeman qualified as a physician in 1887, and in that same year he married. Faced with the twin facts of his new marital responsibilities and his very limited resources as a young doctor, he made the unusual decision to join the Colonial Service, spending the next seven years in Africa as an Assistant Colonial Surgeon. This continued until the early 1890's, when he contracted Blackwater Fever, an illness that eventually forced him to leave the service and return permanently to England.

For several years, he served as a *locum tenens* for various physicians, a bleak time in his life as he moved from job to job, his income low, and his health never quite recovered. However, he supplemented his meager income and exercised his creativity during these years by beginning to write. His early publications included *Travels and Live in Ashanti and Jaman* (1898), recounting some of his African sojourns.

In 1900, Freeman obtained work as an assistant to Dr. John James Pitcairn (1860-1936) at Holloway Prison. Although he wasn't there for very long, the association between the two men was enough to turn Freeman's attention toward writing mysteries. Over the next few years, they co-wrote several under the pseudonym *Clifford Ashdown*, including *The Adventures of Romney Pringle* (1902), *The Further Adventures of Romney Pringle* (1903), *From a Surgeon's Diary* (1904-1905), and *The Queen's Treasure* (written around 1905-1906, and published posthumously in 1975.)

In approximately 1904, Freeman began developing a mystery novella based on a short job that he had held at the Western Ophthalmic Hospital. This effort, "31 New Inn", was published in 1905, and it is the true first Dr. Thorndyke story. In 1907, the first Thorndyke novel, *The Red Thumb Mark*, was published.

From Thorndyke's creation until 1914, Freeman wrote four novels and two volumes of short stories. Then, with the commencement of the

First World War, he entered military service. In February 1915, at the age of fifty-two, he joined the Royal Army Medical Corps. Due to his health, which had never entirely recovered from his time in Africa, he spent the duration of the war involved with various aspects of the ambulance corps, having been promoted very early to the rank of Captain. He wrote nothing about Thorndyke during this period, but he did publish one book concerning the adventures of a scoundrel, *The Exploits of Danby Croker* (1916).

Following the war, he resumed his previous life, writing approximately one Thorndyke novel per year, as well as three more volumes of Thorndyke short stories and a number of other unrelated items, until his death on September 28th, 1943 – likely related to Parkinson's Disease, which had plagued him in later years. He is buried in Gravesend.

If you enjoy Dr. Thorndyke, then you'll love
The MX Book of New Sherlock Holmes Stories
Edited by David Marcum
(MX Publishing, 2015-   )

"This is the finest volume of Sherlockian fiction I have ever read, and I have read, literally, thousands." – Philip K. Jones

"Beyond Impressive . . . This is a splendid venture for a great cause!
– Roger Johnson, Editor, *The Sherlock Holmes Journal,*
The Sherlock Holmes Society of London

The MX Book of New Sherlock Holmes Stories
Edited by David Marcum
(MX Publishing, 2015-   )

Publishers Weekly says:

Part VI: *The traditional pastiche is alive and well . . . .*

Part VII: *Sherlockians eager for faithful-to-the-canon plots and characters will be delighted.*

Part VIII: *The imagination of the contributors in coming up with variations on the volume's theme is matched by their ingenious resolutions.*

Part IX: *The 18 stories . . . will satisfy fans of Conan Doyle's originals. Sherlockians will rejoice that more volumes are on the way.*

Part X: *. . . new Sherlock Holmes adventures of consistently high quality.*

Part XI: *. . . an essential volume for Sherlock Holmes fans.*

Part XII: *. . . continues to amaze with the number of high-quality pastiches . . .*

Part XIII: *. . . Amazingly, Marcum has found 22 superb pastiches . . . This is more catnip for fans of stories faithful to Conan Doyle's original*

Part XIV: *. . . this standout anthology of 21 short stories written in the spirit of Conan Doyle's originals.*

Part XV: *Stories pitting Sherlock Holmes against seemingly supernatural phenomena highlight Marcum's 15th anthology of superior short pastiches.*

Part XVI: *Marcum has once again done fans of Conan Doyle's originals a service.*

Part XVII: *This is yet another impressive array of new but traditional Holmes stories.*

Part XVIII: *Sherlockians will again be grateful to Marcum and MX for high-quality new Holmes tales.*

Part XIX: *Inventive plots and intriguing explorations of aspects of Dr. Watson's life and beliefs lift the 24 pastiches in Marcum's impressive 19th Sherlock Holmes anthology*

Part XX: *Marcum's reserve of high-quality new Holmes exploits seems endless.*

Part XXI: *This is another must-have for Sherlockians.*

The MX Book of New Sherlock Holmes Stories
Edited by David Marcum
(MX Publishing, 2015-   )

Also From MX Publishing

Traditional Canonical Sherlock Holmes Adventures by
David Marcum
Creator and editor of
The MX Book of New Sherlock Holmes Stories

 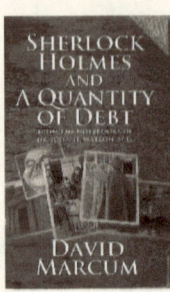 

The Papers of Sherlock Holmes
"The Papers of Sherlock Holmes by David Marcum contains nine intriguing mysteries . . . very much in the classic tradition . . . He writes well, too."
– Roger Johnson, Editor, *The Sherlock Holmes Journal*,
The Sherlock Holmes Society of London

"Marcum offers nine clever pastiches."
– Steven Rothman, Editor, *The Baker Street Journal*

Sherlock Holmes and A Quantity of Debt
"This is a welcome addendum to Sherlock lore that respectfully fleshes out Doyle's legendary crime-solving couple in the context of new escapades . . . ."
– Peter Roche, Examiner.com

"David Marcum is known to Sherlockians as the author of two short story collections . . . In Sherlock Holmes and A Quantity of Debt, *he demonstrates mastery of the longer form as well."*
– Dan Andriacco, Author

Sherlock Holmes – Tangled Skeins
(Included in Randall Stock's, 2015 Top Five Sherlock Holmes Books – Fiction)
"Marcum's collection will appeal to those who like the traditional elements of the Holmes tales"
– Randall Stock, BSI

"There are good pastiche writers, there are great ones, and then there is David Marcum who ranks among the very best . . . I cannot recommend this book enough."
– Derrick Belanger, Author and Publisher of Belanger Books

618

Sherlock Holmes in Montague Street
by Arthur Morrison
Edited, Holmes-ed, and with Original Material
by David Marcum

Separate Paperback Editions

Combined Hardcover Edition

*"It's been suggested that Hewitt was the young Mycroft Holmes,
but David Marcum has a more plausible and attractive theory
– that he was Sherlock, early in his career as an investigator
. . . these are remarkably convincing in their new guise."*
– Roger Johnson, Editor, *The Sherlock Holmes Journal,*
The Sherlock Holmes Society of London

619

MX Publishing

MX Publishing is the world's largest specialist Sherlock Holmes publisher, with several hundred titles and over a hundred authors creating the latest in Sherlock Holmes fiction and non-fiction.

From traditional short stories and novels to travel guides and quiz books, MX Publishing caters to all Holmes fans.

The collection includes leading titles such as *Benedict Cumberbatch In Transition* and *The Norwood Author*, which won the 2011 *Tony Howlett Award* (Sherlock Holmes Book of the Year).

MX Publishing also has one of the largest communities of Holmes fans on *Facebook*, with regular contributions from dozens of authors.

www.mxpublishing.co.uk (UK) and *www.mxpublishing.com* (USA)